## Impulsively,
## She Flung Her Arms
## Around Charlie's Neck . . .

He drew her to him instantly, his arms locking so tightly around her that she gasped for breath. "Oh, Betsy," he whispered, his words getting lost in the tangle of her hair.

Afraid to break the magic of the moment, she didn't answer. Instead, she trailed her fingertips caressingly over his shoulders and pressed her cheek against the bare warmth of his chest. He was all gold and buckskin and strength, and no one in her life had ever set her heart thudding the way he did.

She felt his long fingers gently stroking her cheek and lifting her chin up. She closed her eyes and felt the hot crush of his lips against hers. A warmth of pleasure threatened to melt her bones to tallow, and she clung to him for support.

"Don't let go of me," she whispered. "Ever."

**DAWN OF LOVE HISTORICAL ROMANCES** for you to enjoy

#1 RECKLESS HEART
    by Dee Austin
#2 WILD PRAIRIE SKY
    by Cheri Michaels

Available from ARCHWAY paperbacks

# WILD PRAIRIE SKY

## Cheri Michaels

**AN ARCHWAY PAPERBACK**
Published by POCKET BOOKS • NEW YORK

This novel is a work of historical fiction. Names, characters, places and incidents relating to non-historical figures are either the product of the author's imagination or are used fictitiously. Any resemblance of such non-historical incidents, places or figures to actual events or locales or persons, living or dead, is entirely coincidental.

AN ARCHWAY PAPERBACK *Original*

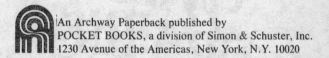

An Archway Paperback published by
POCKET BOOKS, a division of Simon & Schuster, Inc.
1230 Avenue of the Americas, New York, N.Y. 10020

ISBN: 0-671-55154-X

First Archway Paperback printing June, 1985

10 9 8 7 6 5 4 3 2 1

AN ARCHWAY PAPERBACK and colophon are
registered trademarks of Simon & Schuster, Inc.

DAWN OF LOVE is a registered trademark
of Bruck Communications, Inc.

Printed in the U.S.A.

IL 7+

# WILD PRAIRIE SKY

# Chapter 1

JUST BEFORE SUNSET, BETSY SAW A SILVER STREAM winding across the green floor of the prairie. The oxen, thirsty, turned to it automatically, and Betsy gave them their lead.

"We're stopping?" Willa asked hopefully.

Betsy Monroe turned her dark eyes on her sister. *You'd think I was the elder, not the other way around,* she thought. But then, she was used to making the decisions. Ever since she could remember, she had felt older than Willa. "Of course we're stopping," she said, bouncing down from the seat of the covered wagon.

Betsy knelt beside the stream and buried her face in the sweet water. Cool fingers of wetness brushed her cheeks and played in the thick tangles of her chestnut hair. She came up dripping, shaking herself like Toby, the big yellow hound that lapped the water beside her.

"Honestly, Bets," Willa said, her voice full of gentle disapproval. "You look a sight." Betsy laughed to see her sister standing primly on the stream bank. Willa must be as thirsty as she was, but she had gone to the

1

trouble of bringing the dipper from the wagon. "What are you laughing at?" Willa demanded.

"You," Betsy said. "I think you're trying to civilize the West single-handed."

Willa sniffed. The setting sun splashed against her pale blond hair, turning it gold. "No need to act like savages," she replied, "even if we *haven't* seen another human being for weeks."

While Willa drank, Betsy pulled the heavy harness off the oxen. Then, with a broken-bladed jackknife, she made a long scratch on the side of the wagon. It joined the other scratches she'd made, one each day at sunset. She counted the scratches. There were twenty-one of them all together. That meant it was Sunday evening and that the calendar had changed from April to May. It meant that she would turn sixteen before the month was out. It meant that she and Willa had been on their own for three full weeks.

"Willa," Betsy called, turning away from the scratches. She saw her sister gazing dreamily off at the prairie. Its green-yellow grass rolled away from them in every direction, like an endless ocean. Betsy snorted impatiently. "Don't break your back helping me, Will," she said.

"What?" Willa asked in a distracted voice. She raised one hand and pointed toward the horizon. "Look out there, Bets," she said. "Do you suppose that could be Indians?" She watched a second longer. "No, only shadows, I guess."

Betsy tossed her head. "Honestly, Will, you'll be

seeing lions and tigers next if you don't get hold of yourself."

"I'm sorry, Bets," Willa apologized, relieved now that she was sure the Indians were only shadows. "What do you want me to do?"

Betsy swung herself up onto the wagon and tossed down the heavy black skillet. She hopped lightly down after it, with the blue enamel coffee pot in one hand and a slab of bacon in the other. "Catch," she cried suddenly. Willa turned just in time to grab the coffee pot that came sailing toward her. "You get the water," Betsy said. "I'll start the bacon."

Later on, before they climbed into the wagon to go to sleep, Betsy carefully banked the fire.

"You're not going to have a fire all night tonight, are you, Bets?" Willa asked.

Betsy looked at her sister. "Why not? We've had one every other night. 'Sides, it keeps snakes away."

Willa looked from the fire to the horizon and back again. "Indians might see it," she said.

Betsy put her hands on her hips. "What Indians?" she demanded. Willa had been acting like a frightened child all day, and it had just about worn Betsy down.

"Whatever Indians are out there." Willa's beautiful porcelain-doll face was pale except for the spots of pink that glowed on each cheek.

Betsy caught her breath. "I'm not going to sleep in cold camps all the way west just because you're skittish about Indians," she burst out. Even though she was more than a year younger than Willa, she was the taller and stronger of the two. She took after their father that way. She had his hair color and his height and slimness. And she had his temper too, when it came down to it.

"But I have this *feeling,* Bets," Willa said. "I can't explain it, but I'm scared." When Willa frowned, her soft white forehead showed sudden lines, and her gray eyes darkened.

"Don't look at me that way," Betsy said. "You'll get me nervous and jumpy too, and then where'll we be? We've got Toby with us, and Pa's rifle. You haven't forgotten I was the best shot in Wabash County, have you?"

"Oh, Betsy, sometimes I wonder what goes on in your head," Willa burst out, her fair cheeks reddening. "Do you think any Indian worth his salt is going to ride in here, wake us up, give you time to aim, and say, 'All right, miss, take your best shot'? And don't laugh at me, either," Willa said when Betsy began to grin. "You know I'm right."

Betsy gave her sister an affectionate hug. "Oh, Will, if I missed my shot at the Indian, I do believe you could worry him to death. Come on, let's go to sleep."

In the wagon, Willa carefully hung her dress on a peg and slipped into her sprigged-cotton nightgown. Betsy left her dress in a heap on the wagon floor— "like a snake getting out of its skin," Willa observed— and reached for one of Pa's old shirts.

"That thing hardly covers your knees," Willa said as Betsy buttoned the shirt. She picked Betsy's dress up,

4

turned it right side out, and hung it up on a peg beside her own.

"I like wearing Pa's shirt," Betsy said sleepily as she slipped down into her nest of quilts. "Reminds me of Pa."

Willa was silent. Suddenly, the air under the double canvas roof of the wagon was heavy. Betsy propped herself on her elbow and looked at her sister's face. *I shouldn't have mentioned Pa that way,* she told herself. *Willa gets so down when I do.* Betsy, who wanted to make the air bright again, grinned at Willa. "I like letting my legs show," she said wickedly. "I'm planning to wear tights and sing on a stage and wear skirts this short"—she held her hand up to her knee—"when we get to Oregon."

Willa looked shocked. She wasn't sure whether her sister was joking or not. With Betsy, you just never knew.

"And if I can't sing and dance," Betsy went on, "I'll go off with the Indians. They wear short clothes too, what I've seen of them."

"You've only seen boy Indians, so far," Willa said. "I hear the girls wear long dresses, just like us."

"Who said I was going to dress like the girls?" Betsy asked, her eyes fizzing and sparkling just like the root beer they had tasted—and fallen in love with—in St. Louis.

Willa laughed, sure at last that her sister was joking. "I swear, Bets, the farther west we go, the more I think you really *are* a savage."

"I think I'd make a good one," Betsy said. "Don't you?"

"It depends on what you mean by *good*," Willa answered.

Betsy yawned and snuggled back into the quilts. It might be May, but the nights were still chilly, and they were too far from the fire to get any heat from it. She closed her eyes and listened to the pleasant, comforting sounds of Willa tidying up the inside of the wagon. Willa was fearful under the open sky, but put her inside a house or a wagon and she could do half a dozen things while everyone else was standing still.

After a while, the tidying sounds halted. "Betsy?" Willa asked.

"Hmm?"

"Where do you suppose we are?"

Betsy thought a minute. "West of St. Louis, east of Oregon," she answered in a joking voice. The truth was, she didn't know exactly *where* they were. Willa had asked the one question she had no ready answer for.

Betsy woke with Toby's whine ringing in her ears.

"Bets?" Willa called in the darkness.

"Shh," Betsy hissed. "Listen." Maybe it was nothing—a rabbit or some night animal snuffling around their camp. But a cold snake of fear spiraled through her stomach as she remembered the fearful feeling that had haunted Willa all day. Willa had had feelings before, and they'd often proved to be right. Betsy slid her hand out and grasped the stock of Pa's rifle.

There was a muffled rustling sound. Toby sprang forward, his paws clawing at the tightly drawn canvas flap. Betsy grasped the thick fur at the back of his neck and pulled him back.

"Lord," Willa breathed.

"Keep Toby in here," Betsy whispered, turning the big dog over to her sister. "I don't want some Indian putting an arrow in him."

Willa clutched her sister's hand. "You're surely not going out there, are you, Bets?" she questioned anxiously.

"I'm not going to sit here and wait to get scalped," Betsy answered. Her heart was pounding in her chest, and her mouth was dry as dust. She drew aside the wagon flap and jumped down. Toby barked furiously at something unseen in the darkness.

"Who's there?" she called, raising the rifle to her shoulder.

"Tarnation!" a startled voice answered. "It's a naked girl!"

Betsy glanced down at her bare legs. "Next word and I shoot," she called back.

"No need for that," the voice replied. A young man stepped into the circle of firelight. In the dim glow, he seemed to Betsy to be made entirely of gold: gold-fringed buckskins, dark gold hair, skin tanned the color of new moccasins. The only points of contrast were his blue eyes and his white teeth, which flashed in a smile. "Howdy," he said.

Betsy kept the rifle on her shoulder. "Who are you?" she asked.

7

The stranger, she guessed, couldn't be more than eighteen. But the way he just kept on coming, not paying the rifle so much as a by-your-leave, made him seem so sure of himself—surer than even a grown man would be. "I was just about to ask you that," the stranger said.

Betsy stood her ground. "I asked you first," she said with a lift of her chin. Tall as she was, she saw that he was taller.

The stranger grinned at her. "If you don't know who I am, you must be a greenhorn. Why, I'm Charlie Freeman." He spread his arms wide to take in the darkness. "Mountain Charlie . . . Orphan Charlie . . . Handsome Charlie, according to the girls in St. Louis. The whole prairie knows who I am."

Willa's face appeared in the slit of the wagon flap. "Who is it, Bets?" she asked.

Betsy cocked her head. Her dark eyes reflected the gleam of the fire. "I don't know, Will," she answered dryly. "Some coyote wandered in from the prairie, I guess."

Handsome Charlie Freeman tipped his head back and laughed. "Now," he said, his bold blue eyes sweeping over Betsy's bare legs. "Who are you, and what are you doing out here all alone?"

"Who says we're alone?" Betsy asked warily, raising the rifle again.

"I do," Charlie said. He grinned. "No need to shoot me for being right about that, is there?" Graceful as a mountain lion, he walked over to Betsy. "Where're your folks?" he asked

"Dead," Willa answered. "Three weeks ago."

Charlie looked surprised. "And you've been lost out here all that time?"

"No one said we were lost," Betsy snapped.

"You're a mighty far ways from any trail," Charlie answered genially.

Betsy looked at him. "You know this country?" she asked.

"Like the back of my hand," Charlie answered. "I'm a guide."

Betsy's eyes lit up. "Can you take us a ways? We can pay you."

"On an ordinary day I'd be glad to," Charlie said matter-of-factly. "But I'm headed west."

"So're we," Betsy said. "We're going to Oregon."

Charlie's startled gasp whistled like the prairie wind. "You can't go west by yourselves," he said.

"We can if we have to," Betsy answered. She had surprised him, shocked him even. She was on firm ground now, and she flashed him a confident smile. "Even if you don't take us, we've got the map Pa left us. All we have to do is follow the Platte to the Snake, then follow the Snake right up to Oregon. I only asked you to take us 'cause I thought you might need the work."

"Charlie Freeman never needs work," he bragged. "Every wagon train bound west is begging me to guide them. On my way to join one now, matter of fact."

Willa slid out of the wagon, a heavy shawl hiding her nightgown. "You're joining a wagon train?" she asked eagerly. Willa turned to her sister. "Betsy, maybe we can—"

"Shh," Betsy said, cutting her sister off. "He's booked solid, didn't you hear?"

Charlie squatted by the fire and warmed his hands. "I am," he said. "And it's back east the two of you should be headed, not west. You'll never make it across the mountains, either one of you." He shot Betsy a sudden grin. "Still, I hate to leave you here to feed the wolves. Tell you what. I'm headed to Fort Kearney. I might take you that far."

"Thank you, Mr. Freeman," Willa said.

Betsy wanted to shove her sister into the wagon. *Mister* Freeman indeed! "I wouldn't want you to put yourself out any," she said, her voice crisp with sarcasm.

"Fort Kearney's where I'm headed," Charlie said. Betsy watched as he made himself comfortable beside their campfire, his hands locked behind his head.

"Suit yourself," she called back to him as she followed Willa up into the wagon.

"I always do," Charlie called back genially.

Inside the wagon, Willa's eyes were as round as a child's. "Oh Bets, I'm so glad you didn't listen to me about the fire—otherwise he'd never've found us. Isn't it lucky?" When Willa smiled, her face was as beautiful and serene as a summer day.

Betsy looked at her sister. "You call meeting that varmint lucky?"

"Of course I do. I knew from the moment I saw him he'd take us to Fort Kearney."

"How'd you know that?" Betsy asked.

"*You*, Bets," Willa answered. "He was taken with you. Anybody could've seen that."

Betsy tossed her head. "He's taken with himself, that's who he's taken with." In spite of herself, she felt two spots of rose creep into her cheeks. "Put out the lamp, Will, and go to sleep. More than likely he'll be gone in the morning."

"He'll be there, all right," Willa said calmly as she put out the light. Betsy heard the rustle of covers as she slipped back into bed. "One thing you have to admit, though, Bets," Willa whispered.

"What's that?"

"He *is* about the handsomest boy you've ever seen, isn't he?"

"I haven't seen any boys at all since we left St. Louis," Betsy replied stubbornly. "That doesn't make for much competition, does it?" She'd rather have died on the spot than admit that Charlie Freeman was as handsome as he thought he was.

# Chapter 2

In three days time, Charlie brought them to Fort Kearney, in the middle of Nebraska Territory. More than once during those days, Betsy wished she'd never set eyes on Charlie Freeman. He'd been a plague to her the whole time, never losing a chance to show off his own good opinion of himself.

But now she was almost ready to forgive him. The sight of so many wagons clustered outside the fort excited her. Her eyes sparkled, even when they landed on Charlie, who was riding just ahead of them.

"I didn't know we were so close," Betsy said as they rolled through the swinging wooden gates of Kearney.

Charlie turned and looked back at her over the rump of his horse. "You weren't close at all," he said with a grin. "If you'd kept on the way you were headed, you'd be on your way to Mexico right now."

Betsy pretended not to hear him. She wasn't going to let Charlie ruin her good spirits. Not now, with the Platte River so close she could almost taste it. No, the

Platte was their guide now. They had no need for Charlie Freeman—ever again.

"Did you see how many wagons are here?" Willa asked, her voice light with relief at reaching civilization again.

"Enough for three or four trains at least," Betsy answered. "One of them must be headed to Oregon. All we have to do is—"

"You, Charlie!" A raspy voice cut through the air. "Charlie Freeman! It's about time you showed yourself!"

Betsy and Willa watched as an old man—stiff in one leg, long white hair streaming out beneath a hat squashed flat on his head—limped nimbly toward Charlie.

"He looks a terror," Willa whispered. "Like one of the awful kings in the Bible."

"If he takes Charlie down a peg," Betsy replied, "he's a saint to me."

But the old man didn't take Charlie down the way Betsy had hoped. Instead, he embraced him, lifting him nearly off his feet. Betsy saw that in spite of his lameness the old man had powerful arms and shoulders.

After Charlie had slapped the old man on the back and the two had danced around each other like drunken goats, Charlie turned back to the wagon. "This is Captain Meeker," he said, as proud as if he were introducing President Polk himself. "Captain Mordechai Meeker. It's his train I'm guiding for."

Captain Meeker gave a gallant bow, then winked at

Charlie. "You certainly can meet 'em, Charlie," Captain Meeker said. "I never knew such a one for findin' pretty girls."

Betsy sat straight up. How many pretty girls did Charlie know, anyway? Not, of course, that it mattered to her. "We hired Charlie to guide us here," she said quickly, reaching one hand back into the wagon. "And this is where our paths divide." She opened her hand to reveal a heavy gold piece. "I think this should cover your fee," she said, stretching her palm toward Charlie.

"I couldn't take your money," Charlie said, a grin flashing across his face like summer lightning. "I was just doing my Christian duty," he continued, "saving you two from wolves and savages."

Betsy felt her cheeks glow. If it hadn't been a ten-dollar piece in her hand, she would have thrown it at him.

"That varmint!" she said after Charlie had gone off with Captain Meeker. "I hope that's the last we see of him." She picked up the thick leather reins. "Wouldn't I just love to show him, though!" Willa's bright giggle filled the air. "What's so funny?" Betsy demanded.

"How can you show him if you never see him again?" she asked. "Oh Bets, I think you do want to see him again, even if you won't say so."

Betsy slapped the reins over the broad backs of the oxen. As far as she was concerned, the conversation was closed—and Charlie Freeman was out of their lives for good.

\*     \*     \*

There were five trains provisioning at Fort Kearney, Betsy and Willa discovered. Four were bound for California, and one was bound for Oregon. The train bound for Oregon was to be led by Captain Mordechai Meeker.

Betsy's head snapped forward with indignation when she heard the news. "That *rat!*" she exploded to Willa. "That no-account Charlie Freeman! He knew we meant to go to Oregon, and he never let on that's where his train was headed. Do you remember, Will, that night I asked him—asked him straight out—where his wagon train was headed. And all he did was swallow those beans he was eating and say, 'Well, California, I expect.' *California?*"

"Maybe he really didn't know," Willa offered. "Maybe they kind of decided at the last minute."

Betsy turned to her sister. "Oh, Will, you don't really believe that, do you?"

Willa sighed. "No, I guess not. Are you going to talk to Captain Meeker about us going along?"

"Of course I am," Betsy answered firmly. "It's the only train headed our way."

"It's the only train Charlie Freeman is on, too," Willa said. There was just the slightest hint of teasing in her voice.

Betsy looked at Willa. "That's a cross we'll have to bear," she replied. "I guess if the mountains and the Indians don't kill us, Charlie Freeman won't either."

Willa went with Betsy to find Captain Meeker, but it was Betsy who did all the talking. "Can I talk to you

15

for a minute?" she asked politely, relieved to see that Charlie was nowhere in sight.

Mordechai Meeker grinned. "Well, it's Charlie's little lady, so 'tis." Then suddenly his face turned sober. "But if he's broken your heart, there's nothin' I can do about it. No, Charlie's his own man, and it isn't likely he'll soon settle down. So, young miss—"

Betsy felt a sting of annoyance. Why did everybody in creation think so much of Charlie Freeman? Even Willa, her own sister, seemed charmed by him. "I don't want to talk about Charlie," Betsy said.

"No?" Captain Meeker looked relieved.

*As if he gets broken hearts in here every day,* Betsy thought. She forced herself to smile sweetly. "No," she said. "It's your wagon train I want to talk about."

The old man smiled broadly, revealing a row of jagged teeth. "Finest crew to be had," he said. "Reach Oregon before the first frost."

Betsy knew that wasn't possible. No one reached Oregon before the first frost, because the first frost came high in the mountains when it was still summer down below. Betsy didn't comment on it, though. Instead she said, "That's why Willa—my sister—and I want to sign on with you," she said. "Because you *are* the finest."

Willa had never seen her sister flirt before. Not right out this way, her eyes warming the old man and taking him back over the years to his youth. *It's shameless,* Willa's look told Betsy. *Shameless.* But Betsy already knew it was shameless. She just hoped it was shameless enough to work.

Captain Meeker spat thoughtfully into the dirt. A stream of tobacco juice missed the hem of Betsy's skirt by inches. Betsy didn't budge. "We're already provisioned," she continued. "And we can pay our way in advance. In gold."

The old man studied them as if they were a team of horses he was thinking of buying. "You don't look too hefty, neither one o' you."

"We're strong, though," Betsy said quickly. "Both of us. Never sick, not one day in a thousand. You wouldn't be sorry, Captain Meeker," she hurried on. "We wouldn't—wouldn't die on you, you know."

Captain Meeker spat again. It seemed to help him concentrate. "Well, like as you might not," he said. "Sometimes it's them just your age comes through best—too old to die young, too young to die old. Providing, that is, that neither o' you is expectin'."

"Babies?" Willa gasped in embarrassment.

"My sister and I aren't married," Betsy said.

"My experience," Captain Meeker said, "is that babies don't always know who's married and who isn't. And havin' a baby on the trail is about the worst thing that can happen to a woman."

Betsy believed him. "You don't need to worry about us," she said, thinking, *Ma would die all over again if she knew I was having this conversation with a strange old man who's spitting closer to my skirt every minute*. She caught Willa's eye and smiled reassuringly. *But Ma's not here*, Betsy reminded herself, *and I want to go to Oregon!*

Captain Meeker was thoughtful. "It isn't the trail so

much that weighs against things," he said. "It's my conscience."

"Conscience?" Betsy struggled to hide her surprise. Conscience. She hadn't supposed Captain Meeker had one.

"S'pose I do bring you through," the old man said. "What then? Oregon's no place for two young ladies on their own. I can't have it on my head that I brought you west and then left you there."

Betsy laughed so genuinely that even Willa was fooled. "Didn't I explain that part?" she asked, her eyes warming again. "That's why we've got to get to Oregon. Our folks are there waiting for us. We were coming along with another family—our uncle and aunt—but they got sick and died. If we don't get to Oregon this season, Ma and Pa'll be out of their minds with worry. They won't know what happened to us."

Betsy saw the old man's face soften. "Well, when you put it that way. . . ." He winked at Betsy. "You won't make me sorry I took you on, now? Promise?"

"Promise," Betsy said, and they shook on it. She smiled like an angel all the way back to their wagon.

"That was a terrible lie you told back there, Betsy," Willa said as they walked.

Betsy grinned, revealing a tiny chip in her tooth that she had gotten once trying to shoe her own horse. "I thought it was a pretty *good* lie, myself. It's going to get us to Oregon, isn't it?"

"But what's going to happen when Captain Meeker finds out the truth?" Willa asked, her pale face luminous in the settling dusk. "Charlie's bound to tell him."

Betsy hugged her sister. "Think about it, Will," she said. "What *is* going to happen? Nothing, that's what. Captain Meeker can't very well send us back, can he?" She danced ahead of Willa in the dusk and collided with a firm shape. A pleasant, slightly smoky scent came to her, and she felt two strong hands reach out to steady her. Betsy squinted in the dusk and saw Charlie Freeman's blue eyes staring at her.

"Out enjoying the scenery, I see," he said teasingly.

Betsy squared her shoulders. "As a matter of fact, we were attending to some business," she said.

"Business?" Charlie asked. Betsy could see sparks of curiosity in his eyes.

"We were looking for a wagon train to sign up with," she said.

Charlie laughed. "Can't say I didn't warn you about that," he said. "I told you no trail captain worth his salt'd be fool enough to take you on."

"As a matter of fact," Betsy said, "some fool *did* take us on."

Charlie's eyebrows went up. "Who?" he asked.

"Mordechai Meeker!" Betsy answered.

Charlie was stunned. And, for once, he had nothing to say. If Betsy had to drink alkaline water all the way to Oregon, the memory of Charlie's look would make it taste as sweet as spring water to her.

# Chapter 3

IT WAS LOVELY RIDING THROUGH THE SPRINGTIME prairie. They were the third wagon in a chain of twenty-two, a size Captain Meeker said was just right for westering. "Long enough to scare off trouble, short enough to keep clear o' our own dust," was the way he put it.

Charlie Freeman, of course, had opinions of his own. "Twenty, twenty-five wagons is about right for drawing up quick, 'case Indians come," he observed.

Betsy glared at him. She didn't need anyone to go planting Indian fears in Willa's head just now. "I thought you were our guide," she told him. "What are you riding back here for? Are you lost?"

Charlie laughed and tipped his hat to her. "Why, I'm just making sure you ladies don't drop out of sight."

Betsy wrapped the reins around her fist. "If you're waiting to see us turn around," she said, "you've got a long wait coming." Charlie grinned at her again, his blue eyes flashing. Then he wheeled his horse in a magnificent half-circle and galloped off. "For someone who's supposed to be leading us west," Betsy grumbled, "he sure spends a lot of time at the tail end of things."

Willa, wisely, didn't answer her. Instead she turned her attention to the wagons ahead of them and behind. "It's like living in a house, isn't it, Bets?" she asked. "With neighbors on both sides, I mean."

"I suppose it is," Betsy answered. She could still see the tawny gold square of Charlie's buckskin shirt, circling far out on the prairie ahead of them.

"Let's see," Willa said, counting the wagons on her fingers. "There's the Nilssons ahead of us, and the Fords ahead of them. And the Taylors behind us—"

"And more Taylors behind *them*," Betsy put in. Charlie had disappeared from sight, and she gave her attention back to Willa. "How many of them do you suppose there are?"

"Taylors? Well, there's the seven little ones, and the five older ones. . . ."

"And the parents," Betsy continued, "and that toothless old grandmother."

"And an uncle, I think," Willa said, "and some stray cousins."

"No wonder they keep spilling out of their wagons," Betsy laughed.

It was true. Everywhere you looked there was a Taylor. Already, even though it was only their second day out, Kitty Taylor had spent an entire afternoon making friends with Betsy and Willa. And John Taylor, the oldest and liveliest, had ridden up and down the train looking for pretty girls.

"I'm glad the Taylors' wagons are *behind* us," Willa said.

"Why?" Betsy asked.

"Because if they got to Oregon *before* we did, they'd fill up the whole territory."

It wasn't the funniest joke Betsy had ever heard, but it was the first one Willa had told since their parents had died. Betsy laughed all the harder because of it.

She was still laughing when, ahead of them, Ingrid Nilsson's white-blond head appeared at the back of her wagon. *"Flod!"* Ingrid called excitedly, her thin face flushing with excitement. *"Flod! Flod!"*

Betsy shook her head to show that she didn't understand. Rolfe Nilsson and his wife were Swedish, and the only English words they seemed to know were "hi" and "work," which they pronounced "hay" and "verk." Of all the people on the train, only Willa, by some combination of luck and intuition, seemed to understand them when they talked. "What's she saying, do you suppose?" Betsy asked.

*"Flod!"* Ingrid called again. She climbed down from the back of her wagon and walked toward them, her two-month-old baby in her arms.

Willa studied the young woman's face carefully. "Oh," Willa said, smiling suddenly. "It's the river. We must be near the river."

Ingrid was close enough now to catch Willa's words. *"Ja,* river," she shouted, enormously pleased with herself. "River!"

A thrill of anticipation shot through Betsy. She shaded her eyes with her hand and squinted toward the horizon. The whole wagon train was anxious for their first sight of the Platte River, the highway that would take them a thousand miles west.

"I can't see it," Betsy said impatiently. She thrust the reins into Willa's hands. "Take these, Will," she added as she scrambled to her feet and climbed up to stand on the wagon seat.

"Betsy!" Willa's voice was shocked. "Get down from there—you'll break your neck!"

"No I won't," Betsy answered blithely. She held on to the iron hoop of the canopy with one hand, balancing herself against the jolt and roll of the wagon. She took a deep breath. The view was magnificent. It was like walking on an ocean, a big green ocean starred with wildflowers. In the distance, a winding fringe of cottonwood trees showed her where the Platte was.

"Your ankles are showing," Willa said in resigned despair.

"I may ride all the way to Oregon like this," Betsy cried. "You can see the whole world from up here, Will."

It was almost true. From the wagon seat she could see Captain Meeker riding at the front of the train. Along with him were Jed Marsh, the hunter, and Blue Star, their half-white, half-Indian scout. She could see Charlie Freeman as well. He'd reined his horse to a standstill and was half turned in the saddle, staring straight at her. She saw his hand flash in the air, a signal she decided to ignore.

"Do you do this every day?" a voice called up from below.

Betsy looked down and saw John Taylor on his big bay horse. He was grinning up at her, his dark eyes full of life.

"Every day but Sunday," Betsy answered lightly. From the first she'd taken a liking to John. He reminded her of a big, lovable dog, good-natured and a little aimless. "Why, you can see clear to Oregon from here."

"'S that so," John answered slowly, as if he half believed her.

Betsy planted her feet firmly, adjusting to the pitch of the seat as the wagon bounced over uneven ground. "You know," she said, "there's a real knack to this, once you catch on." She felt a thrill of excitement, riding high above them all. It was special, like flirting with a handsome boy or having a dress prettier than anyone else's. She had no intention of climbing down, no matter how shocked Willa looked.

The clatter of hooves sliced through Betsy's pleasure. Charlie was riding swiftly toward them, a look of disapproval on his handsome, suntanned face. "You break your neck and you slow the whole train down, don't you know that?" he asked angrily, his blue eyes raking over her from head to toe. "What in heck are you trying to do up there anyway? Show off your ankles?"

Betsy's cheeks went scarlet. "It's no business of yours *what* I'm doing up here," she replied with a toss of her head. "You're supposed to be guiding this train, not—"

Her sentence ended in a rush of air. The wagon

jolted suddenly as it rolled over a rock. Betsy lost her balance and felt herself falling. She grabbed wildly but there was nothing to hold on to. She tumbled forward and landed in Charlie's lap with a jolt. His strong arms held her tightly, and his face was so close to hers that she could feel the warmth of his breath on her cheeks. "I'm sorry," she said, her cheeks hot with embarrassment.

Charlie's eyes danced. "No need to be," he said. "Girls have done a sight more than that to get into my arms."

Betsy struggled against him, but he held her firm as his horse moved smoothly beneath them. "You're a coyote, you know that? A conceited, cross-eyed coyote. I can't imagine why any girl in her right mind would even talk to you."

Charlie was unconcerned. "Girls in Oregon love me," he answered.

"There must be a big shortage of men in Oregon then, that's all I can say," Betsy shot back. "And you can put me down now."

Charlie's arms tightened a fraction, bringing his chest close against her. "You sure you want to get down?" he asked, a grin showing his even white teeth. "I'm not exactly sure you do. Why, I think you're *enjoying* all this."

"I am *not* enjoying this," Betsy shrieked, her voice so piercing that Willa, Kitty, and John looked up in alarm. "I don't even *like* you."

"Fine thanks that is," Charlie said, his brow furrowing in pretended hurt. "I was only trying to keep you from breaking your neck." He released her at last, and she sprang to the ground.

"Well, I didn't break my neck," she replied, glaring up at him. "I didn't even come close. I was just getting a look at the Platte, that's all."

Charlie had already wheeled his horse around and had begun to ride off. "You'll see plenty of the Platte soon enough," he called back over his shoulder. "Only a greenhorn wouldn't think of that."

Betsy watched him ride off, her body still tingling from his touch.

A day later, in the middle of the afternoon, it began to rain. Betsy and Willa watched as curtain after curtain of water poured across the prairie. In less than half an hour, both of them were drenched to their stockings. When the rain persisted through the night, it soaked the double layer of oiled canvas that covered the wagon. Rivulets of water ran down the iron ribs of the wagon, and Willa spent half the night moving tins and buckets around to catch the drizzle.

"It's like drowning and sleeping at the same time," Willa complained when a new leak began dripping down onto her face.

Betsy didn't hear her. She was bone tired from the day's drive and lay in her damp quilts as peacefully as if she were in the middle of a huge feather bed. Betsy, Willa noted enviously, was like a cat—she could sleep anywhere, under any conditions.

They rose at dawn in a slow drizzle that, by mid-

morning, had turned into a steady downpour. At noon
it was raining too hard to make fires, so they had a cold
camp. Betsy and Willa, who shared food and coffee
with the men of the train in return for the meat the men
hunted, had little to offer for lunch. Damp bacon, stale
bread, and cold coffee were the best they could do.
Still, no one complained—not even Charlie, who
thanked Betsy for the meal.

"Rain much longer," he said, "and we'll all be fish."

Betsy was forced to admire him. He was the wettest
of them all, riding horseback since dawn without any
protection but the clothes on his back. Water rolled off
him in sheets, and his dark gold hair was pasted flat to
his head, but he didn't seem to mind.

Willa, standing near them, gazed somberly at the
Platte. The soggy brim of her bonnet clung to her head
like the petals of a wet flower. "It looks deeper than
the door to Hell," she said, pushing her bonnet brim
back with one hand and pointing toward the river.
"How are we going to get across it, anyway?"

Charlie smiled kindly at her. "Well, we won't have
to cross it at all for a while yet. Not for a couple
hundred miles. But don't worry. The Platte only looks
deep. It isn't really. It's just muddy."

"Really?" Willa's face brightened. She was terrified
of deep water because she'd never learned to swim.

Betsy joined Charlie in trying to keep Willa's spirits
up. "Didn't I tell you what Captain Meeker said about
it?" she asked.

"No. What, Bets?"

"He said the Platte's just an overgrown stream that's got famous for being too muddy to swim in and too thick to drink."

"Kind of like this coffee," Charlie said, taking a swallow.

Willa laughed. Betsy bit her tongue. She couldn't be mad at Charlie, not when he was doing such a good job of cheering Willa up.

Later that afternoon they had their first real test of the journey. The temperature dropped and the wind rose. Cold rain whipped the wagons, and the ground, churned by hooves and wagon wheels, turned to thick mud. With no sun overhead, Betsy and Willa had no way of telling time. The afternoon became an endless twilight. When Betsy saw Captain Meeker give the signal to halt, she breathed a sigh of relief. Her hands and arms ached from hauling on the reins all day, trying to keep the oxen from miring themselves and the wagon in the mud. She looked forward to the relief of making camp for the night, no matter how wet and miserable that camp might be.

But to Betsy's dismay the halt was only temporary. They weren't stopping for the night at all. Instead, Captain Meeker was preparing to take them across a flood stream.

As Charlie told them later, the captain was concerned that the river would swell even more if they stopped that night. In ordinary weather the stream was nothing but a snake-sized body of water winding toward the Platte. But two days of rain had swollen the stream and sent it crashing over its banks.

Betsy's first glimpse of it filled her with anxiety. The current was swift and strong—the kind of current that could catch you and drag you under. Not that she worried for herself. No, she was sure she could swim the roaring Snake River itself if she had to. It was Willa. Willa wouldn't have a chance in water like that.

The wagons were crossing in pairs. The Fords' wagon, the first in the train, and the Nilssons' wagon were midway in the stream. Rolfe was waist-deep in water, urging the oxen on. Betsy could see Ingrid's frightened face, pale as a quarter moon in the gray rain. Her baby's cry could be heard even above the rushing water.

When the Nilsson wagon lurched to one side, Ingrid grabbed frantically, barely managing to hang on. Again Betsy thought of Willa. Suddenly she scrambled back into the wagon and emerged with a length of rope.

"What are you doing with that?" Willa asked.

"Sit still," Betsy replied. Working quickly, she wound the rope twice around Willa's waist. Then she looped each end under the canvas wagon top and wound it around the iron hoop that was anchored to the side of the wagon. By the time it was their turn to cross, Willa was tied securely to the wagon.

Betsy jumped down and grabbed the harness of the lead ox. Slowly, she began coaxing the team into the cold, swirling water.

She felt a tug as the current caught her skirt. It was so heavy with water that it almost pulled her off balance. She felt her feet ache as she dug her bare toes into the mud. After a long minute, she regained her balance and took a step forward. *Darn this skirt,* she thought to herself as she felt it dragging at her knees.

The first Taylor wagon crossed with them. Betsy heard John and his father "hawing" at the oxen. She saw the wrinkled face of old Mrs. Taylor, the grandmother, above the wagon seat. And slowly—more slowly than she would have thought possible—she saw the wagon twist, tilt, and fall sideways into the stream.

Panic seized Betsy. What if their wagon tipped over? She hadn't thought of that when she had tied Willa to the seat. She glanced at the Taylors' floundering oxen, at the white canvas of the wagon barely visible above the water, and at the old grandmother who had made a sprightly swim to the other side. She thought of Willa under water, tied to the wagon seat, gulping water and death into her lungs.

"We can't tip over, that's all," she told the lead ox. He took a trusting step forward. Betsy patted his wet forehead. The oxen took another step forward, then another and another. Betsy cooed to them above the rain, calling each of them by name and offering encouragement. She didn't believe in yelling at oxen the way most men did. She just talked to them, more gently than she talked to most people because she believed oxen *were* gentler than most people she had ever known.

It seemed to work. While the men were still in the middle of the stream trying to right the Taylor wagon, Betsy's oxen were struggling up the opposite bank.

"Do you need help?" Charlie called. He was off his

horse and wading toward her. His voice, for once, had no hint of cockiness in it.

Betsy shook her head. "I can make it."

He looked at her a long time. "All right," he said slowly.

Betsy looked back at him. His eyes were warm in the cold afternoon. "Thanks anyway, Charlie," she said. The words felt funny in her mouth, and she realized it was the first time she had ever called him by his name.

Once the wagon was safe on the bank, Betsy waded back across the stream. She worked all night long, helping to bring wagons across. Sometimes the water rose above her waist. Once she lost her balance and was carried twenty yards downstream before she could swim to shore. By the time they made camp, every muscle in her body ached, even muscles in little out-of-the-way places like her fingertips and toes.

To everyone's relief, the rain had slackened enough to build fires. The Taylors unpacked their soaked belongings and spread them everywhere to dry. The sight of so many pairs of stockings and underwear, so many skirts, pants, and blouses hanging on the ends of sticks struck everyone as funny. After the tense afternoon, the wagon train was in good spirits again.

"We weathered the storm well enough," everyone told everyone else proudly. "We'll get to Oregon all right."

Captain Meeker said nothing to dampen their spirits, even though he knew the stream crossing that day was nothing compared to the high, cold mountains and the churning, rock-edged rivers beyond the Platte.

Willa built a warm fire for Betsy and baked some cornbread. But Betsy fell asleep by the fire long before the bread was ready. Willa found a dry blanket and put it over her sister. There was no sense in waking her up—the wagon was so wet inside that Betsy would be just as well off on the ground.

While Betsy slept, Willa began setting the wagon right again. She raised the canvas top on one side, exposing the inside of the wagon to the warming fire. She hung their damp clothes and bedding over the edge of the wagon to dry, and she had almost finished when Charlie appeared, carrying a tin bowl in one hand.

"I . . . uh, Mrs. Daily back a ways made some soup. I thought Betsy might like some."

"Betsy's asleep," Willa answered gently.

"Oh." Charlie looked disappointed. His glance fell on Betsy's sleeping form. Her chestnut hair fell across her face, reflecting the red glow of the fire. It seemed like a long time before he turned to Willa again. "Well, I . . . good night, then."

"Good night," Willa answered. She smiled after his retreating form. He wasn't the kind of boy for her, but she appreciated him nonetheless. Charlie Freeman was really very kind. She wished Betsy could see that.

# Chapter 4

THE SPRING DAYS SPREAD OVER THE WAGON TRAIN AS smoothly as silk canopies. There were more streams to cross, but none of them were swollen with rain. Betsy never again took the chance of tying her sister to the wagon during a crossing, and Willa, to Betsy's relief, never asked why.

During the high, sunny days when Kitty Taylor joined them on the wagon seat, all the troubles and dangers of the Oregon crossing seemed very far away.

"I don't know what all the fuss is about," Kitty would say, drawing her bright red lips into a pout. "I think they just talk about how bad it is to scare people off, that's all." Like her brother John, Kitty had glossy black hair and dark eyes that glittered with mischief. She grinned at the two girls. "I'm just glad Pa wasn't fool enough to listen. It's plain that anybody with a brain can get himself to Oregon in one piece and—"

She broke off suddenly, remembering that her new friends' parents had died in the middle of the trail. "I'm sorry," she said, her dark eyes losing their sparkle. "I forgot. I just . . . forgot."

"It's all right," Willa said comfortingly.

But even as she said it, Betsy could see her sister sliding into the murky swamp of remembering. *This is never going to do,* Betsy told herself. She started humming a song—"My Old Kentucky Home"—but realized at once that it was a poor choice. When neither Willa nor Kitty joined in, the song died in the air. Finally, she prodded her sister with her sharp, slim elbow. "You can tell me now, Will, and you too, Kitty," she said with an impish smile. "There's no one here to listen. Have you ever kissed a boy?"

Kitty's eyes lit up like lanterns. Willa turned pink, then a violent shade of red. "How *could* you ask such a thing, Betsy?" Willa asked. "You know Ma said never to—"

Betsy cut her off. "Why are you the color of rhubarb sauce if you never did?" she asked. She scanned the fleecy clouds overhead, as if searching for an answer. "I bet it was Henry Stolz," she mused.

"It was *not* Henry Stolz," Willa protested. "It was Tom—"

Willa stopped, biting down on her lip.

Betsy's shriek of delight rippled through the air. "Tom Deane! I knew it! I bet it was last winter at Lizzie Nelson's wedding—that time you wore my pink dress."

"It didn't fit you anymore anyway," Willa said, hoping to steer the conversation in a different direction.

"No, it didn't," Betsy agreed. It was a backward way of doing things—giving her clothes to her older sister when she grew too tall for them.

"Who's Tom Deane?" Kitty asked eagerly.

Betsy kept after Willa. "What was it like?" she asked.

"The dress?" Willa questioned back, her gray eyes innocent. "Very nice, except for the spot where you'd ruined the hem."

"Not the dress, you idiot," Betsy said impatiently. *"Kissing."*

Now Willa turned a sharp look on her sister. "You mean to tell me, Betsy Monroe, that you haven't already found out all about kissing yourself?"

Willa's serious eyes and Kitty's sparkling ones stared unflinchingly at Betsy. If she lied to them now, the look in their eyes said, they would never forgive her.

Betsy gazed up at the clouds again, a look of supreme unconcern on her face. "Well," she told the clouds, "maybe." A slow smile crept across her face. She looked back at Kitty and her sister. "All right— yes, I do know."

Willa was horrified at first. She had suspected certain things about her sister, but this was her first actual proof of it. "But you're only *fifteen!*" she protested. Then her eyes, like Kitty's, began to dance with excitement. "Who was it?"

"Which time?" Betsy asked, fully enjoying the look of shock her question caused.

"Which *time?*" Willa echoed. "Oh, Betsy, you really *are* terrible!"

"I think it's *wonderful,*" Kitty said, her voice full of awe.

Betsy turned to her new friend. "How about you, Kitty?" she asked.

"Me?" Kitty made a quick, dismissing gesture with her hand. "The boys I kissed back home don't matter now. I'm never going to see them again, so why waste time thinking about them? But I'll tell you what," she said seriously. "I've made a careful study of every boy on this train, and there aren't but a half-dozen with us even *worth* kissing."

"Who are they?" Willa asked eagerly, more than a little surprised at herself.

"Well, I suppose I've got to include John, even though he's my brother and it's a mystery to me what girls see in him, and Rolfe Nilsson, who's already got a wife, and Lucas Martin, who's also got a wife, and George Browne, who asked Pa if he could visit me on Sundays, and Freddy Turner, in the next-to-last wagon, and—"

She paused, purposely heightening the suspense.

"And who?" Betsy asked, thinking that Kitty had named almost everyone even remotely good-looking.

"Who do you think?" Kitty asked, her eyes turning dreamy. "Charlie, of course."

Betsy felt as if she'd been hit between the shoulder blades with a lightning bolt. "Charlie Freeman?"

"Of course," Kitty said. "I think kissing him would be the most *wonderful* . . ."

Betsy slapped the reins on the backs of the oxen. "Myself," she said tersely, "I'd rather kiss a bobcat."

She was disappointed in Kitty. She had thought Kitty was smart—too smart to be taken in by Charlie's swaggering and boasting. And, though she didn't admit it to herself, she was mad, too. The image of Kitty in Charlie's arms made her furious. She thought of Charlie holding Kitty's small, slender form, brushing her dark hair back from her temples, telling her what a sweet and delicate thing she was. "Oh, that liar," she hissed under her breath.

"What?" Willa asked.

"Nothing," Betsy said, struggling to push her anger back into its small, secret hiding place. "I'm just tired from driving, I guess."

What, she wondered, was wrong with her? Why did it matter to her *who* Kitty Taylor had eyes for? And why did the thought of Kitty with Charlie trouble her so?

The only thing that marred those fine early days was the sight of turn-arounds. Four days out of Kearney, they came across two families who had dropped out of the train ahead of them. *We're turning back,* the looks on their grim faces said. *Turning back, so don't ask questions!*

The farther Captain Meeker led them from the civilized oasis of Kearney, the more forlorn and pathetic the turn-arounds became. Some had lost their oxen to poisoned water. Others had lost their beef cattle and horses to Indians. Those were the lucky ones. The unlucky were those who had lost members of their families to illness and accident.

Betsy, Willa, and the other members of the train were full of sympathy, but Captain Meeker forbade them to give their own supplies to the turn-arounds. "Lost their nerve, that's what they've lost," he said unsympathetically, and he spat, dampening the prairie earth with a stream of brown tobacco juice.

One afternoon they came upon an abandoned wagon. It loomed like a ghost on the prairie floor, its cover drawn up on one side and its iron ribs glinting in the sun. Black, slim-winged birds circled overhead, and only after a long time did Betsy realize what had happened: The entire family in the wagon had succumbed to some kind of illness, the Indians had taken the horses and cattle, and only the buzzards—and the bodies—remained.

By unspoken agreement, the train slowed as they neared the wagon. Betsy, like everyone else, reined her oxen to a halt. She looked up in time to see Mordechai Meeker pounding down the line of wagons. "What's goin' on back here?" he demanded. "I didn't call a halt."

Samuel Browne jumped down from his wagon. He already had a shovel in his hand, as did his son George. "We've surely got to bury those folks," he said to Meeker. "Can't just leave them there."

There was a murmur of support, and, almost before he knew it, Captain Meeker was ringed by earnest, well-meaning men, each one holding a shovel. As Captain Meeker dismounted, Betsy strained to catch his words. "Cholera" floated to her over the air, and "contamination."

The discussion went on for several more minutes before the men went back to their wagons. Betsy saw

Captain Meeker return to the front of the train and signal to Blue Star, the scout. Then Blue Star rode swiftly toward the wagon. The whole train watched as the half-Indian scout built the smallest of fires, dipped his arrows into it, and sent the arrows flying into the canvas side of the wagon.

If it weren't so terrible, Betsy thought, it might have been beautiful. Slow flames embraced the wagon, whipping lightly in the wind. Curls of dark smoke spiraled through the air, and a tatter of calico fluttered in the turning, red-gold flames.

When the wagon and its contents crumbled into a heap of cinders, the train began to move again. But Betsy noticed that from that day on people didn't scan the horizon quite as eagerly as before. The ghost wagon had chilled them all.

The trail, like a sea washing endlessly up over the same shore, brought them good things, too. One day they saw what everyone at first thought must be a mirage—a man on a mule so loaded down that its brisk trot was a miracle of strength and determination.

But as the wagon train drew closer, the mirage developed texture and solidity. Betsy, who could now stand on the wagon seat with ease, described the details to those below her. "Whoever he is, he's tall," she said. "Feet almost dragging on the ground. And he's got all sorts of boxes and things packed in front of him."

"What do you mean, *things?*" Willa asked impatiently.

"I don't know," Betsy answered, shading her eyes

and squinting. "Boards or something like that. Big, flat boards."

The boards turned out to be canvases, and the mule's owner turned out to be Nash Whitcomb, an artist who'd set out, as he explained, "to paint the great epic of the American West."

"By yourself?" Charlie exploded with contempt. "What a fool thing to do."

"*I* think it's wonderful," Betsy answered before the artist himself had a chance to reply. She shot Charlie a challenging look. "Anyone can head west these days. Only someone like Mr. Whitcomb can paint it."

Betsy made no attempt to hide her admiration for the newcomer. Nash Whitcomb, older than Charlie by a good five years, was dark and elegantly dressed. In fact, he still wore the silk shirts he'd set out from Boston in. And even if they were a bit the worse for wear, Betsy thought they looked dashing.

Captain Meeker agreed to take the artist on as a member of the company, provided he'd exchange the silk shirts for something more practical and make himself useful during the day. He did, but that was only during the day. At night, the silk shirts came out again, and, with sleeves rolled up to his elbows, he would set his canvases up and begin to paint.

Betsy was especially proud of Nash Whitcomb's first painting. Based on her description, it showed the ghost wagon, alone and burning on the prairie. In the painting, Whitcomb had made the wagon the victim of an Indian attack—Indian ponies moved like shadows on the horizon, and the burning wagon was quilled, like a porcupine, with arrows.

When Charlie saw the painting, he recognized the wagon at once. "Cholera's what they died of," he said flatly, his eyes resting only briefly on Betsy.

Whitcomb smiled, his teeth white beneath his dark mustache. "Cholera isn't very romantic, is it?" he asked good-naturedly.

"Nope," Charlie responded. "It isn't. It's what they died of, though. Cholera kills a whole lot more folks than Indians do." Then, without saying anything else, he walked off. Betsy watched him go.

"What are you smiling about?" Willa asked, nudging her sister.

Betsy looked surprised. "I wasn't smiling," she answered.

"Yes you were," Willa said. She sighed. She knew what Betsy was up to, even if Betsy didn't. "You might as well admit it," she said.

"Admit what?" Betsy asked apprehensively.

"You're trying to make Charlie Freeman jealous, aren't you?"

Her words caught Betsy off guard. "Make Charlie jealous? Well, he certainly deserves it. But you're wrong, Will. I'm not trying anything of the sort."

Willa said nothing. She knew her sister well enough to tell when she'd struck a nerve, and she left it at that.

One night Betsy woke to the sound of voices in the wagon. "What is it?" she asked, jerking her body up so quickly that she banged her head against a skillet that dangled overhead.

"Shh," Willa said soothingly in the darkness. "It's Rolfe. Ingrid's sick, and I'm just going to sit with her a while."

"Oh," Betsy said, relief in her voice as she sank back down in the darkness. People were always getting sick and getting well again. It was part of life, a part she didn't worry too much about. Before Willa was out of the wagon, Betsy was sound asleep again.

The next time she opened her eyes, the sun was slanting through the canvas canopy of the wagon. Groggy with sleep, Betsy gasped like a swimmer surfacing from a deep dive. Something was wrong, but what?

*The sun!* she thought suddenly. It was so high in the sky—the wagon train should have been on the road hours ago. Frantically, she looked out the flap of the wagon, half expecting to discover that everyone else had deserted her. But no, the other wagons were still there. Betsy sank back on her quilts, her head pounding. The bright sun made her feel dizzy.

Suddenly, Willa's face, drawn and tired from lack of sleep, appeared at the wagon flap.

Relief flooded through Betsy at the sight of her sister. She bounced up off the bed.

"Don't come near me, Bets," Willa said warningly. She made no move to mount the step-up into the wagon.

Betsy froze. The heavy nightmare feeling came back

again. "What's wrong, Will?" Blue veins showed beneath Willa's white skin.

"Nearly half the train's sick, Bets," Willa said, her voice a rushing stream of emotion. "Captain Meeker's trying to get enough men to drive the wagons."

Betsy shook her tangled hair, trying to loosen the cobwebs of confusion from her mind. Then it came back to her—Rolfe coming for Willa in the middle of the night because Ingrid was sick. But Willa had made it sound like nothing. Betsy took a step forward. "What about Ingrid?" she asked.

Tears welled up in Willa's soft eyes. "Ingrid's dead," she whispered. Instinctively, Betsy moved toward her sister, arms out. Willa sprang backward, away from the wagon. "Oh, Bets," she pleaded, *"please* don't touch me. You can't—it's cholera."

Betsy was stunned. First Ma and Pa, now Ingrid. The image of the ghost wagon rose before her, wreathed in flames, a burning ship that could carry them all to their doom. Cholera! It was as if the disease itself was chasing them west.

# Chapter 5

THEY STAYED IN CAMP FOR THREE DAYS. WHEN THEY left, a cluster of graves marked their passing. Besides Ingrid Nilsson, half a dozen other emigrants had died, most of them within hours of each other.

During the three days, Betsy had a grim chance to observe cholera in all its swiftness. The disease was like wildfire, striking and flaming through the body with lightning speed. A person could be well at breakfast, dizzy with illness at noon, and dead by sunset. Betsy's own parents had died from it only a few hours apart, and she and Willa had been abruptly orphaned. More than any other disease, cholera was feared for its suddenness. There were no warnings and no goodbyes.

Betsy, like everyone else lucky enough to be on his or her feet, didn't have time to think about her own health. She was too busy worrying about Willa— Willa, who had sat with Ingrid and held her hands all through the last minutes of her life. If ever there was someone courting disease, Betsy thought with an ache of apprehension, it was her sister.

But Willa bloomed as fresh and rosy as ever. Methodically, she set about sorting through Ingrid's belongings, burning the clothes and sheets that must be burned, putting keepsakes away in one of the huge round-topped trunks. It was a task that would have broken Rolfe's heart, just as the cry of Ingrid's baby was sometimes more than he could bear.

Anyone with eyes could see the truth—that Rolfe would never have survived those first few days without Willa's tender, unselfish care. Watching them from a distance, Betsy felt an odd flash of feeling that she couldn't, at first, identify. Then, slowly, she realized what it was—envy. She envied her sister.

It was a feeling entirely foreign to Betsy. She had never consciously wanted anything that didn't belong to her. But now she envied Willa because Willa was needed. Who in the world, Betsy wondered, would ever need *her?* And who would she ever need in return? She pushed the thought out of her mind. Some questions didn't have answers.

The first day they resumed travel, Willa rode with Betsy, bouncing Ingrid's baby on her knee. But the next morning she asked Betsy if she would mind her riding with Rolfe. "He's so lonely," Willa explained, her gray eyes grave. "And having the baby along seems to cheer him some. But I don't want to leave you alone, either."

Betsy smiled. "It's all right, Will. Really. I'll be just fine. You know me."

But driving alone was not the same. The hours

stretched long, and she was aware of her body aching as she bounced on the wagon seat. Betsy felt years older than she had felt just a few weeks ago. Then it struck her, suddenly, that she *was* older—a year older, at least. Her sixteenth birthday had come and gone in the cholera camp, but neither she nor Willa had remembered it. And now that she did remember it, there was no one to tell. Well then, she thought, she would just tuck it away. She would save it for some year of her life when she needed a sixteenth birthday. Then she would take it out and give herself the biggest party Oregon had ever seen.

The thought made Betsy smile, and just as she was smiling Charlie Freeman rode up beside her. "You're healthy as ever, I see," he said teasingly.

It was the first time they'd seen each other in four days, and Charlie's quick smile coaxed a reflex smile from Betsy. "I've never been sick a day in my life," she replied. "I thought you knew that."

"I suppose I did," he answered. "Or I should've. Glad to see you haven't lost heart," he said, and trotted off.

For the first time, Betsy found herself wishing he'd stayed. Something in Charlie's face warmed her, took away the chill of loneliness. Unlike the other faces around her, which had begun to show traces of doubt and defeat, Charlie's grin was as resilient as ever.

The mood of longing stayed with her all morning. It lasted right up until she saw Charlie galloping across the green prairie grass with Kitty Taylor in front of him in the saddle. *Charlie!* she thought in disgust. *I might just as soon tie my hopes to the wind as to Charlie Freeman.*

As the wagon train traveled west, they began to see signs of buffalo—slick mud sloughs where the huge beasts cooled themselves, dung chips that they gathered and used for fuel as wood grew scarce, vast black shadows that crossed the horizon for hours at a time.

Betsy, of course, had seen buffalo before. Everyone on the train had—but not the kind of buffalo that dwelt here on the plains, undiminished by hunters' rifles. When John Taylor told her that the hump of a buffalo cow often stood higher than a horse's ears, Betsy didn't believe him. "Who told you that?" she asked suspiciously.

"Charlie Freeman," John replied.

Betsy snorted. Charlie hadn't been around to see her for days. She might have died miles back, for all he cared. "And you believe him?" she asked John.

"Of course," John answered trustingly. Clearly, he was prepared to believe whatever Charlie Freeman told him. He looked at her quizzically. "Don't you?"

Betsy shrugged. She couldn't think of a reason *not* to believe Charlie. As far as she knew, he had never told her a single untruth. Yet the blind admiration he stirred in everyone annoyed her. She found herself growing tired of the whole conversation. "Buffalo taller than horses? I'll believe it when I see it," she said, setting her mouth in a firm line. "And not until."

True or not, Charlie's descriptions of buffalo and the wild, daring pleasures of a buffalo hunt soon infected every man in the camp. Even Rolfe Nilsson was touched by the fever—so much so that he spent every evening at shooting practice with the other men.

"Between you and me," Willa confessed, shifting the baby, Oscar, from one hip to the other, "it's good for him, all this talk. It gets him out with the other men. Yesterday he even talked about how he can hardly wait for the day to come when he can teach Oscar to hunt buffalo."

Willa's smile was completely satisfied. Betsy wouldn't have believed it, but the farther west they went, the lovelier her sister became. It was Betsy herself who was turning gaunt and thin-lipped. She gave Willa, baby and all, a quick hug. "I'm glad, Will, I really am. But if Captain Meeker doesn't find them some real buffalo to hunt soon, I'm afraid they'll blow each other to kingdom come."

She glanced toward the spot a quarter-mile distant where the men were practicing their shooting. Their wild, enchanted whoops rang in the evening air. Unmistakably, the loudest voice of all belonged to Charlie. "A person'd have to be deaf to miss him," she muttered to herself.

"What?" Willa asked.

"Nothing," Betsy answered. "I guess I'm just in an irritable mood tonight, Will. Don't pay any attention to me."

Together they fed the baby and put him to bed in their own wagon, where he was as accustomed to sleeping as he was with his father. All the time Betsy watched Willa with Oscar, she couldn't shake her mood of irritation.

It wasn't just Charlie, though his ear-splitting shrieks and cheers didn't help. It was Charlie and men in general. *Typical,* she thought as she pounded her pillow into an acceptable shape, looking for sleep that wouldn't come. It was just typical that the men found adventure after adventure while the women stayed behind, tending children and counting the graves they passed.

Betsy sighed. For weeks she had driven her ox team like a man, never complaining and never asking for a lick of help. But had anyone bothered to ask her if *she* would like to go hunting buffalo? Of course not. She was too frail to do anything so exciting. But not too frail, she thought rebelliously, to drag six oxen over half a continent.

She slammed her fist into the pillow. It wasn't fair. Not one bit. And the first chance she got, she intended to do something about it.

Betsy didn't have to wait long for her chance. Two days later, Captain Meeker announced a buffalo hunt. Betsy pulled Kitty aside as the men rode out. "Wouldn't you like to see it?" Betsy asked.

"Of course," Kitty answered. "But I already asked Pa and John if I could come, and they said no."

Betsy snorted at Kitty's lack of imagination. "Well, we're not tied to our wagons, are we? No one said we couldn't go out riding on our own, did they? And no one said our ride couldn't just *happen* to take us in the same direction as the men."

Kitty's eyes glittered with excitement. "Do we dare?" she asked in a way that showed Betsy her mind was already made up.

*"I'm* going to dare," Betsy said. "You can do whatever you like."

They saddled horses and left camp without being noticed. As soon as they were free of the circle of wagons, Betsy felt a thrill of relief. She had felt trapped for weeks, she realized—trapped by wagons and people and work itself. Now, cantering across the plains, she felt freedom budding inside her like a flower. She spurred her horse and shot forward, her hair streaming behind her, delicious fingers of wind caressing her face and neck.

"There they are," Kitty called, pointing to a dust cloud on the horizon.

Betsy reined in her horse. In her wild gallop, she had almost forgotten what they were doing here. She followed the direction of Kitty's pointing finger. In this land of short grass and tawny earth, even a few animals kicked up a heavy cloud of dust. The shadow on the horizon was so large that Betsy realized at once the men must have spotted buffalo.

Betsy scanned the land that spread out around them. To the west, gentle slopes angled up, forming an endless, bumpy backbone in the earth. "Let's stay in the hills," she suggested. "We can watch everything from there."

They picked their way along the tops of the hills. Below them, the men were circling toward a herd of buffalo.

Betsy gasped at her first sight of the giant herd. The huge black and brown beasts, still unaware of the men's approach, covered the ground completely. So thick were they that Betsy doubted if their hooves ever saw the light of day.

Even at this distance, Betsy could see that Charlie had not been exaggerating about their size. The bull buffaloes seemed as big as wagons, their massive humps rising above the prairie like mountaintops. Even the calves, born only a few months ago, were as large as cattle. When Betsy saw the gleam of white horns in the thick, shaggy manes, she shuddered. How easy it would be for one of those horns to reach out, hook a man or a horse, and send him flying.

"I hope they're careful," Kitty whispered, reading Betsy's thoughts.

Betsy nodded silently. She leaned forward in the saddle, her breathing shallow with excitement as the men approached the huge herd.

The head of a giant bull buffalo jerked up, sniffing the air. He snorted and pawed the earth, his alarm spreading to the rest of the herd. Betsy watched in fascination as the herd, like a dark, giant ocean, began to roll away from the approaching men. The sound of their hooves filled the air.

Charlie's horse was in the lead, and Betsy saw his eyes flick momentarily toward the hilltops. Automatically, she ducked her head. Had he seen her? No, she assured herself. That wasn't possible. It had been a chance glance, nothing more.

In the excitement of the next few minutes, Betsy lost track of Charlie and her worry that he had seen her. The men had cut off a half-dozen stragglers and were steadily closing in on them. Betsy saw the flash and gleam of raised rifle barrels and held her breath, waiting for the first shots to ring out.

Kitty's terrified scream split the air beside her. Betsy's horse lurched sideways so violently that Betsy was almost thrown to the ground. Struggling to find the reins that had been torn from her hands, Betsy turned in the saddle. An enormous bull buffalo stood directly in her path, not more than twenty feet away. His head was menacingly low, and his white horns glinted in the afternoon sunlight.

Betsy found the reins and grasped them in her icy fingers. For one long, awful moment she looked directly into the small, bloodshot eyes of the bull. She saw the brief, momentary shake of his head as he prepared to charge. Her stomach rolled with fear. She was trapped against the hills, with no route of escape.

The ground shook as the bull pounded toward her. Her frightened horse reared up, and the reins slipped again from her hands. Betsy felt herself tumbling backward, tumbling toward a sharp, dividing *crack* that sounded as if the earth itself had come apart under the flying hooves of the bull.

\*　　\*　　\*

The first thing Betsy saw when she opened her eyes was the blue sky overhead. And, looking directly down from that sky, were the blue eyes of Charlie Freeman.

"What are you doing?" she asked, struggling to get up. The hard, unforgiving line of the earth beneath her was something her backbone would never forget, she thought.

Charlie grinned and pushed her gently back down. "Saving your hide, that's what I'm doing," he chuckled good-naturedly.

Betsy's eyes flashed with annoyance. Why was it that Charlie always managed to catch her in her worst moments? And why was it that he seemed to enjoy them so enormously? She struggled to get up again, but Charlie held her firmly. "Let go of me," she said. "I'm fine. I just don't understand what happened, that's all."

Charlie grinned down at her. "Let's just say you didn't get your buffalo," he answered.

Betsy glanced sideways and saw a mountain of curly brown and black—the carcass of the dead buffalo. "Somebody got him, I see," she said dryly.

"That's right," Charlie said gently. "Somebody did." He was kneeling on the ground beside her. With a jolt, Betsy realized that his long, lean fingers were probing her bare ankle. "Feel all right?" he asked her, his eyebrows drawn together. "I think you might have twisted it when you fell."

Betsy jerked her skirt down to cover her ankles. She struggled free of Charlie's hands and climbed to her feet. "It feels fine," she said quickly. "And I didn't fall—I was thrown. There's a difference, you know."

"Oh," Charlie said, grinning again. "I'll be sure to remember that."

Now that Betsy was standing, she could see the buffalo carcass clearly. Its massive head lolled to one side, the mouth open enough for her to catch the gleam of a purplish-pink tongue. A thin trickle of blood ran from a hole just below the hump. "I suppose that's your bullet," she said.

Charlie didn't answer directly, just touched his fingers to the brim of his hat and gave her a smile that was full of bold self-confidence. *Darn him!* Betsy thought, squaring her shoulders. She took a deep breath and put her hand out. "I guess you did save me, then," she said grudgingly. "Thank you."

Charlie's eyes were warm and amused as they looked into hers. She felt his fingers lock around her own as he took her hand in his. "Think nothing of it," he said with an ironic grin. "I'm sure you'd have done the same for me."

*Don't be too sure about that,* Betsy wanted to shout, but she bit her tongue. Such an outburst, she was sure, would have sent Charlie into whoops of laughter, and Charlie had already had enough fun at her expense for one day.

Betsy and Kitty were sent back to the train alone. The men were needed to butcher the buffalo that had been killed, and Captain Meeker wasn't in a mood to leave himself short-handed. "You two got out here by yourselves," he said, spitting thoughtfully. "I reckon you can get back all right."

Betsy was relieved that he had said nothing stronger, for she'd expected a full-fledged lecture from the old man. What she had done was reckless, she knew. There was no arguing that. And yet, dangerous as it was, Betsy knew she would do the same thing all over again if she had the chance. Racing across the high hilltops had been wonderful. And it had almost— *almost*—been safe. If only that buffalo hadn't come charging up to them, she thought. If only they had gotten away before Charlie rushed up to save them. "Darn him anyway," she muttered to herself.

Kitty looked at Betsy with a knowing eye. "I hope you don't mean Charlie," she said.

"Why *shouldn't* I mean Charlie?" Betsy burst out.

"Well, he saved your life, for one thing," Kitty answered. Her dark eyes, wiser than her fifteen years, studied Betsy's face intently. "And, for another thing, I think he loves you."

*"What?!"* Betsy almost fell off her saddle. She stared at Kitty. "Where on earth did you get such a foolish notion as that?"

Kitty smiled mysteriously. "I know a thing or two about boys," she said. "You should have seen the way Charlie charged up that hill. He must have seen you and the buffalo both from way down below."

Betsy sniffed. "He was just trying to show off," she said.

But Kitty had the rock-hard logic of a born flirt. "Show off for whom?" she asked. "You were out cold as soon as you hit the ground, and he didn't see *me* until everything was over. No, Betsy, he was trying to save you, and I think he was trying to save you because he loves you."

Betsy felt herself blush to the roots of her hair. Against her will, a deep, delicious feeling quivered inside her. She looked at Kitty for a long time. "Is there anything else you have to say?" she asked.

Kitty's red lips curved in an impish smile. "Yes," she said, slapping the reins suddenly and spurring her horse into a gallop. "I wish it was me!" She laughed, and the wind tore the words from her mouth.

Betsy followed her, wishing the wind would tear her own confused thoughts from her mind. Was Kitty right? she wondered. Kitty knew as much about boys as anyone she had ever met, but did that mean she knew about Charlie?

Maybe Charlie was the kind of boy no one, not even Kitty, would ever figure out for sure. Maybe he was exactly what Captain Meeker had once said he was—a wisp of fog that never settled anywhere and vanished in the morning air.

# Chapter 6

BETSY'S ADVENTURE MADE HER A MINOR CELEBRITY in camp. Other women, who would never have tried such an escapade themselves, looked at Betsy and Kitty with a mixture of awe and envy. Young men and boys winked at the girls' misconduct.

Even Captain Meeker seemed to look at her with new respect, and one fine Sunday morning, with the train camped in the protective shadow of Fort Laramie, he volunteered to teach Betsy to ride bareback. Betsy jumped at his offer, gladly abandoning her morning chores for the chance.

Her first wild, reckless dash across the ground ended in defeat—when her horse stepped sideways to avoid a gopher hole, Betsy automatically clutched for the saddle horn. Her hands touched nothing but air, and she hurtled forward, doing what she hoped was a graceful somersault onto the ground.

Captain Meeker rode up to her. "I don't suppose you want to try again," he said. Betsy was up and back on her horse before he could say another word. "Lean

57

into the horse," he shouted as she cantered uncertainly forward. "Use your legs and feet to guide 'im."

But Betsy's legs were swaddled in yards of calico, and her feet were hidden in stiff leather boots. Without hesitating, she reached down, undid the laces of each boot, and kicked them off. Then she tugged her skirt up and tucked it between her legs, leaving her legs completely bare from the knees down.

Her skin made warm, quick contact with the flesh of the horse beneath her. His warm, satiny hide felt so good against her skin that she sighed with pleasure. Then, because Captain Meeker was still watching her, she pressed her knees against the horse's flanks.

He shot off across the sweep of sun-baked ground, and Betsy shot with him. She felt the wind lift her heavy chestnut hair and send it streaming behind her like a banner. She opened her mouth and tasted cool, sweet air against her teeth. In a moment of reckless daring, she let go of the reins and leaned low on the horse's neck, her hands tangled in his mane.

Gasping with excitement, she raced in a huge circle and came back at last to Captain Meeker. Her face was flushed and triumphant. She knew—and so did Captain Meeker—that she would never again fall from a barebacked horse.

"Right good riding, missy," was all the old man said, but his smile was as proud as if Betsy had been his own daughter.

Betsy was still getting her breath back when she saw two mounted figures approaching them. One, visible by the A-shaped easel legs that jutted out, was Nash

Whitcomb. The other, in dashing buckskins fringed at the arms and decorated with vermilion porcupine quills, was Charlie. Betsy suffered a pang of regret. Why hadn't they arrived a few moments earlier, in time for Charlie to see her exhilarating ride?

Nash Whitcomb, his white silk sleeves rolled above tan arms, began setting his easel up as soon as he dismounted. He got out his paints and uncovered a huge bone-white canvas. Charlie grinned a hello at Betsy and Captain Meeker and dismounted. "Howdy," he said.

"Hello," Betsy replied. She eyed his fine buckskins. They were new and light gold, an antelope color that matched Charlie's hair exactly. Besides the delicate vermilion porcupine quills that decorated the shirt, there were also rows of tiny glass beads. It occurred to Betsy that the outfit—right down to its matching moccasins—had been made especially for Charlie. *And,* she thought forcefully, it had been made by someone who cared for him.

Betsy's mind flew to the Indian camps that lay hidden in the distance. She remembered two days, less than a week ago, when Charlie had mysteriously disappeared. Was there, she wondered, some raven-haired, almond-eyed beauty whose heart belonged to Charlie Freeman? The thought struck her like a rattlesnake. She bit her lip to keep the idea at bay. "I see," she said slowly, her eyes wandering toward Charlie's, "you're wearing your Sunday best today."

Charlie grinned, proud as a peacock. "Mr. Whitcomb wants to paint my portrait," he said proudly.

"What?" Betsy asked, glancing from Charlie to Nash Whitcomb.

"Oh yes," Nash said, his neat mustache turning up in a smile. "It's quite true. I think Charlie Freeman is what the West is all about."

"Certainly," Betsy commented. "Death, fever, frostbite—that's Charlie, all right."

Charlie roared with laughter. As if his sense of humor were contagious, like a fever, Nash Whitcomb and Captain Meeker laughed, too. Betsy felt outnumbered and betrayed. How could Nash, her own friend, be so easily taken in by Charlie? Charlie, Betsy often thought, would make a great newspaper writer or a great advance man for the circuses and spectacles that wandered from small town to small town back in the states. He had a gift for sparking enthusiasm, for creating legends and getting people to believe in them. But the legend he seemed to like the best was the legend of himself.

She watched silently as Charlie struck a proud, stiff pose. He reminded her of an owl she had once seen in a museum, stuffed and glassy-eyed in a little glass case. She stiffled a grin as Nash Whitcomb waved his brushes in the air. "No, no, not like that at all," he called. "You look dead. *Do* something."

Charlie looked embarrassed. "Do something?" he asked. "Like what?"

"Anything," Whitcomb said impatiently. "I need to paint life, not wood." Betsy noted with glee the faint red that crept into Charlie's cheeks. She would not, she thought, have missed this for anything. The artist glanced at the horses. "Why not ride?" he suggested.

"Ride?" Charlie echoed. Clearly, he did not like the thought of sharing his portrait with a horse.

"Yes, yes," Whitcomb shouted, his enthusiasm growing. "You too, Betsy, if you want. I'll call it *Young Hearts of the Prairie!*"

Betsy didn't need to be asked twice. She swung herself onto her horse and tucked her skirt between her legs.

"I think this is a *terrible* idea," she heard Charlie mutter as he mounted his own horse.

Betsy gave him a huge smile. "I think it's rather nice," she said innocently.

For the first time, Charlie glanced at her bare legs. "You're riding bareback?" he asked. Betsy nodded, and Charlie rolled his blue eyes toward heaven. "This ought to be something to see."

Betsy flashed a smile at him. "Keep your eyes open," she called, digging her heels into the flanks of her horse.

She galloped out across the plain, streaking toward a horizon that melted, in a blue and purple line, into rolling foothills. Behind her, she could hear Charlie's horse closing the distance between them. He came abreast of her, and Betsy caught the grin on his face. "You catch on quick," he said approvingly.

Betsy turned and smiled at him. "I try," she answered. A strand of hair lashed against her cheek, but she ignored it. She leaned forward a fraction of an inch and urged her horse into a fast, flat-out gallop. She heard Charlie's delighted laugh and then, as he took up her challenge, the sound of his horse's hooves pounding behind her.

They were friends then, for those few minutes as they raced neck and neck across the tablelands. All the stiff, prickly points that marked their relationship faded, washed away by a current of feeling as strong as a river. For a split second, Betsy believed she would be happy to ride anywhere with Charlie, racing at his side with nothing but the wind to come between them.

They rode for more than a mile, galloping until they reached a row of hills too steep for their winded horses to climb. Automatically, they reined the horses to a stop.

"View from the top of a hill like that is bound to be beautiful," Charlie murmured. "Be a shame to miss it." He looked at her and grinned. "'Course, I'm sure you're not up to doing any climbing."

Betsy slid off her horse. "I don't remember saying I was tired," she answered, her long legs already in motion.

The hill was steep and dotted with sagebrush. They climbed quickly, almost at a trot, and got to the top, panting for breath.

Charlie was right, Betsy thought. The view *was* worth climbing for. From the top you could see the whole prairie spread out below, full of shifting colors. Captain Meeker and Jed Marsh were two distant specks, almost invisible on the horizon. "Glory," she said, her voice flickering like the flame of a candle. "This is about the most beautiful place I've ever seen. I wish Ma and Pa could've made it this far."

Charlie was standing just behind her. Her long chestnut hair caught up the sunlight, filling each curl with flaming reddish gold. He had never, in all his life, met a girl quite like her. She could handle an ox team by herself and ride with the fearless abandon of any Sioux or Shawnee. She could vex him with her stubborn independence and make him sure he never wanted to bother with her again. She could dance through his dreams with her tangle of long hair and fox-bright eyes. And she could dash to the tops of hills like this one and leave him aching to touch her. If he crossed the continent a thousand times more, he thought, he would never find anyone like her.

Betsy felt his arms around her before she realized what was happening. Before her mind told her, *Charlie Freeman is holding you,* her body whirled and pressed against him. His chin nestled in the top of her sun-warmed hair, and her arms automatically circled his neck. A piece of hot prairie sun fell to earth and lodged in her body. She felt its heat spreading through her like fire.

"Oh, Betsy," Charlie murmured. "You're so—so different from all the other girls."

His words struck a nerve, and Betsy jerked back, breaking away from him like a dreamer breaking away from the tangles of a dangerous dream. "Other girls?!" she gasped indignantly. Well, she might have known as much. She'd been warned, by Captain Meeker and by Charlie himself—Charlie Freeman picked up girls as easily as a dog picked up burrs. Her eyes flashed. "I didn't know I was being compared." She started down the hill. The grade was so steep that she had to skate over the dirt and sagebrush to keep from falling.

Charlie floundered behind her. "Wait a minute, Betsy," he called. "I didn't mean to—you got it wrong—I—*darn, you are the most horse-headed girl I ever met!*"

By the time he got to the bottom of the hill, Betsy was already on her horse. "Nice to know I'm horse-headed," she said as he caught the reins of his own mount. "I guess that *would* make me different from all your other girls, wouldn't it?"

"It sure does," he said, turning his horse around.

Betsy turned her horse to follow his. She didn't know why, but she felt like crying. There had been a moment on the hilltop that had been theirs and theirs alone. Charlie's lips brushing her cheek had filled her with warm excitement and a promise of the future. At that moment, she could have turned and walked the rest of the way to Oregon with him beside her.

But it had all been a dream. Charlie was Charlie. Charlie, who drifted back and forth across the continent like a cloud. Charlie, who, in a rare moment of being serious, had told her he would rather die than settle down. No amount of wishing would ever make him otherwise.

To Charlie, Betsy thought with a pang, she was just another girl whose name he would forget in time. Maybe he would remember her a bit longer than the rest, but, in the end, he was sure to go on to another place and another girl. Her image would fade in his mind, and the letters of her name would be erased by the shifting sands of his own restlessness.

Handsome as he was, she wasn't going to forget that. She wasn't going to land in Oregon with an empty, aching heart.

Willa looked at Betsy, her gray eyes full of concern, her fine mouth puckered in a frown. "I thought maybe that scare with the buffalo would knock some sense into you, Bets," she mourned. "Not the other way around." Willa had just seen Nash Whitcomb's painting, *Young Hearts of the Prairie,* and she was horrified. "Bad enough for you to be riding bareback," she went on. "But to get yourself painted that way, bare-legged, for all the world to see. . . ." Willa paused, unable to find words capable of conveying her sense of shock.

Betsy found it impossible to act contrite, even for Willa, whom she loved. A secret smile of remembered pleasure played at the corners of her mouth. "Don't go on at me, Willa," she said lightly. "It isn't the end of the world. Nobody'll ever know it's Betsy Monroe in that painting." She grinned. "Not for sure, any-way."

Willa's needle plunked disapprovingly against the cloth of the shirt she was making for little Oscar. "*I'll* know," Willa said. She let the needle drop and bent forward in the firelight. "Oh, Bets, I wish you could— I wish you could *feel* how good it is, taking care of a man like Rolfe and a baby like little Oscar. If you did,

I'm sure you'd never want to do those wild things you do."

Betsy looked at her sister's earnest, beautiful face. "Maybe it's true for you, Will, but I don't think it'll ever be true for me. How can a body be happy just *sitting* and waiting for some man to take notice of her?" She stopped, afraid of hurting her sister's feelings. "I'll be all right, Will. I promise. And someday maybe I *will* find a man who makes me feel the way you feel."

"I hope so, Bets," Willa said, impulsively squeezing her sister's hand. "Just keep your eyes open."

But finding a man, during the next few weeks, was the last thing Betsy had on her mind. Captain Meeker, she thought gratefully, had taught her to ride bareback just in the nick of time. For now they had entered the sweetest part of the journey. Beyond Fort Laramie the land began to slope up toward the mountains that still lay hundreds of miles away. It was deep summer, but the climbing elevation turned the hot days cool and sweet.

The flaxen yellows and greens of the grasslands vanished, replaced instead by colors Betsy had never seen before—vivid purples and corals, smoky grays, and deep, tumultuous blues. Betsy seldom missed a chance to ride out of the camp at the end of a hard day's driving or on Sunday mornings when they were camped for the day beside some sweet stream. One ride brought her face to face with a bobcat. Her horse shifted nervously beneath her, but Betsy sat perfectly still. Her eyes met the green yellow eyes of the cat, and, for a long moment, the two stared at each other. Then the cat turned and walked off. Betsy felt a thrill of knowing, a sense of belonging to the cat's wild world rather than being a stranger in it. She galloped back to the train, full of a happiness she knew she could never put into words.

Nothing—not Willa's disapproval nor Captain Meeker's reminders to stay close to the train when she rode—could keep her from venturing out across the land. She fell more in love with it with every step west she took, more certain that once she reached Oregon she would never feel the slightest urge to retrace her steps for the comforts of the East. She laughed off the dangers of snakes, sudden hailstorms, and prowling mountain lions. Whipping across the land on the back of her fleet and knowing horse, she was certain that nothing could touch her.

Yet everyone, even Charlie, showed concern over her frequent rides. "We're getting into Indian country now, you know," he said.

Betsy shrugged her shoulders. "I haven't seen any yet," she answered.

"Doesn't mean they aren't there," Charlie reminded her.

His protective, smothering cautions irritated her. "I suppose you know all about Indians," she said, tossing her tangled hair.

Charlie's face was serious. "I know enough," he said.

Betsy remembered his magnificent quill-worked buckskins. Her curiosity suddenly got the better of her. "What are they like?" she asked, her brown eyes throwing off red highlights.

"What do you mean, what are they like?" Charlie asked.

"Well, the way they live . . . you know, their customs and things."

Charlie grinned suddenly. "I know one custom you might be interested in."

"What?" Betsy asked eagerly.

"Well, with Indians, you save a person's life, that person belongs to you."

Betsy gulped. She'd jumped like a fish to the bait, and now Charlie was grinning at her with wicked delight. His meaning was plain. Betsy could not help but remember, as Charlie had meant her to, the time he'd saved her from the charging buffalo. "In that case," she said with as much dignity as she could muster, "I'm glad I'm not an Indian."

She turned and walked quickly away, but not fast enough to escape the sound of Charlie's amused laughter echoing behind her.

# Chapter 7

As June passed into July, the travelers said goodbye to the Platte and started keeping company with the Sweetwater River instead. Betsy felt as if she were leaving an old friend behind, but that didn't spoil her excitement. Like everyone else, she felt as if they had passed through an invisible gateway and entered the great heart of the West at last.

They were no different from other emigrant trains, of course, and passing through that invisible gateway extracted its toll. Grass wasn't as plentiful as it had been before, and they had already lost several head of stock to hunger and the poisonous effects of alkaline water. A man named Mr. Blake had died of fever, leaving his wife as poor as a snake. One of the younger Taylors had gotten her leg crushed under a wheel, and they were waiting to see if infection would set in. Weather had plagued them, and hail had torn through the covers of the more poorly built wagons, ruining everything inside. But even so, they'd been far luckier than most trains on the trail, and they knew it.

On the first Saturday in July, they camped a few

miles away from Independence Rock—that huge, loaf-shaped outcropping that marked, for every emigrant passing west, the true beginning of the Rocky Mountains. Captain Meeker organized an expedition to ride out to it, and Betsy volunteered to take care of little Oscar so that Willa and Rolfe could go along.

Willa's gratitude bubbled out of her like a flowing brook. "Thanks, Bets," she said with glowing cheeks. "I'll make it up to you. I promise."

"Don't worry about it, Will," Betsy replied. She knew, without being told, how much the small expedition meant to the couple. They had toiled and worked and helped each other since the day Rolfe's wife had died, but they had never yet had a minute just to be together. And it was high time for that, Betsy thought, high time for the two of them to see that they were falling in love with each other.

Willa smiled and darted off, the gold of late afternoon sun crowning her pale hair. Oscar whimpered, and Betsy patted the restless baby's back. Already he'd come to think of Willa as his mother and fretted in anyone else's arms. "Shh," Betsy whispered, thinking how much room a baby took up in a person's life. "You just hush, Oscar Nilsson. No need for you to feel guilty about spoiling my trip to that old rock. I plan to ride out there all by myself tomorrow morning anyway."

On Sunday mornings it was the custom for Mr. Quigley, from the tenth wagon, to stand in the center of the ring formed by the circled wagons and read a chapter of the Bible. He wasn't a minister. He wasn't even a strong churchgoer himself. He'd gotten the job simply because his voice was louder than anyone else's, which was important because, as he read, the other members of Captain Meeker's train went about their chores.

It was better than church, Betsy reflected as she mounted her horse. At least you had something to do while you listened, instead of just sitting as she and Willa had had to do on the hard pews of the First Methodist Church at home. She grinned to herself. Yes, it *was* better than real church, but not better than riding off alone to see Independence Rock.

She breathed deeply, letting the clear morning air fill her lungs. The scent of pine reached her, and she smiled at the brave, prickly looking little trees that climbed the foothills. Above the tree line, bare rock jutted toward the sky.

Betsy studied the rock formations carefully. It was funny, she thought. You always thought of mountains as up-and-down things, but these were all crosswise layers—layer on top of layer, like stacks of hotcakes. In some places the layers were worn smooth; in other places they fell away sharply, as if a knife had sliced through them. Charlie had tried to tell her that once, a long time ago, great rivers had rushed between the rocks. But Betsy had only laughed and complimented him on his imagination.

The formation known to every emigrant as Independence Rock sat on the earth like a giant loaf of bread. It was more than a third of a mile long and more than twice as long as it was wide. For people passing west it had become a giant signpost, and Betsy read with fascination the names that had been painted, carved, and written on its surface: "Joseph and Annabel Walker, '44," "Daring Dick Darnell, '46," "Reverend Clem Ableson, West by the Grace of God, July 10th, 1839."

She paced back and forth, curious to see if anyone from her own party had signed the rock. Captain Meeker wouldn't, of course, and neither would Charlie—both of them were sure to consider themselves above such greenhorn pastimes. But with a smile of satisfaction she saw that John Taylor had boldly written his own name down, and the date as well. A tiny heart on the western face of the rock held the initials "W & R." Could that be Willa and Rolfe? she wondered. She would think of that heart as theirs, she decided, whether it was or wasn't—and hers as well, for she had brought nothing with her to mark her own passing.

It wasn't yet noon when Betsy finished viewing the huge rock, and she had no intention of wasting a free day and a fresh horse by going back to camp. A few miles ahead on the Sweetwater, she knew, lay Devil's Gate. Here the river rushed through solid rock, or so Charlie had tried to tell her. The thought of being the first in all their party to see it was irresistible, and she automatically turned her horse in that direction.

Charlie, Betsy realized with a fleeting sense of chagrin, had gone far in understating the magnificence of Devil's Gate. The river had cut a path through solid rock, a channel broad enough to let ten wagons pass abreast. Sheer walls of rock rose on each side, as straight and majestic as the walls of a stone church. Betsy stood on the edge of the gorge, looking at the water that swirled a hundred feet below. Gazing across to the other side, she saw rocky overhangs jutting above the water.

A sudden nervous fear seized her. What if she were standing on such an overhang at this very minute? What if it gave way suddenly under her weight and sent her crashing down into the rocky canyon? She sprang back with a shudder, at first scarcely feeling the arms that reached forward to grasp her shoulders.

Then, suddenly, she whirled and found herself staring up into a grim face the color of dark copper.

The Indian's fingers gripped her firmly, digging into her shoulders and lifting her nearly off the ground. Betsy struggled to twist free, but his grip only tightened. Already a second Indian had appeared from nowhere, and a third, smiling broadly, had taken the reins of her horse.

Fright pounded in her chest. She let out a wild scream, but a broad hand was quickly slapped across her mouth. Betsy bit down furiously, aware of the sharp cutting edge of her chipped tooth. The Indian jerked his hand away, a look of surprised hurt in his eyes. "You varmint!" Betsy shrieked, launching her foot in a swift attack.

The sudden move was a mistake, for, as she tried to kick, the second and third Indians sprang to the defense of their friend. Betsy felt rough hands grabbing her ankles and her wrists. She felt her hands being forced together and a leather thong being tied tightly around them. She felt two Indians lift her roughly and set her on the back of her own horse, speaking and laughing to each other in a language she couldn't fathom a word of.

That was when she understood.

She was never going to see Willa again—or Kitty or John or Captain Meeker or anyone else on the wagon train. She wasn't even going to see Charlie, a thought that filled her with unexpected sadness.

"I hate you!" she shouted as the Indians mounted their own horses and prepared to lead her away. "You're nothing but snakes and cowards, the lot of you. Imagine, three of you and one of me, and you still have to tie my hands." Secure in the belief that they couldn't understand her, Betsy raged on and on. "You ought to 'be ashamed of yourselves," she wailed. "Nash Whitcomb wouldn't paint you if you turned up in beads and feathers and your finest. Why, anyone's better than you, even Charlie Freeman, and we all know what kind of a dog *he* is!"

An unmistakable laugh rang out behind them. Betsy twisted and looked over her shoulder. *Charlie!*

She felt as if she'd been pitched down into the gorge itself, with her emotions tumbling end over end in a swirl of confusion. Part of her was furious, as angry as ever that Charlie had managed to catch her at her worst once again. Yet another part of her—a part she struggled to suppress—wanted to leap forward into Charlie's arms.

While Betsy fought with her warring emotions, Charlie rode steadily forward. He looked at the three Indians, automatically picking out the leader of the group. When he was face to face with him, he dismounted. The tall copper-skinned Indian did the same. For the first time, Betsy saw that a silver dollar swung from a thong on the Indian's neck.

Charlie said something to the Indian in his own language. The Indian, with a look of supreme disinterest on his face, shrugged and turned away. Charlie spoke again. Whatever he said, Betsy noted, got the Indian's attention, for he turned back again to Charlie. But the strange dance was repeated many times, the Indian turning away in disinterest and Charlie calling him back. Only after this had happened several times did Betsy realize what was going on. Charlie was trying to buy—*buy*—her from the Indian.

Her face turned scarlet at the idea. What sin in life had brought her to this sorry position—being traded back and forth between a half-naked savage and an arrogant, and probably illiterate, trail guide?

In the end, Charlie secured her freedom at the price of a knife, five dollars, Betsy's horse, and the shirt he was wearing. It was a good thing he hadn't been wearing his best fringed buckskins, Betsy observed privately. She was sure he would never have thrown *those* into the bargain.

The tallest of the three Indians pulled Betsy roughly to the ground and sent her spinning toward Charlie. Then he grabbed the reins of the horse and held them firmly as he regained his own mount. Happy with their trade, the three Indians rode off toward the western hills.

Betsy watched her horse go with a spasm of anger. It was *her* horse, not theirs. It was the horse Pa had ridden before he died. Betsy glared at Charlie. "Did you have to give them my horse too?" she asked stormily. "Couldn't you have talked them out of it?"

Charlie grinned. "I tried, Betsy. I really did. But for some reason, they seemed to think you were worth a horse. Myself, I thought my shirt was more than enough for you."

Charlie laughed. Betsy could not help noticing the smooth, rippling lines of his chest muscles, taut beneath bare skin. She saw a tiny white scar rising like a question mark above one nipple and found herself wanting to trace it with her fingertips. She moved her eyes quickly away from the scar. "I suppose I ought to thank you," she said.

Charlie grinned and reached for her. "You could give it a try," he replied as he swung her up onto his own horse.

Betsy looked down at him. "Well?" she asked.

Charlie swung up onto the horse behind her. "Well what?"

Betsy tossed her head. "Aren't you going to untie my hands?"

"Nope," Charlie said. "I've had enough trouble out of you for one day. You can ride all right like this."

"I *can't* ride all right like this," Betsy protested indignantly.

"I don't think you have much choice," he replied.

As Charlie reached around her to grasp the reins, Betsy felt the smooth pressure of his body against hers. She struggled against him. "Put me down, then," she said. "I'll walk back to camp if it's all the same to you."

"Haven't got time for a walk," Charlie said thoughtfully. "Tell you what, though—you behave yourself, I might turn you loose once we're back in camp."

Betsy snorted. "You're even worse than the Indians, you know that?"

"Probably am," Charlie replied agreeably. "Far as I can tell, Indians aren't so very terrible."

"No?" Betsy questioned. "Well, these Indians were. They had tomahawks—I'm sure they meant to scalp me."

Charlie's laughter fluttered against her neck like a moth. "Did they tell you that?" he asked.

"How would I know what they were telling me? I couldn't understand a word of it. All I know is they meant to take me off with them. They meant to drag me back to their camp and murder me, in case you're interested!"

Charlie bent forward in exaggerated laughter. The weight of his body crushed Betsy against the horse's neck. "Is that so?" he gasped. "Is that what they were going to do to you?"

Betsy struggled to sit up. "Of course that's what they were going to do to me," she snapped. "I'm sure there're lots of people who'd miss me, too, even if you wouldn't!" Charlie's laughter increased, tumbling around her like a swift river. "What the *blazes* is so funny about all this?" she asked at last.

"Well, greenhorn," Charlie explained between bursts of laughter. "I hate to tell you this, but those weren't murdering Indians at all. In fact, I've known those three for years, and they're about the sorriest excuses for Indians I've ever seen."

"What do you mean?" Betsy asked.

"Well, they make it a practice to watch for stragglers from trains—you know, folks who are so dumb or so pig headed they just have to go off looking around by themselves. So they grab the stragglers, ride 'em around for a few hours, then trade 'em back to their folks. It's a right profitable business, in its own way."

Betsy felt wings of humiliation beating against her cheeks. "I don't believe you," she said. She twisted in his arms, trying to look into his eyes. "You're lying."

"Think that if you want to," he said, "but those Indians couldn't scalp a cactus." He rested his chin on her shoulder. "Come to think of it," he said in an amused whisper, his lips almost brushing her ear, "after they'd had hold of you for a couple of hours, I bet they'd have been more than willing to give you back free, no questions asked. Question is, would Captain Meeker have *taken* you back?"

Betsy squirmed in his arms, and he tightened his hold on her as if he enjoyed feeling her struggle. "I hate you!" she shouted. "I wish some real Indian'd come up and scalp you right now!"

He held her tightly, and his lips grazed the sensitive skin of her neck. "Oh Betsy, you don't really mean that, do you?" he asked in a low voice.

She trembled suddenly. Half of her hated Charlie Freeman, but the other half of her was melting against him. For a split second she relaxed in his arms and felt the responsive power of his body against hers. Then, frightened by the wild, sweet tide of her own feelings, she pulled away from him. "Of course I mean it," she said. "I just hope I'm around to see it happen."

"Suit yourself," Charlie answered. The sting of hurt in his voice was unmistakable, but Betsy ignored it. She didn't say another word to Charlie, not even a "thank you" when he untied her hands just before they reached the camp.

As soon as they entered the circle of wagons, Betsy slid from his horse and headed straight for her wagon. She got out a knife, a five-dollar coin, and the best shirt Pa had left behind. Winding these things into a bundle, she walked back to where Charlie was sitting.

"There," she said, tossing the bundle at his feet. "We're even now. I wouldn't want you to get the idea you owned me."

"Don't worry," Charlie called after her as she walked away. "You're so much trouble I wouldn't take you as a gift!"

Betsy stopped in her tracks and whirled around. "The only gift you'll ever get from me is a *farewell*, and that's when we get to Oregon!"

She stormed off across the circle, her heart clattering and shaking against her ribs. Charlie, squatting by the fire, stared down into his mug of coffee. There were nearly a hundred people watching them, but Betsy and Charlie acted as if they were the only two people on earth. A sure sign, some said, of being in love.

# Chapter 8

ONE EVENING WILLA SURPRISED THEM WITH A bucket of lemon iced cream.

It wasn't real iced cream, of course. And the nearest fresh lemon was thousands of miles away. But the taste of mountain snow mixed with sugar, drops of lemon oil, and medicinal citric acid crystals tasted remarkably good.

"Fresh snow," Charlie said, scooping a finger full of ice up to his mouth—an Indian-style way of eating, Betsy was certain. Charlie caught her frown and grinned in reply. "You know what fresh snow means, don't you, Betsy?"

"I'm sure you'll tell us," Betsy replied.

"Means we're getting close to the Divide."

Spoons stopped in midair. "The Continental Divide?" Nash Whitcomb asked. It didn't seem possible. The upward slope had been too gradual. Was it true they were now dancing on the backbone of the world—the place that divided rivers into east-flowing and west-flowing waters?

"I don't believe it," Betsy said, shooting Charlie a sharp look.

"I'd die of shock if you did," he said. "But it's true."

Willa watched their gentle feuding with a knowing eye. Like everyone else on the train, she had reached the conclusion that Betsy and Charlie were made for each other. And, like everyone else on the train, she knew better than to mention it to either of them.

Willa smiled. Before they had come west, she could not have imagined a person like Charlie Freeman. But now that she knew he existed, she could not imagine her sister giving her heart to anyone else. Only someone like Charlie, Willa thought, was capable of handling Betsy in her wilder moments. She approved of him completely. "Won't you have some more ice, Charlie?" she asked brightly.

As Charlie was dipping the last of the iced cream with his fingers, Captain Meeker joined them. "How be, folks?" he asked, hunkering down on his heels.

"Charlie's been trying to tell us we're at the Divide already," Betsy said. "It isn't true, is it?"

"'Course it's true," Captain Meeker replied, loudly enough to get everyone's attention. "What d'you think we've been doin' all these weeks but climbin' mountains, girl? I figure we'll get to South Pass by the week's end."

The words *South Pass* echoed through the group like rifle fire. Loud whoops went up from the men; relief broke on the faces of the women. More than Scott's Bluff or Independence Rock, more than Fort

Laramie behind them or Fort Hall beyond, South Pass was a turning point. Not only did it mark their passage across the Divide, but it also marked the division of the paths that lead west. From here, trains bound for California turned south, heading for the Great Salt Lake and its vast deserts. Oregon trains, like theirs, angled northwest to Fort Hall, where they would pick up the Snake River.

"We're nearly there then," said Daniel Weiner, bouncing his four-year-old daughter on his knee.

*"Ja,"* Rolfe Nilsson beamed, reaching for Willa's hand. "Up one side of d'mountains, down d'other. Den ve are home." Willa smiled at him, a sweet and secret smile that filled Betsy with a pang of envy.

Captain Meeker looked at the men who were celebrating like children. "Crossed the mountains before, have you?"

"No-o," Daniel Weiner said slowly.

"I crossed the ocean from Sweden," Rolfe volunteered.

"Well," Mordechai Meeker said, packing a finger full of tobacco into his cheek. "I've crossed the mountains. So has Charlie here, and Blue Star, and old Jed." He jerked his thumb at Charlie, then at the scout and the hunter. "Don't see any of them a-whoopin' and hollerin', do you?" Daniel Weiner shook his head. Rolfe's fingers tightened around Willa's. "That's on account o' they know what's ahead. Coming this far, it's a ride on your mama's knee compared to what's ahead. I'll grant we've been lucky enough so far, but no train goes west what hasn't got its share o' bad luck. Myself, I'd rather have had ours back there, where it's easy, than up ahead."

He finished his speech with a stream of spurting tobacco juice. Betsy glanced at Charlie, sure he would be laughing and grinning as always. But he wasn't. His handsome gold-tanned face was serious. A shiver scurried up Betsy's back, colder than all the lemon-flavored snow in the world. These four men—Charlie and Captain Meeker and Blue Star and Jed Marsh—knew the secrets of the mountains. If their faces were grim with remembering those secrets, there was a reason why.

*No train goes west what hasn't got its share o'bad luck.* As if Captain Meeker's words had been a grim premonition, bad luck caught them before they reached the Divide.

They'd stopped earlier than usual in a field of short grass. A trickling stream led away from the campsite—a stream so innocent and beguiling that a child couldn't help but follow it.

That's what they all believed had happened, anyway.

Willa was stirring a big kettle of beans and dried apples when Martha Weiner rushed up. "Is Millie here?" she asked in a feverish voice. "I left her by the stream and went looking for something to get the fire going with. She's wandered off."

Within minutes, the whole wagon train had turned itself inside out looking for the child, the little girl who'd been eating lemon ice and bouncing on her father's knee only a few nights ago.

"How can someone just *vanish?*" Willa asked in a worried voice. The lost child was an ominous reminder to her and to all of them on the train. Life was fragile, easily lost. And what happened to any one of them could happen to all.

Betsy saw her sister clinging to little Oscar as if her life depended on it. Thank goodness the baby was too young even to crawl yet, Betsy thought. She slipped her arm around her sister's shoulders. "Don't worry so, Willa," Betsy said comfortingly. "She's got to be close by."

The men formed a search party that fanned out from the campsite. The sound of Dan Weiner's voice calling to his lost daughter echoed back to the circle of wagons, as full of heartbreak as any sound Betsy had ever heard.

The party stayed out until well after dark and returned to camp hungry and empty-handed. Betsy poured hot coffee for the men and spooned up plates of warm beans. "How could she vanish that way?" she asked, repeating Willa's question to Charlie. The crisis had put a momentary end to their feud.

"It happens sometimes, Betsy," Charlie said, his voice gentle with weariness.

"You mean they might not ever find her?" Betsy asked in alarm.

"Might not. Sometimes youngsters get drowned or bit by a snake. Sometimes the Indians get 'em and sometimes no one gets 'em at all—they just disappear. We looked all down that stream, though, and didn't find anything, so I don't think she drowned."

Betsy didn't know whether she was relieved or not. She thought of the other grim possibilities Charlie had listed and shuddered. Knowing your child was dead was one thing, but just *not knowing* was the worst of all. She shook herself and stood up. "Want some more coffee?" she asked.

Charlie looked up at her. "I'd love some," he answered.

Betsy refilled his cup silently. Charlie must be worried, she thought. He wasn't even bothering to insult her coffee.


They stayed by the side of the stream for three more days, looking for Millie Weiner. The trail grew colder every hour, and the chances of finding her grew more and more remote. Finally, Captain Meeker had the sad job of deciding to move on. Time was slipping by, and, even though it was still late July, winter was closing down on them. If they lost any more time, they risked getting caught in the mountains.

The train set out two wagons short. The Weiners stayed behind, and so did their friends, the Cobbs. They would not go on, they said, until they had searched the far side of every hill and valley—a task that might take another week's valuable time.

Captain Meeker didn't try to change their minds. He had seen too much of grief and stubbornness for that. Besides, he knew the trail here was well traveled. He advised the families to attach themselves to the next train that passed by, whether they had found the child or not.

The loss of the two wagons drove a hole through the high spirits of the train. They were scattered now. Living members of the train had been left behind. And, even though no one came right out and said so, they all took it as a defeat. Instead of reaching South Pass in high spirits, the train was somber and quiet.

"We can't go all the rest of the way to Oregon like this," Betsy brooded to Kitty Taylor. "We've got to *do* something."

"What?" Kitty asked, tapping her finger against her small, pointed chin.

"Didn't Captain Meeker say something once about trains having parties at South Pass? You know, to sort of mark how far they've come?"

At the word *party,* Kitty became as alert as a terrier. "I think he did," she said, although she remembered no such thing.

"Well," Betsy grinned. "We can't let tradition die, can we? If other trains have a party, then we've got to have one, too. Let's ask Captain Meeker."

"You ask him, Betsy," Kitty said. The crusty old mountain man scared her a little. "He thinks the world of you—I know he'll say yes."

Captain Meeker did say yes. Like all good leaders, he knew that play could sometimes be as helpful and healing as work.

Thanks to Kitty and the other Taylors, natural conduits of gossip, word spread quickly through the train.

Trunks were opened and plundered for their treasure—dresses that had last danced east of the Mississippi, fiddles and banjos and concertinas that hadn't seen the light of day for months.

For the first time in months, Betsy put on the party dress Ma had made for her just a year ago. It was pale yellow taffeta, with bands of dark green ribbon circling the hem. More ribbons, tied in bows, flirted at the sleeves.

Betsy sighed as she looked down over the full skirt of the dress. Even without her shoes on, the hem fell short of her ankles.

*I've grown,* she thought, *again!* She inspected the hem to see if the dress could be let down, but there was less than a half-inch of extra material. She wished she had a long, sweeping underskirt of dark green silk or, at the very least, elegant shoes and stockings.

Since she had neither, she decided to go barefoot. As for the dress—well, she would just have to do something to take everyone's attention away from her bare ankles. She looked down at a pile of mountain flowers she had gathered, meaning to make a bouquet of them. Picking up three flowers, she began braiding their stems together to form a rope. One by one, she added more flowers to the rope, weaving a long, delicate belt. When she was finished, she wound the flowers around her hips. They swayed and trembled with each step she took.

*There,* she thought. *That ought to keep their eyes off my feet.* A few flowers fell to the floor. Betsy retrieved them and tucked them into her hair.

"Are you ready?" Kitty called. Her small face appeared in the wagon flap. "Your sister's beat you to the party—she and Rolfe are already holding hands."

Betsy gave her hair a final pat. Willa, who used to be so particular about her appearance, had changed her dress in two minutes flat. These days, she was like a rushing river, flowing wherever Rolfe was. Love, Betsy guessed, did funny things to you.

She jumped down from the wagon. The sun was just going down behind the mountains, streaking the sky with wild pinks and ocean-deep blues. Someone had started to play "The Girl I Left Behind Me" on the fiddle, and the notes floated like autumn leaves in the high, clear air. A throb of longing rose up and filled Betsy's soul. She wasn't sure what the longing was *for*, exactly—just a longing so sweet and painful it almost choked her.

"I hope George Browne knows how to dance," Kitty said with a determined giggle.

"If he doesn't," Betsy replied, "I'm sure you'll teach him."

"Wouldn't I just love to," Kitty replied, her dark brown eyes sparkling wickedly. "And more than dancing, too. I wonder if Charlie's coming," she went on, careful to keep her voice casual in front of Betsy. "I wonder who he'll dance with."

"I haven't really thought about it," Betsy said briskly.

That, of course, was a lie. She *had* thought about it, all the time she was getting ready. If Charlie behaved himself and acted like a human being, well, then she might—just *might*—dance with him. But if he acted like the lord of the mountains, the way he usually did, she would make him sick with not dancing. She would sparkle and dance and laugh with every other man of the train—even Blue Star and old Jed Marsh—but she'd look past him as if he didn't even exist.

It was such a good plan it made Betsy's blood race even to think about it. By the time she and Kitty entered the circle of dancers, her cheeks were glowing with excitement. Her pulse tapped against her wrists as she scanned the crowd for Charlie. She didn't see him and whirled expectantly when a warm hand touched her shoulder.

It was John Taylor. "Can I dance with you, Betsy?" he asked, honest and eager as a hound.

Betsy smiled up at him as she put her hands in his. Just as well to let Charlie see her with someone else right off, she decided. She was sure that he was somewhere in the crowd. *Probably waiting for me to ask him to dance,* she thought. *Well, he'll have a mighty long wait.*

It was easy to slide into the night in John's arms, and the idea that Charlie might be watching fired her steps. She glided and whirled through the patterns of the dance, her bare ankles flashing and the trailing ends of her flower belt swinging in a wide arc. Two large bonfires had been built, one at either end of the circle, and in the flickering light Betsy's tossing hair was the color of fox fur. She caught the eye of every man in the train—young and old, married and single—

and long before John grew tired of her she was whirled out of his arms by someone else.

Betsy's spirits rose with each new partner who came to her. It was a perfect night, she thought, a night that made up for hardship and unhappiness.

Kitty had slipped off into the shadows with George Browne, she noted, while Willa and Rolfe were dancing almost at her side. Oscar, like the other babies, had been stowed on a pile of quilts beneath a wagon, safe from stepping feet. The lively fiddle music filled the air like laughter, and hands clapped in time to the music. Even Captain Meeker joined in the fun, sweeping Betsy into his arms so gallantly that she barely noticed his limp as they danced.

"Thought I'd have to wait all night to dance with the prettiest girl here," the old man said, winking at her. Ever since he'd taught her to ride bareback, Betsy could do no wrong in his book. "You've 'bout danced with every man there is, east o' Oregon."

Betsy laughed. "Not quite *everyone*," she said lightly.

Captain Meeker's iron-gray eyebrows shot up. "You mean Charlie?" he asked, guessing her thoughts. Betsy found herself blushing. She couldn't think of a thing to say. "Charlie rode out o' here a few hours ago," Mordechai Meeker continued. "Don't know 'xactly why or where to, but that's Charlie for you."

Betsy's spirits sank like a stone going to the bottom of a lake. The golden shimmer that had spilled over the evening vanished. "That's too bad," she heard herself saying woodenly.

Captain Meeker tipped her chin up with a rough finger. "You're not missin' him, are you?" he questioned. "'Tis pointless, missy. Like missin' the wind or anything' else you got no say over."

Betsy bit her lip. Captain Meeker was right. It was silly and stupid of her to let Charlie Freeman spoil her evening—and even more silly and stupid to let everyone see that he had. She forced a bright smile. "I don't miss Charlie at all," she lied. "I just wanted to make my record for dancing with every man on the train complete."

Captain Meeker laughed and spun her in a wide circle. He knew Betsy was lying as well as she knew it herself, and he admired her all the more for the trouble she went to. "By God, Betsy Monroe," he said in a rare burst of praise. "You're just the kind o' gal they need in Oregon!"

No one would ever have guessed that Betsy even noted Charlie's absence. She flirted shamelessly and danced until side stitches pricked her ribs. Only when the music came to a halt did Betsy find herself on the sidelines.

"Why'd they stop?" she cried feverishly, sweeping her hair back from her flushed face.

John Taylor held Betsy tightly by the hand, afraid she would slip away from him before the music began again. "Some kind of announcement, I think," he said.

Captain Meeker stepped into the center of the circle

and held up his hands for silence. "Time to time," he said, "I'm lucky enough to act as preacher on this train, same way as a ship's captain. That means marryin' people off, when there's a need, to keep them from mortal sin." A ripple of lusty laughter swept the crowd before Meeker could continue. "So it's my pleasure," he went on, "to invite you all to a little ceremony two Sundays from now, for Rolfe Nilsson and Willa Monroe."

Betsy heard her own gasp of pleased surprise. She rushed forward and hugged her sister. "I'm so happy for you, Will," she whispered, brushing back a pang of puzzling loneliness. What would she do when Willa was married? Would she just go on and on, congratulating others as they fell in love and left her behind? "Really happy," she said again, pushing the unwelcome thoughts away.

"Let's have a dance for the newlyweds," someone shouted.

"*Almost* newlyweds," Willa corrected, but she gave her hand willingly to Rolfe as the music began again.

"How d'you like that?" John Taylor mused at Betsy's side. "I didn't know a wagon man could marry people." He grinned down at Betsy. "Hey," he said jovially. "Why don't we get married too?"

Betsy looked up at him, at his sparkling eyes and good-natured face. He was, she thought, completely incapable of serious thought. She grinned, falling in with his mood. Love and marriage weren't such serious, earth-shaking matters after all. She could live quite happily without either of them, she was sure. "Why, I'd love to marry you, John," she said. "I think I'd make an ideal wife."

John laughed and took her hand. "'S long as we're engaged, then," he said, "how about a dance?"

Betsy was ready to say yes when a gleam of gold caught her eye. Charlie appeared on the other side of the circle. Warm firelight danced over his tawny hair and shoulders. His buckskin shirt was open, showing the light gold of his chest.

He caught her eye and smiled at her in a way that made her knees lock. She couldn't have taken another step if her life depended on it. Instead of moving into the circle of dancers with John, she stood stiff and still, trembling from a breeze that rolled inside her like a tide.

Charlie cut straight through the circle, walking up to claim her with long strides. Betsy felt his strong fingers grasp her wrist, and she felt the power of his deep-set blue eyes on her face.

John's fingers let go of her other wrist. Without protest, Betsy let Charlie Freeman sweep her into the circle of music and wild, flickering light.

# Chapter 9

IF BETSY HAD LOOKED TO HER LEFT OR RIGHT, SHE would have seen Willa and Captain Meeker smiling their approval as Charlie swept her into his arms.

But Betsy didn't look left or right. She didn't look at anything or anyone but Charlie. His eyes met hers in a steady gaze, sweeping away everything that lay between them. The pressure of his hand on her waist made her knees tremble. For the first time in her life, Betsy found herself searching for something to say. "You're a wonderful dancer," she ventured at last.

Charlie smiled down at her. "Well, don't let it get around," he said. "Might ruin my reputation." As he spoke, a lock of golden hair fell forward. Betsy found herself wanting to reach up and brush it back.

"I won't tell a soul," she promised.

"Good," Charlie said, drawing her a fraction of an inch closer.

Words, Betsy thought, ordinary words, but they were edged with magic, punctuated by the pulsing touch of their bodies. As they danced, Charlie's long legs brushed against her, tapping secret wells of pleasure.

The music ended too quickly. When it stopped, they found themselves alone in the flickering shadows, looking straight into each other's eyes. Charlie's hand was still on her waist. "I'm glad you showed up," Betsy murmured.

"Me too," Charlie said.

She smiled. "I thought maybe you were staying away on purpose."

"Matter of fact," he said, "I was working." She shot him a puzzled glance, and he explained, "I heard something about a train behind us and went back to see if those folks—the Weiners and their friends—had joined up with it."

Betsy pictured him riding through the darkness, alone and maybe thinking of her. "Did they?" she asked.

"Yep. Got their kid back, too. Turns out that other train found her and picked her up."

Betsy let out a shriek of happiness at the news. "That's wonderful!" she cried. Impulsively, she flung her arms around Charlie's neck.

He drew her to him instantly, his arms locking so tightly around her that she gasped for breath. "Oh, Betsy," he whispered, his words getting lost in the tangle of her hair.

Afraid to break the magic of the moment, she didn't answer. Instead, she trailed her fingertips caressingly over his shoulders and pressed her cheek against the bare warmth of his chest. He was all gold and buckskin and strength, and no one in her life had ever set her heart thudding the way he did.

She felt his long fingers gently stroking her cheek and lifting her chin up. She closed her eyes and felt the hot crush of his lips against hers. A warm rush of pleasure threatened to melt her bones to tallow, and she clung to him for support.

"Don't let go of me," she whispered. "Ever."

"I won't," he replied.

But Charlie did let go of her when the music began again. He had to. Someone was sure to spot them in the shadows. He took Betsy's hand and led her back to the circle of dancers, his eyes full of secret words and promises.

Nash Whitcomb sketched the two of them gliding in each other's arms and then, in payment for the picture, demanded a dance with Betsy. Charlie waited impatiently on the sidelines, his eyes never leaving Betsy for an instant.

John Taylor came up and stood beside him. "That Betsy's quite a gal, isn't she?" he asked. Charlie nodded briefly. There was no way he wanted to talk about Betsy with anyone just now, but John didn't seem to notice. "I don't guess there's a bigger flirt ever been born," John babbled.

Charlie shot him a knife-edged look. "What do you mean?"

"Why, I guess you must've missed it. 'Fore you got here, she was dancing pretty as you please with everyone." John laughed, unaware of the sudden change that swept over Charlie's face. "She almost stole

George Browne away from my sister, and she as good as told me she'd marry me. Kissed me proper to seal the bargain, too," John went on. He couldn't remember if Betsy had really kissed him or not, but he was almost certain she had.

A muscle worked in Charlie's jaw. "Kissed you, you say?"

John giggled. "Well, we *were* gettin' engaged," he explained. "I mean, I asked her, and she said sure she would." He laughed again. "'Course, I wouldn't be fool enough to believe her. I know how girls get when they're in a flirting mood."

Charlie's pride suffered a calamitous fall. He realized that Betsy had been playing a game with him. Words and looks and touches didn't mean a thing to her—even John Taylor had been smart enough to figure that out. Only poor, thick-headed Charlie Freeman had been fool enough to think she might really care for him.

It hurt Charlie more than he cared to admit to think that all the time he'd been holding her, letting himself fall halfway in love with her, she'd been busily counting the other hearts she'd gathered. Tarnation—didn't kissing mean a thing to that girl?

He remembered the needy, lovesick way he'd called her name. *That,* he thought with a pang of deep humiliation, *will probably keep her laughing all night long.*

The music ended, and Nash Whitcomb, splendid in his white silk shirt, bowed gallantly to Betsy. Betsy thanked him quickly, her eyes already picking through the crowd that stood at the sidelines. *Charlie*, her heart hummed happily. *Charlie, Charlie, Charlie!* More than anything, she wanted to feel the gentle, controlling pressure of his hands and his lips.

She grinned to herself. She'd kissed other boys before, but she counted Charlie's as the first *real* kiss of her life. Her first real kiss, she thought, and already she'd become an addict. A terrible addict who was going to fall down and roll in the dirt in fits if she didn't get another kiss soon. But her craving was cut short, for, search though she did, she found that Charlie was nowhere in sight.

Betsy's eyes flicked open, welcoming the bright morning air. Happiness flooded through her body, spilling and splashing like a forceful river. *Love*. The word painted itself on her mind as boldly as emigrants painted their names on Independence Rock. She knew she was in love—as much in love with Charlie as Willa was with Rolfe. *More* in love with Charlie, in fact, than anyone had ever been with anyone else. She shivered with excitement, remembering the way he had stepped through the circle to claim her.

Betsy slipped out of bed, careful not to disturb Willa, who was still asleep. There were so many things to get done, she thought as she reached for her clothes. The world was a fuller, busier place than it had been yesterday. She combed her tangled hair with her fingers. Then, as if they had a life and a memory of their own, her fingers began stroking her cheek the way Charlie's fingers had the night before. What did she feel like to him? she wondered. Where was he now, and what was he thinking about?

She jumped down from the wagon. It was still early. Dew soaked the sparse grass, and pink fingers of light brushed color into the sky. A baby cried in a wagon across the circle, and a cooking fire scented the air with smoke and coffee. Betsy leaned against the wagon wheel and stroked the broad, bony skull of the dog, Toby.

Now that she was up, she wasn't sure what she meant to do. Oh, she knew what she *wanted* to do, all right. She wanted to tell Willa everything that had happened between her and Charlie. She wanted to laugh with her about how good being in love felt. But Willa wasn't up yet, and she didn't want to wake her.

Besides, talking to Willa was only one of the things she wanted to do. What she wanted to do most of all was to see Charlie again. Already, standing in the slanting morning light, her body was aching and trembling for his touch.

She'd never figured out where he had disappeared to last night or why, but she'd already made up her mind not to ask. If she was going to love Charlie Freeman, she'd have to love him along with his impulsive comings and goings. And if she was going to keep him loving her back, she was going to have to make him feel free, not tethered like a horse.

Betsy smiled, happy and content with her own wisdom. Why did everyone make such a mystery of it? she wondered. Falling in love was really as easy as pie, if you used your head.

By the time the camp began to stir in earnest, Betsy had a fire started and coffee boiling. Inside their wagon, she heard Willa slide out of bed. Anxious for the day to begin, Betsy cut slices of bread and put them in to fry with the bacon.

She looked up suddenly. Charlie's shoulders, wrapped in buckskin and glowing gold in the sunlight, rose above the shifting morning crowd. He was already mounted on horseback, and Betsy caught her breath at the sight of his fine profile etched against the white cover of a wagon.

She set the pan of frying bread and bacon to the side of the fire and rushed across the circle. "Charlie!" she called, a tide of happiness sweeping her right up to him.

"Hello," he said icily, barely looking at her.

Her face, so full of tender eagerness a moment before, showed a trace of confusion. "Charlie, I—"

"What?" he asked impatiently.

She stepped back. "I wanted to talk to you."

He looked down at her from the height of his handsome horse. "Ain't got time for talkin'," he snapped. "But if it's about last night, don't worry—we both got carried away is all. Didn't mean a thing to either one of us, did it?" His eyes flicked over her scornfully. "Heck, Betsy, you ain't the first girl who wanted a kiss to mark her way across South Pass."

"Oh!" she gasped, as stung as if he'd struck her.

Charlie looked down at her. "Isn't that what you were going to say?"

Betsy squared her shoulders and looked up at him.

She'd rather die than let him see how he'd hurt her. "That," she said with a toss of her head, "is *exactly* what I was going to say." She turned and walked swiftly away from him, brushing tears from her eyes as she went.

When she got back to the wagon, Willa had pulled the pan of bread and bacon from the fire. Rolfe held little Oscar on his knee, crushing crumbs of bread between his big, square fingers and placing them patiently in the baby's mouth. Betsy ignored the three of them. She climbed into the wagon and flung herself headlong onto her scramble of sheets and quilts.

*Love!* She'd been stupid enough to lie here just a few hours ago and think that Charlie Freeman loved her. Well, that was a mistake she'd never make again—not if she lived to be a hundred and ten. The next time she was fool enough to think a man loved her, she'd stick her head under a cold pump, the way they did to drunks.

Soft steps sounded on the wagon boards. "Betsy?" Willa asked. "Are you all right? Do you feel sick or something?"

Betsy shot up off the bed. "I'm fine," she shouted, shaking herself resolutely. "Just fine!"

# Chapter 10

BETSY AND CHARLIE MANAGED TO AVOID EACH other all the way to Fort Hall. But three days beyond the fort, on a Sunday morning, they came face to face at Willa's wedding.

The ceremony was held under the open sky with the whole company looking on.

Betsy stood beside Willa and Rolfe as Captain Meeker read the service. Rolfe wore a clean blue shirt, and someone had lent Willa a dress of striped lavender silk. Betsy, unfortunately, had found nothing to wear but her own yellow dress with the green ribbons. It was the same dress she had worn the night she danced with Charlie at South Pass, and each rustle of taffeta filled her with a tide of memories, as sweet and vivid as they were painful.

Tears prickled behind Betsy's eyelashes when Captain Meeker pronounced Rolfe and Willa man and wife. She blinked rapidly and lifted her chin a fraction, trying to ignore the lonely, longing feeling that suddenly swept over her. A single tear, round and cold as a diamond, slipped down her cheek. Betsy turned her head so that Charlie, watching behind her, wouldn't see the splashing drop.

There was a wedding feast after the ceremony—or what passed for a wedding feast in the middle of the mountains. There could be no cake because they had no butter and eggs, but Kitty Taylor's grandmother made a pie by mixing flour and bacon grease into a dough and filling it with cooked dried apples.

Because it was Sunday, there was a brief debate about whether or not it would be proper to have music and dancing as well. The debate was quickly settled in favor of music, and soon the notes of a waltz filled the air. Betsy watched her sister glide lightly over the ground in Rolfe's arms, the borrowed silk dress fanning around her ankles. The same longing, empty feeling she'd felt during the ceremony pulled at her heart again, and she thought of slipping quietly away.

Before she could get away, the music shifted to a lively, familiar tune—the tune that had been playing the first time she danced with Charlie. Automatically, her eyes picked through the crowd, searching for the gleam of his golden hair.

Her heart sank when she saw him. Blue eyes sparkling, arm extended gallantly, he smiled as he swept Kitty Taylor into the dance. Kitty's delicate, heart-shaped face turned up to him, and her fine red lips parted in a smile. Her small feet flew in a wide arc as Charlie locked his hands around her waist and lifted her high into the air.

For a moment, Betsy thought she was going to

storm right into the circle and tear Kitty to shreds. But the terrible, knife-twisting pain she felt wasn't because of Kitty, Betsy reminded herself. It was because of Charlie—Charlie, who would never settle down—Charlie, who would never, ever give his heart to just one girl. Even if she made Kitty vanish, Charlie would just laugh and find some other girl. That was the way he was—hadn't she learned that the morning they left South Pass?

A large hand caught Betsy's elbow and spun her gently around. "How about a dance with the best man?" John Taylor asked with a grin.

Betsy hid her thoughts behind a quick smile. "I didn't know you were Rolfe's best man," she replied brightly.

"I ain't," John said, offering her his arm, "but I'm the best man here. How about it?"

Betsy held out her hands. "I'm yours," she said, and let John propel her into the circle.

She kept her eyes fastened on John's face the whole time they danced. When he joked with her, she tipped her head way back and laughed, shaking her head in a way that made her long hair brush against her hips. She matched her steps to his and rested her hand lightly on the back of his neck.

But all the time they danced, Betsy's thoughts were on Charlie. Her heart jumped and throbbed whenever he brushed by. Once she looked to the side and found his questioning blue eyes fastened on her. Betsy shivered with excitement, then tore her eyes away from his. *Don't be a fool,* she told herself, giving her attention back to John Taylor. *Don't be a fool—not over Charlie Freeman.*

The dancing went on until midafternoon, for Captain Meeker warned them that this might be their last Sunday of rest. From now on, he said, they'd likely have to travel on Sundays and even overnight in search of grass and water.

Charlie vanished midway through the party, Betsy noticed, leaving Kitty to dance with George Browne. Not that Kitty seemed to mind—she danced as happily with George as she had with Charlie. Kitty's light, uncaring attitude was the only attitude to have where Charlie was concerned, Betsy decided. She wished she could borrow a strong dose of it for herself.

It was John's idea to tie pans and kettles to the newlywed's wagon. "We'll tie 'em close together and hang 'em right from the middle. That way, the least little movement'll set up a noise to wake the dead."

*Willa will die of fright,* Betsy thought at first, but she didn't try to talk John out of the plan. The *old* Willa might have died of fright, she decided. But the new Willa—the Willa who'd shown up somewhere along the trail with roses in her cheeks—*that* Willa would take it all in stride.

They were planning exactly how to tie the pans together when Captain Meeker approached and pulled Betsy away from the group. "I hate to drag you away from the celebration," he said, "but there's somethin' needs talking about."

Betsy followed him to his wagon, stopping short when she saw Charlie lounging against the shoulder-high wheel. He was humming a song, but the tune ended in midair when he saw her. For a minute they stared at each other, bristling like two dogs. "You two know each other, o' course," Captain Meeker said over his shoulder as he climbed the wagon step-up. He motioned for Betsy and Charlie to follow him. "I got somethin' I want to say to you."

Betsy's palms began to itch with apprehension. Had Captain Meeker learned about her fight with Charlie? On a wagon train, an unmended feud could be a dangerous thing, and the old man might intend to lecture both of them into a state of truce. Betsy clenched her fists in the folds of her skirts. She didn't think she could bear having Mordechai Meeker tell her how to manage her heart.

"You two can sit right down over there," the old man said, motioning them to a bed on one side of the wagon.

Betsy sat carefully on one end of the bed, leaving a great gap of space between herself and Charlie. Anxious to avoid looking at Charlie, she looked around the wagon and saw that it was as neat and trim as the cabin of a ship. There was a small table across from the bed, and Captain Meeker leaned against it as he talked to them.

"Seems," he said slowly, folding his arms across his chest, "we've got somethin' of a problem here."

Betsy was sure, then, that he meant to bring up their quarrel. She glanced quickly at Charlie, but his eyes darted away from her. "Problem?" she asked, her voice wavering the way it did whenever she lied. "I don't understand what you mean."

Captain Meeker spat into a huge metal pot that sat on the floor. "How 'bout you, Charlie? You see a problem here?"

"No, sir," Charlie said in a subdued voice. It was almost worth it, Betsy thought gleefully, to see Charlie with so much of the cockiness knocked out of him.

Mordechai Meeker spat again. "Well, we got one, that's for sure. Fortunately, I think I got the solution." Betsy held her breath, waiting for the old man to continue. "Your sister got married today, Betsy. And, in the custom of married folks, I s'pose she'll be movin' in with her husband."

"Of course," Betsy said. She didn't see what all this had to do with her and Charlie.

"Well, that leaves two women, two wagons, and one man. Not very good numbers. The logical thing to do would be for you to jump your wagon here—just leave it behind—and go the rest of the way with your sister and her man."

"No!" Betsy cried, jumping up in alarm. "I can't leave Ma and Pa's wagon." She darted an accusing glance at Charlie. "Bad enough I lost Pa's horse—I'm not leaving the wagon too!"

Mordechai Meeker grinned, revealing his crooked, tobacco-stained teeth. "I was just tellin' you what was the *logical* thing to do," he said. "I didn't think you'd be real interested. But have you given a thought to how you're goin' to manage that wagon alone? I know you've done a good share of the work all the way across, but bein' on your own altogether, without even a sister to help you, that's a differ'nt matter entirely. Can't have it on my train."

Betsy glanced up at him. "Why not just leave me by the side of the road?" she suggested, her voice full of challenging sarcasm. "I'm sure I'll manage somehow." Charlie glanced at her as if he thought the idea had a good deal of merit.

"Nope, wouldn't do that," Captain Meeker said seriously. "It'd ruin my reputation." He searched for his plug of tobacco and bit into it. It took him several minutes of steady chewing to work the tobacco into the pouch of his cheek. "Now, you know that when that Blake fella died back there, his widow hired the only lone man worth havin' to do her drivin' for her. Jed Marsh, he won't do any work but huntin', and Blue Star or that painter fella wouldn't know which end of an ox to put the harness on. That leaves you, Charlie."

Charlie, who'd been idly studying a map pinned to the canvas wall, sqawked with surprise. Betsy smiled in spite of herself. The last time she'd heard a sound like that had been the day her father was notching the ears of their pigs. "Leaves me for what?" Charlie asked.

"Leaves you to help out Betsy, o' course," Captain Meeker said.

"Oh no," Charlie said, his tanned face flushing. "Oh no, Mordechai—I ain't no ox driver."

Captain Meeker shot him a sharp look. "You are

now. Got no choice. What else can we do—leave her by the side of the road?"

"It's a thought," Charlie said.

Betsy stood up. "Don't worry," she said. "I'd *rather* get left at the side of the road than ask you to help me." Her eyes flashed. "You probably couldn't handle a team anyhow."

"Now just a minute," Charlie said, rising to confront her. "It so happens I *can* handle an ox team."

"Good," Captain Meeker said, stepping between them. "Then you'll help Betsy."

"I didn't say that," Charlie said stubbornly.

"Well, by God, you'd *better* say that," Captain Meeker roared, losing patience with both of them. "You two make the best of each other from here on out, because if you don't I'll skin the both o' you. Understand?" They nodded, and Captain Meeker continued, "You move your gear to Betsy's wagon, then, Charlie, and do it right quick. I don't want an unprotected woman in my train—not even for one night." He swung down from the wagon, leaving Charlie and Betsy to work out the details of the situation.

Charlie glared at Betsy. "I suppose you're happy with this darn fool arrangement," he said accusingly.

Betsy bit her lip. She *was* happy, in a way, but she wouldn't give him the satisfaction of saying so. "I don't see any advantage to it," she replied dryly.

He was still glaring at her. "I should never have stopped that night I saw your fire," he sputtered. "Could've saved myself a world of trouble if I'd just kept riding. Darn it all, Betsy, you're the stubbornnest girl I ever met. I told you you'd never get to Oregon in one piece."

Betsy's chin went up. "I'm doing all right so far, aren't I?" she challenged.

"Depends on what you call all right," Charlie said. "In my book, 'all right' would be getting yourself a husband like your sister did—then *he* could worry about you, 'stead of me."

Betsy pushed by him and jumped down from the wagon. "I don't need a husband to take care of me!" she shouted. "Or you either—so you can just forget about moving your gear into my wagon, for all I care!"

But Charlie couldn't forget about moving his gear to her wagon—not when Captain Meeker had ordered him to. Betsy sat in her wagon in flickering lantern light, wondering exactly where she was going to put Charlie's gear. The wagon was packed to the top already, and even though Willa herself might have moved to Rolfe's wagon, most of her belongings remained with Betsy.

*Well, he can just stash his stuff wherever there's room,* she thought, unfastening the buttons of her dress and letting it fall in a heap around her ankles. *And as for Charlie himself—*

She stopped in the middle of her thought. What about Charlie himself? Where in the cramped, crowded wagon was *he* going to sleep?

*Not with me, that's for sure,* Betsy thought, remembering the way Charlie had accused her of being happy with the situation. She picked her dress up and flung it angrily into a far corner of the wagon. *That conceited coyote—he probably thinks I'm just dying to share my bed with him! Well, he can go to the devil if that's what he thinks!*

She searched for the box of linens and yanked a large, clean sheet out of it. Then she climbed onto the top hump-backed trunk and hung one end of the sheet across a wagon rib to make a curtain. A thud sounded at the back of the wagon, and she almost lost her balance. Charlie's bedroll came sailing through the canvas flap, followed by a bundle of clothes, a small trunk, and finally Charlie himself.

"Evening," he said, obviously delighted to catch her off guard. He looked her over from head to toe, his blue eyes dancing. "New style of dress?"

Betsy felt her cheeks turn as hot as the glass of the lantern. In her rush to hang up the curtain, she had forgotten to slip into her nightgown. She was wearing nothing but a low-necked petticoat, one that she knew was too tight across her breasts. She pulled the sheet in front of her for covering. "I was just, um—I thought this would—well, privacy, you know." She felt like an idiot, perched on the top of the trunk. She couldn't get down without letting go of the sheet. "If you're not doing anything," she said, "would you mind handing me my nightgown? It's hanging on that peg over there."

Charlie ignored her request. "Interesting customs you girls from the East have," he commented with a broad grin. He was beginning to think that maybe this arrangement wasn't going to be so bad after all. "Now, tell me again, what are you doing up there?"

Betsy sighed at his deliberate thick-headedness. "I already told you," she said impatiently. "Hanging a sheet up—for privacy."

Charlie's eyebrows quivered with amusement. "Privacy from who?"

"Who do you think?" Betsy flared. "From you, that's who."

Charlie looked at her as if she'd gone delirious with fever. "You mean you think I'm going to sleep in *here*—with *you*?"

Betsy clutched the sheet to her. "Well, I—I mean, isn't that the arrangement? Didn't Captain Meeker say you were supposed to move your gear in here?" She felt ridiculous. It sounded as if she were begging him to sleep with her.

Charlie laughed, enjoying her embarrassment. "Well, I hate to disappoint you, Betsy," he said, "especially since you've got your heart set on it, but where I keep my gear and where I keep myself are two different places. The night Charlie Freeman sleeps with a roof over his head'll be the night snow falls in flakes the size of buffaloes." He winked at her. "So if it's all the same to you, I'll make camp under the wagon."

Betsy felt hurt and horribly humiliated. Clutching the sheet to her chest, she jumped down off the trunk. The cloth ripped in half, trailing behind her like a wide bandage. "I think it's *wonderful* that you want to sleep under the wagon," she fumed. "In fact, I think it's just the place for you. The dog usually sleeps there, so you'll be in good company."

Charlie laughed. "You're a charmer, you know that, Betsy? I can't think of a sweeter girl west of the Mississippi."

He hopped down onto the ground. A second later, his bedroll hit him squarely between the shoulder blades. "You forgot this!" Betsy called.

Charlie crawled under the wagon and stretched out next to Betsy's dog Toby. He stroked the dog's ears idly, a wide smile on his face. Heartless flirt she might be, but there wasn't another girl like her. He hadn't been this happy in days.

# Chapter 11

NO ONE KNEW EXACTLY WHY THE STOCK BEGAN TO die. Some said it was from drinking the water of dust-choked streams. Others said it was from eating bread when the grass ran out. A few said it was from just plain tiredness, and Mrs. Holt—an odd, fanatical sort of woman—said it was a curse from God.

Betsy's opinion was that it was the land of the Snake River Basin itself, which was enough to kill anything, people as well as livestock.

She had imagined the Snake to be a broader, deeper version of the Platte. It wasn't. In fact, it wasn't like anything she could have imagined. The crystal-clear, spring-fed waters of the Snake wound through sheer canyons and cataracts. In some places the water purled and gurgled a mere two hundred feet below them. In other places, the river flowed through canyons three times that deep. No matter how thirsty they were, the water was always tantalizingly out of reach, protected by sheer walls that dropped straight down to the river bed.

The land itself was the hardened lava of old volcanoes, graveled with cinders and bare except for rabbit brush and scrub sage. It was no mystery to Betsy that stock died on this stretch of trail. The wonder to her was that any of them lived at all.

Nor were they the only train to begin losing stock along the way. Every mile they traveled was marked with dead oxen and cattle, and sometimes the stench of carrion was so overpowering that they tied rags soaked in clove oil over their mouths and noses to ward off the smell.

Charlie Freeman, of course, would not be caught dead doing such a greenhorn thing. He refused Betsy's offer of a clove-scented rag, made from her last good petticoat. Dead oxen might rise like bloated boulders from the side of the road, but Charlie rode on as if he were picking his way through flowers and sweet meadow grass.

When one of Betsy's own oxen died on the trail, he got down off his horse, unfastened the harness without a word, and led the rest of the team around the carcass. Betsy looked back at the body of the dead ox. It was like leaving a personal friend behind. But Charlie just remounted his horse and began humming his four-hundred-and-thirteenth chorus of "The Girl I Left Behind Me."

"Don't you know any other songs?" Betsy asked irritably from her seat on the wagon box.

Charlie grinned at her. "I s'pose I do, but I happen to like this one. Come on, I'll teach you the words."

"I *know* the words," Betsy replied. "I ought to— I've been listening to them for two solid weeks now."

" 'I'm lonesome since I crossed the hill, and o'er the moor and valley,' " Charlie sang. " 'Such heavy thoughts my heart do fill, since parting with my Sally.' "

It was the "Sally" part of the song that irritated Betsy. She braced herself whenever Charlie came to it. Sometimes he put the name Sally in, but he was just as likely to sing the name of Annie or Katie or Susie or a dozen other girls. Each new name he put into the song caused Betsy's teeth to clatter against each other. How many girls had Charlie left behind, anyway?

"You've got a voice like a bobcat," she told him, slapping at a mosquito that had settled on her arm. Mosquitoes, apparently, were the only life forms that prospered in this desolate stretch of country.

"Glad you like my singing," Charlie answered happily. He didn't seem to mind mosquitoes any more than he minded dead livestock. "How about another chorus?"

"I'd rather have quinine," Betsy said.

Charlie laughed. " 'Oh, never will I forget the night,' " he sang loudly, " 'the stars so bright above me; they gently lent their silvery light, when first she vowed she loved me.' "

The poor condition of the stock didn't help when it came to crossing the mountains. Unlike the broad, gentle slopes on the eastern side of the Divide, the lava mountains were steep and punishing. The trails up the mountains were littered with belongings left behind to make the wagons lighter. Even so, the rise was often so steep that the emigrants had to unharness the oxen, tie ropes around the front axles, and haul the wagons up by hand.

No one in the train was exempt from the effort. Betsy soon got used to standing on the side of a mountain in a line of men, women, and children, grasping and straining at a rope as if she were involved in a huge game of tug-of-war.

A few men always stayed behind with the wagons. They had the dangerous work of blocking the rear wheels with rocks to keep them from rolling backward. Betsy always held her breath whenever it was Charlie's or Rolfe's turn to do the blocking, for she knew that more than one man had been crushed to death beneath the wheels of a sliding wagon.

They were hauling a wagon up a particularly steep slope one day, with Charlie and Sam Browne blocking the wheels. Suddenly, the ropes frayed and split, and the wagon lurched backward. Betsy lost her balance when the rope went slack in her hands. She scrambled to her feet just in time to see the wagon plunge and shatter against an outcropping of rock.

*Charlie!* she thought. In the weeks since Captain Meeker had ordered them to make the best of each other, she had come to depend on him. Without once talking about it, she and Charlie had made a silent agreement to bury their hurt feelings and work together. They were an odd, unwilling team, shouting and arguing with each other as often as not, but they were a team nonetheless.

When she didn't see him, she started running down the hill. The grade was steep and difficult, and she did more sliding and skating than she did running. She came to a stop at last by grabbing the branch of a quaking aspen. Gasping for breath, she leaned against the tree.

A familiar chuckle filled the air. "Glad you stopped yourself, Betsy," Charlie said, rising from a cluster of antelope brush. "I already had to dodge one wagon today—don't know if I'm up to dodging you, too." He grinned. Blood trickled from a scratch on his forehead. He wiped it away with the back of his hand. "What brings you down this way? Just visiting, or were you worried about me?"

Betsy didn't answer him. Sam Browne, who'd also jumped clear of the hurtling wagon, waved his hat in the air to show that no one had been hurt. He started up the hill ahead of them.

Charlie offered Betsy his arm. "Admit it, Betsy," he said, swaying close to her and dropping his voice to an amused whisper. "You *were* worried about me, just for a fraction of a second, weren't you?"

"Worried about you?" she questioned, looking into his eyes. "I was worried about taking time out to bury you, that's what I was worried about."

"Betsy, you're all heart, you know that?" She didn't answer, but a minute later when he slipped his arm around her waist, she didn't pull away, either.

\*     \*     \*

If going up mountains was hard, coming down was even harder. The Fords, who drove first in the train, lost everything when their wagon plunged over the edge of a steep ravine. After the accident, the Taylors took them in, figuring that a few more mouths to feed would hardly be noticed.

But worse than crossing the mountains was crossing the fierce, tumbling rivers that laced through the canyons. This was a land of lost waterways—of springs that bubbled up out of the rock, roared through the mountains, then disappeared into underground channels.

Their joy at finding water in an unexpected place was always quickly followed by worry over getting around it. Sometimes they would follow a river for miles, looking for a place to cross or hoping that it would disappear into the rocks.

More often than not the river didn't disappear. Instead, it broadened and tumbled, fed by hidden springs, shooting and spraying over rapids of sheer rock. So turbulent were the waters that it was never possible to guess how deep they might be. White foam frothed on the surface of all the rivers, whether they were two feet deep or twenty.

Betsy became an expert at urging frightened stock across the river. After the loss of the Ford wagon, Captain Meeker had moved Betsy and Charlie to the front of the train. It was having Betsy lead the stock across, he often told himself, that accounted for the loss of so few head.

With Charlie driving the team, Betsy would climb onto his horse, attach a rope to the horn of the lead ox, and let the rope play out as she rode out into the river. Then, with her skirt tucked up and water rushing against her bare legs, she would signal to Charlie. While he "giddyapped" the oxen from one end, she cooed and called to them from the other, hauling on the rope all the time. Once the first team was well into the water, the other teams would usually follow. Only rarely did she have to go back and swim a balky animal across. Oxen, Betsy saw with relief, believed in the wisdom of the majority.

Each river crossing left her shivering and exhausted. One day, in a place appropriately called Hell's Canyon, she crossed three rivers in the space of four hours. When they came to a third river near sunset, she looked anxiously at Captain Meeker, hoping he would make camp for the night and leave the river till morning.

But Captain Meeker had grown mindful of the calendar—not the calendar he carried in a book, he told them, but the calendar that was printed on the back of every dog and horse and ox. Their coats were thickening early, and so were the coats of the antelope Jed Marsh brought down with his rifle. If winter was going to come ahead of schedule, he didn't want it to find them still struggling through the mountain passes.

Betsy started to untie her shoes in preparation for the fourth crossing of the day. Charlie put his hand on her arm. "I'll swim the oxen across, Betsy," he said.

She looked at him quizzically. "Are you sure?" she asked.

He was almost as tired as she was, but he managed a smile. "'Course I'm sure," he said.

Betsy didn't argue. She was too exhausted to refuse his offer. Grateful for a chance to rest, she sat on the wagon seat and watched him loop the rope over the horn of the lead animal.

Captain Meeker came galloping back to her as Charlie swam the horse into the river. "What's he doin' out there?" he asked.

"He said he'd lead them this time," Betsy answered.

Captain Meeker frowned, and Betsy realized that he wasn't at all pleased with the arrangement. "Next time," he said, "you do it."

Betsy bit her lip. How could Captain Meeker expect her to cross four rivers in one day? Didn't he realize that she, like everyone else, was capable of being so bone-weary that she wanted to lie down and sleep forever?

Charlie gave the signal and called. At first the oxen didn't respond to the unfamiliar voice. Then Betsy flapped the reins over them and called their names, and they took a few steps forward.

It took twice as long as usual to coax them into the rushing water. When they were still more than twenty yards away from Charlie, they came to a dead stop. Charlie pulled on the rope. He coaxed them and called to them and even swore at them, but nothing he did moved them.

Then Betsy saw the lead ox turn his head to the side. She saw the rolling white of his eye and realized that the force of the current rising and beating against his chest had spooked him. She hauled fiercely on the reins, using all her strength to keep the animal from turning and heading back to the bank.

"This isn't going to work," she shouted to Charlie over the gushing water. "Swim back here and take the reins—I'll trade places with you."

Betsy saw Charlie's face working. "Can't I ride the horse back?" he called.

Betsy shook her head. "You've got to keep the rope taut, or the ox'll turn around. I know he will. Tie the end to the saddle horn—Gray'll stand his ground till I get out there."

Charlie was silent for a minute. Then he cupped his hands and shouted to her. "Betsy—I know this isn't the best time to talk about it, but I've got something to tell you."

"What?"

"I can't swim."

"Well, that's just wonderful!" she shouted. "Why didn't you say so before you got caught in the middle of this river?"

"It didn't exactly come up," he called back. Even at a distance of twenty yards she could see the sheepish expression on his face. It was almost worth all the trouble to see at last that there was something that Charlie Freeman *couldn't* do.

She plunged into the water and waded out to the lead ox. While she stood in the rushing water, soothing and stroking the animal, calming him with her nearness and the comforting weight of her body against his neck, Charlie inched his way back to the wagon. He hauled himself along the length of rope hand over hand. By the time he climbed onto the wagon seat, he was drenched from head to toe.

Betsy waited until he'd wound the reins around his fist; then she swam out to the horse and hauled herself into the saddle. *Darn,* she thought as she felt her foot slip out of the stirrup. She'd forgotten all about her shoes. She usually took them off when she crossed a river, but this time she'd been in a hurry. Now she felt the current grab the soggy leather and pull it from her foot with a sucking *whoosh*. By the time she reached the far bank, she'd lost her other shoe as well.

She got little sympathy from Captain Meeker, who found her shivering on a flat rock, trying to dry herself in the last weak rays of the sun. "Like I said," he told her sternly. "Next time, you swim the stock across."

Exhaustion and the loss of her shoes brought her close to tears. Stock—that's all anyone cared about. As long as the stock got across, no one cared a fig what happened to her. If she died, they probably wouldn't even miss her until it was time to cross the next river.

Betsy let a few angry, grudging tears slip down her cheeks. She brushed them away when Charlie climbed onto the rock and sat down beside her. "Where're your shoes?" he asked, eyeing her bare, rock-bruised feet.

"I lost them in that river," she answered, "in case

you're interested." She slammed her fist angrily against the rock. "They were the only shoes I had, too. I'll probably be fifty before I get another pair."

That night, after they finished eating, Charlie disappeared into the wagon and emerged with a buckskin-wrapped bundle. "These're for you," he said, handing the package to her.

Betsy untied the buckskin thongs and unrolled a pair of beautiful deerskin moccasins. They were Charlie's moccasins—moccasins that had no doubt been made for him by some adoring Indian girl. "For me?" she asked, not quite certain she understood him.

"I figure I owe you a pair," he said. "I mean, it was my fault you lost your shoes."

She wanted to fling her arms around his neck and kiss him, but she caught herself. "Thanks, Charlie," she said, kneeling down to try the moccasins on.

Charlie knelt beside her. "They're probably too big for you, but I figure you can stuff up the toes," he said.

"No," she said. "I think they'll be fine." She frowned at her long, slim legs. "I seem to keep getting taller and taller—even my feet."

Charlie watched her tie the laces of the moccasins around her ankles. "Well," he said gently. "I like your feet, even if they are tall."

Betsy caught his smile in the firelight. "You do?"

"Sure," he said, helping her up. "They give you something to stand on."

He held her hand, and for a second she wondered if he was going to kiss her. Then, just when she was sure he was going to, he let her hand drop and walked away. She would never understand him, she thought, not if she knew him another hundred years. She looked down at her feet and wiggled her toes, snug and warm inside her new moccasins. She didn't even try to hide the smile that came to her when she thought of him.

# Chapter 12

ONE DAY A BAND OF INDIAN WOMEN APPROACHED the camp at sunset. Betsy's first instinct was to reach for her rifle, but it was impossible to be afraid of girls no older than she was, with small children tugging at their skirts. She found that the bundle one woman carried in her arms wasn't a baby at all but a huge salmon wrapped in wet leaves. Others carried woven baskets filled with juniper berries. Betsy breathed a sigh of relief—the women had come to trade.

It was Willa who approached the Indians first. She had a natural knack for odd languages, Betsy thought. Figuring out what the Indian women were saying wasn't all that different from figuring out Rolfe's confused blend of Swedish and English. Beside, the Indians seemed more interested in Willa than in any other woman in the company.

Shyly, they came up to Willa and put their hands out to touch her pale blond hair. They giggled and chattered to each other as they looked into her blue eyes. Willa stood calmly, letting them run their fingers through her hair, letting them turn her around and

Dawn of Love

around as if she were a life-sized doll. But in the end the victory was Willa's, for she got the salmon as well as the berries for the price of a comb and a faded calico skirt.

"I don't know why folks are so afraid of Indians," Betsy told Charlie as they ate their share of the roasted salmon. Things between them had improved a lot since Charlie gave Betsy his moccasins. They ate their meals together and even managed to have whole conversations without getting into an argument. "I haven't seen a single Indian that really had murdering on his mind," she added.

Charlie pulled a clean fish bone from his mouth. "That doesn't mean they aren't out there, Betsy," he said.

Betsy shook her head. "You're just trying to scare me," she said.

"Not necessarily," he answered.

But Betsy didn't believe him. None of the Indians she'd met had been concerned with anything but filling his own pockets. Charlie liked to scare her, that was all. He liked to make it seem as if she needed him to protect her from the wild, howling wilderness. She stood up. "More pie?" she asked. "I made it with the berries those murdering Indians brought around." Charlie held out his plate, and she filled it with a slice of pie.

Betsy couldn't resist continuing. "They intended to scalp us with that salmon," she said. "And I'm *sure* they meant to use the berries for bullets—"

"All right, Betsy," Charlie said.

Betsy grinned. "It was a life-and-death struggle. Why, one of their babies tried to bite my ankle and—"

He caught her by the wrist and pulled her down onto his lap. "All right!" he said, but he was laughing.

Betsy kicked and squirmed, but not hard enough to slip out of his arms. "You know what I think?" she asked, laughing.

"What?"

"I think *you're* the only real danger out here."

Charlie's eyebrows went up. "'S that a fact?" he asked.

"That," Betsy said, pulling away from him at last, "is a fact." He smiled up at her, contented as a cat. "I suppose you think that's a compliment," she added.

Charlie smiled. "I s'pose I do."

The next morning Betsy awoke early. The weather had changed overnight. A cool chill had come into the air, and a light mist hung in the sky. When she jumped down from the wagon, she saw that the tops of the mountains were hidden in wreaths of drifting gray clouds.

Underneath the wagon, Charlie opened his eyes, saw the flash of her moccasins—*his* moccasins, he reminded himself—and smiled. He scratched Toby's ears and waited for the scent of Betsy's coffee to fill the air. He had never wished to put off the end of a trail before, but he did now. He wished he could go on this way forever, crossing mountain after mountain with this hard-hearted, headstrong girl beside him.

Betsy lit a fire and set the enamel coffee pot over it.

Then she looked up again at the spectacular mountains and saw the Indians coming down from the clouds. That's how it seemed, anyway. They were far up on the side of the mountain, and they seemed to be dropping down through the clouds.

*Good*, Betsy thought when she saw that they were headed toward the camp. *I hope they've got another salmon.*

But if they were coming to trade salmon, they must have a whole river full of them, for Indian after Indian dropped down from the clouds, a long row of braves on horseback.

Betsy watched them as they drew closer. The smell of coffee began to scent the air. She saw Mrs. Knight and waved across the circle to her.

"Going to be a cool day, thank the Lord," Mrs. Knight called, smiling. "Husband says we're sure to make fifteen miles today."

Betsy smiled back. "Looks like we'll have more fish, too," she called. She raised her hand to point toward the approaching Indians. Something whizzed by her and tore through the side of the wagon. She heard a scream and saw Mrs. Knight clutch her arm. Betsy couldn't move. What was happening? A bullet hit the ground in front of her, making the hem of her skirt bounce.

*"Charlie!"* she screamed, finding her voice at last.

He slid out from beneath the wagon and leaped to his feet. The Indians swarmed down from the mountain. They were clear of the clouds now, and Betsy saw with a start that there must be at least a hundred of them. Their high, whooping cries filled the air. Bullets sang between Betsy and Charlie.

Charlie grabbed Betsy and pushed her toward the wagon. "Get in!" he cried.

Betsy had one foot on the step-up. An arrow whipped by her face. "What about you?"

"Never mind about me," Charlie said, pushing her forcefully into the wagon. "Just get in there and stay low!"

Betsy sank down between the two long trunks that lined the sides of the wagon. Cold sweat trickled from her armpits, and her stomach flopped and quivered. The high, whooping cries of the Indians came closer and closer. Over the pounding of her heart she could hear the whiz and sting of bullets.

She crouched on the wagon floor for what seemed to be an eternity. Her legs cramped and fell asleep, and she shook them impatiently. Why couldn't she tell what was happening? It wasn't just her uncomfortable position that bothered her or the danger she was in. It was the *not knowing*. She grew more frantic with every round of rifle fire. For all she knew, everyone on the train could have been slaughtered. She might be the only one left alive.

She crept to the end of the wagon on her hands and knees and slipped her fingers under the flap. Then, praying a bullet wouldn't find her, she raised the canvas a half-inch and peered through.

Indians swooped in every direction. They were so close that she could see their faces, painted with fierce stripes of red and black and yellow. Each shot of a rifle or arrow was followed by a wild, piercing cry of victory.

As Betsy watched, the Indians moved closer. They raced their fleet little ponies in a wide circle—a circle that, Betsy realized, was slowly tightening around the wagon train.

An arrow plunked into the wood near her fingers, and Betsy jerked backward. The wagon rocked at her sudden movement. "I told you to stay put!" Charlie shouted.

Betsy realized that he was directly below her. He had gotten safely back under the wagon. She breathed a sigh of relief, then found herself listening for the sound of his rifle. Like all men on the train, Charlie slept with his gun loaded and near him. But he had no backup supply of ammunition, Betsy remembered. He must be conserving his shot for the last possible moment.

Working quickly, she filled her apron with extra rounds of ammunition, then tucked the ends up to keep the shot from spilling out. She grabbed her father's rifle, said a quick prayer, and slipped out of the wagon. A minute later, she was on the ground beside Charlie.

"Didn't I tell you to stay in the wagon?" he lectured.

"I know, but—"

"Darn it, Betsy, this isn't a game. You want to get yourself killed?"

She lay on her side, facing him. "Well, don't get so mad that you'll hit me," she said. "'Cause if you do,

I'll explode." She jerked and tugged at her apron. Rounds of ammunition came spilling out over the ground, and Charlie broke into a broad grin.

"Like I said, Betsy," he crooned, reaching for the shot, "glad to see you." Betsy set about loading her own rifle. Charlie glanced at her with raised eyebrows. "I suppose you can shoot that thing," he commented.

Betsy smiled at him. "Just watch me."

They held the Indians off until early afternoon. Then, with a whoop and a cry, the attackers vanished. They lay under their wagons another two hours, wary of a repeat attack, then crawled stiffly out to survey the damage. Mrs. Knight's arm had been broken by the first bullet. Samuel Browne had had his shoulder grazed, and two wagons had been hit with flaming arrows and burned.

Betsy saw with relief that Willa, Rolfe, and little Oscar had emerged without a scratch. So had Kitty, John, and all the other Taylors. Between skirmishes, Nash Whitcomb had even managed to make several impressive sketches of the Indians.

Charlie brought Betsy water from a canteen. It was warm and gritty, but she was so thirsty that it tasted wonderful. "Thanks," she said, handing the canteen back to him. Their eyes met and promised a truce. Then she looked up at the mountains. She would never see them in quite the same way again. "I'll be glad to get out of here," she said, her eyes meeting his again.

"Me too," Charlie answered. "But I don't think it'll be today."

Betsy looked at him in confusion. "Why not?" she

asked. Surely they were going to scurry out of here while they had the chance.

"Well, those were Snake Indians," Charlie said slowly. "They're looking for horses just now 'cause they're in a war against the Crows. They'll be after us again, probably. We've got a better chance digging in here than we do strung out across some mountain."

Captain Meeker agreed with Charlie. The Indians were likely to attack again tomorrow morning. The company spent the rest of the day preparing. The men dug trenches beneath the wagons while the women made barricades of boxes, trunks, mattresses, and whatever else they could drag from the wagons.

That night, instead of putting all the stock within the protective ring of the wagons, Captain Meeker directed them to turn some horses loose to graze. The horse owners stopped complaining when Meeker explained that if the Indians could run off several head of horses, the train would probably be allowed to pass on.

It was an uneasy night for all of them. Most of the women had grown too nervous to sleep in the wagons, so they spent the night burrowed in the trenches like groundhogs. Betsy herself lay down beside her rifle, Charlie on one side of her and the dog on the other. She fell asleep with her hand on the stock of the gun.

Charlie lay awake long after Betsy was asleep. Pale firelight flickered through the spokes of the wagon wheels, lighting up Betsy's face and hair. He'd never had a chance to study her like this before. He looked a long time at the fine curve of her lips and the curl of her reddish-brown eyelashes. Damn, but she looked like an angel this way, he thought. Now why couldn't she just keep a little more of that sweetness when she was awake?

The night was cold, a mountain night with autumn sweeping down on them from the top of the world. Betsy stirred in her sleep and nestled against him. Charlie didn't know what to do at first. He even thought of turning away from her or waking her up. But when an angel came to you in her sleep, he thought with a smile, you didn't turn her away. He stroked Betsy's unruly tangle of hair and let his arm tighten around her shoulders. Holding her that way, he fell asleep at last.

Betsy woke up with Charlie's arm flung protectively around her. Her cheek, warm and flushed with sleep, was pressed against his chest. *Now how did this happen?* she wondered. She lay a minute without moving, wondering what she should do.

Oh, what she *should* do was obvious—she should roll away from him right now; she should break his hold on her and lecture him about the advances he made. But lying in his arms was so delicious that she couldn't bring herself to do anything at all. She was still lying there, enjoying the nearness of his body, when his eyes flickered open.

"Mornin'," he said, and smiled.

"Good morning yourself," she answered.

Neither of them moved. She felt his arm tighten around her. "Aw, Betsy," he said in a sweet voice.

She trembled and touched her fingertips to his cheek. A wild, piercing cry filled the air. For a minute Betsy thought the sound was a cry of joy escaping from her own lips. Then the sound of pounding hooves jolted her back to reality.

Charlie let go of her. "Indians," he said, reaching for his gun. "They sure got a lousy sense of timing."

The skirmish was shorter than yesterday's attack had been. Apparently Captain Meeker was right about the horses, for the Indians stayed just long enough to gather them up and drive them off across the mountains. Then, with a few farewell shots from their rifles, they disappeared. By midmorning, Captain Meeker was convinced that the train had seen the last of them.

"I'm kind of sorry to see 'em go," Charlie said, winking at Betsy. "Seems they got a way of bringing folks closer together."

Betsy looked away. What had happened between them—or *almost* happened between them—beneath the wagon seemed like a dream now. Even so, the way Charlie had called her name lingered in her ears, bold as the cry of the prairie falcons that wheeled overhead.

# Chapter 13

WILLA, BETSY THOUGHT, WAS NOT QUITE THE SAME after the Indian attack. The roses that had been happily blooming in her cheeks died suddenly, leaving her face pale and drawn. Her blond hair grew flat and lusterless. When Betsy asked Rolfe about it, the tall Swede grew silent and replied only that his wife was fine.

"*I* don't think she's fine," Betsy said to Charlie one night. She was sitting cross-legged by the fire, mending one of her dresses. "I've known Willa all my life, and I know when she looks sick and when she doesn't." Without realizing it, she had gotten into the habit of sharing her worries with Charlie.

Charlie shrugged. "Why don't you just ask *her* how she feels?" he suggested.

"I don't want to worry her. You know how Willa is."

"No, I don't know how Willa is," he replied, "but I know how you are."

Betsy looked up, needle poised in midair. "How's that?" she asked.

"Confusin'."

Her needle punched down through the cloth. "I beg your pardon," Betsy said tartly. "I happen to think I'm the *least* confusing girl west of the Rockies." She liked saying that, now that they had crossed the worst of the mountains. She found a way to say "west of the Rockies" at least two or three times a day.

Charlie looked up from the harness he was working on and grinned at her. "Well, that ain't much of a claim," he said. "There aren't all that many girls west of the Rockies yet."

She sighed with exasperation. "Do you think you could stop joking for two solid minutes?" she said. "I really *am* worried."

Charlie's brow furrowed. "I know you are, Betsy," he said. "I'm not so good at talking about serious things as I am at joking. You know that much, I reckon."

For a split second, their eyes met in the firelight. Then Betsy looked down at the dress in her lap. "How'd we get to talking about what I know?" she asked. "It's Willa I'm worried about. I'm *sure* there's something wrong with her."

Charlie wanted to say something comforting but couldn't find the words. "Maybe it's just married life," he suggested at last, hoping to make her smile. "Bein' married's enough to take the life out of anyone, in my opinion."

Betsy's needle flew back and forth impatiently,

punctuating the air with rhythmic "thwunking" sounds as it bit into the fabric.

"I was just giving you my opinion," Charlie said defensively. "Why'd you ask me what I thought if you didn't want my opinion?"

When he glanced up, he saw that Betsy was staring into the fire. "You know what I think?" she asked at last.

"What?" Charlie asked. It was just like Betsy, he thought, to ask you your opinion and then give you hers instead.

"I think she feels betrayed by those Indians."

"That doesn't make any sense at all, Betsy."

"Yes it does," Betsy explained. "You know those women we traded for fish with? Well, Willa heard Captain Meeker say it was their braves who attacked us. Willa was so nice to them—she didn't even get upset when they kept sticking their fingers in her hair. I think she feels those women kind of turned us in. You know, went back to their husbands and told them where we were and how many horses we had and so on. See how much sense that makes?"

Charlie shrugged. "I guess," he answered. The only thing that made sense to him was that Willa should be as complex and confusing as her sister was.

Betsy's needle thwunked on. "Imagine that—those girls being so friendly to us and then going straight back to their husbands!"

Charlie couldn't resist teasing her. "Like I said before," he ventured, "marriage isn't 'xactly the most civilized institution."

Betsy knotted the thread and bit it with her teeth. "I don't see you turning down the comforts of a home, though," she said.

"Like what?" he asked.

"Like getting your meals cooked for you," she said. "Like getting hot coffee every morning."

She started to fold the dress she'd been mending. Something was wrong. When she picked it up, her skirt came with it. She scrambled to her feet. The dress clung to her apron like a spiderweb. All the time she'd been mending, she'd been stitching the dress to her apron.

Charlie rocked with laughter. He stood up and walked around to where she was standing. "What's this?" he asked. He bent over and picked up a sleeve that trailed on the ground. He was laughing so hard he was practically hiccoughing. "Is this one of the comforts you were talking about? Will you do my mending, too? Like this?"

"Oh, hush up," Betsy snapped. "You don't need to tell the whole train about it." She searched for a knife and started ripping out the stitches she had just sewn.

Charlie was still laughing. "Betsy, you'd make somebody a terrific wife, you know that? He might have to go naked, but he probably wouldn't get too bored."

"Good night!" she said as she climbed into the wagon. "And try not to snore again tonight—I don't know who's worse, you or the dog, but it sounds like there's an earthquake underneath the wagon." She could hear him laughing behind her.

Later, long after he was asleep, she lay awake in the wagon. She wondered if he'd meant what he'd said about her making a good wife. Probably not, she decided. But it was nice to think about.

Betsy's feeling that there was something wrong with her sister persisted. Sometimes Charlie would catch her brooding away the hours, her face set in a deep frown as she "geed" and "hawed" and "giddyapped" to the oxen.

Those were the times he longed to take her in his arms and stroke her hair. He wanted to pull her to him and tell her everything would be all right. Just looking at her made his chest ache with wanting to hold her, and sometimes he came close to doing just that. But every time he felt the urge, he hesitated. What if she tossed her head and pushed him away? Worse yet, what if she tumbled into his arms—only to tumble out again and go off with John Taylor the minute the opportunity arose?

No, he'd come close to giving her his heart that night at South Pass, and he'd ended up feeling like a fool. He was better off as he was, a no-strings man with no one to tie him down with her tenderness.

Betsy was so sunk in her own brooding that she never even noticed Charlie's watchful eyes on her. As they started through the steep-sided valleys of the Blue Mountains, she felt as if they were entering a place of no return. Shadows of doom seemed to hang in the air, and Betsy worried that the shadows would come to rest on Willa.

Betsy did her best to shake off the dark mood. Perhaps it was just the weather that dulled her spirits, she told herself. It was certainly possible, for now a permanent chill had come into the air, and the rivers they crossed were so cold that she came out with her teeth chattering. Every afternoon woolly gray clouds gathered above them, spilling rain down onto the emigrants.

The wagon covers that had been stiff and water-resistant a thousand miles back were now in sad repair. Torn and patched, they offered poor protection against the rain. Kitty Taylor developed a hacking cough, and Mrs. Knight, whose arm was mending slowly, claimed that the dampness gave her mule-sized headaches.

To Betsy it seemed that between the rain and the rivers they might well drown before they got to the end of the trail. Even though they caulked the wagons with pitch before each crossing, the boards had grown so loose from jolting up and down mountains that they leaked like sieves.

Willa spent an afternoon in tears when she opened a trunk and discovered their mother's fine linen ruined by mildew. Betsy threw the ruined linen out. She tried not to look back at it, sitting in its little chest by the side of the trail. She did, though—just once—and found tears stinging her eyes. Her mother had a fine hand for needlework. She had spent hours on those tablecloths and napkins.

Betsy blinked hard. It was only linen, after all. Linen could be replaced, one way or another. But telling herself that didn't help. The ruined linen seemed to be an ominous warning, a reminder of how much she had to lose and how easily the mountains could take it away from her.

One day they crossed a river so cold and turbulent that it left Betsy numb and gasping for breath. Instead of making repeated crossings to help with the stock, as she often did, Captain Meeker told her to stay on the bank.

Charlie brought her a blanket and wrapped it around her shoulders. "You look just like an Indian," he said. "Warmer?"

Betsy nodded. "All except my feet. I don't think my feet will ever get warm again."

"Well, we'll see what we can do about that," Charlie said. He pushed her gently to the ground and loosened her moccasins. Then, one at a time, he began chafing her chilled feet between his hands. "How's that feel?" he asked after a few minutes.

Betsy let out a contented sigh. "Like heaven," she said. She smiled at him. "I'm glad to see you're good for something after all."

There was a sudden tumult from the back. Betsy looked down and saw John Taylor's big bay horse plunging wildly in the middle of the river. John was nowhere in sight.

She leaped to her feet and flew down to the water. In the swirl of the current she could see John's head bobbing above the surface. He'd fallen from his plunging horse and was being sucked under by the current. Even in a calm stream John was no swimmer, and this water was so numbingly cold that he was completely helpless.

Betsy plunged into the water. The cold water made her chest ache. Her muscles contracted in protest, and it took all her strength to push herself into the middle of the stream.

She swam to the spot where she'd seen John's bobbing, panic-stricken face. When she got there, he was nowhere in sight. She took a deep breath and dove beneath the surface. She stuck out her hands in the water, searching with her fingertips because she could see nothing in the gloom. John's arm bumped against her face, and she grabbed it.

There was no oxygen left in her lungs, and tiny silver lights popped behind her eyelids. It occurred to her that she and John might both drown, but she refused to let go of his arm. She broke the surface at last, not knowing whether John was alive or not. As fresh air filled her lungs, she heard a watery gasp beside her. Yes—he was alive!

She and John had been carried downstream, but she could see Charlie on the shore, feeding a rope out to her. "John," she gasped, keeping her hold on him. "It's me—Betsy. Just hold on to me till I can catch the rope."

But suddenly he began to fight her. He wrenched himself away from her, kicking her with his foot and sending her ducking under the current. Betsy had heard of drowning folks fighting those who tried to save them, but she couldn't remember having heard what to do about it. She came to the surface and saw John's shadow beneath the cloudy water. Taking another deep breath, she grabbed for him.

Betsy succeeded in bringing John to the surface two more times, but each time he struggled away from her. And each time he fought her off, she grew weaker and more exhausted. On her fourth plunge beneath the surface, she was unable to find him at all. She dove and dove, searching frantically through the cold gloom. Finally she realized that it was no use. And if she dove many more times, she herself would be too exhausted to struggle to the surface.

Charlie waded waist-deep into the water to pull her to shore. She was so exhausted that her knees trembled. She fell against Charlie's chest, tears streaming down her face. "Oh, Charlie," she sobbed. "I tried so hard . . . I tried so hard, and I almost saved him." She cried harder and harder. "Why did he fight me like that? I could have got him in if he'd let me."

Charlie didn't know what to do. He'd never had a girl crying against him this way, and it wasn't something he was especially good at. But this wasn't just any girl, he thought in a rush of feeling. This was Betsy—*Betsy*—trembling and crying against him as if her heart would break.

He stroked her sodden hair. He stroked her shoulders and wrapped his arms tightly around her. Then he picked her up and carried her up the bank to their wagon. He got her into the wagon and pulled her wet clothes off her. Willa brought a pile of quilts and felt

Betsy's forehead. She told Charlie privately that Betsy had been in the icy water far too long. That, and the shock of John's death, had given her a fever.

Charlie sat beside Betsy in the wagon all night long. He made a little light by putting a rag in a dish of bacon fat. Sometimes he held her hand, and sometimes he just looked at her fever-red cheeks. Once her eyes flickered open. "Oh, Charlie," she said. "I'm so *cold*."

That's when he lay down beside her and warmed her with his body. It seemed like the most natural thing in the world to do.

# Chapter 14

BETSY OPENED HER EYES ON AN AFTERNOON TWO days later. Sunlight streamed into the wagon through a split in the canvas top. It fell in a bright shaft, touching everything with gold. Betsy blinked against the bright light. Then a piece of the tawny sunlight broke away and hovered over her. It was Charlie, smiling down at her.

"Howdy," he said. He was holding her hand in both of his. "Welcome back."

Betsy swallowed and tried to smile back. Her lips felt dry and swollen. She was as thirsty as if she'd crossed a desert without water. The air in the wagon was still and sweet. She could have lain there forever, she thought, with Charlie holding her hand. "Hello, Charlie," she managed at last, but the words sounded more like a frog croak than a greeting.

His blue eyes danced at her. Better than all the sunlight in the world, she thought. "Got your singin' voice back, I see," he said with a grin. He handed her a dipper of water from a nearby bucket, holding her head while she drank.

The water made her voice better. "How long have I been—?"

"Asleep?" Charlie filled in. "About two days. You got to stop takin' these long naps, Betsy."

Clouds moved over the face of the sun, plunging the inside of the wagon into sudden gloom. Betsy shivered violently. Charlie took her hand again. "Shh," he said soothingly. "Everything's all right now."

But everything wasn't all right. There was a cold spot in Betsy's heart like a chip of ice. One by one, memories came floating back to her. She remembered the numbing coldness of water swirling around her. She remembered diving over and over again, burrowing into the murky wetness until her lungs ached. She remembered John Taylor fighting her, slipping out of her grasp, and sinking beneath the cloudy water.

Suddenly her fingers tightened around Charlie's. "Where's John?" she asked in a choking voice. There was still one tiny shred of hope, and she clung to it desperately.

But one look at Charlie's face erased that hope forever. "I'm sorry, Betsy," he said. He didn't want to tell her the details—that they had searched downriver for John's body for two days without finding a trace of him.

Betsy turned her face toward the wall. Two huge tears swept down her cheeks. "I tried," she said, turning back to Charlie. "I tried so hard to get him to shore with me."

"I know you did, Betsy," he said softly.

Betsy was silent for a moment. Then she asked thoughtfully, "How's Kitty?"

"As good as can be expected," Charlie answered.

The Taylor clan was in mourning. Charlie told her a little about it, knowing she would keep asking questions until she felt satisfied. For the past two nights they had sat up by candlelight, making their peace with the fact that John was dead. There had been a prayer service, led by Mr. Quigley in his beautiful voice, and the Taylor women had shed a lot of tears.

Betsy lay looking up at the wagon cover. Her body felt weak and strangely peaceful. Her mind, however, was as strong and restless as ever. There was something strange, she thought. Why was the air so still? Why were they stopped—in the middle of the day? "Where are we?" she asked suspiciously.

Charlie forced a cheerful grin. "Still east of the Pacific Ocean, I reckon."

"No, no," she said, clutching his hand. "Where *are* we? Why aren't we moving?" Charlie had promised himself he wouldn't tell her the truth—not until she was well enough to handle it. "We're still at the river, aren't we?" she guessed. *"Why aren't we moving?"*

"Well, we've been waiting for you to get better," he ventured.

That was a lie, and she knew it. "Charlie," she said reprovingly.

"And then, too," he said, "we've been—uh—looking for John's body." Another lie, he thought, but only part of one. They *had* been searching for John's body, even if that wasn't the real reason they'd stopped.

It took Betsy longer this time, but she was still able to see through his deception. Captain Meeker was concerned with getting out of the Blue Mountains as quickly as possible. He wouldn't stop to search the river for a drowned man, she reasoned; he would see to the living first. The only reason he would stop for two whole days was if they *couldn't* travel.

Her fingernails dug into Charlie's hand. "It's cholera again, isn't it?" she cried in terror. She pulled herself up to a sitting position. Her hair tumbled wildly about her shoulders, and her eyes, still lit by fever, blazed at him. "We're all going to die, aren't we?"

Charlie soothed her. "No, no," he said, tucking the quilts around her again. "It isn't cholera. Just a little fever—mountain fever, I guess, just like you got. Comes from gettin' wet and dry and wet again."

Betsy's effort to sit up had completely exhausted her. "Is that all?" she asked, letting herself sink back down onto the bed.

Charlie breathed a sigh of relief. "That's all," he said.

"Oh," she started to answer, but she fell asleep in the middle of the word.

For two more days Charlie took care of Betsy. He fed her and kept her tucked in and even tried to comb her tangled hair. Betsy sat up cross-legged in bed, her back to him, and tried to tell him how to make a braid. He tried three times but each attempt ended in disaster. Finally he admitted defeat.

"Look, Betsy," he said. "Why don't we just do it the way Indian girls do?"

"How's that?" she asked curiously. Now that she felt better, her interest in life was coming back.

Charlie parted her hair down the middle from her forehead to the nape of her neck. Then he gathered her hair into two pigtails and got out two long strips of rawhide. Patiently, he wound the rawhide around each pigtail, binding it securely.

The look of determined concentration on his face as he worked on her hair made Betsy want to laugh. "How do I look?" she asked when he'd finished.

He grinned at her. "Ready for war," he said.

"I didn't know Indian girls went to war," she replied.

"Only with their husbands," he informed her.

Betsy laughed. There was a good chance she looked completely ridiculous in the Indian-style pigtails, but she didn't care. If she wanted something fancier, she would just have to wait for Willa to come and do her hair over again.

Betsy stopped laughing suddenly. She must have gone weak in the head not to have thought of it before. Willa. Where was she? Why hadn't she once come to the wagon? Why was it Charlie—only Charlie—taking care of her?

Charlie could almost see her mind working. Her brows knit together, and she worried her lower lip with her teeth. "Where is she?" she asked him.

"Who?" Charlie asked, trying to look puzzled.

"Willa, of course. Something's wrong with her, isn't it?"

Charlie didn't know what to tell her. "It's just a touch of the fever," he managed to say at last.

Betsy didn't believe him. Her worry over Willa—her feeling that an awful shadow was hanging over her—returned. She swung her legs over the edge of the bed and stood up. "I'm going to see for myself," she said, reaching for her dress.

Charlie tried to pull the dress away from her. "Now Betsy, you know you aren't well enough yet to—"

"Leave me alone so I can get dressed," she said calmly. "I'm well enough to walk from one wagon to another. I want to see Willa."

Charlie was mournful as he watched her go. Betsy had guessed the secret he'd been keeping from her since her fever broke. Willa *was* sick—and with more than a touch of fever, too. At this very moment, Willa was tossing in delirium. No one knew whether she was going to live or not.

Willa's illness burned away the last traces of Betsy's own fever. She sat by her sister's bed for two solid days without sleeping, dipping rags in cool water and sponging Willa's burning forehead.

News reached her that George Browne's mother had died, and so had one of Kitty Taylor's little brothers. Nash Whitcomb had the fever too, but it looked as if he might pull through. Betsy shut all these tragedies from her mind. Nothing and no one mattered to her but

Willa. Charlie worried that if Willa died Betsy might try to die right along with her.

But Willa didn't die. One morning Betsy came in with a bucket of fresh water and saw her sister's blue eyes open. Her heart stopped at first, for she feared her sister might be dead. But when the pale eyelids fluttered once, then twice, Betsy knew her sister was alive.

"Willa!" Betsy cried, setting the bucket down so swiftly that water sloshed over the edge.

"It's me, Bets," Willa said in a weak voice. Then her eyelids fluttered again, and she went to sleep. When she woke up four hours later, Betsy had hot food ready for her.

"I'm afraid it probably isn't too good," Betsy apologized, blinking back tears of exhaustion and relief. "You know what kind of cook I am."

Willa smiled and tried to eat. Rolfe sat on the bed beside her, and Betsy held little Oscar on her lap so Willa could watch him while she ate. When Willa had eaten as much as she could, Betsy took the plates outside to wash. She was about to return to her own wagon for the first time in three days when Rolfe came to get her. "Villa vants to talk to you," he said. His English had improved since he'd married Willa, but it still went up and down, like wagons crossing mountains.

Betsy dried her hands on her apron. "All right," she said.

A lantern glowed inside the wagon. Willa's pale hair

fanned on the pillow like strands of flax. "Sit down, Bets," she said softly. "Here, on the bed beside me."

Betsy sat down and looked into Willa's eyes. They were sunken and rimmed with shadows, but a determined spark burned deep in the pupils. "Do you feel all right, Will?"

Willa nodded. "Considering, I feel fine. There's just something I forgot to tell you. I meant to, before I took sick, but I didn't get around to it. I want to now."

Betsy shivered with apprehension. She remembered how rundown Willa had looked before her illness. Was something wrong with her sister—something even more serious than mountain fever? Betsy ran her palm over Willa's forehead. "What is it, Will?"

Willa's hands took Betsy's. "I'm going to have a baby, Bets. Isn't that wonderful?"

Betsy stared at her sister. It had never occurred to her that Willa might be pregnant. Now, at least, she understood why her sister's cheeks had suddenly turned so pale and flat. She bent down and kissed Willa's cheek. "Of course it's wonderful—just so long as it doesn't happen right away."

Willa laughed weakly. "Oh, it won't be for a long time yet—not until the beginning of next summer. Rolfe promised that we'd have a house by then, and— oh Bets, do you want to come live with us? I'd love to have you, and so would Rolfe."

Betsy didn't answer right away. She'd never considered what would happen once they got to the end of the trail. Most of the time it had seemed as if they'd just go on crossing mountains and rivers forever. "We'll see, Willa," she said at last. "You never know what might come up—I mean, didn't I once say I intended to go on stage and dance in tights when we got to Oregon?" She forced herself to smile. "I might just do that, you know."

She left the wagon in a thoughtful mood. The trail, bitter as it had been, had also been glorious. It was almost over now—in another month they would scatter like leaves in the wind. The hundred-odd people who had shared so much with each other would never see each other again, unless it was in heaven.

And where would *she* scatter to? Betsy asked herself. She loved her sister, and Rolfe and little Oscar too, but the idea of being an aunt in someone else's house didn't appeal to her. Perhaps she and Kitty could go off to some city together. But she wasn't sure if there were cities in Oregon, and even if there were she knew that Kitty was planning on being engaged to George Browne by the time the trail ended. Well, Betsy told herself, she could always stick with her original plan and start a farm by herself. But, oh, how lonely that would be!

The wagon step-up creaked as she set her foot on it. Charlie, stretched out beside the dog under the wagon, called up to her. "'S that you, Betsy?" he asked.

"Yes," she said.

"How's Willa?"

"Awake," she answered. "And going to have a baby."

She heard Charlie's whistle of surprise. "Leave it to

Rolfe," he said. "I always knew those Swedes were dependable."

"It's Willa who's having the baby," Betsy pointed out.

Charlie was silent for a minute. Then he called to her again. "Betsy?"

"Yes?"

"I'm glad you're back. My coffee tastes even worse than yours. I found that out."

It wasn't the same as him saying he missed her, but it was close enough. "Thank you, Charlie," she said. Since Captain Meeker had ordered them to make the best of each other, they'd truly become a team. There was something sweetly delicious about knowing that Charlie needed her and depended on her, even if it was only for her bitter-tasting coffee. She tried not to think about the fact that, in a few short weeks, he would disappear from her life forever.

# Chapter 15

THEIR LOSSES IN THE BLUE MOUNTAINS WERE heavy, and all of Betsy's dark premonitions settled on her shoulders like crows. Besides fever, they had weather to contend with. Betsy woke one morning to discover that a dusting of fine snow had sifted into the wagon overnight.

That morning it was so cold driving that her hands grew stiff and swollen. She had long ago worn out the woolen stockings she might have used for mits, so she tore one of her dresses into long strips of cloth and wrapped the strips around her numb fingers.

The overnight chills were even harder on the gaunt oxen than they were on the rest of the company. Every morning the train woke up to discover two or three of the animals dead. The death of each ox was a domestic tragedy, for the surviving beasts were no longer strong enough to take up the slack. The unlucky family that lost a draft animal had the sad task of discarding enough belongings to lighten the wagon.

Along the passes of the Blue Mountains they abandoned a fortune's worth of dishes, linens, and furniture. When Betsy lost her second ox, she and Willa spent an entire evening sorting through their belongings. The heaviest object in the wagon was the cherrywood chest Pa had made—the chest that Betsy had been using for a bed all the way west. Hauling it down the mountains, Charlie said, would be enough to kill their remaining animals.

But neither Willa nor Betsy could bring herself to abandon the chest. Instead they discarded skillets and kettles and anything else they could think of. Skillets, Betsy said, were just skillets. They could be replaced somehow.

Nash Whitcomb spent hours sketching the piles of abandoned belongings. He painted a huge picture of the emigrants, grim-faced and reduced to rags, plodding along beside their skinny oxen. The picture was so real you could almost touch the ribs of the oxen, and Betsy loved it in a strange way. She was the only one who did, though—almost everyone else felt the painter had betrayed them by showing them so poor and down-in-the-mouth.

Nash refused to make the oxen fatter, and he refused to paint out the rips and tears in the wagon covers. He titled the painting *Almost There*. "Just wait," he told them. "One day that painting'll go in a museum, and people'll come to see what the *real* heroes of the West looked like."

Mrs. Knight sniffed and peered at her image on the canvas. "I should hope *not,* Mr. Whitcomb. I hate to think of strangers looking at me with my mouth set thataway."

Betsy's own image on the canvas was nothing to sing about, either. Her face looked sharp as an old woman's, and her hair hung around her face in dull tangles. Charlie rode beside her in the picture, his hat slouched so low you could hardly see his face. It was a far cry from *Young Hearts of the Prairie,* but Betsy liked it anyway. She wondered if the people who came after her, hundreds of years after her, would look at the painting and guess all that had happened to her along the way.

Life had a way of evening itself out, Captain Meeker said. As if to reward them for all they had been through and all they had lost, the land changed abruptly. They burst out of the Blue Mountains into a wild, sweet land more beautiful than anything Betsy could have imagined. One more hurdle, the Deschutes River, still lay ahead, but that didn't diminish the sense they all had of landing smack in the middle of paradise.

This was the jewel of land, wedged between the Blue Mountains and the Cascades, that everyone meant when they said *Oregon.* This was the land men dreamed about and died trying to get to.

Each day disclosed new wonders to Betsy. The short, spindly trees and scrub brush disappeared, replaced by lodgepole pines and fir trees that rose more than a hundred feet into the air.

The land of the Snake River had been black and barren, but here everything was green and gold with life. Yellow rhododendron and purple heather grew in the high mountain meadows, along with plants Betsy had never heard the names of: Indian paintbrush, basket grass, and something Charlie called avalanche lilies. The avalanche lilies were Betsy's favorites—masses of tiny white flowers that fell like an avalanche of snow through the grass.

Willa had been weak and pale since her fever. The baby, she said, was taking all her strength. So one Sunday afternoon Charlie took Betsy part way up a mountain slope to gather wild huckleberries for her sister. The huckleberry fields, scattered through the cool forests, stretched as far as Betsy could see. Charlie told her it wasn't unusual for a single huckleberry patch to cover as much as a thousand acres.

Betsy had not seen fresh fruit for months. She spend the first half-hour doing as much eating as picking, staining her mouth dark blue from the juice of the huge berries. Then, when she'd had her fill, she set about filling the buckets she had brought with her.

Charlie, picking a few yards away, looked at her over his shoulder. "These'd make a mighty good pie," he said, sucking on one of the berries.

She looked at him in exaggerated disbelief. "You're not telling me you'd actually settle for one of *my* pies, are you?"

Charlie grinned at her. "Your cookin' ain't actually that bad, Betsy. Fact, I've kind of got used to it."

"You have?"

"Sure. 'Course, some folks get used to drinkin' poisoned water, too, if they drink it often enough."

She fired a huckleberry at him and it smacked

against his forehead, leaving a purple smudge. The startled look on his face made her laugh. "Watch out," she said. "I may not be much of a cook, but I'm a terrific shot."

Charlie launched two huckleberries in reply. "Maybe so," he said, "but you've met your match."

It was a challenge of all-out war between them. They fired berries back and forth like children, pelting each other until their clothes were stained with purple. "Surrender?" Charlie called to her.

Betsy grabbed a handful of berries. "Not on your life," she called. "I'm just getting started."

"Stop!" Charlie shouted as the berries bounced against him. "Murder! She's murderin' me!"

He waded through the brush to her and grabbed her hands. She struggled against him, remembering all the fighting tricks she knew from her tomboy days. He tripped over her foot and they went down together in the brush. He didn't relax his hold on her, and they tumbled over and over, laughing and gasping for breath.

When Betsy looked up, Charlie was on top of her. His blue eyes danced. "Now do you surrender?" he asked, his body rocking with laughter.

*"No!"* she shrieked, struggling to get a foot free.

"I think you better, or else—" he said.

"Or else what?"

"Or else—"

His words were interrupted by a sudden snuffling noise beside them. Betsy twisted her head and came nose to nose with a black bear. She felt the bear's wet nose graze her arm, as if he were considering whether or not she was worth eating.

"Boo!" Charlie said, and the bear scampered off. It was clumsy with summer fat, and they could see its black rump and tail bouncing through the brush.

Charlie let go of Betsy and stood up. She got to her feet beside him. "I thought bears were fiercer than that," she said. "What do you suppose he was so scared of?"

Charlie grinned at her. "I don't know," he said. "Maybe he heard about your cooking."

They ate huckleberries for two days solid, and Willa claimed she'd gained weight from the huckleberry pie Kitty Taylor's grandmother, in the midst of her mourning, had made. Betsy couldn't see that her sister had gained an ounce, but at least Willa had lost that sunken-eyed, hollow-cheeked look. A good thing, too, Betsy thought, for they were nearing the perilous Deschutes River.

Betsy had heard all about the Deschutes from Charlie. It had been named by the first white men who saw it, hardy Frenchmen who called it "the river of falls" for its many sets of rock-studded rapids.

"If it's so full of rapids," Betsy asked, "how are we going to get across it?"

"Same way everybody else does," Charlie said. "We'll build rafts and try to float the wagons across. That'll give the stock a few days to rest. Then we'll swim 'em across by themselves."

Betsy looked at him. She'd seen the swirling waters

of the Snake, a hundred times tamer than the Deschutes, according to Charlie. "Does that work?" she asked.

"Sometimes," Charlie said. He grinned at her. "I'm not worried about you, Betsy. You swim like a muskrat."

"It's Willa," Betsy told him. "Haven't you noticed how kind of slow and clumsy she's gotten with the baby?"

Charlie had noticed, but he hadn't said anything. "Rolfe's a good man," he said. "He'll take care of her."

Betsy snorted. "He doesn't swim any better than she does. No, I'll cross with her myself, that's all."

Charlie didn't say anything. He didn't even try to talk her out of it. In fact, he admired her decision. Crossing the Deschutes once was enough for practically anybody. Only Betsy Monroe would think to do it twice.

They camped two days on the banks of the river while the men cut logs and made them into rafts. Captain Meeker's plan was to tie each of the rafts to sturdy ropes and haul them across one at a time, using sheer manpower to power the ropes.

The roaring, churning Deschutes more than lived up to its name, and there were moments when Willa didn't want to cross at all.

"We've seen plenty of good land back that way," she argued, pointing in the direction they'd come. "Why don't we go back there and stake our claim?"

"And keep Rolfe out of the best farmland in the country?" Betsy asked, making light of her sister's fears. "Sure, the land back that way is fine, but the land on the other side's the best of all."

Drizzle fell all morning long on the day of the crossing. Captain Meeker had decided to send the Nilssons across first, to get Willa's nervousness out of the way. Betsy's wagon would be loaded onto the second raft.

As they gathered on the riverbank, Willa's face showed pale and determined beneath the brim of her faded bonnet. Betsy herself was none too sure the rafts would hold them, but she hid her fears beneath talk of the sweet land that awaited them. Even Charlie did not guess that her first step onto the quaking raft made her shiver.

The logs of the raft sank when the wagon was rolled onto it. Cold water splashed up over Betsy's ankles. Willa uttered a nervous little cry, sure they were sinking. "It's all right, Will," Betsy assured her. "Just a little water, 's all." She settled her sister on a trunk beside the wagon. "Don't take it into your mind to go swimming, now," she said with a wink.

Rolfe stood at one side of the raft while Betsy stood at the other. Each held a long pole, which they would use to help keep the raft clear of rocks.

"Ready?" Captain Meeker shouted from the far shore. Betsy could see all the men of the train—even Nash Whitcomb—lined up with the rope in their hands.

"*Ja,*" Rolfe called. "Ve're ready."

Betsy saw Willa's fingers grip the top of the trunk she was sitting on. Then she felt a deep shudder as the raft began to move beneath her.

They slid easily out onto the water. Betsy could feel the suck and tug of whirlpools beneath the raft, but the ropes held them firm. Only once did the raft swing toward a pile or rocks, but they were able to pole away from the outcropping before any damage was done. Long before Willa had time to get used to the floating, swaying feeling of the raft on the water, they reached the shallows on the other side.

"Still want to claim that land on the other side?" Betsy asked her sister with a grin.

Willa shook her head resolutely as she toiled up the bank. "Not when this is my home." She stopped at the top of the riverbank and looked at the sweet land spreading in every direction. Far to the west, the blue-gray Cascades reared up, white snow gleaming on their peaks. "Oh, but wouldn't Ma and Pa have loved to see this?"

Betsy hugged her sister. "I reckon we're seein' it for them, Will."

Betsy didn't wait to watch Rolfe and the other men begin unloading the wagon. She dashed upstream to make the crossing back to the other side. There was a place a half-mile up where huge rocks formed a jagged footbridge. Before she set out, she turned and waved at Willa. Her sister didn't see her—she was too busy directing the men who were unloading her belongings. *Like any other housewife,* Betsy thought with a smile.

She stopped and looked up at the gray sky. *I did it,*

*Pa,* she reflected. *All the way from that place you and Ma died. I got us here. And oh, please look down and see how happy Willa is.*

Charlie was waiting for her on the opposite bank. The wagon was already loaded, and Toby, paws wet and tail wagging, stood on the bobbing logs. "Ready?" Charlie asked, helping her onto the raft."

Betsy laughed and took the pole he handed her. "Sure, I'm ready," she replied with a toss of her head. "Why, I'm getting to be an old hand at this. If farming doesn't work out for me, I figure I can open up a ferry business."

"By yourself?" Charlie asked with a grin. The ropes tightened and began to pull them into the current. He used his pole to push them away from shore.

"Of course, by myself. I could, you know."

"Oh, I know," Charlie answered.

It was the last thing they would do together, she thought. There were no more mountains and no more rivers. This was the last. In a few days he would wave his hat at her and be gone forever.

She looked across the raft to where he stood. His golden hair was tied back with a leather thong. His buckskin pants, light brown at the top, were dark where water had soaked the bottoms. The strong muscles of his chest and arms worked steadily as he plied his pole. Something rose up and caught in her throat. *Love.* She loved Charlie Freeman, even though she'd done her best not to.

They were almost in the middle of the river now. The water ran swift and glassy beside them, but Betsy could see the rings and ripples that indicated hidden currents.

Suddenly there was a crunching, splintering sound. One corner of the raft reared up. The wagon, lashed firmly to the logs, creaked backward. Its weight plunged the far end of the raft into the water. The pole slipped from Betsy's hands as she fought to keep her balance.

As the raft bucked and plunged in the current, Betsy saw the huge submerged rock that had shattered it. Wet spray soaked her from head to toe, and she groped for something to hold on to.

The raft shot straight up in the water. The wagon, which had skidded to the far end, was pulling them steadily under. Toby yelped and spun away from her. She saw his yellow head bobbing, then disappearing, then bobbing again in the water.

*"Charlie!"* she screamed, reaching blindly toward him. But he was already gone. She searched the water frantically and saw nothing, not even a fringe of buckskin.

The raft reared up like a huge animal and began to capsize. When Betsy realized what was happening, she tried to get away from the heaving logs. But it was too late. A second later she was plunged into the water, the raft above her, pinning her under.

# Chapter 16

SOMETHING CRASHED AGAINST BETSY'S SKULL, SEND-ing her spinning dizzily through the water. Her body shuddered from the blow, and knife-edged pain raced from the nape of her neck to the top of her head.

*Get away from the raft,* an inner voice told her. She could feel the logs and wagon—all her belongings and possessions—surrounding her like a tomb. No matter which way she struggled, she bumped against something. She was trapped.

Her lungs ached, and long, sharp pains darted in her legs. A slow, dreamy kind of weakness began to spread through her entire body. That dreamy feeling, she knew, was death. It was the feeling that came when you decided to stop fighting the water and let death in.

She struggled against the feeling, snorting like a horse to squeeze the last drops of air from her lungs. Then she let the current suck her slowly down and away. It took all the courage she had to keep herself from fighting the steady drag of the water, to let it pull her deeper and deeper.

When she finally felt the rocks of the bottom, she doubled her legs like springs and pushed away as hard as she could. The effort was enough to carry her to the surface, beyond the wagon.

White daylight, dazzling for all its gray mistiness, nearly blinded her. For a minute she thought she might have died after all, so pearly and gleaming was the world. But when air began to fill her aching lungs, she knew she wasn't in heaven, for such exquisite pain could only be felt on earth.

The current still carried her, and she looked back to see the overturned raft jammed in the water. Beyond that, she could see Rolfe and Captain Meeker and the other men on shore. They were running back and forth, frantic as rats in a burning barn. She raised her arm and tried to signal them, but they didn't see her. From their place on the bank, she was hidden behind outcroppings of rock. Besides, she quickly realized, they thought she was still trapped beneath the raft.

She raised her voice to call to them, but she could hardly hear herself above the roar and whoosh of water. When she took a few tentative strokes upstream, she discovered that the current was entirely too strong for her.

And if it was too strong for her, what had happened to Charlie—Charlie, who'd confessed back in the Blue Mountains that he couldn't swim a lick? The thought filled her with despair so numbing that she pushed it from her mind. If she admitted that Charlie was dead, she knew she would lose all desire to live herself.

Suddenly the current quickened around her. She

bobbed along like a leaf in a spring freshet, completely unable to steer her course through the water. The banks tumbled past her in a blur, and the water turned colder by degrees.

A sound like steady rain or bacon frying in a pan filled her ears. Within minutes the sound escalated to a roar. The surface of the water turned white and foamy, and rocks—heaps and piles of rocks—were everywhere.

With a jolt Betsy realized she'd been swept downstream to the fierce set of rapids Charlie had told her about earlier that morning. Going down them on a raft or in an Indian canoe, he'd told her, would be risking life and limb. Now she realized that she was going to go down them alone, with nothing to protect her from the sharp, slamming boulders.

Before she had time to prepare herself, she felt herself skitter over a pile of stones. Their jagged edges scratched her legs and bruised her sides. The racing, green and white water churned furiously about her, dragging her with it. Sometimes she managed to keep herself above the surface; sometimes she was pulled under the water. She bounced against rocks and gasped with pain. When she could, she used her arms and legs to push herself away from them, but more often than not she found herself powerless. When the rapids chose to send her slamming against a boulder, she went slamming against a boulder.

Then suddenly she was through the rapids and drifting on peaceful green water. Her skull throbbed from the blow she'd gotten when the raft capsized. She had no idea how far downstream she'd come, for she doubted that she'd been conscious the whole time.

She felt her feet touch bottom and waded to the shore. A strange stillness filled the air. Birds called in the trees, and ground animals rustled in the debris of leaves and pine needles, but the day was nevertheless empty. The world and everything in it felt unreal to her.

Betsy probed the back of her throbbing head with her fingers. A huge lump rose at the base of her skull, and her hand came away sticky with blood. Weak and exhausted as she was, she knew she had to walk back to the crossing.

Upstream, Willa would be frantic over her disappearance. Rolfe and Captain Meeker would be hauling the raft to shore, searching for her body. And Charlie—her heart clamped down at the thought of him. He was dead, surely. If she'd barely managed to struggle away from the raft, he'd never have survived. Suddenly she realized why the air seemed so still and strange. *Charlie was dead!*

Silver light swam in front of her eyes; then darkness rushed up to meet her—soft, comforting darkness, darkness she had no wish to return from.

Betsy woke up with the distinct impression that she was not alone. She lay as she was, face down, twigs and dirt and crumbling leaves pressed against her cheek, eyes screwed shut against the day.

It was raining again, and her wet body was chilled and cramped. She listened alertly to something that crunched through the mire of undergrowth. Then suddenly something wet but warm and living touched her shoulder. She jerked her head up.

Toby! The yellow hound looked at her quizzically, nuzzling her with his wet nose to make sure she was alive.

"I'm all right, Tobe," she sniffed, forcing her aching body into a sitting position.

The dog yelped and whined, and his voice unlocked her own deep, churning grief. Tears began to roll from her eyes, slowly at first but quickening so that they nearly blindly her. "Oh," she sobbed, rocking back and forth, gasping and sniffling like a wounded animal. "Oh, Charlie! *Charlie!*"

She'd never felt grief so deep and painful before. She'd mourned the loss of her parents, and she'd felt sad and helpless when John drowned. But this was different. Charlie's death was like the death of life itself. The world would never again sing for her.

"Oh God," she keened, burying her face against Toby's wet side. "Why didn't I ever tell him I loved him? Even if he didn't care about me—why didn't I just tell him?"

She sobbed on and on, choking and hiccoughing and pounding her fists against the ground. She used up the last of her energy mourning Charlie, and at last lay in an exhausted heap on the ground.

" 'O never will I forget the night, the stars so bright above me, they gently lent their silvery light, when first she vowed she loved me. . . .' "

Betsy stirred in the leaves. *Lord, I must have jolted*

*my mind loose after all,* she thought. *I could've sworn that was him singing.*

" 'In hurried words her name I blessed, I breathed the vows that bind me, and to my heart in anguish pressed, the girl I left behind me. . . .' "

Betsy scrambled to her feet. It wasn't just her mind playing tricks on her. It was him, Charlie, come back from the dead to get her. "Charlie!" she screamed, her voice a wild shriek.

He burst through the boughs of the pine trees that edged the riverbank. He grinned, relief showing in his blue eyes. "Well there, Betsy Monroe," he said. "I told them you'd be too stubborn to drown. What're you doing way down here—trying to beat the rest of us to the good land? I been looking for you for two solid hours."

She turned her scratched, tear-stained face up to him. "Oh, Charlie!" she cried. "I thought you drowned."

He started running toward her then, scrambling down the riverbank to swoop her up in his warm, strong arms. "Oh, Betsy," he breathed, his breath warm and vital against her cold cheek. "I got pulled to shore right off, but you—you gave me such a scare."

She sobbed and shook against him, content to be in his arms at last. "Were you really looking for me?" she sniffed.

"'Course I was," he assured her, his voice tender. "You're a heck of a lot of trouble, but I've kind of gotten used to you."

She was still dazed and exhausted, and when she

tried to take a step forward her knees buckled and swayed beneath her. "I got a bump on my head," she explained as he picked her up.

"Let's see," he said. His fingers were as gentle as feathers against her torn scalp. "Well, Mrs. Knight has something to put on it, I reckon."

Charlie carried her up the bank and found a dry spot underneath the boughs of a huge fir tree. He sat down and pulled her down on top of him.

"Aren't we going back upstream?" she asked listlessly. The warmth of his body was pouring into her, filling her with delicious laziness. For all she cared, they could spend the rest of their lives under the tree.

"In a minute," he said. "We'll start back in a minute." He held her gently in his arms. He warmed her feet with his hands and kissed the top of her head.

"I lost your moccasins," she said. "I reckon we're even now."

"I reckon," he said.

He touched the swelling bruise at the back of her head again. She winced in pain. "I don't know what I knocked it against, exactly," she said, "but it was quite a wallop. Knocked me out of my senses."

"I guess I better ask you now then, before you get back in your right mind."

"Ask me what?" she questioned. Already she felt strength flowing back into her body, flowing directly to her from the warmth of his hands and the nearness of him.

Charlie looked down at her. "Will you marry me?"

Her eyes flew open. "This is a terrible time for joking, Charlie."

His eyes never left her face. "I'm not joking," he said.

She struggled with her different versions of reality. There were two Charlie Freemans in the world, one who said he'd never get tied down and one who was asking her to marry him. "I thought you didn't like sleeping with a roof over your head," she said. "I thought you said you'd rather *die* than have a roof over your head."

He grinned down at her. She was his Betsy, all right. "I reckon that bump on the head didn't do *too* much harm," he said. "Not if you feel well enough to argue."

"Well, a roof's an important thing," she replied. Things were happening so fast she could hardly keep track of them, and fireworks of joy were going off in her chest.

Charlie was still grinning at her. "But I didn't say anything about a roof," he said. "I asked you to marry me was all. I figure we could make a camp under the wagon or in some hollow tree. What do you say?"

She jumped to her feet, wide awake now. "I'm not going to live my life like some savage just because I've got a husband who's too crazy to build a house."

Charlie rose up to stand beside her. "You drive a hard bargain, Betsy," he said. "All right, maybe we *could* build a house."

"Good! And we'll drill a hole over your half of the

bed, so the rain and snow can fall right in on you. It'll be just like sleeping outdoors."

He reached for her, drawing her to him once again. "So how about it, Betsy? Will you marry me? I have to warn you—if you don't, you'll be losing out on one heck of a wedding present."

"What?" she asked eagerly.

"I'm buying that painting, *Young Hearts of the Prairie,* for you."

Betsy drew back. "Nash would never sell that," she said.

"Yes he would," Charlie told her. "I already asked him."

Her eyes grew warm and bright as fox eyes. "What do you mean, you already asked him?"

"Last night. I made up my mind, once we got across this river, I was going to ask you to marry me. I know you're a flirt, and I'm riskin' making a darned fool of myself, but—"

*"Flirt?!"* Betsy exclaimed indignantly. "Me, a flirt? That's certainly a case of the pot calling the kettle black."

He grabbed her wrists playfully. "Whoa, whoa. Just calm down a minute 'fore you give yourself fits. You want to marry me or not?"

"Yes!" she shouted. Then she put her arms around his neck and arched up to him. She kissed him and buried her face against his chest. "What kind of fool do you think I am, anyhow? Of course I want to marry you, Charlie."

She stood for a blissful moment in his arms. She thought of her parents, of Ingrid Nilsson and John Taylor and all the others who'd died trying to get to the very spot she stood on. She would make her life worth it, she promised silently. She would have enough love and happiness and joyous moments for all of them.

Charlie's hands caressed her matted hair. "Glad that's settled."

"What would you have done if I'd said no?" she asked.

"Well, I was going to beat George Browne to the draw and ask Kitty Taylor to marry me. And if she had said no, I was going to ask Dolly Knight, even though she's only eleven. And if her parents wouldn't let her, I was going to ask Mrs. Bates, who ought to be glad of any man she can get, and—"

Betsy struggled away from him. "You're *terrible*, Charlie Freeman. I hate you!"

He pulled her to him and kissed her again, a long, firm kiss that went all the way to her heart. "I know you hate me," he said, smiling down at her. "That's why you're going to marry me, because you're the kind of mule-headed, contrary girl who only marries people she hates. Took me the last two thousand miles to figure that out."

She looked up at him. "All right," she said. "Just this once, I'll tell you: I love you. I love you more than anyone in the whole world." She stood up on her toes to kiss him.

They started to walk back upstream, following the

river that had brought them together at last. Toby danced and leaped ahead of them, running off in circles to chase ground squirrels and gophers.

"Where do you figure you'll want the house, Betsy?"

"Not far from this river," she said. "Maybe the first good meadowland we come to." In the course of the afternoon, she'd developed a strong and lasting attachment to the Deschutes. "And I want the front facing the river," she went on.

"Now what kind of fool idea is that?" Charlie asked. "Who builds a house *facing* a river? River's always to the back."

"I want my—*our* house facing the river!" she cried. "What do you know about houses, anyway? You told me you never even lived in one."

"Well, I know enough about houses to build one, and I know where the front and back doors ought to go."

They quarreled happily all the way back to camp. It was going to be a wonderful marriage, Betsy told Willa later, if she and Charlie didn't start a war first.

# AFTERWORD
## A Historical Note

Betsy and Charlie had youth and good health on their side when they traveled west in the middle of the last century. Not everyone was so lucky, and many people who set out for Oregon or California never lived to reach their new homes. In addition to the ordinary hardships of the journey, much of the emigration west was carried out in the middle of a nationwide cholera epidemic.

Heading west was seldom a woman's idea. More often it was the idea of a husband or father who wanted to find better farmland or try his hand at prospecting. The man who viewed going west as a great adventure was often accompanied by a wife who worried over the health of her family and wept to leave her home, parents, and friends behind.

Once on the trail, women had not only themselves to care for but their children as well. Many young women made the trip overland by foot, sometimes pregnant, sometimes giving birth in a jolting or rain-soaked wagon, often carrying their young children with them every step of the way.

Yet, in spite of the hardships they faced, their fears for the lives of their loved ones, and their general unwillingness to make the journey in the first place, most women who went—like Willa in this story—rose to the occasion with flying colors. For these reasons, I think the story of the westward-bound women, even more than the story of the men, is a story of love and courage.

Disease, weather, accident, and lack of food and water were the major hazards faced by the travelers. Indians attacked some wagon trains, but legends of massacres have been greatly exaggerated. For the most part, the Indians allowed the settlers to pass peacefully through their lands. By all accounts, far more Indians were killed by the whites than the other way around, and the slow, steady, and brutal war waged against the Indians for their lands is one of the saddest notes of our history.

Finally, how do we know what the westward journey was like? We have the women to thank for that. Many of them kept detailed journals of the trip. When they got to their destinations, these journals were carefully copied and sent to relatives back east. It was the women's way of sharing the journey with those they had left behind—friends and relatives who, in all likelihood, they would never see again.

I hope this story has brought you closer to their great and spirited undertaking.

*Cheri Michaels*

# STILL GOING STRONG!

*First Love from Silhouette*

### BLOSSOM VALLEY BOOKS
## by
# ELAINE HARPER

*First Love from Silhouette*

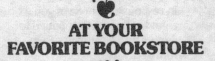

# Is sixteen too young to feel the . . .

Romance, excitement, adventure—this is the combination that makes *Dawn of Love* books so special, that sets them apart from other romances.

Each book in this new series is a page-turning story set against the most tumultuous times in America's past—when the country was as fresh and independent as its daring, young sixteen-year-old heroines.

*Dawn of Love* is romance at its best, written to capture your interest and imagination, and guaranteed to sweep you into high adventure with love stories you will never forget.

Here is a glimpse of the first six *Dawn of Love* books.

## #1 RECKLESS HEART  Dee Austin

The time is 1812, and wild and beautiful Azalee la Fontaine, the sixteen-year-old daughter of a wealthy New Orleans shipowner, is used to getting her own way. There's a war with England going on, and Azalee is warned to curb her reckless ways, but her daring and scandalous behavior makes her a prisoner in more ways than one. While the pirate captain Jean Lafitte can save her from one danger, only Johnny Trent—Azalee's fiery young man in blue—can tame her heart.

Read on . . .

## #2 WILD PRAIRIE SKY  Cheri Michaels

The time is the 1840s; the place is the wagon trail west to Oregon. Headstrong Betsy Monroe knows she can meet any danger the trail offers. But Indians, raging rivers, and stampeding buffalo are the least of her worries. There's also Charlie Reynolds, the handsome young trail guide whose irresistible grin means nothing but trouble. When fate throws Betsy and Charlie together only two things can happen: all-out war or a love strong enough to shake the mountains.

## #3 SAVAGE SPIRIT  Meg Cameron

The Kentucky frontier of 1780 is a wild place, as Catherine "Cat" Brant finds out when she is captured by Shawnee Indians and carried hundreds of miles from her home. Living in the Indians' village, she falls passionately in love with Blue Quail, a white captive who has been with the Shawnee so long he considers himself one of them. Can Cat make Blue Quail love her enough to leave the Indians and go back to her world?

## #4 FEARLESS LOVE  Stephanie Andrews

It is hard to find time for romance during the 1836 Texan War for Independence from Mexico, but fiercely independent sixteen-year-old Lucy Bonner manages to share a few stolen minutes of love with Jesse Lee Powell, a crack young Tennessee rifleman. Lucy risks everything when she tries to save Jesse Lee and the other men of the Alamo and comes face-to-face with the Mexican Army and General Santa Anna himself!

Read on . . .

## #5 DEFIANT DREAMS   Cheri Michaels

The War Between the States? Beautiful Savannah McLairn doesn't want to hear about it. This sixteen-year-old southern belle is not going to let the Civil War ruin what she calls her "prime party years." But swept along by the tides of change, Savannah finds herself behind Union lines, very much in danger of losing her rebel heart to a handsome, young Yankee soldier.

## #6 PROMISE FOREVER   Dee Austin

Yearning for more love and excitement than she can find in 1840 New Bedford, Massachusetts, Tabitha Walker stows away on a clipper ship sailing for California. Once there, Tabitha finds more excitement than she bargained for. She also finds that she must choose between the two young men who claim her love: Alexi, the Russian aristocrat who can give her the world; and Tom Howard, the American sailor who can only offer himself!

**Look for DAWN OF LOVE historical romances
at your local bookstore!**

## THE BIGGER THEY ARE,
## THE HARDER THEY FALL

"Nigel! Down!"

"Huh?" Nigel hadn't shielded himself from the stun grenade. He was blinded from the flash. He clung to Batman's arm and shuddered like a worm on a fishhook.

"Down!" Jane grabbed Nigel by the leg and yanked him down.

The saurus struck even as Nigel came tumbling down onto Jane. She shouted in wordless dismay as she saw the massive head lunging downward at them as she and Nigel slammed onto the ground, all elbows and knees. The smell of rotten flesh blasted over them on the saurus's breath.

Nigel twisted and kicked at the mouthful of daggerlike teeth. The jaws snapped shut on Nigel's foot and the saurus jerked him upward, off of Jane. For a moment, all she could do was watch in horror as the saurus gripped Nigel in its claws and tore his foot from his leg.

*Feel the fear, but don't be it, Jane! Feel the fear, but be Jane, and Jane can kill anything that crosses her path.*

She scrambled up, swinging her rifle off her shoulder. Nigel was in the way for a heart shot, so she aimed for the wide left eye. *Hold your breath. Squeeze.*

Even fifty caliber wasn't strong enough to move the massive head. And like a beheaded chicken, the damn lizard didn't know it was already dead. Something misfired in its brain enough, however, for it to open both claws and drop Nigel. It was all Jane needed. She unloaded the magazine into the saurus's chest.

The massive beast staggered to the right and then toppled with a heavy thud.

# BAEN BOOKS by WEN SPENCER

### THE ELFHOME SERIES
*Tinker*
*Wolf Who Rules*
*Elfhome*
*Wood Sprites*
*Project Elfhome*

### ALSO BY WEN SPENCER
*Eight Million Gods*
*Endless Blue*

To purchase these and all Baen Book titles
in e-book format, please go to www.baen.com.

# PROJECT
# ELFHOME

# WEN SPENCER

BAEN

PROJECT ELFHOME

A Baen Books Original

Baen Publishing Enterprises,
P.O. Box 1403, Riverdale, NY 10471
www.baen.com

ISBN: 978-1-4814-8290-5

Cover art by Dave Seeley

First Baen paperback printing, February 2018

Library of Congress Control Number: 2016018030

Distributed by Simon & Schuster
1230 Avenue of the Americas, New York, NY 10020

Pages by Joy Freeman (www.pagesbyjoy.com)
Printed in the United States of America

# Acknowledgments

I'm afraid that I've forgotten some of the people
who helped greatly with these short stories,
as some were written long before the
thought of a collection occurred to me.
Here are the ones I remember:

Beth Bowles
Andy Bradford
Ann Cecil
Brian Chee
Russell Davis
Joan Fisher
Bonnie Funk
Kevin Geiselman
Ruth L. Heller, DVM
Nancy Janda
Don Kosak
Laurel Jamieson Lohrey
Nan Nuessle
Ellen McMicking
Sue Petroulas
Hope Erica Ring, M.D.
June Drexler Robertson
David Stein
Traci Scroggins
Larisa Van Winkle
N. A. Young

# CONTENTS

# FOREWORD

## *Before We Begin,*
## *I Would Like to Say a Few Words*

I learned how to read before I started kindergarten. I was an avid reader, devouring entire libraries' worth of books. Unfortunately, since I read quickly, as soon as I found something I loved, I would have read all that was available.

Eventually I realized that if I wanted an unending supply, I was going to have to make it up myself. So I did.

The problem with being a writer is it's a skill that doesn't turn off easily once you have it ramped up to novel-a-year speed. It kind of goes into overdrive and every chance it gets, it spits out more ideas than you can possibly use. How did these established characters first meet? How did that person get his name? What was it like building a railroad through virgin forest filled with monsters? What if your brother was half-elf? What would a garden DIY show be like on a world with man-eating plants?

1

I write down all story ideas because a year goes by faster than I ever thought possible. At the end of the year, the next novel has to be queued up. At some point, I decided to make the ideas that didn't fit into novels into short stories. Some of the short stories grew into novellas. Some ideas, however, stayed less than short stories.

Meanwhile I started to read fiction online. Okay, to be totally truthful, I started to read fan fiction online. There were a handful of worlds and characters where I once again devoured everything the author wrote. Other fans, however, had stepped forward to explore all the possible angles. I loved the explorations into lives of characters who didn't have a point of view in the original story. I liked it when the fans took the plot in different directions just to see what it might have been like. And most of all, I was envious of the idea of dribbles and drabbles and such, where a moment is explored and yet not expanded. They were little snapshots of fiction—dependent on the knowledge of the original work—and yet always so vividly drawn.

I wanted to be able to use that freedom to weave something that wasn't a novel, but something more than just a collection. With drabbles and short stories and novellas, I wanted to make a mosaic of the world of Elfhome. I titled it *Project Elfhome* and started to collect bits and pieces.

What you hold in your hands is the end result. This is a collection of novellas, short stories, and drabbles that join together to make a cohesive picture of four worlds colliding in one space. The City of Pittsburgh on Elfhome.

# SINGING STORM OF FIRE

## *Fire Fanned by Wind*

Before you ask, no, I don't know how I came to be. I can, however, discount many of the rumors.

My father, Sword Strike—who is the queen's First and thus the moral compass for the entire holy *sekasha* caste—did not go mad. He did not rape my mother, Pure Radiance, nor did he mistake her for the queen during a drunken orgy. That anyone would even suggest any of the above proves that living forever does not make you wise.

Sword Strike couldn't have. Ignoring who my mother is, the Wyverns would have beheaded my father instantly if he had lapsed into random madness or rape. As for drunken orgies—despite what might be believed of the elfin court, such things are just not done—as in the sun just does not go out.

Besides, one must consider too my mother, Pure Radiance. She is the queen's oracle for a reason. I have seen the female stand blindfolded under oak

3

trees and catch falling acorns. No male could touch
her with force—she would foresee the event a week
before he thought of it.

I wouldn't put a lot of weight in those stories that
my mother tricked my father somehow. Yes, she can
manipulate events with amazing cunning. I've seen
humans set up ten thousand dominoes to trip and
fall in succession, and I thought "my mother does
that with people." But again, one must consider my
father—who could and would—behead her the moment
he discovered that he had been tricked. Since everyone knows that he's my father, there could have been
no trickery involved. (Okay, one could argue that my
father knows that attempting to behead my mother
would be impossible since she could stay twenty steps
ahead of him at all times. I would think, however,
this would infuriate my father, and having dealt with
them my whole life, it is safe to say that the only thing
my father feels toward my mother is bewilderment.)

My own theory, that has stood the test of time and
knowing each of them well, is that my mother saw
my existence necessary for some trigger of events. She
approached my father to act as her stud, and took
away his seed while leaving him clueless as to why.
When I was a young child, I naïvely thought I would
be the center of her plan, the pivot on which the fate
of worlds would hang. For most of my adolescence,
and the first years of my triples, I then became convinced that my mother was the one hiding a mental
illness and I was just the first sign of her madness.

But I digress.

I'd been drowning myself in elfin novels at the time I
met him. An odd and painful way to suicide, to be sure,

but it let me escape my existence without doing bodily harm. Even in my deepest pain, I still believed that my mother had some great plan for me that I merely had to wait for. She was the queen's oracle—the greatest *intanyei seyosa* ever born—surely she had some great, secret reason for bearing a half-caste child like me.

I was in the far corner of the royal garden, hiding with a book, trying to wade through the thick, endless prose of Flame Pen. It bored me to tears, but at least it wasn't me suffering political scandals and lover's betrayal. No one paid enough attention to me to include me in such things.

There he found me, and took notice. "Is that any good?"

I peered over the top of the book, already forming in my mind the title for this episode: *Singing Storm of Fire is Tormented by Yet Another Minor Noble.*

The Wind Clan noble was a young double like I was, maybe a decade older than my fifty years. By his clothes, he was hopelessly provincial. Somehow—as they all did—he'd mistaken me for *sekasha* despite my coloring, and pay court. Some wanted in my pants, thinking I'd be *tenge* and thus safe to bed. Others wanted me to pledge to their Vanity hand. Once they learned I was half-caste, and training in my mother's caste and not my father's, the taunting would start. Why did they all have to act as if I misled them when I tried my best to ignore them?

I'd found, though, that being stunningly rude was the best way to rid myself of unwanted attention, so I responded in low tongue. "It's a load of dung, but better than any company I can expect here at court."

"Ah, that doesn't take much," he responded in kind, not put off by my rudeness. "Have you tried Shakespeare?"

"Shakespeare?"

"He's a human. I'm afraid, though, all his works are in English."

"English?" I cocked my head. "What is that?"

"It's one of the human languages. The humans have quite a few of them."

Was he mocking me? So far, this wasn't going like any of my previous brushes with members of the court.

"What are you doing here?" I snapped. "This area is for Fire Clan only."

"I am Fire Clan."

I scoffed. He was clearly Wind Clan with his black hair and blue eyes.

He spoke and gestured and a flame shield wrapped around him—the heat of it spilling over me.

"Forgiveness," I bowed to him, properly chastised. Remembering my manners, I gave the hated name that my mother had bestowed on me. "Singing Storm of Fire."

"Fire...storm song?" He rolled the conflicting images against each other, for the storm in my name indicates a thunderstorm. "It does not quite suit you—you lack the red hair to pull it off. I would think Discord would be a better name."

I glared at him, regretting not for the first time that I wasn't following my father's path. If I had, I would have had a practice sword and the allowance to answer such pettiness with violence.

"Red hair, indeed! You are one to speak: you look like Wind Clan."

The corner of his mouth twitched only slightly but his eyes openly mocked me.

And I lost my temper. Not that it was a rare thing for me—I'd been warned repeatedly that it wouldn't be tolerated in my mother's caste—but this was the first time I dared to attack a *domana*. And attack him I did. With a curse, I launched myself at him, and we went down in a rolling tangle of arms and legs. I have to give him one thing—he knew how to fight. Within seconds I knew I wasn't dealing with my normal tormentor, who instantly curled into a ball and wailed when struck. He proceeded to deal out blows equal to my own.

Suddenly I was knocked back with a hit that rocked me into darkness. When my vision cleared, I had cooling winds wrapped around me, and my mocker stood between me and my father. Sword Strike had his *ejae* unsheathed and was glaring at me with murder in his eyes.

"Leave her be," the male child commanded, perhaps ignorant of the fact that my father was the queen's First.

"This will not be tolerated," my father growled.

"I provoked her." He stated it as if it was the truth. Stripped clean of anger and left only with terror, I knew that my father wouldn't perceive the child's words as spiteful.

"No harm has been done," the child continued. "There is no need for this."

"You're under the queen's protection," my father snapped. "It doesn't matter whose child she is—attacking you won't be tolerated."

"She is a child, and it will be tolerated," my protector stated coldly. "The Wyverns enforce the queen's law, but it is the queen that sets it and defines its limits. We will take this matter to her, if we need to."

I had stayed tucked in a ball, terrified. My father had the right and ability to kill me where I stood, and I knew it well.

"She's my daughter and part of the queen's household

and has been told that fighting won't be tolerated in the oracle caste."

"Shame on you," the child dared to chide my father, "for denying your daughter the sword that is hers by blood. You let one of your lineage stray from the path given you by God?"

And my father's attention left me to focus on the child between us. I couldn't breathe, not because of fear, but in pure amazement. No one ever spoke to my father so, not even the queen.

"She chose her mother's caste," my father said finally, in a voice that was full of hurt, not anger.

"Can you not see that it does not suit her? A babe screams in hunger even as food is offered to it. You don't strike down the hungry infant. You don't kill the frustrated child. Where is the wisdom of your years? Why do you let her ignorance guide her to ruin?"

Father glanced at me and shook his head. "Why encourage her to take up the sword when no one will have a mongrel such as her? I don't know what her mother was thinking."

"I will take her," the child said. "If she wishes to offer, when the time comes for us both."

"You?" My father looked stunned.

*Him?* I thought, and stared at him, wondering for the first time who this bold child might be. I realized suddenly that while he had cast a fire shield earlier, it was a wind shield that protected me now. He tapped two sets of Spell Stones!

"Who better to take her but another mongrel?" the child said.

My father shook his head. "You are not a mongrel, Wolf Who Rules."

Wolf Who Rules! I gasped. The court had been all abuzz about his recent arrival. He was the son of the queen's sister and the head of the Wind Clan. While the youngest of ten children, he was the only one that was able to access the Spell Stones of both Fire and Wind Clan. He was gifted with a name that foretold a powerful future. You couldn't find a greater opposite to myself—and yet there he was—likening himself to me. And more amazing—offering to take me as *sekasha* if I achieved my sword.

My father glanced at me. "Well?"

"I like to fight," I admitted.

My father took it as a yes, and I suppose, in truth, it was. He sheathed his *ejae* and bowed low to Wolf Who Rules.

"Let it be said, lord, that you are earning your name."

"Thank you, Sword Strike." Wolf Who Rules proved that he knew exactly who my father was.

My father took me by the wrist and dragged me not only from the garden but out of the palace, taking me directly to the Wyvern training hall without even allowing me to collect my fallen book. Not that it was a waste. But I didn't even get to thank Wolf Who Rules for saving my life in more than one way, or get him to promise that he truly meant what he said.

I gazed over my shoulder at him as my father pulled me away, wanting to lock down the memory of Wolf Who Rules. He stood and watched us go, and just before we rounded the bend in the path, waved to me, like I was a parting friend.

## Storm Front

He came to me on winter nights.

Oh, your mind leaps to naughty things, but we were innocents then. Not that we did not know all the words and actions that put passion into deeds, but the need had not fully awakened in either of us. Yes, at sixty, many are already tumbling into the sheets, driven by maturing bodies. What we wanted from each other was to be mind to mind, and heart to heart, not body to body. That would come later.

So he came with hopes and dreams and we would plan to make them true. It was maps that we spread across my bed. It was books that we caressed. We fumbled with Latin, Greek, English, and Mandarin.

The way that time folds and bends and collapses is something that most humans don't live long enough to understand. Memories become islands in a sea of forgotten. So it was months before I saw Wolf Who Rules again, and yet, now, it seems as if after that day in the garden, we were always together. I know that it must have been months, because it was at Winter Court that he first found his way to my bedroom. (It was not a simple task. I spent my childhood housed with my mother, but when I shifted to my father's caste, there was no ready place for me. Sword Strike's place was at the queen's side; there was no room for a half-grown, hot-tempered child in his quarters. My father and I both thought I was fated for the Wyvern training hall but we had not counted on my mother, who quietly had my things moved to a sprawling room in the palace attics. A grand place indeed but difficult to find.)

I do remember that I was about to retire, so I was in my sleeping clothes, when he pounded on the door. I opened it to find him juggling books, maps, and scrolls.

"Discord!" he cried. "My gods, they've hidden you away! It took me forever to find you!"

"Wolf Who Rules?" I remembered my training and stepped back to let him into the safety of my room. I checked the stairs to see if he'd been followed. A Wyvern waited at the bottom of the steps. "What are you doing here?"

"We must plan!" He dumped what he was carrying on my bed since I had no desk.

"Plan for what?" I eyed the materials with dismay. Foolishly, I'd rebelled against the rich furnishings that my mother had piled on me, thinking she was trying to lure me back to her training. I'd carried everything I could to hidden corners of the palace like some anti-thief. At that moment I realized that she knew perfectly well that Wolf would be spending untold hours with me in my rooms. (He later helped me to "steal" them back, laughing at me as we moved them quietly through the halls. As a measure of my mother's influence in the palace, no one ever questioned this bizarre behavior.)

"We must plan for our future!" He spread open the map showing the great expanse of the Western Ocean. Unlike all the other maps I'd seen, though, there was land defined on the other side of the water.

"This is the Far East?" I tilted my head and then tilted the map. The great Far East Seas were missing as were the Dawn Islands. "Where is this?"

"Shortly before we were born, the humans discovered two complete continents. These are maps that they produced of the lands. They called them the Americas. I am calling them the Westernlands. Here, look at this." He spread out a print showing a great level plain cleared in a forest with orderly enclaves being erected. "This is Savannah, Georgia, in North America. A human named Oglethorpe landed here with a hundred and twenty people and within a year had this! And this is New Amsterdam. The Dutch colonized this. Look. Look at the land! A whole world without clan disputes!"

I grasped immediately what he intended. I'd been raised at court, after all; I've watched the circus countless times. When *domana* neared their majority, they would come swaggering to court, expecting riches to be piled at their feet. The hard truth was that nearly every square foot of the Easternlands was tied up with multiple claims. When the Skin Clan fell, there'd been a desperate scrabble for resources that led to the Clan Wars. Well established *domana* held vast amounts but through a network of promises to protect the beholden working the land. They could not share their holdings even if they wanted to; they needed the wealth of the land to protect their people.

A new continent meant Wolf's holdings wouldn't be limited.

It was a stunningly bold stroke but with many inherent risks. No one would trust Wolf to succeed, not without the proper people at his back.

And I was not one of those proper people. I didn't even need my mother's abilities to know that if I was his First, he would not succeed.

He saw the realization dawn on my face. "Oh, come, Discord. Give me at least a decade before you count me as lost."

"Second Hand is good enough for one such as me."

"Discord. My father..."

"I am not Otter Dance. Her modesty does her well but you must realize that her parentage only brings her honor. You need a strong First Hand or you will never get the backing that you need."

"Who of that caliber would follow me into this insanity?"

With my father's knowledge of *sekasha*, I knew who was the perfect fit. "Wraith Arrow."

"Howling's First? Are you serious? Howling could barely talk him into being his First, and my grandfather was a proven warlord. Wraith Arrow would see this as babysitting. He's at High Meadow Temple because he couldn't take a household overrun by ten children."

I considered my mother's training on how to best maneuver people to where you needed them to be. "He will do what is best for the clan; he can be swayed by sheer logic. If you present a strong enough case, he will agree to it. With him, you could take two Hands easily. Three even. We will have to have a solid plan of attack before you approach him."

"So you will follow me into this insanity?"

I had always believed that my mother had some great plan for me. I'd spent my life looking for the reason of my existence. Here, at last, was something large enough to soothe my pride. "Yes. Willing."

## The Meeting of the Storms

I met Galloping Storm Horse on the day he was born. It was on the day I reached majority and formally pledged myself to Wolf Who Rules. The first was a public affair of winning my sword, proving my right to call myself *sekasha*. (The second was between just him and me, a quiet reconfirming of what we'd agreed upon decades before.) Hence my mother was at the Wind Clan Quarters when Otter Dance gave birth to Pony.

It means, of course, that Pony and I were born a hundred years apart to the day. Others might find great significance in this, but I know my mother too well. Just as she planned my birth, she must have planned Pony's too. Nor did I at first attach any importance to his name, for it was my mother that named him, not a random temple priestess who was trying to appease his deadly parents.

Since my father was there to witness my testing, the queen's First Hand was there for support, although I don't know if it was for me or for him, in case I failed. So of course within minutes of delivering her son, Otter Dance was washed, dressed, and proudly showing Pony off.

With my mother right there, it was only natural that Otter Dance present her infant to be named.

Now, one has to understand that during her long

life, Pure Radiance has seen thousands of babies. I think she might be the most experienced person of our race in newborns. When I was young, I had no clue how she could even stand the constant barrage of screaming infants. I realize now that she has some unnatural fascination with them. (I often wonder if she might have invented the entire naming custom to give her access to an unending supply of newborns without upsetting the *sekasha*.) First thing she always does is undress the babies. Normally this makes the infants cry and upsets their parents, who often had never seen a child before in their life. After my mother gets her fill of tiny little feet and amazingly small fingers, the screaming finally wears out her patience and she hands them back to their bewildered mothers.

I stood off to one side, quietly dying. I was a half-blood mutt. I was abandoning the clan of my birth to join the Wind Clan. While Wolf Who Rules accepted me unconditionally, there was no reason for his clan to do so. On hand to witness my testing—and thus also my mother's treatment of Otter Dance and her child—were all the Wind Clan *sekasha* who would be protecting my back for the rest of my life, however long that turned out to be.

And there was my mother, indulging her fetish.

I wanted to snatch up Pony, who was still unnamed at that point, and rush him out of the room. (It turns out that I was suffering needlessly. Otter Dance had helped raise Wolf Who Rules and his nine siblings; screaming babies do not rattle her. Nor did Pony actually cry. He glared up at my mother angrily and aimed a few kicks in her direction.) Still I stood, wallowing in embarrassment and anger at my mother.

Finally Pure Radiance tired of playing with fingers and toes. Or perhaps she remembered that Otter Dance was the Wind Clan First and probably was fairly short tempered after giving birth. Certainly Otter Dance's mouth was pressed into a blade-thin line of anger. (I learned later that Otter Dance had seen this act ten times before, had come to the same conclusion that I had and was not amused by it.)

Placing Pony naked on the weapons table, my mother reached into the sleeve pocket of her white robe and took out the long red blindfold of her office. With a theatrical flourish, she tied it into place.

"Ah, there you are!" She canted her head as if peering down at Pony. "I've been looking for you. Yes, yes, I see now why it's you and no one else."

"What do you see?" Otter Dance asked tensely.

My mother ignored the question as usual. "His name will be . . ." She paused for a moment, obviously seeking the most poetic turn. "Galloping Stormhorse on Wind."

Otter Dance glanced hard at me.

The goddess of war rides a storm horse across the skies, its hooves the sound of rolling thunder. With her fly the storm winds, a thousand winged furies that sing of her glory. In the goddess's wake, like a tornado or a flood, she leaves a landscape changed by her passing.

Until that moment, I never realized what my name became when I changed my clan. Singing Storm Wind. My mother had named me for the furies that accompanied the goddess of war. Now she'd named Otter Dance's infant son after the goddess's steed. With four simple words, she'd tied our fates together in everyone's mind. Worse, there hung the unspoken implication that our path took us to the service of the goddess.

Only today I would pledge myself to Wolf Who Rules Wind. Everyone knew our plans, even though we'd follow custom and say our pledges in private. There was no other reason for my winning my sword at the Wind Clan training hall.

Wolf had a warrior's name. He had filled his First and Second Hand with veterans of the Rebellion. (I was the exception, a mutt newly out of her doubles.) With the strength of those hardened warriors at his back he built a large household with a score of the best *laedin*-caste fighters. In addition to that solid base, he had the support of two hundred or more *laedin* scattered across dozens of Beholden households. Yes, he held a small army, but his dream was of exploration and settlement, not war. A set of Spell Stones had been commissioned and a quarter of the virgin Westernlands had been granted to the Wind Clan. We were to set sail for the river that the humans named the Hudson within the decade.

Wolf had been born to two clans, tapping both *esva*. He could have chosen either at his majority. He'd bonded with his Fire Clan cousins; they, in turn, treated him like their own son. In the end, he picked Wind Clan for sheer political reasons. He even furthered the late king's vision of unity by courting a Stone Clan female to be his *domi*. There were few more bound to the ideal of peace than Wolf.

By our names, however, my mother was suggesting that Otter Dance's son and I were fated to serve the goddess of war. Such a thing would only be possible if I abandoned Wolf. I stood there, feeling utterly slandered and betrayed. If this was the grand scheme Pure Radiance had for me, why did she wait until today to reveal it? After I had committed myself heart, soul and body to Wolf?

I wanted to scream "why" but I knew she wouldn't answer me. The only answer she'd ever given me since I was old enough to ask was "If you cannot see the path, then you cannot know it." It meant that unless I could see the future that she was trying to create, then she couldn't explain it to me. She couldn't risk me tipping the delicate balance of chance.

Pure Radiance handed me the naked baby. Pony and I both glared at her in anger. Never in my life did I want to kill her more, though I knew that even trying was useless. The damn woman was like smoke when trying to land a blow on her. (And yes, when I was a child, I tried many times to do so.)

While I could not score a hit on her, I could thwart her. If she could not tell me the future that she had planned, I could make the one I wanted. If I handed Pony off to Wolf, it would suggest that Pony's destiny (and thus my own) would be tied permanently to Wolf Who Rules.

I marched across the room to where Wolf stood, and I unceremoniously dumped the naked baby into his arms. He accepted the burden with a nod; he understood what I was desperately trying to do.

Still my mother's vision seemed to have already expanded, filling the training hall and holding fast everyone within it. I could see it in their eyes. Simply handing the baby to Wolf was too bare an action. It needed words to counterbalance the name of Stormhorse.

I opened my mouth without knowing what to say and words just came. "This is your blade brother. He will love you well and will guard your heart with his life."

And I felt the words go through me and knew that I had spoken truer than I meant to—and it wasn't the truth that I wanted. I floundered in that moment, wondering exactly who Wolf's heart would be. Surely I didn't mean Jewel Tear. So far she had not impressed me, and her vanity Hand would never be a fit for Otter Dance's child. That much I knew with only my father's blood to guide me.

Wolf knew me well enough to see the truth hit me. He nodded again to me, accepting it. He smiled warmly down at the newborn in his arms. "Hello, Little Horse, I'm your Brother Wolf."

Pony gave him a long serious look, gurgled out a laugh, and then peed on him.

# LITTLE HORSE

"What's he like, this—this brother of yours? Brother Wolf?"

Little Horse could hear the hesitation as Clove Scented Smoke on Wind fumbled with the concepts. Little Horse scanned the sky from the vantage point of the bridge pier; still no sign of a gossamer approaching from the west.

"Blade brother," Little Horse corrected Clove. The apothecary had been sole survivor of a landslide that had reduced his household's estate to rumble. Since the holding had been one of the clan leader's farthest-flung households, Clove had little dealings with the holy caste of *sekasha* and thus wasn't familiar with the strict mindsets. Nor did he understand the relationships between the clan leader and his bodyguards.

"But you should not refer to him that way, nor should you call him Brother Wolf." Little Horse leapt down off the tall stone pier to land lightly beside Clove. "Always call him 'Wolf Who Rules.' There are others—like my father—who would be quite upset if you infer that he is my brother of flesh and blood."

"I don't understand how..." Clove sighed as he touched his face and discovered his spectacles were still perched on his nose. Most conversations with Clove were constantly interrupted as he fumbled with the two small disks of glass joined with a slender piece of wire. Despite Clove's need for them to see anything clearly, the glasses were prone to falling off. "I wish they would just do the spell on my eyes and be done with it."

But the healers wouldn't. Most of the spells that dealt with vision had been developed before the rebellion for the sole purpose of solving the albino emperor's weak eyesight. The spellwork had been ruthlessly tested on thousands of helpless slaves, most of whom were blinded and then destroyed. After the Rebellion, all such spells carried a death sentence for anyone that dared to cast them. Only in the last thousand years had the ban been lifted—mostly from the efforts of Little Horse's grandfather—but no one dared to attempt them. The healers were afraid of people like Little Horse's father.

It left Little Horse nothing to say in reply.

Clove gave a slight laugh as he tucked away his spectacles. "Ah, with my luck, I probably would grow a third eye, right in the middle of my forehead, and start seeing imaginary creatures."

The apothecary's sense of humor was one of the reasons Little Horse liked the male. Clove was also the closest person to his age, although at a hundred and forty, he was twice Little Horse's years.

The bridge had crossed them over to the Stone Quarters. They stopped at a cart selling cold sweet pickled cucumbers on a stick. Mistaking Little Horse for a child of her own clan, the vendor glared at Clove, who was clearly Wind Clan.

"Cause any trouble and I'll call for the Wyverns," she warned.

Clove glanced behind him, put his hand to face to push up the spectacles that were now safe in his pocket, and turned back to blink at her with confusion. "Pardon?"

"I am *sekasha*." Little Horse had learned that it was useless to explain he was actually Wind Clan. His hair and eyes were Stone Clan brown, seemingly giving lie to his words. No one ever questioned his claim to his caste. Apparently no one would dare lie about that.

Clove blinked at him, clearly not following the conversation.

The pickle seller's eyes went wide and she carefully handed over the correct change.

The exchange proved that Little Horse been right to tag along with the apothecary to the spice market. Clove was from a small hold, the isolation making him often seem younger than Little Horse, and half-blind without his spectacles. Clove could get into serious trouble by himself while Little Horse had the protection of his caste.

The cucumber was crisp, sweet and cold. After the first bite, though, Little Horse focused on the crowd moving around them. Excitement shimmered inside him. This was what he spent his entire life training for: to protect a clan member against attack. He realized that he should have his hands free. He finished the cucumber in three large bites and tucked the wooden skewer away.

There was so much to keep in mind. Where was

Clove? Was anyone looking their direction for more than a moment's glance? Any change of body language that warned of attack? What was the nearest point of escape?

The crowd was loud jostling confusion. Over the roar of conversation was the barking of the vendors, hawking their wares. The smell of the multitude of spices was overwhelming; every stall flooded thick scent into the market square. Cinnamon. Ginger. Nutmeg. Cumin.

He was having trouble remembering everything he was supposed to be doing and still walk without stumbling. His parents made it look so effortless. He knew he shouldn't be daunted; they had a thousand years of practice to his handful of decades. Without the protective spells tattooed on his arms, the wyvern scale armor, and the distinctive magically sharp *ejae* that his caste alone could carry, no one recognized him as *sekasha* and stepped out of his way like they would for his parents. Nor did it help that he still hadn't hit his growth spurt and was still a head shorter than most of the adults about them.

Clove made him jump by tapping him on the shoulder. "Little Horse, I never did finish my question."

"What question?"

"How is Wolf Who Rules your brother if not through blood? Did your mother nurse him?"

"No!" Pony laughed. "Because of his name, it was decided that he be trained as a warrior. My mother was the one entrusted to teach him how to fight. She taught him how to tumble shortly after he could walk and almost everything I was taught as a *sekasha*. *Domi* taught him all that he would need at Court and how to protect his Beholden, but my mother taught him everything of the blade."

"Because of his name?"

"Wolf is a warrior's name. It means he will see great battles. It's why the Fire Clan asked that he be raised at Court, close to his cousins." Little Horse realized he was saying too much. "Everyone expects great things of him."

The same could be said of Little Horse. Stormhorse was the mythical beast that the goddess of war rode. Because of his name, given by Pure Radiance herself, everyone expected great things of him.

"What is he like? Wolf Who Rules?"

"He's—he's—" Little Horse stopped the first thing that wanted to spill out of his mouth. Wolf had always acted as Little Horse's older brother, making time to play even as he tried to live up to his name. "Fun" was true but not the thing to say to this near-stranger. "Playful" made Wolf sound like a dog. "Great" seemed to be lacking another word like "brother" or "friend." "Awesome" bordered on overblown.

Little Horse took a deep breath and committed to something. "He's a good leader." That seemed too faint of praise. "He protects his people and always makes sure they're well taken care of."

"Ah." Clove seemed satisfied with the description.

Little Horse sensed a change in the crowd before he saw the source of the disturbance. He noticed that the market quieted with a spreading wave of silence coming from the east. His hand went automatically to his hip before he remembered he was virtually unarmed. His parents allowed him to wear a practice sword within the Wind Clan palace. It wasn't the magically sharp *ejae;* it was only meant to accustom him to the weight and length of an *ejae* riding on his hip. He'd left the practice sword at home, bringing only daggers to deal with anyone outside his caste that started trouble.

Goosebumps rose on his arms as he caught sight of black chest armor: a Stone Clan *sekasha.* The male swaggered through the thick crowd, clearly not bothering to check his stride for the conditions. It bespoke of boorish arrogance. Most of the people within the square were Stone Clan. They still scattered before the holy warrior like frightened chickens.

Knives would be useless against a *sekasha.*

He'd been taught that his caste was perfection in birth. It was their training that gave them the right to be considered holy. Only by blood and by sword did they earn their right to stand outside the law and to judge all those who crossed their path. As the son of Wind Clan's First, though, he also knew that not all of his caste were as perfect as others. He was flawed by inexperience. Older warriors had become too rigid in mindset based on their experiences. Others allowed the desire to excel to become justification for base ambition.

Some thought that perfection meant they could do no wrong.

A wise warrior did not engage an opponent that he could not defeat. The best way to protect Clove was to retreat.

Little Horse started to turn, intending to pull Clove to a nearby alleyway. The apothecary wasn't behind him. He'd been so focused on the *sekasha* that he lost track of the male. Little Horse frantically scanned the crowd, jumping to see over the taller adults, trying to spot Clove.

The young apothecary was easy to spot; he was the only one not scuttling out of the path of the oncoming *sekasha*. While the Stone Clan merchants and clan members carefully kept their gaze averted as they hurried in any direction but toward the holy warrior, Clove stood still, brow creased as he squinted at the dissipating crowd.

"Little Horse?" Clove called, his voice loud against the sudden hush.

With a snarl of anger, the *sekasha* unsheathed his *ejae* and stalked toward Clove. "Arrogant Wind Clan mudsucker!"

Little Horse clenched down on a shout of warning. Surprise would be his only advantage. He lunged through the now-running crowd. It felt like he was swimming upstream. The *sekasha* theatrically flourished his sword, swinging it high for a beheading stroke. Blind to the danger, Clove raised his hand to his face to fumble for his missing glasses.

Little Horse slammed into the *sekasha*, caught hold of the warrior's dominant hand and used his momentum to slash the blade down faster than the *sekasha* planned. The magically sharp edge missed Clove by a hair. The point sliced through the cobblestone, burying the tip inches into the granite. Keeping hold of the warrior's wrist, Little Horse swept his legs out from under him. They went down hard.

He nearly let go in surprise. He hadn't expected it to work. It wouldn't have worked on his mother.

The warrior let go of the *ejae* as he fell, leaving it

upright in the stone. He used his height and weight to take control of their roll and pin Little Horse to the ground. "Going to gut you, little runt! You don't raise your hand to the holy!"

"You don't kill the innocent!" Little Horse wrenched hard and flipped them. "By the blood, I have the right to stop you!"

"Insolent hairless cur!" He tried to break Little Horse's hold and failed. "Catamite! Whoreson!"

Little Horse pressed the male's mouth down into the mud. "I strongly suggest you never say that in my mother's hearing."

He wasn't sure what to do. He wasn't going to be able to keep the male pinned indefinitely. He couldn't even change his hold. If he let go to draw his daggers, the male would regain his sword. The *sekasha's* chest armor protected him from most instant kill hits except those on the head, and those would be difficult to make if the warrior had his *ejae* in hand.

A flash of red out the corner of his eyes warned him that the warrior had just become the least of his problems. He risked a glance toward the far corner of the market squares.

The Wyverns had just arrived in force.

And while *sekasha* were above the law, the Wyverns had made it clear that they'd execute any of their caste fighting in the streets.

*Never let your enemy know what you are thinking.* Little Horse had the lesson beat into him almost every day of his life, so he knelt on the muddy cobblestones with his face carefully locked to neutral. Inside, though, he was grinning. His first real fight and he'd won. His win wasn't completely decisive—the Wyverns arrived to put a stop to it before blood was spilt—but he wasn't the one pinned to the ground getting mud in his mouth.

The Stone Clan *sekasha* had been named Feral Pig-Sticker of Stone who seemed determined to live up to his crude name. Pig-Sticker hadn't realized yet the seriousness of their position. Nor did he seem to recognize the Wyvern standing in front of them.

Not that Sword Strike of Fire carried any badge of his office; he could be a brother to any one of the twenty-one Wyverns in the market square. Truthfully if Little Horse hadn't grown up at Court, he might not be able to tell the tall, red-haired *sekasha* apart. Anyone that could read body language, though, should realize that all the Wyverns within sight were waiting on Sword Strike's command.

And Sword Strike had the right to execute them for fighting in a public place.

"This is not a matter for the Fire Clan." Pig-Sticker was old enough to have the protective spells of their caste tattooed down his arms in black and carry the magically sharp *ejae* that *sekasha* won only after they reached their majority of a hundred years old. He was throwing a snit, though, worthy of a child of only twenty.

"This is Stone Clan business and you have no right to intrude." The male wiped at the dirt on his face, showing his contempt with the narrowing of his eyes and the sneer in his voice. He was from some backwater province by his accent and the fact that he didn't realize that the Wyverns oversaw every aspect of peace at Summer Court.

"Be quiet," Sword Strike said with ice-cold calmness. "It is not your turn to speak."

"Stone Clan settles its own matters..."

"I am Sword Strike, the queen's First," the Wyvern identified himself. He did not add that it made him First for all *sekasha*, Stone Clan included. If he needed to, there was no hope for Feral Pig-Sticker. "I will hear your grievance after Galloping Storm Horse on Wind tells me his side of this."

Little Horse's heart leapt slightly at the knowledge that Sword Strike recognized him. Technically they'd never met, but Sword Strike was the queen's First; their paths had crossed and re-crossed Little Horse's entire life.

The warrior jerked in surprise and then stared at Little Horse hard. "He's not Stone Clan?"

"He was born to Wind. So far, he has not chosen otherwise."

Pig-Sticker blew out his breath in disgust and murmured, "Mutt."

Not the thing to say to a male whose only child was mixed caste.

"Stormhorse will speak first." Sword Strike's voice was ice cold.

Pig-Sticker ignored the tone. "He had first blow."

Sword Strike glanced to Little Horse to confirm this.

Little Horse carefully explained. "He drew his sword first; I landed first blow."

Sword Strike glanced for an *ejae* sheath on Little Horse and then scanned the marketplace. A few minutes earlier it had been crowded with lesser caste. The large square was now empty except for the *sekasha*. Sword Strike spotted the Stone Clan's *ejae* planted like a flag in muddy cobblestones near a bin of garlic. "You are unarmed?"

"I have knives but I did not draw them." Because they would have been useless against the longer sword. His only hope had been to grapple.

"See, he struck..." The Stone Clan warrior started.

"You will wait your turn." Sword Strike pointed at the male and then shifted attention back to Little Horse. "What happened?"

"I was accompanying my lord Longwind's apothecary to market." Little Horse did not add it was because he expected Clove to find trouble. "He did nothing to warrant attack. This one drew his sword without provocation on an unarmed member of my household. I judged his actions to be unjust and I prevented him from killing the apothecary."

"You took no effort to verbally challenge him?" Sword Strike asked.

"I do not have shields or a sword and he had already drawn his weapon. I judged that giving him verbal warning would eliminate the only advantage that I had; namely, surprise. I did not strike with a blade but grappled him."

It apparently was starting to dawn on Pig-Sticker the danger that they were in; he got his face under control.

"Why did you draw your weapon?" Sword Strike asked, with a long, cold stare.

"The Wind Clan scum did not drop his gaze." Pig-Sticker stated as if it explained everything.

Sword Strike's eyes narrowed slightly but he gave no other indication of his thoughts. "You drew your weapon because he did not cower in fear?"

"His eyes are weak; he is nearly blind." Little Horse blushed as he realized that he shouldn't have interrupted. "Forgiveness."

Sword Strike studied Little Horse, face blank. "What is this male's name?"

"Clove Scented Smoke on Wind." Little Horse realized he'd lost track of Clove during the fight. Hopefully the male hadn't found more trouble.

There was a delay as Clove was found and brought forward. The apothecary didn't understand protocol; he tucked himself up against Little Horse instead of staying back.

"Tell me what happened," Sword Strike commanded.

"I'm . . . not . . . sure." Clove took out his glasses, fumbled with them a moment and then perched them on his nose. "They're a human invention; not many of our people have my weakness. These let me see clearly but they tend to fall off. I normally only wear them when I'm sitting down. Without them, everything is a blur. I didn't have them on. I did not see the fight start. Once I realized what was happening, I didn't know what to do. I know nothing about combat. I thought if I could find someone . . ." And he started to cry, which required the glasses to come back off. "Please. This is all my fault. If someone is to be punished, let it be me!"

Did Sword Strike sigh? Little Horse wasn't sure; the Wyvern had perfected his neutral façade.

Pig-Sticker reacted as if Sword Strike had patted the little apothecary on the head. "He is not a child to toddle blindly about the streets. He is an adult; he should learn to be more careful."

"Learn to be more careful," Sword Strike echoed. "Yes. I think that will be the solution here."

"Holy one?" Clove whimpered.

Little Horse went cold inside. If for some insane reason the Wyvern decided to punish the apothecary, there was nothing he could do.

"Feral Pig-Sticker of Stone," Sword Strike said. "Obviously you need more training if you can be bested by an unarmed double. Please go to Cold Mountain Temple. Tell the Stone Clan holy ones there, in detail, about your defeat so they know what you need to learn."

Little Horse could not keep his eyes from widening. His grandfather, Tempered Steel, commanded Cold Mountain Temple. Despite the fact that his daughter chose her mother's clan over his, he was fiercely protective of her. Should Little Horse warn Pig-Sticker not to repeat the "whoreson" insult?

Sword Strike caught the change of Little Horse's expression. He gave a slight shake of his head. No. The Wyvern wanted Feral Pig-Sticker to confess to all his faults. If he survived telling the tale, the training would be quite intensive.

"I just arrived in Summer Court!" Pig-Sticker cried. "I've traveled all the way from Copper Palms. It took months for me to come all this distance."

The island was the southernmost point of the Stone Clan territory. It was nearly half the world away. Worse, to travel to Cold Mountain Temple, the warrior would retrace his steps for thousands of miles.

Sword Strike waved away the protest. "I will arrange for you to travel on a royal packet ship.

"There are two *domana* of my clan reaching their triples this year. They are coming to Summer Court to be acknowledged by the Clan Head and given an introduction to the queen. They'll be taking their first Hand.

"Once it is known that you were pinned by an unarmed double, it is unlikely that you could beat out the other contenders. Those who are trained at Cold Mountain are highly respected. You would be top candidate when the next *domana* comes of age in a decade or two."

All true. Little Horse had even considered finishing his training with his grandfather.

"The packet ship leaves at noon from the royal airfield," Sword Strike continued. "Gather your things and go. Now."

"I-I-I just got here . . ." Pig-Sticker trailed off. He stared at Sword Strike slack-jawed for a moment, and then whispered, "What if they will not train me? It is Cold Mountain Temple."

"I sent you. They will train you. Go."

Pig-Sticker went, radiating his unhappiness.

Sword Strike set a guard on Clove to see that the apothecary purchased his herbs and returned safely to the Wind Clan compound. There was no mention of punishment for Clove, which only left Little Horse's fate undecided. The Wyvern First pointed at him and said simply, "Come."

They crossed into the Wind Clan section of the city but did not head toward the Clan Head's compound. Little Horse walked beside Sword Strike wondering where they were going. What punishment did the Wyvern intend? Not to execute him; Sword Strike would have done that in the market square. Send him to one of the Wind Clan's counterparts of Cold

Mountain Temple? There were four including the one where his grandmother Perfection commanded. Each was as remote as his grandfather's monastery. His life would be fixated on combat and spiritual enlightenment—which was not necessarily a bad thing. He liked to fight. His mother had split her childhood between the two temples. She'd chosen life at court, though, once she reached her majority.

"You will be seventy this week," Sword Strike stated.

Little Horse struggled to maintain his neutral façade. "How did you know?"

"You share the day with my daughter."

Little Horse knew he shared Discord's birthday but he didn't realize that her father was aware of it. It was unsettling information. "Yes, I will be seventy."

"What is your intention? Will you offer to Jewel Tear of Stone?"

"No!" Little Horse blushed at the speed and volume of his answer. He wanted nothing to do with the female. If she didn't love his blade brother, then she should have told him immediately. Wolf Who Rules had spoken purely from his heart when he asked Jewel Tear to be his *domi*; politically the move had been very dangerous. Such courage should have been answered quickly and honestly. Jewel Tear had made Wolf Who Rules wait Little Horse's entire life for an answer. Little Horse could never serve anyone that didn't give her answer to such an offer immediately.

His name suggested that he would serve the goddess of war. He'd never considered that it meant he would offer to an actual female. His mother might be playful in spirit, but she wasn't a dancing otter.

But he couldn't tell all that to Sword Strike. Little

Horse scrambled for a true but less pure answer. "I could not be Sixth to her First; I do not fit."

Sword Strike nodded. "Tiger Eyes does not have the strength to hold against you. There would be a division between her Hands."

Why had Sword Strike ever thought he would offer to Jewel Tear in the first place? Had Jewel Tear finally broken her silence? "Why do you ask?"

"Now that you are seventy, you can change your household or clan to one that better suits you. You could even train with one of your grandparents."

Was the male asking him to choose his own punishment? Pig-Sticker was a provincial nobody but Little Horse was the grandson of two of the most famous and powerful *sekasha* still alive beyond Sword Strike himself. Was the male worried about political backlash?

"I have not given it much thought." Little Horse carefully chose his words. "I know that I can choose to change households at seventy but until I reach my majority, I am not a true *sekasha*."

"You want to offer to a *domana*?"

"Yes." After this morning, he was sure his answer came from his soul. "It will be another three decades before I win my sword and can offer, but yes, that is what I want."

Little Horse couldn't tell if Sword Strike was satisfied with this answer or not; the Wyvern merely nodded. Little Horse was still mystified as to the reason for the conversation. They were far from Longwind's compound; they'd reached the Wind Clan airfield at the edge of the city. There were only open pastures beyond the gossamer's moorings.

Since each clan had their own airfield, he was

surprised that the area was filling up with Fire Clan troops. Nor were they common *laedin*-caste royal marines; it was a dozen Hands of Wyverns.

"Forgiveness, but what is going on?" Little Horse asked.

"Pure Radiance says that Wolf Who Rules will arrive this afternoon," Sword Strike said.

"He's scheduled to return this week." The Westernlands were over three thousand miles away; the ocean took days to traverse. Marauding monsters. Bad weather. Anything could have delayed Brother Wolf, but if Pure Radiance said he'd arrive today, most likely he would.

The Wyverns would only greet the *domana* of another clan if they intended to arrest him. Brother Wolf, though, could use the Fire *esva*. He was a favorite of his cousin, Queen Soulful Ember. He'd been totally out of contact for months. Nor was Wolf Who Rules one to be taken by force, not with his training and abilities. There was no logical reason for armed confrontation.

Pure Radiance did not follow logic.

"What has Pure Radiance accused Wolf Who Rules of?" Little Horse asked.

"Nothing. We're here because of what she needs him to do." Sword Strike pointed at a small young gossamer with the gondola of Wind Clan blue. "There he is. Go meet him. Tell him that he'll be returning to the Westernlands as soon as he's talked with the queen. She'll be here shortly."

The Wyverns had not come empty-handed. They brought weapon crates, a mountain of dried keva beans in cloth sacks, mysterious chests and boxes, and a herd of baby *kuesi*. Little Horse eyed the shaggy beasts currently the size of draft horses. It would take years for the animals to be large enough to do real work. What did Pure Radiance see in store for his blade brother?

Wolf's gossamer drifted to a stop over the moorings. Its tethers dropped to waiting ground crew, the rolls of heavy rope unraveling as they fell.

Brother Wolf was first off the elevator in a show of trust to his cousins. Wolf must have left most his *sekasha* behind to guard the settlement; only Discord followed him. Despite the worry on Wolf's face, he smiled and opened his arms wide to Little Horse. "You've gotten taller again." His blade brother hugged him tightly, as if he had all the time in the world for Little Horse. "Why are you here alone with all these Wyverns?"

*Why am I?*

Sword Strike could have left him with Clove or sent him home. Why did the Wyvern First bring Little Horse here? What was the male doing in the Stone Quarters? It was a wide detour from the Fire Quarters to the Wind Quarters. Was it just luck that Sword Strike was the Wyvern that stopped his fight with Pig-Sticker? Or had Sword Strike been looking for Little Horse? Certainly Sword Strike knew who he was without having to ask his name.

"I'm not sure," he admitted.

His mother had taught him that his name meant nothing; the only measure of his worth was what he did and said. He was aware, though, that most people expected great things from him because of his name.

No one had ever indicated what those great things were going to be.

Was this the eve of his future? Had Pure Radiance sent Sword Strike to find Little Horse?

It was not Sword Strike that escorted Queen Soulful Ember across the airfield but the members of her Second Hand. It meant that her First was overseeing the Wyverns but also was a subtle indication that Wolf Who Rules was a trusted family member. Little Horse steeled himself against disappointment; he would not get any confirmation that he was meant to be there. He told himself that Discord was most likely more disappointed; she'd not seen her father since she won her sword. He could not imagine going so long without seeing his parents. He backed up to take guard position beside Discord as he struggled to keep his face neutral.

"Our dear cousin," the queen greeted Brother Wolf. She wore clothes as informal as her greeting: doeskin pants and a white silk blouse under red-scaled chest armor. She carried nothing to indicate her rank, not that she needed it. The Wyverns at her back were all she needed to claim her right.

"Cousin," Wolf echoed the greeting. "What do you need of me?"

"To be my voice," the queen said. "You are to be my Viceroy in the Westernlands." She waved toward a procession of Wyverns carrying the mystery chests toward the gossamer's lift. "The position comes with a distant voice and five hundred bars of gold bullion."

"Forgiveness?" Wolf glanced at the chests with confusion. They represented nearly as much seed money as Wolf started with. "Viceroy? There is nothing there but my own holdings."

"That will change," she stated. "I need you to have the authority to speak as my representative."

"Who—who will I be speaking to? Has one of the other clans decided to use the land they were deeded?"

She did not explain whom. "There is a place that you know of. You considered it as a site for your settlement. You stayed long enough to clear an airfield. In the end, you did not choose it."

Wolf shook his head as he thought. "There are several such places."

"Two rivers come together to form a great and mighty third river. A tall ridge overlooks that confluence from the south."

He nodded slowly to indicate that he knew what area she meant. "I don't understand. There is nothing there but wilderness. We explored it, mapped several *fiutana* but decided against it."

"You must return to that place. Something is about to happen there. Something beyond Pure Radiance's ability to understand. One thing she has seen clearly: we must not ignore it. It has to be sought out, understood, and controlled, or it will destroy us."

"And the gold bullion?"

"It is important that you can do business as equals with whomever you meet. Gold has always been universal."

His eyes widened. "You think the humans are going to find a way to Elfhome."

"We can only pray for creatures so benign. But yes, your fascination with them will make you invaluable in this. You speak many of their languages. You have studied their history; you know what they're capable of. You must stand strong; do not allow them to think that we are weak. We are not primitives that can be bought with glass beads or bullied with firearms or overwhelmed by smallpox or measles. You are the strongest *domana* ever born; make them respect you."

"Yes, your majesty." Wolf retreated to his warrior-training; his face set to neutral. He bowed low to his cousin.

Sorrow filled the queen's eyes. She laid a hand on Wolf's cheek. "Be careful, my dear cousin. If you're too greatly outnumbered, fall back and send word to me. It is vital that we understand who we face, how they came to our world, and what they want."

Wolf bowed again. "I will be careful."

After the queen had taken her leave, Brother Wolf turned and gave Little Horse a sad smile. "I'm sorry I won't be able to spend time with you. I must go. Give my love to your mother."

Little Horse realized that if Sword Strike had brought him here because of his name, then now was the time to act. "Take me with you."

"Little Horse!" Wolf gripped his shoulders and gave him a little shake. "You're not of age yet."

"I'm old enough to decide my household," he said. "I know my heart. I want to go with you to the West-ernlands. You will need me."

Wolf shook his head. "You are not old enough to fight."

Little Horse fought the fear that he'd run out of time and be swept aside and then left behind. He kept his voice level and chose his words as carefully as time allowed. "A horse does not fight. It bears your weight when you need to be carried. You will do the fighting."

Wolf glanced to Discord.

The female's father might be Sword Strike, but her mother was Pure Radiance. Her mixed caste was marked in her pale blond hair gathered into a tight *sekasha* braid. She looked more like her famous mother than her father. "My mother will not tell you if you ask," she murmured. "Knowledge changes the path taken. It has to be his decision to go and your decision to take him."

"You were given a warrior's name." Little Horse reminded his brother. "We are bound at my birth by my name."

"My mother!" Discord snarled. "She named us all! She uses people like little chess pieces to move themselves over a game board that only she can see."

"If it was just a game," Little Horse said, "your father Sword Strike would never allow it."

Discord snorted.

"He is right," Wolf said. "Nor would Pure Radiance bother if it was not important."

"You don't know my mother..."

"I know she is the most ruthless, calculating female alive. She would do anything to see the future fulfilled: betray her own mother, sacrifice her lover, or bear a child and put her in the path of danger. I know she guided us through the Rebellion and out of the Clan Wars. If we must walk this path to protect our people, then we will."

Wolf leaned forward to press his forehead against Little Horse's. "I love you, little brother. And you're not so little anymore, so I must acknowledge that it is your right to follow your heart. I offer you the protection of my household and when the time comes and you win your sword, I will gladly accept all that you are willing to offer to me. If at that time, your heart takes you elsewhere, so be it."

He wanted to say "never." If Wolf wanted the comfort of allowing him such unwanted freedom as the price for taking Little Horse to the Westernlands, then he would keep his silence. "Thank you."

# ALL THE KING'S HORSES
# AND ALL THE KING'S MEN

Something had gone drastically wrong with the world, Lain Shenske thought, if government agents were kidnapping cripples out of rehab hospitals. They hadn't even let the fact that she loudly refused to go or was dressed in a hospital gown deter them. Pausing only to secure her hated wheelchair, they loaded her from the gurney into a Black Hawk helicopter. They handed her off at Langley Air Force Base, loading both her and her wheelchair into one of several C-17s carrying Army soldiers and tank-like Bradleys.

Yes, something definitely had gone wrong.

They landed an hour later at a tiny little airfield in the middle of farm country. The massive transport jet dwarfed everything in sight with nothing more hostile than corn in view. A sign identified the field as "Butler County Airport" and an American flag flew atop the flagpole. While the Bradleys rumbled out of the C-17's belly, she and her wheelchair were juggled quickly into another Black Hawk with a new sunglass-wearing handler.

"Where the hell are we going?" she shouted as the blades spun up for takeoff.

"Pittsburgh." The new handler was in combat fatigues with insignia identifying him as Army Intelligence.

Pittsburgh? *Pittsburgh?* Lain tried to find some logic in the madness and was defeated.

"Why?" She had meant "Why Pittsburgh" but he misunderstood and thought she had asked "Why me?"

"You're the only fully trained xenobiologist currently available," the officer answered.

That made sense. Xenobiology was still in its infancy. The title had been conferred on only a handful of people with astronaut training and doctorates in biology and astrophysics. Everyone of her caliber had either been killed in the explosion that had crippled her, was in orbit, or had just jumped through the newly activated hyperphase gate that the Chinese had in geostationary orbit over the China Sea.

But "xenobiologist" and "Pittsburgh" didn't add together.

"Why Pittsburgh?" she asked.

Frightening enough, that professionally blank look vanished off his face, replaced with a confounded inability to explain the situation.

What in God's name had happened to Pittsburgh?

"We're coming up on it now," the pilot radioed.

They hauled open the side door, blasting the cabin with spring-cool air. Below, several major highways tangled together. Clustered tight around the intersection was a sprawl of suburbia. Strip malls with massive parking lots lined the access roads with red lights every few hundred feet. Housing plans crowded the hills behind the stores, hundreds of cookie-cutter houses on aimlessly curving streets. The only green was postage-stamp yards and scrub trees growing in areas too hilly to build on.

"That's the Pennsylvania Turnpike and I-79." Her handler indicated the two major highways. "That's Cranberry Township below us; Pittsburgh city limits should be twenty miles south of us."

*Should be.* They followed I-79 south. Military trucks blocked the on-ramps. Eight lanes sat empty of traffic. Despite the ever-present pain in her body and the darkness of her soul, Lain found herself growing concerned for the people of Pittsburgh.

"There." The officer pointed out the door toward a wooded area.

Lain opened her mouth to ask what she should be looking at and then she realized what she was seeing. The highway ended abruptly at the edge of a forest. A thick, uninterrupted green blanket of trees ran as far as the eye could see.

"Oh, dear God," she murmured.

"It's a twenty-five-mile radius," the officer shouted over the green-scented wind roaring through the cabin. "A perfect circle. Gone—with this in its place."

"What about the people?" she shouted.

"We estimate that there are close to three million people missing."

Yes, something was drastically wrong with the world.

The helicopter landed on the highway near where it ended abruptly. Several branches of military were already assembled but, judging by the general milling about, were jointly confounded as to what to do next. Lain had hoped that with all the massed confusion, her arrival would have gone unnoticed until she was installed in the wheelchair and the wreckage of her body covered. A small crowd gathered, though, even as the blades were spinning down, as if her arrival was more interesting than a major US city vanishing.

"Oh, the joys of being famous," she murmured. Her father had been an astronaut, host of a popular science television series and murdered when she was young. Her stepfather was impossibly rich, powerful and notoriously reclusive. Between the two, she'd grown up in the media spotlight but that was standing on two sound legs. Now the stark brilliance was too intense; it laid too much of her body and soul bare for public inspection.

Stripped of privacy, she wrapped herself in the thorns of power instead. "Who is the motherfucker in charge of this mess?"

That checked the crowd that had been gathering. Only one officer kept coming in the cautious half-crouch people used around helicopters. He was annoyingly tall, wide shouldered, and looked like he should still be in college, getting drunk and planning pledge hazing at a frat house. He was in army fatigues with a Pennsylvania Army National Guard badge on his sleeve.

"Ms. Shenske, I'm Lieutenant Perkins. I'm Major General Crocker's aide-de-camp." He put out his hand for a handshake. Considering the wave of army forces slowly following Lain in Bradleys, the National Guard was unlikely to be in charge for much longer.

"So you're the asshole's left butt cheek. Congratulations. It's Colonel Shenske. Some schmucks yanked me out the hospital without a stitch of clothing. I need pants, shirt, socks, shoes, a coat and a blanket. And I want it now. I'm not going to sit around with my ass bare to this wind because you have your head up your ass. Get it for me, or I don't care who the fuck you are, I'll have your ass blistered for this."

Lieutenant Perkins snapped to attention and saluted. "I—I didn't realize—yes, ma'am, I'll have a set of clothes pulled together immediately."

"And if you expect me to be here at this camp for the duration, you better realize that I can't so much as piss by myself. You have at best one hour before this becomes a very real issue. I'll warn you now, if I end up soiling myself because some motherfucker thought up the smart idea to jerk me out of a hospital, heads will roll."

"Yes, ma'am."

"Now tell me—what the fuck is going on?"

"At zero three hundred hours, all contact with Pittsburgh was lost. Satellite imagery confirms that a perfect circle of forest has..." Lieutenant Perkins paused as he ran out of military-speak to explain. "Well—it's here and Pittsburgh isn't. Governor requested a declaration of National Emergency at zero four hundred hours. Unidentified life forms have led us to believe the forest is extraterrestrial in nature."

Her heart skipped at "extraterrestrial" but she clamped down on the jolt of emotions with steel-cold logic. There had to be some reasonable *normal* explanation—although she couldn't even begin to guess at it.

As Lieutenant Perkins brought her up to speed, a knot of soldiers had lifted her hated wheelchair up and off the helicopter. They set the cube of metal down just beyond the spinning blades of the Black Hawk and stood eyeing it in confusion.

"It's not that complicated," she shouted. "Just hit the frigging power button and step back!"

One of them figured out the red button was the power button and there was a sudden scramble backwards as the chair unfolded its eight spidery legs.

"Hold your fire!" Lain shouted as half the soldiers whipped up their weapons and took aim on her wheelchair. "Hold your fire! God-damn stupid idiots."

"What the hell is that?" Perkins shouted.

"It's an AI-assisted wheelchair." She snapped her fingers. The chair skittered around, located her and scurried over to the helicopter. She didn't care what her mother said, it was creepy as hell. The wheelchair was the bleeding edge of robotics, funded by her stepfather's billions of dollars and gifted to her by her mother. The damn thing was full of glitches but was light-years ahead of anything that the VA would provide for Lain. She couldn't blame the soldiers for staring at it, but since she was in a hospital gown, chances were good that she was going to flash anyone standing around when she shifted from the helicopter to the chair.

"This isn't a peep show. Go do your fucking job and let me get decent."

Lieutenant Perkins' eyes went wide and he turned away, barking orders.

"Prepare to load." She waited for the swing bar to extend and lock. The wheelchair took so long to process the command she thought its operating system had crashed again. She checked its screen and realized that it hadn't heard her command over the background noise. "Prepare to load."

The gown covered the scars where her womb used to be, leaving her knees and calves exposed. While her legs were useless, her accident had been recent enough that they still looked normal. She dreaded the day that all she had were withered sticks. The chair's trainer had made the mistake of telling her that once her legs atrophied, swinging her body into the chair would get simpler. She'd given him a black eye. A new, more diplomatic trainer was supposed to start next week; unfortunately, that left her without a personal aide.

Perkins peeked to see if she was in the chair and caught her lifting her useless legs into place.

"Get me some clothes," she snapped. "After I'm decent, I'll look at these extraterrestrial life forms."

The Black Hawk crew provided her with a flight suit to wear. She also secured a pair of binoculars, a two-way radio, and a sidearm complete with a spare magazine. (The pistol proved that her psych evaluation had not been checked prior to her kidnapping, as she'd been flagged as suicidal. Not surprising, as everything she ever dreamed had been blasted out of orbit along with most of the US space program.)

She needed two female privates to act as aides since "bathroom" on the front line was a portajohn. Her wheelchair was clever, but not designed with that limited space in mind. She hated having to let people do what she been able to do for herself since being a toddler. It made her feel weak and helpless and useless.

Once she was dressed, she chased the privates away and tracked down Lieutenant Perkins. "Where are these alien life forms that you found?"

"We put it in a cooler." He started to walk.

"The specimen is dead then?" She followed, trying not to notice how her chair was startling the soldiers as it scurried behind Perkins.

Obviously it bothered the officer as he tried to walk sideways. "Yes, it was killed about half a mile from the demarcation line." He pointed toward the houses clustered together beyond the highway's right of way.

Killing it was the safest thing to do since even small rodents could bite through thick leather and carried everything from fleas to rabies. It was vastly annoying that she'd been dragged all this distance to look at a dead animal. "Did you at least put it in plastic before putting it on ice?"

Perkins looked confused. "Ice?"

"You have ice in the cooler?"

"Oh! Ice! No!" He stopped in front of a forty-foot, refrigerated shipping container. "We just put it in here."

"Oh." She thought he meant the type of cooler you took on picnics. "Oh!" He'd swung open the door and all her annoyance was blasted away. "Oh! A dinosaur! It has the feet and forelegs of a dromaeosauridae but it doesn't have any feathers." It was a beautiful jewel green with streaks of brilliant yellow that probably acted as camouflage within the forest. There were touches of jewel blue round its eyes and toes. There was a round bullet hole in its skull but no exit wound. "Dear God, why did you kill it?"

"It ate two Rottweilers, went through a picture window, and tried to batter down a bedroom door to get to the homeowner. He shot it with his deer rifle."

"The world needs a living dinosaur more than it needs another redneck Pittsburgher."

"Pittsburghers are suddenly in rare supply themselves." Lieutenant Perkins didn't seem to realize what he said. "We've picked out a dozen similar animals using satellites."

"There are more? Still alive?" Life suddenly seemed a lot more interesting.

"Yes. There are two more of these at Monroeville Mall. There's a herd of something loose in the North Hills. Elk or moose or something."

"Mammals?" She threw a glance over her shoulder at the forest.

The trees were taller than coast redwoods, with the bulk and branch structure similar to sequoias, but appeared to be deciduous, which would make them hardwoods. Giant sequoias were the fastest growing trees in the world, but even they only grew between a foot to two feet a year. Physically it was impossible that the trees had grown overnight. It meant that improbable as it might seem, they would have had to arrive—branch, root and soil—from another world.

The forest was showing no signs of distress, so the environment of the planet the trees were from was exact to Earth's. Nearly recognizable dinosaurs, mammals and deciduous forest indicated a nearly identical evolution path. It suggested that they were dealing with a parallel universe.

The military would be worried about the dinosaurs, but the real damage could come from anything. Rats had decimated the entire ecosystem of Easter Island, wiping out a complete forest and a dozen species of birds. Twelve wild rabbits released in Australia had multiplied to millions within decades and led to the extinction of countless native plants. Certain algae caused red tides. One nearly microscopic organism produced toxins that accumulated in shellfish and could cause a paralytic poisoning that lead to death.

She aimed her chair for the abrupt end of the highway. "I need to take samples and build a comprehensive profile of the ecosystem. We need to find out if the alien flora and fauna can thrive here. I suggest that until we know otherwise we treat it as a biological hazard and start decontamination procedures on anyone and anything coming out of the area."

Based on what she was told, the boundary between the two ecosystems was over a hundred and fifty miles. They were upwind of New York City. All streams and rivers in the area fed into the Ohio River. By volume, the Ohio was the largest tributary of the Mississippi River and its drainage basin included fourteen states. Containment was impossible. They could be on the cusp of ecological disaster.

Perkins followed as if tethered to the back of her chair. "What are you going to need?"

*Use of my legs back!*

She bit down on the comment. Precious time had been taken up dealing with her crippled body. If she wasn't stuck in her hated wheelchair, she would already be in a hazmat suit and gathering samples. As it was, she would need to waste even more time trying to protect the hydraulics on her wheelchair from contamination. She couldn't risk taking a biohazard back to the hospital.

She gasped as she remembered the incoming Bradley troop carriers with their tank treads. If the military sent the vehicles into the forest to crawl through the rich moldering debris, organic matter would be embedded into the continuous tracks. If she didn't arrange some way to sterilize the Bradleys before they were loaded back onto the C-17s, they would transfer foreign bacteria, spores, mold, seeds, and insects around the world.

She growled in frustration. Her chair would have to wait. Someone else would have to take the samples while she set up decontamination procedures.

The limousine arrived before the Bradleys. It glided like a black shark through the chaos that was the military camp at the end of the highway. She paused to watch it come. Despite the black tinted windows, she somehow knew that it carried someone she didn't like. Someone that was going to make her life hell.

The limo did not fail to deliver on her expectations. The back door opened and an impossibly handsome man got out as if he owned the highway, the sky and the sun. It was her stepbrother, Yves, whom she unaffectionately nicknamed Crown Prince Kiss Butt. Yves was a testament to her stepfather's power; he was strictly a civilian with no useful ability except as a spy for his father. Yet, here he was, passing through all the various military blockades to arrive like royalty.

It surprised her that the forest drew Yves like a magnet. He was a creature of the city; his idea of "country" was his father's mansion on the Palisades outside of New York City. On weekends he could barely be stirred from the indoor pool, shimmering with reflected light.

She locked down the urge to use his distraction to run and hide. She wasn't a grieving ten-year-old anymore. If he turned his sharp tongue on her, she would give it back a hundredfold.

He stood staring at the forest for several minutes. Finally he tore his gaze away from the trees to look down at the edge of the highway. The end of Earth's ecosystem was marked with a sharp line, mere millimeters in size, where everything was reduced to fine particles. He looked upward where an aurora-like effect danced in the dusk sky.

He turned finally to lock his gaze on her.

Her stepfather had an exotic pedigree. He claimed to be part indigenous Scandinavian Sami and part French. Yves was more of the same with almond-shaped eyes of stunning green and hair that was a rich honey walnut and a face that whispered possible blood ties to the Great Khans of the Mongol Empire. Life had been entirely too kind to him; he still looked twenty.

She certainly was no longer ten. "What the hell are you doing here?"

"We're the largest defense contractor in United States." Yves walked past her, focused on the forest. "I'm here as a consultant."

*Consultant?* Maybe if he'd brought a pet scientist on a leash with him, but he seemed utterly alone. Yves was smart, spoke multiple languages, and had a stunning grasp of history, but advanced physics wasn't in his playbook. What was he really doing here?

She had already heard rumors floating through the camp that the government was grinding to a halt as various factions started to argue over who had control over the area. Homeland Security, FEMA, and the National Guard were all claiming to be top dog. She hated to ask Yves for help; he was the second-to-last person on the planet that she wanted to be indebted to. The entire planet, though, was at risk. Yves had more connections than she did. He had an entire army of employees and a political network spanning multiple countries. If he were busy playing god with them, he wouldn't have time to spare to bother her. It would be a win-win for her.

"Yves, all communities downriver on the Ohio and Mississippi plus probably the Tennessee River need to be warned of possible biological contaminants."

He flicked his hand in negation. "There is no need."

"If this ecosystem can thrive on Earth . . ."

"It cannot," he stated firmly. "Earth lacks what it needs to thrive. There is no danger."

"I have a dinosaur on ice that says otherwise."

"It would die within a week on Earth. Yes, on its own world, it would destroy all in its path, but here it would be betrayed by the very genetics that made it so fierce. It would die a slow and painful death as all its cells cry out for the thing that Earth cannot provide. It is like slowly suffocating."

"And you know this how?" Lain asked. "Or are you just making random guesses and full-out lies?"

"History repeats itself. This is not the first time something like this has happened. Only the evidence has always neatly erased itself, so science has never acknowledged what folk tales hold to be true."

"Fairy tales?"

"Atlantis. El Dorado. Garden of Eden. Avalon. Baltia." Because he knew she didn't recognize the reference he added, "an island that Pliny the Elder described supposedly entirely made of amber. The seven caves of Chicomoztoc of the Aztecs. Alfheim, land of the elves in Norse myths. Hawaiki. Gorias, Finias, Murias and Falias. Irkalla. The Kingdom of Saguenay. Over and over again, all across the world, in every culture there are stories of other worlds. Lost places. Because we've never found evidence of them on Earth, scientists have always dismissed thousands of years of oral history." He waved his hand at the forest. "Once upon a time there was city called Pittsburgh."

Lain didn't recognize any of the names after Avalon and hated that she needed to take his word that so many existed. "Nothing like this has ever been recorded in the last hundred years."

"A hundred years: a blink of an eye." He took a small glass ball from his suit's breast pocket. "Humans started to use stone tools nearly three million years ago. What is a hundred years compared to that?"

He stepped down off the highway and onto the forest floor. Lifting the ball to his mouth, he said a word she didn't recognize. It flickered faintly. Sweeping it back and forth, he walked into the forest.

"It still proves nothing about this flora and fauna being unable to thrive in Earth's ecosystem!" Lain shouted after him. "Where do you think you're going?"

When he didn't answer, she guided her wheelchair carefully down off the thick lip of the highway to follow him. The legs sank deep into the forest debris but her chair was able to pick its way forward.

Yves stopped a dozen feet into the forest, screened from the road by tall ferns. The glass ball gleamed brightly in his hand. He spoke a second unfamiliar word and the light extinguished. Tucking away the ball, he took what seemed to be a piece of glass out of a pouch and laid it on the ground. With a grease pencil, he drew odd hieroglyphs onto the glass.

"What are you doing?" She nudged the wheelchair closer.

"Nothing."

She laughed bitterly at the obvious lie. "I'm not ten years old anymore."

"And yet you still haven't learned to keep your nose out of my business." Yves held up his hand, finger upraised in warning that he wanted her silent. He was the type of person that wouldn't let the fact that she was in a wheelchair stop him from using whatever force he felt necessary to get his way.

She was tempted to ignore his request; she'd learned how to fight in the military. Even in the wheelchair, she could defend herself. She had a weird disquieting feeling, though, that he would seriously hurt her if they got into a fight. They were screened from the road. No one had paid any attention to them leaving the encampment. Another helicopter landed with a loud thumping of blades that drowned out all other noise.

Lain silently reached down and checked that the pistol was still tucked in beside her useless legs.

Yves took her silence as obedience. He dropped his hand and focused back on the glass. He drew several more symbols on the glass then said a foreign word. The symbols gleamed faintly and then a pale dome appeared over the glass and gleaming lines traced an odd pattern underneath.

*What the hell?*

The pattern looked like some type of map. There were a multitude of lines running like water, and a handful of bright motes. The contours hadn't matched up to the three rivers that lay inside the zone. The lines indicated two "streams" in the immediate area, one of which they were standing directly on. She could see no water.

"What is that?" Lain wished she had a camera to capture the image before it vanished.

Yves studied it for a minute longer and then spoke another word and the glowing faded. "Nothing."

He took out a cloth and wiped clean the glass.

*Nothing?* The hell if it was nothing. Yves was looking for something quite specific and apparently found it. He was surprised by the forest but not ignorant of it. He knew it existed. He just didn't expect to find it here.

"Have they identified the power source behind the transfer?" Yves asked.

"No," she said and then the oddness of the question struck her. What was the trigger event? The aurora-like effect that followed the arching path of destruction hinted that the power had come from the atmosphere. She hadn't heard of any large solar flares—but those rarely made even the science news feed. Since her accident delivered its crippling blow to both her and NASA, all the news feeds focused on the Chinese hyperphase gate.

Which had activated last night for the first time.

If the gate worked as promised, it would jump a colony ship to a new world.

She gasped as possibilities hit home. Last night the gate was turned on and created a field through which *something* could travel to another world. Like Pittsburgh. The neat disc of forest was the same shape as the gate, magnified by a factor of nearly one hundred. NASA had been forbidden in its infancy by Congress to work with the Chinese space program, so she knew very little about the gate. Its design was top secret and the actual science unproven. Her stepfather had been heavily involved in the construction via his international businesses. If Pittsburgh's disappearance were caused by men—her stepfather to be exact—it would explain Yves' behavior. She always knew her stepfather was a stunningly powerful man but making an entire city vanish seemed beyond even him. Unless—of course—it was by accident.

Her family just got a thousand times more mysterious—and possibly more dangerous.

She sat in shock as Yves strode back to the encampment. What did she know of the gate's startup? It was supposed to go live for the first time yesterday at noon Beijing time but had been delayed until nearly seventeen hundred. She worked through the time zones. Yes. That would be the right time Eastern Standard Time when Pittsburgh disappeared. The Chinese stated that after a series of tests, powering up and powering down the gate to make sure it was operating smoothly, they'd jump the first colony ship through. It was less clear when they planned those. Were they already testing the gate or hadn't they powered it down yet?

Would Pittsburgh return if they powered the gate down?

There was an odd booming noise, growing louder.

"What now?" Lain spun her wheelchair around, wondering if some idiot was blowing up some other rare specimen.

A huge dark figure loomed inside of the forest. As she watched, it moved into the sunlight and she gasped. It was a tree—walking.

The ground shook with each step.

Lain knew she should be afraid, but all she felt was sudden and complete nirvana. It didn't matter that she could no longer go to an alien world—it had come to her.

The tree's branches were long and slender like a willow, trailing down to brush the ground as the tree walked. It would pry up a massive root foot, shift slowly forward and plant it again in an earth-rattling stomp. The trunk had many rough nodules with the appearance of a bark-covered face but she could see no true visible eyes.

She studied it through binoculars, whimpering as it drew nearer. "No, no, no, turn around." She fumbled with the radio. "Perkins! Lieutenant Perkins! This is Colonel Shenske. You need to stop that tree."

"Which tree? There are thousands of them."

"Are you blind? The one that is walking! It's bearing down on your twelve o'clock. You're going to have to stop it."

"Stop it?"

"It's loaded with seed pods."

"Oh, sweet Jesus." He'd spotted the tree. "I-I-I don't understand. Say again: seed pods?"

"If this vegetation can thrive on Earth, then every one of those seeds could grow into a similar tree. It could be like kudzu."

"Kudzu?" Lieutenant Perkins said.

"Oh good God, man, have you never been outside of Pennsylvania? It's the second worst thing the South ever did to itself. It's a massively invasive perennial vine native to Southeast Asia that was imported as groundcover to prevent soil erosion. It grows unchecked, killing off native plants and trees and covering any building in its path."

"How do you recommend that we stop the tree?"

"At a distance. Roughly half of the plants that have rapid movement are carnivorous."

"So we should shoot it?" He sounded doubtful at the effectiveness. The man obviously knew the result of shooting bullets at trees generally only resulted in ricochets and splinters.

"Do you have any Javelin or Dragon anti-tank missiles?"

He obviously was mentally scanning equipment lists as he slowly answered, "Yes."

"Then get them and shoot it!"

Lain eyed the tree that was closing distance with surprising speed. It was the first living alien life form she had ever encountered and she had just ordered its destruction. If she didn't start moving, she could be hit by friendly fire. First rule of xenobiology was to keep yourself alive. She thought she would never have the chance to apply the rule.

She toggled the wheelchair's control. The chair shuddered. One leg pawed at the ground and then stilled. "Oh, no." She glanced toward the tree. "You've got to work; there's no time for a reboot."

The tree seemed to be following the second bright line on Yves' map. It hit the edge of the highway. The soldiers fell back, yelling in frightened dismay. One of them shot at it with a rifle and triggered a sudden barrage of gunfire. She ducked down and a moment later a bullet ricocheted over her head. An officer shouted to cease fire as the tree surged forward onto the paving. There was a sudden change in pitch in the yelling as the willowy branches lashed forward and snared two soldiers. The shouting went from excitement and fear to horror and pain. It was a sound that Lain had hoped that she'd never hear again. The sound of people dying.

She punched the control pad of her wheelchair. "Come on!" She had to do something, though she wasn't sure what. She was a useless cripple trapped in an unreliable piece of equipment.

Everything went black and she felt like she was falling and suddenly everything snapped back to clarity. The silence was so complete that she thought she'd been struck deaf.

*Oh, God, did I just have a stroke? Did I lose more of myself?* She lifted her hands, wiggled her fingers and tilted her head back and forth.

"The rain in Spain falls mainly on the plain," she said aloud.

No, not a stroke. Nor was she deaf. The wind gusted, making the leaves overhead whisper. The forest was impossibly quiet. No booming footsteps of the willow tree. No screams of pain and terror. No gunshots.

Did the reserves kill the tree already?

The highway wasn't where she remembered it being. She scanned the forest, trying to orient herself.

The base camp was gone.

The highway and all signs of civilization were gone.

Forest continued, uninterrupted.

The Chinese must have turned off the gate. Good news: Pittsburgh was back on Earth. Bad news: she was stuck on whatever planet that the gate was tuned to.

She sat stunned for a moment, and then forced herself to take a deep breath and push out shock. "Well, you always wanted to visit an alien planet. Congratulations. You've succeeded. Now what?"

If the Chinese continued the tests as planned, they should turn on the gate shortly.

If she was right about what was happening.

Logic suggested that she should sit tight and hope that the Chinese turned the gate back on soon. This parallel world, minus man's pollution, was cooler. A few hours after sunset, she would be at risk for hypothermia. All the nearby fallen branches and trees were covered with moss; building a fire with the damp wood was going to take her survival skills. She had no matches but she did have a pistol. If she could find enough dry tinder, she might be able to use the muzzle flare to light it.

Something moved in the forest close by.

Her heart leapt painfully in her chest at the sound, as if it knew something horrible was hunting her.

A deep breathy roar came from downwind. If the beast could smell, it would pick up her scent. She pulled her pistol and checked the magazine. It was a .45 caliber with ten rounds in the magazine. She flipped the safety off. She noticed her hands weren't shaking. Was it because she wasn't afraid to die? This was the death she wanted; on an alien planet, dealing with extraterrestrial life.

If the Chinese never turned the gate back on, there was no way she could survive for long. Not crippled.

"If this is your idea of a joke," she whispered to the God she rarely acknowledged. "I don't think it's very funny."

Something large came crashing through the forest bracken. She steeled herself, knowing that she only had ten rounds, plus another ten in the spare magazine. Twenty bullets until she was rescued. If she was rescued. She couldn't afford to waste even one.

The younger brother of Perkins' dinosaur broke through the screen of ferns. It rushed at her, jaws open. She aimed at its dark eye.

*Why am I fighting so hard? I'm just going to die. Obey the first rule! Stay alive!*

She squeezed the trigger. The dinosaur roared with pain as the bullet plowed through its eye. She flung herself forward, out of the chair, as the beast lunged at her. Its hot breath blasted across her back, reeking of spoiled meat.

There was a clang of metal and the whine of servos as the dinosaur bit down on her wheelchair. She rolled through dead, molding leaves, trying to put distance between her and the beast. The dinosaur shook its head just like a crocodile would to tear chunks of meat from a large prey.

A .45 didn't have the stopping power for a body shot. Getting a head shot from a prone position was going to be nearly impossible. She struggled to sit up, cursing her ruined body.

The dinosaur flung aside her wheelchair. It sniffed loudly, casting about for her.

She levered herself up, took aim on its head, and waited for it to turn.

There was crashing in the forest nearby. A second breathy roar of an adult dinosaur.

*They're pack hunters*, she thought. *Maybe a mated pair, or two juveniles, since this one is smaller than the male inside the cooler.*

The wounded male turned to face her. It spotted her with its one good eye. She shot. The first bullet cut a groove along its heavy bone eye ridge. The second missed. Then she had no choice. She rapid-fired into its body as it loomed over her. The pistol thundered in her hand, slamming her onto her back.

The beast stood over her, its mouth wide to show off massive sharp teeth. And then slowly, gracefully, it toppled over dead.

She had one moment of elation and then the second dinosaur crashed into the clearing. She aimed and fired. The hammer fell onto the empty chamber with a loud click. She was out. She fumbled to roll to the side so she could pull the spare magazine from its pouch. The larger but less decorative female charged, rumbling dangerously. She wasn't going to make it. She wasn't going to . . .

A shrieking bolt of light pierced through the female's chest. The beast crumbled, landing inches from Lain's feet. The last of its breath washed over her.

*What the hell?* Lain rammed the magazine home. She lay in the deep rich moist loam of the forest, panting. Her wheelchair sat twenty feet away, canted on its side, looking extremely battered.

She caught movement out the corner of her eye. She rolled quickly, bringing up her pistol.

A humanoid stood a dozen feet away, bow in hand, string pulled taut, arrow ready. It took her a second to realize that it was nonhuman.

"Shit," Lain whispered. First contact. A lifetime of dreaming of it—all the possible ways it might take place—and her mind went blank. "Shit."

They stared at each other.

He was at least six and a half feet tall, wide shouldered and lean. Pointed ears said he wasn't human but he had to be at least a distant genetic cousin. His black hair and almond-shaped eyes hinted that he was closer to the Asian branch. If she had to guess an age, she would put him at seventeen. Tribal tattoos done in blue ink covered his arms in a complex design reminiscent of Celtic knots. He wore knee-high boots, leather pants and a vest of overlapping scales that seemed more organic than handcrafted. He seemed to be wearing nothing fashioned out of metal; all his weapons were wood, leather and stone.

Primitive as his weapons might be, he could still kill her. It was a basic truth that xenobiologists had always acknowledged—first contact could easily be deadly to both sides.

They stared at each other, weapons aimed.

"I don't want to hurt you." Lain cautiously lowered her pistol. "And hopefully you don't want to hurt me, but I am not going to make my last act in this world killing off an intelligent being."

The male lowered his bow.

Lain breathed out in relief. Mutual destruction averted, at least for the time being. She risked glancing at her wheelchair still lying on its side. She snapped her fingers. Its legs flailed for a moment and stopped. It needed to be righted before it could function properly—if it wasn't totally broken.

She started to crawl toward it, keeping her pistol in position so she could quickly bring it up. "Yes, I might be thrashing around on the ground like a beached whale, but I'm still dangerous. I'm a cripple but I have powerful machines that make me greater than this broken shell. With machines I have flown up to the stars, walked on the moon." She gave a bitter laugh. "Was supposed to swim the seas of Europa—that's a moon to Jupiter, the largest planet in our solar system, although your people might think it's just a star."

She reached her chair and struggled to right it. "Of course it would help if my powerful machine was working."

The male crouched down, cocking his head in what seemed to be puzzlement. She reminded herself that it was dangerous to assign human emotion to the gesture. It seemed, though, that he was curious about her. She knew that she was damn curious about him. Her training, though, stressed that her first priority was to stabilize her environment. Dead scientists learned nothing but the truth of their own mortality.

She finally managed to right her wheelchair. "Load." It whined as it tried to comply. After a second, it shuddered and its operating system crashed. "I am starting to suspect that there is a god and he has wicked sense of humor. He's probably doing all this just to teach me a lesson. I'm just not sure at all what I'm supposed to be learning."

She manually set the chair's armature to load position. "I think part of it is that I'm supposed to remember that it is my mind that matters most, not my body. True, this would all be marginally easier with two sound legs, but not much. Without a gun, I would have been in a bad way with those dinosaurs, crippled or not."

She climbed into the chair and rebooted the operating system. "And I think God was also reminding me that regardless of where I would have gone, I would have needed machines to operate. When I went to the moon, I needed a space suit. In the seas of Europa,

I would have needed a diving suit. And if they ever got that insane trip to Venus finalized—you should have seen that gear. All machines to move this fragile container I have about, because what's important is what's up here." She tapped her head. "It's my mind that makes me special. And there's nothing wrong with it. And machines let me use my mind, be it on the moon, or Europa, or wherever this place is."

"This is Elfhome," the male said.

She slapped her hand over her mouth. He spoke English? She had just ranted on and on. God, what had she said? First contact and she had thrown a hissy fit. Wait—how did he speak English if this was first contact? Maybe she just misheard him.

"Have you really been to the moon?" he asked.

She nodded, hand still over her mouth. He was definitely speaking English with a lilting British accent. He wasn't simply parroting her faint New York accent back at her. Oh God, he had understood everything she had said! What exactly had she said? She had ranted on without thinking. Had she mentioned being on the moon? Yes, she had. She nodded, and then, realizing that he might not know the gesture, added. "Yes, I have. I was—I am an astronaut. That's a scientist that travels to other worlds to study them."

"What's it like? The moon?"

"Very beautiful, in a lifeless kind of way. Rock and dust and cold and nothing more."

He tilted his head to scan the trees above them, as if looking for the moon. "Do you suppose our moon is like yours? Lifeless?"

She floundered in the flood of implications. This twin of Earth had a brother of their moon. A nearly infinite set of identical events that would have needed to happen to form both. And most stunning of all, that he would know that the two planets were so similar. "Statistically speaking, yes."

"Do you find our world more to your liking?"

There was a loaded question. It meant he had a full grasp of the concept of world and that she wasn't a native of his. "Yes."

"My father says it's not much different than Earth."

She considered the implication of the statement. The male not only knew of the existence of another planet, he knew its name and spoke one of its languages. There was only one way she could imagine he knew so much. "Your father has been to Earth."

"Not for several hundred years. I have to say— judging by the city that you sent to visit us—your world has changed greatly since he was there last."

For a moment she forgot how to breathe, and only remembered as she realized she was going lightheaded. Deep breaths. Radically shifting worldview required deep breaths.

"How . . . how . . . how old is your father?" It was the first of the "how" questions she could force out.

The male considered the question for a minute. "The exact count of his age? I do not know it. He has needed four digits to count his age for hundreds of years. I believe, though, that he is still under two thousand years old. Maybe."

"And a year has three hundred and sixty-five days."

He thought for a while longer. "That seems to be a correct number. I confess, one such as I has little need to count the days. I do not watch for winter's thaw to sow crops or such things as that."

Been to Earth. Lived for hundreds of years. Pointed ears. Lived on Elfhome. "You're elves."

"That is what our people are called. You are a human?" It was more question than statement.

"Yes. I am a human. I'm Lain Shenske."

"What does your name mean?"

"It—it doesn't mean anything. Shenske is my family name, given by father's bloodline." She didn't want to explain being Jewish. "Lain is my given name, but neither one actually means anything."

"I am Kaanini-kauta-taeli. It means Lightning Strikes Wind; a brilliance that is there and then gone. My mother was angry when the priestess gave it to me: I will most likely die young."

"That's terrible. Why would anyone even give a child a name like that?"

"Because she saw my future."

She stared at him in horror.

"I do not mind. It has freed me to seize life, live it as I wish now, with no thought of the long future. If you constantly compare this moment with some perfection that you imagined, you are fated to be forever disappointed. Adventure is the unforeseen, not the expected."

Blithe words for someone of sound body who had not had their dreams crushed. But was she not here, on an alien world, far greater than any she expected to explore? Europa would have been a long struggle to drill down through ice to open water and then pray for life. Exploring Elfhome might not be possible without her failure, because with the United States shelving its plans for Jupiter, the world had funneled its energy into the Chinese colony program.

She hated to admit her mother's platitudes of "sometimes bad things have to happen for the good things to follow" had any bearing on her present situation. Lain had snarled in her mother's face for that and every suggestion to use the wheelchair or to push herself in physical therapy. Lain hadn't seen the point; her life seemed over. She couldn't have predicted this impossible event all riding on the flip of a switch.

She cursed. *A flip of a switch*! Sooner or later the Chinese were going to flip the power switch again. If it wasn't for her odd conversation with Yves, she wouldn't have guessed that Pittsburgh's disappearance was linked to the hyperphase gate in orbit. The Chinese would continue testing the gate until it was time for the colony ship to jump to Alpha Centauri. At that point, there would be no reason to keep the gate on. Pittsburgh would return to Earth and the connection to Elfhome would be lost.

If she wanted to stay on Elfhome, she needed to get to a piece of land that wasn't shuffling between the worlds.

# DRABBLE

## *A New Day Dawning*

The sun woke Wojo that morning. Once he realized it was full daylight, he thrashed about for the alarm clock, knocking books off his nightstand. The digital face of the clock radio was blank. The power was off. He swore, scrambling out of bed to check the kitchen's battery-powered clock. Eight o'clock. If he just pulled on clothes, he could make it to work on time. He glanced out the back window to see how traffic on I-279 was...

A forest had replaced the highway.

Wojo leapt back from the window, terror jolting through him. He had to force himself to look again.

Redwood trees filled half of his neighbor's yard—the part where their house used to stand. The driveway, sidewalk, and garden gnome—smiling as if it knew some monstrous secret—stood untouched.

*I'm still asleep*, Wojo finally decided and went to take a cold shower to wake up.

The forest, though, remained. He dressed, looking out various windows as he pulled on clothes. Everything out the front of the house looked completely normal—no stray trees there. The side windows showed the forest stretched east and west in a solid wall.

He used a match to light his gas range and started brewing coffee.

Had he gone crazy? No. The forest was irrational, not him. That was oddly comforting thought. External problems were, his opinion, easier to fix, or at least cope with. He tried the house phone and found it dead. So was, more distressingly, his cell phone. He stood drumming his fingers on the kitchen counter while the tin coffee pot bubbled.

A wolf trotted through the woods. A very large wolf. Pony-sized even.

Wojo made sure the doors were locked and got out his deer rifle.

He filled his travel mug with coffee, added sugar and cream, picked up his rifle, and headed for work.

# WYVERN

Kate Emerson wasn't sure what pissed her off most. Was it being jerked off her first trip back to the states in years, to be shoved into an alternate dimension filled with undocumented zoology, real magic and snotty elves? Or was it that her smattering of ten human languages and knowledge of dozens of Earth's more obscure cultures weren't worth a damn with the Elfhome natives? Or was it that this time around, her native guide managed to always make her look frumpy?

Stormsong came up the mountainside with all the fluid grace of a big cat, annoyingly beautiful in the muggy August heat. The nimble elfin bitch didn't even pant. She paused at the edge of the *kuesi*'s blood, and murmured, "I told you that your 'tracer' would not work," and continued up the rock face in bounds that would impress mountain goats.

"I found this much!" Kate shouted after Stormsong.

"What an idiot couldn't see of the blood trail," the elf's voice came from somewhere above, "a blind man could smell."

Kate picked her way through the swimming pool's worth of viscera to rescue her tracer off of the massive *kuesi* skull. When she'd heard that the railway project manager for the elfin crew was a female, Kate expected to skip all the normal macho butthead stuff.

Stormsong waited on the summit beside Godzilla-sized footprints. The feet of their *kuesi*-snatcher mimicked the structure of birds: three digits pointed forward, one backwards. The talons had gouged the granite as deep as eight inches in places. Old, weathered scratches indicated that the stone outcropping was a common perch site.

"Dragon?" Kate had checked her zoology reports last night, but they varied wildly from gigabytes of data on wargs—frost-breathing cousins of wolves—to three words on phoenixes: *still believed mythical*. The dragon section was nearly as scant, it stated "While apparently dragons vary in size, they are reported to be very large, fire breathing, and dangerous. Approach with caution." Duh.

Stormsong shook her head. "Too small. Wyvern."

Kate tucked into an overhang and scanned the nearby mountain peaks with her binoculars. In the broad valley below them, the railroad right of way cut its straight raw path through the primal forest of the elfin world. Out in the vicinity of Pittsburgh—which fate chose as the human portal into this dimension—they had bulldozers, dump trucks and earthmovers working their way east. The low-tech elves, though, working from the sparsely settled coast, only had hand tools and the *kuesi*. Until a connecting road was complete, trading between the two races was at an impasse. Construction had been going smoothly until the wyvern decided that the work crew was a moveable feast.

Speaking of which, Stormsong had poised herself on a rock projection like a piece of bait.

"Get down." Kate pointed to the protected ledge beside her. That only earned her a cold stare. Damn elves. "Move over here."

"I see better from here."

"The wyvern could take you from there."

The elf made a noise of understanding. "The wyvern. It sleeps. It hunts at night like a *whou*."

"*Whou?*"

Stormsong sighed at Kate's ignorance. "A night bird! It flies very quietly, and calls *whou, whou, whou*."

Kate caught herself gritting her teeth and worked her jaw to ease the tension. What was it about Stormsong that pissed her off so much? Kate wasn't sure if it actually was the elf girl herself, or just the irritation with the general situation finding focus on the only breathing target.

Kate returned to her scanning. "These wyverns. Do they den alone or in mated pairs?"

"Mated pair. Like falcons, females are larger. The nest will be on a peak, high up, on bare rocks with dead branches and such to keep the young in. One mate will stay on the nest and the other will hunt while there are eggs in the nest. Once the eggs are hatched, both will hunt to keep the young fed."

So they were either dealing with a solitary creature, perhaps a youngster, or two beasts—which meant near the nest they'd have to be careful watching their backs.

"Your viceroy wasn't completely clear," Kate said. "What are we supposed to do with the wyvern?"

"Do?"

"The viceroy said this was a royal hunting preserve. On Earth, when an animal on a preserve causes a problem, we trap it and move it to another location where it's not in conflict with humans."

Stormsong shook her head. "Wyverns return to their nesting site, year in, year out. If we moved them, they would return next year."

"Zoos on Earth might take a mated pair."

Stormsong gave a musical laugh. "You might want to risk your life to trap such beasts, but not I. And no. Wyverns need magic to exist. They would die on Earth. Here on Elfhome, they nest on the strongest ley line in their range."

Native guides always believed in magic, but here it was a real, measurable force. Trying to determine reality from superstition was going to be a real bitch.

"What else about this animal can you tell me? What does it look like? Is it a bird?" Damn big bird if it was, carrying off the elfin cousin of an African elephant.

"Wyverns have four limbs like a bird, not six, so they have no front limbs. Their bones are light but strong, as are their scales."

"Scales?"

"These are wyvern scales." Stormsong tapped the vest she was wearing. Kate had never seen the elf without the vest of overlapping scales. Earlier attempts to look at it closer had been rebuffed. From the distance, the stuff looked like steel hammered into seashell shingles, and then somehow dyed blue.

"It would be nice to know what the fuck I'm dealing with here. Can I see the scales?"

Stormsong hesitated and then undid something on her left side and peeled back part of the scales. The scales were attached to a leather undergarment with a slit laced shut. The elf female undid the lacing and then wriggled a bit. If Kate had been a man, the show would have been extremely interesting.

The vest was lined with hard leather. Over it had been tacked a strong cloth, to which scales were sewn into an overlapping pattern. All in all, the vest weighed only ten pounds, but a goodly part of it would have come from the leather. The edges of the scales were sharp and slowly cutting through the leather.

"Why don't you grind down the edges?"

"It is organic carbon. There is nothing stronger that we forge that would grind it down. It can take a pistol bullet at close range without breaking. It is permitted only to the *domana* and *sekasha* caste."

"So this thing...wyvern...is bulletproof?" How the hell was she supposed to kill it?

"It has points of weakness."

"How does it grow? Does it ever shed, like a snake?"

"No." Stormsong wriggled back into her vest and laced it back up. "The young are born with down, which is why the parents are so protective. They are vulnerable until they molt."

So Kate was fighting an armored attack helicopter. Oh golly joy. She wished that she'd thought to bring a missile launcher. She doubted that even her Winchester African with its .458 caliber rounds had enough stopping power for this, but she had nothing bigger back at camp, or on this planet. Kate studied the blood pool. If this splattering of blood and viscera on the southern exposure was from the wyvern arriving from their camp, then the blood trail on the northern exposure was probably from the wyvern taking off. She climbed up to another summit, hoping that Stormsong was right about the wyvern's sleep habits. She'd seen falcons strike like bullets enough times to be nervous as she scanned the northern horizon.

Stormsong stood waiting as patiently as any other native guide Kate had ever used. The wind played with the few strands of golden hair that dared to come out of Stormsong's thick braid down her back.

In the north lay several mountains offering possible nesting sites. Hiking for days through virgin forest without GPS, blindly looking for something that could swallow her whole wasn't Kate's idea of smart hunting.

"You said that they nest on ley lines. That means they're attracted to magic?"

"They will nest where it runs strongest."

"They say magic is measurable. Can you tell, from here, which of those mountaintops has the most?"

The elf girl shot her a hard look and then, reluctantly, nodded. "Yes, of course I can."

Stormsong cleared a flat rock of twigs and dust. From her waist pack, she produced a small, loosely bound, hand printed book, bundled in a layer of suede. She flipped through the pages of complex designs until she found what she wanted. Laying the book flat, Stormsong copied the page out onto the rock with what looked like a grease pencil, only the black lines glittered in the sunlight, like it contained flecks of ground metal.

Kate frowned at the design as Stormsong carefully rewrapped the book and tucked it away. So far it wasn't any more impressive than Earth "magic," although a hell of lot more orderly.

"Stay back," Stormsong whispered, blocking Kate's closer inspection with an outstretched arm. "Do not get metal near it, or make any loud noises."

That annoyed Kate, although she wasn't sure why. Normally natives using magic didn't piss her off, even when it was blatantly nonsense. What Stormsong had copied out looked oddly similar to computer circuit board design.

Taking a deep breath, Stormsong chanted out a series of deep, guttural vowels. As if the mantra had thrown a switch, the black lines suddenly gleamed gold. A glowing sphere appeared over the spell, and slowly a model of the local mountain range took form. From the distinctive stone outcrop, Kate recognized that the centermost mountain was the one they stood on. Watery lines appeared in the model, of varying width and brightness, bisecting the mountains.

Stormsong peered at the model and then looked up, scanning the horizon. "There," she whispered as she pointed at a far peak. On the model, the line crossing over it was the brightest and widest. "That's the strongest ley line in spell range."

The elf extinguished the spell, and smudged out the lines on the rock with her foot.

Kate examined the distant mountain with her binoculars; it looked like the rest of the Allegheny range, an oversized rounded hill. One section of it seemed slightly bald. She unpacked her digital camera and its tripod. She had reluctantly packed these, but it seemed that they were going to come in handy. Training the telescopic lens onto the treeless area, she set the automatic capture on it, took her hands off the camera and let it capture a perfectly still image. Once the timer hit zero, she gave it another second, and then started to enhance the image.

The bald area enlarged to a wasteland of rock, strewn with broken timber.

"Well, what do you think?" Kate asked the elf girl.

Stormsong eyed the picture and then glanced out at the mountain, featureless to the naked eye. "Yes," she said flatly. "That's a nesting site."

*Well, let's not jump up and down with joy.* Kate packed away the camera. "What exactly are the wyvern's weak spots?"

Stormsong picked up a stone and scratched out a rough drawing on the rock. "The joints in the wingtips, here, here, and here. If you can cut this membrane," she indicated the taut skin of the wings, "you can ground it, which will keep it from striking and flying off. Its mouth and eyes are weaknesses. Death magic works, as does light magic."

*Yeah, right.* "Poison? Or does it avoid poisoned bait?"

"It's an indiscriminate eater, but it takes massive amounts of poison to affect it, which we don't have."

"How big is this?"

"They are not as large as a dragon, but they are considerable in size."

*Considerable my ass*, Kate thought, *it has to be huge.* But she kept her verbal opinion to a snort. "How do your people kill these things? Or do you just pick up the scales after they die?"

Stormsong lifted up her bow in answer.

Well, that explained the declining elf population.

"It's stupid to attack it on its own grounds," Kate stated. "We'll lure it to us, and we pick the shots."

"This is not a simple animal."

"The smarter it is, the better. We give it an option. To land in among the trees and hope for a clear takeoff, or take something here on its favorite landing site."

Stormsong gazed at the blood-splattered rocks. "We will try it your way."

Baiting a trap should have been simple. Kate had done it a thousand times before, but she hadn't counted on the size of the wyvern compounding the process. Stormsong maintained that nothing smaller than one of the *kuesi* would do as bait. There was getting the beast up the steep mountainside, and then trying to control it once it smelled the blood. Luckily she thought to bring her tranq pistol, although the dosage, set for a tiger, was only enough to make the massive beast groggy instead of putting it down completely.

"Well, you have some uses," Stormsong said, looking toward the setting sun. "It will not be long. It will come soon."

As a byproduct of working too long in the third world, Kate carried a computer attachment to detect incoming planes as standard equipment. She set it up, unsure if it would work on the wyvern. She liked to cover all bases.

The sun set and the sky slowed deepened into violet and then color leached out to total black. Kate had tucked herself in among the rocks, and as the sky went to dark, tugged on night goggles. She could pick out Stormsong close by, silent, an arrow nocked but not drawn.

From her computer stick tucked in among the rocks, she heard quiet pinging.

"It's coming," she called to Stormsong.

She'd made the mistake of setting it up so she couldn't see the screen, worried only about keeping her hands free. Now, with the gentle chime indicating a closing wyvern, she didn't want to move out of her niche to check the screen for its direction.

Then she saw it, and wasn't about to leave hard cover.

She hadn't accounted for how much space the massive creature would take up on the rock ledge. She'd tucked herself into a niche that seemed a safe distance from the *kuesi*. She scuttled backwards along the overhang as her vision filled up with monster. Stormsong's drawing had been anatomically correct—a wedge head on a snake neck, wings of membrane like a bat's, a lizard leg redone on a falcon template—but lacked scale.

*My God, that can't possibly fly.* But it was. Or to be more precise, plummeting—rocketing down out of the night sky toward the *kuesi*. She planned a shot to the wyvern's vulnerable eyes; she'd expected them to be wide and round as an owl's, specialized for night hunting, done on a more massive scale. In the blur coming toward her, she couldn't see anything remotely looking like an eye.

The wyvern came out of its dive, wings unfurling with an audible crack, legs swinging forward, hooked talons longer than her arm flaring into overextension. Even drugged, the *kuesi* saw death and bleated. The cry cut short with the impact of bodies that she felt through the bottom of her feet. The *kuesi*, that had stood another head taller than her, was suddenly rabbit-small under the wyvern.

"Oh God, oh God," she whispered. Was Stormsong insane? Kill that? With what?

Then like an Earth-born falcon, the wyvern cocked

its head back and forth, examining its kill with its eyes. Protected by a ridge of bone, the solid pupil was a beady black target.

Kate ducked out of her niche, raised her rifle up to her shoulder, and aimed down on the eye. Breathe. Hold it. And she squeezed the trigger.

Even as the elephant rifle kicked, the wyvern jerked its head around, spotting her movement. The bullet ricocheted off the bone ridge, making the wyvern jerk its head aside.

Reflex kicked in, and with icy calm, Kate worked the bolt—ejecting the spent round, loading another bullet, locking the action—and took aim. *Kill it, before it kills you.*

But she forgot about the massive tail until seconds before it hit her.

She saw it whipping toward her, knew she couldn't dodge it, and held position to get off her shot. *Kill it, before...*

And then darkness exploded around her, the actual contact lost in a moment of unconsciousness, and then she was aware of being airborne. Falling. Somewhere close by, she could hear her computer, tucked into the cliff face, pinging again.

*Not off the cliff, oh God, not off the cliff.* And so the contact with solid land only a moment later actually came as a relief. She managed to tumble across the ground, lessening the impact, torn earth filling her senses.

She scrambled to her knees, trying to gain her feet, but her right leg was refusing to move. A bus-sized mouth full of teeth was coming at her—rows upon rows of sharp shark-like teeth.

She was going to die. "God damn it."

With a deep guttural howl, a streak of light flashed through the air, lightning-white in intensity. The light struck the wyvern in the side of the neck, sliced through the armored skin and punched through the other side of the huge neck.

*What the hell?* Kate didn't waste time trying to figure it out. If she lived, she'd investigate closer. If the wyvern was dead, the news hadn't reached its brain yet. It came on.

She rolled to the side, whimpering in pain from her right leg. There was her rifle. The wyvern hadn't turned, and its forward motion began to look like floundering. She could still hear the pinging from her computer, though. The second one was coming.

The tumble hadn't damaged her rifle. It had been fired at some point since she last remembered holding it. She worked the bolt, reloading, and looked up.

Stormsong stood on an outcropping of rock, arrow nocked and bow drawn, sighting down on the wyvern on the ground. What was the little idiot doing? The elf released the string, and the arrow flashed toward the wyvern. Immediately the arrow howled, and light flared around it, growing in size and intensity as it leaped the span. The second arrow struck the wyvern in the back of the skull, blasting the news of its death straight into the brain this time. The wyvern collapsed into an ungainly tangle of giant limbs.

Magic arrows. The damn bitch had magic arrows.

And the damn bitch was going to get nailed from behind. The second wyvern was in a silent dive—aimed at the elf outlined against the stars. The wyvern on the ground probably was the male, because the one in the air was much bigger.

"Stormsong! Move!" Kate shouted, bringing her rifle to her shoulder.

The female wyvern was still in its power dive, wings folded close to its body, mouth closed, its tiny eyes invisible—a great expanse of bulletproof armor. Kate held her breath, waiting for an opening.

And the chance came, as it swung its legs forward, wings spreading to brake its dive. The vulnerable joints of the wings opened up. She squeezed the trigger, and the rifle kicked hard on her shoulder. The bullet struck the joint, jerking the wyvern sidewise, and then its wing folded back at an impossible angle. The wyvern screamed and came tumbling out of the air. It struck the side of the cliff below them in an earth-shaking impact.

Curling in pain on the ground, Kate reloaded the rifle's magazine. *Oh, God, please, let there only be two.*

Silence filled the night. Stormsong stood on her rocky lookout, staring down at the ruined mass of the female. Finally she crossed the ledge to Kate.

"I think my leg is broken." Kate didn't want to whimper, not in front of her.

Stormsong dropped down to her knees and then prostrated herself fully on the ground. "Forgiveness."

"Huh?"

"I have treated you poorly since your arrival, you who have come so far to help us. I believed myself to be superior of all humans and yet found that I was only merely equal. I let it irritate me, and in spite, treated you rudely."

It was as if Stormsong held up a mirror to her soul. Kate suddenly saw her own arrogance and irritation reflected in the elf. *This is what was driving*

*me nuts,* Kate realized, *I saw how I acted with all
other natives. I didn't like what it showed of myself.*

"I wasn't at my best either," Kate muttered, dismayed by the revelation.

"We elves say 'see the beast in yourself and kill it.'
I have slain my beast."

*Kill the beast, before it kills you.*

"Ah," Kate said, and meant every word, "how very
wise of you."

# DRABBLE

## *Storm Winds*

I had been in Pittsburgh, as the humans say, for a coon's age, when I first saw her. We elves say *"nae hae"* but what we're both saying is "we're too shit lazy to figure it out." I think it was a month before everything went to hell and back, so it means that she would have been seventeen.

I had been to the hoverbike races before, had seen her race before, and even knew her name—how couldn't I as the crowd chanted it when she won? But usually she was just a roar of engine, a blur of motion, and a small figure muscling a flying piece of steel through impossible maneuvers.

This time I was down by the pits. I was debating on moving. This close and the bikes flashed by in a heartbeat, and vanished around the bend. And yet, part of my talent was whispering to me, "stay here, stay here, this is important." So I lingered, wondering what could possibly be important in this loud, pulsing celebration of human recklessness?

And then my talent cried "now" and two bikes came flying around the corner. She was down low, hugging the curve, cutting off the leader. She would have made it, but he caught sight of her and dropped down, nearly on top of her. And my heart must have known, even then, even before the rest of me, because it leaped up to my throat. And my hand, guided by my heart, went to my sword. If she had died at that moment, so would have the man that killed her—and what a fucking mess that would have been to explain.

But she sensed him, and slammed into a desperate sideways slide to avoid him. His drive missed her body, but caught her front chain, and the two bikes became a tornado of machines and bodies. The crowd screamed and surged backwards, trying to escape the oncoming wreckage, and I lost sight of her for a moment. Then I spotted her, climbing to her feet on the other side of the track.

"Don't go out onto the track!" She caught a member of another team's pit crew that was about to dart out to check on the other driver. "Get a caution flag up! Call for a caution!"

The pack of bikes came around the corner at that moment and roared through, drowning out whatever commands she was shouting, but I could see her both keeping check on those who would wander out into the race, and organizing clearing the wreckage when the all clear came.

I watched her, wondering why I had my hand on my sword, why I was ready to leap to her defense. My talent is so sporadic that I didn't even realize yet that she was female. I thought she was a boy and wondered at my fickle heart. Wolf Who Rules was my only love—but what was this odd niggling feeling I had that he'd just lost his place?

The other driver surfaced, helmet already off, shouting out obscenities in English. She turned and shouted back in language just as human, just as foul. He made a rude gesture, and she launched herself toward him—only to be plucked out of the air by a very tall man.

That moved me out onto the track. No one could touch her like that—certainly not that man.

"Let me at the bastard, Nathan!" She didn't even seem to be aware that she was being restrained except that it was keeping from her inflicting pain on the other driver. With a curse, she tore off her helmet and flung it at the other driver.

And knowledge pierced through me—there and gone—like an arrow passing through my body. She was to be the one I love above all the rest—the one I would die for.

I stumbled to a halt, stunned and confused. Her brown hair was hacked short, making it easy to see in a glance that she was human. She was small, Stone Clan dark, and howling curse words in English. Her nose was bloody. She was caked with mud. And she was human—which meant she would be dead of old age in a blink of eye.

How could I ever look to her? For all of being a mutt, I was still *sekasha*, by blood and by sword, and only a *domana*-caste elf could hold one like me.

My erratic talent—having shot certainty through me—fell quiet.

"Holy one," someone called me back to myself. A human was bowing before me. He spoke fluent high tongue, a rarity, and he wore a pit crew shirt from the Team Tinker. Over his heart, the word *Oilcan* was stitched in as his name. "I am sorry, holy one, but you must leave the course. The race is about to begin again."

I blinked at the man, realizing that he looked like her male twin.

"Who is he?"

He glanced over his shoulder to verify I meant her. "The small angry one? *She* is my cousin, Tinker."

So I learned the name but I did not learn the means that our fate was to be connected for months to come.

# BARE SNOW
# FALLING ON FAIRYWOOD

Law had just hooked a three-foot *waewaeli* when her phone started to ring. She ignored it as she fought the twenty-pound fish. "Not now, not now, go to voice mail!" Only a half-dozen people had her phone number and at the moment, she didn't want to talk to any of them. It stopped ringing for a minute, only to start again. And again. And again.

"Who the frigging hell?" She'd lost too many phones trying to cradle them on her shoulder and reel in a fish. She would need at least one hand free to answer the phone. Finally she locked the reel and jerked her phone out of her breast pocket.

"What?" she cried as her rod bent as the big fish fought the line.

"Who is this?" a female voice asked.

"Law!" she shouted. "Law Munroe." At least that was the name she was using most recently. The joy of having a mother who had been married ten times meant that even close family friends weren't sure what your real, *real* name was. "Who is this?"

"Oh, good. You'll be a perfect match. Go to Fairy-wood and find snow."

"What?" Law cried. "It's in the middle of freaking June! Midsummer's eve is in less than a week! There's no snow!"

"Fairywood. F. A. I. R. Y. Wood. It's next to Wind-gap. Just out of the Rocks—if there was still a bridge. Lots of urban prairie. You need to find snow. Collect snow up and get someplace safe. All hell is going to break loose regardless but let's not give anyone a nice little goat, shall we?"

The connection went dead and her line snapped.

"Who? What? Hello?" She glared at her phone. Not only had she lost the fish but she lost her streamer fly, too. A Clouser deep minnow. She handmade her flies, so she wasn't out money, just time. She needed one more fish before her ice chests were full and she could visit her customers. If she didn't land another big fish, she'd have to short someone because she could only put off deliveries for so long.

"I thought there was some kind of rule against crazy people on Elfhome!" Grumble as she might, her experiences with her family confirmed it was only diagnosed crazy people who had been deported back to Earth. All the unknown crazies were free to terrorize their relatives and random people. At least with strangers, she could ignore the phone call. "Not my circus. Not my monkeys."

She was standing knee-deep in Chartiers Creek in Carnegie. It was about six miles from where the stream met the Ohio River. She took another fly from her hat and tied it to her line. She'd dropped coolers alongside Campbells Run and Chartiers Creek every few hundred feet. Parking at the end of Glass Street before dawn, she'd walked back to Campbells Run. In the last hour, she'd worked her way down to where the smaller stream joined the larger one, slowly making her way back to her truck. She had her biggest coolers full of trout and crayfish from traps on other streams, but she enjoyed angling for the *waewaeli*. Summer was her favorite time to be a professional forager since she could devote much of her time to the sport of fishing. The dry hot months meant that the Chartiers was shallow enough to wade. She was too far upstream to worry about river sharks and jumpfish; they needed at least four feet of water to navigate a channel. The undergrowth lining the creek screened the ruins of the abandoned neighborhood. The play of water and singing birds masked out any distant noise of civilization. It was her and the fish, one on one, just the way she liked it.

Until her phone rang again. Same mystery number. She sighed and answered, "What?"

"I forgot to tell you: look for the white door."

"Not a red door and paint it black?"

"Oh God no, black would make everything worse. There won't be time to paint it. Just take it with you when you leave."

She knew it was useless to argue about the lack of snow in June. Crazy people didn't listen to logic. Her parents had at least taught her that. "Okay, I'll take the door with me when I find snow."

"Good." And the mystery Crazy Lady hung up again.

Law spotted a big shadow in the next deep pool. She played out line until she could feel the rod load, then cast.

The morning light was still fragile with dawn, the

sun not fully climbed above the hills. It was amazing that anyone was awake enough to be calling her. The woman didn't even seem to know whom she had reached. Had she just randomly punched numbers until someone actually picked up the phone?

She'd just landed the big *waewaeli* when the phone rang again. Same Crazy Lady. Law sighed and answered. "Yes?"

"You only have a few hours to save her. You have to go today."

"Her? Her who?"

"Snow! They're going to kill her if you don't get her to safety."

"Oh, Jesus Christ! Why didn't you tell me that Snow was a person? That changes everything!"

"What did you think? It's June!"

Lawry considered just dropping her phone into the water. No. She knew from experience that didn't really help in the long run. "Who is going to kill her?"

"Do you blame the maker of the gun or the person that pulls the trigger?"

"The person who pulls the trigger."

"Then you would be wrong." And the woman hung up again.

Law waded downstream, replaying all the conversations over in her head. She'd leapt to the assumption that Snow was the name of a person but thinking back, the crazy lady hadn't actually confirmed that. It could be a white dog or cat. And for "where" all she knew was Fairywood—wherever that was—and look for a white door. She had all the fish she needed for her customers and a little time before she needed to deliver them. She could see if she could find Snow.

"Brisbane! We're leaving!" She whistled to fetch him back. Hopefully he hadn't wandered too far from the truck, as the porcupine never moved faster than a waddle.

It took her five minutes just to find the bloody neighborhood on her map. Fairywood was a postage stamp of nothingness even before the first Startup, which was why she didn't recognize the name. She only found it because of the mention of Windgap and the Rocks, meaning McKees Rocks. Windgap had fared no better than Fairywood after Pittsburgh shifted to Elfhome; it had lost three of its bridges in and out of the neighborhood. Far as she knew, both neighborhoods were now uninhabited. There were businesses in McKees Rocks with people clustered around them.

The bad news was it was in the wrong direction for her deliveries, but the good news was there were only a handful of streets officially part of Fairywood. It wouldn't take her long to drive up and down them and see if any white doors popped out at her.

Brisbane came waddling out of the brush. Elfhome porcupines were twice the size of Earth ones and a rich red color. Nothing short of Black Willows and saurus tangled with them, not even pony-sized wargs and steel spinner spiders. As a result, they had one speed. Trying to get them to go faster usually resulted in a couple hundred quills to the face. A porcupine for a pet was the test of true friendship: love me, love my porcupine (and not as a main course for dinner).

"Come on, Brizzy, get your spiky butt into the truck!" She opened the passenger door so he could climb in. A carrot on the seat just out of his reach was incentive to do just that. "We have some kind of damsel to save."

She wheeled the last cooler of *waewaeli* up into the back of her pickup with the help of the winch, strapped it down, and covered it with reflective cloth to help keep it cool. By the time she finished, Brisbane had climbed up into the cab and was chomping down his carrot, squealing with glee. Porcupines were noisy as well as slow and stubborn. She closed the passenger door and climbed in the other side.

There was a time, according to her grandfather, when all the roads and bridges in Pittsburgh had been well maintained. The roads into Fairywood were now a maze of missing bridges and broken pavement. Some of them were only passable because her Dodge had six wheels and massive ground clearance. She wasn't even sure how anyone would get out this far, unless they took a wrong turn off the misnamed Interstates onto Route 60 and then got majorly lost.

"I bet it's a goat. Crazy Lady said 'goat.' Goats are white like snow. Or an indi, they kind of look like goats, only a hundred times cuter. They're like cotton balls with horns."

They crossed into Fairywood and the roads got rougher. Because of the Chartiers Creek and the steep hillsides, there were only three streets that led into the heart of the neighborhood to do the little housing plans circling loop things. With the exception of someone's little yap dogs barking up a storm in the distance, the neighborhood seemed utterly lifeless. The houses looked like they'd been abandoned years before the first Startup. Unlike most of the places in Pittsburgh, they'd been boarded shut instead of left

open to the elements. Weather had blasted all the paint
from surfaces, leaving graying wood. It nearly seemed
like life had been bleached out of the world by time.

Then on the most remote corner of the neighborhood, on a street that ended in a cul-de-sac—there
was a house with a stark, freshly painted white door.

Law pulled to a stop and stared at it. "I guess it
isn't a goat."

She had a variety of weapons in her pickup. She
spent too much time out in the middle of nowhere
not to go armed. She had everything from an easily
annoyed porcupine to a Barrett .50 caliber rifle. The
question was which was appropriate for the situation.
Crazy Lady said that someone was willing to use
deadly force, but Law only had the mystery woman's
assurances. She was going to look like the crazy one
if she went in waving a gun and there was just some
scared female inside.

"Come on, Brisbane, we've got a house to check
out." She tugged on her Pirates baseball cap. "And
maybe a game of ball to play."

She got out a turnip and her bat and off they went.


No one answered her polite knock. The door wasn't
locked. She swung it cautiously open.

The house had never been finished before the first
Startup. Rough-framed stairs led upward without any
nod towards safety. The ceilings were just joists. The
walls were unpainted drywall. With the windows
boarded over, the building was a dark cave, the sunlight from the doorway the only light.

Brisbane trundled in.

"Brizzy!" Law whispered.

The problem with a fearless pet was that he went where he wanted to go, which wasn't always the same place she wanted to be. He didn't come back when she called, which meant he probably could smell something he wanted to eat.

Law hissed a curse. There didn't seem to be anyone in the house. "Hello?" And then considering she was sent after someone with an elf sounding name, she added in, "*Sekia?*"

She should have brought a flashlight. After a morning of sun reflecting off water, she felt blind in the cave-like dark. She took out her phone and shone it into the darkness. "*Sekia?*" And then in English. "Is anyone here?"

Brisbane muttered from somewhere deep in the house. He'd found something to eat but couldn't get to it. There would be no calling him back.

Sighing, she crept forward, panning her phone's light left to right. The house was one of these "open floor plans" that equated into three big rooms downstairs, connected together via large archways. There seemed to be some light shining in the back of the house. "Seriously, Law, why do you keep getting mixed up in shit like this? You don't know even if there's a girl..."

A shadow crossing through the slant of light from the door made her spin around. She couldn't tell what had cast the shadow. She couldn't see anyone. She hadn't heard any footsteps.

"Hello?" She called louder in Elvish, "Snow? This place is not safe." Her high school Elvish classes never covered situations like this. She used Elvish when selling to the enclaves at the Rim but usually the conversations were limited to food, time, money and the weather. Can you get me fish tomorrow? No, you cannot eat my porcupine.

There was a whisper in the darkness to the right of the doorway. As Law stared into the darkness, her eyes slowly adjusted until she could see someone standing there. Somehow she hadn't seen the person tucked into the shadows.

"Hello? *Nicadae!*" Law tried for cheerful while tightening her hold on the baseball bat. "*Sekia?*"

"*Sekia.*" A soft, confused female voice echoed and continued in Elvish, "Who are you?"

"Law." She patted her chest. She hated her full name but elves complained that her name was way too short. "Lawry Munroe. Who are you?"

The figure moved forward into the light. The female was smaller than Law expected. Her baby-doll dress of white fairy silk managed to be very demure for how stunningly short it was. Black curls spilled down her back, nothing like the impossibly straight controlled hair that Law associated with elves. Bare feet. The female pressed a hand to her chest and spilled out High Elvish in a flood.

"Whoa, whoa, whoa!" Law cried in English. "*Naekanain.*" The one Elvish phrase that was useful for all occasions: *I don't understand.* Law was fairly fluent in Low Elvish; she had to be to trade with the elves. High Elvish, though, was a whole different language. "Are you Snow?" She pretended to shiver. "Snow? You?"

That got a long, uncertain look.

"Okay." Law scratched at her back with the baseball bat. She reasoned out the logic of her problem in English. "Crazy Lady got: Fairywood, white door, female. Let's say it's a given that someone is coming to kill any female behind the white door, regardless if you're actually Snow or not."

"*Naekanain*." Snow said slowly, assuming this was actually Snow.

Law simplified—"We have to go"—then realized she'd said it in English. She repeated it in Elvish and used the "come here" hand wave that elves used.

"We have to go," the female echoed the English, but she turned and headed deeper into the house.

Law threw up her hands in frustration and chased after the elf.

Off the unfinished kitchen was an area that probably would have been the mudroom. A spell light illuminated the small rough area. Brisbane was rooting through a pile of travel sacks, grumbling at the fact that he couldn't get to whatever attracted him.

"Brizzy!" Law whistled and held out the turnip. "Come on. We have to go."

The elf gathered up her travel sacks. The look she gave the cave-like kitchen was clear enough: whatever the reason she was there, she didn't like the place. She was perfectly willing to pack up and abandon it, even if the ride came with a porcupine.

The elf's hair was blue-black.

Out in the sun, it was really beautiful. Glossy, loose waves fell down to her hips, coal-black but with subtle dark blue highlights. Human women would either pay hundreds of dollars or sign a pact with a devil for such hair. Her skin was the flawless pale, pale white of elves, even her bare feet. She had long athletic legs. The fruffy baby-doll dress of white silk covered all the naughty bits—barely. Her eyes weren't the vivid blue almost every elf Law ever met had, but a deep stormy gray, the color of thunderclouds.

That said, she looked like she hadn't slept for days, and her beautiful eyes were red as if from crying. But far from being despondent, she explored the Dodge with great interest. She pushed all the buttons, cranked the window up and down and up and down and turned the radio on and off. When she found the maps in Law's glovebox, she gave a happy cry.

Brisbane wanted into the elf's travel sacks and wouldn't leave them alone for the turnip. Once Law explained the porcupine's stubbornness, Snow produced a *saenori* out of the packs. The peach-like fruit wouldn't be ripe in Pittsburgh for another month. It meant Snow had probably recently come from the Easternlands, where Elvish settlements were farther south than those in the Westernlands.

Law's phone rang with Crazy Lady's number again. Law accepted the call and said, "I found her. I think. I found a female elf. I'm not sure what her name . . ."

Crazy Lady cut her off with "Did you get the door?"

"The door?" Law echoed in confusion.

"The white door," Crazy Lady said. "Get it and take it with you."

"Really?" Law was running late and running out of patience.

"People will die if you don't get this right," Crazy Lady stated calmly. "Probably starting with you."

"I'm getting the door."

A quart of white exterior paint was just inside the door still with Wollerton's price tag and an uncleaned paintbrush dried to a solid slab of white. Both looked brand new. The door, though, obviously had hung in place for years. Luckily she had a cordless screwdriver. Doctor Who would approve. After she stowed the door in the back of her pickup, she nabbed the paint can, too.

She wanted to shortcut through Windgap and McKees Rock to get to downtown. It turned out harder than she expected it to be. After the third "fallen" tree, it was obvious that someone had recently used magic to block the streets. Anyone entering the area would be funneled straight to the house where Snow had been. But why?

She was trying to decide whether to backtrack or go cross-country, when her phone rang again. This time it was her mom. Her monkeys. Her circus.

Sighing, Law answered the call. "Hello, Mother."

"Twenty-four years I've been telling you to call me Flo."

"You're my mother—or at least, that's what my birth certificate claims."

"You've checked?"

"Multiple times." She kept hoping it was some kind of mistake. Since her mother had saddled her with a boy's name, she'd gone as far as getting a copy of her birth certificate off of the city. The paperwork ruled out adoption but not switched at birth. The mirror, however, said that was impossible. The older she got, the more she looked like her paternal grandfather; a fact that made neither one of them happy since he had never approved of her mother. "What is it, mother? I'm busy."

"People with real jobs are busy. People that play around and call it work are not."

"Mother, we are not having this discussion again."

"We will continue having this conversation until you realize that you are wasting your life. But that's not why I called."

"It's not?" Law held out the phone to eye it with suspicion. Her mother rarely passed up the opportunity to beat the job thing into the ground in hopes of getting Law to agree just to shut her mother up.

"You will never guess what just showed up at the Scheidemantles' this morning."

"Who?"

"The Scheidemantles. They live down the road, just across of Ginny Czernowski."

"I thought she got married."

"If I said Virginia Mary Elizabeth Frankenwald, you wouldn't know who I was talking about." And people said elves had long complicated names. "She married an accountant that she met in college. They moved into the Donaldsons' old place. They had a little girl last week. They named her Mercy."

With every life accomplishment that her mother listed for her classmate, Law knew that what she really was ticking off were things that Law was lacking in her life. A college education on Earth. A job as a dental hygienist. An accountant husband. Home ownership. Children.

Law had no interest in any of that; especially the whole dental hygienist thing. If you were going to school for something, why pick something that required you sticking your hands in other people's mouths all day?

"Mother, why are you calling me?"

Her mother huffed. "A moving van showed up at the Scheidemantles' this morning. They are moving back to Earth!"

Law almost asked "Who are the Scheidemantles?" but then remembered that they lived down the street from her mother. Had lived. Apparently weren't going to live there anymore. "And?"

"They have that lovely Cape Cod. It's a four bed..."

"No."

"You can't keep living in that drafty old barn."

"Yes, I can."

"You're going to freeze to death one of these winters."

Law knew from experience that her mother wouldn't listen to any of the sane logical reasons why she picked the barn, starting with its being as far as possible from her mother as she could live in Pittsburgh. There was no way she would choose a house just down the street from her. "I have a Tarzan swing in my living room."

And her mother hung up on her.

"Let me get this straight." Ellen McMicking was a customer and good friend. She shared many of Law's views on how to live one's life. She owned two gypsy caravans. One was home to her and her three-legged bobcat, Rigel. (Cool, unusual home: check. Odd pet: check.) The other was set up as a food truck. (Own boss: check.) Normally she parked at the Library light-rail station's vast parking lot. The day before Shutdown, though, she'd moved them into an empty lot in the Strip District. "You stole an elf and a door?"

"I did not steal her!" Law set up her scales while Ellen lined up her coolers. Said elf was in Ellen's little house, eating a second round of breakfast as if she hadn't had food for a week. The hot steel-cut oatmeal with warm berry compote was simply delicious, but Law couldn't imagine having a second big bowl. (By now, though, Snow probably was getting the impression that all humans had very odd pets.) "You don't steal people! You steal things like..."

"Doors?"

"Yes." Law was unrepentant about stealing the door; the house obviously had been abandoned years ago. A quick coat of paint did not establish ownership in her book.

"So you kidnapped her?"

"No! She came with me willingly enough." Still, the female seemed slightly leery, deflecting direct questions with a continuous barrage of questions of her own. The thirty-minute ride into town had been one "What's this?" after another. Still, she hadn't asked for help or to be taken anyplace or to anyone.

Ellen giggled, having entirely too much fun with the situation. "Only you, Lawry, would get yourself into this kind of mess."

"You didn't find it so funny when it was you that I was bailing out of trouble."

Ellen pressed both hands to her chest. "And I'm eternally grateful to you. Oh, those look lovely." She cooed at the *waewaeli*. "I'm going to honey-fry them."

"Fish and chips?"

Ellen sighed. "No chips. My potato supplier from stateside let me down last Shutdown and even if he gets me some this one, I won't have time to prep them. I've spent the last three days making bread. I'm going with sandwiches. I will have parmesan zucchini fries for the adventurous."

"Sounds good to me."

"Yes, but you're adventurous."

"Most Pittsburghers will eat anything that doesn't try to eat them first."

"Yes, but it's the truck drivers from Earth whose rigs are being unloaded that have the time and cash to blow. Please tell me that I can have this whole cooler."

"It's yours." Law was glad she caught the last fish.

They weighed out the fish, transferring them to Ellen's ice chests. Ellen was buying a dozen of the *waewaeli* that weighed in at two hundred and thirty-two pounds. At two dollars a pound, it came out to a little under five hundred dollars. A very good morning's work once she expensed out the cost of gasoline. If she could do it every day of the year, she'd be rich. Ellen, however, could only afford to buy this much once a month for Shutdown. Any other day, she only bought one or two fish. Nor could Law hope for safe fishing in the winter when the streams ran deep enough for the man-eating bigger fish to navigate.

"You don't know who it was that called you?" Ellen asked.

"I just have a number."

"You didn't think to ask?"

"I asked, she didn't say."

Ellen plunged her hands into ice water and then wiped them clean. She took out her phone. "What's the number?"

"It's on my call list." Law turned her hip toward Ellen.

"Is this your way to get me to feel you up?"

"Will that work?"

Ellen slapped her and got Law's phone out of her front pocket without unnecessary (disappointingly so) groping. (Played for the opposite team: no check.)

"You calling her?" Law asked. It was her experience that you never got straight answers from crazy people.

"No, I'm back-tracing her number. The joys of having geeky friends is that they give you wonderful apps. Widget gave me a reverse-number look-up program when she helped me with my bookkeeping software. Oh. Gee."

"What?"

"That's a payphone in Market Square."

Either Crazy Lady didn't have a phone, or she didn't want anyone to trace the call back to her. Law suspected it was the latter. "Tricky."

"What are you going to do now?"

All the girls that Law helped usually asked—if not with words, with a desperate look—for Law to bail them out of trouble. As soon as the girls were tucked someplace safe, they spilled out their stories. Not all the details—usually they were ashamed of their weaknesses—but at least who the hell they were running from. It was possible that the mystery caller knew something that Snow didn't. Maybe Snow didn't even know she was in trouble. (Although the fact that she had dodged all the basic questions seemed to indicate she did.)

It was possible that Snow didn't trust Law simply because she was a human. Elves came to Pittsburgh via the train. The station was downtown, surrounded by skyscrapers. The enclaves where most elves lived were at the Rim, uphill nearly three miles. The most likely scenario was that Snow had been grabbed and taken by humans before she had ever gotten to the safety of the enclaves.

"I need to sell the rest of my fish. I might as well take her out to the Rim; see if she belongs out there."

&#10087;     &#10087;     &#10087;

It was less than twelve hours to Shutdown and the city hummed with activity. The EIA troops were heading out to the border checkpoints. The Pittsburgh Police were going into Nazi mode and towing anyone that illegally parked. The shops downtown and the Strip District were preparing for a massive horde of trucks to pull up and deliver an entire month's worth of goods. Families wanting first dibs on rare big-ticket items were drifting in. In every abandoned lot and empty warehouse, food stands like Ellen's were preparing to feed the incoming masses. Across the street, Gene Thompson had pulled in with his BBQ chicken truck, complete with trailer rigged as a wood-burning fire pit. Gene was splitting hickory with an axe, and smoke already scented the air.

Law checked her truck just the same as if she'd left it parked on an abandoned, weed-choked lot instead of a city block. She banged on the side panels to frighten out small mammals and heat-seeking snakes. She carefully popped the hood and scanned over the engine to make sure no rats had chewed through hoses or belts. She took a few steps back, knelt and scanned under her pickup, looking for the telltale gleam of eyes or brake fluids on the pavement. She opened the driver's door and scanned the cabin to make sure there was nothing up in the dash, under the seat, or behind it.

Snow had been through the routine at Fairywood. She helped look although it wasn't clear the elf knew what they were searching for. Newly arrived humans always teased Law for her caution but they'd never found themselves suddenly sharing a cab with a two-foot-wide spider while going sixty miles per hour.

(Luckily the steel spinner had frightened Brisbane as badly as it scared Law. The spider instantly became a pincushion nailed to the dashboard.)

Brisbane ignored the precautions and climbed up into the cab with his usual disdain.

Law was not one to give credit to rumors. People liked to talk. Just because they ran out of facts didn't stop the mouth from flapping. It always amazed her that people who had never set foot in one of the elf enclaves could go on and on about what supposedly went on behind the high stone walls.

She delivered to the side door that gave access to the motor court, instead of to the front door that led to the public dining areas. Technically, the area was more enclosed than the restaurant part of the enclave. The elves, though, were less careful with the doors and what they said.

Over time it had become obvious to Law that the enclaves operated as tiny little city-states, allied but fiercely competitive. Each had an orchard within the forbidden center courtyard, extensive raised vegetable beds, greenhouses, chicken coops and small herds of *indi*. While humans might gossip about how the enclaves were nothing more than thinly disguised brothels, they were, in fact, cutthroat restaurateurs. If Law sold trout to Caraway's enclave, she would need to sell crayfish to Poppymeadow's. It played into some odd "you're one of us" mindset that the elves had. She was "their" supplier only if she gave them exclusive stock.

Law suspected that the loudest rumormongers were the humans that failed to pick up the cultural subtlety. They made the mistake of trying to peddle one type of goods to all the enclaves and found the door slammed in their faces. Which was fine with Law; it meant more business for her. It also meant she was more aware that she had to walk a tightrope to stay "one of us" with everyone.

Normally, Caraway's side gate stood open all day and she could back right into the motor court. The big doors were shut. She backed her Dodge up so its tailgate nearly touched the inward-swinging gate to make unloading easier. Snow sank down in the seat to peer nervously over the back of the bench seat at the enclave. She had only shown curiosity to the rest of the city, so it was a little worrisome that she seemed scared of other elves.

"Stay," Law said to Snow and Brisbane. The elves thought porcupine was a delicacy and had tried to buy him for dinner more than once.

She knocked on the door by the spyhole. The slot slid aside immediately. Brown eyes so dark they might as well be black inspected her and then the slot shut again.

What the hell? Since when did elves come with dark brown eyes?

She stood a moment frowning at the gate. She could sell her fish elsewhere but she'd promised to deliver trout to Caraway's today. If she failed to deliver, she might lose Caraway as a customer forever. She knocked again and called out in Elvish. *"Nicadae!* Fish! Fresh fish! Very fresh! Very good! You buy!"

The slot opened again and a more familiar set of vivid blue eyes gazed out.

"Law!" The owner of this set of eyes cried. "Forgiveness! Wait!"

And the slot closed again.

Law glanced at her pickup. Snow's stormy gray eyes watched her with surprise and dismay. Snow's blue-black hair and gray eyes should have been a giant clue-by-four whacking Law upside the head. She knew that elves were very much "us" and "them" even household to household. A handful of elves in Pittsburgh didn't have straight black hair; Ginger Wine was a beautiful auburn. The elves that didn't, though, tended to wear Wind Clan blue as if to compensate. Snow was dressed in pure white.

Maybe it was a mistake not leaving the female with Ellen.

There was a clang of bolts being thrown behind the gate, so Law focused back on the enclave.

The dark eyes belonged to a *sekasha*-caste warrior.

Law yelped in surprise and backed up. *Sekasha* were impossible to miss. They had spells tattooed on their arms, wore a special breastplate made of scales from wyvern, and carried a magically sharp, katana-style sword. They were said to be holy and were rare as hen's teeth, usually only showing up in wake of the Viceroy Windwolf. All the elves she'd ever met were scared shitless of the *sekasha* because the caste was legally allowed to kill anyone who pissed them off.

Caraway's majordomo for the restaurant-side of things was a male by the name of Chili Pepper. He was vibrating in place, trying not to get too close to the warrior and still keep her from fleeing. "Law! Law! Forgiveness. Don't leave!" He did a "come" motion with both hands even as he turned to the *sekasha* and launched into rapid-fire High Elvish.

Law glanced back at her pickup. Snow had vanished

and now only Brisbane peered out the window. The holy warrior stared at the porcupine, head tilted slightly in puzzlement. Law caught the word "trout" and the warrior's eyes went to the fish coolers and he nodded once.

Chili Pepper turned back to Law and spoke in Low Elvish. "This is his holiness Galloping Storm Horse on Wind. The viceroy is in residence along with two of his Hands." His eyes flicked sideways to indicate the warrior beside him. He slipped into English. "Plus one. His English name is Pony, but he speaks very, very little English. The viceroy is here so rarely; there is no need for his people to learn it. Still, we have eleven warriors to feed for the next few days. I need all the water produce that you have."

"What?" Was this confuse-Law-with-cryptic-remarks day?

"Tomorrow is Shutdown and we will be here on Elfhome and you will be on Earth. The holy ones need meat." Chili Pepper glanced toward the truck. "Are you sure that we cannot have the porcupine?"

"No!" Law sang and forced a laugh because the *sekasha* was right there, listening, maybe understanding. "I have trout! Lots of meat!"

She opened up the nearest cooler, which turned out to be the one with crayfish. The crustaceans raised up their large spiny claws in the sudden daylight.

Chili Pepper shook his head. "Those are tasty but they don't have lots of meat."

She lifted the lid on the next cooler. This one had trout on ice. "I have several coolers of the fish. The crayfish—" She didn't want to tell him that she had promised them to Poppymeadow. "You are right. Very little meat."

Storm Horse apparently had never seen crayfish before. He leaned forward to poke a finger at the mini-lobsters.

"They pinch," Law warned and then realized that the elf might not understand. "He knows that they pinch, doesn't he?"

Chili Pepper had his hand pressed to his lips, obviously struggling with what to say himself. "I don't know," he finally murmured into his fingers. "He just made his majority in March."

It wasn't like the crayfish could actually hurt the warrior.

Snow in hiding. Holy warrior tempting fate. Time to hurry things up and leave.

Law charged the elves more. She reasoned it was a slight surcharge for dealing with the cultural hurdles. Her life would be easier if she didn't have to catch several different species of fish just because the elves had issues. The elves never haggled. Perhaps because haggling required you to lie about how much you want something and the quality of the item. At the same time, she never tried to really gouge the elves so that they wouldn't balk at her asking price.

Her heavily insulated plastic marine coolers were special-ordered from Earth and top of the line. The elves used wicker baskets. She used an antique scale when working with the elves, made in the 1800s. (She was never sure if they didn't understand her digital scale or thought it was inaccurate.) The first step, though, was to establish that the ancient device was calibrated correctly and that yes, five pounds was five pounds. Chili Pepper used an abacus with cinnabar beads that he flicked up and down. With a hundred fifty quarts of fish, it was tedious. She felt bad that she'd trapped Snow in the front seat of her pickup the entire time. At least with the constant flow of elves carrying off baskets of fish, the *sekasha* was politely shooed away so everyone could work.

If anyone in Pittsburgh knew all the elf politics and skullduggery, though, it was going to be Chili Pepper.

"I found an elf out in the middle of nowhere." Law waved toward the front of her pickup. "She doesn't speak English."

"Yes, I saw." Chili Pepper didn't even look up from his abacus. "I heard about her. Thank you for taking the child in."

Law had saved enough kittens to know what he was actually saying was "No, I don't want it." Not that Snow was a kitten, but obviously the act of finding her someplace safe was going to be the same process. "Who is she?"

Chili Pepper clicked his tongue, which was how elves shrugged. "A mutt. Her name is something like—" He paused to think. "Ground Bare in Winter as Snow Falls in Wind. Or something ill-omened like that. You humans would call her—umm—Dead Winter or Barren Ground or Bare Snow. Her father was Water Clan and she was raised in his household. Her twice-cursed mother supposedly was Wind Clan; not that you can tell."

The attitude at least explained why Bare Snow was hiding in the pickup.

"Twice-cursed?" Law knew that the elves could do real magic but she was a little hazy on what all they could do with it.

"Maybe thrice-cursed. To be stupid enough to leave

your clan for a male. To have the idiocy to agree to give birth to a mutt that no one would want." Chili Pepper glanced at the *sekasha*. "At least, not with a name like that. And then managing to get killed, leaving said child at the mercy of another clan. They tossed her out, of course. A child belongs with its mother's people."

Chili Pepper had called Bare Snow "child" three times. Law knew she was a bad judge of elf ages, but she had thought that the female—nearly as tall as Law and better endowed—was an adult.

"How old is she?" Law asked.

Another click of the tongue to indicate that Chili Pepper didn't know. "She's still in her doubles from what I heard." He glanced to the cab just as Bare Snow peeked over the back of the seat. The female ducked down again. "You humans would say she's a teenager or a fresh man." He meant the first-year university students. The freshmen arrived in Pittsburgh eager to see real elves and made themselves pests at the enclaves. The older students knew better. "She's a little younger than Galloping Storm Horse. Maybe ninety-five. I doubt younger than ninety."

Law had grown up knowing that elves were immortal but it was kind of mind-boggling to suddenly realize that someone nearly four times older than she was could still be considered a child.

"I don't know why she came to Pittsburgh," he stated. "We wouldn't have been able to take her in, not with the viceroy staying with us. I heard about her making the rounds and thought I might bring it to Wolf Who Rules' attention. It isn't right to have a child wandering around in this wilderness alone.

Before I could, though, she'd been turned down by everyone else and had disappeared."

"The other enclaves wouldn't let her a room?"

Chili Pepper stared at Law in confusion. "Let?"

"Rent. Stay. Sleep."

"Oh! No. She wanted to join their household. It's a totally different thing than staying for a short period. No one wants someone from Water Clan. I have no idea why she came all this way without some guarantee that someone would take her."

They'd unloaded both the trout and the *seasi*. It totaled up to two hundred and eighty-one pounds of fish. Hopefully the *sekasha* loved fish because they were going to be eating a lot of it. Chili Pepper lifted the lid to the crayfish and considered them. "Will you bring more, early Startup?"

"Yes! Certainly!" Law cried, wanting to keep her promise to Poppymeadow. As it was, she was going to disappoint Ginger Wine.

Chili Pepper closed the lid. He considered the front of the pickup. "My lord had business out at the aeroport." He meant the airport that was nearly an hour away. "I do not know when he will return. Will you keep her safe?" In other words: I still don't want the kitten, don't you dare leave her here.

"Of course."

"And I can't have the porcupine?"

"No!"

Law sold the crayfish to Poppymeadow. Much to her relief, she remembered that she had four giant snapping turtles tucked way in the back, confined to makeshift cages made out of milk crates and chicken wire. Those she sold to Ginger Wine to keep her promise of "water produce," as the elves called seafood.

Bare Snow stayed hidden in the pickup, watching, learning God-knows-what since most of Law's dealing was a mishmash of English and Elvish.

Traffic was starting to grow heavy as the people returning to Earth rushed through the last-minute errands. She fought her way into Hershel's Exxon on Forbes Avenue, Oakland's only gas station.

During a normal, non-Shutdown day, only two of the pumps were usually in use at the same time. There was a waiting line for all twelve pumps. A frat boy in a Smart car tried to dart in and take the pump she'd been waiting for. She laid on her horn and edged her prehistoric Dodge forward until her grill protector filled his back window.

"Hoi!" She leaned out the window to shout at him. "If you want to use that car to get out of Pittsburgh, you better move it! Your little thing won't even scratch my grill!"

His frat brother beat on his shoulder going, "Dude, what are you doing? The locals are insane! Let him use the pump first!"

They retreated to the other side of the station. Law made sure everything on her truck was locked down and then went inside to pay. It was the other drawback of Oakland. Everywhere else in town, you could pump first. Oakland had too many transients for Hershel's to risk not getting cash up front.

Bare Snow had followed her into the store and was now picking up things randomly and eyeing them closely. All the male eyes were on her. The baby-doll dress showed off as much as it covered up—especially when the female bent at the hip to take things off the bottom shelf. Much as Law appreciated the view, she was going to have to get something longer for the female. (Law had shirts longer than Bare Snow's dress.)

Pat Hershel was working the register. "You've got another stray, Law? An elf this time?"

"Yup."

"Don't go forgetting you're just a girl yourself."

"What does that mean?"

"One of these times you're going to bite off more than you can chew. You should be more careful."

Law clenched her jaw against the first dozen things that came to mind. Pat meant well but she was like most people—they only helped people when it was easy and convenient. As soon as things got messy—usually when the girl was on the verge of drowning in her trouble—they'd back off and let nature take its course. Which was fine and good for them, but why did they always feel like they had to warn her off too? Why were people more concerned about status quo than actually helping?

"I'm filling up both my tanks." Law peeled off twenties she earned from the enclaves. Elves traded gold among themselves, but they took in US currency from their human customers and cycled them back to Law. "And obviously I need some clothes. Shoes. A dress. You got any in the back?"

"Maybe." The gas station also served as sort of a general store for the transients. Hershel's had a tiny assortment of basic necessities to tide newcomers over until they figured out where the real stores were. "The kids tend to take anything that says 'Pittsburgh' or 'Elfhome' back with them as souvenirs. We're normally picked clean by end of Shutdown."

That explained their stock. It had mystified Law why all their clothes had writing like "Elfhome: Nailed it" and "Saw a Saurus, Ate it!" Unlike other stores, they also only carried local snacks and drinks. Iron City Beer. Saurus jerky. Steel City Cola. Honey roasted keva beans. Because everything was locally produced, they were usually well stocked.

Pat had called it correctly, though. The shelves looked like locusts had descended. But they were in luck. There was a pair of cowboy boots that fit Bare Snow. Not one of Law's first dozen choices for footwear but Bare Snow seemed to like them. There was also a Wind Clan blue sundress with Elvish runes spelling out something Law couldn't read. Bare Snow snickered at whatever it said. The sundress was only a few inches longer than the white baby-doll, but they were important inches.

Pat added two slim packs of Juicy Fruit gum to Law's tab. "I was holding those for Stormsong but they tell me she's on Earth with the *husepavua*."

Bare Snow caught the one Elvish word in the mix. "What about the *husepavua*?"

Pat switched to Elvish as she rung up their purchases. "The viceroy is in town because his *husepavua* is on Earth with one Hand of *sekasha*. Normally I keep this aside for the holy one, Singing Storm Wind, but she's with the *husepavua*. You can have the gum."

"Who else is with her?" Bare Snow asked.

Pat clicked her tongue, having lived next to elves long enough to pick up their habits. "I only know the young ones that drive the automobiles. The older elves can't wrap their brains around how to work machines. The 'babies' bring the viceroy's automobiles here for fuel. Stormsong. Cloudwalker. Hawk Scream. Pony. Sun Lance. Oh! I know! Sparrow took Wraith Arrow too."

Bare Snow distracted the conversation away by picking up the gum. "What is this?"

Law showed her how to unwrap a stick and chew on it.

Bare Snow's eyes widened and she gave out a moan that sounded orgasmic. All the males in the store drifted closer.

Pat laughed. "Good luck with that, Law."

"Yeah, thanks, Pat. Can we have the restroom key?"

Law pumped gas while Bare Snow changed clothes in the restroom alone. The elf returned with a wide-brim hat that she'd gotten from someplace. Law could only hope she didn't steal it. With the skimpy blue sundress, the long bare legs and the cowboy boots, she looked utterly adorable. The color of the sundress highlighted the blue of her hair.

A white Ford Explorer at the far pumps caught Bare Snow's attention. One would think that there was no way anyone could miss a gorgeous leggy elf, but the four coeds who arrived in the vehicle never seemed to notice Bare Snow drift about the SUV, peering in the windows.

The female elf scanned the lot while returning to Law's Dodge. "Your vehicle is very different from all the others."

"It's ... it's very old." In theory the 1947 Power Wagon was nearly a hundred years old, but in truth, every nut and bolt been had been restored or upgraded by her grandfather as he converted the antique truck. It had been his pride and joy and he was probably spinning in his grave that she ended up with it. The simple truth was no one else wanted a manual-transmission gas hog. Both of her parents wanted her to sell it for something more practical; it was the one thing that they agreed on. That and that she should get a dog. (Weirdly her father was fine with her dating girls.)

"Some of them look identical, to me." Bare Snow pointed at the coeds' Explorer at the gas pump, one parked half a block down Forbes Avenue, and a third driving past. The older SUVs were popular in Pittsburgh. Most cars on Earth were electric, self-driving, and needed extensive high tech support systems that Elfhome didn't have. The Explorers were designed to be driven off-road. They were easy to adapt to the lower technology level of Elfhome.

"The only differences are these things." Bare Snow pointed at the Dodge's license plate. "What do they mean?"

"Every automobile has a unique code that is written on these." Law simplified best she could. "They're called license plates. None of them repeat. The city uses them to track who owns the automobile, if they've paid taxes, keep the vehicle safe to drive on the roads, and things like that. Why? Did someone take you to that house in an automobile like that one?"

Bare Snow gazed at her, nervously biting at her bottom lip. After a minute of fierce study, the elf took a deep breath. "I don't understand why you took me away from there. You don't even seem to know. You've gone place to place, asking 'who is this' and 'where does she belong' and being turned away. It annoys you not because you want to be rid of me, but because it makes you angry that my people act so coldly toward me." And as if her hands had a will of their own, she reached out to catch Law's shirt and nervously twist it between her fingers. "You've given me food, and clothing, and most importantly hope, and have demanded nothing back. And I don't . . . I don't understand. Why?"

Law had never been asked why. Most people assumed it was simply the way that she was; like the shape of her chin and the flatness of her chest. She looked more like a knight in shining armor than a princess that needed to be saved. Some assumed that she wanted to be a boy, but she didn't. Certainly it would have made a few things easier; like going pee in the woods. Under all the dirt, though, she was as girly as the next woman. A few people thought she might have some secret past, fraught with injustices and horror. She had lived a fairly bland childhood.

"I like feeling strong." She finally settled on something that felt right. "When you're dealing with your own problems, they seem massive and set as stone." Crazy parents. Being a star-shaped peg surrounded by round and square holes. Living on the fringe and liking it except for the fact that it made her feel like the little kid, hands always pressed against the candy store window, looking in but never able to go in and get what she wanted. Not even sure what she would pick if she could get in.

"When you wade into someone else's mess, their problems seem so small and fluid. Do this and that. Hit this guy. Find a new place for her to live. Ask around and find work for her. It all seems so"—she didn't know Elvish for *easy-peasy*—"so simple."

Bare Snow nodded slowly. "Instead of being lost

and alone and insignificant, it feels good when you're finally able to do something. Be important."

"Yeah." The gas pump shut off as the main tank hit full. Law shifted the hose over to her reserve tank.

Bare Snow grinned. "Good! Let's find the white automobile then!" She leaned against Law to draw in the dust on the Dodge's side panel. "Its license plate looked like this."

Most native Pittsburghers were fiercely proud if their plate number started with AAA, AAB or AAC. It meant they were in Pittsburgh immediately after the EIA took charge and the city became a district separate from Pennsylvania. Law had inherited the license plate along with the Dodge. When the wave of EIA workers and other newly arrived humans applied for plates, someone in the licensing department decided to jump the numbering system to BAA. This, of course, led to nicknames like B-plate and B-hole.

Bare Snow wrote "BAD-0001" in the dust. Either some B-hole had gotten lucky in the random assigning of numbers, or they'd bowed to the inevitable and gotten a vanity plate that looked like it could be random. It was a plate you'd remember, though, and Law knew she'd never seen it. She was going to have to pull in favors to find the car. How many depended on what the B-hole had done. Would she just need to kick the shit out of this guy or did she need to get the cops involved?

"Was this the person that took you to that house? Did he hurt you? Steal something from you? Tell me everything."

Bare Snow's eyes went wide. "Everything?"

"Yes, everything."

❖   ❖   ❖

Her name was Ground Bare in Winter as Killing Snow Falls in Wind. It was the root of all Bare Snow's troubles. Named within days of her birth, it was so fraught with ill omens that the temple priestess apologized to her parents even as she bestowed it upon their baby. After that, anything that went wrong was assigned to her presence. A boat lost to a storm? Bare Snow's fault. A red tide? A tsunami wave? All her fault.

Just as Law was starting to wonder if she'd accidently triggered a complete retelling of Bare Snow's life, the female leapt ahead nearly a hundred years. By then Law had finished filling up her tanks, collected her change, and nosed her way into the heavy traffic.

Five years ago, Bare Snow's mother had died while on a trip to Winter Court. At the time, the poor female had felt crushingly guilty. Had her cursed name killed her mother? Her father's death in the spring nearly broke her. Worse, the household she'd grown up in, that of her father's parents, wanted nothing more to do with her. They gave her a handful of coins and asked her to leave.

She had no other family within the Wind Clan. Unsure what else to do, she'd traveled to Summer Court. She arrived to discover that the town stood virtually empty until the Summer Solstice when the queen was scheduled to shift residence to the northern capital. Bare Snow drifted through the vacant city, seeking a household that would take her. The Water Clan enclaves would not take her because of her name. The Wind Clan household refused her for her blue-black hair and stormy eyes.

After weeks of being rejected, a *nivasa*-caste male

wearing Wind Clan blue approached her in the street and quietly told her that she should go to Pittsburgh. She would find people that would accept her there.

At first it seemed as if the quest was blessed. The way to Pittsburgh was far quicker and simpler than she had imagined. She was able to board one of the cargo ships traveling the Western Ocean and then caught the train.

While she traveled she learned more about the Viceroy Windwolf and his household.

"He's of two clans, just like me. His father is Wind Clan and his mother is Fire Clan. He had the support of both clans to set up his holdings in Westernlands. He's asked a Stone Clan female to be his *domi*; although I've heard that has not gone well. She has yet to answer him. Despite his mixed blood, he gathers to him only the best to be his Beholden. Wraith Arrow. Dark Harvest. Killing Frost. His blade brother is the grandson of Tempered Steel and Perfection. And he holds Sword Strikes' daughter, who is mixed caste! But those are *sekasha*; they are perfection despite the circumstance of their birth."

She was sure that Windwolf's people would look beyond her mixed blood and cursed name. Her hopes, though, were quickly crushed. It had only taken her a day to get from the train station to the Rim and be rejected by all the enclaves, save Caraway's, which she'd been repeatedly warned not to approach.

"Why?" Law asked.

"Because of the clan wars." The answer seemed strangely condensed.

When Law was a kid with crayons, she always left the sky paper white unless she did a sunset of yellows and oranges. It was the mythical ocean that Law had never seen, the lakes and the rivers that were blue. To the elves, Bare Snow's answer probably would make as much sense as Wind Clan claiming blue as a color when there was a Water Clan. Bare Snow's last name was Wind; why shouldn't she go straight to the head of the clan in the Westernlands? How did she end up on the other side of the city?

"I had always thought that how my parents met was romantic: a chance meeting on a desolate island. I realize now that the years alone had been sheer torture for my mother. That she had been so lonely that she would risk her life to talk to another being."

Sensing that Bare Snow was about to go off into another long, long story, Law asked quickly, "So you talked with someone here in Pittsburgh? And they took you to the house?"

Just as Bare Snow had been about to break down, a male approached her on the street. He claimed there was a special area belonging to the Water Clan and that he'd been sent to take her to it. Law was fairly sure that was a complete lie. According to her high school civics class, as long as the gate was functioning, the city was to be wholly human-owned. (Which always struck her as odd wording since if the gate wasn't functioning, Pittsburgh wouldn't be on Elfhome. That was the entire reason they called returning to Earth Shutdown.) Elves weren't allowed to claim anything inside the Rim. More importantly, humans couldn't settle outside of it. Newcomers liked to bitch and moan about that since it meant they couldn't go off and dig up emeralds or pan for gold in North Carolina.

"And this human, he had the Ford? The white automobile?"

"*Nae. Nae* human."

"It was an elf?" Law thought Bare Snow had told her it was a human.

Bare Snow considered, screwing up her face as she thought. "Looked human. But he was not human."

"Huh?"

"I'd been to Summer Court. All the households I talked to had spoken in a very austere manner of speech. It is based on the Wyverns' way of speaking, only more formalized. Here in Pittsburgh, there are only Wind Clan households, and specifically those from the highlands. You can tell by the way they talk; it's a very marked accent. Even the *sekasha* at Caraway's had it when he was using the Low Elvish. It means that the viceroy must not use the very formal court language and thus his people feel no pressure to adapt."

Law wondered if she was ever going to find out how Bare Snow got to Fairywood. "I don't understand."

"All the humans I've talked to—Law, Ellen, Patty, Jon—they speak Low Elvish with highland accent."

*Who the hell is Jon?* Law didn't ask. She focused on the mystery human who wasn't a human. "This male didn't have the right accent?"

Bare Snow winced and spoke hesitantly. "It isn't that he didn't have an accent, it was he had too much of an accent. Not even the enclave elves speak as broadly. It was obvious that he was pretending. Once I started to listen closely, I picked up traces of old tongue, that no elf would ever teach a human, not even unintentionally."

"Are you sure?"

"The old ways have been rooted out. Young elves are not taught it. No old one would be so lax to use it without thinking."

"How do you know it then?" Law asked.

Bare Snow blushed and looked down at her hands. For several minutes, it seemed like she wasn't going to answer, and then she said quietly, "The gardener needs to know the weed from the flowers."

Usagi's place on Mount Washington was the kind of playful chaos that only a home with many small children and pets could achieve. The toys started halfway down the block, growing denser as Law neared the front door. She was sure that any home intruder would end up facedown on the floor with a dozen Legos embedded in his feet. Certainly she needed to step over several large Tonka construction vehicles and two Big Wheels to get down the sidewalk. There was no yard to speak of; the two raised planters had given way to endless landscaping projects with said construction toys.

Bare Snow bent to examine the trucks, pushing them to and fro. She probably hadn't seen a cast-metal toy before. She was making motor noises for them just like a child would; maybe it was instinctual.

Usagi's door was painted Wind Clan blue. Law frowned at it, wondering if the white door in Fairywood had been an indication that Bare Snow was Water Clan. Why blue for Wind and white for Water? Law rang the doorbell.

After several minutes, the door opened and Moon Rabbit Warrior gazed up at Law. The little half-elf was in her tweens but she looked six. She was naked except for a pair of butterfly wings strapped to her back and a pink tutu. Her long black hair was up in its customary pigtails, showing off her elf-pointed ears.

In the background, the commune's TV was playing a cartoon video at full volume. The sweet cinnamon smell of fire berries washed over Law; it smelt like Usagi had spilled an entire orchard of the fruit somewhere in her house.

As usual, Brisbane ignored all formalities and waddled into the house.

"Hi, Moon," Law started. "Is Widget..."

"Moooom!" Moon shouted at the top of her lungs. "It's Brizzy!"

"Is his mommy with him?" Usagi shouted from the kitchen.

"Yes!"

"Hi, Law! We're in the kitchen!"

Usagi's was haven to human women who had found their way to Pittsburgh one way or another. They were in love with the idea of magic, elves, and a mystical other world, or maybe just completely disenchanted with Earth. Most of them had the reputation of being "elf groupies," sneaking illegally to Elfhome just to have sex with elves.

In truth, they were taking advantage of a loophole in the treaty. Elf DNA, starting with blood samples but also including children, wasn't allowed to be taken off Elfhome. Elf tradition stated that children couldn't be forcibly taken from their mothers. It created a little known and rarely exploited way to get permanent resident status in Pittsburgh.

It didn't guarantee a living, nor did elves pay child support (although Law wasn't sure if the males even knew of their children's existence). Usagi gathered together other female illegal immigrants with marketable skills to pool resources. They'd taken over an abandoned restaurant building and set up a commune. While each woman shouldered a shift of watching the children, they all also had part-time jobs outside the commune. It was part circus act, part logistical nightmare to get any one woman alone.

Law wanted the commune's newest addition, Widget. She was a cute-as-a-button African-American teenager who wanted to be a translator. She was a whiz with the computer and had learned fluent Elvish online but hadn't actually managed to graduate from high school. Locals would hire someone without a diploma; Pittsburgh had a crying need for people with Widget's skills. The EIA wanted people who had doctorates in linguistics and they controlled the work visas. Unable to legally immigrate to Pittsburgh, the teenager had risked her life to swim the Ohio River at Shutdown in the dead of winter. (Of all the insane things! The girl had thought that river shark hibernated or something stupid like that. Biology was not her strong suit.)

Law had fished Widget out of the water and brought her to Usagi's. The girl hadn't gotten pregnant yet (maybe was still a virgin) so she needed to lay low. Law had been quietly connecting her with people like Ellen who needed part-time computer help and would keep their mouths shut.

Law wasn't going to find out if Widget was home by asking Moon Rabbit—the little half-elf's attention was now locked on the porcupine—nor was it polite to stand at the door and holler like a mad woman. She was going to have to venture deeper into the chaos to find Widget. "Kitchen" meant no work shoes and the like, so Law skinned off her rubber boots.

Bare Snow made an odd noise.

Law turned to find the elf pointing at Moon Rabbit, slack-jawed.

"Tauntiki." Law only knew the word for "child" because Usagi often used it to call her children. As if summoned, Shield of a Thousand Leaves came toddling in after his older sister. Leaves had on a black cape, white mask and a top hat.

"Brizzy!" he squealed in a pitch that could break glass.

The appearance of a second oddly dressed child seemed to have broken Bare Snow. She went down to her knees to examine them closer. Which was good, because the herd of other half-elf children came thundering to the door to see Brizzy. They quickly decided that a new elf was much more interesting. Bare Snow disappeared in a wave of children, babbling in squeaky-voiced excitement. "Oh my God, her hair is blue—" "She's Mercury—" "No, no, it's long blue hair, she's Mars—" "What does your dress say?"

Leaving Bare Snow to the children, Law picked her way to the kitchen. The restaurant had been an expensive French cuisine place with a stunning view of downtown Pittsburgh. The dining room had been done in elaborate crown moldings with massive crystal chandeliers. At one time people had had to pay a hundred dollars for a plate of fancy food and amazing views. The elegant room now acted as the commune's common area. Normally it looked as if a tornado had dumped a thrift store onto a French palace. Today, though, it looked like several toy stores had been added on top of the usual chaos.

No matter what the family area looked like, the kitchen was always spotless. Usagi had gotten the kitchen USFDA approved. The commune made the

bulk of their money selling "Elfhome jams and jel-
lies" on Earth. A surprise inspection when the kitchen
wasn't clean would sink them. Usagi had replaced the
restaurant's original swinging doors between the big
kitchen and the converted dining room with Dutch
doors. The standing house rule was the bottom half was
always, *always* closed to keep out pets and children.

Today obviously wasn't normal for anyone, not just
Law; the kitchen was a disaster zone. The sink had
wicker baskets full of rinsed fire berries. On the two
big commercial-grade stoves were several pots of
bright red jam, a pan of boiling water with lids and a
forest of thirty-three quart water bath canners. With
the exception of the stoves and sinks, every surface
was covered with thousands of canning jars. The bulk
were filled and labeled but scores were still empty.
The heat of the kitchen was staggering. All the windows were open with box fans struggling to move the
stifling humid air.

Usagi was a mini-Martha Stewart: five-two, blond
bob, and the business drive to make millions. Despite
the chaos and heat, she wore a neatly pressed pink
gingham apron and crisp matching kerchief on her
head like some highly starched skull diaper. As usual,
she looked like she could plow through hell while
drinking tea with one pinkie raised. Just the sight of
her always made Law feel like she was too tall, too
awkward, and somehow all boy.

The feeling intensified as Law spotted Widget sitting
in the far corner, right leg up, ankle obviously swollen
by some injury, with an old-fashioned ice pack on it.

"Law!" Widget threw up her hands in an unvoiced
demand for a hug.

Usagi was much more to the point. "Oh, thank gods you're here; we need help!"

Saving damsels in distress: the story of Law's life. "What in the world is going on, darlings?"

"Everything!" Widget smelled of Dove soap as Law gave her the demanded hug.

"It's been the week from hell," Usagi stated. "The *nota inesfa* were late coming in. The day before we started picking, Widget fell down the stairs."

"I'm so sorry!" Widget cried.

"It's not your fault!" Usagi waved off the apology. "I love the ferrets, and with this place we really need them to keep the rats out, but oh my gods, every time you start down the steps, there they are, wanting to play with your ankles."

A timer went off and Usagi turned off flames under the forest of canners.

"You didn't break it, did you?" Law shifted the ice pack to examine the swollen ankle. If it was broken, it could be a hairline fracture.

Widget winced. "Babs thinks it's just badly sprained."

Widget didn't have the golden ticket of being a mother to a half-elf yet, so she couldn't go to Mercy Hospital for treatment. Babs was the commune's midwife. Qualified or not, Babs ended up treating everything from runny noses to broken fingers.

Usagi continued listing their streak of bad luck. "Clover developed edema on the first day of berry picking; her feet swelled up to soccer balls." Clover was nine months pregnant and ready to pop. "Babs ordered her into bed with air conditioning and cold compresses. Hazel has been working double shifts because two of the part-timers at the bakery got caught and are being deported." Usagi windmilled her arms in sheer frustration. "It was just me and Babs and the kids picking. It took forever! We finished two days ago and we've been canning nonstop since then. We're almost done but Clover went into labor. Babs is upstairs with her. We need to have a full pallet packed and ready to go when the truck shows up."

"I'm here for you." It got her a fierce hug that threatened to break bones. For a little thing, the woman had muscles. "Where should I start?"

"Scrub up." Usagi pointed at a clean apron hanging by the door. "Suit up. Build a shipping box, pack it with jars with labels, seal it, and stack it on the pallet on the loading dock. Lather, rinse, repeat."

"Consider it done, but I need Widget to do some database digging when she's free."

Widget threw up her hands. "I'm free right now. I've labeled everything that I can. I have to wait until the seals set up on the next set of jars."

Law knew that by "scrub" Usagi meant under her nails and up to her elbows. Law moved berries out of the way so she could wash her hands. "I'm looking for the owner of the license plate BAD-0001."

"Someone's gonna get it," Widget sang as she fished her tablet out of a messenger bag. "What did this B-hole do?"

"He took a female elf out in the middle of nowhere and stranded her there." Law said.

"Oh my gosh!" Widget cried. "Did he hurt her?"

"No." Law dried her hands and found the shipping boxes. "He might have planned on coming back later, but I found her first." *And have no idea what to do with her.* "She remembers his license plate. I want to find out who to keep an eye open for." Law stated her reason for wanting to identify the man. She wasn't sure why Bare Snow was keen on tracking him down.

"You should tell the police or the EIA or someone." Widget was sometimes hopelessly naïve. Which was why she had needed Law to haul her out of trouble and hook her up with Usagi.

Usagi snorted loudly as she measured jam out into jars.

"What?" Widget asked.

"I had a dickhead of an ex while going to college," Usagi explained. "He got me kicked out of my dorms because 'my guest' wouldn't follow rules. I got a restraining order for him, and moved into an apartment."

Usagi banged around the metal utensils, growing angry as she told her story. "I got kicked out of there because I'd called the cops too many times. The landlord called it disturbing the peace."

"You're kidding!" Widget cried.

"No. The shitty thing was that by the time I'd call the cops, I'd be so scared and angry that I'd be screaming at the world. Dickhead would be calm and smirk and do that male 'must be that time of the month' thing. Like it's unreasonable to be upset by a man who's a foot taller and eighty pounds heavier than you and just won't leave you alone. The cops would end up hassling me more than him. All he would have to say was 'she's my girlfriend' and that would be the end of it. Once upon a time, long past regretting, I'd said 'yes' to this man and that was all that mattered in the cop's head. It didn't matter that I'd been saying 'no' for months, that I'd given up a full scholarship and moved to the other side of the country. It didn't matter that I wanted nothing more from him. We were 'a couple.' This was a 'domestic quarrel' and we were both guilty."

Usagi took a deep breath, eyes closed. "God, sorry, it's been twelve years and it still pisses me off. I finally applied to the University of Pittsburgh and moved an entire planet away from him. I had plans of doing this—" She waved her hand to take in the kitchen and the hundreds of canning jars. "But at the other end of it, I'd be the one living on Earth, calling the shots. In my senior year, he'd gotten my address and started to send me letters. He had plans. Plans that included me. And I just snapped—I was pregnant within a month."

"Wow," Widget breathed. "That sucks."

Law nodded to acknowledge the unfairness of it. Most people were good, wonderful people that would give you anything you needed—time, money, patience. There were, however, one or two people who should be just taken out and shot.

Usagi was probably right for the wrong reasons. If the male that drove Bare Snow truly was an elf pretending to be a human, then neither the police nor the EIA could do anything about it. Even if he was a human (and Bare Snow was mistaken about the accent) he actually hadn't broken any laws. Yet. The man definitely planned something hinky but the police would have their hands tied until someone was hurt or dead.

Someone like Bare Snow.

Law had built, packed, sealed, and stacked thirty boxes when Widget blew out a loud raspberry.

"That doesn't sound good," Law said.

"BAA to BAZ was assigned to the EIA!" Widget cried.

"What the hell?" Law said. "The EIA doesn't have that many vehicles."

"The range numbers are reserved." Widget tapped on her tablet and shook her head. "Basically it lets the EIA generate random plates to put on their cars instead having to go to the city for plates. Kind of independent but cooperative."

Law nodded. "Same old. Same old." The city and the EIA were two huge cog-turning mechanisms, dependent on each other while trying to stay totally separate. The city was a territory of the United States with elected officials and a nonmilitary police force. It maintained the infrastructure of Pittsburgh: the roads, the water, the sewage and the like. The EIA was a United Nations entity created to oversee humanity's presence on an alien world at the edge of Queen Soulful Ember's domain. It controlled access entering and leaving Elfhome and had the final word on everything related to the elves.

Widget frowned at her tablet. "It seems as if the license plate BAD-0001 is on a white Ford Explorer. It's labeled UPU. What the hell is that?"

"Unmarked, private use," Usagi said. "Most of the 'official' EIA vehicles are white with 'U.N.' painted on the hood and sides. But the staff is from all over the world and they occasionally need access to cars for personal activities like shopping. The EIA has a motor pool of unmarked cars for private use. UPU. I could have used one while I interned with the EIA but I never had the need for a car."

"So anyone that works for the EIA has access to them?" Law asked.

"Yes," Usagi said. "You're looking at about five hundred possible males. He would have had to sign for the car, so there's a paper trail."

"Can you find out who used that car?" Law asked Widget.

Widget blew another raspberry. "The city of Pittsburgh has an ancient system. It's easy as pie to get in—actually it's easier than making pie, if you ask me. Rolling pastry is hard! EIA's systems were just updated two years ago with more firewalls than God. I can't get into their system."

"Oh my God, who is she?" Usagi pointed at the doorway. "She's gorgeous!"

Bare Snow peered into the kitchen with curious eyes. A collection of little hands and the tops of heads gathered on the sill of the closed half-door.

"Tell her! Tell her!" the children whispered in Elvish.

Clearly uncertain about her mission, Bare Snow spilled out a long discussion in High Elvish, sprinkled with rote-learned English phrases of "peanut butter" and "chocolate milk" and "I'm not asking. I'm telling."

Usagi covered her mouth to keep in a surprised laugh. "That is not funny," she finally said loudly to the children. She glanced at the kitchen clock. "Oh! I didn't realize how late it was." With her back to the door, she grinned hugely. "I didn't feed them dinner but they know not to get underfoot when I'm working on a deadline."

With practiced ease, Usagi smeared scoops of peanut butter and jam onto slices of homemade bread, squishing them together, and poured glasses of milk, stirring in chocolate syrup, and then lowered each plate and glass down over the other side of the door to a child. "Bring me your dirty plates. Blade and Thunder, you'll have to take sandwiches up to your mothers when you're done eating."

While the children were given their dinner, Bare Snow continued to ask questions. A blush started to creep up Usagi's face even as she tried to control giggles.

"Poor thing. She wants to know where we got all the baby elves—did we steal them or just find them? Why do we have weasels running loose? Why is there a woman upstairs in a bucket of water, screaming? And why doesn't anyone seem worried about that?"

"Bucket of water?"

The giggles won. "It's a birthing pool! Only it's tiny compared to what elves consider a proper tub." Usagi put plates and glasses in front of Law and Bare Snow. "Here, you probably haven't eaten either."

The fire berry jam was like sweet fireworks against the rich creaminess of the peanut butter.

Bare Snow took a tentative bite of the sandwich and her eyes went wide. "Mmmm!" She took another bite, much bigger, swaying back and forth. "Mmmmm."

Usagi explained that Clover was having a baby. She added that all the children were half-elf and had been born to human mothers in the same way. This triggered dozens of questions that Law never had the courage to ask. It amazed her that Usagi actually answered them all.

The father of both Moon Rabbit and Shield was a *laedin*-caste warrior who belonged to the viceroy's household and only visited Pittsburgh occasionally.

Usagi had deliberately chosen a male that wouldn't be able to keep close watch on her. After having Moon Rabbit, Usagi decided that her daughter should have a sibling, so she'd never be alone. Usagi also wanted her children to be full siblings, so she'd sought the same male out a second time. She'd been afraid that he'd only been with her the first time out of curiosity and wouldn't want a reunion. The male, however, seemed eager to be with her again.

Bare Snow didn't seem surprised. "I'd heard that humans are like peanut butter, but I didn't understand until now."

Law had always wondered what the male elves saw in human females. Not to knock Usagi and her housemates, but none of them came close to Bare Snow's beauty. The elf was stunningly beautiful, the way that the sky was always perfect even when filled with rolling storm clouds. Humans, like Law, were like thistles. She supposed some people could like scruffy, but why roll in the weeds when you could have the sky?

Then again, Law did have a pet porcupine.

"I am Ground Bare in Winter as Killing Snow Falls in Wind. Please, call me Bare Snow." She used the English words instead of the Elvish. "I like that name better. I came to Pittsburgh hoping to find a place to belong. I thought that I would be happy with anyone that offered to take a pale shadow of myself. The wind. The ground bare in winter. Now I know that I would be miserable unless I was wanted for all of me."

Widget gave Law a confused look.

Law knew what Bare Snow meant, felt an echo within herself. So many people just wanted part of the package that was Law. They didn't want her to be independent and capable. They called her "male" as if no woman could do what she did and still be a woman. They didn't want her to be gay, while ignoring the fact that they never "chose" to be straight. Or they didn't want her to work as a forager, despite the fact that they hated their job and were envious of her freedom, or to live in a barn, despite the fact that they thought it was cool and had always dreamed about it. She was friends with the people that didn't want to change her, mold her into their idea of "good," but even they had little pieces of her that they didn't want.

Law didn't want to derail the conversation by laying bare her soul, so she looped the conversation back to the whole reason she was at the commune. "So the license plate lead is a dead end?"

Widget stared up at the ceiling, squinting, as if peering into Pittsburgh's Internet clouds. "Well, we could go at it from another angle. I can hit the city's driver's license database. There's a security field on it to denote EIA employees. It also tracks gender, hair color, eye color, height and weight. We could winnow through the males to see if any match up to her perp."

"Perp? Is that Elvish?" Law asked.

Widget ducked her head and blushed deep red. "Sorry, that's what they call bad guys on old cop shows."

Bare Snow described the male. Law wasn't sure she could describe her own father with such exacting details. The female had noted his height, weight, and width of his shoulders, shape of his chin, nose, and cheeks. Bare Snow could even state the exact shade of honey blond hair and green eyes that the male had. It became clear as she described the man that she'd instantly known that he was lying to her and probably meant to hurt her in some way.

"Why did you go with him?" Law asked.

Bare Snow winced and whispered, "Sometimes the only way to learn more about a trap is to trigger it." Then she shrugged and focused on making herself another sandwich. "I know it was dangerous but it made me happy. For the first time, I felt fiercely alive. I thought I would finally matter. I waited and waited for something to happen, but nothing did, so I learned nothing. It made me so sad. Maybe I was wrong; maybe the male was just a human and this was where Water Clan belonged. I cried until I fell asleep. When you found me, I was not sure why you were there. You were clearly not an elf and you had a porcupine. Things became clearer when you took the door."

"It did?" Law was still mystified about the door.

"That there are three forces at work in Pittsburgh. There are those that set the trap. Those that the trap was set for. And the ones that dismantled the trap before it could be triggered."

"Wait. I got there before the trap was triggered? But . . . but . . . you weren't in the trap already?"

Bare Snow shook her head vigorously. "When he left me there, I realized that the trap was not for me. I thought I was to be the bait—although I could not guess for whom. Bait should be wanted, and I am not. When you took the door, I realized that I wasn't the bait. I was the screen. When you set a trap, you seek to erase your presence. You don't want the trap to be detected until it has done its job. And, if it fails to be fatal, you don't want the trap to lead survivors to you."

*"All hell is going to break loose regardless but let's not give anyone a nice little goat, shall we?"* Crazy Lady meant a scapegoat, not a real goat.

"So basically you behind the white door was so that the Water Clan would be blamed for whatever happened?" Law said.

"Yes." Bare Snow took a big gulp of chocolate milk; it left a mustache on her upper lip. "Obviously I needed to change my strategy. I decided to stay mobile until I could determine the players in the game. I believe now that the trap is meant for the viceroy."

"Windwolf?" Law cried.

"Windwolf?" Bare Snow echoed back the English name in confusion.

"That's his name in English." Like all Elvish names, Windwolf's real name was impossibly long and meant Wolf Who Rules Wind. Elvish word order meant that humans ended up calling him "Rules" when they tried to shorten his name. The English nickname kept the local elves from being pissed off when the humans butchered the viceroy's name.

"Windwolf. Windwolf." Bare Snow practiced the nickname and then nodded. "All that I learned today says Windwolf is the target."

"I've been with you all day. No one talked about killing him! He's going to have fish for dinner. That's it!"

Bare Snow tilted her head in confusion. "Oh, you don't know our history. It would not be obvious to you." She thought for a minute. "It is a very long story." She thought for a minute longer. "A very, very long story."

Law went back to building and packing boxes. "This is going to take a while."

❖         ❖         ❖

The female did not know how to condense. Granted, it was an epic tale. Sometime in the past, God knows when because Law didn't, the Skin Clan had an empire that stretched from the Eastern Sea to the Western Sea. There were roads and aqueducts and shipping canals and great dikes built with slave labor at a horrific cost of life. Hundreds of elves died for every mile of a highway that stretched for thousands of miles. The Skin Clan had been all about flaunting its wealth while grinding its slaves into the dirt. Naturally a rebellion swept through the empire, crashing down all central government, leaving behind ruins and memories of a golden age. An hour later, Bare Snow had painted an elegant picture of an era gone by.

"But what about the viceroy?" Law cried finally since his name hadn't surfaced once.

"Wolf Who Rules' grandfather was Howling. He was the first real head of the Wind Clan. We had been the slaves of the King Boar Bristle, whose kingdom was in the highlands. His father—Wolf Who Rules' great-grandfather—Quick Blade had been the bastard son of Boar Bristle and started the rebellion. Quick Blade was but one of many scattered warlords. It was Howling that made an alliance with the *sekasha* and gathered all the Wind Clan households to him. After the fall of the Skin Clan, the Wind Clan claimed all of the Mauhida as their ancestral right. It put them at odds with the Water Clan that long controlled the ports of the Dark Sea."

In other words, her parents were from feuding clans. No wonder neither clan wanted Bare Snow. This explained her situation but not why she thought Windwolf was the target.

"What does this have to do with Windwolf being attacked in Pittsburgh?"

Bare Snow gestured for Law to wait. "It all relates. The war came to the end when Pure Radiance went to Burning Mountain Temple and told the Holy Ones that we were on the brink of complete destruction. Peace must be established and maintained at any cost. So Cinder called a gathering of *sekasha*. Deeming that enough blood had been shed, they chose to complete in games to decide which of the clans would lead the others. Cinder won for the Fire Clan and Ashfall was deemed king of all our people."

Law sighed and glanced to Usagi who spread her hands. Still no mention of the viceroy. "What about Windwolf?"

Bare Snow plunged on with her story. "While Wraith Arrow was attending the summit, Howling was assassinated. The head of clan fell to Longwind, who was barely out of his majority, but had already taken Otter Dance as his First."

"First what?" Widget asked.

"Hush!" Law cried. If they detoured Bare Snow with questions, they'd never get to the end. The damage, though, had been done.

"Otter Dance's mother had been Perfection of the Wind Clan and her father Tempered Steel of the Stone Clan." Bare Snow clasped her hands over her heart and sighed. "Their love is epic. To know in a glance and word that this person shares your spirit." Another heartfelt sigh. "Their daughter, Otter Dance, spent equal time between them, first at High Meadow Temple and then Cold Mountain. She and Longwind were childhood sweethearts. He thought his lot was like many young elves, to be unimportant in the grand sweep of things. His elders never growing old; his time never coming. He let his heart lead him to take Otter Dance as First despite the fact that her father had been Stone Clan. It was his willingness to look beyond bloodlines which made the *sekasha* choose him as Clan Head. Pure Radiance had stated that the only way our future could be secured was by close alliance between the clans. Ashfall's first act as king was to call together the heads of the clans and offer up his children as royal hostages, disguised as unions of alliance."

"Eww!" Usagi cried out in disgust at the idea of using children as tools.

Law was losing track of who was who. "Longwind is the viceroy's father?"

"Yes. He took King Ashfall's daughter, Flame Heart, as his *domi*." Again with the hand clasped over the chest and the deep, heartfelt sigh. "It was love on first sight. They had ten children! Can you believe it? Most people don't even have one! The viceroy is the youngest and the only one that can use both *esva*. He was given a very blessed name of Wolf Who Rules, foreseeing that he would hold all of the Westernlands."

Law thought the whole naming scheme was a load of crap if it cursed one baby and blessed another. "I still don't see how this relates to someone trying to kill him."

"The *sekasha* see truth like a coin; either something is true or it is a lie. Heads or tails. They do not realize that truth is like an onion—it has layers upon layers. Because of that, they can be blinded to a rotten core by an unblemished shell."

Widget started to say something about an onion not having a shell and Law smacked her.

"*Stay on target*," Law growled. "Who is trying to kill the viceroy?"

"When Howling was assassinated, the *sekasha* were furious that someone had gone against their decree of a truce while they were gathered at Burning Mountain. The question was: who?"

Law attempted to jump forward in time because she knew that Windwolf was several hundred years old. If Bare Snow was retelling how his parents met, she could be talking all night. She guessed at how the assassination of his grandfather related to events in Pittsburgh. "The same people that killed Howling are going to try to kill Windwolf?"

"Yes!" Bare Snow cried with delight.

"So—" Law tried to backtrack through the long story. If Bare Snow had named a suspect, Law lost hold of the detail in the flood of information. "Who killed Howling?"

"This is where the onion starts to peel. Rumors surfaced that a warlord by the name of Tornado might have used a Wind Clan household of trained assassins as a bid for clan head. The *sekasha* easily found evidence that he'd hired them. Tornado's *sekasha* executed him and put a warrant out on the Wind Clan assassins who had fled into hiding. They were hunted down and killed, one by one."

"But he was actually framed?" Law asked.

"Framed?" Bare Snow tilted her head in confusion.

Law winced. The word apparently only meant "surrounded with wood" in Elvish. "The evidence was false."

"In a manner of speaking. Someone lied to a *laedin*-caste male. After the *laedin* had passed on the lie as truth, he was killed so it seemed as if he was murdered to silence him. This is the rotten core: the assassins were told that under no conditions would Howling ever bow to a king put in place by the *sekasha*. If another clan head was raised up above him, Howling supposedly planned to kill all the Holy Ones in one massive attack. As *domana*, Howling had the power to do so. The *sekasha*'s protective shields cannot protect them from the full brunt of a *domana* offensive spell. Howling would become what we fought a thousand years to wipe off the face of the planet. No sane person would allow him to go unchecked. That lie, however, was then wrapped in truths. We were in the middle of a war. The assassins could not kill Howling without someone prepared to step cleanly into the void. They chose Tornado to be his successor and then planted the seeds of ambition. He was a proud elf; it was required to make Tornado believe it was his idea. Thus, when the *sekasha* sought evidence of Tornado's crime, they found it. It was true. At least, at the surface."

Law packed the boxes she'd built and tried to understand Bare Snow's logic. The Wind Clan assassins had killed Howling but they'd been tricked into doing it. While they fled into hiding as wanted criminals, the mastermind remained in place.

Bare Snow's mother had been alone on a deserted island when her parents met.

And her mother had been killed when she returned to Winter Court.

This wasn't some epic story of legendary figures; it was the story of Bare Snow's family and how they were connected with the viceroy. Elves don't lie; at least the honorable ones didn't. If it had been an utterly random Water Clan female behind the white door in Fairywood, she could honestly proclaim her innocence, and most likely be believed. Bare Snow had been sent halfway around the world to be in Pittsburgh for this Shutdown. Her cursed Wind Clan name and her Water Clan appearance would lead to questions about her parents. Once her mother's identity was known, Bare Snow's very presence would be damning. It would seem as if she was taking vengeance for her mother's household.

Her family had taken the fall once for the real killer. Obviously someone hoped that it would work again. Considering everything, yes, the trap's intended victim most likely was Howling's grandson.

Law glanced at the kitchen clock. If they left now, they could get to the Rim and warn the viceroy before the border was closed. They only had a few hours left; Pittsburgh was returning to Earth at midnight. All the elves—and only the elves—remained on Elfhome during Shutdown.

But what would she tell Windwolf? If the assassins had known who had set them up, they would have exacted revenge.

*Think, Law, don't just react. That's how you get yourself shit deep into messes.*

This was world-level politics, hundreds of years, if not thousands, in the making. She was just a forager, fishing and hunting for a living because it meant she didn't have to deal with the petty politics of a normal business. And really, the only reason she was involved was Crazy Lady had randomly dialed her phone number and sent her on a fool's errand that only Law would be stupid enough to do. Bare Snow was safe. The viceroy was surrounded by the best warriors of Elfhome.

There was the sudden thunder of small feet.

"Law! Law! Aunt Babs says the baby—the baby has shoulders or something—she needs your help now!"

It was "shoulder dystocia" and it meant Law needed to lift Clover from the birthing pool and get her onto her knees with the baby already crowned. Emergency calm kicked in, letting Law deal with the scared Clover while Babs focused on the baby.

Usagi might be an organized general in business crisis and she could calmly deal with hordes of cranky children, but blood and pain? They rattled her. She became a neurotic little yap dog, barking out useless orders. It was not what either Babs or Clover needed.

Bare Snow got an unintentional education on the whole childbirth process. Afterwards she gazed wide-eyed at the pointy-eared infant. "So that's where they get them."

"Yes, all of them," Law said.

Down in the kitchen, there was a sharp squeal.

"What the hell?" Law hurried downstairs.

Widget was sitting with hands over her mouth, as if to hold in another scream. She lifted her hands long enough to whisper, "Sorry," and then clapped them down over her mouth again. Her stare was locked onto her computer tablet.

"What's wrong?" Law leaned over her shoulder to see what was on her screen. It was a very handsome white man. His hair matched the very exact honey blond that Bare Snow described. The database identified him as Andre Brousseau, a diplomat from France employed by the EIA as a customs inspector. Law picked up the tablet and showed it to Bare Snow. "This him?"

"Yes!" Bare Snow cried.

Law turned back to Widget. "You *know* him?"

"You remember I told you originally I was going to come across the border with another girl? Her screen name was Strawberrie. She never told me her real name. We'd met on this site called Jello Shots. It's a forum for fans of the *Adventures of Soulful Ember* videos. We both wrote Prince Yardstick fan fiction— although she shipped him with Wraith Arrow and I thought that was a total eeewwww..."

"Focus, Widget."

"We e-mailed back and forth for like a year, talking about how to get to Elfhome. We didn't meet up in person until I got to Cranberry. I thought it would be safer to cross with someone else, but when I met her, I could tell within minutes that she had no common sense at all."

This was from someone who'd swum the Ohio River at night in the middle of winter.

"What does this have to do with Andre Brousseau?"

"She'd told me that she knew someone that knew someone that could get us across the border for a thousand dollars. When I got to Cranberry, she took me to this creepy-looking house and there were these really hot-looking guys there." Widget pointed at the screen. "He was the boss of the guy that Strawberrie contacted. They had these coffin-like boxes and they were going to crate us up and supposedly get us across the border. That was until Mr. Brous—Brous—Mr. Fancypants actually saw me. He got all prissy about the fact that I'm black. He actually used the N word!

I never heard anyone actually say it before, outside of history class." She must have come from an extremely well-to-do neighborhood then. "And Strawberrie was all 'I didn't know she was black!' instead of telling him to piss off. And what difference did it make? Unless of course he only wanted some white girl to do who knows what with. As you would say: it felt hinky. So I said I had to pee and then went out the bathroom window. I called 911 and then ditched my phone. I thought she'd be better off arrested than left alone with those guys."

Law knew some of the people that smuggled illegal immigrants across the border. They were all native-born Pittsburghers who drove delivery routes during Shutdown. The ones she knew, you could trust, but then they were risking being deported. Trust went two ways. "Do you know what happened with your friend?"

Widget shook her head. "It didn't make any of the news feeds. I don't know if the police actually did anything. I never heard from her again. I was hoping that she changed her screen name and was ignoring my posts because she was pissed at me. I used the name Elderberry Wine. Elderberry. Strawberrie. Our names were why we started to chat in the first place."

Law gazed at Andre Brousseau's photo. He had that impossible beauty that all the elves had. But his ears were visible. They were definitely round. "Bare Snow, are you sure he's an elf? His ears aren't pointed."

"The Skin Clan made our ears that way so they could tell at a glance who was a slave. It was the first change they made once they realized that we'd become immortal. It means he's a very old elf," Bare Snow said. "His speech pattern says he's thousands of years old. After the rebellion started, the world went into chaos. We were divided into three groups. The Skin Clan and their loyal servants. Their slaves that took up arms against them. And all the others fled from both."

An ancient elf pretending to be French man. A possible kidnapper. A would-be assassin.

"How many 'men' were working for him?" Law asked Widget.

"There were like eight at the creepy house."

A call to the Cranberry police concerning people trying to cross the border illegally would have been diverted to the EIA. Andre worked for the EIA; it was possible that all Widget succeeded in doing was alerting him that she was no longer locked in the creepy house's bathroom. It also meant that Law couldn't contact the Pittsburgh Police about an attack on Windwolf. They'd turn the matter over to the EIA since it involved elves. If Andre had arranged for Bare Snow to be diverted to Pittsburgh from halfway around the world, Law was sure that he had someone covering EIA dispatch to intercept any such calls. Law would bet her Dodge on it.

The problem was that if the shit hit the fan, Brousseau could and probably would start a manhunt for Bare Snow. Enough people knew that she was in town; he'd start the search with "probable cause" and probably make sure that she didn't survive capture.

"We need to get a step ahead of Brousseau. We have a name now." She leaned forward to check the listing. It gave an EIA office as his address. "Bastard. Can you print me a copy of this?"

"Going to the police with it?"

"No, the elves."

"Someone in Howling's household betrayed him," Bare Snow said. "We were never sure who, but the false information that the *laedin*-caste male had could have only come from someone close to him. Windwolf has gathered most of his grandfather's household. Any one of them—except the *sekasha*—could have betrayed Howling."

Which meant going to the enclave could take them face to face with the traitor.

"So we waylay Windwolf. Chili Pepper said he was . . . oh shit!"

"What?"

"He's at the airport." Law leaned over and pulled up a Pittsburgh map. "The only reasonable way to get to the airport is the I-376. If he took the exit at Route 60 . . . follow it to here, turn at Woodmere Drive and again at Roswell Drive and he's in the trap. Three turns."

"That's still really out of the way . . ." Widget protested.

"Route 60 is one of the few roads in that area that still has all its bridges. We're almost to Shutdown. The highways are going to be filling up as people start lining up at the checkpoints so they can be sure to get across the border this cycle."

"So this starts with him looking for an alternate route back from the airport?" Widget started to tap madly on her tablet. "Oh! Blast it all! We have to stop this! Prince Yardstick is the bomb!"

Law growled softly. "The problem is that the elves don't use phones. If I want to talk to the damn enclaves, I have to drive out there and knock on the damn door.

That will take me the wrong direction through all of the Shutdown madness downtown. If I start driving around, hoping that I can run into him and then get him to stop without getting cut down by the *sekasha*..."

"Wait. Wait. Wait," Widget murmured and then flung her hands up into the air and wiggled her fingers. "Muhahahahaha!"

"Is that supposed to be good or bad?" Law asked.

"I have done magic!" Widget gave the evil laugh again. "It's a little known fact that all cars sold in Pittsburgh—with the exception of antique vehicles like your Dodge—still have antitheft GPS systems. Little known because the city is stuck in the last century, technology-wise. Really—I cry at night for the Internet of Earth. I miss it so."

"What is it? This antitheft whatever."

"My point exactly." Widget ducked, grinning. "Simply put, the United States managed to get into the treaty that they could have a handful of satellites up in Elfhome space. They're all hush-hush about it. It's all part of the 'Pittsburgh is still an American city' brouhaha that they're still fighting over in the UN. Since they're American, the satellites aren't under EIA control. Nor can the local police access it."

"Why the hell not?"

"No idea. Probably politics. The University of Pittsburgh, though, has access to them and their security is full of student-made backdoors. Voila!" She held up her tablet to show off a bunch of dots moving on a map.

"And that is...?"

"Our mystery SUV! It's in... Fairywood. Where's that?" She turned the tablet back and zoomed out. "Oh, downstream, our side of the river."

"And those other dots?"

"Um." She put down her tablet to tap on it again. "This one is BAS-0053." She read off another one of the identifiers and crosschecked it. "It's also an EIA UPU vehicle. It looks like they have a whole fleet out in Fairywood. Four at least. Acting weird. They're like ants; crawling around aimlessly."

"They're grid searching," Law said. "Can you pull up the viceroy's cars?"

The elves had a small fleet of the big gray luxury cars for Windwolf and Sparrow's exclusive use. Normally they were kept in coach houses of Poppymeadow's when the viceroy wasn't in town.

"Let's see." Widget closed the window and pulled up a database. She searched for information faster than Law could follow. "Yes, they do have antitheft systems. Oh. Oh. Blast it all!"

A lone Rolls Royce sat motionless in Fairywood, the EIA cars prowling around it like a pack of wargs. This wasn't one lone nutcase elf posing as a human; this was some secret alliance of evil. The other Rolls Royces milled about in Oakland, obviously looking for their lost leader in the wrong place.

"They screwed up their hit on the viceroy." Law watched the markers on the screen move. It was fairly easy to read the activity on the screen since she knew the design of the trap. "He's on foot; running for his life. They probably have people chasing him." She remembered the dogs barking in Fairywood. "Or dogs. Yeah, probably dogs. They're forcing him toward the river." There were only a handful of bridges across the Ohio River and the waters were full of man-eating fish. "The cars will close in from either side, like the jaws of trap."

"Something has changed," Bare Snow whispered.

"What do you mean?" Law asked.

"They have stayed hidden for thousands of years, carefully keeping to the shadows. This is too bold a move. Something has changed."

"Well, someone has dropped a major human city onto the face of the planet."

Bare Snow was shaking her head. For the first time since Law found her, the female looked frightened. "They think they have the upper hand. They would not act so brazenly if they did not know they could quickly take control of all of the Westernlands."

Her history lesson suddenly made sense. She had laid out what it was that these hidden elves wanted: a world where the lives of others meant nothing when weighed against their comforts.

Law was getting that familiar angry feeling that she got from having her nose rubbed in injustice. It was a clenching of teeth until her jaw hurt, and the nails of her fingers digging into her clenched hands.

"We have to go," Bare Snow said in English.

Law nodded in agreement.

Bare Snow threw her arms around Law and kissed her. It was so sudden that Law didn't really get a chance to enjoy it.

"You've got to be kidding," Widget cried. "Really?"

"Um." Law was still off-balanced by the kiss. "Yeah. I'm an expert at getting people out of shit-deep messes."

Pittsburgh had been a city of bridges; nearly five hundred just in the city proper and another thousand scattered in the hills around it. It no longer had the means to keep them all maintained. It lacked the money and the manpower and simple necessity of linking one abandoned neighborhood to another. Main roads linked the city together, but not in a short and direct method. An hour before Shutdown and those main roads were bumper to bumper with several thousand vehicles trying to get into position at the checkpoints or back home before the floodgates of Earth opened up.

Luckily the traffic kept to the main roads, leaving the side streets, backyards, and occasionally shallow streams clear for Law. (Got to love six-wheel drive.) As the crow flies (which was close to the way Law drove) it was six miles to Windgap.

"We need to be careful," Law said. "Just in case we run into the viceroy's guard."

"They were decoyed somehow from his side. They will not know where to even start looking for him."

They reached Fairywood. The viceroy's car sat on the last dead end street, its headlights still shining on the house where Law had found Bare Snow. The driver's and the back passenger doors were open. One of the *sekasha* warriors lay sprawled on the ground beside the big gray luxury car. He'd been dragged from the car and mauled by a large animal.

"Oh no," Law whispered. Was it the same "teenage" male that she'd met just hours ago? She crouched down beside the bloody body and shone her flashlight on the pale face. No. Stormhorse's eyes had been dark brown and this male had eyes of Wind Clan blue. He still looked impossibly young and vulnerable. Pat Hershel had said that it was the "babies" of the bodyguards that knew how to drive.

"He sacrificed himself," Bare Snow murmured sadly.

"The metal within the car kept the viceroy from using his *domana* spells. The holy one drew the attackers to his side of the vehicle so the viceroy could escape out the other way and use his magic."

"Why didn't his shield spell protect him?" Law panned her flashlight over the ground. There were four pug dogs scattered around him. Judging by the massive burn marks on the dogs and crisscrossing the pavement, they'd been killed by lightning. It looked like a thunderstorm had opened up a can of whoop-ass on twenty square feet of Fairywood. The pugs had to be the little yap dogs she'd heard barking earlier. They were just tiny things; the heaviest might have been fifteen pounds. They couldn't have been what mauled the warrior.

Dozens of large bloody paw prints mapped the *sekasha*'s death. They were larger than a warg's, didn't have the wolflike X-shape arrangements of toes and pad, nor were there marks left by the nonretracting claws. They looked like mountain lion tracks, but those were normally only four inches across. These were nearly eight inches, meaning that the beast was freaking huge.

"The shield draws power from the local ambient magic. It can only afford so much protection. Wyverns. Black willows. Saurus. Wargs. If the beast can pin the warrior, its only a matter of time before the spell fails."

Beyond the abandoned car, the dead bodies, the bloody tracks, and the scorch marks, there was no sign of the viceroy. Distantly Law could hear a pack of animals howling. The cadence was wrong for a warg; it was much more the fast baying of excited, little dogs. The sound echoed loud and weirdly distorted.

It nearly seemed like the dogs were at the bottom of a well, the steep sides echoing as well as amplifying the howls. It was coming from Chartiers Creek, a half-mile or so off. She kept losing the sound of it under the rumble of a nearby freight train that followed the creek bottom to the Ohio River.

"Idiots," Bare Snow murmured. "They sprang the attack too soon. They should have waited. Once the city returns to Earth, Wolf Who Rules will be without magic, and defenseless."

Chartiers Creek fed into the Ohio River at McKees Rocks a few miles away. The safety of the Rim lay just across the river. The only safe crossing was the McKees Rocks Bridge. There was a little-known railroad bridge at Brunots Island, but she doubted the viceroy—on the run for his life—would think of it. No, he'd head for the massive stone bridge, lit up for barges on the river and any random plane to see.

Law glanced at her phone. They had less than thirty minutes. "Those dogs are still hunting the viceroy. They haven't caught him yet. We need to find him."

Bare Snow shook her head. "He has every reason not to trust me and none to believe you. He's too dangerous to approach. He'll kill anyone he thinks is part of this trap."

There was a sudden flash of lightning and an immediate boom of thunder.

"Right. Keep our distance from the male throwing lightning."

Law had enough experience with traps to know all their frailties. Even brainless crayfish would escape their cage once all the bait was eaten. She and Bare Snow had the element of surprise on their side. The joy of being quirky-odd was that, even when the jerks saw her coming, they had no idea how much trouble they were in. A lesbian, a porcupine, and an underage assassin. No, there was no way these guys knew what was about to hit them.

They caught up to the first SUV on Creek Road.

Law drove up out of Chartiers Creek just before the water deepened. She plowed through an old chain link fence and fishtailed onto the narrow gravel road that ran along the stream.

She knew she should be screaming scared, but the cool electric rush was settling in. A righteous fight was like hooking a big fish. There was a thrill in the battle. It was as addictive as any drug. That these scumbags were out *en masse* hunting a young male and meant to frame an innocent female for his murder, she felt nothing but righteousness about any damage she dealt out.

She caught the gleam of lights off the creek; there was a car ahead on the road. She flicked off her headlights and used the part in the trees fringing the road, revealing the lighter night sky, to navigate. The road was narrow and rough, just a car-wide beaten path. Around a bend in the creek, where the channel narrowed and grew deeper, the road widened. One of the white SUVs was trying to turn around, taking advantage of the grassy bank where locals fished for river sharks. Even in the distance, Law could make out the lighted license plate. It was BAS-0053. It was one of the EIA unmarked cars.

She threw the Dodge into low gear and stomped on the gas. At the last moment, she blared her horn, seconds before ramming the SUV broadside. The Dodge's grill guard rammed into the lighter truck even as its driver instinctively steered away. The SUV rolled down the bank to vanish into the water, upside down. Only the gleam of its headlights marked it in the glittering darkness of the creek. A large dark figure of a river shark cut through the beams of light.

"That should keep them busy." Law backed up and straightened out on the road.

"Awesome possum." Bare Snow breathed the phrase that she must have learned from the half-elf babies.

Law flicked her lights back on and roared down the little dirt road. She knew the feeling racing through her like electricity. She got this every time she went snarling out to save some girl from a bad situation. There was no murky doubt or fear, just bold determination and a sense of right that made the rest of her life seem like she was barely alive.

She realized that up to this point, all the pressure to conform, to be what other people wanted her to be, had been a huge mountain pressing down on her. It was only at moments like this—when the scales shifted so that what was at stake was someone's life—that she knew, regardless of what everyone else wanted of her, her life made sense. She didn't need to live in a house, have a dog as a pet, work nine to five with a boss telling her what to do, paint her fingernails, fuss with her hair, and lust after some male that would complete her life. All that overwhelming messy little shit didn't matter anymore. She could be herself, completely and totally, and life was good.

She laughed at the knowledge that risking her life was easier than living it.

They caught the second SUV on the bare shoulder of the road, a mile down. It sat a dozen feet from the stop sign where Creek Road branched. The graveled street changed names to Thompson Avenue as it ducked under a low-slung iron railroad bridge to continue following Chartiers Creek or turned sharply and went up the hill. The SUV's interior light was on; its driver was struggling with an actual paper map. The Earth-bound freight train was rumbling over the bridge, drowning out the Dodge's approach.

The map and the train combined to explain why the SUVs were on the odd back roads. McKees Rocks was bisected by the railroad tracks. While a person on foot could scramble between the slow-moving train cars, the SUVs needed to find ways under or over the train. There were only three points were a car could cross and they were nearly a mile apart. The question became: which side of the tracks was Windwolf? The hounds were howling nearby but the sound echoed in the river valley, making it difficult to pinpoint their direction.

Luckily, Law didn't have to find Windwolf to protect him. She only had to derail his killers. She swung in a wide half-circle and rammed the SUV into the driver's door. The Dodge shuddered at the impact, but dug in all four back tires and heaved. The SUV slid on the gravel and then on the grass creek bed beyond. It tipped beyond its center of gravity and tumbled down the bank. It splashed into the dark water.

Her grandfather must be spinning up to mach speed in his grave.

Two down. Two to go. Unfortunately, with the name change, the Creek Road turned to follow the train tracks. There would be no more ramming cars into the water.

Betting that Windwolf wouldn't know McKees Rocks any better than his attackers, Law crossed under the railroad bridge. The viceroy had to be playing a cautious game of cat and mouse, since he had no way of knowing how many people were chasing after him or how heavily armed they were. The east side of the tracks was known as the Bottoms. It was a flat and desolate area, prone to flooding during the spring thaw. Many of the buildings had been abandoned before the first Startup; part and parcel of Pittsburgh's steel-mill age. The only businesses left in the area were a large railroad yard and a sprawling junkyard. It was a maze of hiding spaces. More importantly, it was the shortest distance to the McKees Rocks Bridge.

Law checked the clock again. Minutes were left before Pittsburgh returned to Earth. The hunting dogs were baying close by. They were still miles from the Rim; Windwolf was going to be stranded on the wrong world. She still didn't have a good solid plan beyond "whack them hard." It probably was a good time to start thinking of one.

Obviously she needed to nail the other SUVs before the scattered pieces realized that they were under attack.

A few blocks down she found one of the Fords sitting empty under a lone streetlamp. Law tucked the Dodge in among sumac brushes growing in an old gravel parking lot, thirty feet from the Explorer. The white SUV gleamed bright in the pool of light. Its back hatch hung open, but the SUV had sat long enough for the timer on the lights to click off.

Focused on the Explorer, Law missed Bare Snow's cowboy boots coming off. She became aware that the female was undressing as the elf shimmied off her underwear. "What are you—whoa!"

This was because Bare Snow had pulled her blue sundress up over her head. Elves apparently didn't wear bras; the female was totally naked. The harsh artificial light of the streetlight gleamed on Bare Skin's white skin, picking out a delicate, nearly invisible design on her hips and abdomen. It seemed like someone had stenciled her with Celtic knots across her torso with a concealer pencil. She would have never guessed that Bare Snow had such elaborate tattoos because of how much skin her clothes exposed, but even if she'd flashed panties, the lines would have been covered by her dress.

"What are you doing?" Law managed as she realized that the markings were spells like the ones tattooed down the arms of the *sekasha*. An ink that matched Bare Snow's skin color had been used so that they were almost invisible.

"Going hunting." Bare Snow pulled out two long wooden knives. Where had she been hiding them? They looked like the *sekasha*'s magically sharp swords. Did this mean that the assassins of Elfhome were some kind of holy ninjas? "Stay by the car. I'll engage them."

"By yourself? It will be safer if we tag team—holy shit!"

Bare Snow had whispered something in Elvish. The spell tattooed on her body gleamed for a second and the female vanished from sight. Even the wooden knives vanished. There was a distortion on the seat beside Brisbane like a shimmer of heat.

The distortion vanished as Bare Snow went out the window.

Law breathed another curse in surprise and dismay. It was one thing to know that Bare Snow's mother was a trained assassin; it was another to realize that she had taken eighty-some years to teach her daughter everything she knew before she died. Worse, even if they found Windwolf, Bare Snow's profession was written on her skin. Nothing they could say could outweigh that evidence.

"Yup, stay far, far away from the viceroy while saving him." If they did it right, it should be easy as pie. But as Widget noted: pie really wasn't that easy.

Law cautiously opened her door and stepped out of the Dodge. It was almost midnight. Night had closed in tight. Rimfire washed in ribbons of green and red over the river, marking how close they were to the border, and yet so far. The sumac bushes had taken over the parking lot of the old wire spring and form factory. Beyond the factory's low-slung modern buildings, there were rows of brick warehouses from the 1800s. The windows were a checkerboard of broken glass, empty holes and boarded-over. On the other side of the street, the long train rumbled and squealed and whined to a shuddering stop. The engine must have reached the Rim, miles down the track, and was waiting for Shutdown.

Somewhere nearby were Windwolf, his stalkers, and by the sound of it half a dozen large dogs.

Brisbane took advantage of the open door and scrambled out of the cab, grunting and grumbling at the effort. The problem with having a porcupine as a pet was trying to stop it equaled getting dozens needle-sharp quills embedded into your hand.

"Brizzy!" Law whispered. "Shit." True to his nature of being contrary, he beelined for the white SUV, grumbling loudly as he went. "Oh, Jesus Christ!" Which was both profane and a very short prayer for divine intervention. "Shhhh!"

He wouldn't be quieted any more than he'd be stopped on his waddle to the Explorer. Porcupine grumbling sounds weirdly like a baby trying to talk. She could almost imagine him trying to explain why he was going to get them all killed for the sake of something delicious he could smell in the SUV.

Law jerked her baseball bat out from behind the seat and headed for the SUV. If she could find what was luring him to the Explorer, she could use it to get him back in the Dodge. "That's it. I'm getting a dog. A little one. One I can just pick up and run with."

There was no one in sight. Not the driver of the SUV nor Bare Snow. A block or two away, the dogs were howling with frustrated excitement. They'd lost Windwolf or he'd found a perch spot out of their reach. What was Bare Snow doing? Was she heading toward the dogs or was she looking for the driver?

Brisbane scrambled into the open back. He obviously was following the scent of ripe *saenori*. Someone else had also recently arrived from Summer Court. The back seats were folded down and it looked like a small armory arrayed inside. There was even a shoulder-mounted rocket launcher.

"Shit," Law breathed. Andre and his people had come armed for bear. She suddenly felt outmatched. "Brizzy. Come on. We need to go back and get my shotgun." *And maybe a Molotov cocktail.*

Brisbane ignored her, digging through a travel sack

tucked beside the rocket launcher. "Naaaah, nori, aaah," he muttered and as always her brain desperately wanted to translate it into something understandable. Something reasonable. Something less stupidly stubborn.

Law growled. She leaned into the Explorer, carefully nudged him aside and fumbled with the fabric in the shadowed interior. "Come on. Come on." There were four of the fruits in the bag. She tossed them quickly into the weedy darkness beside the car. Complaining, Brisbane followed the fruit.

Law heard the heavy footsteps approaching; boots crunching on gravel. Bare Snow had taken off her cowboy boots. Law ducked down, gripping her baseball bat tightly. Key to a good ambush was to catch the person totally unaware and make the first hit hard as possible. It wasn't the first time she'd jumped a male with a gun, but never one this heavily armed. It wasn't a case of "a knife" or "a pistol" or "a rifle" but all of the above plus a few grenades to boot.

She rose just as he came around the back of the SUV. Her bat was cocked back as far as she could get it. All her strength and mass went into a line-drive hit. Warned by her movement, Andre started to raise the assault rifle he'd been carrying. The bat hit the rifle barrel with a crack of wood against metal. The rifle flew out of his hands, crashing into the sumac bushes along the berm of the road.

He lashed out faster than she'd thought possible. She tried to roll with the punch but it was like trying to dodge lightning. His fist connected with her chin, and the night flickered to total blackness as she fell stunned to the ground. He shouted something and slapped his hand down onto her chest. There was a crinkle of paper and a flare of light and then it felt like electricity shot through her body, making her shudder.

He stomped down on her chest and pinned the paper to her as she writhed on the ground. He stared down at her like she was a pinned frog in a science class. "Who are you? You look like one of those foragers. Picking weeds and mud crabs."

"Fuck you," she snarled out between her clenched teeth.

He snorted. "Doubtful. That spell works like a Taser on humans. You're not going to be doing anything until I allow it." He glanced about for his rifle. "What the hell are you doing out here in the middle of the night?"

"Going...to stop...you...from killing...Windwolf," Law forced out. Hopefully he might think she had a whole army at her back and flee.

"A little river rat like you?" A laugh slipped out before he frowned at her with worry. "How do you know what we plan? Who have you told?"

Law thought of Widget sitting with her foot up in the air and all the children at Usagi's. "Fuck you."

He pulled out a slip of paper with a spell inscribed on it. "Who knows?"

"Everyone! Andre Brousseau. Everyone knows what you are."

He knelt to slap the paper against her cheek and spoke an Elvish word.

Pain like a hot dagger shot through her face. She screamed.

He leaned close. "Who knows?"

There was the warning rattle of Brisbane's tail. The porcupine might be slow and stubborn but he wasn't stupid. He knew that Law was being hurt. Law cried out louder to cover the noise.

Motion warned the elf. Andre glanced up as Brisbane's spiked butt swung through the air, backed by sixty pounds of muscle. It caught Andre full in the face, driving a hundred of the long barbed quills deep into his flesh. Andre screamed. He jerked off of Law and scrambled backwards with Brisbane in pursuit. The slow-moving porcupine had no hope of catching the male, but Brisbane was at least chasing him away from Law.

"Get 'em, Brizzy! Sic 'em." Law clawed at the spell on her chest, her body still jerking and writhing. Her hand finally obeyed her enough to rip the paper off. The spasms stopped but all her muscles continued to tremble.

She fumbled with her baseball bat, trying to get to her feet. Her hands wanted to stay tight fists. Her legs didn't want to hold her up. Andre's face was full of quills, making him look like he had a massive starched beard, but somehow Brisbane had missed his eyes. He backed up to the SUV and then half-fell into it.

If he picked up one of the many guns inside, she was screwed. She abandoned her attempts to pick up the baseball bat and stumbled toward the SUV as fast as she could make her wobbly legs move.

Andre fumbled in the truck's dark interior. He shouted something over and over again. On the fourth shout, she realized it was an Elvish name. He was calling for backup. He found a rifle, swung it up, aimed and pulled the trigger. The click of the hammer landing on an empty chamber was the loudest noise that Law ever heard.

He swore, snatched up a magazine, and loaded the rifle. He lifted it again.

Law slammed the hatch shut onto his legs.

He screamed and pulled the trigger. The muzzle flash brightened the interior of the SUV. The bullet smashed out the back window and grazed Law's upper arm. It felt like someone hit her in the shoulder with a lead pipe. She lifted the hatch and slammed it down on his legs again, throwing all her weight against the panel. There was a muffled scream from within the Explorer and four more shots fired. Bullets whined over her head. Then there was stillness and the scent of blood filled the air.

*What the hell?*

Law risked glancing through the hatch's shattered window.

One of the bullets had ricocheted and torn through Andre's throat. Blood had sprayed the inside of the Explorer.

"Oh God, what a mess." She'd put men in the hospital before, but she'd never killed a man before. Technically she hadn't killed him; she'd just beat the snot out of him before he shot himself. She wasn't sure if the police would see it that way.

A shout and the sound of running boot steps made her realize that was the least of her worries. Andre's backup was arriving. They were going to be pissed when they saw his quill-filled dead body. There were four of them, lean and dark, racing toward her like a pack of wolves.

"We're so dead, Brizzy." Law heaved the Explorer's hatch door open and pulled the assault rifle from Andre's dead fingers. Her hands were still shaking from the effects of the spell. Blood was pouring down her left arm from where the bullet cut through her, making the rifle slick.

The lead elf suddenly went down as if clotheslined. The others jerked to a halt, weapons raised.

"It's the Death Wind!" one of them shouted. The remaining three drew swords and put their backs together. Law couldn't risk shooting until she knew where Bare Snow was.

St. John's church bells started to ring in midnight. They were seconds to Shutdown. Pittsburgh would return to Earth that had no magic. Bare Snow's invisibility spell would fail; she was about to become visible. The female elf probably didn't even know what the ringing bells meant.

Law shouldered the rifle and trained it on the males as she counted the chimes of the bell. One. Two. At twelve, she'd be able to fire.

Three. Four. Five.

It nearly seemed like time stopped as the bell rang. The swordsmen stood tense, waiting, knowing what would happen next. Their calmness infuriated Law. They had planned to murder Windwolf—perhaps already succeeded—and had lured Bare Snow halfway around the world to pin the killing on her. They were going to stand there as time ran out until Bare Snow was left helpless. They knew they had all the time in the world.

Six. Seven. Eight.

Somewhere toward the airport, someone was setting off fireworks. The distant thunder of the explosives was rolling up the river valley.

Nine.

The dogs howled a block away. Windwolf hadn't made the Rim. A maze of a large junkyard was between him and the McKees Rocks Bridge.

Ten.

One of the swordsmen suddenly fell as if his legs had been swept out from under him. The other two leapt to defend him, furiously hacking at thin air. Law saw the distortion of air that was Bare Snow. The female was lying on the ground. Had she been hit by a sword? Law pulled the trigger. The bullet caught the tallest male in the chest.

A moment later, the other two were on the ground, bleeding, possibly dead from Bare Snow's knives.

Which was a good thing as Law's vision started to blur at the edges from blood loss.

Brisbane waddled over to her, sniffed at the blood dripping on the ground and then stood on his back legs to press his front paws against her hip.

"It's okay, Brizzy." She leaned against the SUV. "Bad guys all dead. I'm going to fall down now." She slid down the side of the Explorer to sit hard on the ground.

Next thing she knew, Bare Snow was kneeling beside her, talking to her about something while bandaging Law's arm. She struggled to pinpoint something very important that they should be doing.

"Windwolf!" Law cried when she remembered. "You should go, find him, and make sure he's okay."

Bare Snow pulled her to her feet. "I will go once you're not out in the open, where you can be easily found. You've lost a lot of blood and there is no magic for a healing spell. You're going into shock. You need to lie down and be warm."

✧        ✧        ✧

Being in shock was kind of like being drunk but not as pleasant. There was a time of dark non-remembering and then she was lying on a floor in a dark building with no idea where or of how she had gotten there. At least she didn't need to vomit.

Gray of predawn was filtering through a massive multipaned window. Brisbane crouched at her feet, muttering happily as he ate something yummy. By scent, Law guessed it was the *saenori* fruit from the Explorer.

As she sat up, Bare Snow ghosted out of the darkness. She was wearing the blue sundress and cowboy boots, looking too beautiful for words.

"Law! You're awake. Oh, good, I was so worried."

"What happened with Windwolf?"

"He was wounded by the dogs, but he was saved by a very brave and clever young female. She's a wood sprite; they are very moral and resourceful."

Law scanned the auditorium-sized, filthy, empty room and realized that they were in one of the empty factory buildings in the Bottoms. They were probably less than a hundred feet from where the fight had taken place. Who the hell did Windwolf stumble into out in this desolated area? "You spoke with her?"

"Oh no! I was careful to keep out of sight. I kept watch until I was sure she was taking good care of him. Much better than anyone else could since we're on Earth. She lives in this little metal house with broken automobiles all stacked on top of each other."

She meant the junkyard. Now that Law thought hard, she remembered that the owner was a young woman and her older brother or cousin or something. They were said to be eccentric but good, honest people. In Law's book, eccentric was a good thing.

Bare Snow settled beside Law with a squeal. "Oh, it was wonderful! I wish you could have seen it." She clasped her hands over her heart and sighed deeply. "You should see the way that he looks at her. He sees her—all of her—and accepts her as she is. He's falling in love; I am sure of it. I wonder if he will ask her to be his *domi*. Wouldn't that be wonderful?"

It did sound wonderful. To be accepted as she was instead of pressured to change until she was a reflection of someone else's idea of right. Only that reflection wouldn't be her. Law would have been erased. There would be some empty shell of a person in her place.

"We can go home now," Bare Snow whispered.

"What about those men? Those males." Elf males weren't men; assuming that all Brousseau's people were ancient elves like himself. "The ones we killed. Are they still laying out on the road?"

"I disposed of the bodies," Bare Snow whispered even softer.

"Oh." Law waited for the guilty feeling to set in and it didn't. The bastards were out for blood; they deserved it. "Good."

"So," Bare Snow spoke barely audibly. Her hands were clenched into tight fists. "Can we go home now?"

*Home. Together.* Law's mind jumped to naughty thoughts and she blushed. A heartbeat later, Law realized why Bare Snow was so quiet. The female was really asking Law if she could move in with her. As much as Law felt she was alone in the world, it was nothing compared to Bare Snow's isolation. The elf was utterly and completely alone. Worse, she had bared all her secrets to Law. The tattoos. Her magical knives. Her assassin training. Everything her name hinted at. The name that made every elf that heard it turn her away. The name that made Bare Snow's grandparents disown her.

And the poor kid was afraid that now Law knew everything, that she would turn Bare Snow away too.

Law reached out for Bare Snow's hand. Part of her felt like she should warn the female about the barn and the Tarzan swing and the roof that leaked like a sieve and the winters in the cave-like milk house. But really, the ugliest, scariest part of Law's life was her inner avenging angel that liked to track down men and beat the snot out of them. Bare Snow met her and wasn't frightened by her. Crazy Lady might have randomly dialed phone numbers until Law answered, but she'd found two soul mates.

Besides, Law was fairly sure that Bare Snow was going to love the Tarzan swing.

"Yeah. We can go home."

# DRABBLE

*Fleeting Impressions*

1. Wraith Arrow had warned me that Pittsburgh was not Earth. I did not understand. It wasn't until we had crossed over the border on the train did I start to know what he meant.

2. I had not expected to hate Earth. I had always thought I wanted to be free of my ability. To be like every other warrior of my Hand. Five fingers moving in unison, not four and one jerked about by some random force. We are all taught to fight blindfolded. On the train through the Pennsylvania farmland, for the first time, I knew what it was like to be truly blind. And I didn't like it.

3. Earth was not what I expected it to be. I thought I knew what it would be like from Pittsburgh, but I did not know what being on stranded on Elfhome had done to the city. It was no longer a creature

of Earth but grown to be a hybrid. A true human city is a screaming loud, dirty, crowded, strange beast. All the human toys that I thought I knew how to work had been changed in subtle ways; I didn't understand how to use them anymore. I was angry with myself for having thought I could be useful without magic.

4. Humans have a fascination with the past that we elves do not understand. Is it because what came before was nothing but horror and enslavement? Because we have no golden age to harken back to? The American Museum of Natural History was like those houses of horrors that Pittsburghers like to stage at Halloween. Less bloody but equally surreal.

5. I was on a boat once in the Inner Sea when a sea dragon passed by. One moment there was only calm water and then something huge rose like a gleaming mountain and undulated past the boat. We were like ants on a leaf beside it. The wake nearly rolled us. Then it was gone. I put out my hands, felt paper under my fingertips and lifted up a cardboard box to find a child huddled underneath. Tears poured down her face; she'd been crying silently for long enough to wet her entire face. She gazed up at me in sheer horror. I'd never seen anyone so scared. And worse, I felt the echo that one dreamer has when they meet another that shares her world vision. She *knew* what was rising up before us. I felt like I was standing on the deck of the boat, watching the coils of something huge and deadly

rise up. I knew—no, I knew nothing—I merely felt the sudden fracturing of the future, that at this moment death could come hard and fast, or slow as drowning, and that all I could do was not draw attention to the tiny vessel I stood on. So I lowered that impossible box of invisibility down over her again, and told her to flee.

# PITTSBURGH BACKYARD
# AND GARDEN

❖⟩══ ⟨══❖

"Welcome to *Pittsburgh Backyard and Garden*. Today, we're tackling a common garden pest, the strangle vine." Hal Rogers grinned at Jane Kryskill's camera and motioned for her to pan right with the slightest tilt of his pith helmet.

"No way in hell," Jane murmured. She did not need eight years' experience of filming in Pittsburgh to know that a half-eaten deer did not make good ratings. It might be sensational news on Earth. It was, however, a fairly typical outcome when an Earth animal met any number of Elfhome carnivorous plants. Eighty percent of their Pittsburgh viewers would not be impressed, and the other twenty would call the studio the next day, pissed off that their dinner had been ruined by the sight.

Hal's grin tightened slightly as he continued. "The strangle vine is a dangerous plant to deal with as it's a master of disguise. It can produce up to five different types of foliage, depending on the type of

181

anchor it attaches itself to. It makes safely identifying this plant very tricky. Thus, it's best to investigate any possible outbreak with weapon in hand. Some people like a machete. Others, an axe. Personally, I like a flamethrower."

He whipped up the wand and gave his signature evil laugh. The cackle inspired the rumors that he had accidently killed someone on his previous show and thus his backslide to obscurity. She'd seen the videos. The only thing he'd killed was the ratings; he'd been bored silly doing curbside appeal remodels and it showed.

"This is a Red Dragon Flamethrower. You can get it at Wollertons on the South Side." Other places in town sold the same flamethrower, but they weren't sponsors of the show. "It comes with this wand with a squeeze trigger and this propane tank backpack."

Hal turned around to show off the ten-pound tank strapped to his back. "Simply turn this valve to *on*." He turned back, his grin widening with glee. "And apply a spark!"

Others might see Pittsburgh as a demotion, but Jane knew that Hal truly loved any excuse to wreak massive destruction. Where else could he routinely play with sticks of dynamite? Of course there was the small matter that his judgment was poor, hence the reason Jane had her job. She had been hired on originally to be nothing more than a glorified gofer. Hal had ignored, shot, or run over (figuratively and literally) everyone else assigned to the show until it was just Jane and her elfhound, Chesty.

Hal nearly took off his eyebrows applying the spark and blackened the rim of his pith helmet so it smoldered as he continued. "The six types of anchor plants that the strangle vine uses are the Elfhome Maple and Beech, the Wind Oak, the Silver Ash, Ironwood saplings, and root-bound Black Willows. For this reason, we advise viewers to clear these native trees from their yards if possible. Strangle vines will use Earth trees for anchors but can't mimic their leaves, which makes them easier to spot."

The yard was filled with native plants, thus Jane didn't notice the vine creeping closer to Hal until Chesty growled a warning.

"Check." Jane silenced the big dog by acknowledging the threat. She pointed at the vine attempting to snag Hal's ankle. "Careful."

"See you!" Hal cried and let loose an arc of flame at the tendril. It recoiled at stunning speed. He laughed again, sounding slightly demented.

Jane's camera chimed quietly as Hal chased the retreating vine across the yard. Locking the focus and the microphone on Hal, she tapped the phone icon. "Hm?"

"You do remember what happens after every Shutdown?" Dmitri Vassiliev, station manager of WQED, asked dryly.

"We all waste our time in a staff meeting as Hal derails brainstorming for new story ideas with suggestions on blowing things up."

There was a moment of silence as Dmitri came as close as he would to acknowledging that she was right.

She continued on with what probably happened at the WQED studios that morning while she and Hal played hooky to film a new episode. "I figure Network just about shit themselves with last month's stories that you dumped on them yesterday and spent all last night flooding our servers with conflicting demands because they couldn't do anything as logical as actually reading your summary first. I also figure that they had ignorant questions like 'why didn't we get any video of the royal wedding' or 'where were the still shots of the new princess in her wedding gown' and 'why did we send them a hundred photos of hoverbike racers covered in mud instead.'"

The answer was that there had been no "wedding" per se, as elves apparently didn't go in for that kind of thing, and the only photos of the bride were of her racing. They couldn't find a single picture where Tinker wasn't covered in mud, so they just sent them all.

"Someone did figure that out. Eventually." Which meant there probably had been several dozen patiently ignored e-mails before the light bulb went on at Network.

Jane laughed bitterly. "This is a large strangle vine in the backyard of an EIA desk jockey who has two little kids. He called his supervisor asking what to do about the half-buried deer under his tree, and his boss called Hal."

Dmitri huffed out as he realized all the vectors of the situation. The United Nations for some reason thought that clerical employees wouldn't encounter Elfhome's hazardous wildlife, so they provided no training on how to recognize lethal situations. The supervisor probably knew there were professional exterminators to handle things like strangle vines, but decided to ask Hal for help. For all his love of explosives, Hal was a political creature, honed by years of clawing through the ranks of network television to achieve in-front-of-the-camera status. That he insisted they tackle the strangle vine at dawn meant that the EIA manager was worth currying favors for—plus Hal would get to use his flamethrower. Lastly was that the lowly EIA employee wouldn't know to keep his children out of the yard until it was safe.

"How soon do you wrap up there?" Dmitri obviously was trying to sound casual while his blood pressure spiked through the roof. The meeting was long over, and Dmitri rarely reamed them out for anything short of setting someone on fire—which they hadn't done yet today—so why was he calling now?

"What else did Network drop on us?"

There was a too-long silence that meant she was going to hate what Dmitri said next. "Network wants us to provide a 'native guide' for a crew filming on Elfhome . . ."

"You want me to play babysitter?"

"No, they asked for a guide, they're getting you as a producer, and you're going to keep them out of trouble even if you need to hogtie them, which I know you're fully capable of."

"I don't do babysitting!"

"It's not babysitting, and you're very good at it, otherwise Hal wouldn't be alive now."

Chesty went to point on a strangle vine staging a surprise rear attack. Jane sighed. When was Hal ever going to learn that these things were more like octopuses than snakes? "That is debatable," she said as Hal went down with a yelp.

"Ouch. Is he going to be okay?"

"Probably." Jane backed up to where she had the tripod set up and a small arsenal of garden weapons and a fire extinguisher.

Hal rolled, cackling wildly, trying to bring the flamethrower to bear on the vine that had him by the ankle. Unfortunately, the plant was much larger than the homeowner had led them to believe. It jerked Hal up into the air even as he squeezed the trigger. He went flying into the tree, leaving a contrail of flame behind him.

"Shit." Jane grabbed the chainsaw.

"Oh, the viewers are going to love this one," Dmitri said and hung up, hopefully to call the fire department.

After Hal was packed off in the ambulance, Jane stopped in the Strip District to pick up supplies for the month. After a morning of fighting a giant man-eating plant with a chainsaw, she didn't want to talk to anyone, and certainly not Dmitri about some stupid babysitting job to some stuck-up New York City network idiots. It was going to be twenty-eight days of useless fighting back and forth until the next Shutdown proclaimed one of them a winner.

She silently loaded her cart with fifty-pound bags of rice, dried beans, coffee, and dog food while considering her choice in career. This wasn't what she thought she was going to do while growing up, but really she had stopped thinking about having a life when she was eighteen.

True, she had always loved filming videos, but it had never occurred to her that she could make money doing it. She had graduated from high school without a plan, vaguely thinking she'd do something like join the Pittsburgh police force or fire department or open a daycare. She lucked into the job at WQED and collided with Hal.

He'd pitched *Pittsburgh Backyard and Garden* to Dmitri as a remake of his network hit lawn-makeover show on a shoestring budget. In truth, though, it had been Hal's way to flee an avalanche of failure on Earth. The early local episodes were boring, mundane and ultimately useless to anyone. Hal zombie-walked through the episodes, sliding toward alcoholism. Jane had been assigned to be Hal's "production assistant" but what she'd really been hired to do was head off his self-destructive tendencies brought on by boredom.

Jane saw the need for change in the show—for Pittsburgh's sake and Hal's. Together they shifted it toward addressing the dangerous species of flora and fauna that crept into people's homes. It was important work. They saved lives at the risk of their own.

Of course they'd had to steamroll over their producer to do it. An imported New York City talent, the man just didn't understand Pittsburgh or how to stay in control of his minions. Her little brothers would have eaten him alive.

After they chewed through two more imported producers, Dmitri had promoted her into the slot. That was six years ago—and all six years they'd been the top show of Pittsburgh.

The checkout girl eyed the sawdust still clinging to Jane's blue jeans, the soot on her face, and the one lone leaf stuck in her braid. "Strangle vine, eh? They're bitches. Gave me nightmares as a kid. You know what Mr. Rogers says on *PB&G*?" She pulled a pair of pruning shears out of her back pocket. "Never go out unarmed."

*PB&G* was the locals' affectionate way of referring to *Pittsburgh Backyard and Garden*. The station ran

with the nickname and changed their logo to look like
a PB&J sandwich. The line was actually Jane's favorite
saying that Hal stole for the show. It reflected what
growing up in Pittsburgh had taught her. None of the
New York imports had ever been able to wrap their
brains around that. They used to mock her—quietly—
for always having a variety of weapons near at hand.

No way she was going back to that.

WQED was one of the three channels still in Pittsburgh, one-time proud home to *Mr. Rogers' Neighborhood*, which made Hal's last name of Rogers faintly
ironic. Originally part of the PBS system, they lost
their funding when the United Nations took control
of the city, which was a bunch of bullshit as most
of the population still considered themselves "Americans." However, since Pittsburgh was now under UN
jurisdiction, the residents only paid city taxes, not
state or federal. WQED currently was affiliated with
NBC since the local NBC station had been wiped
out in the first Shutdown. The other two local TV
stations hadn't fared much better; all three stations
were on equal footing. It was a lose-lose situation for
the television viewers.

As it was, the WQED studio in Oakland was nearly
razed by the Rim as it cut its way through parallel
universes. From space, it looked like a perfect fifty-
mile-diameter circle punched through reality. At street
level, the line wobbled oddly so you couldn't actually
use map and compass to plot its course. She wasn't
sure if it was because the orbital gate shifted over
time or if the Rim varied in thickness at different
points. Whatever the reason, WQED no longer sat

deep within the confines of city, but at the edge of the mile-wide field that was alternately used as a pasture, fairground, or airfield of the big living airships. One of the massive creatures currently floated above the grass, announcing that the viceroy was in town.

"No damage today," she told the studio's motor pool mechanic Juergen Affenzeller as he came out to greet her in the parking lot. She backed the production truck into its assigned space.

"Hey, Jane!" Juergen leaned in the passenger side to pat Chesty. Since he'd been introduced as a friend to the elfhound, he didn't get his face ripped off. "Saw the show. That was epic."

"Really?" He couldn't have seen today's filming but last week's show had been fairly tame for them. They tackled Earth's common poison ivy, oak, and sumac and Elfhome's death crown and bloodied lace, which were both deadly in a very sedate way.

"It was totally awesome! Yoyo Hal!" Juergen bounced up and down as an upright version of Hal falling repeatedly out of the tall wind oak only to be recaught and dragged upwards because he insisted on doing commentary in calm even tones. "It's important to note that a strangle vine can have as many as thirty-seven snare vines. Gak! You need to strike the base of the plant, its nerve center, to kill the strangle vine. Fuck! Never tackle one of these alone. Jane!"

She stared at Juergen in dismay. He'd seen all that? Live? Unedited? With all the embarrassing parts still intact? How?

The mechanic continued to act out today's filming. "And you. Rawr!" He mimed the chainsaw. "That rocked! And then Brian! 'Don't try this at home, hire a

professional pest control contractor.'" Brian was Brian
Scroggins, Pittsburgh Fire Marshal and accidental
guest co-host on a regular basis. "Just epic." She fled
the embarrassing recount, ignoring the belated "So
how is Hal?"

Dmitri was in the break room, stealing all the coffee. Jane would have avoided him otherwise.

"I need some of that." She leaned against the
doorway, waiting for the coffee and the questions.

He started a new pot of coffee brewing. "So?"

It was his way of asking all possible questions at
once.

"The fire is out. Brian isn't going to press charges.
Hal has a broken nose, a dislocated left hip, probably
a mild concussion—once again that damn pith helmet
saved him from anything serious—and first-degree
burns on his foot after his boot caught on fire. Nothing major but we're still out of production until his
face heals."

Dmitri picked up the insulated pitcher full of coffee and tilted his head in a "follow me" signal. "Oh,
didn't know you could dislocate a hip."

"It takes talent," Jane growled as she followed him
through the studio. It would get her coffee faster.

The office area was a kicked anthill of activity
with people on the phone and gesturing at each other
madly. Still, as Jane passed, people would nod and
sometimes cover their headsets to murmur, "Great
job, Jane" or "Great show, Jane."

"What? Was everyone in production with you?"
She clung to anger to tamp down on the hot blush
of embarrassment burning at her collar line, trying
to climb higher. She hated it when she ended up on

camera. It meant she lost control of Hal, which was quickly followed by nearly losing Hal.

Dmitri snatched up the morning *Post-Gazette* and waved it toward her. "Princess Tinker came home last night with the viceroy."

"I saw his gossamer out on the Faire Grounds."

"Well, she just tore the living hell out of Perrysville North, beyond the Rim."

"She what?"

"She strong-armed the EIA into providing bulldozers and dump trucks and started to build something."

"And we don't know what?"

"We sent Mark's crew out to the building site to see what they could find out." Mark Webster was WQED's reporter most fluent in Elvish. "The elves have not a clue; they're just blindly following orders. Apparently asking questions never occurs to them. One of the humans Mark interviewed claimed that they were building windmills out of pickup trucks. Ford F-250s. Another claimed that they're building some kind of supercomputer running on magic. A third said that Tinker kept saying it was something that sounded like 'infrastructure' but he's not sure he was hearing her correctly."

"So, we still don't know."

"We were reviewing the video, trying to guess." Which meant everyone *was* in production with him and had seen the live feed from her camera. Juergen was probably included because of the windmill/pickup truck angle. The entire office had seen her rescue Hal with the chainsaw.

Jane cursed slightly as the hot burn threatened to climb higher.

"You did a good job, Jane." Dmitri flung the newspaper

onto another desk as they passed. "Tinker invented hoverbikes that use magic to fly when she was twelve..."

"Thirteen," someone corrected him.

"Twelve! Thirteen! Who cares? The point is that she's a little mad scientist and the viceroy just gave her complete control of the city because he's in love."

Dmitri opened the door and gestured that she was to go in. He'd successfully distracted her enough that she'd forgotten about the "network surprise" until she was five steps into the office. There were two strangers sitting on his leather couch. Empty cups waited on the coffee table, explaining why he'd stolen all the coffee from the break room.

"I found the coffee, and your new producer." Dmitri shut the door firmly behind him.

"What?" Jane whispered fiercely. She had assumed that the "network surprise" was in the way of a memo, warning of a film crew's arrival during the following Shutdown. She didn't think that they were already in Pittsburgh.

The two men were polar opposites. One was a middle-aged Peter Pan, a schoolboy that never grew up, fair-haired, wiry build, and all grins. The other was a brooding wild man of dark hair and beefcake. Host and cameraman, probably in that order.

"This is Nigel Reid and...Taggart." Dmitri frowned as he realized that he didn't have a first name to stick on wild man. "They arrived late last night during Shutdown. Apparently they had visa problems at the border and were delayed. Almost didn't make it."

"Came across just before midnight, minutes to spare, like Cinderella." Nigel had a slight Scottish burr to his baritone voice. He beamed with the charisma that the camera loved but was pure hell to contain. People like him were sure that if they could just talk long enough, they could persuade anyone into anything. And normally, they were right.

"Apparently our news stories to the network preempted their attention as we didn't hear about your arrival until this morning." Dmitri found a stray cup, inspected it to see if it was clean, and then poured coffee for Jane.

Taggart was obviously the behind-the-camera guy, from his unkempt black mane to heavy five o'clock shadow. His black muscle shirt, worn blue jeans and hiking boots indicated he expected to hit Pittsburgh running and be out filming shortly after arrival yesterday, not holding down a chair in an office today. "We were warned that last Shutdown the viceroy had been attacked and was missing and that we might be walking into a war zone."

Jane snorted at the ancient news.

"It's complicated," Dmitri temporized. "Things are a lot more edgy here but so far, we're not at war with the elves, and we want to keep it that way." He indicated the spare guest chair, meaning he wanted Jane to sit. "This is Jane Kryskill, the producer of our top show, *Pittsburgh Backyard and Garden*."

"Backyard and garden?" Taggart leaned back, body language full of defensiveness that made lie to the vague query in his voice. Hopefully he didn't play poker with that many tells. "Nigel and I do award-winning nature documentaries all over the world. We've been a team for six years. I'd rather not add a third wheel to our machine."

Jane started to protest that the most dangerous

places on Earth wouldn't prepare a crew for Elfhome and then caught herself. If they turned her down, she was free. She spread her hands in a "what can I say" motion to Dmitri. "I'd be a third wheel."

Dmitri gave her a stern look. "They're yours, keep them out of trouble."

"Excuse me," Taggart started. "I thought I made it clear..."

"No, let me make it clear. You're going to be driving around with a great big truck that says you are our responsibility. The elves might not speak English but that NBC logo is fairly universal. If you screw up, every human in this building becomes a target. You've been dumped in my lap without any warning, so you will play by my rules, or so help me God, I'll have the EIA lock you up until the next Shutdown and boot you back to Earth with no chance for a visa approved ever again, understand?"

"I say, I don't think there's any need to..." Nigel started to bring his charisma to bear.

Dmitri stabbed a finger at him. "Shut up! The only thing I want to hear from you is 'yes, sir' and 'thank you, sir.' From now on, Jane is not just your producer, she is your god. You will not go anywhere or do anything without her knowledge and you will do what she tells you to. If you even try to fight with me over this, I will have you locked up until you realize that this is Pittsburgh, and you can't do anything you damn well please."

There was a knock at the door and Michelle Baker leaned in. "Jane, Hal is calling you." When Jane started to take out her phone, Michelle shook her head. "He's got your camera and he's broadcasting live."

"Oh, shit!" Jane leapt to her feet.

"Jane!" Dmitri snapped to keep her from bolting. "They're yours." He pointed at the two men. "Keep them out of trouble."

She cursed and went. Maddeningly, they followed. At least Nigel had the intelligence to wait until they were in the hall to ask in a very quiet voice, "Would he really have us locked up?"

"In a heartbeat," Jane said. She considered telling them about what had happened to the last person who hadn't taken Dmitri seriously. Then she realized that if they were locked up, they'd no longer be her responsibility.

Hal's mask of bruises had darkened to solid black purple from ear to ear. They hadn't cleaned the sap out of his fine blond hair, thus it stood up in wild spikes. He looked totally demented, making a great first impression on the two New Yorkers.

"What the hell, Hal!" Jane cried over the link. "How did you get my camera?"

"I told Johnnie Be Good the code to the truck's locker."

Johnnie Be Good was the slimeball of an EMT who had responded to the 911 call. She didn't trust him near her drinks at parties and she didn't trust him not to be stealing things off her truck.

"Hal! Damn it! Not again! Don't tell people that shit! You know what we have to do to change the fricking codes!" Actually it wasn't that hard, but she made up stuff so he wouldn't do exactly this. She continued while e-mailing a change order to Juergen. "And on top of everything, I'm going to have to come to the hospital and get the camera so no one steals it. You got me out of bed at 4:00 a.m. this morning, Hal. I want to go home, feed Chesty, and go to sleep! It's been a shitty, shitty day."

"They said I could leave if you came and picked me up." He dropped his voice to a whisper and pulled the camera closer. His pupils were little pinpoints. "The angry penguins scare me."

Jane pinched the bridge of her nose, trying to ward off a headache. "They've given you pain medicine, haven't they?"

"My state of medication does not make them any less scary. Tiny, angry little birds."

He was talking about the ancient catholic nuns of Mercy Hospital. They were one of the few things on the planet that actually frightened Hal. She suspected he would be even more cavalier about getting hurt if there was a hospital other than Mercy to go to in Pittsburgh.

"Please, please, please, please, please, please," Hal whimpered. "You've got the Fortress of Solitude. All those empty beds! *Please!*"

"Fine. You can stay at my place. I'll come get you." She slapped down her hand, cutting the feed.

The two men were staring at the display with surprise and amusement.

"Who was that unfortunate fellow?" Nigel asked.

"That's the host of *Pittsburgh Backyard and Garden*, Hal Rogers. We had a rough shoot this morning."

Taggart was clearly confused by the answer. Obviously he thought *PB&G* was a simple landscape show.

Nigel raised a finger in question. "Speaking of beds, where are we staying?"

✧    ✧    ✧

The two men trailed Jane to Ginnilee Berger's desk which was alarmingly clean, as in not only was the desktop cleared of every yellow post-it note, all the pictures of England and peaches-and-cream-complexion people were missing from the cubicle walls.

Jane caught hold of Louis Robinson, the station engineer. "Was Ginnilee fired?"

"No, she's on pregnancy leave. Has been for a month."

"She was pregnant?"

Louis stared at her a moment and then said, "Vespers."

She shuddered as unwanted memories tried to surface. "What?"

"You and Hal were off doing that show on vespers when we had the party for her. Yeah, she was like five months pregnant and planned to have the baby here so it would have Pittsburgh citizenship, but her ultrasound came back showing that the baby was breech. She had to go home; Mercy won't handle high-risk pregnancies for people with visas."

"Home? To England?"

"Yes. England. She'll be back—if she can work out a visa for the baby. She's hoping for joint citizenship, England and Pittsburgh, but it's unlikely."

"But who is doing her job until she gets back?"

"The intern."

"Where's the intern?"

"I think he went home too; it's summer break at the University."

"So who is doing the housing?"

Louis shrugged and backed away. "Not me."

Nigel looked slightly confused and concerned but Taggart immediately grasped the situation.

"So we don't have any place to stay?" Taggart asked. "Network said you would handle our accommodations."

"We would have if we'd had more than," she checked her watch, "fifteen minutes' warning that Network didn't do shit about preparing for your trip. Just to be clear, that includes not letting us know last Shutdown to prepare for you showing up yesterday."

Nigel jumped in to prevent a fight. "We tried checking into a hotel last night after we crossed the border."

"No luck, huh? Welcome to Pittsburgh. Strange thing about disappearing to another planet for a month at a time; really kills the tourist trade." What few hotels remained were booked solid in the summer months.

"We've just spent the last," Taggart paused to count back hours, "seventy-four hours in our truck, sitting in traffic, taking turns sleeping, pissing into a bottle. Three days."

She'd heard that getting across the border was hell on Shutdown. At least it wasn't winter. Taggart certainly looked like he'd slept in his clothes for three days. Nigel must have had a splash bath in the men's room and put on clean clothes.

"Doesn't the University and the EIA have people that stay just for the month?" Taggart asked with desperation in his voice. The man probably just wanted to fall over and sleep in a real bed.

"They have dorms," Jane said. She wondered if their morning of positive karma with the EIA could allow her dumping the two onto them.

"We can stay with you!" Nigel cried with the delight of a nine-year-old being told they were having a sleepover. "Your raccoon fellow says you have lots of beds. We're going to be working together. It would be so convenient!"

Taggart merely watched, knowing the persuasive powers of a TV host. He couldn't keep the smirk out of his chocolate-colored eyes. She really needed to get him into a high-stakes poker game.

"I have a really big dog," Jane said.

"Oh, I love dogs!" Nigel said with all sincerity. "And dogs love Taggart. It's his special talent."

Which apparently annoyed Taggart to all end, judging by the wince.

Housing was plentiful in Pittsburgh but not necessarily safe. They could pick any empty house and squat. Finding a safe place before nightfall would be tricky. She knew better than anyone what could be hiding in an abandoned space. The memory of vespers pushed into her mind and she shivered again.

"Okay, fine, but only for one night. Tomorrow we find you someplace to live."

She'd missed their production truck earlier because Juergen had it in the garage on some pretense so he could climb all over it and drool. Taggart had state-of-the-art cameras to go with it. Everything from battery life to resolution was all a hundred times greater than her camera. It put her ancient truck and ten-year-old gear to shame. Sheer jealousy made her want to kick the truck or something. She could see why, though, Dmitri assumed that they'd be driving the network vehicle all over Pittsburgh: her truck was too old to support their cameras.

The thing had a giant-sized logo of their affiliated network painted on its side as well as *Chased by Monsters*, which apparently was the name of their show.

"Award-winning nature documentaries?" Jane pointed to the show's sharp-toothed logo.

"It wasn't our first choice of names." Taggart obviously hated it.

Nigel, however, was a half-full kind of person. "The name isn't important, it's what we film that is. It is kind of catchy."

Jane didn't want to agree. She hated this sense of being railroaded into babysitting. It opened old wounds. She was going to have nightmares tonight for sure. "I have supplies in my truck that need to be moved to my SUV."

That required a careful introduction of Chesty. He was too well-mannered to growl at them but he gave the men a look that let them know he would cheerfully tear their faces off if Jane asked him to.

Nigel clapped his hands together in sheer joy. "An elfhound! Oh, how wonderful. They're on our list."

"This is Chesty. Don't move while I'm getting him used to you."

"Chesty? As in Lieutenant General Chesty Puller?" Taggart got points for seeming unfazed by having something the size of a bear sniff him over. Even the most avid dog lovers were unnerved by Chesty's size.

"Yeah. My dad was a Marine." He had been a scout sniper to be exact, but she'd found men to be unnerved by the fact. Actually, almost everything in Jane's life unsettled strangers.

Nigel obviously was restraining himself from a petting orgy. "He's a beautiful animal. How old is he?"

"He's seven. The elves say that he'll live to be about a hundred, but he's full grown." She took Nigel's hand and let Chesty know he was to suffer the touch. "Just because he knows you, doesn't mean he trusts you. You have to earn his trust."

"Like his owner's?" Taggart asked.

"I doubt you'll be here long enough for either one of us," she told them bluntly, but for some reason, it only made Taggart grin.

Much to Chesty and Taggart's dismay, she had the cameraman ride with her and Nigel follow in their truck. She had to keep them separated if she was going to keep them from running off and trying to film without her. From what she'd been able to observe, Taggart was the practical details person of the team.

Taggart put his back to the passenger door; either to keep an eye on Chesty in the backseat or to make sure Nigel was staying behind them. Both denoted a cautious outlook, which Jane approved of. It would make her job easier if Taggart was used to keeping Nigel in check.

"We'll see about getting you a place to live tomorrow," Jane said. "Any house that's unoccupied is free to anyone who is willing to take care of it. Its July, you won't have to worry about heating. The station can pull some strings to get you water and power. We watch each other's backs here." Hence the entire show this morning. They do a favor for EIA, and somewhere down the road, they could reasonably call in a return favor. "We're not going to let you screw things up and then drive away next Shutdown. We have to live here."

"Fine," Taggart growled as if it cost him to agree. "But it would be helpful to be caught up to speed. 'It's complicated' is bullshit."

It took her a moment to track back through the morning to find Dmitri's explanation of the current political situation in Pittsburgh. Okay, admittedly it was fairly sketchy.

"Okay, I'll catch you up but you'll have to be patient because it isn't simple."

She waited until he nodded in agreement before starting. She wanted to start laying ground rules of asking for cooperation and getting it. "Earth and Elfhome are parallel universes, mirror reflections with minor differences, the main one is that Elfhome has magic. Geographically they're identical. Recently the elves admitted that they could travel from Elfhome to Earth via a pathway through large cave systems."

"Yeah, we've always suspected something like that. All the legends we have of fae living under the hills."

"Lying is considered a major crime by elves, but not answering the question is an art form that they carefully cultivate."

"And apparently it rubs off," Taggart complained.

Jane ignored him. She'd scripted enough "how-to" bits that she knew that the key to understanding something complex required starting at the important facts that might seem basic but on which all understanding pivoted. "What magic does to the equation is that it superloads the DNA of all the native species. Basically everything on Elfhome could beat the snot out of its Earth cousin. We're genetically close enough to elves that we can interbreed, but they're taller, stronger and immortal. Chesty here will live almost twenty times longer than any Earth breed of his size."

"Do you mind starting with something I don't know? Like if the viceroy is dead or alive? And why he went missing?"

Jane plowed on with her explanation. "There's a third

parallel universe, with yet another mirror world, named Onihida, and it has magic. Its people are the oni."

He didn't startle as much as she expected and his next question explained why. "Whose theory is this?"

She dropped the big bomb. "Twenty-eight days ago, the oni made a very serious attempt at killing the viceroy."

"Wait!" There was the reaction she was expecting. He stared at her, eyes wide. Pure cameraman, though, that was the only body reaction to his surprise. Thankfully his voice made it worth everything, his normal rich near bass went all squeaky. "You mean they're *here*? In Pittsburgh?"

"Yes. Number unknown but possibly in the hundreds, if not thousands. Goal unknown, but obviously hostile to the elves. The elves have reluctantly also admitted that they had a running skirmish with the oni several hundred years ago. It started on Onihida, went across parts of China, and ended in the cave systems that lead to Elfhome. Or used to lead. The oni so scared the shit out of the elves that they blasted the pathways between Elfhome and Earth shut."

Taggart gazed out the SUV's windows at the city streets. Mercy Hospital was in one of the better areas of town since it lay protected on two sides by the river. All the windows had glass in them, the sidewalks were clear of weeds, and no wild animals were scurrying for cover. It could be any street in America. "I thought if the EIA was allowing people in, that the trouble had blown over."

Pittsburgh desperately needed supplies from Earth once a month. There simply were too many people and too little farmland for the city to feed itself, even in the summer months. It would have gridlocked incoming traffic completely if the EIA had tried to turn back everyone not transporting food.

Jane didn't point out that they'd downloaded all the information to Earth at midnight yesterday. The network had twenty-four hours to realize they were sending their people into a war zone and call them back.

Hal normally was excitable with a quirky sense of humor. On painkillers, he was manic and loopy. Most people thought Hal was funnier with all politically correct safeguard brakes stripped off and the engine running at full. The nuns of Mercy Hospital, however, were not among that number. If anything, "loathing" was probably an accurate word to how they felt about him. Over the years, they had abandoned all "family only" rules for Jane in order to facilitate her taking him away. As far away as possible. They had hinted that his returning to Earth—permanently—would be a good thing for everyone.

Today was no exception.

Mother Superior of the Sisters of Mercy herself was lying in wait for Jane at the foyer.

"You have to keep in mind we only can restock our supplies once a month. Frankly it always stresses our supplies of medications when Mr. Rogers is having a streak of bad luck. With fighting breaking out right and left..."

"Mother Superior, this is Nigel Reid. Nigel, Mother Superior is head of the nuns that oversee this hospital. Anyone attacked by a monster is brought here to be treated."

Which of course was all that took. TV hosts were kind of like napalm. You threw them at any major infestation and they cleaned out the area of all hostiles.

Nigel lit up as if introduced to Santa Claus. "Oh, how simply wonderful to meet you!"

Taggart caught what she had done and his eyes glittered with his smile. "That was pure evil."

"Judicious use of resources is always appropriate."

For reasons that she could never understand, they always put Hal in pediatrics, as far from the nurses' station as possible. It was possibly because it was usually the least occupied floor, or perhaps it was a statement on what they thought his mental age was.

He was standing on the window ledge, hospital gown flapping open in the back, as he waved her camera around.

"Hal! What the frick are you doing with my camera? Get down! And don't you dare break my camera!"

"Jane?" Hal glanced over his shoulder. His two black eyes made him look like a startled raccoon. "Jane!" he cried with joy and then realized he was holding evidence of his crime. "Jane!" And that he was currently mooning her. "Jane!" And in trying to hide the evidence while pinning the flaps of the hospital gown together, he started to wobble dangerously on the window ledge. "Jane!"

Cursing, Jane caught the wrist of the hand holding the camera and jerked him toward her. In what was an unfortunately well-practiced move, she pulled him into a fireman's carry over her shoulder. "I swear, Hal, I'm going to tell them to tie you to the bed if you pull this shit again!"

She delivered him to said bed.

"But there was this huge bird! It was bigger than me! Black like a crow! Wings this big!" He was attempting to show her by spreading his arms. She, however, was prying her camera free. "Ow! Ow! Ow!"

"You break my camera, and we can't shoot for two months. I break your hand, we can still shoot tomorrow."

"Letting go!" Hal cried. "Letting go!"

She checked the lens for scratches. Camera parts needed to be ordered from Earth. They'd have to wait until next Shutdown to order replacements and then another month for the lens to arrive. If he'd screwed up her camera, she was so going to kill him.

"I was just sitting here when this freaking huge bird came swooping out of nowhere." Hal was attempting to use his charisma to talk his way out of trouble, only because he was on drugs, he derailed quickly into incoherence. "At least I think it was a bird. Might have been a superhero. I am Batman! Only more like Hawkman—without the goofy cow." He meant cowl. He put his fingers to his head to make odd points on Hawkman's cowl. Obviously he hadn't seen himself in the mirror yet; he already was masked by deep purple bruises. "Cow. Cow. Mooo." He noticed Taggart for the first time and he went wide-eyed. He tilted his head, still making horns. "My God! You're Taggart with the unpronounceable first name."

"Yes, I am." Taggart rubbed at his face to cover a smile. "And you're Hal Rogers from *Pittsburgh Backyard and Garden*."

"I am." Hal slowly frowned as he tried to think through the confusion of the painkillers. He glanced about the familiar hospital room, the Boulevard of the Allies just outside his window with the Monongahela

River beyond the steep cliff. "This is Pittsburgh. What the fuck are you doing here?"

"I'm wondering myself," Taggart said.

Hal suddenly lunged at Jane and wrapped both arms around her. "No. You can't have her!" He hissed like snake. "Jane is mine!"

Normally she didn't think of Hal as a small man. His personality could fill a room to claustrophobic level, making him seem seven feet tall. In truth, however, he came right to boob-level on her.

"Hal!" Jane worked at prying him off her. "If you want to get out of here, you better get dressed, because I'm not taking you out of here with your ass flapping in the wind."

"What's he doing here?" Hal whispered fiercely.

"Get dressed!" She gave him a shove and turned around so she wouldn't be flashed as well as mooned. Although after eight years working together—and various plant-assisted disrobing and the subsequent ambulance rides—she'd seen the entire package more times than she could count.

"Does Dmitri know he's here?" Hal asked and then answered himself. "Of course Dmitri knows. Dmitri knows everything. He's freaking omniscient. That's just an act when he calls right in the middle of something amazing and goes *what are you doing?* like he doesn't damn well know you planned a glorious explosion. Just freaking glorious."

Hal was rambling on about his recent misadventure with high explosives. If Taggart weren't standing there, she would take advantage of Hal's drugged state and quiz him on that, because she still was trying to figure out where he got the C4. More importantly, if the source was going to supply him with more in the future.

The network cameraman was eyeing Hal over her shoulder with open surprise and dismay. "What exactly happened this morning? He looks like he's been flogged."

"We were victorious!" Hal shouted. "We looked that thing in all seventy-four eyes and burned out its heart!"

Jane sighed and pinched the bridge of her nose. So many things wrong in that sentence, she wasn't even going to try. God, she prayed that Nigel wasn't anything like Hal. "Right, let's get going. I want to get home before dark."

Technically she lived in Pittsburgh, but barely. The true city's edge was another mile or so north. Once the township of Coraopolis, the nearly unpopulated neighborhood, however, was one of the points where the Rim had migrated inward via invading Elfhome vegetation. What had been sprawling neighborhoods gathered around Pittsburgh International Airport were now collapsing homes among ironwood forest. The trees were still considered "saplings" but already towered a hundred feet over her driveway. The harsh sun instantly softened in a way that seemed magical.

Chesty jumped out his open window the moment she parked and started a perimeter patrol of the front yard. The cost of living so close to the Rim was that she had to be ever vigilant. Only after he'd made a full sweep of the front yard without signaling danger did she get out and take a deep breath of the green stillness.

Taggart slid out of her SUV and stood taking in her ancestral home in the sun-dappled forest. The massive stone walls. The turrets. The gables. "Wow."

"Welcome to Hyeholde."

"This is not what I expected," he said quietly, as if not to disturb the peace. "A castle? Here?"

"When my great-great-grandfather proposed to my grandmother, he promised her a castle. He never mentioned that they'd have to build it with their own hands. It took them seven years just to finish the West Room."

He laughed. "So you are a native guide."

"You can't get much more native without being an elf."

"Mine!" Hal cried from the backseat for the zillionth time since leaving the hospital.

"So, you live here alone?" Taggart obviously was asking if Hal lived with her.

"Yes." She hoped the brusque answer would stop any more questions, but she hoped in vain.

"Your family went back to Earth?"

"Don't ask personal questions." Jane added a glare so he'd get the point.

"She's got lots and lots and lots of family in Pittsburgh," Hal shouted. "And they all drive her nuts, so she hides out in her Fortress of Solitude."

"Shush, you." Jane considered duct tape for Hal's mouth. God knows what he might tell the New Yorkers. She keyed open her gun safe and took out her assault rifle. "Stay with the SUV until I've checked the house."


Her great-great-grandfather had built the castle to be a restaurant, so it had an industrial-sized kitchen. She'd opened it up into one of the smaller dining rooms to add in a small eating and living room space.

She got Hal settled on her big leather couch and assigned Nigel the task of keeping him there, one way or another. For the next hour as she squirreled away her supplies, fed Chesty and made a simple dinner, Hal ranted at hyperactive speed about his time doing network television.

She knew the pain medication was wearing off when Hal grew quiet.

When she paused to check on him, Hal asked, "Why are they here?" in a small miserable voice that sounded nothing like the normal Hal.

She opened her mouth to answer and realized that she really didn't know why the two were there. She'd been so caught up in trying to wriggle out of responsibility and taking care of Hal that she hadn't actually found out the details.

He probably hadn't asked Nigel because, despite the friendly banter, he didn't trust the man. The common thread of his stories, she realized, was that on Earth he'd been betrayed, and abandoned for more famous stars, by people he thought he could trust. Wives. Producers. And ultimately fans. Had he kept to old Earth stories in order to keep from playing up anything connected to *PB&G*?

"They've got a network show called *Chased by Monsters*, and Dmitri wants me to keep them out of trouble," she explained.

Hal frowned and looked at Taggart, who was now slumped in the matching chair, looking exhausted. "You're not here because Network is betting on a war?"

"Depends on who you ask," Taggart said. "Ask me, no. I'm never doing that again. I've had enough of the stench of blood. I wouldn't put it past Network though; certainly they suddenly green-lighted our show after months of having us on hold."

"Wait. What?" Jane had missed something important.

"Taggart is an award-winning war correspondent," Nigel said because Taggart apparently was modest and Hal was falling into a stupor. "Network probably okayed our show because it created a win-win for them. If there's a war, they have one of the best men trapped inside. If there isn't, they get what promises to be a hit show."

It suddenly made sense why Network hadn't warned Dmitri last Shutdown about the men's arrival and yet had given them a freshly painted truck. The decision had been made to send them after they'd processed WQED's last news dump, and then it was too late to send an e-mail to Pittsburgh.

Jane swore. "Bastards."

Nigel spread his hands slightly in a "what are you going to do" motion. "It gets us what we wanted, so we can't really complain."

"We've been trying to get onto Elfhome to film documentaries for years." Taggart scrubbed at his face. "The UN has a chokehold on information coming out of Pittsburgh. Most people wouldn't notice it. We notice because there's a huge black hole where things like wildlife documentaries should be. Jane Goodall's work produced sixty years of film. Jacques-Yves Cousteau alone had thousands of hours of documentaries. Oxford Scientific Films did four seasons on meerkats. What do we have from Elfhome in nearly thirty years? A whole new world with fascinating people, plants and animals? Zip."

"Maybe the networks don't think they'll sell."

Taggart snorted. "Documentaries are funded differently. Production companies like ours often fold their profit back into the next film, along with money from private investors, government grant money and philanthropists who have a special interest in the source material. Normally we make a film and then market off the rights to networks. It gives us creative control over what we do."

Nigel nodded along with Taggart's explanation. "We've had the money for the last three years, but our visa applications kept getting turned down. We just didn't have the clout to force them through. So we decided to see if a major network would have better luck—and they did."

"But you're stuck filming crap now." Hal snorted. "*Chased by Monsters*? Better be damn good at running."

"And exactly how do you get hurt filming a landscaping show?" Taggart retorted.

"If it can't kill us, we don't film it," Jane said, to stop the fighting before it could start. "There's a lot of dangerous flora and fauna in Pittsburgh and it doesn't stay beyond the Rim. It comes into people's backyards and sets up shop. We teach our viewers how to deal with it, but it means we have to actually get close enough to get hurt."

"Deal with, as in kill?" Nigel seemed flabbergasted.

"This isn't Earth. These aren't endangered species. This morning we were dealing with a very large strangle vine in a neighborhood with lots of children. There's no way to move it to someplace where it isn't a danger, especially while it's actively trying to kill anything that stumbles into its path. Pets. Children. Automated lawnmowers."

"That one is always amusing to watch but it always ends badly for the lawnmower," Hal said.

"Well, yes, the idea behind 'chased' is that we aren't hunting the creatures," Nigel said.

She remembered that they'd mentioned a list when they first met Chesty. "Which creatures?"

They had a list that made *Pittsburgh Backyard and Garden*'s fare look tame. She stared at it in horror. Half the animals were mythical—possibly—and certainly never seen near Pittsburgh. Did they have the pull to get them all the way to the Easternlands to find out? Humans were discouraged from leaving Pittsburgh city limits, with the exception of the train crews, who actually got to travel to the East Coast. The elves normally forbade humans from traveling to the other continents. Fame, however, opened many doors.

"What, exactly, did the network set up for you in terms of visas?" she said.

"Why?" Taggart asked.

"Many of these animals aren't native to the Westernlands." She scrolled down and a laugh of disbelief or perhaps fear slipped out. "Basilisk? Bigfoot?"

"We thought we should list all legendary animals," Nigel said, explaining—apparently without realizing it—why they had visa problems. "Can't hurt to ask. Dragons are real, right?"

"Elves say they are." Jane desperately wanted a Scotch, but if she had one, Hal couldn't resist having one, and she didn't want go back down that road. "This list is suicidal if you're not willing to defend yourself. This isn't Earth, where you can sit in your Jeep and take pictures of lions, or go sit in the middle of a bunch of apes. Most of these things will peel open a

SUV like it's a can of sardines and make a snack of everything inside."

"It would be amusing to watch but it would end badly for you," Hal murmured. It was hard to tell if he was making a play on his previous statement or if he didn't realize he was repeating himself.

"The list is a starting point." Nigel leaned forward, face lighting up with inner fire. "To get us in the door. What we want is all of Elfhome. To revel in all that it has to offer. The virgin ironwood forest. The beautiful immortal elves. The strange and magical beasts. And the humans that live peacefully side by side with all this."

Jane shook her head, trying to resist the power of a TV host beaming at her one-on-one. "Don't snow-job me."

"I've seen this kind of shit before," Taggart said with quiet intensity. "When a country goes dark, its means someone has something it's trying to hide. And often what they're hiding is horrible war crimes like mass graves and attempted genocide. Someone is keeping the media out of Pittsburgh."

The knowledge that there were people sharing her house, people whose safety she was responsible for, weighed heavily on her. It sank her into the murky waters of old nightmares, where well-founded grief blurred into something strange and nearly unrecognizable.

She bolted awake with Chesty nosing her face.

"I'm fine!" She pushed him away and sat up. Her alarm clock read six in the morning with the sky just lightening with dawn. Hal's soft snores invaded the normal quiet of her house. "I'll be even better when I get rid of all these men."

She stomped across the hall and pounded on Hal's door and got an "I'm up!" yelped in reply. She stalked down the hallway, shouting, "Daylight is wasting, ladies! Time to get up!"

She wasn't prepared to find Taggart already in the kitchen. Judging by the smell, he had made coffee and toast. He wore low-slung pajama bottoms and had been standing in front of the bank of televisions she'd set up so she could watch all three Pittsburgh channels at once.

He had dark curls on his chest that matched his long black mane, which only served to underscore her first impression of "wild man." Judging by his muscled abdomen, he visited a gym often in New York. She could also tell in a glance that she was very much into dark-haired wild men.

She opened her mouth to tell him to get dressed and nothing coherent came out.

He gazed at her with open worry. "Are you okay?"

"Just . . . just . . ." Needed to remember that she was extremely pissed at him for invading her life. "I had a nightmare."

He quirked an eyebrow.

"Lawn gnomes had taken Hal. I couldn't find him."

"Ah, so you don't really hate him?"

She was caught off guard by the question. "No! Why would you say that?"

"Friendship is a rare beast in our line. Most people only fake it."

"I don't fake anything."

"I'm starting to understand that." His gaze made

her blush because it seemed to suggest he was into tall blondes. Then again, most men were, at least at first meeting. Usually after they met her father's ghost, though, they realized that tall and blond only stretched so far.

"Tell me, who exactly is Tinker?" He nodded toward the televisions.

All three channels were covering the same story from slightly different perspectives. Jane swore as the details filtered in, painful in the familiar cadence, as if time had wound back eight years. *Vanished without a trace. No witnesses. Missing since yesterday. Jumpfish and river sharks made finding a body unlikely.*

"Oh, God." The cameras of the news crews picked out all the same trappings as when Boo disappeared. The police cars. The EIA river patrol boats. The family waiting on the shore for news. The only difference this time was that it was elves gathered into a protective circle. The viceroy's face was full of unbearable grief.

"You know him?" Taggart asked.

"Her. Tinker is a girl." Not much older than what Boo would be now, if Boo was still alive. "Everyone knows her. She's famous." Jane thought of all the photos of the muddy hoverbike racer that they had sent Network. In every one of them, Tinker had blazed glorious. Determined in battle. Joyous at her wins. Grinning even in defeat.

"I'm sorry," Taggart said quietly, and Jane realized that there was a tear rolling down her cheek.

"I don't really know her." Jane wiped at her face. "She's just eighteen; she's still just a kid." According to certain juvenile betting pools, Tinker had barely started to date before meeting the viceroy. "But

Pittsburgh is a small town. Everyone has dozens of points of commonality. My cousins are on her crew. My younger brother hangs out with her cousin. My mechanic's little brother is her best friend."

The impending ripple of grief moving through the city, touching everyone, made Jane's throat tighten up. She focused instead on the chaos on the screen trying to understand when and where Tinker had disappeared. Last Jane had heard, Tinker had been building something out beyond the Rim. How had she disappeared with all those people at her beck and call? She wasn't a first grader with five older brothers to distract everyone. Tinker might be barely five foot tall but her personality expanded to fill the room. Jane had noticed that any time she'd crossed paths with Tinker, everyone in the area had tracked her movement.

Maddeningly none of the three reporters were actually covering what had happened. Chloe Polanski hated working with a crew (and from what Jane had heard, the feeling was mutual) and used an eyepiece camera. Her shots were either close-ups of herself or confusing sweeps of the river. The woman was good for interviews but sucked when there wasn't a warm body to tear into pieces. Kimberly Shotts was going for the human-interest angle and her cameraman stayed focused on the viceroy. Only Mark Webster's cameraman was showing enough of the surroundings for Jane to get her bearings as to where the elves and humans were gathering. They seemed to be at the old Greyhound parking lot off of Second Avenue, about six hundred feet from the footings of the 10th Street Bridge.

Jane swore as Mark's camera showed the wreckage of Tinker's famous hoverbike in the emergency pull-off lane of 376, just feet from the Monongahela River. "What the hell did she hit?"

As if to answer her, the camera panned upwards to the Boulevard of the Allies at the top of the cliff beside Second Avenue. The drop from the highway above was straight down several hundred feet.

"Looks like she went off the cliff," Taggart said.

"Not by accident," Jane said. "She could make a hoverbike do anything. She could fly..."

Jane realized that Mark was showing the edge of Mercy Hospital. "Oh, freaking hell."

She scrambled to her camera charging station. She'd swapped out memory cards before stowing her camera in the truck. If Hal had actually recorded anything yesterday, it would be the only thing on the fresh card.

The first thing was Hal's "call" to the studio. She had missed out on him thanking her profusely for her promise to come and get him.

"Thank you, Jane. You wonderful, wonderful girl. A true goddess! You magnificent Valkyrie! I love you..."

She hit fast forward, swearing softly, as she started to burn with embarrassment because Taggart had followed her from the televisions.

"Is that your main camera?"

"It's our only camera."

"That ancient thing? I thought you were the top show."

"Welcome to Pittsburgh," she growled. The truth was that Hal killed too many cameras to let *PB&G* have the newer equipment, not that what Mark's crew were using could be consider state of the art. Jane paused as she found Hal's "big bird." Hal wasn't the best cameraman so it blurred in and out of focus. At first the scale was impossible to judge until a hover-bike suddenly soared out into the air near it. The rider and bike separated even as they both plunged toward the ground.

Jane gasped in horror. The rider was Tinker. Falling.

The black bird dove and caught Tinker in midair. Only did then the size of the creature become obvious. It was huge.

"What is that?" Taggart asked.

"I don't know. I've never seen a bird this big."

"Is it a bird?"

"I don't think it's a wyvern. Its wings look feathered. Wyverns are lizardlike with batwings."

"Are you sure?"

"There's a wyvern stuffed in the Carnegie Museum, just down the hall from the dinosaurs. Every other year in school we went there for a field trip because there's not much else to see in Pittsburgh."

Tinker thrashed in the bird's hold and then went heart-stoppingly limp. The black bird flapped away. Hal attempted to keep the bird in sight with zoom and things blurred in and out of focus again.

Swearing, Jane pulled the chip out of the camera and slotted it into her home video editor. She flipped through the frames until she found the cleanest shot of the creature.

"Does that look like a winged man to you?" Jane said.

"What exactly do these oni look like?"

"Tall. Strong. Red haired. No one said anything about wings."

"So there's another player in town."

Jane cursed, dropping F bombs, and she found the clearest picture of Tinker being caught by the winged man and sent it to her printer. "They're searching the river for her body and she never went into the water."

"Congrats on the scoop."

"Scoop, hell." Jane snatched the picture off the printer. "We're telling her family what really happened to her."

"Really?" He looked surprised and pleased by the news.

Jane pointed across the room at the center television where the camera dwelled on the viceroy's open grief. "He thinks his bride went into a river full of man-eating fish. If anyone should know that Tinker was still alive, it should be him."

It was like having two children in the car with her. Okay, one child and a young adult that kept backsliding. Hal was attempting to prove he was really only eight years old. Taggart could resist the taunting part of the time. Nigel was the senile grandmother who never noticed that the children were fighting. He sat in the backseat, smiling serenely at the passing landscape. What made things worse was that Taggart called shotgun so he could film through the front window. That made it so she couldn't reach Hal to swat him into silence. She found herself tempted to hit Taggart just because he was beside her. And because he'd changed into a dark blue silk shirt and cologne that smelled so good she just wanted to roll in it.

"I can kill us all," Jane growled, gripping the wheel tightly, and resisted the urge to drive the production truck into the ditch to prove her point.

Somehow they reached downtown without her killing anyone.

The EIA had Hummers blocking the on-ramp to 376 and then again at Second Avenue where it ducked under the Boulevard of the Allies. She avoided the EIA for the outsiders that they were. She cut up Forbes Avenue to the Armstrong Tunnels. There was a Pittsburgh police cruiser and a wooden barrier blocking the inbound lane. Luckily it was Bo Pedersen. He started to wave her away until she rolled down the window. The motion turned into a greeting.

"Didn't recognize the truck. What happened to yours? Hal blow it up?"

"I didn't do a thing to our truck, Bowman!" Hal shouted from the backseat, leaving out that he'd set himself and a good portion of the neighborhood on fire.

"He's still on pain meds," Jane said.

Bo laughed. "Yeah, I heard that Hal set himself on fire yesterday."

Hal started to say something. Jane held up a hand to silence him without looking. Now that they'd stopped moving, she could and would climb into the backseat to beat him. Judging by his quiet, he knew this.

"I need through, Bo," Jane said.

Bo shook his head. "The elves are on the warpath, Jane, and that means EIA is being pissy about who has access."

"Oh, Jesus, Bo. Just open the gate and let me through, or I'll drop Hal on you and let you babysit him."

"Hey, hey!" Bo backed away. "My wife's expecting. I'm going to be a daddy. You keep Hal."

"Congrats, Bo. Tell Patty to let me know if she

wants my place for the baby shower." The price of taking over Hyeholde was constantly being asked to host family weddings, showers, and birthday parties. Since every single party triggered old nightmares, she hated the invasions. Still, if offering up her house would get her through the tunnel, she would just have to suffer.

Bo's huge smile indicated she'd just made someone very happy. "Will do!" He glanced toward the tunnel. "I suppose since WQED is on the 'approved' list, I can let you in. Just be careful! Tie Hal down or something."

"Thanks! I just might do that." Jane waited for him to move the barrier and then drove into the tunnel.

"I take it you know him," Taggart murmured.

"His wife is my second cousin." Far enough out that Patty probably wouldn't have asked Jane but would be overjoyed at the invitation.

"Jane is related to everyone," Hal said.

"Not everyone," Jane growled. "It just seems that way. Most of the people who stayed in Pittsburgh after the first Startup did so because they had a shitload of family staying. My family on both sides has been here for hundreds of years."

"Anyone that she's not related to went to high school with her or one of her five brothers."

Boo would have started high school soon. No one would have the chance to sit beside her in class, write in her yearbook, or ask her to the prom.

At the end of the tunnel, Jane turned left onto Second Avenue and drove down to the parking lot. The elves were still clustered around the viceroy by the river's edge. At a safe distance were the human camps: the police, the EIA, and, of course, the news

crews. Jane really didn't want to park near the reporters. They were bored and looking for something of
interest. Taggart and Nigel were something new. If
she avoided the reporters, though, it would be like
blood in shark-infested water. She pulled in and parked
beside the WQED news van.

Leaving Chesty to guard the *CBM* truck, she got
out with her camera in hand. Hopefully she could get
to the viceroy without attracting attention. The more
people who knew that she wanted to talk to him, the
more likely she would be blocked by them. After the
news crews there were ranks of police, the EIA, and
the viceroy's guards.

Complicating her attempt was the fact that Hal,
Taggart and Nigel chose to trail behind her. Mark
Webster already knew everything about Taggart and
Nigel. He recognized their truck and waved in unin-
terested greeting. Kimberly Shotts was intent on filming the elves. She glanced over, saw Mark wave and
dismissed them.

Chloe Polanski, however, locked on target. She was
the type of person that gave reporters bad names.

"What are you and Hal doing here?" Chloe closed
on them quickly. "You're not news—unless you run
over your own cameraman."

"That was an accident," Hal said.

"Hal!" Jane tried to get around the woman but
Chloe kept shifting at the same time, blocking her. "It's
none of your business what we're doing here, Chloe."

"I want to know because I am news. What do you
two walking accidents think you're going to do? Help
kill river sharks?" There was a huge booming explosion and water fountained upwards nearly a hundred

feet and came raining down with dozens of silvery fish of all sizes. "Because the viceroy is doing well enough on his own."

"It's none of your damn business," Jane repeated, gripping her left fist tight. She normally didn't hit women, but normally women didn't need hitting. Chloe had been a bitch after Boo had disappeared, something Jane had worked hard to ignore at the time. She'd been under the mistaken impression that news coverage would actually help find Boo. All it did was make everyone in Pittsburgh think her mother was a horrible person, her mother included.

Chloe flicked her gaze down to Jane's fist and smirked. "What? Are you actually going to try and hit me? You do realize I'm filming this?"

Jane snapped her fingers over her shoulder at Taggart, trusting that he still had his camera in hand. "Film this. There, now so are we." She gave her camera to Hal. "Either get out of my way or I'm going through you."

"Oh, the college dropout is going to try and make me move."

"Was that supposed to make me mad? I've seen your interviews, Chloe; you can do better than that." Jane gave a "come on" with both hands. "You want to fight, we can fight."

Chloe smirked and shifted into a karate stance. Being that the reporter knew all about Jane's upbringing and high school sports medals, her confidence could only mean that she was even better trained.

For a moment Jane was sure that she was about to get her ass kicked but was equally sure that if she could get one good punch landed on Chloe's face, it would all be worth it. But then Chloe dropped out of ready stance and slid sideways, alarm filling her face.

Jane shifted, bracing for whatever third party was joining the "discussion."

One of the viceroy's bodyguards was suddenly in their midst, a tall female with her hair dyed the same color as the protective spells tattooed down her arms like Celtic knots. Anyone with half a brain cell skittered backwards, hands raised in the universal sign of being unarmed. The female elf was one of the *sekasha*-caste, a holy warrior thought to be perfect, and had the freedom to kill anyone that pissed her off.

"What's going on here?" the female snapped in English that sounded pure Pittsburgh.

"We have something that the viceroy needs to see," Jane said.

"It's important that I see it." The female held out her hand.

Jane reluctantly gave her the photograph of the winged man holding Tinker. There was no way she could fight her way past the female.

The warrior stared at the photo and then gave Jane a hard look. "If this is faked, I'll kill you myself. How did you get it? When was it taken?"

"I took it!" Hal leaped forward. "I was at the hospital." He pointed at his raccoon eyes as evidence. "And I was completely stoned. Still am slightly. Pain medication. Makes me all loopy."

"Hal," Jane cried, "you're going to get yourself killed!"

The female caught Hal's chin with her hand and turned his head this way and that. "You're the silly grass man."

"Yes!" Hal cried and then, "No! I'm not silly."

"Yes, you are," Jane growled. "Trust me on that. That's a single frame of a video he took while he was in the hospital."

"Why didn't you come forward earlier?" the warrior snapped.

"Because he was drugged, I thought he had only imagined a giant bird. I didn't hear about Tinker's disappearance until this morning. Once I realized that she went off the Boulevard right beside the hospital and that Hal had a clear view of that, I checked the footage. When we realized what it showed, we came straight here."

"We want to see this video."

Jane had never been this close to Viceroy Windwolf before. All the elves she knew were young looking; immortality made them practically ageless. Surrounded by his hardened warriors, though, Windwolf looked like a lost boy.

He took a deep breath and breathed out, "Oh, thank gods, she didn't go into the river."

"It's a tengu," Wraith Arrow, head of Windwolf's bodyguards, said. "An oni spy. Their masters made them from crows; they like to flock together. If there's one here in Pittsburgh, there's more. There's probably several watching us now, laughing at us."

"He appears to be drugging her." The blue haired female was the only one of the elves that seemed familiar with the concept of "camera" and had explained it in detail while showing the video. She'd stopped it now on one of the frames and zoomed in on where the tengu held something white against Tinker's face. "So she would stop struggling and be easier to carry."

The female advanced a dozen frames and then turned, holding up the camera to align it with the lay of the land. "He took her upriver."

"He probably was trying to get to the tree line." The viceroy's personal assistant, Sparrow, pointed out that the tengu was flying toward the closest edge of the forest without crossing the heavily populated section of Oakland. "Away from witnesses. From there he could have flown along the Rim and crossed back into the city where there're few humans."

Windwolf looked to the blue-haired female. "Discord?"

She looked, frustrated, down at the ground. "I don't know. This." She waved at the river. "This has always felt like a waste of time but short of racing blindly about, hoping for something to hit me, no. Nothing. Forgiveness."

"She's alive," Windwolf said. "That is what is important. And she is more useful to them alive."

The looks on older elves' faces said that death might be more pleasant than being at the mercy of the oni.

"The sooner we find her, the less damage they can wreak on her," Sparrow said. "We can cover more ground if we split into several search parties."

Having plowed through all three channels' news crews, it was no surprise that Dmitri called moments later. Jane winced at her phone's screen and glanced toward Mark's cameraman to verify that Dmitri was probably *watching* her as well.

"Hm?" Jane tried for innocent-sounding.

"What are you doing?" Dmitri asked totally deadpan.

"Omniscient," Hal sang quietly.

Jane snorted. Nothing supernatural about Dmitri's

ability when half the time they were beaming straight to the studio, just in case Hal managed to blow up the entire neighborhood. She explained about Hal filming Tinker's kidnapping.

"And you didn't think to share this with our news crew?"

"Her family had the right to know first," Jane said.

There was a long pause on the other side. "Jane, I know that you're going to want to help but you of all people can't."

"Why can't I?" Jane tried to keep her voice neutral but it came out cold and hard.

Dmitri sighed. "To make a long story short, because I said so. Do you really need the long story?"

"Yes." Her voice had gone colder and harder. Her father's voice when he was truly angry. Hal was retreating, quickly.

"I've tried several times to syndicate *Pittsburgh Backyard and Garden*. I know that the American audience would love it, but every time I get close to closing a deal, everything suddenly goes south for no reason. Nigel and Taggart told me yesterday about the troubles they've had getting visas to come in to film, so I checked with the other stations. They both have run into similar news blackouts. This *Chased by Monsters* got past whatever gatekeepers are blocking us. We need for it to succeed because so far it's going to be the only voice Pittsburgh has on Earth if the elves and the oni go to full-out war."

"You think there's enough oni here to start a war?"

"If the elves didn't want news leaking out, they'd be creating roadblocks for us here in Pittsburgh. EIA Director Maynard was handpicked by the viceroy and he's proved himself loyal. To keep you and Hal off American televisions, they'd simply keep you from filming. Everything we know about the oni suggests that they're getting to Elfhome via Pittsburgh during Shutdown. If someone is blocking us at network level in New York, it's the oni, not the elves."

"You really think the oni care if humans watch *Pittsburgh Backyard and Garden*?"

"This is about politics, Jane. The number of troops sent to support a peacekeeping effort could be influenced by the fact that thirty percent of all Americans recognize the name Hal Rogers and know the faces of a handful of Pittsburgh homeowners."

In other words, whatever they could get out, in whatever form, was actually propaganda.

"Tinker is not your baby sister. The elves will look for a thousand years if they have to. I need you to make sure *Chased by Monsters* is our voice on Earth. Nigel and Taggart only have visas for two months and then they have to take whatever they have and leave. If they don't have enough footage for an entire season, the whole thing is canned. Do you understand?"

"Fifty-six days, counting today, to do an entire season?"

"You're the only one that has any hope of doing this because you're only one with the right experience with the kind of shit Elfhome can throw at a film crew. I need you focused."

"Fine." She hung up on him just to salvage some pride. Fifty-six days. They would need to do approximately one episode every three days to meet the network's minimum. "Taggart, Nigel! Set up! We're doing a shoot here."

"Shoot what?" Taggart asked.

"You want to do river sharks and jumpfish. There." She pointed at the dead fish piled on the shore, the larger fishes cut open so their stomachs could be searched for the missing princess. "That's the entire ecology of Elfhome rivers."

"We were hoping for living examples..." Nigel started.

"We will get to those. Right now everything within miles is probably dead or stuffed. This is a once-in-a-lifetime shot. We'll get this now. *Now!*" She shouted to get them moving.

"Right." Nigel clapped his hands and turned to Taggart, who was already filming. "Here we are with an unexpected bounty. In one place, a full selection of all the fish found in the rivers around Pittsburgh. This massive example here is known as a river shark. They are believed to have evolved from an ancestor similar to the fresh water sharks of the species 'requiem' on Earth. Like their cousins, these sharks have round eyes and their pectoral fins are completely behind the gill slits, which normally are five in number. While Earth cousins are normally found in warm seas and mouths of rivers, the Elfhome river sharks have slowly worked their way the entire length of the Mississippi and the Ohio, an amazing one thousand, eight hundred and eighty-one miles, to find their way to Pittsburgh."

Nigel crouched beside the shark that dwarfed him. "While the largest of Earth's requiem sharks rival the Great Whites, Elfhome's river sharks are remarkably larger. This one here is nearly five meters long. The record here in Pittsburgh is an unbelievable 6.4 meters. What do these massive creatures eat? Let's see!"

In a move rival to one of Hal's, Nigel plunged his whole arm into the slit cut into the shark's stomach. He jerked back his hand wrapped in the pulsing glowing mass of a water fairy. "What do we have here?"

"Put it down!" Jane cried in warning.

"I'm trying to," Nigel said calmly, despite the wince of pain that flashed across his face.

"That's a water fairy." Hal whipped out his ever-present expandable grab-stick. Joining Nigel in the frame, he used the tool to pry the gleaming mass from Nigel's hand. "It's a distant cousin of the cuttlefish that has been crossed with a jellyfish. This one is just a baby, but still a sturdy little critter, despite its appearance."

"How poisonous is it?" Taggart murmured as the water fairy was peeled free to expose a massive welt on Nigel's hand.

"Not very. Keep filming." Jane headed to her truck for her first aid kit.

"Dmitri wants to know if you gave me a chip yet." Mark met her at the jersey wall. Chloe and Kimberly trailed in his wake, hoping to glean what they could. "What chip?"

"This one." She thrust the memory chip at him and kept going. Kimberly paused, unsure which of them were the hotter story.

Chloe kept pace with Jane. "Jane Kryskill, you're the camera woman of *Pittsburgh Backyard and Garden*."

"Field Producer," Jane growled her official title, which Chloe probably damn well knew.

"You're working with award-winning war correspondent Keaweaheulu Taggart."

Did everyone in Pittsburgh but Jane knew who the hell Taggart was? *Keaweaheulu?* What kind of name was that? It sounded nearly as bad as an untranslated elf name. Jane ignored Chloe and unlocked her truck. She needed to get back to Nigel before his hand swelled up to the size of a baseball mitt.

"How is it that he's here on Elfhome with footage of Princess Tinker being kidnapped? Did your network have foreknowledge of this? How did your network know to send an award-winning war correspondent this Shutdown?"

The questions started to sound damning when left unanswered. It was almost lunch time, which meant Chloe might be broadcasting live, giving little opportunity for damage control by the channel managers.

"Our network knew nothing about the kidnapping until it happened. By dumb luck, Hal Rogers happened to witness it and get footage. Surely, all your viewers know Hal and his dumb luck. Taggart is not here as a war correspondent."

"Then what's he doing here?"

"Trying to get eaten!" Jane turned to face Chloe square on. "Taggart is here is with world-famous naturalist Nigel Reid to film a network show called *Chased by Monsters*. They want to film Nigel coming face to face with Elfhome wildlife and hopefully surviving the experience." She let her sarcasm drip through since most Pittsburghers were slightly disdainful of newcomers. "If any of Channel 5's viewers hear of any monsters in the Pittsburgh area—other than reporter Chloe Polanski—please let us know."

They ended up drinking Iron City Beer and eating blackened river shark and grilled water fairy in the Neighborhood of Make Believe.

"I didn't realize you could eat water fairy." Jane had been dubious as Taggart carefully grilled the skewered pieces over the charcoal grill in the studio's parking lot. She wouldn't let him feed any to Chesty until he'd proved it wasn't fatal by eating some of the tentacles.

"Both cuttlefish and jellyfish are common street food in East Asia." He waved his beer to take in the surrounding sets of fanciful puppet houses. "Can't believe I'm drinking beer in the Neighborhood of Make Believe. It almost feels blasphemous. King Friday's Castle. The Museum-Go-Round. The Platypus Mound."

"The Platypus family was why I become a biologist." Nigel was eating left-handed as his right was still swollen from the water fairy sting. "Dr. Bill Platypus and Elsie Jean and little Ornithorhynchus Anatinus."

"I thought her name was Ana," Jane said.

"It was Ana for short. Her full name was an injoke. It's the Latin scientific name for platypus. I identified with them at first because they were Scottish, like me, and then because they were so not like anyone else." He pulled up his pants legs to show off the fact that both his legs were artificial. "Like me. I wanted to know everything about platypuses. And then to understand how unique they are, you have to understand the rest of the animal kingdom. One thing led to another and, voila, Dr. Nigel."

"The only egg-laying venomous mammal on Earth," Hal said. "God knows what the hell their cousin is like here on Elfhome. Can you imagine?"

"Have the elves even been to Australia?" Taggart asked.

"Not that we can tell." Jane tapped on the table beside her tablet to draw their attention back to why they were at the studio in the first place. "Focus. We need to figure out what we're shooting tomorrow. I've got all the monster tips that were sent to the station. We take the most mobile first, any warg or saurus sightings, if there's any. Then work down by mobility."

Taggart lifted his eyebrows in question to what she meant.

"Black willow and will-o-wisps are slow moving and will be in the same general area for a couple of days. Last on our list will be completely stationary creatures. Steel spinners. Strangle vines."

"They're also most common." Hal read off his lot of the tips. "Strangle vine. Strangle vine. Spinners."

"Loch Ness?" Nigel said. "Elfhome has a Nessie?"

The viewer had spotted "something huge in the river" from the I-79 Bridge. "What the hell was he doing down there?"

"What do you mean?" Taggart asked.

"Oh, I-79 is practically a road to nowhere since it's right on the Rim. Oh, it was right after Startup. He was coming home."

"A Loch Ness sounds promising," Nigel said.

Jane shook her head. "No. He probably saw two sharks close together or just one really big shark. We don't need more sharks for now. Besides, anything in the river is going to be hard to find and bloody dangerous since we'd have to beg, borrow, or steal a boat."

"That would be fun," Hal said.

"No!" Jane snapped. "We'll do spiders before river monsters that may or may not be there."

"Gossamer?" Taggart said.

"What?" Jane held out her hand for the tip. The caller pointed out that no one had ever been able to coax the elves into a close look at their living airship. "Now that has merit. I'll see if Dmitri can get us onto the viceroy's gossamer."

"I can call the homeowner from this morning," Hal offered. "He and his boss owe us."

"The viceroy owes us," Taggart said.

Not that their video had led to Tinker being found. Jane had checked for updates on the search all day. The EIA confirmed rumors that Windwolf had sent word to his cousin, the queen, requesting for royal troops to help find his bride. The Pittsburgh Police were asking for people to avoid known deserted areas. The updates accounted for everyone involved except the oni. It made it seem as if everyone in Pittsburgh was battling an invisible giant.

Jane put the gossamer tip aside. "Okay, that goes near the top, pending permission from the elves to tour the viceroy's airship."

"Oh, I can try out my call," Nigel said.

"Your what?" Hal asked.

"Gossamer call." Nigel got a shy, embarrassed grin. "We've spent the three years of waiting for visas on researching everything known on Elfhome. The oddest thing was that the most comprehensive videos on Elfhome are a series of animated shorts by a strangely secretive production company known as Lemon-Lime JEl-Lo."

"Actually their name is the only thing anyone knows about them," Taggart added.

"Animated?" Jane wondered if she had heard them wrong.

The grin got even shyer. "The videos use a fairly crude method, blending modeling and CGI work, but they're hysterical. Each is about ten minutes of pure farce but the storylines interlock creating a very detailed world. The thing is, if you check their facts, they're spot on."

"What you can check," Taggart said.

Nigel nodded. "Which loops us back to the idea that all information about Elfhome is being strictly limited. One of their videos mentioned a gossamer call and indicated that it was ultrasonic in nature."

"What exactly is a gossamer call?"

"What they'd discovered was if you analyze video tapes of the gossamers arriving and leaving Pittsburgh, you can isolate the ultrasonic commands that the elves use to control the living airships. They've also pieced together information that any creature bioengineered with magic—such as wargs—have similar 'call commands' embedded at an instinctual level."

A month ago, Jane wouldn't have believed it was possible, but then the undeniable evidence had surfaced that the elves could manipulate DNA at fantastic levels via magic. "They had enough information to build one of these calls?"

Nigel's grin went from shy to incandescent. "I can't wait to try it out."

Jane made a note to herself to steal Nigel's gossamer call before they toured the viceroy's airship.

"Oh! Oh!" Hal cried. "A saurus!"

Secretly she was hoping that they wouldn't get any tips on saurus sightings. With Hal, the filming was fairly simple: find it; kill it. They would pad the footage with how to tell if a saurus was in the area, the type of guns needed to successfully drop the big lizard, the dangers of bringing too small of a gun to the fight, the merits of such tactics as shooting from second story windows or tree stands and any other bullshit they could think of.

Nigel and Taggart, though, probably wanted to do something stupid like film the saurus without trying to kill it first. Things could get messy fast.

"Where was the saurus spotted?" Jane hoped the location was near the Rim where the T-Rex's Elfhome cousin might wander back off radar.

"Dormont," Hal said.

"Dormont?" Jane said. "That's nearly downtown!"

"It says Dormont," Hal read. "Sleepy Hollow Road. Where old Mount Lebanon golf course used to be."

Jane took his tablet to read it. The tip had been sent by "Beef4U." The name sounded slightly pornographic and juvenile. Was it a joke? "That's Castle Shannon."

"Another castle?" Taggart asked.

"It's a town," Jane said.

"Was a town," Hal muttered.

She pulled up a map to double check her memory. "Yes, for some reason the early settlers in this area all wanted castles. Castle Shannon was a farm that grew into a town."

"Pittsburgh never lets go of the past," Hal continued to mutter. "You get directions by what used to be there. Castle Shannon is mostly empty row houses."

Nigel sprang to his feet. "We go now?"

"No!" Jane cried. "It's already dark."

"It would be very atmospheric," Nigel started for the door.

"Sit!" Jane barked and pointed at the chair he just vacated.

He wavered and glanced to Taggart.

"You're hurt. I'm drunk." Either Taggart was a lightweight or exaggerating, as he was only on his third beer. Jane always kept count of other people's drink so she knew when to shut them off. She had thought Taggart would be good for at least four beers before hitting "drunk." "Hal is on pain killers. It's dark out. And there's a fucking war brewing. Jane is right. We finish setting up a shooting schedule, get another good night's sleep and start out at dawn."

They transferred everything she thought might be useful from *PB&G*'s production truck to the *CBM* truck. It would be a week until Hal's face healed enough that they could film, so they could focus first on the network show. They hadn't resolved the housing issue except to verify that no one in the offices was actually handling those duties. She really didn't have any choice but to take the men home again.

It was ten o'clock when they left the offices, a full fifteen hours since they left her house, but it still felt like she was slacking. Part of her soul wanted to be out looking for lost little girls. Even if Tinker were found, though, her soul wouldn't be satisfied. She would need her Boo back for her to be at peace and the nightmares to end.

As she pulled out of the parking lot, she turned on the radio and tuned to KDKA. Her cousin Sean was doing the news before leading into his show on local fusion music. Their video clip of the tengu was still the headline story. Pittsburgh Police had set up a tip line for anyone who might have spotted a black winged man flying over the city. Director Maynard of the EIA reported that he had requested additional

troops during Shutdown. As Dmitri pointed out, the
United Nations would have to approve the request,
influenced most strongly by the United States. Sean
repeated the news that Windwolf sent for royal troops.
Once again, everyone in Pittsburgh was reporting in
except the oni.

Sean transitioned to commercial with "You're listening to Sean Roach on KDKA."

Taggart chuckled quietly. "He's using the name
Roach? Seriously?"

"There's nothing wrong with Roach," Jane growled.

"They're cousins," Hal sang from the backseat.

"Your cousin's name is Roach?" Taggart said.

"Yes, my Uncle Bill Roach is a very successful
businessman. All his kids are business savvy."

"And they stayed here in Pittsburgh?" Taggart asked.

"New York is not the center of the universe," Jane
said.

"I didn't say it was. In fact I don't really like
New York." He stared out the window at the forest
to the north of the city as they drove down Bigelow
Boulevard. The streetlights went up to the Rim and
stopped abruptly. Beyond it elf shines drifted over
the dark canopy, a million earthbound stars. "I like
quiet and solitude."

"Mine," Hal grumbled quietly in the backseat.

"What is that?" Nigel leaned forward to point
through the windshield.

She glanced to see where he was pointing. They
were crossing the Fort Pitt Bridge. Downriver was a
glimmer of lights moving in the dark water below.

"Water fairies," Hal said. "Lots of them. I've never
seen anything like it."

It was probably the most dangerous section of road in Pittsburgh. Five lanes of traffic fed onto the bridge from three directions and had approximately five hundred feet of road-planning insanity to merge to two lanes into the tunnel or take the off-ramp to the river-hugging Route 51.

During the day, Jane wouldn't have thought about stopping, but traffic trickled to a halt at night. She checked her rearview mirror. There wasn't any other traffic following them. She put on her flashers and stopped at the center of the bridge.

"Stay off the road," she warned.

A large truck rumbled across the inbound deck overhead.

They scrambled over the jersey wall to the sidewalk and set up tripods for the night shooting. The mass of water fairies flowed inexplicably closer, coming upriver.

"We could go to the Point," Hal murmured in the darkness beside her. He pointed across the water at the fountain set in the wedge of concrete that marked where the Mon and Allegheny River flowed together to create the Ohio River.

Jane shook her head. "It would take us fifteen minutes to drop down to 51, swing across the West End Bridge, come back across the Fort Duquesne and get into Point Park. Another three or four minutes to walk through the park and set up."

"We could U-turn—there's room enough and—" Hal started.

"Hal, last time I listened to you, I nearly lost my license. No!"

"If they go up the Allegheny, we'll miss them," Hal said.

Nigel suddenly blew a loud piercing tri-toned whistle.

It made Jane jump and swear. "What the hell?"

"Am I supposed to hear it?" Hal asked. "I thought it was ultrasonic."

"It has four tones. Only one is..." Nigel started to explain.

The last of his explanation was lost under a deafening roar, seemingly in answer to his whistle. It was stunningly loud. The deep rumbling noise echoed off Mount Washington, making it impossible to pinpoint the exact origin.

Chesty leaned out the window of the truck and growled.

"What the hell is that?" Taggart asked.

"I don't know." Jane peered into the dark. The glittering school of water fairies darted suddenly to the left and flowed up the Allegheny River. There was another roar and it seemed closer. Louder.

"You think it might be the Nessie?" Nigel asked.

"What the hell is the Loch Ness?" Jane said.

"The most popular theory is that it's a plesiosauria, about the size of a sperm whale."

"Shit!" Jane cried. The last thing Pittsburgh needed was a huge river monster.

Nigel blew his whistle again. The answering roar from the dark waters sent shivers down Jane's back.

"Nigel!" She snatched the whistle from Nigel's hand. "What the hell are you thinking?"

"That we get a picture of whatever it is." Nigel's tone indicated that he had no clue why she was angry.

"Is that it?" Hal was leaning far out over the railing to point at something arrowing through the river, coming at them at alarming rate. It seemed comfortingly small—barely a dozen feet in length—until Jane realized that she was just seeing the creature's head. There was another wedge behind it, easily adding thirty feet to the creature. Suddenly the forty-some feet that the bridge deck was from the river's surface didn't seem far enough.

Chesty had gone full-throttle warning snarl.

"In the truck." Jane reached out and jerked Hal back. A second later, electricity flared in the water like a Tesla coil discharging, outlining a massive crocodilelike body. The monster was nearly fifty feet long from nose to tip of tail. "Truck! Truck!"

"How wonderful!" Nigel cried. "Shouldn't we be filming this?"

"Too dark." Taggart shoved him into the backseat, earning Jane's love. "We'll film it tomorrow!"

They cautiously looked for the river monster the entire next day, careful not to stray too close to the water's edge, with Chesty on watch. Jane kept hold of the whistle and refused to let them use it.

"We could call Nessie to us," Nigel pointed out many times.

"No!" Jane kept shouting back.

Taggart finally broke the pattern. "Can you at least explain why?"

Jane growled. God, she hated being outnumbered. This was like riding herd on her little brothers, only worse because "I'll beat you if you do" wasn't an acceptable answer. "First rule of shooting a show on Elfhome." She grabbed Hal and made him face each of the two newbies so there was no way they could miss the mask of dark purple bruises across Hal's face. "Avoid getting 'The Face' damaged. Viewers don't like raccoon boys. Hal is out of production until the bruising can be covered with makeup. We've got fifty days and a grocery list of face-chewing monsters to film. We have to think about damage control.

"Second rule!" She let Hal go and held up two fingers. "Get as much footage as possible of the monster before you kill it. People don't like looking at dead monsters if you don't give them lots of time seeing it alive. Right now we have got something dark moving at night in water. No one has ever seen this before, so we can't use stock footage to pad. We blow the whistle and it will come out of the water and try to rip your face off—violating rule one—and then we'll have to kill it and thus break rule two."

"Sounds reasonable," Taggart said.

"Would we really have to kill it?" Nigel's tone suggested he equated it to torturing kittens.

"If it's trying its damnedest to eat you? Yes!" Jane cried. "And if we just lure it out of the river right now, without some way to keep that from happening, we will have no other option. Until we know which of the three rivers this thing is in now, even setting up a safe perch to film from is going to be a waste of time. We don't have time for this. I can get people to keep an eye out for it and call us if it shows up."

She had Hal too well trained to argue with her. Nigel looked to Taggart instead of her.

"I think Jane's right," Taggart said. "Our end goal is to get enough great footage that we can get an open pass to Elfhome. We haven't shot anything but water today."

Nigel nodded reluctantly. "Okay, let's do the saurus tomorrow."

❖    ❖    ❖

It came as no surprise that her nightmares had gotten worse. Between Tinker's kidnapping, the lack of any progress at finding her, and quiet sounds of someone else in her house, she had no hope. At three a.m., she slipped out of her room and padded down to the kitchen to find something to drown them out.

There was light on in the kitchen. It was in an odd place. She paused to feel Chesty standing beside her, not growling, before swinging the door the rest of the way open.

Taggart was holding her refrigerator's door open, studying its contents, wearing only his low pajama pants.

"Do you not have shirts to sleep in?"

"Actually, no." He eyed her milk as if there was something strange about it.

"It's fresh."

"I've never seen milk in a glass bottle before."

"I get it from a dairy down the road. It's easier for them to recycle glass bottles than plastic."

"It's like I've gone back in time." He poured the milk into her smallest saucepot. "Do you have any sugar and cocoa I can put into this?" As she handed him her sugar bowl, he explained his lack of shirts. "Network wanted us in L.A. first before coming to Pittsburgh to do pre-production work. Design the logo, hire on the people that will be doing the graphics for titles and end credits. Mostly what we spent the month on, though, was having it drummed into us that we were going to film monsters. The bigger and more fantastic, the better. Then we flew to New York to drive to Pittsburgh—and half my luggage didn't make it."

"Ouch."

"Luckily it was just my backup boots, some extra

pairs of jeans, and," he motioned to his bare chest, "the shirt I sleep in."

"We do have clothing stores." Jane put the cocoa on the counter beside the saucepot. "We can get you something tomorrow evening after filming."

"Thanks. Sorry about waking you up." Then reluctantly he added, "I have bad dreams. If I go back to sleep, it's like I just hit pause when I woke up."

"Been there, doing that. You didn't wake me. I've got my own little demons."

He did his eyebrow quirk, which was stunningly sexy since he had the most striking eyes she'd ever seen.

She found him a teaspoon to keep from blushing. She grew up with a small testosterone-driven army, but never had to deal with man alone in her kitchen, half-naked, in the middle of the night. At least, not one that wasn't related to her.

"I have five younger brothers." She stumbled for an explanation.

"Hal said something like that."

"Yes, well, what Hal hasn't mentioned is that I had a baby sister too. When I was eighteen, she was six."

He realized the implication and his face filled with sorrow for her. With the look, all the raw grief that been building up the last few days seemed to expand to fill her. Feeling like her heart was about to explode with the anguish, she found herself talking.

"My dad died when I was twelve. My brothers were ten, eight, six, four and two." Not that she had their ages memorized for that year alone; it had always been simple to figure out. "I'm not sure what the hell happened in June, but every other March, regular as clockwork, my parents had a baby."

Taggart nodded while mixing sugar, cocoa and a splash of milk into a dark paste. The fact that he continued to make hot cocoa, albeit in a very odd manner, made it easier to spill out her grief.

"I'd always spent a lot of time watching my brothers, but after my father died, it was like I became the dad. Mom had just had Boo and needed to be the mommy, so I took care of everything Dad used to do. Cut the grass. Fix things that got broke. Teach my brothers how to run and climb and shoot and fight. I didn't really mind it. It was just how things were. I didn't know anything else."

He stirred the paste in the hot milk. She realized that he'd made enough for two people. She got out two coffee mugs and set them down on the counter. As if she'd opened up floodgates, the words kept spilling out. There was something comforting about the dim kitchen, the quiet of the night. For once, not being alone was a blessing.

"My brothers. It was like they had a death wish, and every time I turned around, I had to fish them out of the river or cut them down from a strangle vine. Boo was smart. She was curious as a cat but she'd always get someone else to do stuff for her. She'd be there in the thick of things but she was never the one stuck and screaming."

He poured out the steaming cocoa, dividing it neatly, and then turned to wash out the saucepot.

"The summer that I was eighteen, our freezer quit working. Here in Pittsburgh, you have to have a freezer, especially with eight people in the family. You shoot a deer. You catch a shark. You butcher a cow. You can smoke some of the meat, but the rest, you have to freeze it or it will go bad. The thing is, they're harder than hell to get. There's one little appliance store down in the Strip District, just a hole in the wall. Every Shutdown they get one truck full of things—washers, dryers, refrigerators, hot water heaters—and there are only one or two freezers per month. You can put money down and order one in advance and wait two months. Or you can be the first person in the store as they unload the truck. Mom didn't want to be out the money and have to wait, so she decided that we'd go into the Strip District the night before Shutdown and just camp there until a truck came in and we'd get one. You know all the 'could have' and 'should have.' She still tears herself apart blaming herself. She could have ordered the freezer. She could have left us all at home. She should have left Boo with my aunt. It just eats at her. It eats at all of us."

"What happened?"

Jane lifted her shoulders. "We don't know. One minute Boo was there, with us, and then the next, she was gone. All the delivery trucks trying to get into the Strip District, unload and get out of the city before they get stranded on Elfhome. It's a crazy time."

"Been there. Done that."

"The police thought at first that maybe she went to the river's edge. We told them that she wouldn't do that. She was too smart. Then they thought maybe she tried to get home. We'd come all piled in my mom's pickup but there were other times we'd come in on the light-rail. We were all sick of being stuck in the Strip District, waiting for the big trailer to be unloaded down to the freezers. But she was about the only one of us kids that wasn't whining about going home. It was the first time she'd been in town for Shutdown. All those different trucks all being unloaded, some of them right there in the street. Whole families carrying everything into their stores fast they could. She was fascinated.

"And then, the police suggested that maybe she'd gotten into one of the empty trucks. At least, that's what they said in front of me and my brothers. And then they took my mom quietly aside and said what they really meant. That one of the truckers took her.

"That got the EIA involved and they stopped all the trucks that had deliveries in the Strip District that hadn't crossed the border already and searched them.

"You know when they first disappear, you're angry. You told them just to be good, stay close, and not get into trouble and now they're nowhere in sight. You look and you look and you look—just so angry you could hurt someone—and you're rehearsing what you're going to say when you finally figure out where the hell they are. Then slowly this fear takes root, and starts to grow, and you try so hard to hold on to that anger, because it's so much safer than the fear.

"But it leaks away and all there is left is fear. And then that goes away too, because you know, whatever horrible thing that was going to happen has happened. It's over. It's done. It can't be undone. And you walk around feeling like a big hollow drum with no idea how you're supposed to feel."

The hot cocoa was the best she'd ever tasted, hinting that Taggart had spent many sleepless nights perfecting it. Her dreams for the rest of the night were unsettling in a totally different way and featured a wild man with chocolate-colored eyes.

The tip from Beef4U had specified the old Mount Lebanon golf course. Jane hadn't been back into the area for years, so she had expected to find it overrun with possibly dangerous brush. She was surprised when they arrived in the early gray of dawn, to find the grass looking regulation height.

"What the hell?" She pulled to a stop to peer out over the lush rolling green. She was driving her SUV with Nigel following in the *CBM* production truck. "Don't tell me someone actually still plays golf."

"Wouldn't surprise me." Hal surprised her by volunteering to ride with Nigel, but based on the chatter over the voice-activated headsets, they were bonding over a mutual love of flora and fauna.

Taggart was in her passenger seat, smelling good enough to eat. She never met anyone that could be so distracting without saying anything. He was wholly focused on filming.

Something moved in the fog. She tensed. They couldn't be so lucky as to spot the saurus immediately—could they? The answer was no, as the forms resolved into cows grazing lazily.

She swore softly. "Shit. 'Beef4U.' A damn farmer sent in the tip."

Taggart laughed, his voice dipping down almost to bass.

Jane snorted out in disgust. "Okay, the good news is spotting the saurus just got a hell of a lot easier. Plus we've a ton of free bait."

"The bad news?" Taggart asked.

"Smart boy. Cookie for knowing that there's bad news." Jane eased her SUV across the worn dividing line to drive along the berm. "Bad news, Pittsburgh beef cows are the meanest son-of-a-bitches."

"So, we have to dodge several tons of pissed-off sirloin while filming one hungry dinosaur?"

"Welcome to Pittsburgh." She drove slowly along the converted golf course. "Keep an eye out for oncoming traffic."

"What are you looking for?"

"Tracks."

The farmer had gone to town on fencing, putting up eight strands of barbwire to create a six-foot wall around the golf course. Jane suspected that Beef4U was trying to keep animals out as well as in. Considering that wargs were a growing problem in the area, she couldn't blame him for trying.

"There!"

She automatically jerked back to her side of the road and then realized that Taggart hadn't spotted an oncoming car but a monster. He had his camera already trained on the massive creature poised to attack.

"Oh! That's where that went," Jane said.

Truth was sinking in on Taggart. "That's . . . not real, is it?"

"No, that's a proper T-Rex. Saurus are more velociraptor in shape, although just about the same size. I think that's from a miniature golf course that was like ten miles away. Yes, this is Sunset's stuff. There's Skull Mountain and Batman. I wonder where they found the pirate ship. Oh, God, they've got the dragon den statue from Sandcastle!"

"Pittsburghers love castles."

"It's an abandoned water park down on the Mon River. They couldn't keep the water fairies out. And yes, we do; it's part of the American dream." She was going to drive past but realized that Nigel had pulled into the parking lot. "What are they doing?"

"Oh, we can't pass this up." Taggart motioned for her to go back. "It's far too surreal. This is what we came to film. The real Pittsburgh."

"This makes us look like redneck nutcases." Jane backed up so she could pull in behind the production truck. Nigel and Hal were already out, gesturing at all the statues visible from the parking lot.

"We've got to get this, Jane!" Nigel cried as she and Taggart climbed out of her SUV.

"All right." She waved to get them to keep Hal from chiming in. They only had a vague tip on the saurus and so far they hadn't seen any sign of one. Certainly the cows seemed unconcerned and the fence hadn't been breached. Most likely the putt-putt was as safe as any other place in Pittsburgh; which was to say, only somewhat harmless. "Set up so the T-Rex is in frame and you can do basic biology comparisons." She turned to Taggart. "Keep an eye and ear open. I'll be in the truck."

She would have liked to put Chesty on guard duty, but he would only guard her. Elfhounds were very loyal to a very small set of people and she'd never been able to get him to include Hal into that unit.

Because she and Hal killed their show's subjects every week, often with fire, they used the production truck to make sure they had good footage before fully engaging the creatures. After the actual fighting started, whatever they got, they got. They'd also learned that while a smoking body afterward rarely made great material, it was worse to come back the next day and discover that predators had found the corpse.

She flicked on screens and put in an earpiece to link her with Taggart and Nigel. "I'm set."

Taggart had a perfect frame already. Nigel waited until Hal got a light reflector in place.

Nigel stood a moment in profile, looking up at the T-Rex looming over him and then turned toward the camera. "No more than this statue can capture the true essence of a dinosaur can our cameras convey the primal silence of this place. We're standing in the heart of the displaced zone on a Saturday morning. At one time two million people lived in this area. A sunny day, like today, would have heralded thousands of lawnmowers growling to life. Cars coming and going to one of a dozen malls. And across the street, people would have been lining up to tee off. Cows graze there now. We haven't seen another car for half an hour. All there is to be heard is the rustle of the wind through the trees."

*Hopefully just wind,* Jane thought.

"This miniature golf place stands *almost* abandoned. Someone is keeping the grass trimmed. There's clubs and a bucket of golf balls and a sign that reads 'play at your own risk.' Someone has added 'be careful of the water trap on third hole.' This place stands as a monument to what is quintessential Pittsburgh. The people of this city adapt and go on."

Jane was impressed that Nigel had managed to take in all those details since they'd arrived. Judging by the torn earth around the dragon statue, the owners of the park had only recently looted the abandoned water park in Homestead and dragged it halfway across town. Apparently, there was enough interest in the putt-putt to improve it but not make it a viable business.

"This fellow is Earth's Tyrannosaurus, or T-Rex. He was a theropod dinosaur, which means he's bipedal, or walks on two legs. He's been extinct for sixty-five million years. We are here today seeking something very much alive. The Elfhome saurus.

"This distant cousin is very much like this fellow here. The saurus grows to a massive forty feet in length from nose to tip of tail, and fourteen feet high at the hips." Nigel raised his hand and demonstrated that if his knuckles were the dinosaur's hips that the saurus would be considerably taller if it straightened up from its running stance. "This effectively doubles its reach. And unlike the T-Rex, the Elfhome saurus has very functional forelegs that can reach and grasp."

Nigel lifted his right hand slightly.

"Done?" Taggart asked.

"Done," Nigel said. "For now. I could talk for hours about the saurus but it would only be worth it if we catch one on film."

"How was that, Jane?" Taggart asked.

She checked lighting and sound. "It was perfect."

"I want to do the water trap." Nigel pointed past Mario and the mushroom castle of the second hole. The moat of the castle extended out into a small pond with stepping stones out to an island that acted as the tee for the third hole. The cup lay somewhere on the shore beyond the larger-than-life Batman standing guard on the flat roof of an old-fashioned police station.

"What do you think is in there?" Taggart filmed the water trap on the third hole.

"The mind boggles." Jane eyed the murky green water on her monitors. "The most dangerous things are in the river, not ponds."

Hal pulled out his grab stick and gave the water an experimental stir.

"Hal!" Jane barked.

"I'm being careful." For Hal, these were often famous last words.

"Just stay out of the water and keep back from the water's edge," she ordered.

"We could just throw a stick of dynamite in," Hal said. "Just to be sure."

"We don't have any liability waivers signed, so no dynamite."

Taggart gave a bark of surprised laughter. He was getting hauntingly beautiful shots at amazing speed. The nearly abandoned golf course in the early dawn light seemed luminous and yet achingly sad through his lens.

"Hush, you," Jane grumbled, feeling mildly jealous. She wanted to be outside, filming too, but time didn't allow for that.

The men carefully picked their way around the water trap to where rooftop Batman stoically guarded the cup.

Nigel reached up to pat the statue's foot. "The stories you could tell."

And hopefully they wouldn't add any new interesting ones today.

Nigel leaned against the miniature police station and grinned with boyish glee. "It's really starting to hit home. I'm on Elfhome. I was eight when Pittsburgh suddenly vanished from Earth. It was like Christmas.

The first Startup was in the middle of the night and we woke to a changed world. I remember how all the television channels for days played endless footage of the forest that sprang up without warning where the city once stood. How completely and totally dumbfounded the world was on how to explain what had happened. And after the first few hours of the wall of trees, the stories of the strange and wondrous animals rampaging through the suburbs that remained on Earth. For me the most amazing were the two saurus that made it to the Monroeville Mall parking lot . . ."

Jane saw a movement in the background. Something big and black was charging down the hill behind the Batman statue. "Cow!"

"What?" Nigel asked as Hal took off running, reflector held over his head.

"*Cow!*" Jane shouted again.

A big black angus bull came thundering toward the men, who scattered in all directions. Jane swore as she realized that the loose bull could only mean a break in the fence, which meant something had taken the eight strands of barbwire down. Worse, Taggart and Nigel weren't heading toward the safety of the trucks. They looped around Batman with the bull chasing them.

The idiots didn't understand that the bull wasn't the real danger.

"Stay!" She gave Chesty the command to keep him out of her line of fire. Snatching up her weapons, she charged from the production truck. She ran toward the water trap, shouting as she ran. "Nigel! Taggart! Stop looping!"

Taggart shouted, waving his arms to get the bull's

attention as Nigel scrambled up onto the roof with the Batman statue. Once safe from the bull's charge, Nigel yelled and kicked at the passing bull, trying to lure it away from Taggart.

"No, no, no. *Incoming!*"

Jane flung the stun grenade ahead of the bull and then ducked down, hands on her ears. Even with sight and hearing shielded, the explosion was a loud brightness on her awareness. The bull staggered backwards, disoriented by the light and noise.

Luckily, Taggart still had his combat reactions. He'd shielded himself from the blast. Unfortunately, he still seemed flabbergasted into inaction. "What the hell was that?"

"It's a flashbang."

Taggart swore, uncovering his ears. "I know what the hell it is! Why?"

"Because I can't shoot the damn bull without having to pay for it! Get to the truck!" She pointed toward the production truck. Hal knew the drill; he was already clambering into the back.

"Nigel?" She turned to order the Scot down off the low roof.

A saurus loomed over the Batman statue.

"Nigel! Down!"

"Huh?" Nigel hadn't shielded himself from the stun grenade. He was blinded from the flash. He clung to Batman's arm and shuddered like a worm on a fishhook.

"Down!" Jane grabbed Nigel by the leg and yanked him down.

The saurus struck even as Nigel came tumbling down onto Jane. She shouted in wordless dismay as she saw the massive head lunging downward at them as she and Nigel slammed onto the ground, all elbows and knees. The smell of rotten flesh blasted over them on the saurus's breath.

Nigel twisted and kicked at the mouthful of daggerlike teeth. The jaws snapped shut on Nigel's foot and the saurus jerked him upward, off of Jane. For a moment, all she could do was watch in horror as the saurus gripped Nigel in its claws and tore his foot from his leg.

*Feel the fear, but don't be it, Jane! Feel the fear, but be Jane, and Jane can kill anything that crosses her path.*

She scrambled up, swinging her rifle off her shoulder. Nigel was in the way for a heart shot, so she aimed for the wide left eye. *Hold your breath. Squeeze.*

Even fifty caliber wasn't strong enough to move the massive head. And like a beheaded chicken, the damn lizard didn't know it was already dead. Something misfired in its brain enough, however, for it to open both claws and drop Nigel. It was all Jane needed. She unloaded the magazine into the saurus's chest.

The massive beast staggered to the right and then toppled with a heavy thud.

Her ears ringing from the gunfire, she reloaded and then caught hold of Nigel and dragged him back, keeping her rifle aimed at the still monster. Nigel's booted foot stayed beside the dinosaur even as she pulled him to safety.

"Hal! Call 911!" she shouted. "Get an ambulance out here."

"No, no, I'm fine," Nigel said weakly. "Just a few scratches." He had parallel furrows on his back, seeping blood. He tried to sit up and she pushed him down.

"Lay still!" Jane jerked off her belt and slapped it around Nigel's thigh and twisted it tight. There was surprisingly little blood. No blood actually.

"Jane. It's all right." Nigel gave a weak little laugh. "I don't have feet."

"What?" Jane cried.

"I was born without all the bones in my legs. The doctor amputated them at the knee when I was baby. I've never had feet."

Right. She knew that.

It was a typical *Pittsburgh Backyard and Garden* production in terms of content: angry creatures trying to eat them, explosions, screaming, yelling, occasional gunshots, and eventually a dead monster. The actual saurus attack was gorgeously filmed. A true professional, Taggart had locked back on Nigel moments after the flashbang had gone off and kept focus on him despite the fact that he could have been filming the man's death.

Jane comforted her pang of jealousy in the knowledge that Taggart had only been able to get the footage because she was dealing with the saurus. If she and Hal had an actual crew, they could get shots just as good.

"It's good!" Jane reported to the others. "Let's film a closing."

Nigel's wounds had been sanitized and bandaged but he opted to put the torn shirt back on to wrap up the episode. He thought it counterbalanced the "very dead" state of the saurus, and Jane had to agree. The men set up to film. With Nigel sitting on the ground beside the massive head and the foot it had torn free, they started to film.

"This is not how I wanted this segment to end," Nigel said. "Considering the alternative, I'm happy to be alive, thanks to our brave and wonderful producer, Jane Kryskill."

Jane blushed hotly. She would have to edit that silliness out.

"Unbelievably, this is an adolescent male," Nigel continued on a more professional vein. "The elves say that saurus typically live about a hundred years, which makes them fairly short-lived for an Elfhome species. This male is probably ten years old and would have reached full maturity around fifteen. That's lucky for us, since if he was an adult, he probably would have had a mate and up to a dozen young nearby."

There was an odd noise over the microphone and after a few seconds, she recognized it. A police siren echoed off the hills as the squad car raced toward them. Had someone actually called the cops on them?

"Hold up, guys. We're getting company."

A few minutes later a Pittsburgh Police black-and-white came down the road, braked hard when it spotted their trucks in the parking lot and came up the driveway at a cautious speed.

Jane went out to meet it, careful to leave all her weapons in the truck.

The responding officer was her best friend, Brandy Lyn Pomeroy-Brooks-Abernethy, which could be a good thing or very bad. Brandy had grown up with a burning desire to be Wonder Woman, complete with golden lasso and bullet-deflecting wrist guards. She'd settled on policewoman as the nearest thing, much to the dismay of Honorable Lissa Pomeroy, her grandmother and Pittsburgh's only judge. Brandy gave out tickets to anyone that pissed her off, friend or foe, on the theory that it made it easier to find out who her true friends were. At any hearing, the offenders would find themselves locked in a legal battle between Judge Pomeroy and Brandy, as if it were a contest for Brandy's soul.

Thus Brandy was the only cop in Pittsburgh who would arrest Hal and anyone else rather than ask for an autograph.

"Hey, Jane. We got a call that a war was breaking out. Are you okay?"

"We're fine. Things got a little hairy, but I've got things handled."

Brandy looked at the *Chased by Monsters* truck, then at Jane, and then back again. "Is Hal okay? I heard he set himself on fire the other day."

"He's fine. Network just has us working on this show for a few weeks."

Brandy eyed the *CBM*'s sharp-toothed logo and shook her head. "What do they think you are? A Monster Hunter?"

"Yeah, that's just about right."

Brandy caught sight of Taggart. "Spend all day filming that? Your life is so hard." She noticed then Nigel's bloody, one-foot condition. "What the hell happened to him? I'll call for an ambulance."

"No, don't!" Jane waved her down. "The scratches look worse than they are and he's got a spare foot in the truck."

Brandy's face went to neutral. "A spare?"

"Yeah." Jane felt giggles coming on. It had been a stressful hour. If she laughed, though, Brandy would go into Wonder Woman mode and arrest them all.

"It's supposed to come off like that. We'll just pop the other one on."

Brandy put her hands on her hips and glared at Jane. "You didn't shoot any of the cows, did you?"

"We haven't touched the cows!" Jane covered her mouth to keep the giggles in. Technically, they hadn't *touched* the bull. "I shot the saurus; many, many times. We're just wrapping up."

There was the rumble and snarl of a big diesel engine, and a half-ton Ford pickup came growling up the road. It turned into the drive and stopped behind the police car. For a moment, the truck seemed to have no driver. Then the driver's door swung open, a set of steps unfolded, and a tiny old woman climbed down out of the truck, muttering obscenities the whole way. She looked like she was several inches under five feet tall, seventy pounds wet, and close to a hundred years old if not over it. She slid a cattle prod out from behind the pickup's seat before walking over with a gait that belied her age.

Jane didn't know the woman but Brandy did.

"Hi, Grandma Gertie," Brandy said.

Oh, this was famous Grandma Gertie Betts, and she was over a hundred years old, having been born in the late 1920s. She'd been slowly annexing large sections of the South Hills to her farm, producing everything from apples to zucchini. She didn't have any children but a horde of adopted "grandchildren" that helped her run her various businesses.

"Well, God damn it, you could have fucking told me that you got my fucking e-mail!" Gertie came to glare at Jane. "If I'd know it was *PB&G* down here, making all this fucking noise, I wouldn't have called the fucking police!"

*Note to self*, Jane thought, *make an effort to swear less. I so don't want to grow into this woman.* "We're sorry. Thank you for the tip."

"I would have shot the fucking thing myself but it's always such a hoot to see Hal be Hal." Yes, all stories of Grandma Gertie fully indicated that she would. If nothing else, there were two rifles on the gun rack in her pickup. "You two didn't smash up anything, did you? This is Hal we're talking about."

Jane considered a moment. Normally they did do property damage but today they'd been fairly conservative. "No. We didn't damage anything."

"Good. It's been a pain in the ass to get some of these hauled in from all over Pittsburgh but it makes a nice place for all my kids to come play."

Brandy escaped, leaving Jane to fend with Grandma Gertie. Jane in turn handed her over to Hal to keep busy while they finished shooting. Unfortunately the tiny woman reminded Hal of the nuns of Mercy Hospital and he kept sending Jane pleading looks to rescue him.

Once they wrapped, she rescued Hal with an auto-graphed official WQED slickie on the show.

Jane escorted the old woman back to her pickup. "Thanks again for the tip. New York gave us a very tight schedule which we'll only be able to keep if we can find subjects to film."

"I'll tell my kids to keep their eyes and ears open." Gertie slid the cattle prod in behind the seat and used the stepladder to climb the several feet up into her pickup. "But now, I've got a bull to find and chase home."

There was a little troll doll in the shadows of

Grandma Gertie's dashboard, slyly grinning at Jane. The sight of it made Jane's heart go heavy and sink. She was about to pull back when the other details sunk in. The troll doll was wearing a little Viking helmet.

"Oh my God! Helga!" Jane snatched up the doll. There was a black smudge on the upturned nose and the cascade of white hair was dirty and ratty, but it was Helga. On her bare toes were the touches of purple paint for nail polish. Jane could barely breathe. "Where did you find her?"

"Those troll dolls used to be popular way back. I never saw a Viking girl before though."

"Where did you find it?" Jane shouted.

"I didn't find it, it found me." Gertie touched old thin fingers to the doll. "A few weeks ago I gathered up a herd of the kids and took them all to Sandcastle to get the dragon. I didn't think anyone would be there and everything would be free for the taking, but there were a bunch of people squatting there, using the swimming pools as fish tanks, although God knows why. There's been plenty enough fish in the river since we took to visiting Elfhome. We pulled the ride apart to get the statue and took it. Sometime in the confusion, the doll slipped into my truck."

For first time in her life, Jane abandoned Hal and her schedule. She wanted to head straight to Sandcastle, but her father had trained her too well to go alone. She raced after Brandy, knowing that this close to lunch she'd stop at the only food place still open.

McMicking's was a little deli at the Arlington light-rail stop. It was actually two tiny houses built on trailers. Ellen ran a tightly stocked deli and lunch counter out of one while she slept in the other. She made her store mobile just in case business became too poor she would be forced to move. Arlington was her third location. She had started at Library and worked back toward Pittsburgh, keeping to the light-rail tracks.

Brandy was perched on the hood of her squad car, finishing off a bowl of Ellen's famous pumpkin and spinach curry over jasmine rice.

Jane waved the troll doll. "Look! Look!"

"Yeah, I see it." Brandy twiddled her fingers in a "give me" sign. "It's a doll. An ugly doll. Use your words. Tell me why it's important."

"Boo had this when she disappeared." Jane pushed the troll into Brandy's hand. "It showed up in Grandma Gertie's pickup when they were at Sandcastle. Boo is at Sandcastle."

Brandy examined the toy, shaking her head. "How can you know it's the same one? We had a couple of these when I was a kid. They all look alike. Same beady eyes, big grin, pug nose and wild-looking hair."

"With a Viking helmet?"

"No. But my personal experience isn't a true statement of how many Viking trolls there are in Pittsburgh."

Jane snatched the doll back and smacked Brandy with it. "Stop talking like your grandmother!"

"You come roaring up, waving a doll, talking all crazy about your little sister? I know what comes next. You're going to want me to go busting down doors and get ugly in someone's face. I'm just telling you what my grandmother is going to say when this hits her court."

"This is Sergeant Helga Teufel Hunden. She was my mom's doll before she gave it to me." All their toys were hand-me-downs and secondhand store finds.

Everything had been battered and ugly and half-broken even before they got hold of it. Helga had the virtue of being seemingly indestructible. "Before I gave her to Boo, I replaced her hair and repainted her helmet, and I made her a purple dress and I painted her toes to match. I can guarantee that even if there is a shitload of these dolls in Pittsburgh, this is the only one with purple toes."

"Good enough. But it's been eight years. Someone could have found it lying on the ground in the Strip District the day she went missing and it's been drifting person to person since then."

"Someone put it in Grandma Gertie's truck when they were at Sandcastle . . ."

"It could have been put into her truck at anytime, anywhere, by anyone. You know she doesn't lock her truck and has dozens of kids underfoot all the time. Everyone calls her Grandma for a reason."

"Why are you being so pig-headed about this?"

"Because I've watched your family tear itself apart and then have to rebuild itself every time we find anything even remotely connected to your sister's disappearance. That girl's body that we found in the woods two years ago. And the boy's skeleton two years before that. It's suddenly the day that she disappeared and you're all blaming each other for not keeping close enough watch on her."

"So for peace of mind, you want us to just say 'she's dead, end of story.'"

"No, that's not what I said," Brandy growled. "Look, it doesn't make sense. If Boo was the person that put the doll in Grandma Gertie's truck, why didn't she just stay there?"

"I don't know!"

"Jane, I love you like a sister, and if this was any other time, I'd round up some people and go tear Sandcastle apart. No one seems have noticed, but the shit hit the fan thirty days ago. A week after Windwolf was nearly killed, EIA started major housecleaning. They have two NSA agents going through all their personnel files and they started Gestapo-level seizing EIA employees and throwing them in jail."

"I—I haven't heard that."

"No one has. Someone is keeping a tight lid on the news. They opened up the county jail to hold them all."

"Wait? They're holding them? Why didn't they ship them to Earth for trial?"

"Because they're not human. The EIA has been infiltrated by the oni. It went as high as Director Maynard's personal assistant, who turned out to have a tail and dog-ears. The oni were using magic somehow just to look human. The EIA was spending too much time trying to keep more oni from slipping into Pittsburgh to transport the ones in holding to the border."

"Why didn't you tell me this?"

"Because it's coming down from on high that hush-hush is best for Pittsburgh. Let the EIA clean house. The thing is that the EIA did most of the heavy lifting, and we have been picking up the slack. Now Tinker's been kidnapped and we do not have the resources to follow ghost leads."

"Please!"

Brandy looked away, shaking her head. "Jane. I can't. I can't drop everything because of a toy found in a pickup truck weeks ago. Grandma Gertie is getting old. That doll could have been in the truck for days before she noticed it. She could have been anywhere when it was put into her pickup. And why would a little girl who disappeared eight years ago put a doll in a truck, and do nothing else?"

"Brandy!"

Brandy's shoulder radio crackled and her dispatcher directed her to head to a shooting and added that an ambulance was responding. "I have a job to do! I have to do it because no one else is going to!"

The *Chased by Monsters* production truck pulled into McMicking's parking lot just as Brandy raced away.

"How'd you find me?" Jane snapped. She didn't want them there, reminding her that she had her own job to do, one that no one else could do.

All three men tapped their right temple to indicate the headset she was wearing.

"Oh, freaking hell!" Jane cried. "Don't tell me you heard everything I said?"

"Okay. We won't." Hal pointed at the deli. "It's lunch time. Let's do food." He turned to Nigel. "This place has amazing food. Good as anything you'd find in New York."

"Gypsy wagons!" Nigel clapped his hands in delight. He'd attached his backup set of feet, so only the faint blood staining through his clean shirt remained as proof of how close a call they'd had. "Oh, how charming."

"Are you okay?" Taggart asked.

Jane nodded mutely as tears started to burn in her eyes. Somehow last night had broken down her defenses around him and it left her emotionally fragile.

He carefully took the doll out of her hands. He brushed the ratty, dirty hair back from its impish smile.

"People used to ask if Boo was half-elf because she was so beautiful. She had hair so pale blond that it looked white, the bluest eyes and skin like china. When she was clean and still—which was usually only when we were at church or a wedding or something—she was like an angel that had fallen from heaven. But with us, most the time, she was half-naked, muddy, and grinning. To me, she was just as impish as this doll. And her hair. Her hair would be this mass of untamable curls. When I fixed Helga for her, I made the hair just like Boo's."

"We'll find her," Taggart said.

Jane shook her head, taking back the doll. "I can't put you at risk."

Hal came back carrying biodegradable takeout containers that perfumed the parking lot with the smell of rice and pumpkin curry. "I say we film a show."

Jane smacked him.

"Ow! I mean it! Everyone in Pittsburgh knows *PB&G*. Even if you don't own a television, there are those billboards of me all over town. We just do our normal shtick."

"Shtick?" Jane echoed.

"Come in with cameras, walk all over the homeowner, and blow the hell out of their property."

Jane stared at him for a moment as she realized that he was right. Shy of the viceroy and the director of the EIA, the various TV personalities were the most famous faces in Pittsburgh. Unlike some of them—like Chloe Polanski—Hal was well liked. People sensed that at his core, what Hal wanted more than anything, more than ratings, was to honestly save people. It was the main reason that Jane put up with his craziness. Despite the homeowners' misgivings and the chaos *PB&G* caused, they kept the dangerous flora and fauna from killing countless people.

But would his fame actually protect him?

Jane shook her head. "I can't ask you . . ."

"You're not asking," Hal said. "This is my plan and I'm quite proud of it."

"I think it's a good plan," Nigel said.

She glanced at Taggart and he gave a sheepish grin as he nodded.

Oh, God, this was what she was most afraid of: she was outnumbered by crazy men. Vague plans to call her little brothers evaporated as she started thinking of damage control. The fewer crazy men she needed to corral, the less chance of something going wrong. Hopefully.

Pittsburgh was full of forgotten corners. It was nearly two thousand square miles of space transported to Elfhome. For every handful of empty houses there was an empty quickie mart, gas station, dry cleaners, Starbucks and McDonalds. And with every failed business, there came another handful of empty houses. Desolation grew like a cancer. Homestead had been home of the famous steel mill, a fairly new mall, the sprawling water park of Sandcastle and sixteen hundred households. When she was little, there had been a strip of houses clustered around West Street, eking a living from the still-open Sandcastle. When the park closed, the neighborhood went under.

The entrance of the park looked no different from all the abandoned buildings that they'd passed coming in. Jane's heart sank. The squatters must have moved out after Grandma Gertie's tribe descended on them.

"What is it?" Taggart's question made her realize she had sworn softly.

"It's empty," she said.

"How can you tell?"

"There's no takens."

"Takens?"

"Pittsburghers do stuff to show that a building is taken. Set up a planter with flowers. Paint the door Wind Clan blue. Put out a welcome mat. Install an obvious doorbell. Or put up a new mailbox, even if they can't get the mail delivered. It keeps other people from trying to move into their space."

"What if they don't want people to know they're here?" Taggart said. "They've got a little girl they've kidnapped and God knows what else. They don't want to be noticed."

He had a point.

On the theory that Hal was the recognizable one, he got out and pushed open the gate. It swung easily and silently open. Beyond them was the massive parking lot, cracked and weed-choked. The tall waterslides towered on the other side like twisted dreams.

Everyone but Nigel cautiously got out of the truck. Silence reigned, broken only by the calls of crows.

Jane shouldered a backpack stuffed with every tool she imagined she might need for a jail breakout. She hefted the big light reflector like a shield while her heart hammered in her chest. There was a tiny little voice deep inside her that she currently was ignoring. It whispered that the only reason she was letting the men talk her into this was because she was being selfish. She was supposed to be the smart, level-headed one who knew when it was time to ditch and run.

Taggart glanced at her and read her face. "Oh, you can't back out now." Taggart brandished his camera like a weapon. "You promised us."

She didn't remember making any promises. In fact, that was so unlikely that she knew he was lying. It felt weirdly better, though, to know control had slipped from her hands, and with it, responsibility.

Hal took his place out in front, his pith helmet on, and his grab-stick tucked under his arm like a riding crop. He was grinning hugely like he did just before he got to blow things up. Probably because explosives were well in the realm of likely outcomes of their rescue attempt.

Chesty stood at her side in heel. The elfhound scanned the lot with open suspicion, which meant they weren't as alone as they seemed.

They went through an over-the-top mime of setting up to shoot. *Don't mind us, we're harmless.*

Hal, however, seemed slightly confused what their real mission was. "Should I intro as *PB&G* or *Chased by Monsters*?"

Jane bit down on the automatic "We're not actually filming!" No need to announce that to anyone who might have very sharp ears. Besides, she was fairly certain that Taggart was filming—in fact probably would keep filming even if gunshots and explosions occurred. "Do both. Depending on what we get, we'll use the video for one show or other."

"Welcome to *Pittsburgh Backyard and Garden*. I'm your host, Hal Rogers." Hal paused and straightened nervously. "Welcome to *Chased by Monsters*. I'm Hal Rogers." He half-turned, giving the camera his handsome profile, the raccoon mask of bruising covered up with half a bottle of concealer. "And this"—he waved a hand at the twin square towers that made up the front entrance; the landlocked builders had tried to combine Cape Cod, lighthouse and castle themes for the gatehouse and utterly failed—"is Sandcastle: an eighty-seven-acre water park with fourteen water slides and multiple swimming pools located on the banks of the Monongahela River. Opened in 1989, it bravely continued operating even after it found itself on Elfhome. It closed its doors..." Hal paused to shove open the accordion steel gate stretched between the two towers. "...in 2020 after a sudden outbreak of deadly Elfhome water creatures in its water supply. Despite heavy chlorination and an extensive filtering system, creatures such as river plankton, elf shrimp, and water fairies took over."

And in they went.

No one came forward to stop them. The place looked completely deserted. Jagger bushes grew waist high in every inch of lawn. Weeds choked the cracks in the cement sidewalks. Chesty nearly quivered at her side, nostrils flared, jerking his head from one target to another. They were being watched by half a dozen things that Chesty considered dangerous.

So Boo's kidnappers wanted to pretend that Sandcastle was deserted? Fine. Jane and her crew would play ignorant.

Hal marched forward a dozen feet, pointing out the park's three large pools and the fact that the river lay just feet beyond. The pools had been covered by some kind of odd-looking tarps.

"Camo netting," Taggart murmured.

More evidence that someone was hiding something.

Behind the buildings that lined the boardwalk, Dragon's Den lay dismantled by Grandma Gertie, the massive statue at the slide's heart missing. All that remained was the two stories of open wooden stairs leading to the now-vanished launch point. Considering how big the dragon was, Gertie must have had dozens of people with her. It was little wonder they could come in and go without a fight. But why hadn't Boo just gone with them? Hidden herself in the truck instead of the doll?

Eighty-seven acres of possible hiding spaces.

"What monster do we track today?" Hal said as he paused at the decision point. Go into the gift shop? The park offices? Head for the buildings closer to the river or go on to the boardwalk? "Indeed, that is the question: what is out there?"

Hal pointed out at the open river on the other side of the mushroom pool. Hopefully he could keep attention away from what Jane was doing. "The other day we spotted a creature never seen before in Pittsburgh, a massive river reptile generating a storm of electrical discharge. It had been described by one of our viewers as a Loch Ness monster."

While Hal gestured and info-dumped about the river monster, Jane leaned the reflector against the wall and pulled out a Ziploc baggie. The first things that had gone into their new freezer were several pieces of Boo's clothing to be used by scent dogs. They'd used most that first summer, but she'd found one still buried at the bottom. One last chance to find her baby sister.

"A long-standing theory has been that the Loch Ness is a plesiosauria, which is a marine reptile that first appeared during the early Jurassic period and is thought to be now extinct. These massive predators reached lengths of forty to fifty feet in length. What we witnessed the other night, though, seems to classify the Pittsburgh Nessie as a type of electric eel."

She pressed the cloth to Chesty's nose. "Seek. Seek."

Chesty whuffed in the scent. Dropping his head, he started to track.

"Electric eels get their names because they can generate up to six hundred volts of electricity." Hal managed to make his stroll forward, matching Chesty's progress, seem totally natural without losing track of the information he was presenting. "This powerful amount of voltage is five times the normal output of a household outlet. Those, however, are Earth's electric eels. The largest of these only reach about seven feet in length. How much voltage could a creature that is fifty feet long generate? The possibilities are staggering!"

Chesty headed to the boardwalk that once was lined with food stands with names that made it clear what they sold: Potato Patch, Uncle Tony's Pizza, Philly, Healthy Hut. The eateries had steel grates rolled down to cover their storefronts. Chesty passed the rows of locker rentals and went still at the first steel grate cover. Jane knelt beside the grate and gave it an experimental tug. It rose up an inch on well-oiled tracks. There was a large room beyond, dimly lit by celestial windows.

"We're going in." Jane lifted the grate two feet. Chesty crawled under and she wriggled in after him and let the door close behind her.

At one time, the place had been a café. Chesty beelined through overturned tables and broken chairs to the swinging doors into the kitchen full of large stainless steel appliances.

There was a startled squeak and someone ducked around one of the counters. The move, however, had backed them into a corner. They stared at Jane and Chesty with eyes wide, hair a wild tangled bloom of unruly white-blond curls.

"Boo!"

"Jane!" Boo skittered away from her outstretched hand, ducking through the shelving under the counter. "Go away!"

"Boo, I'm here to take you home!"

"They'll kill you if they find you here!"

"Who?" Because now that Jane found her baby sister, she wanted to know whom she was going to kill.

"Lord Tomtom's warriors."

"Who?"

"You have to go!"

"Carla Marie Kryskill, come here now!"

"Jane!" It was the little girl whine she remembered so well. "I can't leave Joey! He's my responsibility."

"Fine, we'll take Joey too." *Who the hell is Joey?* Jane couldn't remember ever hearing of a missing "Joey." Maybe it wasn't another kid.

"They have him in a spell so he can't be found and he's chained."

"We'll get him out. Where is he?"

Boo stared at her for a long moment as if staring into her soul. After eight years, did Boo still have the ability to trust anyone?

"I promise," Jane whispered. "We will not leave without the both of you. Okay? Semper Fi. Leave no man behind."

Boo's eyes filled with tears and she gave a tiny nod. "Take me to Joey."

Originally built as a row of isolated shotgun-style buildings, Boo's captors had cut doors between the restaurants and built up walls until the structures were one big maze. In a dim back room, they found a little black-haired boy, chained by one foot, inside a gleaming hologram-like spell. Jane stared at shimmering lines of power that wove from the floor to a matching design in the ceiling, creating a cage out of nothing.

She knew nothing about spells except they were much like lamps—they needed a power supply and a continuous loop to function correctly. In theory, breaking the circuit turned off the spell. She tapped the bar quickly. It felt as cold and hard as steel but it looked no more solid than light beamed through smoke.

"What's going on?" The little boy sounded very American. He looked like a kindergartener. "Who are you?"

"This is Jane." Boo reached through the bars to lace fingers with him. "She came! She's here to save us. Both of us."

Jane dug frantically through her backpack. "Taggart, I found them. I'm going to kick the beehive to get them free. Get ready to move fast."

"Okay." Taggart answered steadily.

She took out the bolt cutter and laid it aside where she could find it quickly. Once she started, they'd probably only have minutes to get to safety. She found the foam package of whack-a-moles. They'd developed the little explosives to force vespers out of their holes so they could be filmed. They worked on the same principle as a nail gun, driving a spike straight down into hard packed ground. She'd never tried them on concrete; hopefully they wouldn't explode like a pipe bomb instead.

"Here." She passed the light reflector into the cage. "Hold this up like a shield. Boo, get behind that counter."

She used clay to create a seal between the explosives' barrel and the concrete over the spell etchings.

"Fire in the hole!" The explosion was deafening in the small room. Thankfully, though, the bars of the cage vanished.

"Jane! Incoming!" Taggart shouted. The grate rattled up back at the café's entrance. There was the loud whistle of the monster call. As the grate clattered down and gunfire broke out, there was a distant roar of the river monster.

Swearing, Jane snatched up the bolt cutter and scrambled quickly to Joey. The chain was stupidly short, only a few inches between a loop on the floor and the shackle around his ankle. The metal cuff had chafed him raw and bleeding. She'd thought that there was something horribly wrong with his foot until she realized that it wasn't deformed. He had a bird's foot. Instead of a human foot with five little toes, he had a bird's with four scale-covered talons. Three long talons faced forward. A shortened fourth splayed out in place of a heel. Not as long as a true crow's foot, but long enough to allow him to grip a branch solidly with his foot.

Jane gasped as the image of Tinker's kidnapping played out in her mind's eye. The boy was a tengu. Boo had been taken by oni? The oni had been in Pittsburgh all these years? How many of the missing children—thought dead of jumpfish and strangle vines just like Boo—had the oni taken?

"Jane! They're coming!" Boo tugged at her arm. "Just go away. They won't hurt us; they need us alive. They want the call for the tengu flock! They need the blood of the Chosen to take control of the flock."

Jane's breath caught in her chest as she saw for the first time Boo's feet. The ghost-white scales of her talons that matched her pale hair. Jane looked up into Boo's face. Her baby sister's face. Her baby sister's blue eyes.

"What did they do to you?" Jane cried.

Hurt filled Boo's face. "Just go away!"

"We're all going, now shut up." Jane cut through the chain.

"Jane?" Hal shouted over whistle blast and gunfire.

"Over here!" Jane started to unload her backpack of weapons.

A minute later, Taggart found them. "That door won't hold for long. Do you have any weapons?"

Jane laughed, checking the magazine and handing him a pistol. "For generations, my family has been Marines, police officers, moonshiners, and local mafia. Do the math."

"You've got guns. Lots of guns."

"My family all but bleeds bullets." Jane took out two more pistols. She held the little twenty-two out to Boo. "You remember how to use these?"

"Don't point it at anyone you don't want to kill." Boo took the gun. "Which is a lot of people right now. Aim down the barrel, hold your breath, squeeze."

"Good girl."

There was a roar, this time sounding far too close, and the whole building shook as if hit by a freight train.

"Where's the back door?" When Boo only stared at her in horror, Jane groaned. "Please tell me there's back door."

Boo shook her head. "They're nailed shut. That's the only door in."

"Shit! Shit! Shit!" Jane scanned the room. What should they do? She realized that there were too few of them. "Where's Hal?"

There was a sudden explosion from the hallway beyond the cage room.

"I've made us a door!" Hal called.

"Hal! Damn it, how many times have I told you to warn people before you blow things up?"

They went out the hole that Hal had blown through the back wall. A back service alley ran the length of the boardwalk, lined with boarded-up loading docks. Electricity was crawling over the building like a lightning storm had been anchored to the storefront. They ran toward the truck that seemed a million miles away.

Jane realized that the whistling was growing quieter. She nearly stumbled as she looked over her shoulder and realized that Taggart was running in the opposite direction, still blowing the whistle and leading the river monster away. A muffled roar came from inside the building and screams of something that could have been human.

"Idiot!" The park was a maze of deep waterways to anyone who didn't know the area. Once he was beyond the corner of the building, he'd be out of sight. Nor was there any guarantee that there weren't oni coming around the other way to cut them off.

"Hal, get Chesty and the kids to the truck."

"What?"

"Truck! Go!" Jane shouted and pointed. "Chesty, follow!"

She headed for the stairs that one time led to the top of the Dragon's Den ride. "Taggart, you idiot, what the hell do you think you're doing?"

"Giving you a chance to get to the truck and into it without a horde of monsters on top of you. Five people and one large dog and only three doors."

He had a point.

The river monster came crashing out of the building into the back service alley. It looked like a weird cross between a catfish and a crocodile. Its mouth was a snout filled with teeth with long whiskers on either side. It had four stubby legs and a long whip-tail. Electricity snarled and leaped from it to every nearby object.

Taggart whistled and the thing turned and crawled at stunning speed after him.

"Don't go left at the end of the buildings, Taggart. Swing right!" Jane ran up the steps keeping track of both Hal and Taggart as they both ran in opposite directions. "And stop blowing that stupid whistle. It turned already. Let it go chomp on someone else!"

Taggart's laugh came across the channel.

When Jane reached the second floor deck, she saw that a big male was running to block off Hal. She lined him up and only thought about how they'd taken her sister. Twisted her sister's body against her will until she wasn't even human anymore. She killed him like she'd kill any other monster trying to stop Hal.

She turned and picked off a male coming out of the building, carrying a rifle. A third that she hadn't seen took a shot at her from the boardwalk's roof.

The bullet whined past her. She didn't miss with her return fire.

"Jane, we're at the truck," Hal reported.

"Get out to the street and head toward the mall to pick us up. And be careful, Nessie might be out there with us."

One of the oni, however, cooperated nicely in drawing the monster's attention. She scrambled over the wall to the city street to join up with Taggart just as Nigel drove up.

"That was stupid," she said as she scrambled into the backseat with Chesty, Boo and Joey.

"Yeah, a little." Taggart squeezed into the back from the other side. "I spent three years as a war correspondent. My nightmares are all about sitting and watching people die and doing nothing. I don't think I could stay sane if I'd stood and watched you die."

"Mine," Hal muttered darkly.

Whatever she might have said was cut short as Boo snatched up Helga from the dashboard.

"Look, Joey!" Boo cried. "I told you someone would find Sergeant Helga Teufel Hunden and Jane would come for us."

"Why didn't you just go home with Grandma Gertie?" Jane asked.

"I told you!" Boo pulled the little boy into her lap. "Joey's my responsibility. I couldn't leave him. Big sisters take care of their little brothers."

Jane recognized her father's ghost even though he had been dead before Boo could talk. She'd imprinted him into her little sister without meaning to, but this was all kinds of wrong. "Boo, he's not your little brother." The boy wasn't even human.

"Yes, he is!" Boo tightened her arms around Joey and glared at her with cold hard eyes. Her father's eyes. "You always said that you can't pick your family but still had to do right by them. The oni made us brother and sister. I'm Joey's big sister and I won't let anything bad happen to him."

From within Boo's protective hold, Joey blinked up at Jane. He looked only five or six but he'd been chained and caged like an animal. The only real difference that she could see between him and any of her brothers at his age was that like Nigel, he'd been born with odd feet. This might be all kinds of wrong, but it wasn't this little boy's fault. She nodded. "Okay. If he's your little brother, then he's mine too."

A quiver of Boo's bottom lip was all the warning Jane got before she had her arms full of bawling little girl with poor Joey squashed between them like a teddy bear. Boo cried as if she'd had her heart torn out.

"Hey, hey, big girls don't cry," Jane said, because any moment she was going to lose it. If she started, she wouldn't be able to stop, and she knew from experience that her tears would burn like liquid fire. "It's okay. You're safe!"

"I was so afraid!" Boo wailed. "I prayed and prayed that you'd come for me, but I thought—I thought when you saw what they did—I thought—you'd say that we weren't s-s-s-sisters anymore!" She had been so scared that she could barely even say it.

"You are my baby sister." Jane held her tight. "Nothing anyone could do to you, no magic, nothing, could change that. You will always be my baby sister."

Once Jane got Boo and their new little brother safe, she was going to war. Not with her rifle, although she dearly wanted to, but with her camera. The oni obviously were gearing up for guerrilla warfare because they couldn't stand against the joint forces of humans and elves. The news blackout was their doing; keeping the two allies from uniting. She wasn't going to stand back and let them get away with it. She wasn't going to let them turn her city into a war zone. She was going to find out their every secret and broadcast it across two worlds. They were about to learn the meaning of "no better friend, no worse enemy."

# CHASED BY MONSTERS

Jane missed how it started.

She went out to set perimeter alarms and came back to find that they were comparing feet.

The children, of course, had crow feet, complete with scales and talons. Little Joey's scales were black as his spikey hair. Jane's baby sister, Boo, had white scales to match her pale blond curls, but her feet were otherwise identical to the boy's. Since neither child had shoes, most likely they had triggered show and tell.

Taggart was holding his camera on his lap, viewfinder tilted up. He was filming the comparison of feet without being obvious. Jane locked down an automatic kneejerk hate of being in front of the camera. If they were going to get the news out to Earth that Pittsburgh needed help against the oni, it was stories like Boo's that would win over hearts.

Nigel had taken off his boots to show off his prosthetics that looked like pieces of curved metal. The naturalist was discussing feet in his faint Scottish burr. "The heel is essentially a finger pointing backwards. See, the leg comes down and connects to the ankle, which is a pivot joint like the wrist. From there, the foot shifts out in two directions. Forward are the toes and backwards is the heel. This bone is called a calcaneus. Because it has to bear the weight of the entire body, though it's evolved over time to a large, strong bone."

Hal was not to be outdone. Hal had his cross-trainers off, and as he unveiled his feet, everyone but Nigel recoiled slightly. "It's called Brachymetatarsia. It's a condition in which there are one or more abnormally short metatarsals. I have the most common form, which affects the fourth toe."

"Oh, that's weird looking," Joey whispered, not old enough to realize it was rude, however true it was.

Luckily Hal had thick skin. "In my case, it's acquired, not congenital."

"I thought only women developed that," Nigel said.

Hal shrugged. "It means that I am truly unique and special."

Taggart was slowly taking off his hiking boots, apparently bullied into joining. "I have hobbit feet. Big and hairy." And he did. They were epic.

All eyes turned to Jane.

"The kids need baths," Jane announced to keep from being roped into this odd display.

Taggart tilted his head slightly to indicate she should look at her sister.

Unshed tears shimmered in Boo's eyes. The whole foot display, then, was for her sake.

Jane sighed and sat down on the edge of her battered coffee table. She pulled off her boots and socks and reluctantly put out her feet for inspection. Five heads bent over her toes to inspect them.

"Uh," Taggart breathed in surprise. "I didn't think you were the type to paint your toenails."

Boo gave a wordless squeal of delight and launched herself into Jane's arms. "Purple!"

"Yes, purple just for you." Jane hugged her baby sister tight. Over her mass of white blond curls, she saw Taggart raise an eyebrow in question. "It's her favorite color."

In the weeks leading up to Boo's kidnapping, the little girl had begged and pleaded with Jane to have a full manicure. Jane never knew what had triggered it, but had resisted because she had tried it *once* when she was eleven and loathed the results. Her right hand had looked like she dipped her fingers into the polish, and in less than a day, she'd picked most of the polish off.

On the morning Boo had gone missing, Jane had bought a bottle of purple nail polish. They'd sat on the tailgate of their family pickup truck and painted all their toenails as her younger brothers slept off a night of trying to kill one another. It had been a quiet moment of ritual girl bonding.

Two hours later, Boo vanished out of their life. Taken. Presumed killed.

Every week after that, for eight years, Jane had painted her toenails the same exact purple.

If Jane had a quarter for every time she'd washed one of her younger siblings, she could invest in an automatic baby washer. With the exception of his feet and the fact he didn't act like the shampoo was acid, Joey proved to be no different than any of her younger brothers. It was a little unsettling when he used his feet like a second pair of hands; he could even unscrew bottle tops with them.

Boo surprised her by asking for help with washing her hair. It scared Jane what evidence of abuse she would find under Boo's dirty clothes. Jane silently called herself a coward as she filled the tub with fresh water and added lavender-scented bath salt. Seeing scars would be nothing compared to the pain of wearing them.

It was a relief, though, that Boo had no noticeable scars. Only her birdlike feet marked what damage her kidnappers had done to her. Boo kept them under the surface of the foamy water. Either she was still ashamed of them or it didn't occur to her that she could use them like hands.

Boo's hair proved to be just as wild and curly and white as when she was six. It surprised Jane since most of her family had been towheads as children but by fourteen their hair had changed to honey gold.

"He liked my hair pale." Boo pulled one of the wet locks of hair forward to gaze at sadly. "He did a spell so it would never change color."

"Who did?"

"Kajo. He did that first. Just the color. He was going to make me an elf next, but then Danni said I was too dangerous of a toy to keep. That he was only keeping me because of some sick mommy obsession and he should get rid of me before I could hurt him."

Jane felt like someone had just punched her hard in the stomach. "He took you to be a toy?"

Boo shook her head vehemently. "No. I was stupid. I'd seen Kajo with Danni. Her hair was just like mine. I wanted to meet her, so I followed them all the way to a warehouse where they were meeting with Lord

Tomtom. He has cat ears and a tail. Even a six-year-old can tell he isn't human. He was going to kill me, but Kajo stopped him. Kajo liked my hair."

"Kajo and Lord Tomtom are both oni?"

Boo wrinkled up her nose. "There's all sorts of oni. There's the purebloods but there's not a lot of those in Pittsburgh. Some of the officers are purebloods; they wear face paint to make themselves scarier. And then there's the lesser bloods who'd been bred with animals. They don't need face paint to be scary. And then there's the greater bloods like Kajo and his Eyes. They look almost human."

"What do you mean by Eyes?"

"They're women who can see the future." Boo said. "I think they're related to Kajo. Danni calls him 'big brother' when she's mad at him."

The mention of brothers drove all other thoughts out of Jane's mind with the sudden realization she was going to have to tell her family that she'd found Boo. Jane shuddered a little at the thought of how their five brothers were going to take the news.

How long could she put it off?


Jane threw away the dirty rags that Boo and Joey had been wearing. Luckily she had a massive closet full of kid's clothes. Her mother and aunts had kept every stitch of clothing that Jane's generation had outgrown. The price for taking over the family estate was storing all the clothes until the next generation could grow into them. Jane enforced military order on the closet to keep it from being reduced to pure chaos every few months. She standardized on twenty-seven gallon, airtight, stackable, heavy plastic bins. They were labeled and organized by sex and sizes. She pointed Boo toward the handful of girl containers and then pulled down one labeled "Boy's size 5" for Joey.

When she opened up the bin, Joey gave a cry of joy and snatched up the topmost piece of clothing.

"Ravenclaw!" He held up a black shirt. "That's my house!"

"It is?" The long-sleeved shirt had a large bird that looked more like an eagle than a raven.

He hugged the shirt to his chest. "At Hogwarts there are four houses: Gryffindor, Hufflepuff, Slytherin, and us! Ravenclaw! Our element is air and we're smart!"

"Oh! Harry Potter!" Her brother Geoffrey had gone through a phase when he was about ten. It was what inspired him to learn magic, which led to his carpentry since ironwood could only be crafted with spells and magically sharp tools. He was the only human in the city that could work with the wood. He shipped his furniture as far away as New York and Los Angeles. The shirt most likely had been his.

Joey nodded enthusiastically. "Riki read to me every night before bed. When we would finish a book, we'd watch the movie." The smile faded. "We'd just finished *Prisoner of Azkaban*, but we didn't get to see the movie." He held up the shirt. "Can I have it?"

The shirt was in the wrong bin; it was at least three sizes too big. Jane couldn't say no. It really didn't matter that the shirt didn't fit; after what Joey had been through, he deserved any little thing that could make him happy.

"Sure." She helped him pull the shirt over his head. It came to his knees and his hands were lost in the sleeves.

"There, you look like a true Ravenclaw now." She rolled up the sleeves until his hands appeared.

"I'm just like Harry," Joey tented out the shirt so he could study the decal. "The oni killed my parents when I was just a baby. I live with my Aunt Katsumi and Uncle Hiro, but they're not mean at all. I have three cousins instead of one; Riki, Mickey and Keiko. None of them are like Dudley. Aunty Nori is Mickey's aunt, not mine, just like Marge Dursley, but she's not mean either. She always brings presents for all of us and plays Sturdy Birdy with me. We live hidden in among muggles, who don't know anything about magic or monsters."

Jane gazed at him, so tiny and helpless. It was starting to hit home that she'd taken a child. Being that he had been chained to the floor inside a cage, it seemed a perfectly justified action. But keeping him was filled with moral ambiguity. Boo said that she was now genetically his sister, and certainly their matching crow feet seemed to support that claim.

*You can't pick your family*, Boo reminded Jane, *but you still have to do right by them.*

For Jane, "do right" was to return Joey to the family that obviously loved him if they were reading nightly to him. The only problem was that it didn't sound like Joey's family lived in Pittsburgh. If they did, the people around him would know about magic and monsters. "Do you know where your aunt and uncle live? What is their address?"

"Three eight three five Startouch Drive, Pasadena, California, nine one one oh seven."

"California?" Jane echoed with dismay.

Joey nodded.

Returning him to his family wasn't going to happen any time soon. She had no idea how she was going to get him back to Earth. With the EIA infiltrated by oni, she couldn't use official channels. She knew that there were people that smuggled in illegal immigrants, but for the time being, she could trust no one but family. Jane couldn't even call Joey's aunt and uncle. She would have to wait until Shutdown when Pittsburgh returned to Earth to contact them. The poor people. She knew firsthand the grief that they must be going through.

That her family was still going through. Jane sighed, deciding to at least call her mother. She would still be at her café downtown. Jane would have to wait until her mother closed up; otherwise there might be strangers there to overhear the conversation. Actually, Jane realized it would be best to just ask her to come to Hyeholde and not to go into details on the phone.

Said conversation did not go as planned. Her mother was tired and already upset. Jane's youngest brother, Guy, had been in yet another fight at summer school.

"Mom! Mom! I'll knock some sense into Guy! Just... please...I need you here. It's really important."

"Can't you come to the house?"

Her mom still lived on their old street. The world's biggest gossips, Mike and Mitsuko Barker lived in the house next door. The Barkers were the type of people that you could trust with your kids but not your secrets. The standing joke was "Telephone, telegraph, tell a Barker."

"Mom, my boss saddled me with two new people..."

"Yes, Mitsy Barker was telling me about them. She

saw you on the television with Chloe Polanski. Nigel Reid! What's he like?"

What her mom was really asking was "do you find him sexually attractive?" and "can I start asking about grandchildren?" One would think raising seven children was enough for anyone, but apparently it was the people who had lots of kids that looked forward to a houseful of even more.

For some reason all Jane could think of was Taggart wearing only his pajama bottoms and the arrow of dark hair pointing down to his beltline. And the fact he smelled heavenly at all times.

"Jane?" Which really meant, "You didn't say 'no' like usual."

"There's someone I really want you to meet," Jane said truthfully. "Not Nigel. Someone else. But I'm really tied up here and can't bring them to the house."

"Okay." Her mother's voice was fully of surprise and curiosity. "I'll be there as soon as I can. I'll stop and pick up something to cook."

Translation: I'll properly welcome this mystery man into the family.

"That would be good." Jane hung up. She leaned her head against the kitchen wall and considered banging it a few times. Why was it easier to deal with the heavily armed oni than her family?

Taggart chose that moment to walk into the kitchen. "Are you okay?"

"Yes." *My mother is coming to pin* someone *down and force them to propose. And she's not picky as to who.* "No." Considering the last forty-eight hours, maybe that was the wrong thing to say. "I'm not sure." Jane didn't want to explain her mother's pending siege, so she tackled the other thing that had her unbalanced. "I never thought it would turn out this way. I mean, this is the way I wanted it to. Prayed it would. But I always thought that if we were lucky, the most we'd ever recover was a few gnawed bones that we'd never be totally sure were hers. This? This is too good to be true. I keep thinking I'll wake up and find out it was a dream."

Taggart smiled gently at her and leaned in close. "It's not a dream. You're awake and she's in the other room, safe and sound, watching a movie. Harry Potter, I think."

Chesty stood up, alert but not growling.

"We're getting visitors." Jane went to her gun rack and got down her rifle.

Taggart glanced to Chesty. "Trouble?"

"Probably not, but I wasn't expecting anyone. Stay put."

Outside she could hear the deep rumble of a big truck coming. As it neared, the timbre grew familiar. It was her brother Alton's Ford pickup. She swung her rifle onto her back, but stayed hidden from sight while he slowed and turned into her long drive.

When she was sure it was only Alton, she drifted out to meet him. He took note of the rifle on her shoulder. He lifted his rifle out of his gun rack before swinging down out of the cab.

"What's wrong?" He scanned the woods around Hyeholde. Alton had been as fair as Boo as a child. Since their baby sister had disappeared, he'd grown increasingly dark and scruffy. His honey-blond hair was down to his shoulders, and recently he'd stared to grow a beard.

"Nothing's wrong," Jane said. "Just being careful."

"Ah." He sounded unconvinced. "So Brandy called me for no reason at all to tell me to hunt you down and sit on you."

"Like that would work."

He shrugged. All her brothers were tall and strong but they'd had a lifetime of being whooped by Jane. They were naturally reluctant to get her riled up but pride made them equally reluctant to admit that they were scared of her.

"I got an elk while picking blueberries," Alton said. "I figured I'd come out and check on you."

Alton made a living by foraging for fruits and nuts that grew wild now that half the farms in Pittsburgh were abandoned. He sold his finds to the elf enclaves and the handful of restaurants still in business. When it started to snow, he'd switch to hunting big game. It was early in the year for him to bag an elk; the midsummer heat made it difficult to properly age the meat. What he wasn't saying was that he needed to borrow her garage which been converted out of Hyeholde's old springhouse.

Jane nodded but added terms. "I want some of the blueberries and meat."

Alton put out his hand to seal the deal with a fist bump. "Brandy said you're working with a new crew." He pitched the last as a question, tilting his head toward the *Chased by Monsters* production truck. "Is Hal okay? I heard he set himself on fire."

"He's fine." Jane glanced into the back of his pickup. A young red elk bull filled the truck's bed. The big male was a cousin to the Eastern Elk, which had gone extinct in Pennsylvania in 1877. She hadn't known that fact until she and Hal had done a *Pittsburgh*

*Backyard and Garden* episode on a young bull that was terrorizing Observatory Hill. A herd of elk might make a good show for *Chased by Monsters*. The oni were suppressing information out of Pittsburgh in preparation for a guerilla war with the elves. To build human support for the city, Jane and her crews needed to show the interesting upside of living on Elfhome. Bountiful big game would win the hunters over. "Where did you bag it?"

"Down by Brownsville, almost to the Rim. There's a mated pair of saurus with little ones or a warg pack or something pushing herds into the South Hills. I could have dropped two or three but I'm not sure where I'd age all the meat. Want me to bag you one?"

She shook her head. "I want to film a herd."

"Ah, okay." He circled back to the start of the conversation. "So why does Brandy want me to sit on you?"

There was no avoiding it so she might as jump to the truth like ripping off a bandage. "I found out who took Boo and where they were holding her."

"What?" he shouted. "What are we doing here? Why haven't you gone after her? Why didn't you call us? Why would Brandy want me to sit on you?"

"Whoa, whoa, whoa." Jane was glad that she'd left her brothers out of the rescue mission. "I need you to calm down and promise me..."

"No," Alton snapped. "I'm going after her, with or without you."

Jane punched him in the stomach. He clamped down on a cry of pain and took a swing at her but she'd already ducked out of his reach. He really needed to learn to keep his guard up. "Listen to me."

He unleashed a string of curses as he staggered back, rubbing his stomach.

"And stop swearing; you sound like a whore. I've already went after her."

"Oh, freaking hell, Jane, you could have started with it was another false lead!"

"Shut up and listen. I need you to promise me that you won't tell a soul about Boo."

"What?"

"You need to keep your mouth shut. No one can know about Boo and Joey. Promise me."

"Who the hell is Joey?"

Jane sighed. It would be easier to explain this only once to all of her family but that was a recipe for sheer chaos. "You've been listening to the news? Did you hear that besides Earth and Elfhome with the elves, there's a third parallel universe where the world is Onihida and its people are called oni. There used to be ways to go from universe to universe via caves."

"Yeah, yeah." He made a motion that she should jump to her point. "Magic resonance through the rocks, blah blah blah, same effect that transfers Pittsburgh to Elfhome. Wormholes between mirror worlds. Some with magic, some without. Wait? You mean the oni took Boo?"

Jane signaled for him to wait. "The oni and the elves had a war three hundred years ago. It started on Onihida but it spilled onto Earth in China. The oni managed to push a small army through their pathway before the elves pulled down the caves. Part of that force were tengu; humans who had been merged with crows as punishment."

"The tengu took Boo too? Why? I could see them taking Tinker now that she's a . . ."

"Just shut up and listen!" Jane cried. "The tengu had been normal humans. They couldn't easily find their way back and forth between the two worlds, but they were doing it. Onihida was like the Aladdin's treasure cave and giant's castle in 'Jack and the Beanstalk' and every fairy tale you ever heard. It was filled with monsters but if you were cunning and brave, there was gold and treasure. Or at least, that's the legend that lured the tengu to Onihida."

"What does this have to do with Boo?"

"Do you want hit again?"

"No!" He backed away from her, hands up. "I just don't see where you're going with this fairy-tale stuff."

"It matters. Trust me."

"Fine. Can we string up my elk while you tell me 'once upon a time' bullshit?"

Hyeholde been built by hand by Jane's great-grandparents in 1930s stones and timbers salvaged from a big old barn. The sprawling house looked like a castle and the old springhouse had been built to match. Thus it had been built with two-foot-thick foundation stones and a vaulted ceiling that could double as a hayloft. Most of the year it was a perfect place to hang deer and boar to age. The heat of mid-July, though, meant that Alton would need to break the elk down to something that could fit into a walk-in cooler.

While they used his truck's hoist and a pulley anchored to one of the roof joists to lift the half-ton beast, Jane explained who Joey Shoji was.

"So this guy Joey..."

"He's six, Alton. He's a little boy, not a guy."

This made her younger brother look even more

confused. "So this little boy is like a prince of the tengu."

"More or less. His uncle Jin is the Chosen One." Jane was a little unclear what all that entailed beyond making Jin something like the pope, only more so. "If his uncle dies, then Joey or one of his cousins will become the next Chosen One. Apparently selection isn't as simple as oldest inherits; it sounds like a roll of the dice. One in four it's Joey. Maybe one in five." The oni had used magic to transform Boo into a tengu; specifically they'd made her part of the Chosen bloodline by using Joey as a blueprint. The boy seemed sure that made Boo a valid candidate.

"Okay." Alton meant he was still completely lost but didn't want to admit it. "But why can't I tell anyone this shit? Why the hell would I even want to? And what does this have to do with Boo?"

"Promise me that you'll keep your mouth shut. You can't even tell our cousins. Just us can know."

"Know what?"

"I found Boo, and I killed people to get her back."

He worked his mouth, too stunned to form a coherent word, then finally forced out, "What? You? Where?"

"Promise me. You know what will happen to me if I'm arrested? I'll get sent to Earth and locked up." Maybe even executed, but she didn't want to put that on him. Once he got over the shock he'd fall into "oldest male syndrome." He'd alternate between being pissed off that she didn't call him and feeling guilty that he wasn't the one that found Boo.

"Fucking hell, of course I'll keep my mouth shut. You really killed someone? Where did you find her? Where is she now?"

"In my living room, watching a movie."

He pointed wordlessly toward the house.

She nodded.

Without a sound, he ran to find their baby sister.

One down, four more to go.

Jane reluctantly called her younger brothers, saying that she was holding an emergency family meeting. She thought she knew the shape that the evening would take. As they arrived at her house, they all surprised her by their reactions. She never realized that they had been hiding their true selves.

Alton never cried. He'd been stoic through their father's funeral and the weeks after Boo's disappearance. Over the years, he'd been increasingly distant, disappearing into the wilderness for days on end. Jane knew he'd be happy to see Boo, but she didn't expect him to bawl like a baby until Jane took him awkwardly in her arms and comforted him.

Geoffrey always seemed so confident and sure of himself. He'd taught himself furniture-making and started a business specializing in beds and tables made from ironwood. Yet he stood in the dimness of the foyer, smelling of sawdust and bruised green, too shy to approach Boo.

"She won't know me." Still Geoffrey couldn't take his eyes from their baby sister. "I was never home when she was little. I always stayed late at school, working in the wood shop."

Jane caught him by the wrist and pulled him to Boo's side. He sank to his knees and whispered, "Do you remember me?"

Boo flung arms around his neck and hugged him

tight. "Of course I do. You used to make me toys and leave them on my pillow. Betsy the cow. Billy the goat."

"I was making you a barn to put them in." Geoffrey's voice broke. "I never got to give it to you."

Jane expected Marc's reunion to be equally quiet. He was so taciturn and solemn that his nickname in school had been Stone. Much to the family's dismay, but no one's real surprise, he'd turned down a football scholarship on Earth to enroll in the police academy. A cop's "just the facts" façade seemed to suit him well. Marc burst into laughter, though, and couldn't stop. He swung Boo in circles and tossed her up into the air like she was still six. "Our baby girl! Our Boo!" he kept shouting and whooping.

Duff brought fresh cannolis from the bakery he worked at during summer vacation, which Jane expected. Normally the family clown, instead of laughing and joking loudly like he normally would, he was quiet and gentle. Later, he took Jane aside and insisted that they take Boo to a shrink to a deal with all the trauma of being kidnapped and held prisoner. "We have to make sure we do the right thing by her. We screwed up bad once. We got to get this right. We have to do everything to make sure she can put this behind her and have the life she should have had."

Sixteen-year-old Guy roared up on his hoverbike. He'd been going through a teenage rebellion phase and had been surly for the last few months. He listened to Jane's story of rescuing Boo and Joey with quiet concentration. He hugged Boo with the same adult focus, the angry teen temporarily banished.

Her mother arrived and chased them out of the house in order to be alone with her baby. Jane suspected that her mother planned to find out how badly Boo had been abused and if she needed medical treatment. It was a discussion that her older brothers shouldn't hear and Jane couldn't bear.

They had retreated to the garage on the pretense of helping Alton skin the elk. Only Duff was actually helping. While the two of them sharpened their knives on whetstones, the rest of them sat watching with beer in hand. Hal, Taggart and Nigel had retreated upstairs for their turn at the bath and to deal with their various war wounds.

"We need to go to Sandcastle!" As the youngest, Guy tended to talk loudest. He was compensating for a lifetime of no one paying attention to what he said. "We need to go now."

"No." Jane had been afraid that once her brothers heard the full story they'd want to go take revenge on the oni. She had confessed to shooting Boo's kidnappers so that they would have no one to attack.

"We need to get rid of the evidence," Guy continued. "Your fingerprints are on the casings and it would be easy to match the bullets to your rifle if the police do ballistics."

Marc grunted in agreement.

Jane jerked around to stare at Marc in surprise. "You're agreeing with him? What kind of cop are you going to be?"

Marc pointed in the general direction of Sandcastle with his beer bottle. "This isn't Tom, Dick and Harry getting overzealous about defending their marijuana crop. They're not even slimeball pedophiles that grabbed two kids off the street. This was a heavily armed, well-trained, carefully hidden terrorist encampment. The EIA have linked the oni to that gunfight on Veterans Bridge in June. They carjacked a minivan and the driver is still missing. They threw a VW off the bridge, killing the passenger. And they jigged a load of C-4 to blow in the middle of a traffic jam that they caused. They've brought a war to us. Far as I'm concerned, Sandcastle was a combat zone. It's even more righteous than any of Dad's kills in Afghanistan, because this is our city."

Their father had been a sniper for the Marines. He'd taught Jane how to shoot before he'd died. After that, she'd taken his place and taught her brothers.

"That's right!" Guy shouted. "The elves and the oni are at war. We don't have to worry about anyone finding out. Right?"

Marc shook his head. "From what I can tell, the mayor is mandating a true neutral stance. Killing an oni—at the moment—is being treated just like killing an elf."

"What the fuck?" Guy cried. "Why?"

"Because there's a shitload of Pittsburghers who hate the EIA and the elves, in that order," Marc said. "They see Pittsburgh as American soil, not United Nations. They hate all the treaty-based laws against immigration and expansion. They want a land rush like what happened with the Louisiana Purchase or the opening of Oregon. Screw the native population. Because Elfhome is a mirror of Earth, we know where to find matching deposits of silver in Nevada, gold in the Yukon and all the oil in Texas. The expansionists are pissed that they're here on Elfhome and yet still as dirt poor as they were on Earth."

Guy sputtered with teenage rage. "The mayor is siding with the oni because he'd lose the expansionist vote?"

Marc made a rude noise at the idea. "He's afraid there'll be riots in the street just when the elves are already pissed the hell off. It would be one thing if the EIA was at full strength, but they've discovered that more than a quarter of their force are actually oni moles. The EIA is so busy housecleaning that it would be just the eighty of us cops dealing with several thousand idiots."

"The expansionists would really back the oni if push came to shove?" Taggart asked as he walked into the garage. He jerked to a stop, hands up, as six pistols were leveled at him. "Sorry. It's just me."

"Make more noise when you walk up." Jane tucked her pistol back into her kidney holster. "No, they wouldn't back the oni, but they wouldn't back the elves either. A lot of people say that the elves are dogs in the manger. They're not developing the planet's resources, but they refuse to let humans claim land outside of Pittsburgh city limits."

"It's their planet," Taggart pointed out. "It isn't right that they lose control of their home world because we can outnumber them."

"We were born here," Duff growled. "We have friends with kids. How many generations until it's ours too? Never?"

"None of that matters," Alton said. "What matters is keeping Jane and Boo safe."

"And Joey," Marc added firmly before Jane could. "We're not letting anyone screw with a six-year-old boy, regardless of his race or species."

"And Joey." Alton and Geoffrey both nodded in agreement.

"So we clean up the mess at Sandcastle," Duff stated.

And all five of her brothers started to ready themselves.

"Whoa, whoa, whoa!" Jane shouted. "Not tonight."

"Why not?" Duff whined.

Jane didn't say, "Because we left a very big monster stomping around Sandcastle. Something new. Something freaky." That wouldn't slow her brothers down. Instead she said, "Because we need to make sure Boo and Joey are safe here at Hyeholde first."

The kitchen screen door squeaked open and their mother whistled sharply.

"Besides, if we don't eat as a family tonight, Mom will skin us all alive."

It was the first time that WQED's station manager Dmitri woke Jane up. He was fairly hands-off with his top show; he only called if they'd set something on fire or accidently shot someone. She stared at her phone screen and then cautiously answered with her normal, "Hm?"

"I just got off the phone with Maynard. He wants *PB&G* at Sandcastle."

"Maynard? Us? At Sandcastle?"

"Yes, I believe those are all the salient points," Dmitri said and hung up.

Jane was completely and totally awake out of sheer adrenaline.

What would the Director of the EIA want with them? If it were merely because they had wreaked havoc on Sandcastle while rescuing Boo and Joey, Maynard would want both TV crews, because they had gone in the *Chased by Monsters* truck.

❖       ❖       ❖

"What is Maynard like?" Taggart asked as they drove to Sandcastle.

Alton had taken Boo and Joey out berry picking with Guy as backup. Since Alton could go weeks without seeing another human, the kids would be safe with him. It was agreed that her mother and other three brothers would go about business as usual.

It meant that the *Chased by Monsters* crew could come with her and Hal to Sandcastle. Jane hadn't been able to dissuade them. Since their last visit to the water park made it clear that what worked best was for Taggart to operate the camera while Jane laid down suppressive fire, it was hard to argue. Hal pointed out that if Maynard were laying some kind of trap for them, it would be very unlikely he'd call the station manager and arrange the meeting.

Which circled back to why Maynard wanted to see them. Dmitri probably had hung up on her simply because he didn't know and something else was demanding his time, something with questions he could answer. Or in a moment of distraction, he forgot he wasn't talking to one of his investigative reporters whose job was to find out what the story was without guidance.

"I've never met Maynard." Jane glanced in the rearview mirror at Hal in the backseat.

"I only met him once." Hal put up his hands as if he expected her to hit him. "And that didn't end well."

"I told you not to take animals to a black tie event," Jane snapped.

"It what we naturalists do." Hal pressed a hand to his chest to include himself in the rarefied group. Nigel's influence on him; Hal had never called himself a naturalist before. He had, though, the degrees to support the claim. "People expect it. Besides, it wasn't an animal *per se*. It was a plant. And I had it on a leash."

"It was a black willow seedling!" Jane cried. "It tried to eat the mayor!"

"He shouldn't have knelt down like that," Hal said calmly.

Jane glanced to Taggart for support.

He gave her a look of sympathy. "Been there. Done that. Banned from the *Today* show."

"I still say she had peanuts or something up her skirt," Nigel murmured from the backseat.

They were so screwed.

Jane sighed. What did she know about Maynard? "The EIA has around five thousand employees in Pittsburgh. It's a United Nations agency, so English isn't always their first language. Only a couple hundred are combat; they man the checkpoints and patrol the Rim. The rest are all pencil pushers. There's over four hundred 'delegates' alone representing the nations of Earth since the bigger countries have more than one. It means one tenth of the city's population are outsiders who have power to kick anyone—even people that were born here—off the planet. And it pisses off most people."

"Yes, outside police forces tend to do that." Taggart had been a war correspondent; he had probably been to UN-policed areas on Earth.

"Elves are easy to live with. They're good neighbors. I think because most of the ones here in Pittsburgh are excited about living with humans. They're young for elves, open minded and interested in our culture, and yet stay mostly on their side of the fence. The only elves you find living within the city are ones who have close relationships with a human, usually of the opposite sex."

"Only because ninety-five percent of the Pittsburghers are straight," Hal murmured from the backseat. "Elves are more bisexual than papayas."

"Papayas?" Jane cried. "What the hell does that mean?"

"We'd like to meet some elves," Nigel said. "Everyone on Earth is wildly curious about the elves but there's so little information on them."

Jane nodded to indicate that they could work on it. It made sense that the oni would block information on the elves to keep humans from sympathizing with the elves once full war broke out.

"I might have met Maynard," Hal said. "But Jane really knows him better than me, since she was born in Pittsburgh."

Jane snorted. "That's not really the same." The man was a legend in Pittsburgh; legends were fairy tales told to children that rarely reflected the truth. "We're taught the story of how Maynard became the director in school along with the story of Paul Revere's ride and Paul Bunyan and his blue ox. It gave us a really messed up idea of what is real. I honestly thought there was a breed of giant blue cows on Earth."

Taggart laughed.

"Think Pocahontas and John Smith without the sex," Hal said.

"Hal!" Jane made a cutting motion over her throat. She knew from experience Hal could maintain TV host commentary even while sedated. He wasn't coherent while drugged but he could keep talking through most insanity without missing a beat. "You threw the ball into my court, let me talk."

"Sorry." Hal didn't sound at all contrite.

Jane decided to stick to the grade school version. "You wouldn't know by looking at him but Maynard's maternal grandfather was a full-blooded Native American. Maynard is one-quarter Iroquois. He spent half his childhood on a reservation in upstate New York."

"Which makes him Pocahontas in this story," Hal murmured.

"Hal!" She reached into the back to prove she could hit him if he didn't shut up. "His father was from a long line of military, so as a teenager, he went to West Point. After graduating, he'd been a second lieutenant assigned to a unit that was supposed to be deployed to the Middle East. A few days before they shipped out, the Chinese activated the orbital gate for the first time for a battery of tests. Maynard was with the first troops to arrive, a few hours after the Pennsylvania State Police set up a perimeter."

"The rest of the story is like Paul Revere's ride. All we were ever told in school was lanterns in the bell tower, and Paul yelling 'the British are coming.' If you read military history, though, Paul didn't shout anything because it was a covert mission. Every place he warned dispatched riders to spread the word. Halfway through the night, he and another man, Sam Prescott, were stopped before they reached Lexington. Prescott, who had been out sexing up a lady friend before he got dragged into the craziness, escaped and he was the actual person to reach Concord. The main reason Revere is famous was because of Longfellow's poem that credited him with what really was a forty-man effort."

Taggart laughed. "In other words, who knows if the short version you got is actually based on truth at all?"

"Yeah. The glorified version is that Maynard and Windwolf met in the woods, just the two of them, and became friends. It's doubtful because Windwolf always has his bodyguards with him and Maynard would have been with his unit. Whatever. The story goes on to say that the viceroy ran into another unit of American soldiers, this one packing more weapons and under the command of someone totally spooked by all the Elfhome weirdness. The officer in charge tried to use force to corral the elves into some kind of holding area. Next thing you know, Windwolf is totally pissed off and nuking the hell out of the Americans. Maynard stripped off his weapons and walked out to talk to Windwolf. Between them, they made peace. When the UN stepped in, Windwolf insisted that Maynard be put in charge of the UN forces and that's the way it's been since year one. Basically most people consider Maynard the god of Pittsburgh in terms of what can and can't be done."

"Is he trustworthy?" Nigel asked. "With all these moles, can he be counted to be still on the elves' side?"

"The expansionists think he spends too much time kissing up to Windwolf, but I think they're missing the point. Maynard knows that we're stranded on Elfhome ninety-eight percent of the time and there's an entire world of elves that could wipe us off the map in the twenty-nine days between one Shutdown and the next. He has several thousands of idiots to mess things up and tens of thousands of innocent people to protect from their stupidity. He operates on zero tolerance and that doesn't make for a lot of friends."

And it meant that if he knew that Jane had wreaked havoc at Sandcastle to get back Boo, he would...

Jane wasn't sure what he would do. And it scared her.

The Sandcastle parking lot was crawling with EIA dressed in combat camo and armed with assault weapons. It unsettled Jane to see them. It was one thing to know that Pittsburgh had a small army made up of outsiders; it was another to witness them out in force, knowing that they'd been infiltrated and couldn't be trusted.

She slowed to a crawl, scanning the troops through the chain-link fence.

"What is it?" Taggart asked.

She spotted Maynard among his people. He was easy to pick out, as he was a tall, blond man dressed like an elf. "Just making sure it was actually Maynard that called Dmitri and we weren't walking into a trap."

She pulled into the Sandcastle parking lot and parked as far as she could from the troop carriers. The Pittsburgh Coroner's van sat tucked between the military vehicles, indicating that the EIA had found the males that she'd shot.

One of the things that annoyed expansionists the most about Maynard was he always adopted elfin fashion when Viceroy Windwolf was in Pittsburgh. They thought he should wear a business suit or his dress uniform. Despite the elegant clothes, there was no missing the military stamp on him. His long blond hair might be pulled back into a ponytail by a Wind Clan blue ribbon, but he stood at parade rest.

Because Maynard had asked for Hal, they'd gone

in the *PB&G* production truck. Jane flipped on the remote recording as they locked up the truck. Taggart was carrying *PB&G*'s ancient camera; Jane's truck couldn't handle the *CBM*'s newer cameras. Jane had her pistol in its kidney holster, but she really didn't want to have to shoot her way out of any mess. She carried the light reflector as a prop. With Hal in the lead, they all walked across the cracked and weed-choked parking lot to where Maynard waited.

Hal's superpower was his charisma; like most TV personalities, he refined it to megawatt power to reach through the camera and charm the audience no matter where they were. Face to face, it was kind of like being run over by a train. "Director Maynard!" Hal extended his hand, smiling broadly, beaming at full power. "Hal Rogers of *Pittsburgh Backyard and Garden*. Glad to meet you."

Maynard did a slight double take as he shook Hal's hand. Hal had broken his nose just days before and still had the raccoon mask of two black eyes.

"We were filming a segment on strangle vines." Hal gingerly touched his nose and theatrically winced in pain. "Got a little too close."

"I see," Maynard said.

"My studio manager said that you wanted to see me and my crew." Hal waved to take in Jane and the others to explain the extra bodies. His tone was mildly curious and unconcerned. *We've done nothing wrong.*

"I want you to tell me what happened here," Maynard said.

Hal managed to appear only mildly confused while Jane's heart leapt up her throat. "And I could do this—why?"

"You do have a doctorate in biology, do you not?"

"Yes, as a matter of fact, I do," Hal beamed with pride. "UC-Davis." Jane couldn't tell if the confusion that followed was faked or not. "I don't understand what that has to do with anything."

"For reasons I have never understood, the University of Pittsburgh chooses to take its break in the middle of summer instead of the dead of winter."

"Horace Mann," Nigel stated. The r of "Horace" was trilled by his Scottish accent.

"What?" Maynard and Jane both asked.

"Horace Mann is why the American schools follow the European standards," Nigel stated. "In 1843, he toured the schools of Europe and returned to the states to publish a paper on his findings. It was very influential and set many standards that the schools of America follow to this day."

Jane had no idea why Nigel might know this odd tidbit of information, but she really wished he'd kept his mouth shut as Maynard was now staring at Nigel and Taggart with fierce concentration.

After a minute, Maynard tilted his head slightly and pointed at the naturalist. "You're Nigel Reid, aren't you?"

"Yes, I am." Nigel smiled, turning on his hosting superpowers. "Glad to meet you, Director."

Maynard pointed at Taggart. "And you're Keawea-heulu Taggart."

Taggart's eyebrows went up with surprise. Probably not very many people tried to pronounce his first name and succeeded. "Yes."

"Nigel is here to film a new series for NBC," Hal explained. "We're showing them the ropes."

"Very gracious of them." Nigel didn't sound at all like a man that had nearly been eaten by a dinosaur only twenty-four hours earlier. Only a slight tightness around his eyes gave away the fact he was in pain from his rough handling. "Wonderful people. It's only been five days and already we've seen *amazing* things."

Taggart tried for unconcerned and failed. He covered by bringing up the camera to pan over the wreckage of Sandcastle. By the looks of it, the monster must have chased the oni all over the water park as a path of destruction crossed and re-crossed the midway.

Maynard eyed them with surprise. He took out a mini tablet computer and checked something. "Forgiveness, the last few days have been exceedingly . . . hectic. Yes, my people have Reid and Taggart entering at Shut-down. Good. Good. As I was saying, the University of Pittsburgh is on summer break and I'm scrambling for biology experts. I have something to show you."

He led them past the coroner's van to a line of dead bodies stretched out on the ground. The first three had each taken a bullet to the head. They had the gravitational strength of black holes on Jane's focus. She'd killed these people. All three were big brutish-looking males, but so had been her father. They wore face paint to look fiercer. What kind of souls had the paint hidden? Did they leave behind wives and children?

Taggart put a hand to her shoulder to steady her. She realized that he was telling Maynard that he was a war correspondent and used to dead bodies laid out in a row, but that Jane had never experienced it before.

"I'm afraid it's going to become a common sight before this comes to an end," Maynard said.

"They have horns." Hal seemed unaffected by the dead. Considering his degrees, he probably had experience dissecting human bodies. "If elves were the basis of our fae legends, I wonder if the oni are our demons."

"The Japanese use the word 'oni' to denote 'ogre' or 'demon,' depending on the translation," Nigel said.

Pittsburgh's coroner, Tim Covington, and his staff noticed the camera on Taggart's shoulder first, blazoned with *PB&G*'s logo. All activity ground to a halt as they were starstruck by Hal's presence. There was a moment of boyish silliness as Hal clowned with the men and women wearing rubber gloves and face masks. Jane was happy that it took all attention off her and gave her a chance to recover her balance.

After five minutes, though, she flicked her hand across her throat and Hal used his superpowers to gracefully turn the humans back to work with "I should let you get back to wrapping this all up."

"My own experts will deal with the gunshot victims." Maynard indicated the coroner's staff who were putting the oni that Jane had killed into body bags. "This is why I called you in." He crossed to a second line of bodies—or, more correctly, random body parts. He pointed down at the upper torso of a male. The body was torn in two, exposing the bottom of the ribcage. The lungs and heart had gone with lower half—most likely down the gullet of the river monster.

"Something went through this area last night. Judging by the bite marks, it's huge." Maynard walked forward, pointing to other half-eaten bodies. "And hungry, or maybe travels in a pack. And there's this." He stooped to indicate a feathery-looking vinelike pattern marking the chests, arms and legs of the various dead.

"Covington says that this is indicative of lightning strikes. Only it didn't storm last night and there's no power lines down in the area."

Jane was counting the dead. Boo had told them that there were fourteen oni guarding over her and Joey. Jane had shot three. If the river monster had killed the rest, then there were no witnesses to their rescue mission. The bits and pieces gathered together, though, seemed too few. Had they escaped or were they eaten whole?

"The elves can throw lightning," Hal said. "Are you sure that one of them wasn't the cause of these burns?"

"Only Windwolf can do that and he was with me last night." Maynard pointed toward the river. "There are tracks of something large."

"We had asked viewers to phone in sightings of monsters so we could film them." Jane worked on their alibi as Hal and Nigel examined the tracks. "We were in the South Hills yesterday filming a saurus that Grandma Gertie e-mailed in. It nearly ate Nigel. One of our tips was a sighting of a large river monster. We thought we spotted it from the Fort Pitt Bridge the day after Startup, but when we searched for it the next morning, we couldn't find any trace of it."

Maynard gave her a hard look. "You didn't think to mention this to anyone?"

"Actually we asked both your river patrols and the police to keep an eye out for it."

He consulted his tablet again and sighed. "Forgiveness. I see that you did. What did you see?"

"Not much," Jane lied and prayed that the man never saw their footage. "When we saw this thing, we didn't realize it could leave the river. That's why we went after the saurus; a dinosaur in the suburbs seemed more dangerous than something confined to the water. This is a game changer; we need to find this thing and stop it."

And Jane meant every word of it. Because of the jumpfish, no one strayed too close to the riverbank. Downriver of Sandcastle, though, there were thousands of people living just outside of jumpfish range of the water. It was one thing to have this thing rampaging through an abandoned water park in one of the emptiest neighborhoods in Pittsburgh. It was quite another if it came ashore on the North Side or downtown.

With the Pittsburgh Police spread thin and the EIA busy trying to find the kidnapped princess while cleaning house of oni moles, there was no one else able to deal with such a large, dangerous monster.

"We'll take care of this," Jane said.

"You sure?" Maynard asked.

"We've been solving problems like this for years." Hal could truthfully claim it, too. "We can handle this."

Maynard raised his hand to his ear and listened to some report over an earpiece. His eyes narrowed and he glanced toward the parking lot. A lone hoverbike was coming at breakneck speed.

Jane didn't realize she'd growled with anger until Taggart asked quietly, "Who is that?"

"Wicked Witch of the West on her broom stick," Hal said.

Jane backhanded Hal with her free hand. "Chloe Polanski." Maynard knew *PB&G*'s reputation, but he'd called Dmitri for Hal's help. He'd only recognized the men who appeared in front of the camera, not Jane who normally stayed behind it. Nor had she introduced

herself—she rarely did. Thus he probably didn't know
her father had been a sniper. The three perfect head-
shots meant nothing to him. Chloe, though, had covered
Boo's kidnapping and gotten to know Jane's family well.
If she saw the bodies . . .

Jane had to be sure that Chloe was too preoccupied
to notice until the oni were safely body-bagged. "Do
you mind if we film a public announcement warning people to stay away from the river and to report
anything unusual they see?" Jane shifted so that her
back was to the dead oni.

Maynard nodded after moment of thought. "Yes,
that would probably be a good course of action."

Jane waved Taggart to aim the camera at Maynard
and lifted the reflector. "Hal . . ."

"Raccoon boy." Hal pointed at his face.

There wasn't time for makeup. "Nigel. Highlight
the basics: unknown beast wreaks havoc at Sandcastle, multiple dead, size of beast estimated to be
quite large, able to move both in the water and out.
People are to stay away from the river and report
any sightings. Go!"

Nigel hit his mark beside Maynard, squared off
with the Director, set his face on "serious" and the
moment that Taggart indicated he was rolling, launched
into commentary. "This is Nigel Reid, coming to you
from Sandcastle Waterpark for NBC. I'm here with
Director Maynard of the EIA."

Nigel glossed quickly over the oni, suggesting only
that those dead were killed by the monster. Taggart
gave Jane a questioning glance but any discussion would
be picked up by the camera's microphone. Silence was
ingrained into the cameraman.

Jane watched out the corner of her eye as Chloe dismounted her hoverbike. *Take the bait. Take the bait.*

"Director, obviously this is a massive creature." Nigel managed to guide the director even farther from the coroner's van by indicating the tracks leading down to the river. "The footprints are nearly two feet wide. We can see the wide, smooth drag mark that is classic for crocodile. This creature appears to be long and low to the ground."

Maynard took out his tablet and started to take notes. "What else can you tell me about this creature?"

*Everything.*

Nigel continued on as if they hadn't actually seen the monster in question. "The largest known crocodile is the saltwater crocodile which can reach up to twenty-two feet and weighs up to four thousand, four hundred pounds. They are aggressive hunters and are considered very dangerous to humans in areas where they are found. The creature that attacked Sandcastle is easily twice the size of the largest known crocodile."

"Twice?" Maynard echoed with dismay.

"Yes, that's what these tracks indicate." Nigel pointed to the large footprints in the dirt. "We're looking for an animal that is over forty feet in length. It's most likely a very strong swimmer and able to leave the water at any low point in the river and walk inland for—well—until it decides to turn around."

Chloe kept coming, laser-targeted on Maynard. She walked past Tim Covington without even glancing at him.

"And the electricity burns?" Maynard checked on Chloe's progress. He kept his face expressionless but clearly he didn't like the woman any more than Jane did.

"I would have to say that this creature must be electrogenic, or capable of generating an electric field. Fish that are electrogenic have an electric organ, which is made up of modified nerve or muscle tissue. These flat, disklike cells number in the thousands and they're stacked, each one of them producing 0.15 volts. So in essence, they're like little batteries, carrying a charge from the exchange of positive sodium and potassium ions within the animal's body. The cells individually generate a very small amount but this is multiplied by thousands of cells. A six-foot electric eel can generate six hundred volts; this is comparable to the third rail of a mass transit system."

"So the Sandcastle monster could be seven times more powerful?"

"Yes, it could be. It's obviously generating not only more voltage but also more amps, which makes it quite deadly. By the entry burns on these bodies, the electricity appears to be arcing through the air to its victims, much like a bolt of lightning."

Chloe might have arrived on a hoverbike wearing a helmet, but not a hair of her blond bob was out of place. Jane had no idea how she managed it; the only reason Jane kept her long hair in a ponytail was otherwise it looked like a rat's nest by the end of the day.

Chloe surprised Jane by waiting until Nigel paused before she started to talk. "What are you idiots doing here?"

"Taping a show." Jane tried for the intelligence level that Chloe assigned them. *Don't mind us, we're not running around wiping out enemy camps.*

"This is not a backyard or garden." Chloe waved toward the hole that Hal had blasted into the back of the one building during their last visit. "And someone already beat you to blowing this place up."

"Giant man-eating fish is what we do." Jane ignored the bit about blowing things up. Behind Chloe, Covington was zipping up the first body bag. Two more to go. "We're filming this segment to air during the news. We need to warn viewers to keep on the lookout for the creature."

"You're going to stir up mass hysteria when you don't even know what caused this?" Chloe sneered. "All you have is a set of tracks..."

"And some well-chewed bodies," Hal muttered in Jane's shadow. She suspected that the woman frightened Hal by her sheer ruthlessness.

"Only an idiot would believe you could know what type of animal it is from its tracks."

"My grandfather was a tracker, Ms. Polanski," Maynard stated quietly. "He could tell everything about an animal—how big it was, how healthy it was, how long ago it had passed through the area and at what speed—just by its tracks."

Behind Chloe, Covington zipped up the second bag.

"The police and EIA are spread thin still looking for Tinker *domi*." Jane shifted to the side to keep the coroner's activity out of Chloe's peripheral vision. "*Pittsburgh Backyard and Garden* has agreed to track down and kill this creature, but we need help. One of *your* viewers gave us the original tip on this beast. He saw the creature in the river by the I-79 Bridge. Not only do we have to warn people about this thing, but we need all eyes looking for it."

"And the credit will all go to WQED?" Chloe asked with scorn.

"Ms. Polanski, I require your cooperation in this." Maynard stated it simply but it was fraught with implications. He was the god of Pittsburgh. Anyone that didn't play by his rules found themselves exiled back to Earth. "I want this thing dead."

Chloe gave him a cold, annoyed stare but then looked away with a slight huff of frustration. Thankfully she glanced not toward the last oni dead by bullet but at the hole that Hal had blown through the wall. "Fine. I want an exclusive interview."

Jane relaxed slightly as Covington zipped up the last body bag for the headshot victims. All the evidence of their involvement was now covered up. Only the half-eaten bodies remained.

Maynard glanced at his watch. "You have five minutes."

Chloe tapped her eyepiece. "This is Chloe Polanski with Director Maynard at Sandcastle Water Park." She glanced down at one of the bodies. All that were on display were the monster-dismembered ones. "This appears to be an oni encampment hidden here at Sandcastle. How many warriors did you find here?"

*Yes, how many?*

Maynard blocked them both. "We haven't matched up all the body pieces yet to come to an exact number yet. We will be issuing an official report later."

"Were they all oni?" Chloe asked. When Maynard frowned slightly at the question, she went into more detail. "Were there any humans or elves . . . or tengu?"

Jane's heart flipped in her chest. They had fled the scene so quickly that they had no chance to scrub away any sign of Joey and Boo.

"There was no sign that Tinker *domi* was held here."

Maynard leapt to a different but more obvious end of the questioning. "Tengu" was only linked to "Tinker's kidnapper" for Maynard and not to "helpless children."

Chloe wasn't easily deferred. "So no signs of a prisoner possibly killed along with the oni? Is it possible that anyone being held captive—like Tinker—was eaten by this thing?"

"Tinker *domi*," Maynard corrected her firmly. "The elves will not tolerate anyone being so informal with her title."

Chloe flicked away the comment with her perfectly manicured fingers. "Yes or no?"

"There is no sign that Tinker *domi* was held here," Maynard repeated coldly.

Chloe pressed her lips together into a tight, unhappy line but otherwise didn't let her frustration show. She was being amazingly restrained but this was Maynard, not some poor grieving family who had lost their baby.

The oni in body bags were being loaded into the coroner's van. Jane controlled a deep sigh of relief.

"Did you take anyone prisoner?" Chloe asked. "Oni or otherwise?"

"No." Maynard wouldn't lie about it. Probably. He had a reputation to uphold with the elves. That he would not tell a lie was part of his legend.

"So all you will discuss is this mythical beast?" Chloe asked.

"This is an unexplored continent on Elfhome. Not even the elves know what lives in the rivers." He glanced at his watch again. "Any other question before you let your viewers know about this new creature?"

Chloe glanced around and eyed the body bags. Jane held her breath.

"I think we should dig around and see if we can turn up some tissue samples to run DNA scans off of," Nigel said into the silence. "See what this blighter is made of. Surely there's a lab somewhere in town that can do a rush job for us."

"Maybe," Hal said. "Or the elves could magic us something. Bibby-bobby-boo."

Jane punched Hal in the gut for saying her sister's name.

Chloe whipped around to stare at them. "What?"

"Nothing," Hal whimpered.

Nigel continued as if Hal hadn't slipped. "We can't assume that this is a solitary creature. Depending on the species of crocodile, they lay anywhere from seven to nearly a hundred eggs. Electric eels can have up to three thousand young hatch from one clutch of eggs. Really it's a matter of physiology. It would be helpful if we could get some DNA and see which species this monster is most closely related to. Scans would let us know what we're dealing with."

Chloe laughed. "Don't you think we would notice three thousand giant electric crocodiles swimming around the Mon?"

"The hatchlings could be wee things compared to their mother." Nigel measured out something only inches across. "In the water, if they swim in school, they'd be like piranha. The question is, how quickly can they walk on land?"

"Don't be ridiculous." Chloe tapped her eyepiece. "Reporting one monster is fine—certainly there's undeniable evidence that something big went through here—theorizing a swarm of tiny man-eating fish walking around on land is too much."

Jane hated that she secretly agreed with Chloe, at least at a gut level. Pittsburghers had enough on their plate being caught between warring nonhuman forces and their main ally, the EIA, filled with traitors.

"Just make sure you thoroughly warn your viewers about the adult creature," Maynard ordered. "If anyone is harmed because you're negligent, I'll have you escorted back to Earth on the next Shutdown."

Chloe huffed but nodded her understanding.

Maynard pointed at Jane. He'd figured out who actually was in charge. "Do whatever you need to do to kill this thing."

Jane vetoed using Nigel's whistle to call the monster to Sandcastle while the EIA were there. She didn't want to risk the lives of all the men if they lost control of the situation. (Actually the idea that they would have any control with so little planning was laughable, so collateral damage was almost guaranteed.) She wanted a foolproof plan and an empty playing field—and a cannon—before facing the monster again.

She owned a chain-fed auto-cannon—well, technically Bertha belonged to her entire family—but waving it under the EIA's nose would get her locked up faster than shooting oni.

Much as she wanted to gather up her crew and flee, they still should try to erase any evidence that they left behind.

Maynard refused to allow them to poke around in the water park's boardwalk restaurants where Boo and Joey had been held. He stated firmly that if the buildings collapsed on them, he didn't want to waste time digging them back out. His men were already cautiously searching the restaurants for clues to where the oni were holding Tinker. Jane could only hope that her team hadn't left anything behind that would link them to the attack on the encampment.

It left them with only the camo-net-covered swimming pools to film while discreetly collecting gun casings. The Mon-tsunami wave pool was the closest to the tower where she'd covered their retreat. The oni had created a grating of chicken wire to cover it completely. The water was dark and smelled of river but wasn't stagnating. The oni were aerating the pool to keep alive whatever lived in it.

"What do you think they have in here?" Hal pulled out his extendable grab stick and poked at the wire. "Jumpfish?"

Jane caught Hal by the collar and hauled him away from the edge. A second later a dozen bodies plastered themselves to the screen covering, tentacles gripping the wire, sharp beaks attempting to find an opening in the grid.

"What the hell?" Jane breathed in surprise. "Are those water fairies?"

"Not quite," Hal stated calmly. "They seem to be a larger, more aggressive version than any we've seen."

Taggart panned the camera over the pool and then focused on the far end. The oni had dug a ditch that led toward the Monongahela. "I think they planned to release these into the river."

"Why the hell would they do that?" Jane growled in anger. Water fairies were annoying but they were fairly timid.

"To drive humans out of Pittsburgh," Nigel said. "The oni have been planning this war for years. The fewer humans in the city to side with the elves, the better. Monsters in the river. Monsters in the woods. Who would want to stay?"

"Those of us who were born here." Jane looked around. "We're not leaving here until everything in these pools are dead. We are not letting these things get into the river."

Nigel nodded reluctantly. "After seeing what the oni did with your sister, there's no telling what they might have done to these to make the water fairies more deadly. We can't let them out into the wild. If nothing else, they'd probably replace the original species."

"How do we do this?" Jane asked.

"Dynamite," Hal suggested.

"We're not going to start blowing things up with the EIA still here," Jane whispered fiercely.

Hal spread his hands. "If they watch the show, they know that's how we handle a lot of things."

Taggart snorted with what sounded suspiciously like barely muffled laughter.

Jane pointed a finger at him. "This is not funny." She switched targets to Hal. "At this time, I don't want to go reminding the EIA of that."

"When we were..." Nigel caught himself and dropped his voice to a whisper. "When we were here yesterday, I noticed that there were several carbon dioxide canisters for the drink fountains still sitting about. If we dispense the gas into pool, the water fairies will suffocate. It would be mostly painless, and very quiet."

"Quiet is good." She pointed up at the tower behind them. "Let's go up, do an aerial shot of the park, and pick up casings. Then we'll see what's in the other pools."

❖          ❖          ❖

The rest of the day was surreal. The Mushroom Pool with the giant bright-colored sprinklers had river shark pups. The Tad Pool had baby jumpfish that flung themselves out of the wading pool like evil rain. Wet Willie's Water Works was filled with large red, jellylike orbs the size of apples.

"What are those?" Jane asked the naturalists.

"Roe?" Nigel guessed.

"Yes, I think they are eggs." Hal plucked one out of the pool with his grab stick. "Wonder if they taste like caviar."

Jane smacked him in the back of the head before he sample it. "Don't eat things when you don't know what they are. It could be poisonous."

"There's thousands of them." Taggart knelt to examine them closely with the camera.

"They're extremely large," Nigel said. "And freshly laid. The larvae are just developing. After about three days you normally can make out the eyes and the beginnings of the spinal cord."

"There's no camouflage netting over this pool." Hal pointed to the set of monster tracks that led up to the edge of the concrete surrounding the shallow wading pool. "I think the monster laid these last night."

Nigel eyed the evidence and then nodded. "It was returning to the place it was spawned."

Jane laughed. The men looked at her with confused surprise. "Karma's a bitch," she explained. "It literally bit the oni in the ass. We couldn't have called the monster here if it wasn't already returning."

"If it spawned here, it's not a natural creature." Nigel's burr thickened with his anger. "It's clearly a beast of war. We cannot let these hatch either. If we drain the water out of this pool and leave off the cover, the heat will kill them."

*And a few gallons of gasoline, just be sure.* Jane could tell that it tore at Nigel to destroy life. Hal was much more pragmatic about it. He knew that humans rarely left the tiny pocket of Earth ecosystem that Pittsburgh represented. Beyond the Rim, there were no Earthborn species. They couldn't compete with their magic-reinforced cousins. If the humans didn't aggressively protect their ground, the flora and fauna of Elfhome would wipe them from the face of the planet.

"Let's make sure we document all this before we start."

The saurus had battered Nigel the day before. It hadn't done serious damage, but under his clothes, he sported massive bruises and shallow claw marks. The pain was starting to show as they set up to film the roe. The EIA crews were still carefully searching the rubble, looking for the viceroy's bride. It was a weird kind of torture, wanting them to find something, afraid that they would find the wrong thing.

"This is a nursery of monsters," Nigel started with his indignant anger carefully controlled. "River shark. Jumpfish. These are large dangerous predators—known man-eaters—in a city fronted on all sides by water. Thirty percent of Pittsburgh lives within a thousand feet of a river. Pittsburghers have spent years trying to reduce the population of river sharks and jumpfish. As we saw the other day, the number of these predators in this area is staggering. The only logical explanation for there to be so many river sharks and jumpfish is that the oni have been restocking them from this hatchery."

He gestured toward the other pools. "The water fairies here have obviously been genetically engineered into something larger, more aggressive, and perhaps more poisonous. In this pool, there are several hundred eggs, just like this one." Nigel hefted up the egg held in Hal's grab stick. "Consider that a salmon can reach to nearly five feet in length and its roe is smaller a pea. Imagine the size of the creature that hatches out of this egg. Such a monster killed and ate an unknown number of oni before laying these eggs. The oni planned to unleash thousands of these massive predators onto an unsuspecting city, unprepared for the onslaught. It represents bio-terrorism at a horrific level."

In the end, she convinced the men to set the roe on fire using the gasoline in the *PB&G* spare gas can. If only all her problems were as easy to solve.

Brandy showed up in a Pittsburgh police squad car as they were stowing their gear. Brandy slammed her door and came storming across the parking lot like the goddess of justice.

Jane figured that she'd better beat Brandy to the punch. "Why did you call Alton and tell him to sit on me? You know how my little brothers are. I had to deal with all five of them last night. They wanted to know why you wanted me sat on. You know if I'd told them, they would have gotten their guns and come here! Do you know what kind of mess that would have been?"

"You didn't do this?" Brandy pointed toward the flaming egg pool.

"I have a temper but I don't tear people in half and eat them." Jane shoved the reflector into the production truck. "The oni were using Sandcastle to breed things like river sharks, and releasing them into the Mon. We think one of their monsters turned on them. Director Maynard called us in as consultants."

"Oh." Brandy deflated at the news. And then deflated a little more. "Oh. I'm sorry."

"You're sorry about what?"

"Your sister! Boo! You thought she might be here."

*Yes, Jane, you should be more upset.* Anger was easier than pretending to be disappointed. "No! She's not here!" Jane remembered then that the EIA was still searching the rubble for clues to Tinker's location. "They're checking to see if any survivors are trapped inside the buildings. Any news about Tinker?"

"Nothing good. The viceroy's 'blade brother' disappeared last night."

"His what?"

Brandy spread her hands to indicate ignorance. "It means adopted brother or foster brother or something like that. The kid is the youngest elf in Pittsburgh; from what I can tell they consider him not much older than your baby brother Guy. He'd been at the hospice; they were testing him to see if he'd been drugged or had a spell cast on him or something. That part really isn't clear; something about seeing things that weren't real. What's clear is he was forcibly taken."

Jane cursed. Losing Boo had torn her heart out. If Guy had vanished too, it would have killed her. She couldn't even imagine what Windwolf was going through. The damnable thing is that the humans were reporting on the viceroy's movements. The oni could easily be moving Tinker from camp to camp, staying one step ahead of the elves.

Jane breathed in deep as she realized that Boo might know where all those camps might be.

Unfortunately Brandy noticed. "What?"

Jane stared at Brandy, fighting to keep dismay off her face. *What the hell do I tell her?* Jane caught sight of Taggart pretending not to be listening into the conversation. A lie spilled out, seeded in the truth. "My mom has this crazy idea," she turned slightly and dropped to a whisper. "She thinks that I'm interested in Taggart. So she wants to do a big family dinner tonight and I'd forgotten until just this moment. It's a 'welcome to Pittsburgh' dinner that is really a thinly disguised 'welcome to the family' thing."

The family dinner wasn't a lie. Her family was going to be gathering at Hyeholde, trying to make up for lost time and sharing the responsibility of protecting Boo and Joey. Jane had to go back to her place to get the cannon. If her brothers found out about the river monster, they'd want to help. The last thing Jane wanted was to have to ride herd on Hal and her brothers at the same time. Since her family would be at Hyeholde when they returned, they were going to have to wait until full dark to unpack the cannon.

Brandy glanced toward Taggart. "Oh, girl, if you don't want to tap that, let me know."

Jane opened her mouth and didn't know what to say except, "Hey!"

"So your mother's idea isn't so crazy after all?" Brandy laughed and headed back to her car. "Call me! Let me know how things work out!"

✧          ✧          ✧

One of *PB&G*'s early shows dealt with a steel spinner nest at a farm in the South Hills. The appreciative farmer gave Jane two dozen newly hatched banty chicks. Jane had been caught off guard by the gift and simply stuck them in the back of the production truck while she dealt with Brian Scroggins, the fire marshall. (It takes a flamethrower to safely clean out a nest of the giant spiders. Brian eventually agreed with Jane that the farmer should have warned *PB&G* that he used the remote shed to store wood pallets, used engine oil, and nearly a hundred half-empty cans of spray paint. The damn aerosol cans went off like bottle rockets for an hour.)

By the time she remembered the chicks, they'd imprinted on Chesty. The big elfhound was doing the best he could, but clearly the golf-ball-sized chicks threw him into confusion as they attempted to tuck themselves under their "mother."

Cuddling wasn't something her family did. Most acquaintances knew that the Kryskills weren't the touchy-feely types and kept out of striking range. Joey was as determined as the chicks to tuck himself up against his new family. Every time Joey hopped up onto the lap of one of her brothers, they went wide-eyed with surprise. They understood that Boo would see them brushing Joey off as rejecting her. They knew too that Joey desperately wanted the comfort of knowing he was loved and protected as their "little brother." It helped that he was a sweet little boy. So her brothers soldiered on despite being clueless how to "mother" the little boy. It would be comical if it weren't so sad. Alton was doing the best, but then he'd ended up with the chicks too.

Yesterday had been a very impromptu meal of

spaghetti heavily supplemented with vegetables raided
out of her garden. Today her family came prepared to
cook, because that was what Kryskills did to celebrate.

Jane's mother made her famous fried chicken (but
only after Boo and Joey gave her puzzled looks and
asked "Chicken is yummy, why wouldn't we eat it?").
Geoffrey grilled corn on the cob while mixing up jala-
peno butter. Marc made baby red potato salad with blue
cheese and bacon. Guy tossed a salad of mixed greens
and fresh-picked tomatoes with strawberry vinaigrette
dressing. Duff made sauerkraut, sharp cheddar cheese
and potato pierogies with caramelized onions. Alton
used the blueberries that Boo and Joey helped pick for
berry-and-cream-cheese turnovers dusted with confec-
tioners' sugar. In the spirit of "we're all one big family,"
the kids braided friendship bands with leather cord and
red silk twine and tied them to everyone's left wrist.

Jane answered all the "where do you keep" questions,
washed pans as they were done being used, and kept
Hal out from underfoot. Seriously, the man was like
a three-year-old in the big kitchen, wanting to lick
bowls and steal bacon. One would think he knew not
to get close to her brothers while they wielded knives.

Nigel had the good sense to anchor down one of
the barstools at the island. He asked quiet leading
questions to keep the conversations going. Taggart used
mad ninja-stealth to film the cooking. Their videos
were to be Pittsburgh's voice on Earth; her family's
pain had to be recorded and shared.

It reminded her of the viceroy standing grief-stricken
by the river. The oni had kidnapped his bride. And
Boo might know where she was being held.

❖      ❖      ❖

On the pretense that she wanted help setting the great table, Jane got Boo alone in the main dining room. Last night they'd eaten in turns in the kitchen, as Jane's everyday table only sat her mother and brothers comfortably. Jane's family had moved on without Boo, unconsciously sizing their lives to six siblings, not seven. Luckily the addition of Joey, Hal, Nigel and Taggart helped keep it from being painfully obvious to Boo.

Jane unlocked the windows and rolled them up to air out the room. A summer thunderstorm was blowing in; the wind was picking up. It caught the sheers and made them dance in the gloaming. She would have to close the windows quickly if it started to rain. "You went blueberry picking with Alton?"

"Berry picking. Berry eating. Tree climbing." Boo's voice came from up high.

"It was so nice to go in any direction I wanted." Boo stood on the railing of the second floor balcony that overlooked the main dining room, arms outstretched to feel the wind. "No one to stop me but me."

"Like hell! Get down from there! What the hell do you think you're doing up there?"

"I've always liked being high." Boo walked barefoot quickly along the railing to the bannister, making Jane stutter with fear and anger. "I'm getting down!" And she came sliding down the bannister like she was six again.

Was it a tengu thing to be high? Was Boo afraid that being too much tengulike upset Jane? Well, it did. Jane didn't want Boo to know it.

"You're just like your brothers," Jane focused back on the windows so Boo couldn't see her face. "Trying to give me a heart attack with Kryskill craziness."

Boo hugged her from the back, pressing her face against Jane's shoulder blade. "It's so hard to be stuck on the ground," she whispered. "It's like I've been buried alive."

So it was a tengu thing. *Cope with it, Jane, cope with it.* Jane took a deep breath. "You need to set a good example for Joey. At least until we can get him back to his aunt and uncle."

Boo whimpered softly. "We can't. They're dead. The oni killed them."

Jane breathed out a curse. "I thought—the way he talks—"

"He doesn't know. I haven't told him. The oni wanted to capture the whole family. With just Joey, they could only make copies of him. If they'd gotten the entire family, they would have taken one or two apart to see how they were put together. I've seen Kajo do it with fish at the hatchery; shatter animals down and put them together differently. Make monsters."

Boo trembled, her voice breaking. "But they killed all of Joey's family. That's why they made me tengu. With a copy, they had someone they could sh-sh-sh-shatter . . ."

"You're safe!" Jane turned and gathered her into a hug. "I won't let anyone hurt you. You're safe!"

Only after the tears were dried, the table wiped free of dust, a trolley of the good dishes and silverware wheeled out and placed on the table did Jane remembered why she'd gotten her sister alone. By then the cooks were finishing up the food and Nigel was bandaging Hal.

Why had the oni taken Tinker? To shatter her down? Jane felt sick at the idea.

"Do you know where any oni camps are?" Jane asked quietly and at the farthest point from the kitchen she could get Boo.

"Not anymore. Danni made Kajo move all the camps because Pure Radiance came to the Westernlands. A deadly game of hide and seek, she called it. All the camps that I knew of were abandoned. The hatchery was the only one of Kajo's that stayed in place. I don't know if Lord Tomtom moved his; I never knew where they were in the first place. Kajo and Lord Tomtom never got along."

Jane breathed out in disappointment. At least she didn't have to decide what to do if Boo did know where Tinker was being held.

The food cooked, they sat down to eat. Hal tried to start before blessing and both Jane and her mother slapped him. It was a wonder he'd survived her family for so many years.

It was all good and happy until the last crumb of the blueberry turnovers. Family tradition said that the youngest three had to clear the dishes, generally because they'd been spared from having a cook a dish. Guy bussed the table with the ease of a trained waiter. Boo scrambled to keep up, wanting to help but without the years of experience. Joey carried a plate at a time into the kitchen with exaggerated care. Everyone else leaned back from the table and drank equal parts of fresh milk and strong Assam tea. (After years of being smacked, Hal stopped asking for coffee after meals. Nigel and Taggart seemed to relish the tea as much as her brothers.)

With deceptive calm, her mother lifted up her cup

and said, "Mitsy Barker called me this afternoon. She said Nigel was on the noon news. Something about a giant river monster?"

The table went silent and her family all stared at Jane.

*Telephone, telegraph, tell a Barker.*

To be fair, Jane had to expect someone to tell her family after warning the entire city. She was really hoping, though, it would be after she killed it. She wanted it to be like rescuing Boo; the Kryskill family circus wouldn't know what Jane was planning until after all the shooting was over.

Jane spread her hands. "We're filming dangerous stuff that lives in the backyard like we always do. It's kind of like a saurus that lives in the river. It's not like river sharks because it doesn't stay in the water. You could call it a jumpfish with legs."

"You're going after the *namazu*?" Boo cried with obvious horror.

Jane inwardly cringed. She'd forgotten that Boo probably knew exactly what they were hunting. Nor could she smack her baby sister to keep her quiet. She tried glaring at her instead.

"The what?" Alton asked.

"The *namazu*!" the two kids cried.

"The god fish!" Joey stood on his toes and held his arms wide as possible.

"It is a very big, crocodilelike fish thing!" Jane stated loudly to override the kids. "Hal and I have been dealing with shit like this for years."

Which was a mistake as her brothers all turned to Hal. While Hal could host-dazzle Maynard, he was intimidated by her family. "It is a smidge larger than our typical fare." He turned to her and saw her face.

"I-I-I have all confidence that Jane can handle this. Given a big enough gun and a hunting stand and the monster call."

Chaos erupted. Her brothers' main focus started with "You're taking Bertha?" After Boo informed the table that "It can throw lightning," their concern forked to include the dangers of hunting the monster *alone*. (Her brothers did not count Hal because they'd helped teach him how to shoot. There was a reason Hal liked dynamite to solve problems.) Jane tried to squash the idea that the Kryskill Family Circus would join her on the filming. It was bad enough that they would be creating video evidence of the illegal firearms that her family owned; she didn't need her brothers on film too.

Her mother's loud whistle cut through the conversation.

Jane, her brothers and Hal snapped to standing attention. After a heartbeat of silence, Nigel and Taggart also stood up, looking slightly bewildered.

"I went and listened to the report myself," her mother said calmly into her cup of tea. "I know how big you believe this thing to be. You will need Bertha but you're not taking her out by yourself. She's a family resource. You'll need to mount her on a vehicle and brace the vehicle against recoil. You'll need someone to drive that vehicle and someone who is a better shot than Hal as your backup."

Her mother took a long sip of tea; chaos returned. Jane said nothing. There would be no arguing with her mother. Besides, she was completely right. They'd need to take the *Chased by Monsters* production truck with Taggart filming. Hal was as good a driver as he was at shooting, which was to say only adequate. Nigel was still moving gingerly from being almost eaten by the saurus just the day before and was unfamiliar with the area. Someone from her family would have to drive the gun platform.

Her brothers were all stating loudly why they should be the ones to accompany Jane. Alton was playing the "oldest son" angle. Geoffrey was the most mechanically minded, thus able to deal with any problems with the chain-fed cannon. Marc stated that he was a cop, and thus the one able to get her around police detection. He was also the best driver among them. (Also his decommissioned EIA Humvee was already modified to be a gun platform. It was the most logical vehicle to use.) Duff was the best shot of her brothers (though Jane beat him three out of five shoot-offs.) Guy pointed out that as a minor, if they did get caught, he'd get into the least amount of trouble; besides, he just had summer school while everyone else worked.

Her mother sipped and listened, her eyes narrowing slightly as she considered the arguments. As she lowered her cup, the Kryskill boys all went silent. Her empty teacup chimed loudly onto the china saucer. "Marc and Geoffrey, you will back up your sister." She raised her voice over the wordless outcry from the other three brothers. "Alton, you'll be responsible for the safety of Boo and Joey. Duff, since you'll be the only one at the bakery tomorrow morning, you'll be the communication hub. Set up code words before you leave tonight. All calls are to go to Duff to coordinate activities and use the code words he provides. Guy, you can stay one hour and then head home and play the stereo loud enough to make your ears bleed."

"What?" Guy cried.

Their mom clarified. "Stick to your usual Sunday schedule." Their mother checked her phone and stood. "Tonight is bingo night at the fire hall. I'll have to hurry or people will notice that I came in late. The oni have to consider the possibility that Boo and Joey escaped in the chaos last night. The most reasonable thing for Boo to do is to contact her family. The oni might be watching us to see if there's any change in our schedules that would indicate that she's returned. Last night we had the excuse that Jane had guests to feed, one of which had been attacked by a saurus. Tonight we have to return to our regular routines. Go do what you normally do. Not a word to anyone, not even your cousins. Is that understood?"

"Yes, ma'am!" the Kryskill's siblings answered.

Guy gave Joey a nudge and the little boy cried out, "Yes, ma'am!"

"Keep your eyes open, your heads down, and your guns close," their mother said.

"Yes, ma'am!"

"Make your father proud." Their mother flicked her hand to indicate that they were free to start. "Dismissed."

"Who or what is Bertha?" Taggart asked quietly after her mother had kissed and hugged everyone including him and Nigel goodbye. (Normally her mother didn't take to strangers so quickly but they had returned Boo to her family. She didn't usually kiss or hug either, but she wanted an excuse to linger on Boo, cuddle Joey again, and size up Taggart for son-in-law material.)

Jane's brothers were starting their traditional dish-washing activities, which meant the dishes and kitchen would be spotless and her brothers would be sopping wet. (In the winter, this usually required a traditional clothes-washing activity afterwards.) Jane had pulled Taggart aside to keep his camera from being damaged when the water volleys started.

"Do you know what a M242 is?" Jane asked. Most people wouldn't but he was a war correspondent.

Taggart *stared* at her. Obviously he knew the gun. "Why does your family have a chain-fed auto-cannon?"

"I'll take you to the museum sometime to see the wyvern they have mounted. It could carry off the saurus we killed the other day. Dragons are supposed to be bigger. My dad didn't like surprises. Bertha was his answer for any surprises that cropped up."

"And we do have a big surprise to deal with," Hal murmured, as he brushed between them, clearing a path for Joey who was still carrying dishes from the dining room to the kitchen. Hal was surprisingly good with kids, having done a year of children's science programming. (Apparently he focused too much on blowing things up and setting things on fire for the comfort of PBS lawyers.) Hal added in "Mine" before disappearing into the kitchen.

"Yes." Jane didn't like the idea of pulling Bertha out of her hiding place but she wanted something that would definitely kill the high-voltage, massive jawed beast before it had a chance to close on her team.

Taggart glanced after Hal, eyes narrowing slightly. He caught Jane by the arm and pulled her into the quiet of the entry hall.

She guessed what he wanted. "No, I don't know where my dad got Bertha. It was before Geoffrey was born . . ."

"No, that's not what I wanted to know," Taggart said quietly. "Are you in love with Hal?"

"What?" Jane cried. "No!"

"He's in love with you."

She wondered why Taggart would think that and then remembered the video from Hal's "phone call" from Mercy Hospital where he thanked her profusely. At the end Hal had stated that he loved Jane. "He was drugged. He gets loopy and says shit that he doesn't mean."

"Oh, he meant that. You can't spend a day locked in the car with the man and not know that he's afraid of losing you."

"Afraid of losing his producer. I've been the only person that can work with him without getting maimed. That includes filming on Earth too; he once set a PA on fire."

Taggart scrubbed at his face, laughing. "I almost pity the man. Look, I learned through several painful experiences, that when I start liking a woman, the first thing I need to find out is if she's already in love with someone else. There's nothing worse than falling head over heels for someone, and then have them go 'I'm sorry but I've realized that he's the love of my life.' Losing something makes it suddenly clear that it's very important to you. So, step one, clear the playing field. Quickly. While there's still a chance to back out without the desire to go drown myself in a metric ton of whiskey."

They stared at each other in silence a moment.

"Are you?" Taggart asked.

"Am I what?"

"In love with Hal?" Taggart cried.

"No!"

"Are you sure? Think about it."

"Are you hitting on me?"

"Maybe."

"It seems like a stupid way to go about it. Don't you normally ask if the girl likes you first? Just because I'm not in love with Hal doesn't mean I like you."

He nodded slowly, hunching his shoulders. "Can you qualify 'not like?' Is that in 'I'm not attracted to you' or 'I hate your guts' or whatever?"

Jane blushed and looked away. "I didn't say that I didn't like you. It just seems like an ass-backwards way of going about things."

"It's just that I'm pressed for time," he whispered. "We only have two-month visas."

Her insides flipped weirdly at the idea and she realized what he meant about losing something making feelings clear. "Oh. Shit."

He leaned close to her. "I have tried very hard just to like you, but I've failed completely. These last few days have been an utter free fall. No parachute. No safety net. With totally, hopelessly in love at the bottom."

Her insides flipped again, but differently, all fluttery and weird. She wasn't sure that she liked the feeling. "Sounds painful."

"Potentially." He leaned closer so that she could feel the heat of his body nearly touching hers. "You're the most amazing woman I've ever met and I love you and I think this is going to kill me."

She put her hands up to keep him from leaning closer. This was all too fast. She couldn't wrap her mind around it enough to come up with anything intelligent to say or do. "What do you mean?"

He laughed bitterly. "It's taken me years to get here and in a very short while, I'm going to have to leave, and I don't think I'm going to be able to talk you into coming with me."

"Like hell!" Jane stomped firmly on that idea.

"Yeah, I figured it was that way. Part of your appeal actually."

"Really?"

"I've been to the most war-torn places on Earth. A lot of times people saw me as a way to escape. I like that you're happy where you are and comfortable with who you are. That you change anything that you don't like. You're a very strong and capable person and I find that amazingly attractive."

She blushed and looked down at their feet. Every guy she'd dated—mostly in high school before her brothers started to open carry—those were the reasons that guys ran away from her. They'd ask her out because all they knew was she was a tall leggy blonde that brooded quietly in the back row. Once they got to *know* her, they were scared of her. By her senior year, all the boys drawn to her build kept a safe distance. She'd gone stag to her prom with Brandy and three of their other intimidating female friends.

Taggart wore leather hiking boots. Good quality. Obviously not new but not so worn as to be scruffy, recently cleaned and polished. Stonewashed jeans. Rugged smartwatch. Dark linen shirt, top button undone to show off a dark curl of chest hair, and dog tags on a chain.

Her mother always said that you could learn a lot about a man by his choice of friends, how he treated strangers, and how well he took care of his equipment.

With the exception of Hal, Jane hadn't had much of a chance to apply that advice since high school. She'd known Taggart for five days. He'd been quiet almost to vanishing from her awareness. Often she knew where he was only by his wonderful scent and the heat of his body next to her. There was very little there to judge him by.

Just as quiet was his friendship with Nigel. The other man radiated gentle, warm charm, intelligence and boundless enthusiasm. Taggart rode protective herd on Nigel's fearless curiosity just as she did with Hal. Nigel accepted it without questioning. They obviously trusted each other and respected each other's judgment.

They'd risked their lives to save her little sister.

She raised her eyes to look Taggart in the face. He was actually very good-looking in that wild-man way. His black hair had a healthy shine despite needing a trim. His dark eyes look steadily into hers. His thick eyebrows gathered into a slightly worried look. His mouth could be considered very kissable.

"I—" She what? Love was not a word her family used lightly and she barely knew the man. Hell, she wasn't sure she could even pronounce his first name. "I like you." *Oh, that sounded lame.* "I think I more than just like you." *Okay, she was digging a hole here.*

Relief flashed over his face, quickly followed by amusement.

"Don't laugh at me." She pointed a warning finger at him.

He rubbed his face to cover a grin. "I'm not laughing. I'm happy. It's actually easier to know that you don't lightly use the word 'love.' If you do use it, you mean it, in a very deep and meaningful way."

If. Hard enough to decide how she felt without knowing that the clock was ticking on her answer.

Hell must have frozen over because the dishes were done without the normal water battle. This was her brothers focused on someone other than each other. Normally Jane would pity the fool who managed to get all the Kryskills' attention but not this time. She needed her family acting as a unit.

They moved out into her barnlike garage that still smelled faintly of elk blood. While Geoffrey readied the block and tackle, Alton lifted up the floorboards to expose Bertha's hiding place and Marc backed his decommissioned Humvee up to the doors. Jane powered up the *Chased by Monsters* production van. They might need to seriously edit the video but they should get it, just in case.

"Are you sure?" Taggart asked over his headpiece.

"From what I can tell from imported reality shows, Americans love heavily armed country folk."

"Och!" Nigel cried as Alton pulled back the canvas covering and revealed the cannon. "You are seriously heavily armed."

The gun's barrel alone was over eight feet long. It fired bullets nearly an inch thick at a maximum rate of five hundred rounds per minute. Its effective firing range was nearly two miles. They didn't have to worry about hitting the monster—what they had to worry about was missing and hitting something else.

"Oh, this is going to be glorious!" Hal cried.

"Forget it, Hal." Jane logged into her work account to pull down the e-mails from viewers reporting monsters. "This thing is meant to take out armored vehicles and small ships. I'm not letting you strafe downtown by accident."

"I'll be careful."

"You don't even know what careful looks like." Jane trusted that her brothers would be able to mount the gun to the Humvee and keep Hal from attempting to test fire it while she was busy. They might resort to tying Hal to a post, but that was fine with her.

Guy slumped into the chair beside her. He'd been doing teenage sullen since their mother declared he was to go home and act like nothing important had happened.

Jane pushed a map toward him. "We need a place that's totally open, nothing to trap us in. It needs to be along the river and as far from any people as possible. We have to be able to open fire without worrying about stray bullets hitting a house half a mile away."

Guy grunted, ignoring the map. "Do I really have to go home?"

Brandy's news about Windwolf's kidnapped blade brother flashed into Jane's mind. She would give just about anything to get back Boo, but not Guy. "No."

"What?" Guy cried. "Really? You're kidding. Right? You're not really serious—are you?"

"I don't want you to go home. I have no idea what Mom was thinking. The oni need Joey to control his people. Without him, they risk losing control of all the tengu. Anyone with half a brain cell would think to go to Mom's on the off chance that Boo wasn't eaten by the monster. I don't want you there all alone. You can stay here until Duff is ready to go."

"I'm not . . ." Guy caught himself and ended with a low growl of anger.

"You're not what?"

He glared at Jane until he realized who he was talking to. He glanced away and lowered his voice. "I'm not Boo. Ever since she disappeared, everyone keeps babying me as if I would vanish too. Duff would do something and it'd be 'idiot', and I do the same exact thing and it'd be 'Oh, be careful! You could be hurt! Stop it. Come here. Be a good little boy.' But no one would ever say what they really meant, which was 'you're next.' I'm not. Never was."

"They kidnapped the viceroy's baby brother last night," Jane snapped. It had to be tearing Windwolf's heart out. "A *sekasha*. One of the holy, kick-ass SEALs of elves with magical shield spells tattooed on his arms, trained every day of his freaking life for a hundred years, armed to the teeth including a sword that will cut through just about anything. The oni went into a building filled with elves and took Windwolf's brother right out of his bed. The oni are dangerous people and we just pushed them hard. They're going to push back."

"I'm not scared."

"I'm not asking you to be scared, I'm asking you to be careful. That means not going out alone. Everyone should pair up as much as possible. And when you do go home, stop a block from the house, make sure you've got a bullet in the chamber, safety off, and go in with caution."

He stopped looking sullen and nodded slowly. "Okay. Assume that the house has been breached."

"Better safe than sorry." She tapped the map. "Find me a kill zone."

She was hoping for at least three e-mails from

viewers so they could triangulate the direction the monster headed out of Sandcastle. Thousands of messages scrolled across her screen. She was going to need help to filter through the e-mails. Picking up her tablet, she headed into the garage to enlist the others.

The viewers didn't just stick to reporting monster sightings. They had questions and they didn't trust the answers that other sources were giving them. They trusted Hal, so they were turning to *Pittsburgh Backyard and Garden* for information.

They wanted to know more about the oni and the tengu that kidnapped Tinker. Those that had questions about the river monster wanted to know why Hal was dealing with it instead of the EIA and the police. Displaying a great lack of scientific understanding, several wanted someone (implying Hal, which only boggled Jane more) to contact the hyperphase gate in orbit and have it do a Shutdown so Earth forces could reinforce the EIA.

"Because it's in another universe," Jane growled at the tenth such e-mail. "The gate is in orbit around Earth! Different planet, people! How can you live in Pittsburgh and not know the basics? They teach this in grade school!"

"They're not locals," Hal said as if he'd been born in Pittsburgh. "They see the moon and it looks the same to them even though it has slightly different craters. The sun comes up and goes down in the same directions, and they lose sight that they're not in the same universe. To them it's the same moon, same sun, same stars."

"The stars are totally different!" Jane cried. She only

saw the stars of Earth once or twice a year but she could tell they were in different places. Then again, her father taught her how to find her way home at night, armed only with a knife.

"Most people can't see the stars on Earth," Nigel said. "There's too much light pollution. The children don't learn the constellations. They can't tell the difference."

Reason one thousand why Jane had no interest in moving to Earth. She glanced up to locate Taggart before realizing what she was doing. He stood beside the Hummer, recording her brothers lowering the cannon into place. Unlike Hal, he was as tall as her brothers, but wider in the shoulders, like he'd spent his youth swimming. The memory of him without his shirt flashed through her mind, followed quickly by curiosity of what he looked like without anything on.

Jane looked back down, blushing. *Focus, Jane. We've got a monster to kill.* "Assuming the . . . the . . . what are we going to call this river monster?"

"Nessie?" Hal used the name they had stuck on it for lack of another name, before they'd gotten a good look at it.

"Ach, that isnae Nessie." Nigel's Scottish had thickened noticeably. He held Alton's flask; it was filled with her brother's experiments in making Scotch. It was also proof that Jane was losing control of the situation. *If she ever had control.*

"*Namazu*," Boo and Joey both stated firmly.

"*Namazu* is a legendary giant catfish, in Japanese myths," Nigel explained, rolling his *r* as he lost his BBC accent and the Scottish took over. "Its thrashing is what causes earthquakes. The gods have pinned it

under a massive boulder in an attempt to minimize
the damage it can cause. The *namazu* is considered
a metamorphic catfish; the accepted image of the
creature does not match up to any real species. There
are several species of catfish with an electric organ."

"The monster's barbels"—Hal put his hands to his
mouth and twiddled his fingers—"which is what the
whiskers are called, would indicate that the creature
might be related to a catfish since there's only a handful of fish that do have them."

"Kajo named them *namazu*," Boo said firmly. "He
made them."

"Made?" Nigel and Hal asked.

"Them?" Jane and her brothers cried.

"How many did he make?" Jane asked.

Boo shrank back from them. "I don't know! I only
saw him release the last one five years ago. And it
wasn't that big when he did." She held up her hands
and measured out something only about four feet long.
"At least, Kajo said it was the last one, so it meant that
there were others, right? He said it needed time to grow
into something more impressive. Like me. He said that
a few years might seem like a long time to me, but in
a few decades, I'd start to see the world the way he
saw it. That forever was like drifting on an endless sea,
everything constantly changing and yet everything stays
the same. But after all that, he made me tengu."

Having admitted that she was no longer human,
she curled into a small, sniffing ball.

Duff recovered first. He pulled Boo into his lap.
"It's okay, baby girl, it's okay. No one is taking you
away from us ever again. You're our baby sister and
we love you."

Over Boo's head, he gave Jane a look that said: *We need to get her help.*

Jane had no idea how to get her help and keep her safely hidden at the same time.

"The roe indicates that there's at least two," Nigel's pointed out. "Normally a male catfish is the one that makes the nest and invites the female in. After she lays the eggs, he drives her out and guards the nest himself."

Nigel took another swig from the flask and started to pass it on to Hal.

Jane intercepted the flask. For this planning stage, she wanted her two experts functional. Hal would not stop at tipsy with Scotch, even if it was stuff as bad as Alton's homebrew. Beer he could handle, but not the hard liquor.

Luckily, Hal was caught up in the excitement of the upcoming hunt and didn't notice. "That would explain all the half-eaten oni! The carnage makes more sense with two predators going on a feeding frenzy instead of just one."

Nigel nodded in agreement. "The great white shark are believed to only need seventy to a hundred pounds of meat every two weeks. All those torn-apart buggers was much more than one beastie could reasonably down in a sitting, even at forty feet long."

Jane realized that her brothers were staring in surprise at the naturists.

"What exactly happened at Sandcastle?" Marc asked.

They showed her brothers the video from the day before. It was surprisingly viewable even as Taggart ran for his life, dragging the *namazu* away from Hal and the children. It had been stupidly brave of him.

She had worried that her brothers would cheer the oni dying but they were better than that. They flinched every time one died.

"The *namazu* is big but fairly slow when you compare it to a saurus or a warg," Jane listed out the river monster's strengths. "What makes it dangerous is the electricity. We first spotted it on Fort Pitts Bridge Outbound. You know how high that is? The discharge was arcing to the point where it almost reached us. I don't think we can do a second-story shoot as we would for a saurus. We're going to have to treat it more like a pack of wargs on steroids." The magical cold of the warg's breath made houses fragile boxes to trap anyone inside. Killing wargs normally required a running fight. "The vehicles should be safe from the electricity."

"Assuming you can get just one at a time," Alton muttered darkly. He had the most experience dealing with Elfhome wildlife. "It doesn't seem to be able to turn in a tight area. See, it backed up there instead of twisting around. You might be able to use that to your advantage."

"You left eleven oni alive." Marc took out his phone. "I'm going to see if anyone on the force knows what the EIA found. If the guards aren't all dead, you might have to deal with them at the same time."

"Don't ask too many direct questions," Jane warned. "The oni have moles in the EIA. They probably also have some in the police department."

Marc snorted and gave her a bemused look. Right. He was the one known as "Stone" by most people. He walked out into the night, saying to the person that answered, "What do you know?" After that, there was no more from his end of the conversation except occasional grunts.

"Because of Bertha's range and rate of fire, the only 'safe' place to film this will be in the passenger seat." Jane tapped the back of the Humvee. "We can mount some smaller cameras for more coverage; they'll be insurance on getting something on film. Everything is going to be fairly choppy as soon as Bertha opens up."

"Annnnd I'll be where?" Disappointment filled Hal's face as he realized that he wasn't going to be driving or shooting.

"You and Nigel will be in the production trucks. We'll have the mobile antenna up for both of them and cameras feeding to both, just in case we end up out of range of the *Chased by Monsters* truck."

"Jane!" Hal whined.

"If we have ammo left over, I'll take you out to the quarry and you can play with Bertha while we get additional footage to pad the episode. I'm expecting that most we get won't be useable."

"How much ammo do we have?" Taggart asked.

"Hopefully enough," Jane didn't want Hal to know the exact number because she planned to limit him to a few hundred shots. "She fires five hundred shots a minute, which is a good thing and a bad thing. We have to be sure we have the *namazu* in the crosshairs when we open up or we'll chew through everything before we kill her."

By "we" she meant herself. She just didn't want to have to fight every male within hearing about it.

Marc returned to the garage, his face set, which usually meant he was unsettled by what he learned.

"Well?" Jane asked.

He leaned close and whispered, "The EIA just found someone alive in the rubble. She's hurt. They're taking her to Mercy."

"Her?" Jane whispered. Boo hadn't mentioned that any of the oni were female. Not that it mattered, but Jane had gotten the impression it was a strictly males guarding the two children.

Marc lowered his voice even more. "They think she's tengu."

"Oh, shit." All of the guards were oni because Joey was being kept hidden from the tengu. Kajo couldn't trust his hold on Joey's people if there was any chance that they could free him. The only reason that a tengu would be at the hatchery was because she'd been attempting to find and rescue Joey. The boy had at least two aunts and a female cousin prior to the attack on the house in California. Boo had said that they were killed but it was possible that one had escaped, and thus good as dead for Kajo's needs. Was this one of them?

It was easy to think of Joey as their new baby brother. He was a sweet little kid that desperately wanted to be safe and loved. An adult who was "extended family" was something else. Jane had some cousins she wouldn't trust any further than she could throw them. (Her mom's side of the family reflected a sense of law and order, but her father's side showed their moonshiner background.)

If Joey was now Boo's brother, and by that tedious blood link, their new baby brother, what did it make his cousins? No one would blame them for ignoring that implausible connection—except Boo, who'd suffered too much already.

Then again, the enemy of your enemy is your friend.

If the oni only controlled the tengu through their hold on Joey's family, couldn't Jane use the same leverage to get Tinker and Windwolf's baby brother back?

But there was the small matter that the female would be under heavy guard with the elves probably quickly closing in to take custody of her.

"Alton, stay with the kids." Jane pointed at her oldest brother. She wasn't sure what she was going to do, but she didn't have time to sit and think. She needed to act now if ever. "Marc and Geoffrey, finish with Bertha. Duff and Guy, go through the sightings and find me a kill zone." She would need the *Chased by Monsters* team for an excuse to get access to the tengu. "Nigel, Taggart." And then because if she left Hal, he'd get into trouble, her garage possibly could be destroyed, and he'd end the night tied in a chair, she pointed at Hal. "Come."

It was a forty-minute trip to Mercy Hospital. By the time Jane parked in their special reserved parking space—Hal's slot of shame—they had a plan. A simple plan. Alarmingly simple. Claiming that they were seeking medical attention for Nigel's saurus wounds, they'd enter Emergency and start to ask lots of questions on the guise that they were gathering material for a show. Technically they wouldn't even be lying.

Once they determined where the tengu was located, it should be just a matter of pushing their way in for "an interview." After that, they'd be purely winging it.

The last part of "the plan" had her stomach doing somersaults. Her family had been put right. She wanted to salvage Joey's and save Windwolf's, but it put Boo into jeopardy. How were they to know if they could trust this tengu female? Why would she believe anything that Jane had to say?

Dr. Nan was on duty. The petite blond doctor knew them too well. She laughed as she caught sight of Jane. "What did Hal do this time? Ah, he's at least upright this time." She snapped on a pair of latex gloves. "Come here, my pretty."

"No, no, no, no, not me. Him!" Hal hid behind Jane.

Dr. Nan clapped her gloved hands together. "Fresh blood!"

"Nigel Reid, this is Dr. Nan Nuessle." Jane waved to the naturalist. "Yesterday, he was roughed up by a saurus. He's not feeling good."

"Yesterday? Oh, good lord, you people!" Nan pointed at Nigel. "You, on the gurney. Show me where it hurts."

Nigel gingerly peeled off his shirt. "We cleaned the wounds and applied antibiotics and plasters."

"Plasters?" Dr. Nan looked a little alarmed.

"Bandages," Jane clarified, having been through this exact discussion the day before. It was the difference between American English and British English.

"Oh, I see." Dr. Nan ripped off the bandages, making everyone wince. She was wonderful with children; she just didn't suffer fools, which meant Hal. Poor Nigel was suffering from association. "Oh, no. You call this clean? Saurus are meat eaters. They have nasty stuff living under their claws, which they embed deep into any wound. Salmonella. Botulism. Leptospirosis." She started to assemble supplies on a stainless steel tray beside the bed. To a nurse, she said, "I'm going to need two grams of Ceftriaxone."

"Two grams?" everyone echoed. Experience had taught Jane that shots were usually given in milligrams.

"These wounds are inflamed. Infection has already set in. You can't pussyfoot around once these babies get started. You got to slam the door shut on them hard."

Having Nigel treated was supposed to be a pretense. That he was seriously at risk made Jane feel guilty. She should have made sure he was fine last night, or this morning, before heading to Sandcastle. She had noticed him slowing down. She should have checked him earlier.

"Do you mind if we film this?" Nigel explained that he was in Pittsburgh for his show, *Chased by Monsters*, hence the reason he'd been attacked by the saurus. "The show name is misleading. Ouch. We really want to focus on what it's like to live on Elfhome. Ow. Your experience in emergency medicine must be extraordinary. People like myself attacked by exotic plants and animals. Treating elves and oni."

"Elves are *verboten!*" Dr. Nan ruthlessly scrubbed at the long, inflamed scratches while she talked. "They go to the hospices out beyond the Rim. Even human adults and children react differently to drugs. There's no way we could safely treat elves."

"Oni?" Hal asked. "Have you treated any of them?"

"Oh, you just missed that circus. We got a tengu in this evening along with half a dozen EIA grunts. They were digging her out when the building collapsed on all of them."

"Were any of them badly hurt?" Nigel asked.

"Various broken limbs, concussions, cuts and bruises. I think two of the grunts are still on their feet and pulling guard duty. I tossed the tengu to the surgeons; let them figure out what to do with her. I do not do birds."

Which meant that Dr. Nan probably didn't know where in the hospital the tengu was now. Security, though, would know where a prisoner was located.

The guard on duty was new to Mercy Hospital. His boyish face made him look impossibly young despite a sparse beard, probably grown in the attempt to appear older. Jane nearly felt bad unleashing Hal on him as Dr. Nan finished cleaning and bandaging Nigel.

"You're Hal Rogers!" the guard cried.

Hal beamed with happiness at being recognized. "So a fan of the show?"

"Am I ever!" The guard patted his pockets until he came up with a little pad of sticky notes and a click pen. "Can I have your autograph?"

"Sure!" Hal took the paper and pen. "Who do I make it to?"

"Jade Tinnerman. It's spelt like it sounds. T. I. N. N. E. R. Man."

"Jade?" Hal said.

Tinnerman gave an embarrassed smile. "My mom was saved by an elf at Startup, so she named me after him."

"So you're a real Pittsburgher: born and bred!" Hal had a practiced signature that included a little cartoon likeness of himself in a pith helmet and safari jacket. When he had a chance, like now, to take his time giving out his autograph, he went big.

"This close to being an half-elf." Tinnerman held up his thumb and forefinger nearly pressed together. "But then my mom met my dad and I got stuck being only human."

"Oh cruel fate," Hal cried.

Jane kicked Hal to get him to hurry up.

Hal edged away from Jane. "I heard that the EIA brought a wounded tengu in tonight. Did you see her?"

"Oh yeah, that was freaky." Tinnerman held up his hands, curling his fingers into claws. "She had big chicken feet! And she was wearing these, these, things—they were like Freddy Krueger's gloves but for her feet or something. She had on blue jeans and in her pockets were car keys, a driver's license, and a pack of Marlboro 100s. And get this, the license says she's from California."

It took all of Jane's control not to ask if she was from Pasadena.

After a patient's clothes were taken off, their personal effects went to security. (Unless there was a spouse in attendance, or in Hal's case, Jane.) Jane wasn't sure what security normally did with the items, but it was possible that Tinnerman still had access to them.

Luckily, Hal realized that too. "Are you sure it's a real license? When I was a freshman in college in California, the big thing was fake ID. The drinking age is twenty-one. There you are, in college, everyone drinking around you, and you can't buy beer until you're almost ready to graduate."

Pittsburgh conformed to European legal drinking ages instead of those of the United States, a reflection of the EIA influence over the local laws. At a private residence, there was no minimum age, and sixteen-year-olds could buy beer and wine.

"Get out!" Tinnerman cried in disbelief. "You have to be twenty-one to buy beer?"

Hal spread his hands in a "what are you going to do" gesture. "Right. Beer?"

"That's unreal," Tinnerman said.

"So this tengu's ID might have been fake," Hal said. "If you want, I could look at it and tell you if it's real or not."

Tinnerman looked uncertain.

Hal pressed the boy. "Once the EIA gets ahold of it, they're not going to tell us anything. They're keeping us in the dark for most of this oni thing. We were at Sandcastle this morning because the oni have been releasing monsters into the rivers. Lots of them. And the EIA is too busy looking for Tinker *domi* to deal with them, so they called in. Pittsburgh has a right to know what's really going on. We can tell them."

The young guard nodded slowly, glancing around to see if anyone was listening. "Yeah, you're right. Let me grab it."

"Make sure you show the camera," Jane whispered while the boy fetched the ID.

Hal nodded, still focused on the guard.

Tinnerman returned and furtively showed Hal the ID. "Does it look real?"

Hal didn't grab it from the boy. "At first glance, yes. But not everything is what it appears. Rub your finger over the signature. With a real one, you should feel the letters because they've been raised."

Tinnerman's eyes went wide. "You're right!"

"Also there's an outline of a brown bear when you shine a line from behind it." Hal produced a small flashlight and twiddled his fingers for Tinnerman to hand him the ID. Hal shifted slightly so Taggart could film the card and pressed the light to the back of the card. The dotted outline of a grizzly appeared on the right hand side. "Yup, there. See."

Tinnerman whistled and took out his wallet to find his Pittsburgh's driver's license. "Do we do anything that fancy?"

"That's nothing. Watch this." Hal flipped the flashlight over. "It looks like her picture is on here twice, right? But actually it's on the card three times. The third only visible under ultraviolet light."

Jane read the name on the card as Hal demonstrated the hidden photo. It claimed that the pictured woman with black hair was Yumiko Sessai. Jane hadn't thought to ask Joey if the rest of his family shared his last name of Shoji. His cousin's aunt, though, definitely wouldn't have his name. Yumiko looked like she could be related but she also looked like she could be related to most of the people in Japan. Her address was Pasadena. It wasn't Startouch drive, it was Ranch Top Road.

Jane poked Hal to move on. Quickly. There were at least two EIA guards on duty. If *PB&G* was going to "interview" Yumiko, they'd better do it before more guards could arrive.

"So where is this tengu?" Hal asked.

"She's up on the top floor, right hand corner. It's the room furthest from the nurse's station, just in case trouble breaks out." It would be the room that Mercy Hospital routinely put Hal in, most likely for the very same reason, only two floors up. Usually the rooms around Hal were empty. Mercy was the only hospital in Pittsburgh but anyone that could put off surgery went Stateside to get it done. "Although I can't see what trouble could break out since the tengu is still unconscious and Sparrow will be here to collect her before she wakes up."

"Sparrow? The viceroy's secretary?" Hal asked.

Tinnerman nodded. "Yeah, the grunts told me that they'd called Maynard and he was with Sparrow down in the South Hills, nearly to the Rim by Brownsville. She's on her way. They wanted to be sure I knew it so I could keep an eye out for her and make sure she got to the top floor when she arrived." He straightened proudly. "I'm fluent in Elvish. I got straight A's in high school. Busted my butt and got rank three translator qualifications."

Hal made appreciative noises, as it was fairly impressive. Rank four required a Master's degree; it also was the minimum level for official EIA translator positions. It meant that most Pittsburghers couldn't get a job with the EIA despite conversing in Elvish their entire lives.

Nigel came down the hall, walking gingerly as he rebuttoned his linen shirt, but otherwise beaming with delight as normal. Hal caught sight of him and did a quick wrap-up, thanking Tinnerman for his help.

"This way." Jane started them toward the correct bank of elevators to get up to the patients' rooms. "Since the EIA had a building dropped on them, we only have to get past two guards who have had a very shitty day." And it was about to get worse. Jane tried not to feel guilty. "If Sparrow shows up while we're talking to Yumiko, let me do the talking." Hal's Elvish sucked. "I'll let her know that Yumiko might know where Tinker *domi* is being held. If we can get Yumiko to trust us..."

Jane yelped with surprise as Nigel suddenly dragged her and Hal sideways into a janitor's closet. "What the hell?" She whispered because the man probably had a good reason for cramming them into a five-foot-wide space.

"Jane, there's something I haven't told you that you need to know." Nigel turned on the closet light, dragged Taggart into the closet too and shut the door.

"What?" Jane fought with a rag mop trying to fall into her face. "Seriously, what are we doing in here?"

"Turn the camera off," Nigel told Taggart. "This cannot be recorded. It is a matter of life or death."

Taggart looked mystified but hit the power button his camera. "Okay. It's off. What's this about?"

"Sparrow was the one that arranged to have Windwolf killed," Nigel said quietly.

"What?" Jane cried.

Nigel held up his hands to quiet her. "Sparrow conspired with the oni to have the viceroy killed. If she had succeeded, she would have been in control of Pittsburgh until the queen decided who would rule in his place. Since these are elves, that could have been longer than any of us could imagine. It would have handed complete control of the city to the oni."

"Shit!" Jane hissed.

Taggart was looking lost and confused. "Why didn't you tell me this?"

Nigel sighed. "Because I'm protecting the ones that told me. Also there's no proof to those allegations, but I believe them to be true."

"Who told you?" Taggart growled.

"No one can know this," Nigel said. "It must never be repeated, particularly on camera. It must remain a secret to our deaths."

"You know you can trust me," Taggart said.

"I met the wee lasses who are Lemon-Lime," Nigel

said. "Och, they are clever little ones but they're in over their heads. They trusted me with their lives; I cannae betray them."

It took a moment for Jane to remember that Lemon-Lime was the name of the film company that gave Nigel the monster call. "How little is little? College age? High school?"

"They are not that much older than Joey. Eight. Nine." He measured off a child that would only come to slightly above Jane's hip. "Twins. At first I couldn't believe them; Lemon-Lime videos are extensively researched and the humor is cunning, albeit often juvenile. It didn't seem possible for such wee lasses to produce them. But then they explained the gossamer call. They weren't repeating information that they barely grasped. They'd taken the barest of clues and created a device that uses magic—a power not found on Earth—to control beasts that live on another world. But by doing so, they had stumbled across a horrific secret. They trusted me with their lives by telling me what they'd found out."

Jane had six younger siblings; she didn't completely trust anything coming out of a child's mouth. "Two nine-year-olds uncovered a conspiracy between an elf and the oni while on Earth?"

"They did a video of Windwolf being saved by a human man and woman, although the details ... Oh! Oh! Oh my!"

Jane glanced around the tiny closet to see what was triggering Nigel's wide-eyed look of surprise. "What?"

"They released this last month, immediately after Windwolf's attack and disappearance hit the news. It was assumed that Lemon-Lime had some inside knowledge." He pulled out his phone, and played a video. It was animated but accurately showed the attack on Windwolf by Foo dogs. And then it got weird. Windwolf was chased onto Grandma Gertie's putt-putt golf course, menaced by a bull, attacked by a saurus, saved by Jane and Hal then taken to the Neighborhood of Make Believe.

"What . . . what . . . what . . ." Jane sputtered. She grabbed his phone and played it again. In the video, Jane was wearing something that looked like a Valkyrie costume but they'd nailed Hal from his pith helmet and safari jacket. "This is what happened to us! The events are out of order. We ate at the studio the night before, but this was yesterday morning! Bull. Flashbang. Saurus. Rifle."

"I think we should consider anything they told me to be deadly accurate," Nigel said.

Jane played the video a third time. "This is so creepy." It was so wildly unlikely that she wanted to believe that the events had been staged to match the video but everything had been too completely random. Her argument with Chloe that led to her asking for viewers to call in monster sightings. Nigel wanting to stop at the putt-putt golf course. Her decision to use a flashbang to scare off the bull. No one, not even Nigel, could have guided them into this exact fight.

Add in the fact that they were having this discussion in a janitor's closet and her life suddenly felt completely surreal.

"The elves say that they have oracles that can accurately see the future," Nigel said. "We've dismissed those claims as native superstitions. Obviously we were wrong."

Boo had said that the Eyes could see the future and that Kajo had moved all his camps because Pure Radiance had come to the Westernlands. Hide and seek.

"The twins had no proof because they simply 'saw' the truth." Jane handed back the phone. "It means we won't have evidence to give the elves. We can't accuse Sparrow."

Taggart growled softly. "If Lemon-Lime is right, then Sparrow is probably also behind the kidnapping of Windwolf's bride and foster brother. She stood there on the riverfront and pretended to help lead the search. Most likely she was directing the elves away from the oni camps."

"Sparrow can't let Yumiko talk to the other elves," Jane said. "Wraith Arrow said that the tengu are the spies of the oni. Sparrow can't be sure what Yumiko knows. One wrong word and the *sekasha* will kill Sparrow right after they kill Yumiko."

"We have to free Yumiko before Sparrow arrives," Taggart said.

Jane dropped her voice to a whisper. "The EIA is not going to let us free their prisoner."

Hal grinned. "We're not going to ask them."

"What's that supposed to mean?" Jane said.

He grinned wider. "Accidents happen."

Jane followed Hal down the hall wishing it wasn't a good thing they were known for their mayhem. She wasn't sure how Hal planned to cause an accident but normally he could do it by simply breathing wrong (his excuse for the fire in the WQED's break room although there was a cake and candles involved). It just felt wrong to let him lead. Normally letting him have free rein led to bad things. They wanted a distraction, not to level the hospital.

Mercy was one of the places where Hal's super hosting powers worked in inverse. (The WQED station was the other.) Familiarity breeds contempt or fear or something. Everyone that saw Hal, and recognized him, veered to get out of his path.

"Remember, Hal," Jane whispered. "This is the only hospital on Elfhome. If you get banned or something, we are going to be screwed. And do not burn it down. Pittsburgh needs it."

"I'm not going to burn it down." He was, however, nearly bouncing like Tigger with anticipation, which usually meant bad things were about to happen.

"Get ready for anything," Jane warned the other two, which for some reason only made Taggart grin too. "Nigel, we're going to try and get footage for the show. This is a member of a third intelligent race. So far as I know, no one's been able to get a living oni on camera. This is huge news, so of course we're interested in anything we can learn about the tengu. Also we've told Maynard that we'll kill the *namazu* and we believe the female might have important information on the number of monsters released into the rivers."

Nigel nodded.

"We'll keep the camera and hopefully the focus of the two guards on you while Hal does . . . what he does best."

The guards stood at the door, one just inside the room, the other in the hall. They were in full battle gear and covered with dirt and sweat and blood. Jane had her pistol in a kidney holster but she didn't want to get into a gunfight. The two obviously recognized Hal despite the broken nose and black eyes.

"Mr. Rogers, what are you doing here?" His name badge identified him as T. Talley. He was big man and imposing looking. Unknown to him, the effect was weakened by the fact that his shorter partner went a little bug-eyed (his glasses unfortunately compounded this greatly) and edged away from Hal.

Hal's reputation was known. Good. Maybe. This could be a two-edged sword.

"This is Nigel Reid, world famous naturalist. He's here in Elfhome to film—well, everything! The network has asked me to show him the ropes. Smooth the waters, so to speak. And keep him from being eaten. This is Pittsburgh, after all."

The other, identified as P. Tapper, laughed nervously.

Nigel clasped his hands together and beamed at the men. "So good to meet you. We hear all about the EIA on Earth. Lone peacekeepers deep in the virgin ironwood forest. Hal is right; we want to know everything about Elfhome. Would you be up to an interview on what it's like to be posted on Elfhome?"

"What?" Talley cried.

"Now?" Tapper asked.

"Well, after we've had a peek at your prisoner. It's extraordinary that we've made contact with yet another intelligent race. Millions of years of just humans and now a plethora of other beings."

"Yes . . . what?" Talley obviously wasn't keeping up.

Jane glanced past the two into the room. It was one of the private hospital rooms looking out over the Mon River. They were on the top floor, two flights up from the window where Hal had filmed the male tengu kidnapping Tinker. Yumiko lay in her bed with a dozen tubes and wires connected to her body. She seemed unconscious. She was a tall, lean, small-breasted female with only a blanket to keep her decent. There was a bloodstained bandage on her left thigh. From where they stood in the doorway, the only indication that she wasn't human was the tips of her black crow feet.

Jane's heart dropped to see that Yumiko was shackled to the bed. She'd known there were strict government rules about using restraints in hospitals that meant patients were rarely bound by straps to their beds. (Yes, Hal was the reason she knew this. No, Mercy would not make an exception for Hal, no matter how much both she and the nuns thought it was a good idea.) Police-applied shackles, however, neatly bypassed those rules. She'd hoped that since the EIA brought the female unconscious to the hospital that they wouldn't have restrained her. Apparently they were taking no chances with their prisoner.

Jane had thought she could fireman-carry Yumiko out of the hospital, depending on how hurt the female was. Between the elevators and their special parking spot, it wouldn't have been too difficult. Jane knew that the railing on the beds could be partially dismantled. (Hal took things apart when bored.) It took time, though, to unscrew all the posts. (And to screw them back together.) They were going to have to steal the entire bed. This was not going to be easy.

"I'm—I'm not sure if we can allow..." Talley was trying to wedge into the narrative flow that Nigel was directing more to the camera than to him. He was trying to lock a steely gaze on Nigel but the camera kept distracting him.

Nigel wasn't giving him the opportunity to derail

him. "... wounded tengu was brought to Mercy Hospital and treated. Sergeant Talley, were you the one that rescued her from the trapped rubble?"

The EIA officer leaped for the opening. "Private Tapper and I were part of the team that was sifting through the rubble at Sandcastle."

"We saw you there this afternoon!" Tapper added. "We heard you're going after the monster that ate all those oni."

Talley continued, steamrolling forward now that he found a safe subject. "The subject was pinned via a pipe through her thigh. We cut the pipe above and below her and brought her here to Mercy for it to be removed. This brought down the building on us."

"And surgeons removed the pipe?" Nigel asked.

*Oh, God, please let it have been removed already!*

"Yes. They were all freaked out by her though; she's half-bird."

The conversation jerked to a halt as they all stared at the unconscious female.

"Brilliant!" Nigel stated. "I notice, though, she has no wings. Didn't the male that kidnapped Tinker *domi* have very large wings? They were quite remarkable. I was hoping that I'd have a chance to see them in person."

"Yeah." Talley drawled out the word. "She didn't have wings. We're hoping to ask Sparrow when she gets here."

Tapper had been nodding and shaking his head along with Talley's responses. The blue EIA helmet was making him look like a bobblehead toy. "Her insides definitely are all bird."

Nigel had been gradually moving them closer to the

bed. It was unhurried, baby steps through the door, into the room, and then drifting nearer and nearer to their objective. Sergeant Talley drifted with them while the fearful Private Tapper (who obviously knew Hal better) stayed at the door. Jane ignored Hal, trusting him to do something, hopefully soon. Looking at him would only draw the guards' attention to him. She was starting to secretly writhe inside with anticipation and fear. "Trust" was not a word she used lightly and usually never in connection with Hal except in some sarcastic meaning of the word. The only thing she actually trusted Hal to do was hit his mark, keep track of the camera, and maintain an informative and coherent monologue, even while being eaten alive.

Yumiko had all the normal contraptions connected to her: blood pressure cuff, IV drip, heart monitor, oxygen nose line and a finger clamp. Most of them would trigger alarms the moment they were disconnected. If the monitors were simply turned off, then the alarms wouldn't sound. There remained, though, the problem that all the tubes and wires tied the bed into place. Without stripping off all the miscellaneous medical equipment, they wouldn't be able to move the bed more than a few feet.

How to do this without getting caught?

Luckily Nigel had drifted to the foot of the bed and focused Talley's attention on Yumiko's crow feet by flicking the sheet to one side, uncovering them fully. Taggart shifted, blocking the officer's view of Jane.

"Brilliant!" Nigel cried. "Her foot is anisodactyly!"

"Hey, hey, don't . . ." Talley cried. "What?"

"Anisodactyly. It means she has three digits pointing forward and one back. It's the most common of bird feet among passerine, or perching birds. And she has scales, just like a bird. They're made of keratin; it's the same material as hair and fingernails in humans and scales in snakes. In a bird, it also forms beaks and claws. This form of scaling is cancella. It's really just a thickening and hardening of the skin to form a protective coating."

With everyone's attention firmly on the foot of the bed, Jane clicked off the blood pressure monitor, the oxygen monitor, and some other weird thing that had never been connected up to Hal all the times he'd been in the hospital. She slipped the IV bag off the stand and laid it beside the female's head.

Out in the hall—finally—there was a startled yelp of pain and fear from Private Tapper.

"Stop, drop and roll!" Hal shouted. "Stop, drop and roll!"

*Oh, God, he'd set the private on fire.*

There was another scream, louder, and the fire alarm went off.

That was her cue to kick into high gear. She leaned over to pull the nose tube off the tengu.

Yumiko caught her arm and stared at Jane's left hand.

"Sparrow is coming." Jane tried to tug her arm free.

Yumiko's gaze lifted to Jane's face. Her eyes were the same electric blue as Joey's. She frowned up at Jane.

"Shit, please tell me you understand English," Jane whispered and then realized two important things. The first was that the IV needle had already been removed from the back of the female's hand. The second was that the tengu was no longer shackled. "How the hell..."

The tenor of the screaming changed out in the

hall as Private Tapper was blasted past the doorway by the high-pressure spray of a fire hose.

"Turn it off!" Sergeant Talley shouted, trying to swim upstream to reach Hal. "He's not on fire anymore! Turn it off!"

"What?" Hal shouted back.

"What's going on here?" A female shouted in Elvish. "Where is the tengu spy? Why are you playing with water?"

Sparrow had arrived.

"Jane, watch out!" Taggart shouted.

Yumiko had produced a scalpel from the folds of the sheet and stabbed at Jane's hand. The blade sliced down her forearm. A foot-long thin line of blood welled up along the cut.

"Oh, shit!" Jane caught Yumiko's hand holding the scalpel while trying to jerk free her arm. She realized that Taggart was about to put down his camera to help her. "Keep filming."

"You're bleeding!" He stated the obvious.

"Yes, I know." Jane normally could easily beat any woman and most men at arm wrestling. The skinny female was stronger than she looked. "Give. Me. That. Scalpel."

Yumiko head butted Jane full in the face.

Jane staggered back, tasting blood. She was, however, free of the tengu. She kept backpedaling, putting distance between her and the blade. Taggart caught hold of her and pulled her even further back.

Yumiko moved with inhuman speed and strength, vaulting from the hospital bed. She rolled across the floor and came to a halt beside the overbed table. The female stood, sweeping up the table, and flung it at the window. The glass shattered.

"We're on the top floor!" Jane cried as Yumiko leapt to the sill of the broken window. For a moment, the female paused there, glancing back at Jane. She seemed unconcerned that she was dressed only in a bandage about her thigh and a black tattoo across her back. Nor that she teetered sixty feet up from the sidewalk.

She spoke a word and leapt out into the sky. Massive wings appeared on her back out of thin air. The wings swept downward with a loud rustle of black feathers, checking her fall.

For a moment, she hung in the sky, a huge black bird eclipsing the sun.

And then she was gone.

"What the hell? Where did she go?" Jane cried.

"Who cares? You're bleeding." Taggart put down his camera and focused on staunching the blood.

Sparrow came through the door like a storm trooper, an assault rifle leveled and ready to shoot. "Where is she?"

"She went out the window." Jane waved her free hand.

The elf glanced at the broken glass and then pointed the rifle at Jane. "You let her go?"

Jane gripped Taggart's arm to keep him from shifting in front of her. "No! She'd picked the locks on her shackles and escaped. We came to question her about the river monster that killed all the oni at Sandcastle. Director Maynard asked for our help killing it."

"She had a knife," Taggart growled in passable Elvish. "She stabbed Jane."

"What did the tengu tell you?" Sparrow asked.

"Nothing," Jane said. "I don't think she understood English."

A slight tightening around Sparrow's eyes made Jane think that Sparrow knew that the tengu was fluent in English and thought Jane was lying. Yumiko did have a California driver's license, which would indicate that she probably knew enough English to pass a test.

Jane had learned that the best way to stop an attack was to put the person on the defensive. "Do your people know anything about this monster? We've never heard of anything like it. Is it native to Elfhome? Do you have it in the Easternlands?"

"Why would I know anything about an oni spell-working?" Sparrow stalked out of the room.

Because she knew that the oni used spells to create the monster.

With Sparrow gone, Taggart turned his attention back to her wound.

"I'm fine," Jane said.

"I know you're fine. I also know it's easier to do this with two hands instead of just one."

Jane breathed out her annoyance. He was right. "Okay."

"Let's wash it first." He unbuttoned his shirt cuffs and rolled up his sleeves. He was wearing a quietly elegant, state-of-the-art smartwatch. In Pittsburgh they didn't do much more than tell time, but most newly arrived people wore them out of habit. The friendship band that Boo and Joey made looped across the watchband.

Jane frowned at the bracelet and then her wrist. Hers was gone. "Damn." She crossed to the bed and picked through the linens.

"What are you looking for?" Taggart ask.

Jane crouched down and scanned the floor under the bed. "It's gone. Damn it! Did she take it?"

"Take what?"

"The bracelet that Boo and Joey made." Jane tossed the sheets again. She was leaving bloody fingerprints on the white linen. "I had it on in the truck. It's gone now."

"Let's bandage your cut before you lose more blood, and then check the video."

The cut proved to be shallow and only alarming because it ran the whole length of her forearm. Taggart washed it with an antiseptic, applied antibiotic ointment, placed gauze over it and then wrapped her arm with tape.

Taggart had kept the camera trained on Nigel up to the last minute. Then as Hal started his distraction, Taggart had caught the flash of the blade sweeping upwards. He'd jerked the camera toward Jane, following the scalpel even as he called warning. Despite the suddenness of the attack, he'd caught the blade's path on film. The braided bracelet had been on Jane's wrist and then, as a line of blood marked the scalpel's passage, it was not. The twisted leather cord dropped onto the white sheet and, a moment later, was snatched up by the tengu.

"She wanted the bracelet," Taggart said.

Jane caught Taggart's wrist and examined the bracelet closely for the first time. She'd only glanced at it when Boo had tied one to her wrist; she'd been too busy getting ready for dinner to actually study it. Taggart's looked identical, with three strands of cording, two of which were leather and one red silk. She'd thought the bracelets crudely made because there was no symmetry to the knots and braiding. She remembered now a documentary she'd seen once where the Incas had an entire language of knotted cords. "Yumiko looked at my hand first. I thought she was disoriented, but she wasn't. I bet these are some kind of secret tengu message. She saw it and knew that Joey had made it. She took it as proof."

"That's—that's a stretch." Taggart rolled down his shirtsleeves and buttoned his cuffs.

"Why else would she take it?" Jane tossed the linens again.

"It doesn't make sense that she'd take it once she had a good look at it. If she hadn't taken it, you wouldn't be worried now."

Taggart had a point: she wouldn't be aware of the bracelet's importance if Yumiko hadn't taken it. With his sleeves buttoned, his bracelet was hidden, as were Nigel's and Hal's. Since she was wearing a tank top, hers had been the only one visible. She realized why the tengu female had taken the bracelet.

"Yumiko took it so Sparrow wouldn't see it. Sparrow is an oni double agent; she probably could guess that the bracelet meant that we have Joey. She probably would have shot us all."

"That makes sense," Taggart agreed slowly. "I think the only reason Sparrow didn't shoot us was because you were obviously hurt."

Jane glanced about the empty hospital room. "We should head back home and talk to Joey. We need to know who Yumiko is. If we can trust her."

"What the hell happened to you?" Geoffrey cried when Jane walked back into her garage an hour later. Since both Nigel and Hal were soaked from head to toe, she didn't bother hiding her bandaged arm.

Her brothers must have finished installing Bertha on the Humvee as a canvas tarp had been draped over it. They'd raided the toy bins in the storage room for plastic dinosaurs and matchbox trucks. The reptiles dwarfed the vehicles; unfortunately it probably was the correct scale.

"Hal was Hal," Jane temporized, getting a "hey" of indignation from Hal. "What are you doing?"

"Tactics," Marc said without embarrassment while Duff and Guy distanced themselves from the toys. Joey was hanging on Alton's back like a monkey.

Jane held up her phone with the downloaded capture of Yumiko Sessai's driver's license on it. She didn't want any of her family seeing Yumiko attacking her. "Joey, do you know this person?"

"That's Yumiko!" Joey cried.

"Is she related to you?" Jane asked.

Joey shook his head. "She's a *yamabushi*."

"She's a what?" Jane asked.

"*Yamabushi!*" Joey cried. "They're the seven loyal servants of Wong Jin who were given magical powers by our guardian spirit, Providence, so they could protect his daughter."

"They're like super ninjas that guard the Chosen bloodline," Boo translated, and then gave a condensed version of everything she knew about them. "There were five living in the house behind the Shojis'. The two places shared backyards, so they acted like one big home. The *yamabushi* all used the name Sessai and pretended to be Mom and Dad and kids. One was around my age. His name was Haruka."

Joey nodded enthusiastically; he didn't realize the significance of the past tense. "He goes to school with Mickey and Keiko. Yumiko goes to Caltech with Riki."

"And these?" Jane held up Alton's wrist to show off his since hers was gone. "What are they?"

Joey leaned over Alton's shoulder and probably would have fallen if Alton hadn't tightened his grip. "The charms? They're for protection."

"What kind of protection?" Jane said.

"Against tengu!" Joey said. "It tells tengu not to hurt you because you're under the protection of the Chosen line."

Boo caught Jane's hand to inspect her wrist. "What happened to yours? You didn't throw it away, did you?"

"No. I gave it to Yumiko." Jane wasn't sure if this was a good thing or bad. If all of Joey's family was dead, the *yamabushi* most likely saw herself as his next of kin. Jane didn't see it that way; it seemed too much like giving him to the first stranger who thought they had a right to him. It might become a custody battle fought at night with guns.

There was a chance that Yumiko might also want Boo since she was now genetically part of the Chosen bloodline. *No way in hell.*

Jane didn't want to discuss the possibilities with her brothers. They might be tempted to shoot Yumiko on sight. Jane wanted to give the female the benefit of the doubt. The enemy of Jane's enemy was her friend—at least until they need to be coldcocked, tied up and handed back to the EIA for questioning.

Jane tucked away the phone as she turned the facts over in her mind. If Yumiko was a bodyguard, then it explained Yumiko's actions. The female had been at Sandcastle searching for Joey. Captured, she'd been playing dead, waiting for a chance to escape. Jane showed up wearing the bracelet. To protect Joey,

Yumiko would need to erase all trace of him, which meant taking the bracelet.

"Where is Yumiko?" Joey asked.

"I don't know," Jane said truthfully. "She disappeared before we could talk to her."

"*Intonjutsu!*" Joey cried.

"What?" Jane asked.

"That's the ninja skill of disappearing," Nigel murmured. "The *yamabushi* were a sect of warrior monks that live in temples deep in the mountains. The Japanese believe that the tengu are protective, yet dangerous, mountain spirits. They are often depicted in the distinctive robes of the *yamabushi* monks."

Joey was nodding along with this. "When the Chosen was brought to Earth, his servants hid him among the *yamabushi*. They took the name to honor the monks."

"The oni don't know that the *yamabushi* exist," Boo added. "The tengu managed to keep the Chosen bloodline hidden on Onihida. Only after they came to Earth did the oni find out about the Chosen."

"Are you sure?" Jane asked.

Boo gave her an annoyed look. "Kajo had a fight with Lord Tomtom about it. Tomtom didn't believe there were *yamabushi*. He said that it was a myth to frighten the other lesser bloods; to keep them from trying to prey upon the tengu. He thought that any tengu that was particularly fierce encouraged people to think they're *yamabushi* to boost their reputation."

If half the oni command doubted Yumiko's existence, then the female could have the other members of Joey's family safely hidden someplace. Somehow they had to have a long conversation with Yumiko.

First things first: the *namazu*.

Her brothers had raided more than just the toy box. They'd also managed to round up a half-dozen wooden sawhorse barricades and Team Tinker's headsets.

Jane eyed the equipment with dismay. They would be spread across three vehicles with Duff fielding monster sightings from viewers, monitoring police activity, and coordinating the running fight. They needed seven linked headsets. Because the *PB&G* equipment was so old, her set of four weren't compatible with the four that the *Chased by Monsters* crew had brought with them. She'd told her brothers to solve the problem; she didn't expect this. "You didn't tell our cousins about Boo or Sandcastle or anything?"

"I bribed Andy with cannoli and beer," Duff stated. "He didn't even think to ask."

That sounded like their youngest Roach cousin. His older brother was the business manager of Team Tinker. He would have held out for the piece of whatever action the Kryskill boys were gearing up for.

The headsets were custom made by Tinker herself. They used voice-activated microphones to create a full-duplex tac net and had more bells and whistles than God. There were ten in all, so there were more than enough for their needs.

Duff was scared that he pissed her off. "They don't use an open channel like the production truck's headsets. We'll still use code words—because yes, the oni could be monitoring the phone systems—but this is going to be much more secure. Plus I can patch in anyone with a cell phone, so if I need to, I could even call Alton or Mom at any point and link them in."

"Don't you dare call Mom!" Jane wanted to stay in control. Last thing she needed was her mom wading in and taking over. "I don't care what happens, you do not call Mom."

Duff nodded his understanding.

"Do we have a kill zone?" Jane asked.

"Hays Woods," all her brothers answered.

"Here." Duff picked up his tablet and flicked through some satellite pictures. "These images are really old but Pittsburgh hasn't changed much in terms of roads and such. This is Hays Woods. It's about seven hundred acres of forest on a steep hillside."

Alton pointed out narrow dirt road meandering through the woods. "There's lots of walking trails through it that've been widened so that foragers like me can get trucks in and out. Between the river and South Hills, the woods are isolated from the Rim, so they're mostly Earth flora and fauna and are fairly safe. I hunt squirrels, deer, and fish. Some people cut hickory for smoking meat."

"Oak for carpentry," Geoffrey stated to prove he knew the woods as well. "There's some cherry too."

"Good. Good." Jane headed off a flare-up of sibling rivalry. She studied the map. The woods occupied a steep bend in the Mon River with Hazelwood across the water. The trees would hem in monsters, but the width of the trail would also make turning difficult. They needed to stay out of range of the monster's electricity attack. If they called in more than one monster, they could be trapped between the two with nowhere to run. As long as they fired downhill toward the river or east toward Sandcastle, it would be unlikely they hit anything important. Downtown, however, was within the gun's four-mile range to the west.

"Viewer tips get us any sightings?" Jane asked.

"There were two from the Hot Metal Bridge." Duff swept a finger down river, around the bend, to the first bridge across the Monongahela. The historic landmark used to carry crucibles of molten steel from the blast furnaces on the south bank to the rolling mills on the north bank. Originally a railroad bridge, it had been converted just prior to the first Startup. It was one of the bridges that linked the heavily populated South Side to downtown and Oakland.

"Shit," Jane breathed. "Do we know the range of the monster call?"

"Not really," Nigel confessed. "I was told that it might be up to a *mei* since it uses magic, but there's no way to confirm that. So far, we've been practically on top of the monster when we used it. We were lucky that we've hit on the 'come here' command."

"There's a very steep dirt road here off of East Carson," Alton pointed out. "It was a power line right-of-way for the electric company but it's been expanded so you don't need to drive all the way around to Glass Run to access the walking trails."

"There's also this path off of Becks Run Road," Geoffrey added.

Jane shook her head. "We would have to drag the monsters under this railroad bridge. If they damaged the bridge, the connection to the East Coast would be cut short of the city proper. That could be critical if this goes to full out warfare."

Jane hated everything about this fight. That they didn't know how many monsters were in the river. That she needed to involve her brothers. That they were the only ones who could call the monsters out of the river. Short of handing over the monster call to the compromised EIA, no one else was as heavily armed as her family. "We're doing a running fight. We'll use the monster call here East Carson. Once we have incoming, we'll head up this dirt road into the woods. We'll pull the first one to this clearing and open fire. Lather, rinse, repeat."

She ran her finger down East Carson. South Side Flats was about a square mile of flood plains beside the Mon River. Because of the steep hillsides that edged the river, East Carson had very few side streets beyond the flats. "If we set up the barriers here just after South Thirty-Third Street and here at Becks Run Road, and then here where it ends at Eight-Eighty-Five, then we can have two or three miles to ourselves to work with."

Jane wished they could take advantage of the night cover but she didn't want to fight blind. "We'll head out at four-thirty. The production trucks will find hard cover at the top of this hill. The Humvee will set up the barriers, make sure the area is clear of bystanders, and do a dry run of shifting from East Carson to the walking trails."

"What about me?" Hal had been studying the map intently. "How am I going to see anything with so many trees in the way?"

Jane smacked him. "You're to stay behind hard cover in case we accidently fire in your direction."

Alton zoomed in on the map to find a small side street. "There's a vacant private school here. It's all brick, so it would provide lots of cover for the production trucks. The walking trails edge the property, so the cameras will be in range."

"I won't be able to find that," Hal stated firmly.

"We've never filmed in that area. There are no back-yards and gardens. It's all abandoned and, knowing Pittsburgh, there were never street signs, even before the first Startup."

Nigel eyed the maze of side streets they would need to take from Becks Run to the school. "Och, neither could I, not in the dark without GPS."

Jane considered not filming the hunt.

If she just left Hal, Nigel and Taggart at Hyeholde...

No. That wouldn't work. She'd have to lock them into the basement or something. If it had been just Hal, it would be fairly simple to just pick him up and carry him squirming and kicking to the bath-room and handcuff him to the sink. (She'd done it before when she decided his drinking needed serious intervention. The bathroom gave him access to water and a toilet.) She had four bathrooms (Hyeholde was a restaurant after all), but she only had one pair of handcuffs. It would be a mistake to underestimate any of the men. They were all intelligent and used to getting themselves out of all sorts of odd trouble. (Mostly because they also seemed to have the same level of common sense—which was to say very little.) Taggart and Nigel were wild cards; there was no tell-ing what they might know. They could be black belts in martial arts and have Houdini-level escape skills. Locking them up could be tricky. If one got free, he'd free the other two.

Earth needed to see what the oni were doing in Pittsburgh. They had to see the forty-foot walking electric catfish to believe it. If she was going to put her little brothers at risk, she'd better reap the maxi-mum gain out of it.

"I know Hays Woods," Guy said. "I've gone with Alton a bunch of times. I can guide them."

Jane scanned her brothers. Alton was going to keep Boo and Joey out of the mess. Geoffrey and Marc were going to be in the Humvee with her. Duff was handling communication; with three vehicles in motion, they were going to need someone outside the action as backup to keep things clear. Nor did Duff know the area any better than Hal and Nigel.

"Come on!" Guy cried. "I can do this! I won't be in any danger if I stick with the production trucks."

If Guy was with the production truck, he could keep Hal in check. Without someone babysitting Hal, there was a strong possibly that Hal would try to see the fight somehow. Typical Hal stupidity would follow.

If it was anyone but her baby brother . . .

But that was the source of all of Guy's rebellion. No one was letting him be anything but the baby while he knew full well that all his older brothers had been treated as adults long before they turned eighteen. It was part and parcel of being allowed to handle a gun.

"Fine," she said. "I want you take your rifle with you."

"Yes!" Guy went bouncing off to do a victory lap around the Humvee, arms upraised.

Her four other brothers glared at her.

"Someone has to sit on Hal," she explained the most obvious point. Understanding dawned on their faces. Taggart looked amused by it.

"Hey!" Hal cried.

Guy leapt at Hal and grabbed him in a chokehold, proving he'd grown taller than Hal sometime in the last month. "Consider him sat on!"

"Let's get some sleep and head out at four-thirty."

Jane ignored the fact dragging her brothers into this fight meant she was going to have monster-sized nightmares.

At a little after five in the morning, with sunrise still an hour away, they rolled into South Side Flats. Most of the windows in the row houses and three-story apartment buildings were dark. Graveyard shift hadn't ended and dayshift workers weren't awake yet. Jane prayed silently that the hunt went fast and they could kill whatever was out there quickly and quietly. She hated that all but one of her brothers was in harm's way.

Marc drove the Humvee in the front. They'd covered Bertha with a heavy tarp but anyone with two brain cells could tell what was underneath. While Marc stopped to set up the police barricades, complete with flashing warning lights, Guy and Nigel continued on down East Carson in the production trucks.

"Can't I at least drive?" Hal complained yet again over the channel.

"No!" Jane, Duff, Geoffrey, and Guy all snapped.

Jane continued with reasons why. "Chaser One knows where he's going and he's a better driver than you." *And it will be easier for Guy to ignore Hal from behind the wheel than on the passenger side.* "He can't babysit the incoming feed and make sure all the backup cameras are online. You have to do that. We're only going to be able to do this once." *Hopefully.* "You'll let us know if any of the cameras go out and we'll do what we can to fix them." *As long as Bertha is operating, since our lives will ride on keeping the cannon firing.* "And I told him that he can punch you if you don't listen to him."

"Jane!" Hal knew that her brother only lightly smacked him when they thought he needed to be hit. "Punching" was a whole different ball game.

"Chaser Two, you already have a broken nose," Jane ruthlessly pointed out. "Another hit to the face means nothing."

"Jane!" Hal pleaded that she not be so cold to him.

"I'm trusting you with my baby brother. Don't you dare screw up! And stick to the code words—stop using names."

"Jane—ow!" Hal cried.

"Just checking my reach." Guy hated "baby" and probably felt the need to prove he could keep Hal in line.

After that, silence came from the *PB&G* production truck.

Beyond the wide flats of South Side, there ran only a narrow ledge at the foot of the steep hills that edged the river. The bank was thick scrub trees and the old cracked pavement of the Heritage Trail. Jumpfish made the old walking path too dangerous to use since it lay only feet from the water and well within the big fishes' range. On the other side of the road were the railroad tracks that headed straight east to the coastal elf settlements.

Pre-dawn started to lighten the sky to fragile gray. Mist hazed the Monongahela. The river lay nearly a thousand feet wide at this stretch, dark water hiding all sorts of evils. In the 1950s, a B-25 bomber had crashed into this section of the river. Fifty feet of airplane with a wingspan of seventy feet, swallowed up by water, never to be found. How many monsters were hidden in the waters?

They stopped to put up the barrier at Becks Run Road and continued downriver to erect the last blockade.

Her hand brushed against Taggart's. She glanced down at the seat between them. If she shifted slightly, she could take hold of his. If she did, would he see it as her committing? She huffed out. Commit to what? Hand holding? Not like they're going to be making out in the back of the Humvee with her little brothers in the front. It was a stupid time to even be thinking about it.

If they killed the monsters, would Maynard repay them by extending Taggart's visa? Would a few extra months actually make any difference? Two months. Two years. Sooner or later the visa would run out and he'd be gone. Unless of course they got married.

She glanced at Taggart. He studied the misty river through his camera lens. A giddy warmth and painful shyness surged through her, making her want to take his hand and at the same time edge away from him like he was a dangerous thing.

"Stupid, stupid, stupid," she whispered. "Thinking of that? Now?"

"Hm?" Taggart looked toward her.

"Nothing," Jane whispered. She covered her microphone and whispered a half-lie. "Just nervous. Hal and I deal with this kind of shit all the time but we always know what we're fighting. How many. And we don't get other people involved."

He took her hand and held it in silent comfort. He said no platitudes; he knew her fears were well grounded. His hand was warm and comforting.

"Keeper, this is Chaser One and Two," Guy reported, using the code words that Duff came up with. Joey and Boo had helped. "We're in position. Waiting on the Seeker."

"Do you have hard cover?" Duff asked before Jane could.

The tone of Guy's voice indicated he was giving a teenage roll of eyes at the stupidity of the question. "Yes, there's a large cinderblock garage in the back. We've got full cover."

"Set up and check the feeds on the cameras..." Duff read from "the plan."

"I know what we're supposed to do," Guy snapped.

Duff skipped over what was written to add, "and keep an eye out for normal shit like steel spinners and wargs."

"I know," Guy growled.

God as her witness, she had to be insane to get her brothers involved in this.

They hit the end of East Carson. Jane gave Taggart's hand a squeeze and left his comforting presence to set out the last barricade. Luckily since this was the abandoned part of town, it was unlikely any real police would stumble across their fake roadblock.

The world was pale and still and silent. The sun hadn't risen and the birds hadn't started their morning serenades. The only noise was the Humvee's motor and the dark gurgle of the river.

"Oh shit! Oh shit! Oh shit!" Duff cried over the headsets.

"What is it?" Jane started to run for the Humvee. Her heart climbing into her throat. Had something happened to Alton?

"They're in the city!" Duff cried. "They're on Liberty Avenue! There's two—maybe three. Bo is yelling

for help. One of them overturned Bowman's car and
he's pinned!"

Bo Pedersen was married to their cousin Patty.

"Damn it!" Jane climbed onto the Humvee and
stripped the tarp off the cannon. "Change of plan!
We're intercepting them in the city! Move!"

"You sure?" Geoffrey asked even as Marc punched
the gas pedal. The Humvee leapt forward. "We're
going to be seen."

"Yes!" Jane snapped. "Liberty Avenue is nearly the
heart of downtown. If you've ever had to chase a flock
of damn turkeys all over downtown, one thing you
learn is that unless you can fly, you can't get from
the river's edge to Liberty Avenue. There's a damn
maze of jersey barriers, bridge abutments and retain-
ing walls in the way. For more than one *namazu* to
show up in the middle of downtown, they're being
led through the maze. The damn oni have a monster
call just like we do and they're using the *namazu* to
terrorize the city."

"Seeker?" Guy cried over the com. "What's our
orders?"

"Move to Mount Washington and find hard cover.
Do not come into downtown!" And because he wouldn't
listen to that, she lied. "I want those trucks safe! We
need them intact."

"Okay." Guy sounded like he'd swallowed her lie.
"We're rolling!"

The morning sun was just starting to peer over the
hills as they roared toward the skyscrapers of downtown. The very tips of the PPG glass castle gleamed
brightly while the rest of the city was full of shadows.

Jane was up in the gunner's stand, growling out curses. They couldn't sit by and let the damn things wipe out the remaining police force. Bertha, though, would chew the hell out of downtown if they open fired at street level. Almost every building had big glass storefronts. If they missed the monster, the bullet could plow through blocks before hitting stone.

Whoever called the *namazu* into the city had the advantage; they knew the real commands that the monsters were bred to obey. Jane's crew wouldn't be able to drag the *namazu* out of the city unless they were the only ones commanding the creatures.

"Keeper?" Jane cupped her mic to cut down the howl of the wind. "Somewhere downtown is an oni with a monster call just like ours. I need eyes on him!"

"Okay. Okay. How do I find him? Shit! Shit! Shit! Seeker, can I bring in outside help?"

"Yes! Do anything you need!"

The communication line went silent for a few minutes until a stranger's voice suddenly joined.

"I'm patched into..." A young female voice paused to yawn deeply, "the cameras downtown. Explain again what I'm looking for."

Duff explained quickly and quietly. "Someone downtown at this minute with a whistle that they're blowing."

"You woke me up to find a flutist?" the unknown girl asked sleepily.

"It's more like a bosun whistle," Jane snapped. "Find it!"

"Who is that?" the female asked the question that Jane wanted to ask.

Duff kept to protocol. "You don't need to know now. I'll explain later. Lives are on the..."

"Holy crapola!" the girl shouted. "What the heck are those things?"

Well, the girl had just proved she had the ability to access downtown's cameras.

"The oni with the whistle is controlling them," Jane stated as calmly as she could while wondering who the hell this girl was. "Find him!"

"Okay," the girl said before the words totally sunk in. "Wait! An oni? What does an oni look like?"

"It's five-freaking-thirty in the morning!" Jane shouted. "He's going to be the only person downtown blowing a freaking whistle!"

"Working!" the girl cried. "Working! Jimmy Crickets, those things are—whoa! Oh no, oh no, it's trying to eat a cop!"

"Where?" Jane, Marc, and Duff all cried.

The girl made all sorts of sputtering noises and then cried, "Market Square! Market Square. We got to do something, D—"

"No names!" Duff shouted to drown out the stranger. "No names! This is an unsecure line! I'm Keeper. You're Beater One."

"Keeper!" Jane snapped.

Duff understood the unasked question. "She's the newest bunny, Seeker!"

The bakery that Duff worked at employed illegal immigrants who all took rabbit names for some unknown reason. Babs Bunny. Clover. What was the new one? Widget No Problemo. (Jane could not understand how this was a rabbit name but the girl was nevertheless one of the bunnies.) It meant that the girl couldn't go to the police or the EIA without endangering herself.

There were more squeaks from the bunny that

boded ill for Bo Pederson. They were still on the wrong side of the river, a mile away from Market Square. Jane couldn't help but remember that the last time she saw Bowman, he had announced Patty was pregnant. Guy had grown up with no memory of his father. It left a hole that even four older brothers couldn't fill. "Marc?"

"Got the pedal nailed to the floor." His voice was tense. He was the one that knew Bowman the best.

They reached Smithfield Street Bridge and turned hard without slowing. The tires screamed in protest and the Humvee leaned.

"Don't roll us!" Jane leaned into the turn to counterbalance Bertha's weight.

"Working on it," Marc stated calmly.

In theory the bridge had two lanes of traffic inbound and outbound. Jersey barriers and high curbs, though, limited the inbound to one lane at the turn. They overshot it, ending up in the outbound lanes as they headed into the city.

"Wrong side," Geoffrey murmured to their little brother. "Get over."

"Not going to happen," Marc replied. "Not at this speed."

They whipped past the first arch of steel girders that marked the start of the center lenticular trusses. Beyond that point, there was no way to cross back to the correct lanes.

"Forbes Avenue has only three lanes," Geoffrey warned.

"Well aware of that," Marc said.

"Let the man drive!" Jane shouted. This was another reason why she didn't want to get her brothers involved.

Her brothers might be afraid of her, and they might do what she told them, but they'd fight with her and among themselves at every decision point. She had Hal trained to jump when she said jump. Her brothers might decide to override her at the worst possible moment. "Make sure we're locked and loaded!"

"We can't fire Bertha in the city!" Marc shouted, confirming her fear that her brothers wouldn't listen to her.

"The hell we can't!" Jane shouted back. "We're not going to let these things eat Bowman! I've seen what they do to people!"

"There's going to be responding police and paramedics!" Marc shouted. "We'll hit them with friendly fire!"

She was normally the one urging caution to her younger brothers; of all the times for them to suddenly grow up! "We'll be careful! Keeper, find me another kill zone! One-mile radius!"

"What? What? What?" Widget cried in confusion and then must have spotted the Humvee incoming on the city's many cameras. "Oh! That's the cavalry? Oh, that rocks! You've got four targets in Market Square and two more on their way up the other end of Forbes Avenue."

Six total?

Jane cursed and covered her mic. "Marc, take us through Market Square so we can save Bowman's ass, and then head out of town. The plan is to pull them out of the city if we can." She let go of her mic. "Beater One! Get eyes on the oni with the whistle!"

"I'm looking!" Widget cried.

They hit the end of the bridge and flashed into the city proper with towering buildings lining the street.

They tore down Smithfield Street. Marc slowed for the sharp turn onto Forbes Avenue. The roar of the *namazu* came echoing up the artificial canyon. The *namazu's* discharge flickered like a Tesla coil within the still-dark street, reflecting off all the big glass storefronts.

Ahead was the full city-block-wide Market Square, bisected by Forbes Avenue and Market Street. It was a mix of brick and cobblestones and patches of grass. A dozen lampposts that looked like old-fashioned gas lamps still gleamed in the pre-dawn darkness. A clutter of trees, parking meters, trash cans, and café tables combined to make the kill zone a navigation hell. Lining the left hand side of the square were the half-dozen slick, black glass castles that been the Pittsburgh Plate Glass headquarters and now housed the EIA offices.

This was going to be a running of the bulls through a china store.

"Seeker, we're in position!" Guy reported from across the river on Mount Washington. "We have hard cover and we've got eyes on you. We confirm that there are six targets. I repeat: six."

The EIA was *not* going to be happy with them.

The piercing trill of the monster call echoed up the street. Somewhere ahead was also the oni commanding the *namazu*. A deafening roar of answering monsters washed over them in reply to the whistle. A moment later, a squad car went flipping past where Forbes Avenue opened into the square.

"Bowman!" Marc cried.

A *namazu* appeared at the intersection, blocking their way. Marc stomped on the brakes and they went skidding forward, several tons of metal about to meet several tons of angry electric fish.

Jane opened fire.

The big gun thundered as it shook in her hold, spitting out bullets faster than the eye could follow. The bullets slammed into the *namazu*, knocking it sideways as blood misted from the rapid-fire projectiles tearing it open. She strafed left, down the *namazu's* body, away from the squad car.

Marc veered hard to the right, gunning the Humvee. They shot past the nose of the *namazu*. It lunged at Jane in the gunner's seat. She poured bullets into its open mouth.

"Hold on!" Marc shouted.

They swerved the other way at whiplash speed. There was a wall of scales and arcing electricity and a flash of teeth.

Widget was making all sorts of yips and yelps over the com channel. "Nonononono! Yes. Yes! Watch out!"

Geoffrey blew their monster call but the *namazu* seemed to pay no attention to him. "Come here" apparently didn't work when practically standing on the creature. Either that or the oni's commands took precedence over Geoffrey's.

"Find the oni with the whistle!" Jane fought to control the gun. The great glass castle of PPG was shattering under the hail of bullets that had missed the monster. She prayed that Widget was right about no one being in the line of fire. What direction was Bo? She risked a glance over her shoulder.

The squad car had landed upside down. Roof crumbled, Pedersen was trapped inside. A *namazu* lumbered toward the car, guided either by hunger or the oni with the monster call. Jane couldn't risk opening fire on the beast; the chance of hitting Pedersen was too high.

"Seeker!" Duff shouted over the thunder of the bullets. "The only kill zone within a mile is inside the stadium! Three Rivers Stadium is the kill zone! Do you copy?"

"I copy on the kill zone!" Jane shouted. "Three Rivers Stadium. Find me the damn oni!"

"He's on top of the PPG building!" Widget said. "Not the big one. Number Two. The little one all by itself on Market Square! I don't think you can see him though! He ducked back behind one of the little pointy things on the roof."

Jane would blast the glass castle into shards but it could kill any innocent bystanders in the apartment buildings beyond it.

"I can see him!" Guy announced from Mount Washington. "I have a clear shot straight down Market Street."

*No! Not Guy! She didn't want her baby brother to kill someone. He was only sixteen.*

"Take the shot!" Marc shouted. "They're going to kill Bowman!"

Jane gave a wordless shout in dismay and protest.

"Damn it, I missed!" Guy cried. "He's ducked down. I can't see him."

There was a sudden fury of black wings overhead and a scream as someone plunged from the rooftop of the nearest glass castle.

"She threw him off the roof!" Guy cried while Widget had been reduced to an endless stream of "Oh my God, oh my God, oh my God..."

"I have a shot of the tengu." Guy's voice cracked and he sounded younger than sixteen. "What should I do?"

"Hold fire!" It might be Yumiko. Jane prayed that it was Yumiko and that the female was helping them.

The shrill notes of the whistle cut through everything. The *namazu* stopped, lifted their heads, and then started to move away from the overturned squad car.

"What is she doing?" Geoffrey reloaded.

"She's leading them away," Jane said. "Keeper, ETA on paramedics for Pedersen?"

"Three minutes," Duff reported.

"Get ahead of the *namazu*. We'll take them to the stadium and open up on them."

Yumiko must have heard Jane shouting out the kill zone because the tengu headed toward Stanwix Street, which was the most direct route to the stadium. Marc raced across the Roberto Clemente Bridge as the *yamabushi* called the monsters up the on-ramp of the bigger Fort Duquesne Bridge.

"Oh! Oh!" Widget cried over the com from wherever she was. "Guys! Guys! I don't know if this is good or bad but we're getting company. It's the EIA; a whole platoon of them. They're coming out of the Liberty Tunnel right now."

It meant that if the EIA had any clue what was going on downtown that they'd be on the Humvee's tail in a matter of minutes.

"What's the plan?" Marc asked.

"Do we have a plan?" Geoffrey asked.

"We get the door open to the stadium," Jane said. "Get the monsters inside and then shoot the hell out of them."

"That sounds like a plan." Geoffrey said.

"Then we look for nests," Hal added.

"Nests?" Jane asked.

"I want to try some of that roe." In typical television host fashion, he was using as many words possible to explain something simple. "Cautiously, of course, but I'm curious as to what it tastes like. It looks much more like salmon roe than sturgeon caviar."

"What nests?" Jane shouted.

Nigel explained clearer. "If the oni are anywhere near intelligent, they made the *namazu* at least fifty percent female. There should be two more nests at minimum."

"We will deal with that later," Jane growled. Hopefully. If they weren't in jail. The fact there were nests, though, gave her an idea. "Chaser Two, call Maynard."

"Me?" Hal's tone was clear that he didn't think it was a good idea. "Maynard?"

"Yes, you! Tell him that we're doing what he asked and killing the monsters. Be charming. Tell him about the nest at Sandcastle and tell him that we need to be free to look for more."

"But I want to watch you—ow!" Hal gave a cry of pain even as Jane shouted, "Now!" Guy must have hit Hal again. "I'm making the call. See. The phone is ringing!"

"Take off your headset!" Guy snapped and Hal disappeared out of the conversation.

Marc hit the end of the Clemente Bridge, turned hard onto General Robinson Street and flew down it. Three Rivers Stadium loomed straight ahead, a great concrete donut on the North Shore. It been scheduled to be torn down months before the first Startup to make way for two stadiums dedicated to football and baseball. Since all the professional sport teams had fled the city, it had sat abandoned for years. If

Yumiko actually got the *namazu* onto the vast playing field, it would be like shooting fish in a bucket. Giant electric fish.

Only Jane had no clue how they were going to get the *namazu* into the stadium.

"Keeper, is there an entrance large enough for the targets inside?"

"I-I-I have no idea. Beater One?"

"If it's a normal stadium, it should," Widget babbled. "Back in the States, they have these monster truck rallies at stadiums all the time. I don't understand the concept but people like them. And if they can drive jacked up pickup trucks into the stadiums, there has to a monster-size entrance somewhere. The question is: where. Where? Where? There! It's in the back, opposite of the River Front Entrance."

Yumiko was darting in and out of sight as she led the monsters out of downtown. Jane could barely keep track of her despite the massive black wingspan. The tengu needed to stay aloft, away from the arcing electricity from the *namazu*, while keeping hidden from any snipers. Yumiko used what little cover the Fort Duquesne Bridge afforded as the five remaining monsters lumbered across the top deck. It was only a thousand feet but the on-ramp and off-ramp easily doubled the distance.

From Jane's position, it certainly looked like they were all hurtling toward the same point, but it was difficult to be sure. She wanted to believe that Yumiko had realized that they were on the same side. It would be dangerous to assume that they were now trusted allies. The tengu woman could be leading Jane into a trap.

Widget was right about the vehicle entrance. There was a massive steel garage door protecting a tunnel that would have allowed a tractor-trailer to drive onto the playing field. Jane wasted a dozen bullets to shoot it into shreds. Marc smashed into the weakened barrier. The door caved and they drove down the short corridor to a second door. They downed that one. Beyond it was the weed-choked playing field.

Jane swiveled in the gunner's chair, aiming back down the tunnel. She could see across the river to the first floor of Gateway towers. No. She couldn't simply open fire while the *namazu* were bottlenecked in the tunnel.

"Do we have time to film a pass of the stadium?" Taggart broke his silence.

"Chaser One, how close are the targets?" Jane asked.

"You've got two minutes, tops," Guy reported from Mount Washington. "We've lost sight of you."

"Understood."

They plowed through the tall weeds to the fifty-yard line. Taggart scrambled out of the Humvee and did a quick pan of the silent, abandoned stadium. The empty seats. The shadows heavy on the eastern end of the field. The slice of sunlight just touching the top lip of the western rim. They sat in the silence and let him film despite the fact that their instincts were screaming for them to run. They needed film clips like this one to tie together all the confusing action pieces to make an understandable narrative. Taggart understood what would convey the desperation of their situation more than Jane, just as Earth-born Widget knew the general layout of stadiums when Duff did not.

"Backup camera three is out," Nigel reported.

"I'll check it after I reload." Geoffrey shifted the big ammo cases around and fed a new chain up into the gun.

Jane kept aimed at the tunnel, heart thudding at the knowledge that they were unarmed until Geoffrey finished reloading.

"Seeker!" Guy cried from his advantage point. "You've got incoming!"

"Let's go," Jane said.

Taggart slid back into the Humvee.

Outside the stadium, there was the trill of the monster call. Yumiko flashed overhead; a rustle of black wings and then nothing. From some hiding space within the stadium itself, she blew the call again. The five *namazu* roared in answer, the noise echoing up the entrance tunnel.

"Get us room to maneuver," Jane said.

Marc grunted. There wasn't going to be a lot of spare area once the playing field was filled up with giant monsters throwing lightning.

The *namazu* lumbered down the tunnel faster than she expected. Electricity crawled along the seats near the entrance, flashing brilliance in the still pale morning sunlight. It startled a flock of pigeons that winged upwards. One vanished in a sudden puff of feathers.

Jane held her fire; she didn't want to block the tunnel with a dead body.

The beasts rushed toward the Humvee, spreading out as they came down the field.

Jane opened fire. She focused on the far right, creating an escape path. The monster flailed under the rain of bullets. "Come on, die! Die!"

She couldn't tell if it was completely dead but she

switched to the second monster. "Move!" She shouted over the thunder of the cannon.

Marc sped toward the opening she made even as the left-most monster closed on the goal end. The other two split up, moving to cut them off even as the third gave chase.

"Left," Geoffrey muttered as they raced directly at one. "Left! Leftleftleftleft."

"Shut up!" Marc jerked the wheel right.

They dodged the *namazu's* head and Jane strafed down its flank as they passed the long body. The other lunged at them. It slammed into the Humvee, making it tip. Electricity arced and crackled around them.

"Don't roll us!" Jane fought gravity.

"Kill it then!" Marc shouted.

It snapped at Marc, smashing his window.

She opened fire without thinking of anything but her little brother. The recoil tipped them the rest of the way over. The Humvee hit hard on its side. They plowed through the deep weeds.

"Jane!" Geoffrey slapped her safety belt buckle and jerked her out of the gunner's seat.

"Oh, damn, Bertha!" Jane cried.

"Forget Bertha!" Geoffrey shouted.

"Fire in the hole!" Marc shouted.

They covered their ears and ducked their heads.

There was a roar of noise as a flashbang went off.

Taggart cried out in surprise.

Jane's heart flipped. Oh God, if he was stunned and blinded the monsters were going to kill him. "Are you okay?"

"I'm fine," Taggart called. "I just forgot your family owns stock in that company."

The Humvee lurched as the blinded *namazu* slammed against it. They were grounded; they had to get out before its electricity could strike them.

"Go!" Jane shouted.

They scrambled out of the Humvee. She must have killed the *namazu* that tipped the Humvee. It wasn't moving. The remaining beast was reeling from the flashbang.

"Get to the upper levels." She led the way across the field toward the high wall surrounding the field. Of course both her brothers wanted to cover their retreat. "Move it!"

The *namazu* roared. It came crashing through the weeds toward them. She hit the wall first and scrambled over it. All instincts were screaming for her to stop and make sure the others got to safety. The hard truth was that her best chance of protecting them was to kill the monster.

She turned, swinging her rifle off her back and up to her shoulder. It was heart-stoppingly close to Marc and Taggart. *Losing something makes it suddenly clear that it's very important to you.*

"Don't think of that now," she whispered. She sighted on the *namazu*'s small beady eyes, held her breath, and pulled the trigger.

The crack of the rifle was weirdly comforting. The beast staggered and then slowly crumbled.

The silence was surreal.

"Okay," she said to fill the silence. "That's a wrap."

The EIA officer in charge was a big, square-jawed idiot from Eastern Europe. His nametag identified him as Lieutenant Juhan Kukk. He spoke with a heavy accent and lapsed into his own language when addressing his men. He quickly proved that in addition to being a newcomer to Pittsburgh he was both racist and sexist. He ignored Jane because she was a woman and Taggart because he wasn't white enough. He focused all questions and demands at Geoffrey. Jane really wanted to punch him but kept her fists close to her side.

At least the idiot didn't try to take Taggart's camera. He did take all their weapons and had Marc handcuffed after failing to stare down her younger brother.

Worse, Sparrow appeared with *sekasha* in tow. With elves in attendance, Jane didn't dare lie but the one person she didn't want to tell the truth to was Sparrow. Not with the steely-eyed *sekasha* at her back.

Elves weren't gender-biased. The female elf knew Jane was the one to deal with. The focus was unnerving. The knowledge that Sparrow could order the *sekasha* to kill them fluttered fear through Jane. It was one thing to subject her younger brothers to the slow grind of the human legal system, another to expose them to the elves' swift justice.

"Where did you get this?" Sparrow held up the gossamer call.

The question was in English but Jane answered in Elvish, hoping that any oddity of her story would be discounted as a lack of fluency. Jane cluttered up the story, hiding the truth with other truths. "There was an oni calling the monsters into the city with a whistle. He was making them attack Bowman—the police officer—he's married to our cousin. The daughter of our mother's aunt. They're going to have a baby. The oni was on the roof of the PPG building. My people shot at him, trying to stop him before the monsters killed our cousin's husband. He fell from the roof."

She stopped there, leaving it to seem as if they'd gotten the oni's whistle.

If Sparrow had given the oni the gossamer call, she would realize that Nigel's instrument didn't match the oni's. She wouldn't be able to prove it without exposing herself. It was a dangerous game of bluff poker.

Sparrow studied her with maddening calm. The female was like some snow queen, dressed in a tight frosty-blue fairy-silk gown and blond hair braided with ribbons and flowers. What was going on behind that beautiful exterior? This female had tried to murder Windwolf and most likely had been behind Tinker's kidnapping. Yet she stood unconcerned among the deadly *sekasha*. She had to be very good at this game.

Sparrow flicked a hand to indicate Bertha. The EIA had righted the Humvee. The cannon looked undamaged. "Where did you get this weapon?"

"My father left it to his children. I do not know where he got it. He was afraid that a wyvern or a dragon might attack the city while Wolf Who Rules was not nearby."

Kukk's bigotry meant he wasn't happy that the elves had taken over the conversation. "It doesn't matter how they got it, it's illegal. The treaty states that individuals can't import heavy weaponry onto Elfhome."

"I didn't import it," Jane stated calmly as she could.

Kukk plowed on with the charges. "It's against city ordinances to fire weapons within a hundred and fifty yards of any residential structures. Our downtown headquarters looks like Swiss cheese. There's a dead man—who may or may not be oni—splattered on the sidewalk."

If this idiot got her brothers killed, Jane would make sure he was dead before she went down. "What does it matter if he was an oni or a human or an elf? He was calling the monsters into Market Square. What other reason would he be on the rooftop of that building before dawn?"

"Why were you there?" Sparrow countered.

"We'd promised Director Maynard to kill the monsters. When we heard the report that our cousin's husband was pinned, we rushed to save him."

Sparrow pulled out more damning evidence. "You were at the hospital when the oni prisoner escaped."

The *sekasha's* eyes narrowed dangerously. Jane realized that the conversation served no purpose except to sway the holy warriors into acting. If that was the game that Sparrow wanted to play, then Jane could too. In fact, as a TV show producer, she could play it very well. This was, after all, media propaganda.

"Like we told Director Maynard, one of our people had been wounded by a saurus two days ago. His wounds became infected and we took him to be treated. The staff there told us about the tengu. The people of Earth have no idea what the elves are fighting. The only pictures of oni are dead ones. If the people of Earth are to help the elves protect their world, then they have to know what the elves are fighting. An interview with a human turned into a crow, her body twisted by magic, would have been compelling evidence against the oni. She'd stolen a scalpel and gotten free of her restraints before we arrived."

"Hal Rogers set one of my men on fire," Kukk complained.

"Hal set himself on fire earlier this week," Jane pointed out. "He's accident-prone. I normally don't allow

Hal access to anything that can start a fire because of it. Your man provided Hal the flammable materials. We put him out. He was relatively unharmed."

"Relatively?" Kukk growled.

"It was an accident which Private Tapper was equally responsible for." Jane came as close to lying as she dared. She was sure, though, that Hal couldn't have started the fire without a lighter from the private. "We promised Director Maynard to hunt down and kill the monster. We've killed six. There might be more." Sparrow's face tightened and Jane knew that was the right track to take. "There was a nest with several hundred eggs at Sandcastle. We're fairly sure there are two more nests. There could be as many as four more. Those need to be located and destroyed."

"You have broken the treaty..." Sparrow started.

"If these humans were born in Pittsburgh," the leader of the *sekasha* stated quietly, "then they have not broken the treaty."

"I am the *husepavua*, Dark Harvest," Sparrow said.

"And I'm Second of First Hand." Dark Harvest cut her short. "We are at war. My decision stands. She and her younger brothers were born here. They are 'natives' of Elfhome. As such, they are allowed any weapon needed to defend their home."

"That section refers only to the rights of elves," Kukk said.

"If you believe that, then you have misunderstood the wording," Dark Harvest said.

Jane gasped as she realized that traitorous Sparrow had most likely had a hand in translating the treaty into human law. Of course the oni would want the humans only lightly armed.

"Let them go," Dark Harvest commanded.

"They broke multiple human laws," Kukk stated.

"Idiotic laws." Dark Harvest waved away Kukk's objections. "Monsters do not cooperate and stay outside of the limit you stated. They had no choice. You will not punish them for this. Take off the restraints."

They fled the North Side. After a stop at Market Square to film the dead *namazu* there, they headed to Mount Washington to meet up with the production trucks. Jane was glad that Marc was driving; her mind was in a whirlwind. What did she really know about anything? What did the treaty really say—at least as far as the elves were concerned? How many Pittsburghers were actually oni? How many nasty surprises like the *namazu* did the oni have scattered in the abandoned corners of the city? She wasn't even sure of things like how Maynard ended up as director of the EIA, which left the question of his loyalties dangerously unclear.

One thing was clear: the elves considered themselves to be at war and most of the humans in Pittsburgh didn't realize it.

Taggart startled her by taking her hand. Apparently once you breached the hand-holding threshold, the door was always open for more. It felt good though in all the confusion to have something solid to cling to. He and Nigel were good people. She couldn't have gotten Boo back or killed the *namazu* without them. Yet in less than sixty days, she was going to lose Taggart.

Unless she solved his visa problems.

"Marry me," Jane whispered.

"What?" Taggart's eyes went wide.

"If you marry me, you don't need a visa to stay on Elfhome."

His eyes went dark and sober. "If you don't love me . . ."

"I think I do." She squeezed his hand tightly. "It might take me a while to be sure, but we don't have that time. I trust you. You're a good man. I think you're hands-down the sexiest guy I've ever laid eyes on. And you didn't run screaming from my family. I think given time, I will come to love you more than anything in the universe. I'm willing to take the risk that it won't work out if you are."

He stared at her open-mouthed for a full minute.

"Well?" Jane wondered if maybe she should have waited until they weren't covered in *namazu* blood and reeking of gun smoke.

He kissed her. He was just the right height so that they interlocked perfectly. Under the wonderfully soft fabric of his silk shirt, he was warm hard muscle. He kissed even better than he smelled, which was amazing.

"I'll take that as a yes," Jane said.

Her mother was going to be ecstatic. Her brothers probably would be relieved that she wasn't marrying Hal. (They liked Hal but had no respect for the man.)

Hal.

She knew him as well as she knew her brothers. She had, however, no idea how he was going to react to the news. Would it be best to tell him immediately or wait—like until the day of the wedding—or maybe a few weeks afterwards?

On second thought, she was fairly sure he was going to lose it. Taggart was right; Hal loved her. Maybe if he hadn't caught himself on fire the first day they met, things might have gone differently with them. Putting a man out immediately slotted him into the "younger brother" category, despite the fact he was ten years older than her. She didn't want to think of herself as the shallow type of woman that only liked macho-looking men, but the fact that Hal came to shoulder-level on her had always led to embarrassing face-plant moments.

Marrying Taggart only solved half the problem. What were they going to do about Nigel's visa? He was very good-looking in his own right and a sweet-natured, intelligent man. Did she know anyone desperate to get married?

Brandy? No, the police officer only wanted a sexual partner, not a husband.

Until they found someone for Nigel, they had to assume that they only had fifty-some days to film the first season of *Chased by Monsters*. They needed to find any hidden *namazu* nests, make sure that the rivers were free of the monsters, and do the paperwork for Taggart to become an official Pittsburgher via marriage.

God, her mother was going to want a real wedding: church, priest, white dress, and a big reception afterward with a table full of several hundred cookies. Her family would want to start baking as soon as possible. They were going to want to use her ovens. Hyeholde was about to become overrun by every relative that could be drafted into the effort.

Maybe she shouldn't tell her family either.

Her mother would kill her if Jane went behind her back.

She was still wrestling with logistics when they pulled into Hyeholde's long driveway.

First step obviously was to find the hidden nests, since they had no idea how long the eggs took to hatch. Second was to fill out the paperwork to keep Taggart in Pittsburgh. Third was to find a woman for Nigel—assuming that the man was straight. The realization of how little she knew about the *Chased by Monsters* team scared her slightly now that she was planning to marry one of them.

She forced herself to put all thoughts aside. The price of living out in the middle of nowhere was to be vigilant to danger. They'd left the house empty for hours; she needed to be sure that nothing deadly had wandered into the area.

The morning had her so ramped up that Hyeholde felt like the abandoned and forgotten corner of Pittsburgh that it was. She stood in the driveway, rifle in hand, listening carefully to the wind move through the trees.

Jane eyed the forest that pressed close to the yard. Were the woods too quiet? Or had the morning just ratcheted up her paranoia to new heights? "Stay on watch. I'm checking the house."

Her front door was still locked, none of the windows were broken, and nothing seemed to be stirring within the house. The back door and both side doors were barred as well as locked. She couldn't shake the feeling, though, that someone had been in the house.

She looped back to the trucks.

Her brothers were all standing guard with rifles. Hal was up in Bertha's gunner seat, pretending to fire the big gun, complete with sound effects. "Pew! Pewpewpewpewpew!"

"Bertha doesn't go 'pew,'" Guy complained. "*Star Wars* lasers go 'pew.' Bertha goes 'Powpowpowpow-pow!'"

"More like 'Boomboomboomboom,'" Geoffrey stated.

Should she tell Hal that she was marrying Taggart before or after letting him shoot the cannon? If she told him beforehand, he would probably demand more shots. They didn't have ammo to waste.

Taggart stood silently to one side, camera on his shoulder, letting her decide when to spill the news.

Alton's pickup came rumbling up the driveway.

Guy reached up and yanked Hal out of the gunner's seat. "You don't point guns at people you don't want to kill." Apparently Guy considered himself still on the job of sitting on Hal.

"Hail, the victorious heroes!" Boo called, leaning out the window, waving.

"Hoi!" Jane called back.

Joey launched himself at her as soon as she opened the door. "You were on the radio!"

"We were?" Jane let herself be hugged tight and kissed on the cheek by the little boy.

"Sean saw it all." Alton climbed down from his truck. Their cousin Sean Roach was the late-night DJ at KDKA radio. He must have been pulling an all-nighter to be at the station so insanely early in the morning. From the studios in the Gateway Center skyscraper, Sean would have had a front row seat to the Market Square action. "Sean bumped the morning show programming so he could do play-by-play. He knew it was you; he recognized Bertha. He was doing damage control. He kept saying things like 'the unknown heroes have saved the pinned and helpless police officer!' Speaking of which: Bowman is at Mercy with a concussion and minor lacerations."

Jane laughed with relief, kissed Joey on the forehead, and handed him off to Marc. "EIA wasn't happy but the *sekasha* made them let us go. I think we need to seriously go over the peace treaty and find out what it really says."

"We need to find the nests," Nigel stated firmly.

*We need to plan a wedding. We need to get a girl for Nigel. We need to break the news—gently—to Hal.*

Joey squealed and giggled as Marc tossed him up in the air. "Higher!"

Marc complied, throwing him higher and higher, making him shriek with laughter.

"Whoa! Don't put him into orbit!" Alton snagged Joey out of the air. "Come on, we got to make our fresh dough and mozzarella cheese for the pizza."

"Pizza!" Joey cried. "Yay!"

Taggart gave her a questioning glance. He clearly was wondering when she wanted to break the news.

Geoffrey misunderstood the look. "We survived! Now, we cook!"

Taggart grinned. "I like this tradition."

While her brothers started dinner, Jane covertly scanned the laws concerning marriage and immigration. The proof of identification didn't fall on Taggart but on her. She had to provide a Pittsburgh birth certificate and proof of continued residency. Otherwise it was fairly simple. File for license. A blood test for God-knows-what. Pick out a date. Tell her family.

Alton had fresh milk from Grandma Gertie's Dairy. The process of transforming it into fresh mozzarella fascinated Joey. Geoffrey worked on turning tomatoes from Jane's garden into sauce. Marc made dough.

Guy scoured her pantry and refrigerator for possible toppings. "How do you live this way? There's barely anything in here! What do you eat?"

Jane smacked him instead of answering. She enjoyed cooking but it felt like too much effort to cook just for herself. She ate with family on Sundays, and on Fridays with her friends. The rest of the week was hit or miss. She crossed the kitchen to help him locate suitable toppings. "Kalamata olives. Anchovies. Chorizo. Done. Go pick some spinach and fresh basil."

Chesty stood up with a deep growl, looking toward the front door. A moment later the doorbell rang.

"Hyeholde has a doorbell?" Guy asked in surprise. No one ever used it.

"I didn't hear a car," Marc stated.

The doorbell rang again.

Jane pointed at her brothers. "Stay." She motioned Chesty to follow her out into the foyer. Who the hell was at her front door? She put her right hand back so she could quickly pull her pistol and cautiously cracked the door open.

Yumiko stood on the doorstep. She wore a loose, black tank top and capris. Her crow feet were bare. There was no sign of her massive wings. "We need to talk."

"Yes, we do." Jane agreed without opening the door wider.

"You have Joey Shoji."

"Yes. I consider him family. I won't allow him to be harmed in any way; that includes being used as a figurehead by a religious fanatic."

Yumiko snorted. The edges of her lips might have twitched with a smile. "He seems happy here."

"You've been watching."

"We couldn't risk Joey being hurt."

*We?* As in Yumiko wasn't alone? *The truth or a bluff?*

"Joey doesn't know what happened to his family after he was taken," Jane said.

Yumiko's eyes narrowed. "And?"

Was she being clueless or cautious? Jane realized that if the oni hadn't succeeded in capturing all of Joey's family, then Yumiko wouldn't want to leak their location.

"I don't know who survived." Jane caught herself from adding that she didn't care. "My father died when I was twelve. I can't imagine losing your entire family. Joey's a little boy. He needs people, lots of people that care about him, to help him over this. If it's just you here to pick him up—then—no, you can't have him."

Yumiko studied her in silence for several minutes. Jane really hoped that they weren't going to start shooting at each other. Yumiko stepped back and waved at the treetops. There was a rustling and then two small figures winged down out of the trees.

It was a tengu girl, probably only fourteen years old, and a boy around ten.

The girl hid behind war paint and a fierce glare. The boy hid behind Yumiko.

"We're here for Joey," the girl announced. "You better give him to us."

"This is Keiko Shoji." Yumiko nudged the boy and gave him a comforting smile. "And Mickey."

Joey's cousins. Not what Jane expected but they certainly looked like Joey.

"We're making pizza. Do you want to join us? It would be easier on Joey."

"Pizza!" Mickey cried, full of eagerness.

Keiko gave Jane a teenage look of disgust that said she couldn't believe that Jane had stooped so low. Yumiko obviously was looking for a trap.

There was a slight noise behind Jane. Yumiko reacted instantly, pulling Keiko behind her and reaching for her pistol.

"Stop it!" Boo shouted.

Yumiko went unnaturally still. It was as if Boo's words had turned her to stone. Then slowly the tengu woman cocked her head in puzzlement. "Who are you? You're one of the Chosen."

"This is my baby sister," Jane said. "We have lots to talk about."

Joey's reunion with his cousins was at first joyous and then heartbreaking as they explained to the little boy that his aunt and uncle had been killed. He cried uncontrollably until he took refuge in Boo's arms. Boo rocked him, hugging him close and singing "Skyfall" just like their mother would have. "Let the sky fall, when it crumbles, we will stand tall, face it all, together, at skyfall."

"Any of the Chosen bloodline can command an individual tengu. The Chosen One—Jin Wong—can command the entire Flock. For centuries, we've kept the existence of the Chosen One and the *yamabushi* secret from the oni. We'd thought that the raid on the Shoji house had been nothing more than the oni rounding up tengu that had slipped from their grasp.

They'd staged similar attacks on other houses. That they changed your sister means that we were wrong. Riki had been cooperating with them while I searched for Joey." She dropped her voice to a whisper. "He's had to do some horrible things to keep up the impression that he's cooperating with them."

Like kidnapping the viceroy's bride and brother?

Riki was the cousin that nightly read the Harry Potter books to Joey. Jane had assumed that he'd been killed. She understood being willing to do anything and everything to get a family member back. Hopefully now that Joey was safe, the tengu would listen to reason. "I want to free Tinker and Windwolf's blade brother."

"Riki doesn't think that's wise. He's learned that Pure Radiance foretold Tinker being the lynchpin to stopping the oni. The greater bloods think they understand dreaming; they believe this means they can use her to do the opposite. Kajo's Eyes are strong but they're young, untrained and overly confident. They think they have outmaneuvered Pure Radiance. What they don't realize is that Pure Radiance rarely makes her prophecies known nor has she ever left court since she ended the Clan Wars. She obviously wanted the Eyes to act on her prophecy."

"Pure Radiance set Tinker up?"

"Yes. She's played to the Eyes' weakness; they have human lifespans. They are very good at the short game; they can easily keep one step ahead of someone who thinks day to day. Pure Radiance is Vision's daughter, the oldest of the *intanyei seyosa*. A decade is a child's game to her. She can plot out a century, guiding full civilizations toward an outcome that she wants. I think she's giving the Eyes enough rope to hang themselves."

"And Tinker is just an expendable tool?"

"Possibly to Pure Radiance. Not to us. We are attempting to keep her safe."

It was a politically safe, wise thing for Yumiko to claim but not necessarily the truth. "Attempting" indicated that the tengu were far from in control of the outcome. If they were, half the Shoji family wouldn't have been butchered.

"The oni will come looking for Boo." Yumiko detoured the conversation to something closer to home.

"I am not leaving my family." There was a tremble of fear in Boo's voice.

"We can keep her hidden." Alton said.

Unless we have a big-ass Kryskill wedding.

"If you come with us, we'll be able to give you wings," Keiko said.

Boo gave her a look of utter want and glanced to each of her siblings. "I've lived without wings for fourteen years. I can live another year or two without them."

## *Author Note:*

*I had the strangest dream, and you were there.*

I dreamed in cartoon one night. Seriously, instead of normal people, everyone was animated. What's more, it was like the ending credits of a Japanese anime. In Japan, there is a strong tradition of doing group dances, kind of like country-western line dancing. Entire towns will turn out to do their regional group dance. As a reflection of this tradition, most animes have a dance which they show in the ending credits.

In my dream, Tinker, Oilcan, and Roach of Team Tinker were dancing away, doing the 1960s dance, the Monkey. (It's one of the simplest sixties dances; the dancer basically pumps their arms up and down in time with the music.) Roach was in the middle, between the two cousins.

Suddenly Tinker *transformed* into an elf. Roach startled but kept dancing, eyeing her with surprise. Pony, Stormsong, Jin and Providence popped into scene, dancing to the right of Tinker. Roach edged away but kept dancing.

Then Oilcan *transformed*. Roach startled in the other direction. Thorne Scratch, Merry, Baby Duck and Impatience popped in, taking up left of Oilcan. Roach was starting to look panicked.

Pop! The twins appeared in front of Roach who looked like he was trying to climb an invisible ladder out of surprise. The twins had Joy and the Jawbreakers dancing on the ground, and Nikola and Chuck Norris flying in the air in little mini hover-dance platforms.

Roach jaw-dropped. He slowly backed up until he was waaaaay in the back and then bolted out of sight.

I woke up laughing. I'm not sure what my subconscious was trying to tell me.

# DRABBLE

## Three Ways the Twins Do Not Meet . . .

*I've always enjoyed fan fiction where the fan authors reinterpret characters and events. One of my favorites is where a main character goes through the same event but with different supporting characters for different outcomes.*

*As I started to plan the fifth book of the Elfhome series, one of the naturally reoccurring events is how the twins would meet various people. Who would they meet first? How would they meet? How would the established characters react to the sudden arrival of the twins? Unfortunately, while there were many possible "first meetings," because space is limited, probably only one will make the final cut.*

*After two or three introduction scenes occurred to me, I decided to go ahead and write out possible fun meetings.*

*Be aware that the point of the exercise is merely to have fun.*

*None of This Really Happens!*

# 1. How the Twins Do Not Meet Lain Shenske

Lain Shenske had discovered long ago that the only sane way to talk with her niece was face to face. On the phone, Tinker's attention was on whatever was at hand; most of the girl's remarks were addressed to the piece of machinery that wasn't cooperating, or the math formula that she was scribbling, or whatever other pursuit was occupying her mind. Over time Lain had trained her niece to come and talk to Lain about mundane things. Telephone calls, thus, were when Tinker was knee deep in trouble and sinking fast. Those were crazy-making conversations with improbable events playing out and the expectation that Lain could actually do something to solve the problem at hand.

Over the years, Lain had learned that the first tinge of a headache often was just a forewarning that her peaceful life was about to implode. She had to train herself to wait for the phone to actually ring. Occasionally she would slip and pick up the phone before it rang. Due to some oddity in the phone system, the connection was made prior to her phone ringing. Not that it mattered much; Tinker rarely noticed that she'd been dropped into silence. She would normally launch into full expository mode before Lain could get the receiver to her ear.

But once in a great while, there would only be puzzled silence on the other side. This was one of them.

After a moment, Tinker said, "That's weird, it didn't ring, but the graphic changed."

"Did you dial the right number?" Tinker asked herself.

"It came up with Lain Shenske on the connection ID," Tinker answered herself.

Lain covered her mouth to hold in a gasp of surprise. It was Tinker's voice from years ago, when she was a child. There had been a subtle change in timbre that Lain hadn't realized until this moment. Puberty and years of shouting over the noise of large machinery had deepened Tinker's voice slightly so it wasn't child-squeaky. It wasn't Tinker on the phone.

"Maybe you got her voicemail," the child said. "Maybe it's broken. We should try calling Orville again. We still don't know if Esme told Lain anything about Alexander. If she didn't, then Lain isn't going to believe we're her nieces."

*Nieces?*

"And nephew," Niece One added.

"I can hear breathing," Christopher Robin interjected, or at least, a young nephew that sounded like him.

"My breathing?" Niece One asked while Niece Two said "Her breathing?"

"Someone else," Christopher said firmly.

"Hello?" one of the girls said.

"Who is this?" Lain asked.

There were two startled squeals on the other side and the connection was broken.

*Oh, good God, Esme, what have you done?*

## 2. How the Twins Do Not Meet
   Director Derek Maynard

With Pittsburgh trapped on Elfhome and one major dragon fight in the downtown section of the city, plate glass was becoming scarce. Thus it took nearly three weeks for Maynard to have all the windows of his office replaced.

He sent his secretary out for coffee and collapsed into his chair. He had hopes that his life was returning to something that resembled order.

That hope, along with two of his new windows, were shattered by the sudden arrival of the Dufae twins. He knew what they were immediately; he learned who they were much later. At that moment, he was too surprised to greet them properly. Tinker always had that effect on him; doubled, it was only more so.

They didn't seem to notice him as they pushed up goggles and eyed the broken glass sprayed across the wood floor.

"I told you that the building was in the way," one of them complained. They were inches shorter than Tinker but otherwise twins to her. Same spiky brown hair, dusky skin, and destructive ability.

"Details, details, details," the other twin cried as she crunched across the glass to peer out the bank of windows on the other side of his office. "There, see, we'll make it easy with the next jump."

"I don't know." The first girl joined her twin. "I think we'll just plow into the hillside."

"We'll clear it!"

"That's what you said about this place." The doubting twin clapped her hand. "Recall!"

They turned and watched the window that they had smashed through with an air of expectation.

Maynard was just about to say something polite but firm when an Easter Island moai statue smashed through the window beside the two broken ones.

"We're not sure we like this," the statue complained in a little-boy voice. "It seems a very awkward way of traveling."

"Well, we can't move you any other way," the optimistic twin said.

"If we had a big enough lever..." the pessimistic twin said.

"Jumping!" her sister cried. She clapped her hands. "Shields!"

The other sighed and wrapped her left hand tight around her twin. With her right, she aimed at the top of Mount Washington. "Jump!"

They soared out the window as if on a bungee cord anchored on Mount Washington, twin screams of fear or delight or both. A moment later a puff of smoke and a sudden scattering of birds marked their landing a few feet shy of the hilltop.

"Oh, you're Director Maynard," the moai statue said. "Nice to meet yooooou!"

The last word was yelped as the statue shuddered across his wood floor, gouging a massive groove into it. It hit the edge and vaulted into the air to soar after the twins.

Maynard stood staring after them. Oh God. Two more Tinkers.

## 3. How the Twins Do Not Meet
## Team Tinker's Business Manager, Roach

It was a sign of the times that a trip to Pittsburgh Salvage made Roach wax nostalgic. Yes, refuse and salvage were both perceived to be bottom of the food chain. Garbage in the summer could be insanely offensive to work with. Both businesses, however, gave access to money, materials, and time to do less profitable activities. Because the landfill smelled (and, around some of Tinker's experiments, was explosive) Team Tinker had spent years hanging out at the salvage yard, plotting world domination.

It was a wonderful time. Yes, Tinker nearly killed them all with her "toys" several times but that was part of the fun. Living on the edge. Never totally sure what was going to explode next.

Roach *carefully* poked through Tinker's workshop, telling himself that it was inevitable that the racing would come to an end. People grew up. Got married to people that didn't understand the addiction. Had kids too young to be at a noisy and often dangerous pit at the racetrack. After the Team Providence mess, Tinker wanted to mass-produce the Deltas, so Team Tinker was losing its advantage as well as its riders. Of the two, the loss of their riders was actually the more damaging. Despite what people thought, it took brains to race. The best riders could calculate the most effective move at any instant.

An odd squealing noise from the back of the salvage yard stopped his reflections. He drifted out of Tinker's workshop, head cocked. It sounded like kids screaming in fear or delight; you could never tell with kids. There was a weird accompaniment to the screaming, a grinding of metal and a low roar. What the hell was that?

Suddenly a small figure whipped around a stack of wrecked cars and collided with Roach.

"Ow!" the child complained.

Roach blinked down at the girl. He knew her—five or six years ago. It was Tinker. She was the age she'd been when he'd first met her, maybe a little younger. Still human. She didn't have the pointed elf ears or almond-shaped elf eyes yet.

"Tinker?" he asked. "Is that you?"

"Duh." The girl sounded like Tinker used to. "Who else would it be?"

Roach knew that Tinker and Oilcan didn't have any other family. "What the hell happened to you—this time?"

"What does it look like?" She gestured up and down.

Anyone else, he'd be looking for holograph projectors or something. This was Tinker though: weird shit just always seemed to happen with her.

"Are—are you okay?" Stupid thing to ask but he'd just been blown out of the water in terms of logical, reasonable things to say.

He jerked back a step as a second Tinker whipped around the corner and squeaked with surprise.

Tinker One slapped a hand to her face and sighed.

"What are you doing?" Tinker Two cried.

"It's Roach." Tinker One pointed at him. "Roach!"

"I know it's Roach. Unless he's got an anti-gravity spell in his back pocket or some kind of shrink ray in his truck, we don't have time for chit-chat."

Yup, this was an authentic Tinker conversation. Based on experience, Roach figured this would be a good time to start running.

# BLUE SKY

Two weeks after Pittsburgh became permanently stranded on Elfhome, the war between the elves and the oni reached John Montana's gas station. John had been greasing the CV joint of a Honda he had up on the rack when the bell on the pumps chimed, announcing someone had pulled up for gas. He listened for the sound of his little brother's feet moving across the ceiling above him, but could only hear the rumble of rock music. He ducked out from under the Honda, walked to the old fireman pole that dropped down from their apartment, and yelled, "Hey! We've got a customer down here!"

The bell chimed again and again, like someone was jumping on the air hose, making it trigger. Just kids messing with the air hose, John thought, and headed outside, still carrying the grease gun.

He hadn't been expecting trouble. It had been a summer of hell since war had broken out between the elves and the oni, with humans like John caught in the middle. But with the recent dramatic events, he thought that the elves had won, and the war was over.

Looking at the sea of elves in Fire Clan red massed outside his gas station, John realized that he was mistaken. Most of them were common garden-variety *laedin*-caste soldiers, but sprinkled among them were the holy *sekasha*-caste warriors, with spells tattooed down their arms. The elves had been distracted by the chime, playing with the novelty of the air hose like kids. When they noticed him at the garage's third bay door, though, all play died from their faces, and the eyes they turned toward him were hard and suspicious.

"Oooohhhh, shit." John felt his stomach tighten into a cold knot. The evening news had covered what had happened in Chinatown just days before, showing the blood-washed sidewalks and the headless dead of the oni flushed out of their hiding spaces. The elves weren't taking prisoners.

They saw the grease gun in his hands and they drew their swords.

"It's not a weapon!" John cried out in low Elvish, dropped the tool, and stepped backwards. "It's not a weapon!"

"Get on your knees!" one of the *sekasha* shouted in high tongue.

John raised his hands, holding them out to show they were empty and got down on his knees. *This can't be happening.* "It's not a weapon," he continued in low Elvish because he was more fluent in it. "I fix automobiles. It's only a tool for applying oil to the automobiles."

The *sekasha* nudged the grease gun with his toe and watched it leak. Satisfied it was harmless, he signaled to the *laedin*-caste elves to search the garage. "Is there anyone else in the building?"

"My little brother. He's just a child. Please don't hurt him."

"If you're both human, you have nothing to fear."

That was the problem—they weren't.

One of the other *sekasha* produced a sheet of fine handmade paper, a spell inked onto its surface. John knew what this was. The oni used spells to disguise themselves as humans. The paper held a counterspell to break the illusion. The elves pressed it to John's forearm, spoke the verb component and a static charge ran over him like low voltage electricity. The hairs on his arms and back lifted and stayed standing.

"John, who was playing with the..." His half-brother, Blue Sky, came sliding down the old fireman pole, landing in the center of the chaos. He stood only chest-high among the armored elves, thankfully looking younger than he was. He glanced around at the strangers, unafraid, until he saw John on his knees in front of the sword-wielding *sekasha*. "John!"

"I'm not hurt!" John cried. "Everything is—no, no, no, no!"

Blue had launched himself at the *sekasha*, shouting, "Get away from him!"

John surged up, reaching for Blue, but an elf caught him by the back of the head, jerked him back to his knees, and pressed a sword blade against his windpipe.

"Don't move!" the elf behind him snapped.

The *sekasha* dodged Blue and tried to sweep out the boy's legs. His brother back-flipped over the sweeping foot. Without even turning, or looking, the *sekasha* slashed backwards with his sword.

"No!" John screamed and fought the hold on him. "He's a child! A child!"

The sword hit Blue Sky in the head, smashing him to the ground. John shouted out in wordless dismay.

"Hush!" the *sekasha* commanded, sheathing his sword. "I used the back of my blade. He's only stunned."

The *sekasha* held out his hand for another spell paper and placed it against Blue's arm. He activated it and a distortion of air flowed over Blue and vanished. The boy groaned as the *sekasha* turned him, carefully, gently, to examine him.

His gaze was suspicious when he looked back at John, but he signaled to the others to free him. John didn't bother to stand, just scrambled on his hands and knees to Blue and made sure that his little brother wasn't hurt. As a testament to the *sekasha*'s skill with his sword, there was only a slight bruise on Blue's forehead, and his eyes weren't dilated. The boy glared at the *sekasha*, so John locked him in a hold.

The Fire Clan *sekasha* grunted. It was hard to tell if he was amused by Blue's glare or annoyed by it. "What are you doing with this child? Where are his parents?"

"We share a mother," John said. "She is sick. She went back to Earth. His father is dead."

"Who was his father?" The *sekasha* asked.

The one thing you didn't do was lie to elves. As much as John wanted to say that he didn't know, if would be worse to be caught in a lie. "Lightning Strikes Wind."

Unfortunately, the warrior recognized the name. "He was one of the Wind Clan *sekasha*?"

John nodded.

"He is—fourteen?" The *sekasha* tried to guess Blue's age.

"I'm seventeen," Blue answered for himself. It was a sore spot for him, because he'd been mistaken for as young as ten.

"Shhhh," John hushed him.

"You don't feed him right; he's too small." The *sekasha* stood and walked about the bay, studying the old fire hall that John used as a garage, from the fire pole that Blue had slid down to the gas pumps outside. He stomped on the air hose, making it chime again.

Blue was shaking with fury in his hold. John, however, was terrified that the worst could just be starting.

"Wolf Who Rules," the *sekasha* named the head of the Wind Clan. "Does he know about the child?"

"No." John had lived in terror of this day. He didn't know how the *sekasha* would react to their holy bloodline being mixed with human. Even if they didn't kill Blue Sky outright, there remained the chance they would take him from John.

The *laedin*-caste warrior appeared to sketch a bow to the *sekasha*. "The building seems clear, holy one."

"Clear!" the *sekasha* shouted.

Profound silence filled the garage as the elves went still, waiting. John had heard that the Stone Clan, newly arrived to Pittsburgh, was using spells to find oni hidden within the walls of buildings and secret tunnels underground.

"Clear," someone outside shouted. The elves relaxed.

The *sekasha* signaled for the others to move to the next building down. "If he was not *sekasha*-caste, I would not care what you do with him. My duty here is clear. He is of the holy blood. His clan must be told. This is no way one such as he should live."

Blue jerked in John's hold.

"I'll take the child to Wolf Who Rules." John struggled to keep his brother checked. "I swear I will."

The *sekasha* looked down the street to where his people searched for oni. As John hoped, he deemed it easier to let John handle the problem than to abandon his duties. "I will know if you break your vow. I will not be kind."

"John always keeps his promises," Blue snapped.

The *sekasha* smiled. "He has his father's reactions."

"What do you mean?" John asked.

"We *sekasha*—we protect those we love."

"You shouldn't have promised." Blue swung up onto the counter of the old fireman's kitchen as John opened the fridge and dug through it, looking for a beer. "It means you have to do it."

"I didn't want him taking you with him."

"He couldn't have done that!" Blue cried.

"He's a *sekasha*." John found an Iron City beer, opened it and drank deeply. He was still shaking from the encounter. In the stainless steel surface of the fridge, he could see the line where the sword blade had pressed against his throat. "They're allowed to do anything they want. They're considered too holy to be bound by law made by mortals."

All his life, John had watched the Wind Clan *sekasha* prowl the city like lions among lambs. Even other elves watched them with fear. Thus, he'd been terrified when his mother brought a drunk *sekasha* home. At thirteen, he was just beginning to realize that she wasn't fully sane and that he couldn't trust her to keep them safe. John spent the night sure that the warrior would kill her when he sobered.

After Blue Sky was born, their mother grew more and more erratic. The treaty with the elves banned criminals, the insane, and orphans; the elves didn't want the dregs of humanity littering their world. The same treaty, however, meant Blue Sky couldn't travel to Earth. Caught between the two rules, John struggled to keep his mother's insanity hidden until he was eighteen. At that point, John sent his mother to Earth and stayed behind to become Blue's guardian.

Until today, his greatest fear was that the elves would kill Blue out of hand, deeming his human genetics a stain on their holy bloodline.

Now, he was afraid that even a half-blood like Blue was too holy to be raised by a mere human.

"So, what do we do?" Blue asked.

John sighed and put down his beer. He'd put this off for years. There was one glimmer of hope. "Come on, let's go."

"Where are we going?"

"I'm going to see if Tinker can do anything about this."

Tinker and her cousin, Oilcan, could be called good friends. At one time, when the cousins could still be called children, they played daily with Blue Sky. Eventually they had grown up and grown apart. Still, they had the same interests, traded business, knew the same people, and went to the same parties. Like John and Blue, the cousins were orphans and only had each other. John would like to think it created a bond between them—but he'd learned in the past that when things went horribly wrong in your life, the people you thought you could trust sometimes turned their backs on you.

Luck, courage and a good bit of ingenuity had landed Tinker in a position of power as the wife of the clan head, Wolf Who Rules. If anyone in Pittsburgh could help them, she could.

But the question was—would she?

The elfin enclaves lined where the Rim used to cut through Oakland. Each a block wide and half a mile deep, the high-walled residences acted as both hotels and restaurants. Since everything about the clan head was tabloid fodder, everyone in Pittsburgh knew that Tinker and her new husband were living at the Poppymeadow enclave.

John and Blue Sky passed through three checkpoints on their way to Oakland. Each time they were questioned in depth, searched for weapons, and checked by spell to see if they were oni. It took them two hours to work their way to the enclaves. John parked his pickup, and they walked to the tall garden gate that normally stood open, but they found it shut and locked. He tried knocking.

A slot gate opened and an elf peered out at them.

"Forgiveness," the elf said. "The dining room is not open."

"I need to see—" John realized that saying Tinker's name without her proper title would be considered rude. Elves set store on that kind of thing. He frowned a moment, trying to remember her new title. "*Domi*. I beg you. May I speak with Tinker *domi*?"

"Who asks?"

"John Montana," and then, quickly, he added, "It's clan business! I'm here to see her as the clan's *domi*."

"Wait here."

Blue had been kicking pebbles. When the slot shut, he scoffed. "Clan business."

John smacked him on the back of the head. "Behave."

"I don't like you groveling to them."

"It's not groveling, it's fitting in. At the race track, you fit in by acting tough and saying you've got the best team. Different place—different set of rules."

"At the races, we're all equal. Elves are all about keeping people under your thumb."

"You sound like half the rednecks of Pittsburgh."

"I am one, that's why. My father never cared enough to see how I was doing. I don't see why we have to do this."

"Your father didn't know about you—"

"Because he was a murdering psychopath of a *sekasha* and our mother was a nutcase."

John ignored that little rant. "At the races, you know that if anyone on the pit crew didn't do what I told them, they'd be off the team. Every place has rules—and none of them are better or wrong—they just are."

There was a rattle of metal on wood—the bar on the gate was being drawn. They were being let in.

"Now be polite and don't screw this up—or you might be staying here when I go home."

Blue gave him a terrified look, but was polite as they were frisked for weapons and, once again, checked to see if they were disguised oni.

Tinker was just a year older than Blue—thus John had known her all her life—and yet, when they were escorted into an orchard courtyard, he barely recognized her. Oilcan had told him about the physical transformation. John had guessed that power would probably also change her—but he hadn't been ready for this.

He had known a coltish girl dressed in dirty hand-me-downs. She enjoyed her solitary junkyard existence because it allowed her to play mad inventor. Famous for her virginity, she unknowingly blew away all would-be suitors with aggressive intelligence, fierce independence, and stunning naivety.

This stranger wore a dress of fairy-silk green that shimmered against her dusky skin. With magic, her eyes and ears—along with her underlying DNA—had been changed from human to elfin. She lay on a blanket in the dappled shade, her head resting on the lap of a young male *sekasha*. Four more *sekasha* watched John intently, while pretending polite disinterest. It was difficult to judge the ages of elves, but John thought that all five seemed young, as if Wolf Who Rules tried to match up his wife with guards who were just "teenagers" themselves. Despite the tranquil setting, the three males and two females bristled with weapons. Whereas the Fire Clan *sekasha* had been redheads, the Wind Clan *sekasha* were dark-haired and blue-eyed like Blue Sky. Their spell tattoos and scaled chest armor were in the deep blue which identified their clan.

"*Domi*, wake up," her pillow murmured. "They are here."

She woke slowly, yawning and rubbing at her eyes. Her actions were innocent, but the skin-tight dress made them sensual. It wasn't until she blinked at John and said his name that he realized that her arm was braced and inked with healing spells. He hadn't heard that she'd been hurt, but considering her last fight with the oni had nearly leveled the city, he shouldn't have been surprised.

She really shouldn't arch like that as she stretched awake. He glanced away, feeling like a pervert—she was young as Blue! "Sorry, the healing spells..." She yawned. "They make me really tired. What's wrong, John?"

John had hoped for a private talk with Tinker. Apparently that was impossible. He worked on ignoring the *sekasha*. Blue leaned against him, glaring at the guards.

"The Fire Clan *sekasha* were just at the garage. They've ordered me to talk to Wolf Who Rules. I was hoping you could—be in our corner. We could use some help."

"I don't understand." Tinker ran her hand through her short brown hair, grabbed a handful and tugged at it. The familiar gesture comforted John that something remained of the girl he knew. Under the clean skin and beautiful dress, he could see the core of the compassionate person he knew—now weighted down with responsibilities. She had gone from being accountable only for herself to having all of Pittsburgh on her shoulders and, judging by the weary sigh, fully aware of it. "Why did Wyverns send you here? To talk about what?"

Blue pressed tighter against John's side and shook his head.

John sighed. Having promised the Fire Clan *sekasha*, he had no choice; he had to broach the subject. "Blue's father was Lightning Strikes Wind."

Tinker looked confused but the *sekasha* attending

her went from polite disinterest to staring at Blue Sky with startled amazement.

"Stormsong?" Tinker turned to the blue-haired female who had her hand pressed to her mouth. "Who was Lightning Strikes?"

Stormsong blinked away tears and composed herself. "He was killed by a saurus at the Faire Grounds five years ago. He was barely out of his doubles."

"Oh!" Tinker made a little sound of hurt. "I saw him die. I didn't know he was that young. All elves seemed so old to me then—but I guess that would only make him seventeen or eighteen if he were a human."

Elves became adults at a hundred, when they needed three numbers to write their age. John had always assumed it included a much extended "holding pattern" much like the gray zone for humans between the age of sixteen and eighteen, when they were old enough to drive and to drink but not legally adults. It suddenly occurred to him that he had been wrong all along. Elves didn't mature quickly and yet remain legally a child. They matured slowly through the ages that corresponded with the human range of twelve to eighteen.

John stood there in shock. He had expected that Blue would continue growing up, slower than humans, but reaching maturity within the next ten years or so. But he was wrong—Blue would not be growing up for a long, long time. "Blue Sky's half human," he finally managed to say. "He might grow up faster."

Tinker's guards shook their heads.

"If his father had not been *sekasha*, that might have been so," Stormsong said. "But we breed true; ours is always the dominant gene. He will be his father's child much more than his mother's. He won't be able to deny his nature. I know from experience, it will be better if he accepts it instead of rebels against it."

John struggled with all the implications flooding over him. He remembered how as a teenager, he'd grown like a weed. Blue was seventeen but still looked like a ten-year-old. "What do you mean?"

The *sekasha* exchanged looks, and then the male at Tinker's side said, "Forgiveness, *domi*, but as Lightning Strike's child, he belongs to Wolf Who Rules' household until he's an adult. It is the clan's responsibility that he be raised correctly."

*At least I was right about something—this was exactly the reaction I was afraid of.*

"Pony!" Tinker cried. "We can't just take Blue Sky from his brother!"

"Sooner or later, *domi*, it must be done," Pony said. "He will be a child long after his brother dies of old age."

"I am seventeen!" Blue cried. "I'm almost full grown! I'm top hoverbike driver in Pittsburgh, and I put in forty hours a week helping John run the shop."

"I have to say, I know how he feels," Tinker said. "I'm not happy that the queen has said that I have to wait until I'm a hundred before being considered an adult."

"His case is much different from yours, *domi*," Stormsong said. "There are hormone changes that affect the development of the mind, and those come with aging. A child, no matter how mature, still views the world with a child's mind, and reacts to it in the same way. You matured to an adult before being made an elf, *domi*, but have been given the protection of a child until you have learned all you need to know about our society. Your lack is of knowledge alone. Much as he wants to be viewed as adult—as much as he must hurt seeing others his age treated as almost adults—he will not be one for a long time."

"John, say something!" Blue cried. "They can't do this."

It all matched so well with what John had been ignoring. Blue had dropped out of high school, complaining that everyone suddenly seemed like alien creatures. The problem was that Blue had continued to have elementary school interests, while the others raced to embrace all things adult.

"The problems will truly start when his *sekasha* nature joins the natural aggression of puberty," Stormsong said.

"We like to fight," Pony clarified. "And we're very good at it."

Blue loved the fierce competition of hoverbike racing. While in high school, Blue came home with bloody noses—and reports that his taller opponents were the worse for wear.

"And he needs better nutrition," Pony said. "He's too thin, his hair is brittle and his fingernails are ridged; all signs he's not eating right. If his diet doesn't change, his adult bones won't be as strong as they should be and his eyesight might be impaired. A *sekasha* child needs twice the meat and milk as a normal elfin child."

"I'm fine!" Blue shouted. "I'm not too small! I eat fine! I'm not violent, and I'm sick of everyone acting like I'm not here! You can talk all you want, but I'm not living here!"

And he bolted out of the orchard though a gate that John hadn't noticed.

John shook himself out of his daze. "Blue! Blue!" Oh great, so much for showing his wonderful parenting skills! "Tinker, please, he's only half elf. He's still half human, and that part makes us brothers. Our blood has to count for something. I don't want to give him up."

"*Domi*," Pony countered. "It is not possible to raise a *sekasha* child alone."

Tinker, however, seemed to be listening intently to the whine of a hoverbike's lift engine spinning up. "That's coming from the motor court, isn't it?"

"That little turd is taking my bike!" Stormsong cried in English, and took off running in the direction Blue had gone.

John's heart dropped down through his stomach. Oh, no! He took off after Stormsong, keenly aware that she had a pistol as well as her sword. Beyond the courtyard was a motor court with a dozen garage bays open showing off a fleet of gray Rolls Royce Phantoms. Just outside the last bay, Blue sat astride a top-of-the-line custom delta hoverbike.

"Blue! No!" John shouted.

The boy maxed the lift and popped the bike over the high demesne wall in one easy leap. On the other side, he dropped all power into the spell chain and roared off.

Oh, God, how could Blue be so stupid? John spun to face Stormsong, holding up his hands to warn off her anger. "I'm sorry. I'll get it back, and fix anything he breaks on it." He edged around her, heading back to the orchard. "I promise you, I'll make things right."

He echoed the apology to Tinker as he passed her, heading for the front gate and his pickup.

Tinker trailed after him. "He'll just go home, won't he?"

"I don't know," John admitted. "But I'll get the bike back. Please don't call the police."

"Fuck the bike," Tinker snapped in English and then dropped back to low Elvish. "It isn't safe for him to be alone in the city right now. There are still pockets of oni troops. The humans are upset at the elves. And if the Wyverns think the Wind Clan isn't handling Blue right, they will take him."

John stumbled to a halt. "But you said that Blue was part of Wolf Who Rules' household."

"The Wyverns are head of the *sekasha* caste," Pony explained calmly. "They have ultimate responsibility for Blue Sky."

John was at his pickup before he realized that Stormsong was following him.

"I'm coming with you." She opened the passenger door.

John stared at the tall, leggy female. "Why?"

"Because I can get you around all the roadblocks that the royal troops have set up, and protect Blue Sky from anyone that might try to hurt him."

She had a good point, but it still seemed wrong to get into the truck with one of them. John still wasn't totally convinced Blue was in no danger from the *sekasha* beyond being taken from him.

"I'm not going to hurt your brother." She read the disbelief on his face. "I swear to you, by the blood and the sword that makes me a *sekasha*, I will never harm Lightning Strike's son."

An elf would never lie. To them, there was nothing more important than their personal honor.

"He's really a very good kid." John slammed shut

his door and started the engine. "He's just upset and angry. He's never done anything like this before."

"I know that."

"How can you know that?"

"It's why we're considered holy. Virtue is not a choice for us; it's encoded in our genes, on the same level as the color of our eyes. Under stress, Blue Sky might falter, but he'll never stray far from righteousness."

"Morality is not a genetic trait."

"What the fuck do you know?" Stormsong snapped back in English. "Elves didn't start out immortal. We were made that way while we were slaves to the Skin Clan. For thousands of years, they perfected bioengineering, using what you know as elves as their guinea pigs. Each caste is a different gene pool they set up. They wanted the perfect guard, one that they could trust absolutely, so they made the *sekasha* virtuous without measure."

"I've never heard of the Skin Clan."

"Because we *sekasha* carved their fucking evil hearts out—each and every one of them."

*So much for trusting their guards absolutely.* "And I'm supposed to hand my brother over to you to raise?"

"That's what we want." Stormsong shrugged. "But you've asked *domi* to intercede—so it is possible that is not what will happen."

John studied the female, trying to tell how serious she was. "If she decides in my favor, you'll obey her?"

"Yes." Stormsong saw the surprise on his face, and added, "She's our *domi*," as if it explained everything.

"I don't get it," John said. "You're these holy warriors of God, each of you hundreds of years old, and you roll over and listen to..."

"Do not go there." There was a razor edge in her voice. "I will forgive much, but not a slur on my *domi*."

John swallowed down anything that could be taken as negative toward Tinker. He couldn't believe that they would so blindly obey her judgment. "After the Skin Clan, why would you listen to anyone? You're the ones who are 'virtuous without measure.'"

Stormsong smiled. "Because we like to fight."

"That's bullshit."

"No. It isn't. We prefer to solve all our problems with violence—but might does not make right."

"So you let someone less vicious run the show?"

"More or less."

"I still don't see why you would listen to Tinker," John said as they rolled up to the first checkpoint. "Compared to the rest of you, she's just a kid."

"I thought you knew her—I guess I was wrong."

With Stormsong in the truck, John was waved through without the prolonged questioning, being tested with spells, and being searched for weapons. It also turned out that Tinker had called ahead. Blue hadn't been shot at when he ran the roadblocks. The news chilled John.

*Let him be home, safe and sound.*

There was no sign of him at the gas station. John raced through the building, checking all the rooms. Everything was as they left it.

The bell on the pumps chimed, summoning John back to the garage.

"He's not here." Stormsong said it as a statement, not a question. She bounced on the air hose again. "He doesn't want to bring trouble down on you, so he won't come back."

"Shit, shit, shit." John tried to think of where Blue would run to as Stormsong walked through the garage, giving it the same careful study that the Wyvern had. "Go ahead and say it."

"What?"

"'This is no way one such as he should live,'" John quoted the Wyvern.

"Actually, this is cool." She touched the fireman's pole lightly. "But there's nothing of us, the people who will still be here when you're gone. The oldest living elf is close to twenty thousand years old—that's a long time to be alone."

"I've taught him what I could." John headed for the door, trying to ignore the guilt taking root in the center of his chest.

"I told you—we see things in black and white. What we don't embrace, we reject. We don't do the middle ground. You're teaching him to hate himself."

"I am not!" John cried.

"Yes, you are."

Was he? Everything they claimed to be *sekasha* had fit Blue Sky so well. Could this be true too? Guilt grew through John like a dark weed. He went out to his pickup and got in but still had no idea where to head.

Stormsong got in beside him. "He's that way." She pointed west.

"How do you know?"

"I'm mixed caste—much like Blue Sky. My mother is the queen's Oracle. I spent my childhood trying to deny being a *sekasha*. I went through much of what Blue Sky is going through now. Even hating myself."

John considered west. A large chunk of Pittsburgh still

lay in that direction, from their gas station in McKees Rocks to out past the airport. Even Tinker's scrap yard lay in that direction. "Can you be more specific?"

"He's feeling helpless right now. He's heading someplace where he can feel powerful."

The racetrack.

John could hear the whine of a hoverbike being pushed through the curves and loops of the racecourse even as he parked in the big empty lot. As a team captain, he had a passkey into the track.

"It will be important to get him off the bike." Stormsong followed close on John's heels. "He might hurt himself."

"He won't wreck the bike by mistake," John assured her. "He's one of the best drivers in Pittsburgh. See."

Stormsong gasped as she watched Blue Sky tear through the complex twists and turns. "Oh, shit. I didn't connect the name. You're Team Big Sky!"

"Yeah, we are."

She laughed. "Oh, Lightning Strikes would have been proud. Team Big Sky has always been the clan's favorite team."

John trotted down the concourse steps, trying to escape the remorse he felt, but it followed him. He should have told Lightning Strikes that he had a son. If it had been John, he would have wanted to know before he died. *I couldn't be sure, though, that Blue would be safe!*

Blue flashed past, spotted John, and pulled in a sharp loop, heading back toward him.

"What do you think you're doing?" John walked out to meet him.

Blue slid away, keeping out of grabbing range. "I don't want to be one of them! If I can't be with you, I won't be with anyone!"

"Blue, this isn't solving anything. Cut the engine and talk to me."

Blue frowned and started to reach for the keys and then spotted Stormsong tucked in the shadows of the stands. "What is she doing here?" He gave John a look full of pain. "You're just going to give me to them?"

"I don't want to, Blue, but it might be the best thing for you."

Blue twisted hard on the power and shot away.

"Blue!" John shouted.

Stormsong made a sound of disgust. "You know— you suck at this."

"I'm just doing the best that I can. It's not like I had a great model to work from. When I was little, if I was bad, my mother would say *'I just can't take it anymore, I'm taking you to the EIA. You can go live with another family on another world.'* And after Blue Sky was born, it became *'take care of him, or I'm taking you both to the EIA.'* Okay, so I'm not the best parent in the world. I really don't have a clue what I'm doing, but I have never, never threatened to give him up."

"You should have given him to us! We would have done a better job than this!"

"I wasn't willing to risk his life to find that out!"

"If you're worried about his life, then stop fighting with me and do something about him!" Stormsong pointed upward.

Blue Sky raced up the tallest ramp that climbed skyward. At the summit, he popped up and landed on the very rim and balanced there. As the bike teetered on the narrow ledge, Blue killed the engine.

When Stormsong had said "hurt himself" she wasn't meaning by accident.

"Blue!" John shouted. "Don't be insane! Come down!"

"I won't be one of them!" Blue shouted.

Stormsong kneed John in the balls. Surprise made him scream at the pain. He didn't even see the second hit. He went sprawling in the dirt, with black closing in. Distantly he was aware that Stormsong had drawn her pistol and was taking careful aim down at him.

"John!" Blue shouted and the hoverbike's engine snarled to life.

The gun thundered over and over again, the shots echoing off the stands.

Somehow Stormsong had emptied her gun and missed him. John scrambled away from her, aware that she was drawing her sword. Blue was roaring toward them.

"You promised!" John held out his hand, pleading to her. "You promised not to hurt him."

"And I'm not going to," she said quietly as Blue leapt at her. She spun, caught Blue in midair with her left hand. As his weight spun her around, she sliced the hoverbike's spell chain. The engine's power diverted into the lift and the hoverbike soared upward on maximum lift. She continued the turn, slamming Blue against the ground and pinning him there.

Blue thrashed in her hold. "You murdering whore! I'm going to kill you!"

"Blue, she didn't hurt me." John's head was clearing; his balls ached and he felt like vomiting, but he was basically unhurt. "Shut up before you make her mad."

Blue went still in surprise, and then squeaked, "John!"

Stormsong let Blue go. The boy scrambled to him. John hugged him tightly, relieved that he hadn't self-destructed. The *sekasha* looked on with sadness in her eyes.

"Why the hell did you do that?" John asked her.

"We protect those we love," Stormsong said.

Meaning she knew that Blue would come to John's protection. John supposed this was what she meant by solving all problems with violence.

Blue kept himself between John and Stormsong as they pulled down her floating hoverbike, maneuvered it to his pickup and killed the power. After they strapped the bike down, they drove back to Poppymeadow's enclave in silence. Blue huddled in the middle, a small ball of hurt. Stormsong cleared them through checkpoints. Thunderclouds gathered, threatening a downpour.

The same servant opened the gate at Poppymeadow's, letting them in. "*Domi* is sleeping in the garden room."

"Again?" Blue sneered.

Stormsong cuffed Blue on the back of the head. "Tinker *domi* moved heaven and earth to save all the people of this city. She is a good and just leader. But until her injuries are fully healed, she will have to sleep often."

Apparently they were now considered trustworthy; they weren't searched, nor escorted through the enclave. The garden room turned out to be a small conservatory filled with a riot of blooming flowers. Tinker slept curled on a chaise with only Pony in attendance. Stormsong knelt beside Tinker, and kissed her forehead to wake her. "We're back, *domi*. We found the child and brought him back."

"Hm?" Tinker opened her eyes sleepily. "Oh, good." She yawned and reached out for a hand up. "I was worried. Thank you for keeping him safe."

Tinker hugged the female *sekasha*. The depth of Stormsong's affection showed on her face.

*We protect those we love.*

The *sekasha* weren't standing guard over Wolf Who Rules' wife—they were protecting their beloved *domi*. She had won their hearts. Nor was the fact all that surprising. Blue had always bordered on puppy love for Tinker. She was courageous in a fight, fiercely loyal, never lied, and kept all her promises.

John supposed that if Blue had to go to someone else, at least it was someone he knew he could trust. "Tinker, I've thought about this, and I'm willing to do whatever is best for Blue Sky. I ask that he stays in Pittsburgh, and I want to be able to see him."

"You don't want me?" Blue fought to stay stoic in the face of the news.

"This isn't about wanting you, or not wanting you. This is about what's best for you. They're right. You probably would have been better off with your father from the start."

Tears filled Blue's eyes and he bowed his head to keep them hidden. "Why does everyone want me to be an elf?"

"Because you are an elf." John tapped him on his pointed ear tips to remind him. "And without meaning to, I've poisoned you against yourself. I know this hurts, but I really think you should come and live with Tinker."

Blue bowed his head lower, shaking it. "If I become one of them, you'll be afraid of me. You will hate me."

"Blue, I swear to you, nothing you can do or say or be will ever make me hate you."

"I don't want to lose you!" Blue whispered.

Tinker put her arms around Blue. "When I was thirteen, and Oilcan was seventeen, he moved out. I felt like I was losing him, but I wasn't. We're even closer now, because we don't have to fight over all those little annoying things that come with living with someone. What to watch on the TV and whose turn it is to take out the trash. He's still there for me anytime I need him. You're not losing John. You're gaining a very large family."

Blue scoffed. "Just what I need, a dozen more people to tell me what to do." But he turned and hugged Tinker tightly.

The elves had said that Blue was free to come and go as he pleased. John expected that Blue would put it to the test. He didn't expect that it would be so soon. Close to midnight, Blue sulked into the shop.

"What are you doing here?" John moved his bowl of popcorn so Blue could sprawl on the couch beside him.

Blue made a sound of disgust. "Do you know that Stormsong is the only elf in Tinker's household that speaks English?"

"You're fluent in Elvish."

"It's a pain to have to speak it all the time. And besides, there's so many things in Pittsburgh that Elvish doesn't have a word for!"

"True."

"What are you watching?"

"Something Oilcan loaned me." John suspected the loan had been an excuse to make sure he was coping with Blue being gone. "It's a season of a reality TV show called *American Chopper*. This family custom-builds motorcycles."

Blue usually disliked gearhead shows, so John was surprised when he exclaimed, "Oh, cool," and settled in to watch, apparently contented. Two handfuls of popcorn later, Blue added, "You know, the enclaves don't have TVs, computers, flush toilets, or electricity."

"Barbaric," John said.

"And get this! No showers! You're supposed to bathe in this big heated swimming pool with everyone else. Males and females together!"

John laughed at the disgust in Blue's voice. "Was there anything you liked?"

"I got to watch them sparring with practice swords. It was really cool." Blue gave a sigh of happiness. "You should see how they can move. They say I'll be able to fight like them someday. And they gave me this cool bow. I can't wait until you see it. You should come eat breakfast with me tomorrow. The food is amazing."

The cold knot in John's stomach dissolved. John had thought he was losing his baby brother. He'd been afraid that the damage he'd accidently done to Blue Sky was permanent. The *sekasha* obviously knew how to coax Blue Sky toward accepting his elf heritage.

"Breakfast. Sure, sounds good." John mussed Blue's hair. It actually sounded as if they were gaining an extended family.

# DRABBLE

## *How Oilcan Does Not Meet Team Mischief*

"Oilcan," the tiny voice whispered in ultrasonic range. "Oilcan!"

He opened his eyes and blinked.

And blinked again.

There were four mice on tiny hoverbikes on his nightstand. They had racing goggles perched on their heads and scarves of various colors wrapped about their necks.

"We did it!" One fist-pumped its little paw. "Hooyah!"

This made the other three cheer and clap their hands.

"Hello?" Oilcan whispered. Was he dreaming, or had his life just gotten a whole lot odder?

"We have an important mission for you," the pink-scarfed mouse stated.

"Life and death!" the green and red mice cried.

"Me?" For the life of him, he couldn't imagine what he could do for talking mice.

"You are Orville Wright, correct?" the blue mouse

asked. Unlike the other three, this one sounded male. Like Christopher Robin to be exact.

"And you hate your name, correct?" Pink asked. "Orrrrville."

Which was exactly how the kids in grade school used to mangle his name.

"Yeah," Oilcan said. "But what does that have to do with anything?"

"You have to find us wonderful names!" Red and Green cried. "Orville Oilcan, you're our only hope!"

"They don't want to call me Chuck Norris," Pink explained. "They want to call me Charlene!"

"And they say we can't be Jawbreaker!" Red and Green cried.

Jawbreaker?

"By the time we can do anything about it, it's going to be too late," Pink said. "We'll be stuck with horrible names."

Their point wasn't completely off since he still had people that refused to call him anything but Orville. All the tax forms and legal documents, too, required him to use his "real" name.

"We want cool names!" The Jawbreakers cried.

"And I want to be Chuck Norris. If Alexander can be Alexander Graham Bell then I can be Chuck Norris Dufae."

"Okay." Somehow this had to be Tinker's fault. "What names do you want?"

"Crimson Death!" Red cried.

"Cthulhu!" Green cried.

This wasn't going to be simple as it sounded.

*And no, this doesn't happen either!*

# PEACE OFFERING

Since war broke out between the elves and the oni, the stories in the *Pittsburgh Post-Gazette* had gotten a lot more bizarre. Walking trees loose on the North Side. Dragons terrorizing Oakland. A spaceship crashing into Turtle Creek. Flocks of men with crow-wings mobbing downtown.

The *Post-Gazette* was still printed on paper complete with non-scalable fonts. Olivia had to wear her secret identity glasses to read it. She looked like a prim and proper librarian with them on, auburn hair twisted up into bun, a vintage blue gingham sundress on. No one could tell she was an illegal immigrant, a runaway teenage bride, and a whore. She and Superman. Both from Kansas. Both hiding behind the glasses. Both not what they appeared to be.

"Oh, I love this war." Peanut's moaned comment sounded like pure sex.

Olivia glanced up from yesterday's newspaper. They were waiting for the keva bean handout on Penn Avenue, a block and a half from the head of the line. Earth Inter-dimensional Agency personnel and Pittsburgh Police officers had been on crowd control since dawn. A flood of red uniforms, though, signaled that the Fire Clan had arrived with the keva beans.

Everyone had gone tense as the elves fanned out, even the police and EIA personnel. The royal marines were *laedin*-caste and proved to be a surprisingly friendly and laid back group. Unfortunately Prince True Flame of the Fire Clan had also brought with him nearly fifty of the holy *sekasha*-caste warriors known as Wyverns. Because they were considered morally perfect, the Wyverns were above the law. They could and would kill anyone that pissed them off, even other elves. The humans scanned the incoming troops, looking for the scale-armored vests and protective spells tattooed down the Wyverns' arms in Fire Clan red.

After a few minutes, it became apparent that there were no *sekasha* among the elves. The crowd seemed to take a collective sigh of relief.

Only Peanut had been unfazed by the arrival of the royal troops. She eyed the marines like they were red-frosted cupcakes. Until the war broke out, all the male elves in Pittsburgh that were interested in intercourse with human women had already been claimed. Peanut had been up against the window of a bakery, drooling at what she wanted and couldn't get. Every day now brought more elf troops to the city. "Oh, I need to get some of this yumminess."

"Don't you get enough at night?"

Peanut laughed. "That's all men. It's the difference between a stale Twinkie and one of those hot fresh-made coffee rolls loaded with cinnamon and topped with icing." She mimed licking her fingers. "Elves. They live forever and they see nothing wrong with sex, so they do it all the time, and they do it oh so well."

Olivia wondered if it was also why half of the marines were female. Certainly her life would have been very different if her family hadn't considered sex connected to sin and a woman's weakness.

She'd arrived in Pittsburgh during the last official Shutdown in mid-July. It was the farthest from Kansas she could get; a totally separate universe from the one she'd grown up in. Elfhome was the world of elves that was a mirror to Earth, with Pittsburgh the only human outpost. It seemed like a perfect place to hide from her husband.

She'd gotten a job, found an empty house to squat in, and everything seemed good. Three weeks later, war broke out. Pittsburgh found itself lost deep in virgin forest, three hundred miles from the nearest elf settlement and an unknown number of oni hidden within the city limits. All contact with Earth and its bounty had been cut off.

Olivia had always believed that if she worked hard and used her head, she'd land on her feet. The writing on the wall, though, told her that she wasn't going to survive this war. She might be from Kansas but she wasn't Superman.

Certainly she was no longer surviving with any virtue intact.

Before the war, there was actually a shortage of workers for low-paying jobs. The city had needed people like her to fill the gaps. She'd been working at a bakery on third shift. She was paid under the table, so even though she was only making minimum wage, nothing was being held out for taxes or benefits.

A week after the war started, though, the bakery was out of flour, sugar and salt.

Since then, she'd been walking Liberty Avenue with the other hookers, trying to keep food on her table.

"Oh, I want that one." Peanut pointed at a clump of elves standing nearby. Olivia couldn't tell which one had caught the girl's eye. The elves looked like they could be brothers or cousins. Tall. Lean. Red haired. That they were impossibly handsome went without saying; they were elves. "Save my place?"

"Don't be stupid," Olivia whispered as Peanut shifted into full streetwalker mode, pulling down the neckline of her tight shirt to show off almost all of her breasts. "This is going to be the only handout. The food is here. The line is going to start moving any minute."

"I'll make it quick." Peanut started to broadcast her interest at the elves and they received her message loud and clear. "Isn't he gorgeous?"

"All elves are gorgeous."

"That old one with the messed up face; he isn't."

The newspaper had carried candid photos of the new elf lords as they had arrived in Pittsburgh. Only one hadn't been Paris model beautiful. "Forest Moss on Stone?"

"Yeah, him, he's freaky looking. They say he's a complete nutcase."

Three of the male royal marines drifted over to peer down at Peanut. Olivia was a fairly tall woman but the elves were all a foot or more taller. They were armed with rifles, swords, and daggers. She'd been raised with ten stepbrothers and could probably match any human male in a fistfight, but the combination of the males' height, weapons, and their sexual interest made her shift away from Peanut.

*I'm not really with her. I'm a librarian. Can't you tell by my glasses?*

"I'm Peanut Butter Pie." Peanut slid her mini-skirt up high enough to flash her red panties. The elves' eyes dropped from Peanut's sizable breasts to her lace-covered groin.

"I have heard that peanut butter is very, very good," one of the males said.

Which was, of course, why Peanut picked her name. Something about the spread made it insanely good to elf taste buds. Peanut claimed her real name was boring and stupid. Not that Olivia really had the right to judge; all the girls walking Liberty Avenue knew her only as Red.

Peanut caught the male's hand and tugged him toward the tiny dead-end alley called Mentor Way. "Let me give you a taste."

Olivia shook her head. It was still early morning; only a handful of dumpsters and some fading shadows would screen the two from the curious eyes. Olivia studied the distant head of the line. People seemed to be stirring a block and a half down. Had the handouts started?

"Damn you, Peanut," Olivia whispered. "I'm not going to starve because you were off getting boinked silly."

"Forgiveness." The marine's friends were still hovering over Olivia.

She'd hoped that if she ignored them, they'd go away. She considered pretending not to know Elvish, but then decided she should figure out what they wanted. "Yes?"

"Are you an adult?" the taller of the two asked.

She considered how to answer. She had been told

that no matter what, never lie to an elf. Her forged paperwork showed she was eighteen, but the truth was she was only sixteen. "*Naekanain.*" She fudged by pretending to not understand. "I live alone. I am one person—how do you say—my household."

"You're old enough to marry?" he asked.

"Yes." She didn't even have to lie for that one. It wasn't her fault that she wasn't "legally" married since the state of Kansas didn't allow a man more than one wife, and a judge would have had to approve the marriage of a fifteen-year-old. She hadn't wanted to get married in the first place.

"Like I told you, Dart." He pointed to Olivia. "They're tiny even when they're fully grown."

Olivia was the tallest human woman in sight, but she was still a good eight to ten inches shorter than any of the female elves.

Dart waved off the proof. "The Wind Clan *domi* is smaller than this female."

Olivia didn't know the meaning of the word *domi*. Without a doubt, though, they were debating the maturity of the girl being hailed as Princess Tinker. The girl was two years older than Olivia but six inches shorter. Even with the war on, everyone was talking about Princess Tinker. Pittsburgh's own little Cinderella. Pictures of her were being plastered all over the city. Olivia had been surprised at how small and scruffy-looking the girl was.

"Did you hear, Ash?" Dart said. "One-eyed thinks he can get a human female to be his *domi* since no elf will have him."

Ash laughed. "He is insane. You heard this one." He pointed at Olivia. "Humans live alone."

Dart nodded. "I heard he's been pawing all the

*nivasa* at the Wind Clan enclave. Male and female alike. The holy ones won't put up with that forever. Especially Thorne Scratch on Stone."

Olivia was relieved that the conversation had shifted off her. She wished the marines would move away. Everyone around her was obviously made just as uncomfortable by the elves' presence and their discussion. There was a five-foot gap on either side of her.

There was a call from down the street and the elves echoed it so it traveled up Penn Avenue.

The two elves glanced down Mentor Way. Olivia could hear Peanut's muffled yelping. She'd spent weeks working as a streetwalker and yet the sounds of sex still made Olivia blush.

"Hoi! Blaze!" Ash called. "The handout is starting! Shoot your gun and get it out of that girl."

Olivia lifted her newspaper and pretended to read even as Peanut's moans grew louder. The elves laughed. Out the corner of her eye, she could see that Dart was pretending to be holding a girl by the hips and thrusting into her.

"He's only a hundred this year," Ash said. "I remember that age. Fucking anything on two legs that bent over for me."

"I'd feel like I was taking a child," Dart said. "That girl looked sixty or seventy."

Ash laughed. "You idiot, humans are dead of old age at eighty. She's probably . . . forty." He'd missed Peanut's real age by at least twenty years or more.

"Forty?" Dart frowned at the alley. "Good gods, that's indecent."

"She's probably an adult, although it's hard to tell with them. Blaze! Come on!"

There was a deep male groan and then silence from the alley. A minute later, the two came out from behind a dumpster. The male was trying to refasten his pants as Peanut towed him to Olivia's side.

"I'm on the next street over," Peanut was saying, pointing toward Liberty Avenue. "Come find me anytime."

Peanut pulled him down and kissed him hard before letting him go.

Two consenting adults agreed to have fun together. No money was even exchanged. Still it seemed wrong for intelligent beings to be screwing in an alley like dogs. Olivia sighed, recognizing herself as a prude. A stupid trait to have considering that her survival depended on having sex with men in alleyways. Everything would be easier if she could just be more like Peanut.

Peanut laughed. "Go ahead and say it, Red."

"I wish I could be more like you."

"No, you don't." Peanut caught her hand and squeezed it. "You can forgive me, but you'd hate yourself. You've got grit, Red, and you're proud of it."

Lately it's all she liked about herself.

"Besides, if we get a bunch of elves trolling Liberty Avenue, maybe girls will stop being killed." Peanut winced at the surprise on Olivia's face. "You did hear about Cotton Candy? Right?"

"No." Olivia's stomach did a sickening roll. In the last three weeks, six girls had been killed. The streetwalkers lived too close to the underbelly of the city where the oni were hiding. Only Roxy, buried in rubble when the dragon fight smashed through downtown, could have been any one of the sixty thousand humans in

Pittsburgh. The other five girls were killed because they were whores working the streets, dealing with the city's lowlifes. "What happened?"

Peanut spread her hand. "She was up by the train station. No one saw what happened exactly. She took a shotgun to the face. They think she leaned into a car, trying to come on to the driver. She must have seen something she shouldn't have. He was an oni or something like that."

Olivia's stomach did another sickening roll. Ever since she'd lost her job at the bakery, she felt like she was slowly falling to her death. The irony was that she decided to come to Pittsburgh because it would be so hard to crawl back to her husband if things turned ugly. "I can't keep on doing this. I need to get off the streets."

Olivia had been afraid that they would be refused a share of the handout since their names weren't on any database. She used "Red" to make it harder for police and EIA johns to check if she was a legal resident. Like most of the other streetwalkers, Peanut used her nickname for the same reason; she was the only girl willing to risk being arrested to stand in line with Olivia.

When they reached the front of the line, they discovered that the elves in Wind Clan blue were passing out the dried beans, not the EIA as they expected. The elves weren't concerned with official citizenship—they were only checking for magically disguised oni. They'd already found one warrior hidden with the humans; it had been dragged to the other side of the street and beheaded. The stench of fresh blood in the late summer heat made Olivia's stomach roil.

She fought the urge to throw up as the elves took a piece of paper with a spell written on it, pressed it to her arm, and activated it. After the magic confirmed she was as human as she looked, the elves stamped her hand bright red and weighed out her allotment of keva beans. The handout was ten pounds, measured out on scales. Olivia watched the beans spill into her canvas tote, knowing that the beans were really time. If she rationed herself to a cup a day, she could live off them for weeks. The problem was that when the beans ran out, there might not be food to buy in the stores. She needed money now to buy what little remained before war and winter could disrupt the food supplies from the coast. Much as she wanted to stop streetwalking immediately, she should keep the beans for an emergency supply.

"This is going to be the only handout?" she asked the Wind Clan elf that was doing the weighing.

"Yes. Beloved Tinker *domi* commanded that it be given out to keep people from panicking. The next shipment will be sold to wholesalers for resale."

Which meant first come, first served, at whatever price the stores decided to set.

Wiley's was a little mom-and-pop grocery store two blocks from her house. Olivia shopped there daily to spend all her money from the night before on what little food was left in the store. Wiley's carried local produce and dairy, staying open while the Giant Eagle down the road had closed. Everything that was in cans and plastic containers—basically everything imported from Earth—was sold out.

A small, refrigerated case held fresh milk and eggs.

There was also butter in little canning jars. It reminded her of the ranch. With thirty mouths to feed, every day meant a new jar of butter. She hated the reminder but it couldn't be avoided. Butter wrapped in paper came from Earth. Wiley's got their dairy from a little farm in the South Hills.

She winced at the prices listed on the case. Everything was twice what it cost a month ago. She checked her wallet trying not to think of what she'd done to earn the twenties inside. If she got a bottle of milk, butter and a dozen eggs, she'd have enough money left over for a bag of apples and potatoes and three zucchini. The apples and potatoes would keep if she kept them cold and dark. The zucchini would give her something other than milk and eggs to eat.

There was a small rack of slickies in the back of the store. One of them was labeled "Princess Tinker" and "all new photos!" She picked it up and flipped the images.

According to the slickie Tinker had invented hover-bikes and been one of the star riders on the racing circuit. One picture showed her flying around a corner of a racetrack, head-to-toe mud. Another she was standing after a race, face muddy except where the goggles had protected her eyes. There was nothing elegant or regal about her. How did she get to be a princess?

The next page showed her about to step into a gray Rolls Royce. She wore a rich bronze-colored gown of fairy silk. A fortune of diamonds adored her throat and left wrist. A small wedge of blue marked the center of her forehead like a beauty mark. Her husband and his guards towered over her, emphasizing that she was just a tiny thing.

Clothes, apparently, did make a princess. The caption was in Elvish, and read "Beloved Tinker *Domi*."

Was "*domi*" then the Elvish word for Princess? Certainly "she commanded it to be given out" suggested that Tinker was more than just a concubine. The marines had said that Forest Moss wanted a human *domi* because no elf would have him. Why not? And what exactly would the job entail?

Aiofe was in her backyard, taking down her laundry. Olivia could see the girl from her kitchen sink. She'd avoided the anthropology student since she'd found out that Aiofe was doing an internship with the EIA. The UN police force had ultimate power in Pittsburgh in regards to humans. They were the ones that deported illegal immigrants. People were saying that with Pittsburgh stranded, the original treaty with the elves was void and that the EIA no longer had any authority.

If anyone could tell Olivia about Forest Moss, it was Aiofe. Olivia put on her librarian disguise; auburn hair twisted up into a bun and reading glasses balanced at the end of her nose. She felt vaguely guilty when Aiofe brightened at the sight of her.

"Ah, Red! I've been worried about you." Aiofe had a slight Irish lilt to her voice. "I'd been meaning to come over and knock, but your light is never on."

"I'm still working night shift," Olivia partially lied. Out of habit, she joined in taking down the clothes and folding them neatly. She avoided the indecently frilly panties and bras to focus on the T-shirts sporting logos from the University of Pittsburgh. "You're not working today?"

"They let me go early since I'd been up all night getting things coordinated for today's handouts. At dawn they gave me my share and told me to go home. To be truthful, I think they may be afraid that rioting might start and they didn't want a wee Jackeen to be underfoot."

Unlike the elves, most of the human forces were male. Obviously the men thought that Aiofe couldn't defend herself. Unfortunately they probably were right. While Aiofe was as tall as Olivia, she'd been an only child and gone to a girl's school where the "contact sport" was soccer. Good little girls only learned to defend themselves when they were exposed to little boys who had been taught that roughhousing was how real men acted.

"Everything seemed to be going well when I left," Olivia reassured her. She liked the familiar comfort of doing chores with another woman. She'd been so lonely lately.

"That's Pittsburghers for you." Aiofe shook out a towel and folded it. "They're so used to reality standing on its head that they're taking it all in stride. I figured that was the case and so I came on home. Can I ask you something?"

Olivia's heart leapt as she thought of all the questions she didn't want asked. There were so many truths she'd been keeping from everyone. "What is it?"

"How do you grow beans? I was thinking of planting some of what they gave me."

Olivia laughed in surprise and relief. "You can't grow those keva beans now."

Confusion filled Aiofe's face. "Aren't dried beans just the seeds of bean plants? Why can't I put them in the ground and have them grow?"

"We're less than a month from first frost."

"What's that?" Like Olivia, Aiofe had no family and her college friends had been on summer break when the war broke out. The girl was only marginally better off than Olivia in that she had a respectable job translating for the EIA, but there were times she seemed dangerously young and naïve.

"When it drops below freezing, most plants die. In Pittsburgh, the first frost is usually mid-October. That's why the leaves are starting to turn." Olivia pointed to the sugar maple that straddled their backyards. The edges of its leaves were tinged with yellow. It served as a reminder that despite the late summer heat, autumn was officially only days away.

"I know why the leaves change," Aiofe complained. "I just don't know anything about growing stuff. I was born in the farming country of Whites Cross Ireland but we moved to a flat on College Green in Dublin when I was little. I don't know these things. Food always comes from the market."

"I don't know how long keva beans take to mature but they seem a lot like kidney beans and those take three or four months to grow. If we'd planted some back at the start of the war, then maybe there'd have been time, but now is too late. You'd just waste your beans."

Aiofe blew a raspberry out. "The story of this war." She threw her hands up in the air and waved a pair of red silk panties in the air. "Yay." She dropped her hands. "Boo."

"Huh?"

Aiofe tossed the panties into her plastic laundry basket. "Oh, the elves haven't allowed humans to travel

out of Pittsburgh, so everything we knew about them
was what we could learn from the ones here. They
were all Wind Clan beholden to the viceroy because
he owned this half of the continent. With the oni
invasion, though, he had to call on the other clans
for reinforcements. Yay! We have this massive flood of
new information." Aiofe waved a black pair of panties
this time. "Boo! Pitt is a ghost town because we were
on summer break. None of the anthropology profes-
sors are on Elfhome. It's only me and five other grad
students with internships here in Pittsburgh. We're
taking notes like crazy."

"The Fire Clan and the Stone Clan?"

Aiofe nodded, plucking down her bright underwear
with no outward sign of embarrassment. "The Fire
Clan is here as a neutral party because the queen sent
them. From what we've been able to gather, she's the
only one with a true standing army. It's a force that
she normally uses for peacekeeping missions between
the various clans. They're not getting anything out of
the war except keeping Elfhome safe from invasion.
The Stone Clan sent a small mercenary force and the
Wind Clan is paying for the mercenaries' help. That's
the tale, cut and dried, but every day we're learning
all sorts about the political nastiness between the
clans. Yay!" She threw her hands up in the air. "Only
Pittsburgh is now in the middle of it." She dropped
her hands with a sigh. "Boo."

"Forest Moss. What's the story with him? What
happened to his eye?"

Aiofe scooped up her basket and nodded toward her
backdoor to indicate that Olivia should follow her in.
"What we didn't know until recently was that the oni

and the elves went to war before. Apparently all three planets had ways to go through caves to get from one to the other with Earth smack in the middle. Forest Moss and his household were the first elves to find Onihida. That's the oni's world. The oni took them prisoner and tortured them all, trying to find out how to get to Elfhome. They tied Forest Moss down and burned his eye out. He's the only one that survived."

Olivia shivered as she thought of the sunburst of scars circling Forest Moss' empty socket. How long did they burn him with hot knives before they actually plunged the tip into his eye? Were there more scars hidden by his clothes? "Is he really crazy?"

"He's not the full shilling, as my da would say."

Aiofe hadn't prepared for winter yet, so her kitchen seemed spacious and airy. She'd spent her spare time painting the walls butter yellow and putting up crisp white curtains instead of bracing for freezing winds and a possible loss of electricity or gas. The kitchen table was doubling as a desk, overflowing with actual paper books, newspapers, datapads and slickies. Aiofe obviously trusted the EIA and the elves to keep Pittsburgh functioning until the peaceful end of the war. Olivia glanced about, feeling guilty that she hadn't taken the girl under her wing and shown her how to prepare her place. Olivia wasn't even sure that Aiofe would take her suggestions; she was nearly five years younger than the grad student. She probably would think Olivia's mistrust of the government was hopelessly militant redneck.

"So, have you gotten a chance to meet Princess Tinker?" Olivia asked instead.

"Tinker *domi*!" Aiofe corrected with a laugh. "The

Wind Clan elves get really cheesed off if you call her Princess."

"Why?"

"She's their *domi*! They've been in Pittsburgh long enough to know what 'princess' means. The two words are worlds apart."

"Really?" Olivia's heart sunk.

"In English, 'princess' means basically a pretty girl that has no power in government whose only value is to produce children for the bloodline. We don't have anything close to the absolute authority of a *domi*. She could order her guards to kill any elf in Pittsburgh and no one would question it. It's her right. To call her Princess Tinker is a sign of disrespect."

"Oh."

"One of the boyos gave me this." Aiofe opened a small lunch cooler, took out a plastic bag and held it open. There was a dead rabbit inside. Someone with a great deal of skill had killed it with a rifle bullet to the head. It'd been field dressed but not skinned. "I think he's sweet on me, but I don't know what to do with it."

Olivia's stomach rolled at the smell of blood, recalling the dead oni on Penn Avenue. She swallowed hard, reminding herself that it been weeks since she had protein beyond eggs and milk. "I'll help you cook it for dinner."

Aiofe grinned. "I'll wet the tea."

According to the newspaper, the newly arrived Stone Clan elves were staying at Ginger Wine's enclave. The elves' businesses gathered just over the edge of where Pittsburgh abruptly ended, as if a giant blade had sliced through the city. Beyond the thin line of cement dust and sheared-off guardrails was virgin forest as far as the eye could see.

Olivia took a bus out to the University of Pittsburgh and walked the last few blocks to the Rim. The enclaves faced humanity with tall, blank stone walls. Each compound was a block wide and hundreds of feet deep with two- and three-story buildings forming a sheltered orchard courtyard. While the enclaves acted like hotels with restaurants, she'd never actually been inside one of them. They were supposedly very expensive.

She walked down the street, reading the names printed in Elvish over the front doors. Ginger Wine's door was shut and locked. When she tentatively knocked, a spyhole slid opened up and blue eyes gazed down at her.

"We're not taking new guests." The male obviously learned English from a native Pittsburgher.

Olivia steeled herself against the fear that was jangling through her. "I would like to talk to Forest Moss."

The eyes went wide with surprise. "That nutcase? No, no, you should avoid him. We all do."

At least it made her fear turn to annoyance. "You shun him?"

"I do not know this word: shun."

"You don't talk to him? You don't look at him? You pretend he doesn't exist?"

He tilted his head. "He's *domana* and Stone Clan and insane. It is best that we avoid him. Even the Stone Clan people avoid him."

"So absolutely no one talks to him?" She knew it was silly to be angry on his part but she'd lived through being shunned. It'd been an agonizingly lonely three months before she caved to the shunning. She had thought she could easily deal with not having to talk to the silly idiots who filled up her life, but she didn't realize that her own family would join in to break her will. At the time, she thought it was because they believed her marrying Troy would be the best thing for her. Only after she caved in and agreed—so she couldn't call her wedding night a rape—she realized that they were only concerned that they wouldn't end up sharing her punishment.

"He is dangerous," the elf said, as if that forgave everything.

And she'd been "stubborn," "stupid," "sinful," and a host of other things muttered behind her back but never to her face, and always just loud enough for her to hear.

"I need to talk to him."

"He's not here. He's off with my lord, Windwolf. They're out hunting oni and won't be back until late. You should go home; the streets aren't safe after dark anymore."

If she left Oakland, it would only be to go walk Liberty Avenue to turn tricks. "Can I wait inside for his return?"

"We're considered Stone Clan territory for the duration." He did not sound happy about the fact. "I'm not allowed to let strangers in without one of them giving me permission. Go home."

He closed the spyhole, effectively ending the conversation.

Hours later the elves returned to the enclaves in force. Hundreds of them poured into the area from somewhere to the east. Most of them wore the Fire

Clan's red, and then there was a small clump of Wind Clan blue. A Stone Clan female was marked by a handful of elves in black. Olivia missed Forest Moss until the last moment. He walked apart from the others, completely alone despite the throng. Five Wyverns moved with him, seemingly guarding over him while not actually interacting with him. They kept out of reach, always with their back to him.

She hurried through the crowd of elf warriors, trying to reach his side. But he'd entered the enclave and the door was firmly locked.

Her place had been too silent in the mornings. It reminded her too much of when she was being shunned. She'd splurged on an old digital clock radio within a week of arriving in Pittsburgh. After two days of failing to talk with Forest Moss, she woke to the news that Ginger Wine's had been attacked during the night. Dozens of elves had been killed in the attack; their names, however, weren't being given out. With her heart looping through her chest like it was on a rollercoaster, she took a bus out to Oakland.

Ginger Wine's was a smoking rubble. Oni bodies were stacked on the street like cordwood. There was no sign of the dead elves. In the summer heat, the slaughterhouse stench was nearly unbearable.

A work crew from the EIA were loading the oni bodies onto trucks.

"Do you know which elves were killed?" Olivia asked one of the men. "What happened with their dead?"

The man pointed toward the Faire Grounds where black smoke was billowing up. "Elves cremate their dead; say it frees the souls to pass on. Ginger Wine only lost two of her people. The rest are all Stone Clan." He obviously thought she was friends with the Wind Clan elves that ran Ginger Wine's establishment.

"Was Forest Moss killed?"

"The *domana*? No. He wasn't here. He had been out with Windwolf. He totally lost it, though, when they got back. He wandered off screaming." The man gave a vague wave toward downtown. "Completely out of his head."

Forest Moss was on the top floor of Kaufmann's. She'd found him only because of the concentration of Pittsburgh Police, EIA and Wind Clan elves gathered around the department store. Olivia apparently missed Tinker *domi* by minutes. In her wake, the elves and humans were trying to come to an agreement about what should be done with Forest Moss. None of them were happy about the elf lord occupying Kaufmann's but no one wanted to risk trying to get him to leave.

She cautiously worked her way through the store, dodging the Wyverns who were searching the aisles. Judging by their speed, they were using it as an excuse to keep a distance between them and their charge.

Forest Moss was in the back corner of the children's department. He'd collected all the mannequins around a child's tea table with a toy china tea set. The dolls gathered around him, smiling brightly, holding out stiff white hands to welcome him. Somehow Forest Moss had reduced a half-dozen various mannequins to plaster dust. It hazed the air and covered everything with fine white powder.

Why was he here of all places? Why was he destroying the dolls even as he treated them to tea? There was so much she didn't know about him, not even his age. From the photos she'd seen of him, she knew that his hair was always pure white, even without the fine dust. It poured down over his shoulders and was gathered in a loose ponytail just about his hips. She couldn't tell his age from his profile, it was so marred by the scars encircling his empty eye socket. His eyelid had been sewn shut, the scars vivid white as his hair against his dusky skin.

"It's all your fault," Forest Moss wailed as he clutched an eight-year-old girl mannequin to him. "You were supposed to protect them. They whispered little lies to you and you believed them all. Our beautiful lovelies, all dead, because you failed them."

She took a deep breath as she felt a wave of sympathy toward him. She still felt responsible for Tyler's death even though she had been helpless to prevent it. She'd been overruled at every turn. His "real mother" let him play with the rough older boys. As "men" the teenagers didn't need to listen to her arguments that Tyler was too young to play in the hayloft. She couldn't talk her husband and sister-wives into taking the four-year-old to the hospital after he'd fallen. In everyone's eyes, she was old enough to fuck, but too much a child to make any demands on how her "children" were raised.

How much more guilt was Forest Moss feeling because he hadn't been helpless?

Maybe Forest Moss needed her as much as she needed him. Certainly she would have given anything for someone to reassure her that she had done everything she could to save Tyler and that his blood was on other people's hands.

Taking another deep breath to steel herself, she closed the distance between her and the tea table.

Forest Moss whipped about to see her, hand pressed to his mouth, fingers cocked oddly. He paused, his brow knitting together. Unlike his hair, his eyebrow and eyelashes were dark brown. Judging by what was left of his face, at one time, he'd been very handsome. And he seemed much younger than she expected. If he were human, she would have guessed him to be in his mid-twenties.

She'd spent days trying to arrange for this conversation but she hadn't considered exactly what she would say. At least, not in Low Elvish. When she ran through this moment in her head, everything was in English with a lot of slang and curse words thrown in. "I heard that you—you—you want a someone to be your *domi*? A human *domi*. I'm—I'm—" Willing sounded too much like a marriage vow. "I want—I need you."

He stared at her for a full minute as if he couldn't see through the dust that drifted through the air. His good eye was dark brown, the eyelids almond-shaped in a way that looked almost Asian. "What magic is this that all that I want suddenly lives and breathes? Do I dream? Ah, if I do, I wish to die before I wake."

He still had his right hand up the shirt of the girl mannequin, the buttons straining.

She reached out and cautiously unbuttoned the brightly flowered blouse, exposing the large brown hand against the white plastic skin. The dark eyebrows rose in surprise.

She wet her mouth against her nervousness. He was just another male, like any other john. Normally she wouldn't allow a free touch but there were language barriers to cross. Elves normally didn't have to pay for sex with humans; there were too many elf-obsessed women willing to give it away. And Olivia wanted something more than just money.

His good eye went wide as she guided his right hand to her hip. She had on low-rider jeans and a midriff; his hand rested on bare skin. He breathed out shakily, his gaze riveted on where they touched skin to skin. His large hand made her look like she wasn't much bigger than the mannequin he'd been molesting. He swallowed and put his other hand on her and watched vividly as he ran both hands over her stomach. The half-naked girl mannequin teetered from its sudden abandonment and then toppled over.

With a low moan, Forest Moss dropped to his knees in front of Olivia. He pulled Olivia close so he could mouth her belly as he pushed up her shirt.

Weeks of selling her body and Olivia still wasn't used to that moment of when the protection of clothes was pushed aside, leaving her exposed and vulnerable. She swallowed hard on the fear that surged through her, as if it was a wild beast that wanted to scramble up her throat and come howling out her mouth. She locked down on whimpers.

She had learned the hard way that it was dangerous to close her eyes. She forced herself to watch him carefully, watch him for the start of an attack. He cupped her bared breasts reverently, tears streaming from his one good eye.

After several heart-stopping minutes of worship, he murmured, "Water to a male dying of thirst. Nay, heavenly cream. Once I start to lap it up, will I be able to stop? Do I dare? If the thirst is not quenched, then does the tentative sip make the need all the more torturous?"

It seemed the best time to open up negotiations. Normally she wouldn't let a guy get this far without talking price, but this time, she was asking more than twenty bucks. "I'm not just for the taking. I need something in return. Make me your *domi*."

He leaned forward, his lips nearly touching her. It made her wince despite the fact she should be well used to this by now. "But I have suffered this thirst so long, I think if I do not drink deep and long, I will die."

"Make me your *domi*." She hated every word coming out her mouth. It was ironic she'd fled to Pittsburgh to get out of the mockery of marriage that she'd been forced into. "Promise me that you'll make me your *domi* and you can do what you want."

He looked up at her, his one eye searching her face. "This sweetness could be for one as wretched as me?"

"Only if you take me as your *domi*."

Fear filled his face. "I—I am not prepared for *pavuanai wuan huliroulae*. I have nothing to give you."

She didn't know the phrase but she was afraid it meant he was broke. "You don't have money?"

"Money?" With shaking hands, he pulled out a small beautiful silk pouch. Undoing the drawstrings, he poured several large coins into his hand. Elf bullion. Her heart leapt at the coins. According to yesterday's newspaper, they were trading for five thousand American dollars per coin. She expected him to give her just one but he spilled all the glittering gold into her palm.

She gasped, instantly torn. This was much more than she expected but with it, she wouldn't have to fear winter. As long as there was food to be bought, she could afford it. Did she take it? Did she give some back? Did he even know the value of what he just handed to her? Was it spare pocket change to him? Or was it all that he had?

When she considered the condition of Ginger Wine's, it might be all that he had.

"Do you accept?" he asked breathlessly.

Did she? Her breath caught as she realized that she was on that verge of no return. Like when she went to her mother and told her that she'd marry Troy. When she walked down the aisle of the Zion church to where Troy waited with his other wives. When she looked at the pregnancy test that she'd bought at the drug store with hoarded cash and realized that she needed to flee Kansas or doom her baby to a life at the ranch.

And that had worked out so well.

Was she about to make another horrible mistake?

But really, could she truly continue to run all the risks of being a streetwalker through a Pittsburgh winter as she got bigger and bigger with child?

Work or starve her unborn child along with her or this.

She closed her fingers on the gold coins. "Yes. I accept."

He crushed her to him, and with desperate whimpers, seemed to feed on her. He lifted her off her feet, laid her back on the low table with the tiny china teacups and little platters of cookies. The child mannequins all grinned silently as they watched him move over her, weeping and whimpering.

When he pulled away from her, she thought it was to pull down his pants. Instead he fumbled out a leather bag and produced a thick pencil.

"No, no, no. Must be careful. Must be sure or they'll use their swords to put things right."

He held her still with one hand pinning her hard by the shoulder. With the fat greasy point of the pencil, he drew something on her stomach.

"What are you doing?"

"Shhhh." He pressed the pencil to her lips, his one eye bright. He drew another line and said something in Elvish that she didn't recognize. The drawn lines gleamed momentarily and fluttered. He whispered another word and the light faded. He pressed his free hand to her belly, smearing the lines. "Perfect! Perfect!" He glanced around at the watching mannequins. "But not here. They'll be back and they will not want to stand around and wait for me to have my fill."

He meant the Wyverns. No, she'd rather not have them watching. She wasn't that brave.

She guessed the location of the freight elevator and that the newly arrived elves wouldn't know enough about department stores to cover it. She took Forest Moss down to the delivery docks and out onto the street.

Where could she take him? Ginger Wine's was nothing but rubble. She wanted bank rate of exchange on the bullion, not whatever a hotel would give her because she didn't have enough American dollars to pay for a room. Which left her house.

Feeling like she had just stolen an elf lord, she guided him to her home.

❖     ❖     ❖

The only highlight of the worst summer of her life been finding the Victorian house on Mount Washington to squat in. Yes, it was too big for her but the kitchen had a wood-burning stove, a sitting area big enough for a bed, tall windows that faced south, and high ceilings that made the room seem even bigger. She would be safe and warm all winter in the one room. If the war hadn't broken out, it would have been perfect.

She hadn't realized that she'd be bringing Forest Moss home with her. She nervously scanned the room after she'd pulled him inside and bolted the door behind him. Luckily she'd washed her breakfast dishes and left them drying in the rack. Her bed was a twin-sized futon on the floor. She'd washed her sheets and air-dried them just the day before. The half-finished quilt she was sewing by hand out of fabric remnants even managed to make the futon look like a real bed instead of sheets spread out on the floor. She had black-eyed Susans in a Coke bottle by her bed and herbs growing on the windowsills. Her place wasn't pretty as Aiofe's place but it felt cozy to her.

She had had sex with all of her other johns in their cars and back alleys. She'd never brought any of them home. What did he think? She nervously put her keys on the counter and turned to Forest Moss.

He was still staring at her as if she was the only thing in the universe.

Her purse was heavy with the elf bullion. It thumped when she put it down on her battered table. He'd given her more than enough money to survive.

It was time for her to keep her part of the deal.

She turned off the light and stepped into his arms.

❖        ❖        ❖

Peanut was right.

Elves were damn good at sex.

After six months of marriage and weeks of turning tricks, Olivia thought she knew everything about sex. The orgasm took her by surprise. She felt the familiar flutter of pleasure that she normally felt but then it grew and grew and then went stomach-flexing, bolt-of-lightning good with all sorts of little aftershocks and jolts.

Not to say that she didn't know what she'd just experienced. She'd watched every man that had ever been with her ride through the whole show. To finally know how good they'd felt every time made her feel used and cast aside like a condom. The injustice of it filled her with rage at the entire gender and she smacked Forest Moss.

"Is something wrong?"

"Yes." She didn't want to explain how screwed she'd been to have been born a human female. "If my johns are feeling that great, I don't charge enough."

"I don't understand." The shadows hid his ruined eye. In the dim light, he was as beautiful as any other elf. There was a glimmer on his cheek. When she touched his face, she realized he was crying.

"You did nothing wrong," she reassured him.

He whimpered like a puppy as he slept, curled around her. In the morning, he wanted to stay naked, stay in bed, stay skin to skin. Since the baby books said that getting up slowly helped prevent morning sickness, she lay with him, embarrassed by the sunlight pouring through the windows, leaving her no place to hide.

At least Forest Moss was gentle with her. Troy had been all impatience and hardness, leaving bruises as he took his pleasure. Everyone from her older sister-wives to her mother all told her to be silent and endure it. A man's right to his wife. The men in the alleys and the cars had been no different.

Forest Moss seemed content to just lie in the warm sunlight, wrapped around her, so close they seemed to share the same breath. She had never experienced so much intimacy. Troy had six wives before her. He came to her Friday nights, took his pleasure and hogged most of the bed, stealing the blankets. It was so much rutting in the dark.

Forest Moss seemed to want to see every little part of her. He held her hands, one at a time, up to the light.

"So small," he murmured. "Like Wolf's child bride."

She blushed. "I'm much taller than her."

He considered her, smiling gently. "Yes, you are right. You are older?"

Her blush deepened. "I need to eat."

Another key thing that the baby books said would prevent morning sickness was to eat many small protein-rich meals.

With Forest Moss hovering nearly close enough to touch, she scrambled up her last eggs. He frowned at the nearly empty fridge and then opened the cabinets that she had nothing to put into. When she tried to share the food with him, he refused it.

"I've been living fat on the Wind Clan coin." He pushed the plate toward her. "A week's worth of missed meals would not hurt me."

Troy was always served first and given the best

Wen Spencer

cuts of meat. It made her eyes burn with long-held, previously unshed tears.

"The coins you gave me," she approached the subject tentatively. Money was normally the domain of men. "Is it all you have?"

Worry filled his one good eye. "For now. I have land that the Wind Clan paid as restitution for my fighting. I will receive funds from our clan when we establish our household here."

Our clan. Our household.

"Where is this land?"

"I—I'm not sure. I did not have the means to clear it and build anything, so I did not bother to view it."

She had read in the paper something about the division of land. She pulled out all the newspapers since the Stone Clan's arrival a few weeks back. She found the story that ran last week. The accompanying map showed how the land was divided up. The size of the parcel took her breath away. It could have swallowed up the Zion ranch in Kansas a hundred times over. It was, however, all virgin forest. It afforded no shelter from winter and certainly nothing to eat except squirrels and deer.

They would need to stay here at her place until spring. At that point, if the war was over, they could hire someone to cut and lumber. There were most likely abandoned houses near that area they could squat in until they had money enough to build something like a small farm.

She realized then that for the first time in weeks, she felt like she was going to live to see spring.

He pulled her close and after a moment she relaxed against him and let herself feel the comfort of no longer being alone.

"I have prayed so long for you," he whispered.

She laughed into his shoulder. "Someone like me. Any girl would have done."

"You alone had the courage to face my demons and quiet them."

She wished she could believe him. She knew that any number of women in Pittsburgh would have eventually set their sights on him. She was fortunate that she was the first to hear of his plan to take a human partner.

When she sighed, her breath caused fine white dust to drift from his hair.

"You need to wash your hair," she said.

"A bath! Yes! Certainly!" But when she showed him the shower, he frowned at it for several minutes. "This is not a bath."

"You just stand here, water comes out from this part, you adjust the heat of the water with these knobs . . ." She fell silent as he continued to look confused and unsure. Did the elves not have running water?

As she fussed with the shower, she glanced at the mirror and froze in surprise. Almost hidden under her bangs was a small black diamond. It looked like the blue triangle Tinker had in the one slickie photo of her entering the Rolls Royce. Olivia rubbed at black spot and then used soap and water. It didn't come off; it seemed tattooed into place.

"Did you do this to me?" she asked Forest Moss.

He cringed back at her tone. "It is the custom. The *dau* tells others that you've accepted my offer and that you're my *domi*."

"So, it won't come off?"

Alarm filled his face and he looked ready to cry. "No."

"I don't want it off." She stopped trying to wash

it away as it was obviously distressing him. In some ways he was like a child. It was good that she loved children. Maybe she was exactly the type of human woman he did need. She cautiously asked, "When did you do it?"

"Last night. It is a simple spell."

For part of the shower, he remained childlike, letting her wash his long silky white hair. And then he turned, and suddenly was all male, and proved yet again that Peanut was right about elves. It was embarrassing how the much the tiles in the bathroom amplified her cries right up to the point she couldn't think of anything but the pleasure jolting through her. Afterward there was something pure in relaxing in his arms as the warm water beaded down over them.

She woke late that night with someone tapping her palm. A strange male elf crouched beside the futon, a spell light cupped in his hand. He put his finger to his lips, indicating that she should stay silent. She jerked back in fear. Forest Moss was wrapped tight around her, still asleep. The stranger frowned at her and shook his head silently to rebuke her.

As she grabbed at the sheets, she realized that he wore the red scale vest armor and arm tattoos of a Wyvern. Nor was he alone. There were four more Wyverns in her kitchen, all watching silently.

Her breath caught in her chest and she leaned back against Forest Moss.

The crouching Wyvern looked at her sternly and crooked his finger in a universal "Come here."

Piss the Wyvern off or leave the protection that

Forest Moss may or may not provide her? Why were they here? Why did they want her to leave Forest Moss? The Wyverns could and would kill anyone they wanted. So far their kind had killed one of the elf lords, a Pittsburgh policeman and dozens of people that may have been oni or humans.

And the Wyverns were now frowning at her and repeating the "come here" motion.

If she hid behind Forest Moss, and he came to her defense, would the Wyverns kill him out of hand? They had killed his clansman, Earth Son. If she wanted his help, then she had to protect him.

She nodded reluctantly and started to extract herself without waking Forest Moss. He lay with his ruined eye pressed against the pillow, leaving only his beauty heartrendingly vulnerable.

As she slid forward, the Wyvern didn't reach for her but started to step back, giving her room. His eyes went suddenly wide and he threw up his hands to protect his head and a moment later, the room exploded.

Forest Moss was awake, howling wordlessly. He gestured and another explosion blew out the far wall. The Wyverns went flying backwards, vanishing into the rubble.

"What are you doing?" Olivia cried. She wasn't sure how he was doing it but he was going to bring the house down on top of them. "Stop it!"

"No!" Forest Moss shouted. "I won't let them take you away. I won't! I won't!"

There was a loud groaning complaint as the room lurched.

She caught Forest Moss by his hair and dragged

him backward through the dining room and out the
front door and onto the sidewalk. He howled the
entire way like a dog caught in a bear trap, a sound
of pure bestial pain.

"Stop. Stop!" She put hands on either side of his
head and tilted his head until he was staring into her
eyes. "Look at me! No one will take me away. I won't
let them. I choose where I go and I'm not leaving
you. Now calm down."

Brave words. Truth was, she was scared shitless. Had
he killed the Wyverns? Obviously they had known he
could blast the shit out of everything and had been
trying to defuse him. Why hadn't they brought drugs
and a straightjacket? Because those things would have
made him even harder to handle?

She wrapped her arms around Forest Moss and
crooned to him, trying to get him to calm down. She
wanted to ask him a million questions but she was afraid
he'd lose it completely if she pushed for answers now.

The Wyvern that woke her appeared at the corner
of her leaning house, seemingly unharmed. She wasn't
sure how he survived the blast.

She tightened her hold on Forest Moss. "What do
you want? You don't break into someone's house in
the middle of the night and drag them out of bed."

"Who are you?" The Wyvern watched Forest Moss
carefully.

"I'm his *domi*!" She pushed back her bangs to
show him the *dau* on her forehead. "And you're not
separating us. Just deal with us both."

The warrior stared silently at her as if weighing
his options and then he nodded. "Very well, but you
must come with us."

"Without clothes?" Olivia realized that she'd left her purse with the bullion lying by their bed. In her panic, she'd saved Forest Moss but not the money that would keep them both alive through the winter. "All our belongings are still in the house. We can't just leave them."

The Wyvern shook his head. "It is not safe for you to return to the house."

Olivia growled out the one Elvish curse she knew, making his eyes go wide. "You destroyed the only place we had to live and now you're going to steal everything we own? Leave us naked?"

He looked anyplace but her face as he considered her charge. In the end he slowly nodded. "We will do what we can to salvage your belongings. Keep him here. Keep him calm."

They saved her purse with the bullion, the food from the fridge, Forest Moss' clothes and her blue gingham sundress before the house groaned and collapsed in a sudden thunder of broken timbers.

The elf encampment lay beyond the enclaves, just across a stone bridge that was still under construction. A large clearing had been cut in the towering ironwoods, leaving only five massive oak trees standing. Elfshines drifted under the dark canopy, glowing bright enough for them to walk easily through the camp.

Prince True Flame of the Fire Clan was in one of the white silk tents that gleamed like a lantern from the outside. He was leaning over a table, studying maps, as the Wyverns escorted Olivia and Forest Moss in. He looked up and relief went across his face when he saw Forest Moss.

"Good, you found him," he said to the Wyverns and turned his attention to the maps again.

"No, they terrorized him," Olivia snapped.

"They were in a bed together," the Wyvern reported. "They'd had intercourse..."

"I'm his *domi*." Olivia tried not to shout the words.

"And she is not *naekuna*," the Wyvern finished.

Forest Moss started to wail.

"Tell me what is wrong," Olivia said. "Can't you see that you're torturing him? You've shut him up in silence with his grief and his guilt until you've driven him mad! He needs me."

"It is against our laws for *domana* to have half-caste children. It's for the protection of their entire clan. If you were fertile when he coupled with you..."

"I was already pregnant when we met."

"She is perfect!" Forest Moss wailed. "Beautiful and fearless. I can drink deep and fill my thirst. Perfect! Perfect!"

Prince True Flame sighed and looked to the Wyvern beside him. "I do not want to start the clan war again over the idiocy that the Stone Clan is committing here. You are our moral compass, Red Knife. What say you on this?"

"She quiets his madness," Red Knife murmured. "If she was with child prior to their union, then there has been no harm done. I say allow them to continue until she bears the child."

"That will buy only a little time."

"He has offered. She has accepted. There is no risk she will bear a half-caste child. Those are our laws. We cannot deny him what we've allowed Wolf Who Rules."

"She is human," Prince True Flame pointed out.

"We determined that humans were intelligent creatures with souls when we first found our way to Earth. For that reason alone, we have trusted them to enter into a treaty with our people. We cannot recognize that they are as we are—with souls and minds—and not treat them as equal—for to do so would judge them on their bodies alone. If we deny them equality, then we can't claim that our souls and minds are proof that we are shaped by God. To diminish them is to diminish ourselves; one follows the other as day follows night."

Prince True Flame nodded and sighed. "What is your name?"

"Olivia."

"Olive Branch above Stone," he translated her name to Elvish. "We need him sane and fighting. See that it happens."

She grabbed Forest Moss by the wrist and dragged him from the annoying elf before she said something angry and got them both into trouble. The set of five Wyverns followed cautiously at the distance. Knowing that they were safe for now, she ignored them. She didn't stop walking until they were back to Pittsburgh proper, comforting in its familiar human city streets.

"What are we going to do?" Forest Moss asked when she paused in the shadow of the Heinz Chapel.

No one had ever asked her that before. She'd always been told the shape of her life, ignoring what she wanted. She hadn't come to Pittsburgh to escape sex, marriage, and having a baby. She hadn't been running away from anything. She'd been running to the right to choose such things for herself.

Maybe some would scorn the shape of the life she was building, pointing out that Forest Moss was a tormented, scarred, one-eyed insane elf. But he gazed at her as if she was clever and good and wise and strong. He stood waiting patiently to hear what she thought. She leaned her forehead against his chest and marveled at how comforting it felt to be with someone who believed that his life was better if she had her own thoughts and desires.

"I need to find someplace to live," she said.

"Together?" he said with such fear that she realized that, unlike "wife," the term "*domi*" didn't come with the expectation that she had to live with her mate.

"Yes," she hugged him tightly, wanting to heal him. Wanting to be as strong and powerful as he believed her to be. As she always could have been, if just given the chance to be herself. "Together."

# PRICE OF PEACE

Less than a mile from the Rim, where the enclaves of Wind Clan elves were backed by virgin forest, one lone façade blazed in defiance. The red neon sign proclaimed fearlessly ESSIE'S ORIGINAL HOT DOG SHOP. A small blue sign stated firmly, HOME OF THE 'O' FRIES, WINGS AND BARBECUE, SUBS AND BEER. A rich perfume of grilled hot dogs, fried potatoes, melted cheese, and cold beer flooded out of the open door. How it managed to serve this bounty of food while stranded on an alien planet, under siege during a war between two inhuman races, Olivia had no idea.

It was, however, a welcome human refuge. She paused just inside the door, blinking at the sudden unforgiving light of ancient halogen overheads. The busy cooks ignored her entrance, lifting baskets out of the cooking oil, turning hot dogs, and delivering up paper-lined baskets while chanting out filled orders.

Olivia pushed her way into the crowd waiting for their food, beers in hand. The day had been a blur and her stomach was clenching up into a tight knot that lately was followed with vomiting. She was vaguely aware of the wave of silence and widening eyes.

"Next!" the girl at the counter cried, slapping the last slip onto the counter by the cooks.

Olivia was fairly sure that she was jumping the line, but the line seemed to be in the process of trying to escape what was trailing behind Olivia. Nothing she could do about the situation, so she was determinedly ignoring it for now. She scanned the menu. No wonder the restaurant still had food after a month of being stranded on another planet. It featured jumpfish, saurus, stag, and something called indi. The fish was breaded and fried, the indi was served as kabobs, but the other meats were made into sausage as substitute hot dogs. Her stomach nearly revolted at the idea of mystery meat on a bun.

"Can I have a large fries with cheese?" The menu board proclaimed them as homegrown potatoes, which meant they most likely came from one of the South Hills farms. She might have problems with the grease if she just ate fries. She scanned for a safer option and spotted a turkey sandwich listed at the bottom. Until a few weeks ago, there were large flocks of the wild Earth birds everywhere, flourishing in the abandoned backyards all over the city. By the end of winter, though, they might be extinct on Elfhome. "Can I have a turkey sandwich with lettuce, tomato, onion, and pickles? And a ginger ale."

"Turkey hoagie with the works. Large fry . . ." The girl trailed off as she glanced up and then behind Olivia. "Oh crap."

Olivia ignored the curse and the temptation to turn around. Nothing she could do. She pushed a crumpled twenty across the corner. She tried not to think of what she had done to make the money. Shame, however, burned hot on her cheeks.

The girl continued to stare until Olivia waved a hand in front of the girl's wide eyes. "Oh! Yes!" She made change, counting out bills and coins. Halfway through, the girl paused and frowned at Olivia. "You're not Princess Tinker."

"No, I'm not," Olivia said.

The girl continued to look at Olivia, obviously expecting a name. Olivia had abandoned her human name when she fled Kansas. For weeks she'd been introducing herself only as "Red." (Her hair was more auburn than carroty-red; besides, the nickname of "Ginger" pissed her off.)

What was the name that Prince True Flame had given her? Somehow he'd known that "Olivia" was Latin for "Olive Tree" and then twisted it slightly. "I'm Olive Branch Above Stone."

"Stone?" The girl's frown deepened. Her fingernails and lip polish were Wind Clan blue and she was wearing a Team Tinker T-shirt. Her glance flicked to over Olivia's shoulder. "Eeeewww."

Olivia clenched her hand tight on her change. It would be one thing if the girl was simply a bigot, but her reaction was much more selective than blind prejudice. Obviously elves were fine as long as they were pretty. *Turn the other cheek…with my fist.* But Olivia resisted the urge. She had to think about "them."

"Is something wrong?" a deep male voice said in Elvish.

Olivia sighed and turned around. So much for ignoring "them."

Elves were impossibly tall, broad shouldered, and handsome even to the human eye. The holy caste of *sekasha* was no exception. The elf warriors added in "heavily armed" and "extremely dangerous" to that description. Considered above the law, the *sekasha* could and would kill anyone that pissed them off. In the last few weeks, they'd mowed down oni soldiers and spies, suspected human collaborators, a Pittsburgh police officer, and one of their own lords. Advice on the street was to stay as far as possible from the *sekasha*.

Which was impossible when five of them were intent on following Olivia around.

The ones quickly clearing out the hot dog shop were Wyverns; *sekasha* from the Fire Clan and part of the royal troops that came to Pittsburgh with Prince True Flame. They looked like identical quintuplets to her, all red haired and stunningly green eyed, and exactly a foot taller than her. Besides the scale armor vest and the protective spells tattooed down their arms (both in Fire Clan red), their caste was identified by their long swords said to be magically sharp and able to cut through anything. (Nothing was said about the rifles and multitude of knives that they also carried.)

She wasn't sure which of the Wyverns had spoken. She could barely tell them apart. Unsure, she fixed her gaze on the one that seemed to be the leader of the five. At least, he was the only one that addressed her directly all night.

"It's been a hard day and I'm easily upset." She kept to the truth since elves thought lying was the ultimate sin. "It's in the middle of the night, in a war zone, I no longer have a house to go back to, and I'm going to..." She had no idea how to say vomit in Elvish. "Hurl."

"Hurl?" the elf repeated the English word.

"*Saemata*." The counter girl murmured. "Forgiveness!" she squeaked when both Olivia and the holy warrior glanced hard at her. "I—I—I couldn't help but overhear."

"You're ill?" the elf asked Olivia.

"I'm pregnant!" she snapped. "And my stomach is empty. I need to eat something."

"Holy shit!" the girl breathed. Another hard look made her tear off the order and slap it down in front of the nearest cook.

"And this place serves food?" The Wyvern's tone suggested that he doubted that was the case. He eyed the sizzling basket of French fries cooking in hot oil.

"Yes," Olivia growled and turned back to the counter. "Can I have my ginger ale now?"

"Oh, sure, here." The girl pulled a cold bottle from the standing cooler and popped off the metal lid. A tiny cloud rose out of the top of the chilled bottle like an escaping genie.

*Careful what you wish for.* Olivia had wanted safety for her unborn child; she'd gotten a twenty-four hour guard of the scariest elves on the planet. The damnable thing was that they weren't really guarding her. They might even consider it convenient if she was killed.

She realized that only the leader of the Wyverns was focused on her. The other four were paying strict attention to their true charge, Forest Moss, while maintaining the most distance that the small restaurant allowed. He was rocking in place, muttering darkly, while braiding and unbraiding a handful of his pure white hair. The rest of his long hair flowed loose as spun silk over his shoulders and down his back to past his hips. It covered his rich clothes and beautiful good eye, leaving only the empty socket of his left eye, sewn shut with a starburst of scars radiating out from it, visible.

Her heart ached at the sight. He wasn't old enough to deserve white hair; at least in elf years. He'd been betrayed and tortured and then abandoned to total isolation for hundreds of years. A weaker person would have killed themselves. Forest Moss had simply gone slightly but not completely mad. At least, not until this week. The war and the royal troops seemed to be bent on destroying what little sanity he had left.

"Hey," she reached out and caught his hands. "Let me." She gathered up the marvelously silky stuff and tied it into a ponytail with a blue bandana from her purse. He leaned down as she worked and rested his forehead against her shoulder. "There, there. Everything will be fine."

He took a deep breath and whispered, "My *domi.*"

"Yes, yours." She felt like she was lying as she offered what little comfort she could. If she understood the conversation between Prince True Flame and the Wyverns earlier that evening, though, their union was temporary. Somehow they needed to find a way to make it permanent. He needed her as much as she needed him. Maybe more.

But first, food, and then someplace to live.

Not surprisingly, their food order was given top priority. Within minutes the counter girl handed over a small mountain of French fries and a torpedo-shaped turkey sandwich that she called a hoagie.

Olivia and Forest Moss took over a hastily vacated

booth. The Wyverns remained standing, watching for attack.

Her first bite explained why the diner was packed so late at night. The fries were amazing: hot, crispy goodness with a cheese sauce that tasted like food of the gods. Knowing that her tummy would make her regret pigging out on them, Olivia switched to the turkey hoagie. Thankfully it was its own bundle of awesome: crusty fresh bun, wonderful smoked turkey breast sliced thick, and sweet homemade pickle chips. The nausea passed and Olivia was able to consider the future with slightly clearer mind.

Pittsburgh had a population of something like two million people living in the metropolitan region at the turn of the century. It now had less than a hundred thousand. Vast sections of the city were standing empty. Finding a place to live was at once easy and very difficult. Some areas were safer than others, thus more densely populated. She had been on the fringe of South Side, which had the river to protect the neighborhood from saurus and wargs. South of that, people clustered close to the light-rail system with only adventurous types setting up farms beyond. The commute from the South Side, however, required two bus rides, one to downtown and a second up Forbes Avenue to Oakland. True Flame made it clear that the elves needed Forest Moss nearby and fully functional.

Oakland would be a better place for their new home. It would put them near to the royal troop encampment and the Wind Clan enclaves. The triangular neighborhood, however, was another popular place for humans to live. The Monongahela and the Allegheny Rivers protected two of its three flanks from dangerous animals. The Wind Clan enclaves at the Rim created a barrier along its third. At the heart of this zone sat the third largest employer, the University of Pittsburgh. Unlike the rest of the city, Oakland had very few empty buildings.

Since illegally entering Pittsburgh, Olivia had only been in the neighborhood three times. The first time was a full day of looking unsuccessfully for a place to squat. The second was a few days ago, seeking out Forest Moss, sight unseen, to propose to him. The last was now. She knew only the three main streets: Forbes Avenue that the buses came up, Fifth Avenue that the buses went down, and the Rim that bisected them both. She didn't want to go wandering around in the middle of the night in a strange part of town, looking for something that might not exist.

Forest Moss was watching her as if his life depended on her. And perhaps it did. At least, his sanity seemed to.

She realized with a flash of guilt that she forgot to ask him if he was hungry. He skipped their last meal because there hadn't been enough for two. She pushed the mountain of french fries toward him. "Eat some while they're hot."

She had to show him how to pick them up with his fingers to eat them. Did elves not do finger food? She had no idea what was normal table etiquette for elves. Did they eat with forks and spoons? Chopsticks? Sporks? Surely elves weren't so lazy as to make one utensil do the work of two.

There was so much she didn't know about elves. She had only taken Elvish through online homeschooling as an act of rebellion. All ten of her stepbrothers and her four stepsisters were learning Spanish, a practical second language when Kansas was just a few hundred miles removed from Mexico. Unlike the other whores on Liberty Avenue, she had no obsession with elves.

It was the distance of Elfhome to Kansas that lured her to Pittsburgh. She thought that she would only be totally free if she could hide on another world. All she had managed to do was trade one set of problems for another.

.To be fair, things had gone well at first. She found a good solid home in a safe neighborhood. She had a job at a bakery. She was starting to make friends. It had seemed like she would be fine.

Then the war started and her life went down in flames.

Currently she had the clothes on her back, a ten-pound bag of keva beans, and a purse full of elf gold bullion.

Forest Moss reached out his hand and took hers.

*And one half-mad elf lord with a very scary personal guard.*

She was exhausted. The Wyverns had dragged them out of their bed to go talk with Prince True Flame. It would be hours until dawn. She just wanted to go to sleep and deal with everything in the morning.

The elves, however, had made no suggestions as to where she could find shelter.

She collected the empty paper french-fry boat, the paper wrapper from her sandwich, and the greasy napkins onto the plastic tray.

The Wyvern leader, however, was standing between her and the trash can.

"What is your name?" Her Elvish wasn't up to knowing how to *politely* ask someone to move out of the way.

"Forgiveness," he bowed slightly. "I'd forgotten that you do not know our ways. I'm Glaive Smites the Sun."

"I need to put this stuff into the bin behind you." Olivia refrained from jabbing him in the stomach with the tray. That never ended well with her stepbrothers; usually she would have to then pick everything off the floor. Their justification was that women were supposed to be meek and mild and kept in their place.

Glaive stepped aside. He watched with interest as she tilted the tray to send the paper items into the bin. It was possible that he'd never seen paper napkins and plates before. They were objects of her "sinful" youth when she'd lived with her father, wore halter-tops and blue jeans, and sang Katy Perry songs. Little freedoms that she'd rediscovered after she'd escaped to Pittsburgh.

With life and death in the balance, she hadn't considered her independence when she approached Forest Moss. For the few hours when it had been just the two of them, he'd patiently and unquestioningly followed her. It was a day of sweetness that often took her breath away. She thought she'd stumbled into a paradise of safety without tyranny.

After dragging her to Prince True Flame, the Wyverns had done nothing else except to loom behind her. They felt menacing. Their reputation was fierce.

So far the Wyverns had done nothing to hinder her, not intentionally. Their abrupt appearance had triggered Forest Moss into blowing up her house. She couldn't blame it on them. It'd seemed that the last thing they wanted to do was upset Forest Moss.

The Wyverns, however, had done nothing to help. They loomed silently; watching without comment.

She'd forget that they were behind her except for the reactions of the people around her. Late night customers kept walking into the diner, then turning on heel as they saw the Wyverns and fleeing back into the night.

She couldn't stay at the diner without driving away other customers. She marched out into the dark empty street. The night was sticky hot but the weather report had called for thunderstorms in the morning. They would need shelter.

The tip of the Cathedral of Learning gleamed above the neighboring building like a lighthouse. Spotlights bathed it with light. The massive limestone tower rose thirty or forty stories higher than any other building in Oakland. It drew Olivia's gaze like a beacon.

*"He's a queer hawk. He's always on the doss. Either he's knackered or schlossed or both. I'm not a squealer but it's murder to root around all the empty floors to find him every time he wants to kip."*

Olivia remembered the tidbit of information mostly because it took her so long to translate Aiofe's Irish slang. The grad student had been complaining about someone that worked at the Cathedral. When drunk or tired, the man would slip away to sleep. Aiofe explained that she would have to check half a dozen empty floors to find him.

Without thinking, Olivia started to march toward the Cathedral. Behind her was a multitude of heavy boot steps.

"What is this place?" Forest Moss asked as they stood within the massive, three-story-high Commons Room. The limestone vaults arched far overhead, looking more like a gothic church of Europe than an American university. Only a handful of lights were on so most of the room was lost in shadows.

"It is a school." She wondered if she used the right word because he looked even more puzzled by her answer.

"Like Oxford?" Forest Moss asked.

"Yes, exactly." Olivia had picked that much up from Aiofe, who had abandoned a chance to attend the English university for the more exotic Elfhome-based one. The difference was that Oxford apparently was an entire village of old stone buildings whereas Pitt just had the Cathedral. The American university had started as a little log cabin. They'd walked past a replica of that original building out on the lawn.

"It looks like the churches your people have on the continent." He waved toward the east. He meant Europe. "Stone palaces to your gods, where only your priests live."

She nodded, distracted and unsure if he meant that God didn't live in the churches or if he simply meant that the buildings stood empty of humans most of the time. Her grandmother had always told her that God made his own temples.

They were the only people awake and moving in the giant space. Their footsteps echoed loudly off the limestone columns and vaulted ceiling. Certainly there was lots of space for them, but it looked very cold and uninviting.

"This room is too open." Glaive finally spoke his mind. She couldn't tell if it was a command to find something else, or merely an observation. She agreed with him.

There was the scrape of metal on stone, a jangle of

keys, and then a male voice singing a mix of Elvish and English words. *"Naekanain! No. No. Naekanain! Don't play for that team. Don't swing that way. Don't you understand the words I'm saying? Naekanain!"*

They found the janitor around the corner, loading supplies onto a cart, bobbing his head to music playing over ear buds. He was in his twenties but seemed too old to be a college student, which probably explained why he was cleaning in the middle of the night. Certainly he wore the sturdy boots, worn blue jeans, and belt knife that the locals favored.

"Shit!" he cried in surprise when Olivia tapped him on the shoulder. "You scared me. What are you doing in here? You're not allow..." He looked beyond Olivia and saw the Wyverns. "Oh, holy hell!"

"We need someplace to sleep." She noticed the open door behind him. The room beyond had crystal chandeliers, beautiful mural paintings on the ceiling, elaborate gilded moldings, a long gleaming table and red velvet upholstered chairs. "Oh, this is nice. What is this?"

"The Austrian Room. It's one of the Nationality Rooms. All the classrooms on this floor are decked out as a different nations...Wait. Did you say 'sleep?' You-you-you..." He glanced toward the Wyverns. "I'm going to have to call someone."

The room was luxurious but lacked anything remotely looking like a bed.

"Before you call anyone, open up the rooms so that we can see them."

He considered her and the Wyverns for a minute before pulling out his keys. "They don't pay me enough to say no."

❖     ❖     ❖

The Scottish room had a crown molding of thistles. The Swiss room was clad in wood and had a large tiled object that might have been a wood stove. The Yugoslav room had ornate, carved wood wainscoting. All the rooms were beautiful in their rich decorations. They were, however, stark and uncomfortable. Most of the rooms had only old-fashioned, wooden chairs with desk armrests.

Olivia felt like Goldilocks, trying out rooms, looking for a perfect fit. She was dragging the bears along with her to witness her attempts at finding a comfortable bed. At last they found the Syria-Lebanon room, which had satin sofa pillows on top of marble benches.

She sank down onto the cushions. Forest Moss settled beside her, seeking the comfort of her touch. The Wyverns stood waiting to see if she approved the room, or like the others, rejected it and moved on.

It was the most beautiful room she'd ever been in. The walls were elaborately gilded with silver and gold leaf. The floors were white marble inlaid with red stone. The gold-and-white-striped pillows were soft and shimmering. Every square inch of the ceiling was carved, inlaid, painted and gilded. "Lush" only began to describe the room. The deep U-shaped sofa, however, lined the walls, leaving only a small square of floor space free. The addition of six tall male elves made the room claustrophobic.

It was starting to freak her out that the Wyverns just stood there. They'd followed her around without speaking among themselves except occasional hand signals. They showed no surprise or dismay or even interest on their faces. It reminded her of when she was being shunned. She hated their silence but their disapproval might be worse.

She closed her eyes so she wouldn't have to see them. She decided it was a good thing that they were so patient. Troy would be shouting at her by now. Next step would be grabbing hold of her so hard it would leave bruises and dragging her to where he wanted her. Certainly, in her Bible, a holy being was patient. *"With patience a ruler may be persuaded, and a soft tongue will break a bone."*

She would believe that the Wyverns were just until she had evidence otherwise.

She woke up hours later with no memory of falling asleep. She simply failed to open her eyes after closing them. Sometime during the night, the number of elves standing around watching over her multiplied. Ten of the *laedin*-caste royal marines had joined the party. They brought with them blankets, food and news that since it was pouring down rain, Forest Moss wasn't needed by Prince True Flame.

Breakfast came in little wooden baskets; warm to the touch and fragrant with hot food. Her stomach, however, roiled at the smell. She cautiously opened the basket that Forest Moss handed her. It contained a thick oatmeal-like substance that tasted like walnuts and honey.

"Do you like it?" he asked anxiously.

"Yes. It's good." One less thing she needed to worry about. The only food they'd managed to save from her house were keva beans and potatoes; both needed cooking.

He opened his basket, revealing smoked eggs and dark rye bread. "This is Fire Clan cooking. The royal marines have their own field kitchens. Battle rations are plain but filling. They'll be good for your baby."

She tried not to feel upset by the fact that he called it that: her baby. She was barely able to think of her baby as more than an upset stomach. She knew that her feelings would change once she could feel it kicking and moving. Right now "it" was like the tail end of a bad case of food poisoning. She couldn't expect him to see her baby as his. The moment it was born, it would be obvious that Troy was the father. Her baby would probably be blond or red-haired, freckle easily, and have round ears. In a single glance, people would know that nut-brown Forest Moss had nothing to do with producing the baby.

She'd hoped that he would consider it "their" baby. Certainly she always thought of the man that raised her as her father. The lack of blood ties only mattered when he tried to keep custody of her when her mother married her stepfather. She never considered her stepfather as her parent; he was a narcissistic dictator who saw her as a rebellious piece of property.

What type of father would Forest Moss be to her baby?

There was a sudden shift among the elves as someone came walking quickly down the hallway. The janitor's late night phone call was finally bearing fruit.

The woman had her gray hair pulled back into a long braid, and wore a chocolate brown silk damask dress not as long as an elfin gown but certainly just as elegant. Aoife had told Olivia about the head of her college enough times that Olivia recognized the woman by description alone. She had to be Agnes Fisher, Dean of Elvish Studies.

Olivia was sure that the dean was the one interceding on the University's behalf because she was an expert on Elvish culture. The woman, however, ignored

Olivia and the Wyverns and tried to interact solely
with Forest Moss. The dean spoke rapid fire High
Elvish, which Olivia didn't understand. Forest Moss
stared at the woman, confusion growing on his face.

All her life Olivia had people tell her to shut up
and stay invisible. Her mother had told her "be a
little ghost" until Olivia cut eyeholes in a bed sheet
and wore it around the house, moaning. Her experience last night at The O and later with the janitor
had taught her that the male elves all expected her
to lead. It was at once frightening and intoxicating.
It made sense why Forest Moss deferred to her, but
why the Wyverns? Were they waiting for her to make
a mistake so huge that they could rightfully kill her
for it? Certainly that level of pettiness was what she'd
learn to expect from "holy" people.

The dean carried on at length in High Elvish,
which Olivia didn't know.

"Oh, please, stop that," Olivia finally snapped in
Low Elvish.

The dean glanced at Olivia for the first time.
"Forgiveness?"

"I'm Forest Moss' *domi*. He doesn't understand
human customs and technology so you're going to
have to deal with me and I don't speak High Elvish."

The dean glanced at her forehead where Forest
Moss had marked her with the *dau*. Her gaze dropped
down, taking all of Olivia in. Her dismay was clear on
her face. "How old are you? Do your parents know
what you're doing?"

Olivia couldn't lie with the elves listening in so she
ignored the question. "Our house collapsed. We need
temporary shelter."

The dean opened her mouth and then reconsidered whatever she was going to say and closed it. She studied Olivia for a silent minute. "Until the middle of June, I had no idea who Tinker was," the dean said in English. "I'm told that she was quite well known with the hoverbike racing fans. The last two months has been an education on how much the elves hold that teenage girl in esteem. The entire tengu race has gone from hated enemies to trusted allies by her word alone. It is compelling evidence that any young inexperienced female who gains the position of *domi* can be a power to be reckoned with. That said, Tinker is *domi* for the head of the Wind Clan, deep in their territory. I believe it would be a mistake for you to assume that you wield similar level of command among the elves."

"I assume nothing." Olivia was very aware of her ignorance. "But it's kind of rude to come busting into here, getting all high and mighty, when you haven't even told me who you are."

"I'm Dr. Agnes Fisher, Dean of Elvish Studies. And I'm sorry, but I need to ask you to leave. I heard what Forest Moss did at Kaufmann's; blowing up all those child mannequins. We're responsible for the safety of our students. We can't..."

"What students?" Anger made Olivia raise her voice. "You went on summer break just before the gate failed and you delayed fall registration because of the war." She flung out her hand to point at the empty Commons Room behind Fisher. "There's no one here!"

"What is wrong?" Forest Moss raised his hand, cocking his fingers. "What did she say?"

"Nothing is wrong." Olivia hugged him. "Hush.

Everything is fine. I'm still exhausted from last night and it makes me short tempered."

It wasn't a complete lie. Pregnancy was making it feel like she'd spent the night wading through quicksand. She'd gotten up with the sun out of habit; she hadn't had the luxury of sleeping in since she was a little girl.

"You should rest." He swept Olivia up into his arms. "She needs to rest; she is with child."

Olivia blushed, knowing that the dean would jump to the wrong conclusion as to who the father of her child was. Why did it matter what the woman believed? If the rumors were true, there were half-elf children scattered all over the city. They were kept hidden away so the elves couldn't take them from their mothers. The hookers on Liberty Avenue could talk of nothing but how Blue Sky Montana had been forcibly taken from his older half brother. Olivia hadn't thought the problem would ever be applied to her. She realized that one day it might.

Suddenly the dean was a welcome distraction. "I should finish talking to her." Olivia wished she hadn't exaggerated how tired she felt to excuse her anger. It would be nice to be good and angry instead of lost and confused.

"You can do it tomorrow," Forest Moss said. He'd lived for hundreds of years; tomorrow probably seemed only minutes away.

Behind them, she heard Glaive telling the dean to return the next day. The woman didn't argue. Olivia was torn. They had no right to squat in the university's building, even as temporary shelter. If she insisted on talking with the woman, Olivia could possibly lose the argument with her. That would mean they'd end up out in the rain, trying to find someplace safe to live. The woman had already conceded for the day and was walking away. Forest Moss laid Olivia down on the sofa cushions that were newly covered with lavender-scented sheets.

"You must not wear yourself out or you'll become sick." He covered her with a soft blanket that felt like angora. "There is no place we need to be. Rest."

There was no place for them to go, so he was right that there was no place they needed to be.

Confrontation with authority: round two.

The dean's gown was Wind Clan blue and she had with her a thick book titled *United Nations Elfhome Peace Treaty*. Twenty-four hours had given the woman time to prepare. The dean tried for "friendly, nonthreatening meeting" by taking a seat on the sofa across the room from Olivia and Forest Moss. It was difficult for Olivia to judge the dean's age. The skin on her hands was tissue-paper thin; her veins mapped their way over delicate bones. They were grandmother hands. Olivia's mother looked older but life on the ranch had been hard on her mother.

At one time Dean Fisher had been stunning; she was now merely regal-looking with black hair that aged to a lush dark silver. Her eyebrows were still dark bold wings, although that might be due to makeup. She silently studied Olivia with rich amber brown eyes.

In Olivia's experience, silence was a weapon.

Olivia focused on braiding Forest Moss' hair. It calmed him when she fussed over him. Forest Moss sat at her feet, threading pieces of black silk ribbon through his fingers, humming happily. She wove the three strands of his white hair. Over. Under. Over. Under. She ignored Dean Fisher, stealing the power of the woman's silence.

"I've checked the treaty," the dean finally stated quietly in Elvish. "Pittsburgh, including these buildings, will be considered Wind Clan when and if the treaty is declared null and void."

Forest Moss' humming faltered slightly but he gave no other indication that he was listening to the conversation. He hadn't even looked up when the woman entered the room.

"I believe Prince True Flame—" Olivia paused, not sure how to say "trumps" in Elvish, "—is of higher power than the viceroy. He wants Forest Moss close at hand, ready to fight."

"I understand. What I don't understand is why you haven't sought out shelter elsewhere. The enclaves are better suited at hosting *domana* and *sekasha*."

Olivia blushed and focused back on braiding. No one had suggested that to her and she hadn't thought of it herself. If it was an option, why hadn't the Wyverns said something sooner? She peeked up at Glaive who was standing quietly within striking range of the dean.

Amazingly, the male took her glance as a demand for information. "Ginger Wine's is uninhabitable until the support walls are repaired. The viceroy is using Poppymeadow's. Forge will be staying with his grandson; Iron Mace will also be guarding over the children. The distant voices say that three more Stone Clan *domana* will arrive shortly with their households. They will be housed at two of the Wind Clan enclaves and that requires all their current guests to be shifted. Forest Moss on Stone and his *domi* must find other lodgings."

Olivia hadn't heard that more *domana* had arrived in Pittsburgh. She wondered if Forge and Iron Mace were Stone Clan or Wind Clan. She didn't want to detour the conversation. "Forest Moss needs to be in Oakland but there's very little in the way of empty houses. It will take time to find something suitable. In the meantime, we need access to restrooms and shelter from the rain."

"I understand." The dean's response annoyed Olivia because it seemed by her tone that she was actually saying "You can't stay."

"Your school currently isn't holding classes," Olivia snapped.

"The chancellor has decided that we will start fall term on Monday. We have to assume that Tinker *domi* will not be able to reestablish a connection with Earth. It isn't even clear how she severed it. To continue as a school, the university must hold classes and give our students the education that they were promised."

Olivia breathed out her anger. She'd slept an alarming amount yesterday. She didn't want to be bullied out of a place with electricity and running water when she wasn't sure of her own health. "I know that there are multiple floors in this building standing empty. There are subjects that you no longer teach, so they are no longer used."

The dean glanced at Forest Moss. "This is a delicate, historic, iconic building..."

"Then one of your dormitories. They're probably half empty as it is. You used to be bigger than University of Kansas. Your student population is a fraction of what it used to be and you were on summer break."

"You have to understand, long before the first Startup,

we stopped being able to house our entire student population. The university decided that instead of trying to build more dormitories in an increasingly crowded area that it would guarantee housing only to incoming freshmen. For decades, our upper-level students have lived off campus in apartments. To save costs, they've recently started to take over abandoned buildings to operate households modeled after the enclaves. We do not oversee those structures."

"So you're saying you don't have empty buildings?"

The dean controlled a glance to the listening Wyverns. It was nearly unnoticeable, just a flick of the eyes and then her face going tight. The woman wanted to lie but couldn't. "We might. I am unaware of any but housing is not my responsibility. I would have to look into it."

"Until then, we could move upstairs to one of the empty floors."

The dean sat still and poised while considering her options. Finally she accepted defeat with, "I'll call buildings and grounds. They'll turn on the lights on one of the empty floors."

The Wyverns did not like the elevators. There were several, each dedicated to different levels of the tall building. The cars were large and clad in feather-pattern bronze and polished until they gleamed.

The holy warriors eyed the elevator to the twentieth floor like it was a great gaping mouth that was going to swallow them whole.

"Death trap," one of them murmured.

"It's like the lift on the gossamers." Forest Moss walked into the gleaming car. Olivia stepped in after him.

The warriors exchanged glances, sighed, and boarded. They rode up in silence.

The janitor waited in the twentieth-floor lobby, wiping his greasy hands on a rag. He bobbed, doing a quick bow, and started to edge nervously toward the elevator. "I got all the lights working. Had to fiddle a bit since some of the bulbs were older than I am."

The dean blocked his escape. "Go downstairs and make sure the rest of their party know how to work the elevators." When his eyes went wide, she sighed. "No, the others aren't Wyverns, they're *laedin*-caste. Just tell them you're their escort and don't let them get off on other floors."

He got onto the elevator, muttering quietly, "Sure. Sure. Just tell a bunch of sword-happy elves to behave like they're a bunch of stateside freshmen."

The dean ignored him and waved a hand toward a big wooden desk that reminded Olivia of the checkout counter of her childhood library. "You can use this floor; it's been empty since shortly after the first Startup."

"Is the elevator the only way up?" Olivia didn't want to be trapped this high if the power gave out.

"There are stairs." Dean Fisher motioned toward double doors at the end of the hallway. "Students sometimes use the thirty-six flights of stairs for exercise, so don't be alarmed if you hear someone in the stairway."

"Exercise?" Olivia couldn't imagine what the students would be doing on the steps. Surely they didn't walk up thirty-six floors. Weren't there machines that let you climb stairs without leaving one spot?

"It's safer than many of the side streets and alleyways," the dean said. "We're close to the Rim even with the enclaves to buffer the city. Our security routinely sweeps all the floors to make sure we don't get any stray plants or animals."

The dean indicated the hallway behind the imposing reception desk. "Elvish Studies was going to expand into these offices next year. The restrooms on this floor have been updated, but not much else. I'm afraid that the mass exodus during the first year on Elfhome meant that anything that could be bought easily on Earth was left behind. Feel free to use whatever you find here."

Dean Fisher moved down the hallway, flipping on lights, opening blinds, and pointing out the restrooms. All of the rooms looked like the occupants had fled in the middle of the night. Papers covered the desktops and floors. Drawers hung open, some empty, others half-full. A cup of coffee sat on one desk, a layer of mold growing on the surface of an ancient pool of liquid.

"All the phones should be hooked up." Dean Fisher paused to pick up one old-fashioned headset and listened for a tone. "Yes." She switched to English and held out a card. "These are all my phone numbers. If you need anything during the day, just dial my extension. After office hours, I'm at the second number. That's my private cell phone number. To dial out, you'll need to enter '9' first. It's ancient." She paused as if realizing that Olivia might not understand the antique system. "Have you ever used a landline?"

"Yes." Olivia didn't bother to explain that she never owned a cell phone. The ranch considered them something sinful that only men could use safely. There was a phone system in place similar to the university's so

that all incoming phone calls could be screened prior
to connecting the caller with the right person.

"Most students are baffled by our ancient technology.
Their phones are tiny flat things that they carry in their
pocket and do everything from take pictures to send
e-mail. We need to give the freshmen detailed instruc-
tions on how to use the university's phone system. They
grasp it quickly; they're used to the fundamental idea
of using a tool to speak with anyone. Elves do not have
anything similar to telephones. They don't see the need.
If they want to communicate with someone, they write
a letter. The days that it takes for a message carried by
hand to travel back and forth, to them, are like minutes to
us. If the need for communication is great enough, they
go themselves or send someone from their household."

Olivia had gotten enough allegories drummed into
her that she recognized one dressed up in different
clothes. The lesson of this particular one, however,
eluded her. "Your point being?"

"You are young. Frighteningly young."

Olivia expected the dean to ask her age again, but
the woman glossed over that detail.

"I have found that the younger the student, the
more they believe that they understand how the world
works based on their very limited experience. They
don't realize how subtle reality truly is; there are layers
to the world. What seems to be the truth is only the
reflective surface, mirroring back their perceptions."

Olivia fought to keep her voice level. "And I've
found that the older the adult, the more sure that
they know what is better for the child, even when
what they believe kills the child."

The dean's eyes filled with sorrow. "Yes, I realize

that is true too." Nevertheless, she plowed on. "There is much we don't know about the elves; we've only had contact with fairly young and adventurous individuals of the Wind Clan. Even the viceroy should be considered a teenager. Everything has changed. We can't take for granted what the elves want is something we can easily understand."

By "we" the dean obviously meant "you."

Which might be true but it certainly applied to everyone else in Pittsburgh too.

"We," Olivia stressed the pronoun, "will only be using this floor until we can find a house."

They cleaned.

Which was to say that the Wyverns stood around guarding them from God-knows-what, the royal marines established where they were supposed to be and promptly disappeared, and Forest Moss picked up random items and studied them for an hour before setting them back where he found them. Olivia worked quickly and efficiently; cleaning was the one thing that the ranch taught her to do well.

She set her sights low; she limited her cleaning to just one section. She and Forest Moss would be camping in the space only until she found something in Oakland where they could safely live. The rooms had been the offices of Nathan Yocum, Dean of Children's Literature, and his administrative assistant. The larger room had a charming but dusty window seat, a big leather sofa, two wingback chairs, a massive wooden desk, and large built-in bookcases as befitted the offices of a dean. Someone had taken the desk chair, which was fine as there were plenty of other places to sit.

The royal marines loved the elevator. They rode up and down and up and down in it all morning. Much to the university's dismay, they used it to explore all the floors—abandoned and occupied. They would circle back to the twentieth floor bearing gifts from the startled university staff and found treasures from the abandoned offices. The elevator would ding, the doors would slide open and they would spill out, laughing and talking loudly like excited schoolchildren. They would track Olivia down in the warren of offices, show off their latest discovery, and ask her to explain it.

They laughed at her Elvish, saying that she sounded like someone from the Wind Clan. Apparently the creators of her online language classes had never spoken with elves from the other clans.

The marines were an equal mix of males and females. They were all over six feet tall, red haired and green eyed. From a globe they found, she learned that they were all from an area that matched up with Northern Italy. They'd arrived just days ago via the train. Prior to that, they had never seen a diesel engine, an automobile, an electric light, or even a human before. They brought her staplers, tape dispensers, staple removers, binder clips, and bubble wrap. The last, once she showed how the bubbles could be popped, triggered a running game of keep-away.

"They seem so young," Olivia said as the game charged down the hall, popping and cracking.

"They're about your age." Forest Moss believed that Olivia was eighteen or older. "They are fresh out of training. The more-experienced troops were deployed to protect the Spell Stones. Neither Aum Renau nor Aum Hearn was heavily guarded prior to the oni's first attack of the viceroy. There was little need. They are shielded against everything except traitors. Since the Spell Stones are our greatest weapons, they are also our greatest weakness."

The Spell Stones were "our" while her baby was "yours." It would not be so galling if she actually knew what the stupid things actually were.

It exhausted her to simply clear the larger room, dust the bookshelves, and explain every possible piece of office equipment known to humankind for the last fifty years. At least the marines had done more than explore the cathedral; they brought cots, more blankets, and baskets of hot food. The warriors all had ironwood forks and spoons in kit bags. During the day, however, they'd found plastic sporks for Olivia and Forest Moss to use. Inside the baskets were grilled fish fillets, more of the dark rye bread, and a roasted root that tasted vaguely like turnips that had been sweetened with honey.

"Are we paying for this?" She hadn't seen any money exchange hands but that didn't mean that someone wasn't keeping track of what they were eating.

"Oh, yes, close accounting is kept. Wind Clan bleeds heavily for this war."

She didn't understand if that meant they would be charged or not. She glanced to Glaive.

The Wyvern explained in more detail. "The Wind Clan is responsible to house and feed the incoming *domana* from other clans. Wolf Who Rules Wind will cover any expense incurred within reason."

This was good news since she only had the keva beans salvaged from her house. With two mouths to feed, the food would not last long. Considering that the marines had grown to twenty in number, she was thankful that they were feeding her instead of the other way around.

"For how long?" she asked.

"For the duration of the war." Forest Moss pressed her hand to his cheek. "It's all bookkeeping. Extremely petty of us to quibble over money when our world is at risk, but that is how we keep the peace among us. Otherwise we would be like pigs fighting over table scraps while the butcher looks on."

"So the Wind Clan will feed us as long as the fighting continues?" Olivia said

Forest Moss smiled gently. "Do not worry; the war will not last long. The oni have been cut off from their world, so they have no retreat and no reinforcements. Every day more elves arrive in Pittsburgh to fight. We will quickly root out these oni. I was given land. We can build a holding and gather people to us. We will soon be a proper household."

God forgive her, but she didn't want the war to end quickly. At least, not until next summer, when they'd had a chance to plant crops and harvest them. All the food from Earth was running out. It was only a matter of time before the elves were the only source. For her unborn child and all the people of Pittsburgh, she didn't want their survival to be dependent on the good will of the Wind Clan. It would be a simple matter of letting Pittsburgh starve in the dead of winter.

She hoped that the Wind Clan would be better than that. She prayed that they were. But she couldn't afford to assume that they would be.

They only needed to be in Oakland during the war. The moment it ended, they could settle anywhere in the city. They could stay at the Cathedral of Learning. The important thing was to find winter clothing and start stocking up on food.

She yawned deeply.

Tomorrow.

She woke up late at night, the moon shining light through the windows on the ranks of cots around her. The Wyverns, who stayed up the night before, slept while the marines kept watch down the hall.

It made Olivia feel like she'd awoken in preschool during nap time and found her classmates still asleep. She wondered why. She spent years sleeping with all her stepsisters, stacked like cordwood in bunk beds. Maybe it was because the Wyverns were unknown elements; possible allies instead of known enemies.

She didn't have the luxury of seeing the world as a child. Currently her worldly possessions were exactly a pair of underwear, a pair of sensible shoes, a gingham sundress, and a purse full of gold. She needed clothes not only for herself but for Forest Moss too. He had lost everything at Ginger Wine's; his rooms had burned the night of the oni attack.

She tiptoed to the restroom. Forest Moss didn't stir but all the Wyverns woke long enough to watch her pass. Half of the marines were gathered around the elevator; the rest were in cots scattered about the twentieth floor. They grinned sheepishly at her as if she'd caught them doing something wrong. They bowed repeatedly, like a flock of drinking bird toys.

What had she interrupted?

They didn't seem to be drinking or smoking (if elves smoked), or even roughhousing more than normal.

They must have been talking about something they didn't want her to hear. She let the restroom door squeak closed behind her, clunked across the tile floor, coughing to make more noise. Then, slipping off her shoes, crept back to the door. At the ranch, eavesdropping was the only way she ever learned anything. During the day she'd learned the individual voices of the marines so she was able to identify the speakers.

"See," Dagger whispered loudly. The female was the brassy leader with a little too-friendly hands. "All this strangeness and she's calm as ice on a lake. No amount of wind is going to be ruffling her."

"Two different things." Ox didn't bother to whisper. He tended to be blunt to the point of rude, but not in an intentionally mean way. "He could shatter again at any moment. She's still human; there's nothing she can do to stop him."

"She calms him right down." Coal sided with Dagger. "Ice on rough waters."

"No, he's like a keg of black powder," Ox stated. "One spark. Boom. Everyone dead before they can stop the explosion. He'll probably just kill her by mistake."

"He's too valuable!" Rage lived up to her name; her voice was rough with her anger. "We need him. The oni have powerful human weapons and dragons and wargs. Forest Moss is a seasoned warrior, something that Wolf Who Rules is not."

Coal made the sound of agreement. "It was Wind Clan *domi* that killed the oni dragon, not the viceroy. Do you think, once she's *dashavat*, she'll be as fearsome in battle as the child bride?"

Olivia didn't know the meaning of the unfamiliar word. *Once she was what?*

"I don't think it will come to that. Forest Moss is going to shatter and the holy ones will put him down. You'll see. Just like Earth Son." Ox whistled, imitating a sword cutting through the air. Earth Son had been beheaded by his own guards.

"Wyverns don't want to do that," Dagger said. "We're spread thin and Forest Moss has fought bravely so far. Earth Son was a coward."

"At that place with the children statues that he was blowing up, they were discussing putting him down like a mad dog when she slipped him away. They might not want to do it, but they will."

They meant Kaufmann's. The Wyverns had been that close to writing Forest Moss off as a lost cause?

"I would like to go to that place," Lynx said. Apparently Elvish didn't have a word for "department store." "They say that the stairs moved and would carry you up and down without you moving your feet."

The conversation changed to the rumored sights of the city that the elves would like to see. Olivia backed away from the door, her heart beating madly. The Wyverns planned to kill Forest Moss? The only reason he was still alive was because she kept him sane enough that the elves felt safe around him?

Were they right? Could Forest Moss lose control enough to accidently kill her?

She used the toilet because the need was real and ignoring it wouldn't solve any of her problems.

Somehow this was worse than when Troy first unleashed his anger on her. She'd been scared then because she knew no one would stop him from hitting her until he felt like stopping. This time the Wyverns would stop the person hurting her by killing him.

It should make her glad that someone was protecting her. Had she become one of those women that expected abuse as part of a relationship? Or was it because she didn't want to believe that Forest Moss would ever hurt her?

She finished, washed her hands, and then stood staring at her reflection.

Shouldn't she be comforted by the fact that she was being protected?

The door squeaked open and Dagger leaned in. "Are you okay?"

"I'm fine," Olivia said automatically.

The Wyverns woke again as she made her way back to her cot despite the fact she was trying her best to move silently. Forest Moss stirred, sought her warmth and fell back into deep sleep.

She imagined that she felt the eyes of the Wyverns on them. Judging them. At any moment, the holy warriors might decide to take a sword to Forest Moss. They could even do it with her beside him, spraying her with blood. She shuddered, remembering how it felt when they butchered the lambs. The small thrashing bodies that had to be held still for the knife. The stench of blood and the slickness of it on her hands. The cries of fear. The distress of the ewes wanting back their lambs.

Olivia wrapped her arms around Forest Moss, hugging him protectively.

Anyone could be dangerous; even the smallest of children could pick up a gun and pull the trigger. It was the nature of God's creations; the will to survive included the ability to kill. Even bacteria could murder. What set humans apart from animals was the moral understanding that ability to kill others didn't equate to the right.

The Wyverns might be just and holy, but they had no right to kill Forest Moss.

She couldn't let them, but she knew she couldn't stop them. Somehow, she had to find a way to keep them from harming Forest Moss.

Olivia and her private army went shopping the next morning. By some minor miracle, the nearby Giant Eagle had managed to stay open while the rest of the chain had closed. She trundled through the big supermarket, pushing a cart with one squeaky wheel, followed by a herd of Wyverns and royal marines. Imagine Dragons' "Radioactive" played over the sound system, the deep thumping bass accompanied by the cart's squeaking. "It's a revolution I suppose," the male lead sang. "We're painted red to fit right in."

She eyed the sea of red behind her in the mirror over the vegetable bins labeled "local produce." Fitting in was not what they were doing. Employees and other customers were scattering before her like flocks of frightened pigeons.

She raided the bins for produce that would keep. Apples. Potatoes. Winter squash. The next aisle that used to be canned goods was picked clean. Not even dented cans of spinach remained.

"Welcome to the new age, to the new age," the PA system sang.

It felt like the apocalypse had hit Pittsburgh. It reminded her that she needed the elves to survive the winter.

At least the next aisle, which was paper goods, was

still well stocked. Pittsburghers hadn't considered what life without toilet paper was going to be like. She picked up a mega-pack and handed it to the nearest marine. The male elf eyed the package decorated with the cartoon bears as if he'd never seen toilet paper before. She ignored him, handing a second and third mega-pack out to the bewildered elves. The marines huddled around the newly burdened soldiers, examining the packages and making guesses as to what they contained.

"Bear cloth?" one guessed, pointing at the bears.

One could read French. "*Ne bouche pas sur pour les systemes septiques. Septiques. Septiques.* I don't know this word. Ah! *Paper hygiénique.* Paper for health."

This only mystified them more.

She wanted cloth diapers but there were only disposable ones in the next aisle. Savvy parents had bought out the larger sizes, leaving behind only three packages for newborn. Those would last her a week. She was going to have to find more before her baby was born.

The next few aisles were as empty as the canned goods. Only the overhead signs hinted at what had been shelved there. Pasta. Soup. Cereal. Soda. Spices were largely untouched. Her budget didn't allow her to buy to her heart's content, not when anything beyond salt and pepper came at a dear price. Beyond iodized salt, nothing was required for survival.

Before she could stop him, Forest Moss had picked up a bottle of Chinese Five Spice and broken the seal.

"Anise." He intermixed English words with Elvish. "Cassia, which is the bark of Cinnamomum trees. Cloves." He sniffed again. "Gingibre. Badian, which is sometimes called star anise. I used to trade herbs for bronze and then steel."

She swallowed down a whimper. The bottle cost over ten dollars for just one ounce. She had never tasted the spice mix, let alone used it. She couldn't put the open bottle back on the shelf; the spice would start to degrade once the seal was broken. It would be unfair to anyone else to pay so much money for an open bottle.

"This would be very good on fowl," he continued. "You need more meat for your baby to be healthy. When we find our own place, I will see that we are given live chickens instead of prepared meals. That way we can quickly have a whole flock. I will cook for you. I've gotten very good at it."

If he cooked as well as he made love, then it would be a feast beyond her imagination. She blushed furiously and added the spice to her cart.

The cashier rang up her purchase with shaking hands. It was more than Olivia had ever spent on anything. She reluctantly handed over all her American cash. She had the elf gold bullion but each coin was worth thousands of dollars. She was going to have to exchange one to buy winter clothes.

The next morning, their fragile peace fell apart. Orders came from Prince True Flame for Forest Moss to report for combat. Glaive insisted that Olivia be left at the cathedral.

"I want my *domi* to come with us!" Forest Moss cried. "I was not at the enclave to protect our people when the oni attacked. I will not leave her behind."

"Ginger Wine's was taken by treachery, not by simple force." Glaive used the same tone one would use with a willful child. "You would have died if you had been there."

"She is with child. I cannot *dashavat* her until the baby is born." Forest Moss used the same word that the marines had used. By the look of distaste on the Wyvern's face, it wasn't a good thing. "She cannot defend herself like Wolf Who Rules' child bride."

Olivia ducked her head so her face wouldn't show. She was actually two years younger than "Princess Tinker" but she hadn't told Forest Moss that. She had allowed him to believe that humans considered her an adult. Since she had been forced into a marriage at fifteen, she thought of herself as "adult" even if most of the humans in Pittsburgh would disagree. Made to grow up, she wasn't going to let herself be stuffed back into the bottle of "child." It was her experience that the only difference was children had to do what they were told.

"The kitsune made the oni invisible to everyone at Ginger Wine's," Glaive continued. "The oni killed nine of our Stone Clan brethren and took Jewel Tear before anyone could react. Your presence would not have made any difference to the outcome."

"The child bride . . ."

"Would have also been taken. We have no defense against mind tricks. The Wind Clan *domi* survived only because the oni limited their ambush to Ginger Wine's."

Tears started to run from Forest Moss' one good eye. "I cannot abandon my *domi*. She is defenseless!"

"The oni have no reason to attack her," Glaive said. "She is only *domana*-caste via her *dau* mark. Taking her would not give the oni access to the Stone Clan's Spell Stones. She has nothing of worth."

She had a small fortune in elf gold bullion in her purse but she didn't want to point that out.

"If you drag her along," Glaive finished, "she will be in direct line of fire for all the oni forces."

Forest Moss started to rock in distress.

Glaive put his hand on his sword, his eyes narrowing in calculation.

"Please." Olivia stepped forward and cautiously stretched out a hand to the rifle on Glaive's back. "Can I have this?"

Glaive's eyes widened in surprise but he didn't stop her as she took it from his back. It was a true military-issue full automatic, a little heavier than the semi-auto that her stepfather owned. It seemed as if the construction wasn't of regular gunmetal, but it functioned exactly the same.

She checked to make sure it had a full magazine. "I'm not defenseless."

Forest Moss paused, startled out of his panic.

"I don't want to be part of the fighting." Olivia still wasn't sure if she understood what the war was about, and what the oni planned for the humans in general. If she was going to kill someone, she wanted to be sure it was the right people. God had been fairly clear on "thou shalt not kill" but then he muddled the waters with lots of smiting of enemies. Olivia was fairly sure that anyone trying to kill her intentionally became "the right people," but if she was merely unintentional collateral damage, the morality of defending herself was uncomfortably gray.

"You can use that weapon?" Forest Moss asked.

"My mother," she fumbled with the Elvish. She didn't know the word for divorce, remarry, or stepfather. She wasn't sure elves had such things. "When I was a child, she joined a group of people that don't see eye to eye with almost everyone on just about everything. They own a great deal of guns." Probably more than was legal considering the effort they went to keep their gun purchases secret. "They taught me how to use this weapon."

Target practice was the one nondomestic activity that she was allowed to do, so she learned to do it well. She also learned a great deal about brawling but that was never "taught." It was a natural result of making her stepbrothers look bad on the firing range.

"I should stay..." Forest Moss started.

"No, you need to go." It had been the one qualifier Prince True Flame put on their union: Forest Moss had to continue his duties. "The oni know nothing about me. They don't know my name or what I look like. I can mix into any group of humans and disappear."

His eyebrows quirked as he considered it.

She leaned against him, lending her strength to him. "I will be fine. You need to do your duties."

He needed to be useful or the Wyverns would kill him.

Forest Moss wrapped his arms around her and they stood while he grew calm with the assurance that she would be safe.

She thought that the Wyverns would take all the royal marines with them. To pacify Forest Moss, however, they left all twenty of the marines with her. There was no way she could blend in followed by a flood of red. Yes, she could go shopping with them in tow, but she'd hoped that she could see a doctor for a prenatal exam. She suspected that a pelvic exam with the circus in tow could be dangerous for the doctor's health, but she wasn't completely sure.

She set to work cleaning, hoping that they'd go exploring again. Within an hour, they'd scattered throughout the building. They'd figured out the various access points to the twentieth floor and were guarding them in rotating shifts. What they didn't realize was that they'd missed one. Children's Literature had once spanned two floors with an ample library on the floor below. Hidden behind a panel in one corner was a dumbwaiter to ferry book trucks between the two. It was a tight squeeze, but she could fit inside.

She took with her one of the elf bullion coins that Forest Moss had given to her. She left the machine gun behind because humans with guns drew attention, especially when they visited banks. She meant it when she said that she could easily blend in with the general population. She'd been doing it for weeks.

Olivia was waiting on the corner for the downtown bus, elf-free for the first time in days. She was reading the newspaper with her hair up in a bun and her reading glasses on. It felt good to be able to blend in with the crowd of other humans waiting for the next PAT bus to come lumbering down Fifth Avenue. Did Superman ever feel like this? The relief of being just like everyone else?

She recognized the wave of change go through the crowd before even looking up. The quick scuffling and inward breaths of fear. Wyverns were coming. What now? She looked up as a familiar number of Fire Clan red bodies came marching up the street, but she didn't know any of the faces. This wasn't the group that had gone out with Forest Moss.

How did they even find her?

Were they even looking for her?

For a moment she thought they were going to walk past her but then they stopped a few feet past her.

"There you are," a female voice said in Elvish.

The female was short for an elf, dusky-skinned and dark-eyed like Forest Moss. Her dark brown hair had been hacked short so it stood up in uneven tufts. She gave Olivia a predatory grin.

*Oh, joy, another crazy elf.*

They stood for a few minutes, taking study of each other. The female wore a bright yellow high-low dress that was cut above the knees in the front but trailed down the back to almost the ground. It nicely showed off her little slouch boots of black and silver snake leather. Her bare arms and legs were covered with fading bruises. She looked like someone had dragged her through hell and back.

After the third or fourth minute of staring silently at Olivia, the female raised a finger and tapped it downward, ending with a point at Olivia's chest. "Right. You have no idea how to act. When you meet someone for the first time, you tell them your name."

"But you know my name, because you were looking for me." What name did the elf expect her to give? Red? Olive Branch?

"Consider it practice," the female said.

*Freaking crazy elves.*

"Why aren't you telling me your name?" Olivia asked.

"Practice," the female repeated. "If you don't learn, everyone will think you're uncivilized."

"What if I don't care what any of you think?"

The female reacted as if she never considered the possibility. The bus came trundling down the street.

"I'm getting on this." Olivia pointed at the incoming bus as she had no idea what the Elvish word for it was. Did elves even have a word? They lived like fairy-tale people with swords and horses and massive flying fishes.

"Where are we going?" the female asked.

"We?" Olivia put away her reading glasses and took out her coin purse.

"I've sought you out in order to speak with you."

The bus rumbled to a stop with a growl and hiss of hydraulic brakes. The door opened. All the people waiting on the corner froze in place, waiting to see what Olivia decided.

"Oh, hell." She muttered in English and stomped up the steps of the bus. The driver's eyes widened as the Wyverns and then the battered female elf boarded after Olivia. There was a sudden mass exodus via the back door of the bus. None of the other humans waiting at the corner got on.

Olivia fed quarters into the coin box. "Can I have a transfer?"

"Are they with you?" the driver murmured.

"No." Olivia took the slip of paper that the bus driver handed her and slumped into one of the bench seats a few feet back. As she dreaded but expected, the female settled beside her and the Wyverns took up stations around them.

The handful of brave humans still on the bus clustered in the back.

"Do you really not care what the others think of you?" the female asked.

"No," Olivia said as calmly as she could.

"They can kill you," the female said.

"Why would they?" Olivia believed the elves would but she needed to know the triggers. She had never been totally sure that Troy would kill her, but she'd learned what would drive him to dangerous rage. "I'm unarmed and much smaller and younger than any of your people."

"Our people," the female corrected her. "You are to be considered one of us now that Forest Moss has marked you."

Joys of marriage, or whatever the elves called it. Fine, Olivia would stick to this female's semantics. "Are there no laws against killing?"

"There are laws," the female said. "But if you're challenged to a duel and do not fight, they will call you a coward."

"Fine," Olivia said.

"Have you no pride?" the female asked.

Pride was her biggest flaw, according to Olivia's mother. "I pride myself at being much stronger-willed than the bullies that seek to dominate me. I would be shamed if I sink to their level where violence is necessary to display my character."

"If you're to be *domi*," the female stated, "you must protect those you hold."

Olivia wasn't sure if they had totally strayed from the point or not. It seemed like playground-level mentality. Did the elves do double dog dares? "If someone attacks me, it is my fault for being weak, and not theirs for being cruel?"

"But how can you protect your people if you do not fight?"

"Are we discussing what other elves think of me," Olivia said, "or the oni attacking me?"

"Elves," the female said.

"And why would elves attack elves? Aren't the oni the enemy?"

The female stared at her, head tilted in confusion. Considering the fact that she was hundreds of years older than Olivia, it took all of Olivia's willpower to keep the practiced "just trying to clarify" look on her face. Really, years of defending her vision of Christianity had made this an easy exercise.

"I'm Jewel Tear on Stone," the female finally introduced herself.

"Oh." Olivia felt bad. She should have guessed. The Wyverns didn't protect normal elves, just the *domana*-caste, and there were only a handful of those in Pittsburgh. Just days ago, the female's household had been butchered by oni and she'd been kidnapped. Yes, Jewel Tear would consider protecting her people important. Olivia might have misunderstood the entire conversation. The straight As of her home school language classes really hadn't prepared her for nuances of actual conversations.

"I'm Olive Branch over Stone." Olivia gave her elf name and put out her hand for handshake.

Jewel Tear eyed her hand with suspicion. "Humans keep doing that around me. What does it mean?"

"It is a gesture of friendship and trust." Olivia held her hand steady, waiting, even though she was fairly sure that Jewel Tear wasn't going to shake her hand.

"Oh. We do not do that. Our hands are our weapons. We do not entrust them with those we do not love."

Forest Moss would often take her hands in his and entwine their fingers. Olivia hadn't realized what an act of faith it was for him. It made her feel oddly giddy. She dropped her hand into her lap, embarrassed by the rush of emotions.

Jewel Tear didn't seem to notice. "You should know that two of the incoming Stone Clan *domana* are Harbingers. They earned their reputation during the Rebellion. They are powerful and dangerous enemies."

"They are Stone Clan?" Olivia was missing something in the translation.

"Sunder is an old, old elf born at the dawn of the Rebellion. To hir, the Clan War was a short and messy affair, insignificant to the thousands of years that shi fought. If shi thinks that you are dangerous to our people in any way, shi will kill you despite your being Stone Clan."

Olivia had learned the gender neutral pronouns in high school but hadn't realized she'd ever use them. "I see."

Jewel Tear lowered her voice. "Darkness is the one you should fear. His great joy in life had been his niece, Blossom Spring from Stone. His beloved younger sister died giving birth to her and he raised Blossom Spring as his daughter. Blossom Spring had been with Forest Moss when he was captured by the oni. He escaped. She did not."

"She was killed?" Olivia hoped that Forest Moss didn't abandon the female.

"Her First, Granite, drowned her in a chamberpot."

Olivia stared in horror at Jewel Tear. "Why would he do that?"

Jewel Tear leaned in to whisper. "She'd been raped by the oni. They had made her pregnant."

Olivia reeled at the implications. Did this mean that the Wyverns would have killed Olivia if Forest

Moss had slept with her while she wasn't pregnant? And what did this mean for Jewel Tear, who been kidnapped by the oni? "Why?"

"Granite needed to kill her unborn oni bastard to protect the Spell Stones."

Those things again. "What are those? The Spell Stones?"

"They are our greatest strength but also our greatest weakness. Granite could not allow the oni to gain access to them."

"But what are they?"

"It's how the *domana* cast their clan's *esva*. Forest Moss will teach you. Until you can protect yourself, you should keep your distance from Darkness. So, where are we going?" Jewel Tear asked.

Olivia didn't know the words for what she planned for the day. Since Jewel Tear's presence meant Olivia once again had a Wyvern guard, she couldn't visit the OB/GYN as planned. Nor did Olivia know if she could trust this female. She learned the hard way that a few minutes of kindness often meant nothing. It would be a mistake to assume that Jewel Tear saw them as "friends" or even "allies."

Luckily, while the conversation had been short, the bus had gone straight downtown without stops. Olivia wasn't sure if this was because there hadn't been anyone waiting on the corners as the driver approached or if he'd had flipped the sign to "out of service" in order to expedite getting the Wyverns off his bus. Either way, they were nearing the first stop on Sixth Avenue. She reached up and hit the "request stop" button.

"We're going here."

✧        ✧        ✧

Mellon Bank's sole building sat in the heart of downtown. It was an old building from the nineteen hundreds with marble floors, tall columns and three-story-high coffered ceilings. Olivia attempted to stand in line, but once again the line evaporated because of the presence of the Wyverns. Gritting her teeth, she stepped up to the suddenly not busy teller's window.

"I need to exchange this for American dollars." She pushed the gold ingot across the counter.

Apparently this was not a common request. The teller needed to get his supervisor who was an older woman. She in turn fetched another woman, older still.

"Miss...?" The manager paused for Olivia to fill in the missing name.

In for a penny, in for a pound. "Stone."

"Stone?" the manager echoed with confusion.

"S. T. O. N. E." Olivia spelled it slowly.

The manger's gaze flicked to the collection of elves waiting behind Olivia and then down at the long oval gold ingot on the counter between them. So far, none of the bank employees had even touched it. It sat gleaming on the polished granite like some dangerous trap.

"I'm going to have to see some ID," the manager stated.

Olivia pointed to the *dau* mark on her forehead. "I'm Forest Moss on Stone's *domi*, Olive Branch above Stone."

The manager glanced again to the Wyverns. Olivia could almost see the gears grinding through the logic in the manager's head. The bank most likely only dealt with the elves' gold-based standard at a computerized report level. They probably didn't have any way to verify the gold content of the bullion. Elves didn't lie. The Wyverns were the most morally straitlaced of the elves—as well as the most dangerous. The Wyverns wouldn't allow Olivia to lie and might be offended if the bank suggested that she wasn't trustworthy. The enclaves all used American currency as agreed upon by the UN treaty. If the bank refused to accept the ingot, they could jeopardize the entire economy of the city.

If Olivia weren't so dependent on the outcome, she would feel sorry for the manager.

"You wish to exchange this *one* gold bullion for American currency?" The manager verified her risk level.

"Yes, this one." Olivia didn't mention the others, which would obliviously rattle the manager's cage.

The manager took a deep breath and asked calmly, "And how do you want that?"

"Tens and twenties please."

Jewel Tear had been silent until they left the polished marble of Mellon Bank behind. "Can we talk now?"

She had planned to go to a doctor's office next and get her first real prenatal exam, but she didn't want to go with a horde of elves in tow.

Shopping was nearly as vital and this way she wouldn't have to worry about how she was going to carry everything back home.

"We can talk as we walk." Olivia led the way down the block to Kaufmann's.

Odd how one afternoon would suddenly endear the place to her. This was where she'd met Forest Moss. He had not been at his best, but perhaps it was better that way. Her husband Troy had been careful only to show his good side until after the wedding.

Olivia had arrived in Pittsburgh with just the clothes on her back. She had pieced together the barest of necessities by shopping the secondhand store in the South Side. Cheap dishes. Battered pots. Summer dresses. Threadbare sheets, blankets and towels. She needed to quickly replace all that she lost when her house collapsed, and more. Native Pittsburghers would be stocking up on food. It was the scientists and college students and EIA employees on temporary assignment that would need more. Sooner or later, they would realize that they were on Elfhome to stay and would need coats, boots, hats, and blankets to make it through winter.

But first, she was feeling queasy. She might as well start with the drugstore in Kaufmann's basement.

She went down the baby aisle, scented with baby powder. There were only two boxes of Preggie Pops. She dropped one box into her basket and opened the second one for a lollipop to suck on while she shopped.

"What is that?" Jewel Tear took the first package out of Olivia's basket and eyed the obviously pregnant woman on the cover.

"It's medicine." Olivia tore the plastic wrap off the lollipop. "For pregnant females. I'm going to have a baby." And then to make things perfectly clear, she added, "A human baby."

"Is that why she's fat?" Jewel Tear continued to stare in fascination at the box's art.

"Yes."

"But you are not fat." Jewel Tear held out the lollipop package to compare Olivia's profile to the woman's on the box.

Olivia sighed. "I'm only two months pregnant. I'll look like that when I get to be—" She eyed the picture,—"about six months pregnant." Which was kind of stupid since most women had morning sickness mostly in the first trimester.

"Six months?" Jewel Tear echoed in surprise. "Half a year? How long will you be pregnant?"

How long were elves pregnant when they had babies? They were immortal. Did that mean they were pregnant for years? Was that why the Wyverns weren't worried about Olivia being with Forest Moss at the moment?

Maybe answering Jewel Tear's questions was a mistake. Olivia cleaned the store out of prenatal vitamins, and then added in diaper cream, diaper wipes, pacifiers, and rattles until the basket was overflowing. She pushed the full basket at the Wyvern hovering nearby to get rid of him.

"Go get me another basket," she ordered.

"How do you know that you're pregnant without magic to tell you?" Jewel Tear whispered.

Olivia eyed her. What did this crazy elf want? She'd been silent at the bank and through the first floor of the department store, and even the first few aisles of the drugstore. And now this whispered question and fearful glance to see if they were overheard.

The Wyverns only agreed to Olivia staying with Forest Moss because she was already pregnant by a human. *Domana* weren't allowed to have half-caste babies. Olivia wasn't sure what they were going to do once she had her baby and was fertile again. Until a few days ago, she wasn't sure if she would survive the winter. She would worry about spring when it arrived.

What would pregnancy mean, though, to Jewel Tear? The elf had been kidnapped and dragged off into the wilderness for days. Olivia glanced down at the bruises on Jewel Tear's arms and legs. Had she been raped? Was she worried that she was carrying an oni bastard? Did elves permit abortions? Some Christians believed that a woman's life was secondary to a handful of cells that someday might be something that could exist outside her body. Did the elves use the reverse of the same twisted logic? Jewel Tear should die along with the half-oni fetus? Like the female drowned in the chamberpot?

"Come with me." Olivia went down the aisle to where the condoms were displayed and snatched up the same test she'd used two months earlier. "Where's the nearest restroom?" Olivia asked the sales clerk as she pushed money across the counter to pay for the test.

"Down—Down the hall, to the right." The clerk was staring over her shoulder at the Wyverns.

She collected her change. "I'll be back to pay for the other items."

They had to let the Wyverns check the bathroom for assassins and escape hatches before achieving privacy.

"I don't know for sure this will work." Olivia ripped open the test. "It detects a human pregnancy hormone. I'm not sure if elves have the same hormone. Weirdly enough, I know these don't work for animals like horses and cows. But humans can interbreed with elves, so we can't be that different."

"Like the Wind Clan half-breed, Blue Sky?"

Olivia nodded. She'd read about the boy in the newspaper. "Yes, his mother was human and his father was one of the Wind Clan *sekasha*." She uncapped the test. "See this part. Pee on it."

Jewel Tear eyed the test and then looked at her. "I'm sorry, your Elvish is sometimes hard to follow. Did you say 'pee on it'?"

❖          ❖          ❖

The digital readout on the little plastic stick read "pregnant."

Jewel Tear would have thrown it in the toilet to flush away the evidence if Olivia hadn't stopped her.

"No, no, that won't work." Olivia knew from experience. "Here, wrap it up with toilet paper and shove it into the bottom of this trash can."

They both washed their hands afterward. Olivia studied Jewel Tear in the mirror. The elf seemed to be running through some intense interior dialogue and was oblivious of her. Every emotion from fear, to uncertainty, to amusement chased over her face but she didn't seem devastated by the news.

"You are two months pregnant, yes?" Jewel Tear whispered.

Olivia nodded.

"So it takes several months before someone can look at you and tell?" Jewel Tear asked hopefully.

"Do you want to have the baby? There are ways to stop it."

"Yes, there are," Jewel Tear whispered.

"Humans have safe ways to do it," Olivia explained more clearly, just in case the elves' way involved something like swords and chamberpots.

Jewel Tear wrapped her arms about her, almost seeming protective of the child she carried. "I don't know what I want to do." She stood a moment, rocking in place, staring off into the distance. And then her gaze snapped to Olivia and sharpened. "No one can know about this."

"I won't tell anyone." Olivia had enough troubles of her own. Jewel Tear's problem, however, could be her own in less than a year. "What would they do to you if they found out?"

"They would kill it," Jewel Tear whispered. "Half-caste, they might show mercy to, but not half-oni."

"What about half-human?"

Jewel Tear looked surprised. "I thought your child was full human."

"It is," Olivia admitted. "But I don't know what will happen after I have the baby. Will they take Forest Moss from me?"

Jewel Tear looked surprised. "You love him?"

"Yes."

Jewel Tear waved away her concern. "After your child is born, he will make you an elf, like Wolf made his *domi* an elf."

"What?" Olivia cried.

"Forest Moss cannot change you now. The risk is too great that your child would be horribly deformed or killed in the womb. Nor is it entirely safe to *dashavat* children. He will have to wait until the child is mature before making it an elf."

Events of the summer made more sense. "Windwolf made Tinker an elf because he could not take her as *domi* otherwise?"

"Yes, his *sekasha* would not allow him a non-*domana* lover."

They returned to the drugstore, silent in their fearful worries. Olivia collected her basket and took it to the front counter to pay for the contents. There was a mirror behind the cashier. She found herself staring at her reflection as he scanned all her items.

*"She is with child. I cannot* dashavat *her until the baby is born,"* Forest Moss had said when arguing with the Wyvern that morning.

Olivia reached up and touched both of her human ears.

Tinker had been a human girl. Windwolf had changed her into an elf.

The Wyverns expected Forest Moss to *change* Olivia after her baby was born.

"Miss?" the cashier said. "Miss?"

She stared at him, hands over her ears, still reeling. *They expected me to become an elf!*

"Do you want anything else?" the cashier asked.

If she wasn't changed, the Wyverns wouldn't let her stay with Forest Moss after her baby was born. Forest Moss would be crushed if he lost her. And if he snapped again, the Wyverns would kill him.

"Miss?" the cashier asked again.

She pulled out her fat envelope of bills from exchanging the gold bullion. Forest Moss had already paid her to stay with him for forever. She didn't fully realize the terms. She had thought that being a *domi* was like getting married; you promised to cook and clean and have sex. She should have realized the catch; Tinker had been born a human but been transformed somehow into an elf.

But Olivia didn't want to be an elf.

Moving on sheer automatic response, she tucked her change into her purse, accepted the heavy bags filled with her purchases, and moved away from the counter for the next mythical customer to check out. She and the elves had the drugstore to themselves. Everyone in Pittsburgh knew how deadly the Wyverns were—even to their own.

She forced herself to focus long enough to troop upstairs, back to the children's department where she first made her deal with Forest Moss. She'd thought she had known all the possible ramifications of becoming his *domi*. She thought it could be no worse that prostituting herself to nameless men on the street in the middle of the night.

She'd spent years resisting pressure from her family to become someone else. To believe in their narrow-minded, bigoted God. To see herself as a flawed creature whose soul depended on her husband's virtue because that's how they interpreted God's words. To become meek and submissive before all men because that's how they twisted God's will to suit their desires.

She knew in her heart that they were wrong. She clung to her God through all of the years of beatings, verbal abuse, belittlement, and shunning. Her God didn't see her as a lesser creature because of her birth as a female. Her God didn't want her to grovel at the feet of others simply because they had been born men. No one stood between her and Him. She was like an infant on her heavenly father's shoulder, loved and not judged, and no one could convince her otherwise.

But she'd been born a human with a human soul. To warp her entire existence so that she was something else? Something immortal? She would never die and thus never go to heaven. Never rest on her heavenly father's shoulder, surrounded by his love?

She had offered herself to Forest Moss. There was no denying that he needed her like air. Without her, he could very well die.

Fear made her stomach churn. She got out another lollipop to quell the sudden need to vomit. *I've got months before this is really a problem. And so far,*

*the Wyverns have been puppy dogs compared to the
men of Zion Ranch.*

Jewel Tear held up the tiny onesies. "Will it—*your*
baby—be this little?"

The female might be pretending to ask about Olivia's
baby but she meant her own. Jewel Tear flicked a
glance toward the Wyverns who were all looking at
the tiny clothes with equal dismay. Honestly, all the
elves seemed to be spectacularly clueless about babies,
for being hundreds of years old. She was starting to
think that none of them had ever seen a baby before.

Was that why Jewel Tear was even considering
keeping her baby? Because she was afraid she'd never
get a second chance to have one? The poor thing had
no clue what she was getting into. Olivia had been
terrified of going into labor all alone. Of having to
take care of a newborn with no one else to help keep
food on the table. No wonder Jewel Tear had tracked
Olivia down; she had no one else to ask for advice.

"It—my baby—needs to be small enough to—"
Olivia's Elvish failed her. She picked up a stuffed
rabbit and demonstrated a baby dropping down out
of her pelvis.

Jewel Tear's eyes went huge. "Oh!" Apparently she
hadn't considered "pregnant equals giving birth" before.
Jewel Tear eyed the rabbit and then clearly fought
the urge to press her hand to her womb. "Doesn't
that hurt?"

"Yes." Olivia tossed the rabbit to the nearest Wyvern.
"A lot." She added two packages of cloth diapers. By
the time her baby was born, the stores would have
been picked bare. On second thought, she added
another two packages for Jewel Tear. "Most women,

though, seem to forget how much it hurts in a short period of time. I think if the memory stayed sharp, they wouldn't have a second baby."

"I see. And it stays little for how many years?"

*It.* Obviously Jewel Tear hadn't started to think of the baby as a person yet.

Olivia handed the Wyvern a pile of yellow onesies, two packages of caps, and a dozen receiving-blanket gift sets. "It's about a year before a human baby can walk or talk." God knows how long it took elf babies because elves obviously had no clue. "Babies mostly eat and sleep at first. They cry a lot. They throw up constantly. They pee and poop and you need to clean that up. They can only drink milk from your breast." Olivia assumed all supplies of formula would be gone by the time she had her baby in April or May. "You can't leave your child alone, ever. You must carry it with you everywhere you go."

Jewel Tear picked up another one of the stuffed rabbits and eyed it. "It sounds horrible. Why do you want one?"

Olivia hadn't really wanted to have a baby. It all came with the package deal of being forced into marriage and unprotected sex. Jewel Tear was right, though. Olivia could have gotten an abortion as soon as she reached Pittsburgh. She felt stupid to admit why she decided not to, but Jewel Tear had trusted her with her greatest secret. The female elf had earned some of the truth. "I love little children. They're sort of sluglike when they're first born, but by the time they're two, they're just so full of wonder at everything. Everything is marvelous to them and it's a joy to share each new experience with them. And they love you so fiercely and completely. You are their entire world."

Blushing, she picked out the rest of what she needed, loading down the Wyvern. Jewel Tear, she noticed, hadn't put down the stuffed rabbit. As if it was a test run for taking care of a baby, the female continued to carry it as they checked out and headed home.

They collided with the cathedral's unit of royal marines once they returned to Oakland. The marines greeted the Wyverns with relief, ignoring Olivia until it was revealed that she hadn't been kidnapped and then rescued. Then they turned toward her like her stepbrothers who she'd outfoxed and made to look bad.

Jewel Tear kept her eyes down, staying out of the conversation, still cradling the stuffed bunny in her arms.

"Oh, be quiet," Olivia finally snapped.

"Why did you leave their protection?" one of the Wyverns asked.

Olivia threw up her hands and pushed through the soldiers to the line of humans who had paused to watch with interest. They froze in fear as they became the focus of all the elves' attention. "Without the marines, I'm a human, one of sixty thousand, helpless and thus harmless." She stepped back beside Dagger. "With them, I'm one of four females. I am a target, but I'm still helpless."

"She cannot offer protection until Forest Moss changes her," Jewel Tear added quietly without looking up. "Can you blame her for not yet wanting the responsibility of her position?"

She really wished Jewel Tear hadn't used the word "blame." It was her experience that people were more than willing to blame the most innocent of people merely because they could. Her sister wives used to blame her for bad weather, uncooperative animals and misbehaving children.

The Wyvern breathed out frustration and shook his head. "The enemy might not be able to pick you out of a crowd today, but they will learn your face, and you will be a target even if you have not been changed yet."

She nodded her understanding as her stomach flipped queasily. The elves were obviously assuming that she would become an elf.

She had hated Kansas, from the endless sky to the narrow minds of the ranch. Despite that, she'd been homesick; she missed the comfort of Christian fellowship. She'd thought about joining a church after the first month in Pittsburgh. Any decent person, though, would wonder where her parents were, and a truly good person would need to know how she was surviving on her own. If she was safe. If she had enough to eat. If she was ready for the winter. Her life didn't stand up to the scrutiny that a close-knit community would bring.

It brought her to tears when she thought about Christmas without belonging to a church. She got goose bumps singing carols in evening services. The soft light of candles filling the church. The scent of pine trees and beeswax. Voices raised without an organ's accompaniment; a unison of love and devotion. "O Holy Night." "Silent Night." What Child is This?"

She'd told herself it was only for a year. Once her baby was born and she was firmly rooted in Pittsburgh, she'd start carefully vetting the churches in Pittsburgh.

Once she found one like her grandmother's in Boston, she'd have the community she desperately wanted.

When she had tracked Forest Moss down, she thought she could continue on that timeline. Instead of walking Liberty Avenue, selling her body to random strangers, she would be safe at night in a familiar bed. Everything else would stay the same. She should have taken Tinker's life as a warning. The girl had been yanked out of her life, flown to Aum Renau, and things had never been the same for her.

Olivia had lost her entire life once. She was twelve when her mother decided to return to the ranch. They left behind her father, paternal grandmother, aunts, uncles and a herd of younger cousins that were as close as sisters and brothers to her. The church she'd attended since she was born. The middle school full of kids she'd known since kindergarten. The library where all the librarians knew her name and fed her wonderful books that expanded her mind.

They had driven for days, the sky growing larger and larger until the world was just wheat and sky. She felt like she'd been reduced to a speck of dirt and dropped on a foreign planet full of aliens.

So lost...

Like she felt now.

She curled up on the window seat and stared out through the glass. What was she supposed to do? She needed Forest Moss' support to survive in Pittsburgh through the winter and the war. She wouldn't be able to keep turning tricks to earn money as her pregnancy got more and more obvious. For her baby's sake, she needed to eat well and stay warm and safe. And Forest Moss needed her. Without her, he'd unravel. The

Wyverns would decide he was too dangerous to live, especially with other *domana* arriving in Pittsburgh that made him less vital to the city's defense. Forest Moss *needed* her and she owed him and was fairly sure that she loved him.

But she was scared of losing herself.

She'd spent so many years fighting her family as they tried to beat her into their mold of a good and proper woman. They had wanted her to be a docile, obedient baby machine. If they could have arranged for uneducated, they would have worked for that too, but the state of Kansas tested their home school students.

What the elves wanted was worse. They wanted to change every cell of her body, and in doing so, strip away her mortality. If they took her basic humanity and then isolated her from everything human, how could she possibly stay herself? On top of it, they had bound her willingness to change to Forest Moss' life. All the beatings and shunning and days with nothing but bread and water paled in comparison.

It would be one thing if Forest Moss wanted her to change; she would never change for anyone's selfish desires. All that he wanted, though, was to be with her. It was the Wyverns that would force her to decide between the two.

They needed to separate themselves from the Wyverns. How?

The Wyverns hadn't come to Pittsburgh until the war broke out. They would leave once it was done. Hopefully. She could pray for a quick and speedy end. If they left before she had her baby, then the elf sense of time might mean that no one would try to change her until it was far too late.

They would need a better place to live, one that would provide through the winter.

She stared out the window at Fifth Avenue and the sprawl of city beyond the Cathedral's wide lawn. There had to be a simpler way to find an empty place than walking up and down the streets, checking every door.

Movement on the lawn caught her eye. Some of the students were playing Ultimate Frisbee. A handful of the marines had gathered on the sidelines to watch. The humans were as curious as the elves. The game halted to teach the marines how to throw the Frisbee.

It made her remember that Dean Fisher had said that the university assumed that their students would find an apartment in their sophomore year. How? The students would be coming from Earth with everything they would need for an entire school year. They wouldn't be roaming the streets for days on end. There had to be some way for offworld students to line up housing before they crossed the border.

Elfhome Real Estate had an office on Forbes Avenue that whispered "luxury." A big picture window. Thick pile carpet. Large ironwood desk. Leather visitor chairs. The cornered agent gazed at her with wide, wide eyes as she explained that she needed someplace to live. Forest Moss sat silently in the chair beside her, staring at the ceiling. The Wyverns stood quietly at her back. The marines milled outside, occasionally peering in through the picture window.

She finished with the most important part. "The Wind Clan will be paying for our quarters as part of the Stone Clan compensation for coming to Pittsburgh and fighting the oni."

"But—but—but," the real estate agent stammered. "I don't understand what you think I can do about this."

Olivia considered the lettering on the window that stated: Elfhome Real Estate. She scanned the photos of apartments decorating his wall. They had captions such as "studio with view" and "one bedroom with balcony."

"You are a real estate agent, right?" she said just to confirm it. He could have been a secretary or a very well dressed janitor.

He put up his hands as if to ward off a blow. "We're property managers for several Earth-based real estate companies affiliated with the University of Pittsburgh. Pitt maintains dormitories for undergraduate student housing. We handle the temporary and permanent housing for graduate and doctorate students, faculty and some of the postdocs who are doing field work in the area."

Olivia huffed impatiently and locked in on the key words. "You handle housing."

"For people *associated* with the University of Pittsburgh." He stressed the word "associated."

She countered with, "Pitt was on summer break when the gate failed."

He paused for a moment, obviously sensing a trap. "Yes."

"So there are apartments with occupants coming back to them—right? They're on Earth and we're on Elfhome and there's no way to get from one to the other."

"Yes." He drew this word out as if he suspected that he shouldn't admit to the truth. His eyes darted to the listening elves that probably couldn't follow the English conversation.

Which might not be to her benefit.

Olivia switched to Elvish. "I need someplace to live close to Prince True Blood's encampment. You have empty apartments. I don't see the problem here."

He took a deep breath and glanced to the Wyverns again. After a minute, he wet his lips and stated carefully in Elvish. "We demand that people meet certain requirements. They have to be employees or students of the University."

"I can take a class," Olivia said.

He opened and shut his mouth a few times.

Olivia scanned the apartment offerings on the wall. They would need room for her and Forest Moss and eventually the baby. A scrape of boot against tile added in a horde of elves, at least at the start. Three bedrooms. There was only one such offering on the wall.

"That one." Olivia pointed to the flyer. "I want to see it."

"The penthouse at Webster Hall Apartments?" The agent's voice threatened to break.

"Yes."

He named the monthly rent, which given another situation would have had her fleeing the building. It was thousands of dollars a month. How did anyone afford such a place? She swallowed down her fear. First things first: make sure it was acceptable and then see if the Wind Clan truly would foot the bill.

"Show it to us."

His gaze flicked to the Wyverns again and then slowly he half-bowed. "Yes, certainly."

Webster Hall was a stately sandstone building on Fifth Avenue next to St. Paul's. Olivia suppressed a familiar twinge of guilt at the sight of the cross on the steeple. She hadn't wanted to get married to Troy, had resisted months of bullying before agreeing, had been legally too young, and he had six wives already. She had, however, said vows before God and witnesses. She meant those oaths at the time. And yet, here she was, more or less married to an elf.

Troy's God might have been the type that damned an abused child to hell for adultery, but Olivia's God didn't. In fact, her God might be the reason there were so many tornadoes in Kansas.

Squaring her shoulders, she marched into Webster Hall. Forest Moss, the five Wyverns, and a real estate agent trailed behind her. Thankfully the marines stayed outside.

There was a spacious lobby with expensive-looking leather sofas and a wall of gleaming bronze mailboxes for the tenants. Beyond a locked security door, there was an elevator to the upper floors.

They left two Wyverns in the lobby and squeezed into the elevator car when it arrived. It deposited them in a tiny hallway on the penthouse level.

The front door opened into a small foyer. A small galley kitchen was immediately to the right with a small refrigerator, electric range and a microwave. Closed off to make the most of wall space, the room would be pitch black in a power outage.

Olivia walked into the living room, trying not to like the fact that it was one long wall of high windows. They'd been having Indian summer and the sun baked the room in warmth. Come winter, though, heat would escape through the glass at an alarming rate in a power outage.

"How is the building heated?" Olivia asked.

"There's central heat and air conditioning."

All electricity-dependent then. Olivia knew that electricity was fairly easy to take out. One good storm or a well-placed bomb, and a section of the city could be without power for hours, maybe days. The oni had tried to take out the city's power plant once. There was no fireplace, wood burning or gas, so there wasn't another way to warm the apartment. She wished she had thought to ask before demanding to see the apartment.

There were three bedrooms, just as stated, but the smallest would hold little more than a crib and a dresser. If the Wyverns continued to sleep within sword's reach, then the apartment was far too small. Since it had been the largest apartment listed, then this was a dead end.

Olivia sighed and leaned her forehead against the glass. The wall of windows gave the apartment a better view of the Rim than the taller cathedral. She could clearly see the line of destruction running from horizon to horizon in a sweeping arc, marking where a fifty-mile-diameter circle had been punched out of Earth and dropped onto Elfhome. The Rim sheared through city sprawl, streets and buildings reduced to rubble by the transfer. To the northeast lay virgin Elfhome forest: towering ironwood trees and nothing else for hundreds of miles. To the southwest, Pittsburgh lay, under siege by oni and alien vegetation, and losing the battle.

Looking at it made her feel completely alone.

She closed her eyes. *Please, God, help me. I don't know what to do.*

The real estate agent had gone into professional

mode, babbling about the benefits of the apartment. "It's an amazing view of the old CMU campus. I have always loved Hamerschlag Hall. It's the one with the rotunda on the roof."

She opened her eyes to peer at the far hillside. There were several large old classical-looking stone buildings. The one with the rotunda was stunningly beautiful. She hadn't heard of a second school in Oakland. "CMU campus?"

"CMU was Carnegie Mellon University. Well, still is, only it moved to Earth."

Maybe she was thinking too small. She had a small army trailing behind her. They could take over a large building. Not this one; it was too dependent on electricity. Something they could install wood stoves in. They could do radical infrastructure changes on a big building. Fortified areas. Escape routes. Hydroponics.

"Hammerslag?" She pointed because she knew she was butchering the name. "Is that empty?"

"No, no." He shook his head. "The EIA uses the campus as overflow offices and barracks. Director Maynard's offices are downtown at the PPG castle, but during Shutdown, there's an EIA-only access road open directly to the campus. That way their personnel aren't caught in the traffic jams."

She had her hands full with the elves; she didn't want to add the EIA. Still there were dozens of old stately buildings on the hillside. "The EIA uses everything over there?"

"Everything except the old Phipps Conservatory; that building way to the right." He pointed to the glimmer of glass through the trees.

"Like a greenhouse conservatory?" she asked.

"Yes."

"How old is old?"

He spread his hands to indicate ignorance. "Over a hundred years old. I think it was built in 1890—so—a hundred forty years. It didn't fare well after the first Shutdown. It was very dependent on admissions to stay open. It was a big drop from a population of two million people living within an hour drive time to sixty thousand."

"So it's closed?" she asked.

"Yes, it closed a few years ago."

"Perfect."


The Phipps Conservatory was like something out of a fairy tale, an elegant and fanciful expanse of glass that glittered in the Indian summer sun. It sat on a hill by itself, separated from the rest of Oakland by a deep ravine spanned by a wide stone bridge. Remnants of banners rustled in the wind as they hiked up the hill toward it, offering hope that the neglect to the building wouldn't be too extensive. She could make out vague shapes of towering plants within.

Getting past the locked front doors proved to be simple for impatient elves with magically sharp swords. Better yet, once they could unlock the doors from the other side, Forest Moss was able to repair the damage done to the door with a few gestures and words.

The front of the building was set into a hillside and capped with a great glass dome that washed the area in sun. Judging by the dozen round tables, each hosting four chairs, there had been a café on one side of the foyer. A quick exploration revealed a small working kitchen. Across the hall was a denuded gift shop with one giant garden gnome looking forlornly at the empty shelves. There were also bathrooms with multiple stalls.

The next area was a courtyard with palm trees, moist and green. Just as she was wondering the source of the water, a sprinkler head popped up and misted the area.

She did a little victory dance. So far, perfect.

The more Olivia explored the conservatory, the more perfect it seemed. While the greenhouse areas were vulnerable, there was a large brick building in back that housed offices and classrooms that could be converted into an easily defendable living space for a large number of people.

Room after room of wild splendor teetering on the edge of ruin but not completely lost. Hard work could salvage it all but pretty plants weren't what she needed. She needed crops to eat. It seemed like a shame to tear out the cultivated gardens to grow vegetables. The last and largest room, however, was labeled "Production Greenhouse" and was nothing short of a miracle. With the large bag of keva beans, she had everything needed to grow all the food they would ever need. It meant that no matter when the war ended, they could survive the winter and still have seed for next summer.

Her God was watching over her. He would provide.

She pressed her hands together and bowed her head in prayer. "Thank you for your wondrous bounty."

# THREADS THAT
# BIND AND BREAK

❖⇥═◉═⇤❖

Gossamers filled the skies over Pittsburgh. Translucent as jellyfish and shimmering with thousands of tiny fractured rainbows, the massive beasts defied all logic.

Law watched the gossamers with new eyes. She grew up with the sight of the great living airships swimming above the skyscrapers. As a child, she'd accepted their existence without question; impossible creatures lurked in every corner of Pittsburgh. Since June, though, she'd learned many dangerous secrets and dark truths. The Skin Clan twisted sea creatures into flying airships by using powerful spells. There were larger, more dangerous beasts scattered across the planet that they'd made for war. Nor did the Skin Clan limit their biological tampering to animals; they carried out countless experiments on their slaves. They were cruel and immoral masters and they were in Pittsburgh. Somewhere. Carefully hidden.

Law studied the airships, aware for the first time of the menace that they represented. She never realized before that there were differences between the beasts and the gondolas slung under their bodies; most likely because she'd only seen the viceroy's airships coming and going. The one lone airship over the airfield was being untethered to make room for the incoming ones. It was the viceroy's surviving gossamer, as the other animal had been killed earlier in the summer. Its gondola was Wind Clan blue, the importance of which she never knew until June. The color turned the wooden craft into an unmistakable war flag.

The incoming airships were carried by larger beasts. The gondolas were black, trimmed with red or green, and bristled with weapons. The Stone Clan had arrived in force. The prows of the black-and-red gondolas jutted out with saw-like teeth gleaming like blood. The largest drifted toward the Wind Clan gossamer with the menace of a river shark.

The viceroy's airship fought its tethers, dragging the dozens of elves holding onto the mooring ropes.

Law had three coolers full of fish in the back of her Dodge for Caraway's majordomo, Chili Pepper. Alton Kryskill's Ford pickup was backed into the motor court and they were off-loading two wild boars. Normally another forager at an enclave meant that Law had screwed up her delivery time and had lost a customer. Yes, she was running late. Caraway's enclave, though, was bracing for an invasion from the Stone Clan; they'd buy from both foragers and beg for more.

Law sat on her tailgate, listening to the conversations around her. Since June, she'd had a second unofficial job: freelance spy. She wanted to find the Skin Clan before they could engineer the downfall of Pittsburgh. Nearby gunfire as they arrived had lured Bare Snow

off to investigate. Law remained to find out what the
enclaves knew about the incoming Stone Clan *domana*.

The Kryskills all had that wild and wooly Norse
god look going on. Alton had slipped a few notches on
the scruffy scale since she last seen him in May; his
dark blond hair was down to his shoulders and he'd
let his chronic five o'clock go to full beard. Alton was
getting bad news via his cell phone. He didn't want
to be overheard; he'd drifted to the farthest corner
of the motor courtyard. Law could barely make out
his snarled questions. "Who? When? Why?" Judging
by Alton's free hand, coiling into a fist, someone was
in for a serious beat down. The Kryskills were not
people you wanted pissed off at you. His family had
pulled an actual cannon out of thin air and kicked
monster butt in July. Law wanted to know what had
Alton looking so angry.

Not that Alton was the only one upset in the motor
courtyard. The elves weren't happy about their incoming guests.

"Harbingers!" Caraway's cook worried at the skirt of
his white apron. "Harbingers! I can't believe they sent
Harbingers. Here! To our territory! They mean war."

Chili Pepper focused on counting out American
dollars to pay Alton. "You need to wet age the boar
and then cook it slowly over a low temperature; you
will not be able to serve it tonight."

"Don't tell me how to cook," the cook snapped.

"Then focus on your duties and not on things you
cannot change." Chili Pepper tucked away his leather
billfold. He re-counted the bills he'd taken from it.
"We are hosting Darkness of Stone. We cannot bring
dishonor to Wolf Who Rules by doing it poorly. The

distant voices say Darkness will have his six Hands plus three Hands from Cold Mountain Temple and another hundred *laedin*-caste on top of that."

Law clenched her jaw to keep her dismay off her face. The warriors with Darkness alone could easily overwhelm the viceroy's force. The combined might of the three incoming Stone Clan *domana* might even outnumber the royal troops.

"We don't have enough meat to feed that many warriors!" the cook cried.

"Calm yourself. Law is here with water produce." Chili Pepper waved to her. "You can serve the *wae-waeli* tonight and roast the boar tomorrow."

Alton glanced her way and his eyes narrowed in what might be anger.

*What did I do to piss off the Kryskills?* The monster fight stated the Kryskills' alliance fairly clear. She thought they were on the same side. Then again, no one knew what side Law was on. She nodded at Alton, wishing that he'd lose interest in her.

One of the saw-toothed airships drifted over the courtyard, filling the sky and throwing everyone into deep shadows.

*Speaking of not knowing which side a person was on . . .*

Alton glanced upward and then focused back on his cell phone.

The cook whispered a curse as the gondola slid overhead, revealing rows of mysterious hatches. Judging by the way all the elves stepped back under the eaves, they were most likely some type of gun ports. The Wind Clan's reaction to the weapons was unsettling; they didn't trust the incoming forces.

One thing she'd learned about being a spy was that occasionally you had to risk a few questions to understand everything going on. "Is that his? Darkness?" Law pointed upward.

Chili Pepper nodded in reply to her. He snapped fingers to break his household out of their panic. "The Wyverns will guarantee that the Stone Clan does not harm us. This will be no different than Winter Court. We have done this before *domou* took Caraway as Beholden, we can do it again."

"He is a Harbinger?" Law had never heard the word before. "What does that mean?" How trustworthy could he be if all Caraway's people were scared?

Chili Pepper pursed his mouth like he didn't like answering, but he did. "Harbingers are our greatest warlords from the Rebellion. For thousands of years, they battled the Skin Clan, taking us from slaves to freedom."

"Ruthless," Cook muttered. "Harbingers would level cities. Streets would run with blood."

"Shush," Chili Pepper whispered. "We don't gossip to outsiders about guests."

There was a loud snap of ropes from the airfield.

"Get her! Get her! There is no one on her!" a distant voice shouted in Elvish.

Law spun around to see the Wind Clan gossamer flying away, trailing broken mooring ropes. As she watched, a dozen tengu rose up from the city, black wings laboring to gain altitude to chase after the airship.

The elves of Caraway's enclave cried out in wordless dismay.

"The tengu are *domi*'s Beholden." Chili Pepper snapped his fingers again. "They will fetch back the gossamer. Get these wild pigs to the slaughterhouse, and carefully. Don't spill any blood on the cobblestones. Our guests will be here in minutes and it would be in poor taste to have bloody paving."

While the elves struggled with the big dead pigs, Alton walked over to Law's Dodge. Normally Law didn't hang out with men. Most guys didn't deal well with a woman that could out "man" them at hunting, fishing, shooting, and fighting kind of things. They seemed to think that all those activities were pissing contests where women shouldn't enter because they lacked a penis. To compensate, most guys turned into loud-mouthed jerks. Alton Kryskill was a rare exception, probably because he had an older sister that could kick the teeth out of any moron who said women should act like the weaker sex.

Law and Alton had gone to high school together and been in the same clubs. Ecology. Rifle team. It made them friends of sorts.

"Hey." Alton put out his fist to bump hers. "Where do you stand in all this? You do know it'd be bad if the oni came out on top in this?"

The oni were the least of their problems but Law kept her secrets to herself. "I'm with the elves in this." By that she meant the elves that could be trusted. The secret traitors among the elves were their biggest problem. Who were these incoming Stone Clan *domana* really?

Alton nodded as if it was what he expected her to say. "Look, we're trying to get everyone that we can trust in on this. Tinker *domi*'s cousin, Oilcan, was taken, we think by his elf grandfather. Tinker *domi* is freaking out over this. We're going to find Oilcan, even if we have to tear the city apart to find him."

"Who exactly is 'we'?" Law asked since Alton was the last person she expected to call Tinker by her correct title. The Kryskills were a wild and woolly bunch, even for Pittsburgh. Someone had been drilling protocol into Alton. If Law weren't living with an elf, she wouldn't have picked up the difference. Most humans in Pittsburgh called the girl Princess Tinker even though it wasn't her title.

"Team Tinker. My cousin is the team's business manager. We only want people we can trust looking for Oilcan; people we know are human and aren't working with the oni."

That did narrow the field down to kids that they went to school with. Assuming that the Kryskills could actually be trusted. The question remained why Alton was being all so proper.

"I'll keep my eyes open." Law waved toward the bed of her Dodge. "I've got to stop at Station Square. A bunch of friends called needing help with their booths at Oktoberfest. I promised them I'd gather stuff for them."

"They're still holding Oktoberfest?" Alton pointed toward the crowded airfield. "With all that going on?"

"They moved the location because of the war, but yeah, the shrine gets installed today."

Alton nodded his understanding. He held out his phone. "Here's my number. Call me if you find anything. Be careful. The oni might be behind Oilcan's kidnapping but just the same, his grandfather and great uncle are serious heavy hitters."

Law was weaned on videos of what Windwolf could do if pissed off. "Just your family and Team Tinker against two *domana* and how many *sekasha*?"

Alton dropped his voice to a whisper. "Jin is flying into the city to personally supervise the search. If you spot them, call me, and the tengu will have our back."

The Kryskills were allied with the tengu. That was an interesting piece of information. How did that happen?

"Will do," Law promised.

The wild boar had been carried off.

Chili Pepper made shooing motions at Alton. "Go! Go! Make room for Law! Bring more tomorrow. As much as possible."

Alton waved as he pulled out, making room for her Dodge. Law backed into the motor court thinking about Oilcan's kidnapping. Bare Snow had told her about Forge and his missing son and beloved dead wife. Rumor had it that Forge planned to stay in Pittsburgh for Oilcan's entire life, however long that may be. It didn't make sense that Forge would take Oilcan to harm him. The kidnapping had all the fingerprints of the Skin Clan; they most likely wanted a war between the Wind Clan and Stone Clan. Oilcan was merely a pawn in a hidden game.

It was her experience that grandfathers couldn't be reasoned with; that part of their brains had atrophied from disuse. Someone could use their prejudice to manipulate them into stupidity; Law's Aunt Rosie excelled at that. Admit that they were wrong? No, grandfathers didn't do that. At least, neither one of hers would.

Having Team Tinker tracking down Forge might be a bad thing. If Tinker refused to take the bait, the Skin Clan might settle for a war between the elves and the humans.

"Forgiveness." Chili Pepper interrupted Law's thought. "I need to ask you about the mutt."

"Who?"

"The half-breed with the ill-omened name. The female child you found at midsummer's eve." He meant Bare Snow. "I don't remember her name exactly. Something about death."

"What about her?" Law struggled to keep her voice level.

"Tinker-*domi* exiled one of Steam Vent's household. He was in charge of the Union Station since the disguised oni were discovered working on the trains. *Domi* was quite angry with him for allowing harm to come to the Stone Clan children. She has made it clear that anyone that allows a child to be hurt will be exiled from Pittsburgh."

Technically, Bare Snow was still a child, since she was a few years shy of her majority. It made her approximately seventeen. She had begged all the enclaves to take her in and they'd turned her away. Nor had anyone bothered to find out if she found a safe place to stay. Heads would roll if Tinker found out.

"I found her someplace to live," Law said vaguely.

"Alone?" Chili Pepper's tone indicated that wasn't acceptable.

"No, it's a human household."

Chili Pepper's eyes narrowed as he considered the ramifications. "Can they be trusted? They are not abusing her?"

As if anyone could abuse Bare Snow without getting a knife to the throat.

"They can be trusted," Law said.

"They are not using her for sex?"

Law blushed, thinking of last night. "What—what do you mean?"

"How do you say—pimping her?"

Obviously Chili Pepper had not a clue that Bare Snow had been trained to be an assassin. "No! Nothing like that! She seems very happy. She picks apples and such."

"Ah! Good. Good. *Domi* would be pleased." Apparently that was all that mattered in his mind as he focused on more pressing matters, like the incoming Harbingers.

"Ok-to-ber-fest," Bare Snow chanted in English, as she pulled on her panties. She'd slipped into the Dodge's passenger window just as Law had pulled away from Caraway's. The spell tattooed on her torso required her to be naked in order to be invisible. "Oktoberfest. At Oktoberfest, we will drink bear."

"Beer," Law corrected her. It earned her a hug and a kiss on the cheek. For a trained assassin, Bare Snow loved to cuddle. It was distracting when she did it mostly naked.

"At Oktoberfest, we will drink beer and eat pierogies," Bare Snow stated firmly despite the fact that she couldn't stand the taste of beer. There would be plenty for elves to drink; all sold under their Elvish names.

"Yes."

The female pulled on her blue sundress that covered all her tattoos but not much else. Law rarely could get her to wear much more; the elf liked the ease of undressing. Law wasn't sure what they were going to do come winter.

Bare Snow dropped back to Elvish. "What are pierogies again?"

"Potato and cheese dumplings." The elves didn't have potatoes, as keva beans were firmly established as their main starch crop before potatoes were introduced in Europe on Earth. Nor did they have peanuts, which probably explained their fixation with peanut butter.

"Ah, yes, pierogies are good." Bare Snow unbraided her long blue-black hair, taking out long sharp ironwood needles as she did. They were going to see Usagi's kids, who loved to play with Bare Snow's hair.

Law explained what she'd learned from Alton.

Bare Snow added what she'd found out. "The gunfire was Tinker *domi*'s troops clearing the oni invaders out of her cousin's enclave. I arrived too late to help, beyond saving a puppy. It was so sad; she loves her cousin so much. She was very upset but Prince True Flame kept her from taking her grievances to the Stone Clan. That would not have gone well for the Wind Clan."

Considering what she learned at Caraway's, no, it would not have gone well. "Can these Harbingers be trusted?"

"They are old and clever, with ancient grudges. They are like a blind swordsman filled with rage; they will attack anything that moves. It could make them easy to manipulate. The Harbingers might have sided with Tinker *domi*. They abhor spell-working. Cana Lily, though, abhors the Wind Clan. He is a warlord from the Clan War. He would have gladly given Tinker the fight she sought and the Harbingers would have backed Cana Lily."

"Oh joy."

"What's more, since the Skin Clan attempted to prolong the Clan War, it is possible that Cana Lily has always been one of their pawns."

❖          ❖          ❖

Law admired her fellow Pittsburghers. Hell or high water, they were determined to live their normal life. Oktoberfest was an ancient Earth festival imported from Europe ages before the first Startup by immigrant steelworkers. Law believed that the original festival had been held in October (hence the name) but it had been combined with the elf harvest celebration that started a week or so before the fall equinox. (Elves did not have holidays but holy weeks.) Since it featured drinking large quantities of beer, the humans aimed for Friday and Saturday instead of a set day, thus the date was fluid.

The festival was normally held at the fairground that doubled as the gossamer airfield. The war made that impossible, so the powers that be had moved it to the converted railroad station of Station Square. It was a trade-off between access to the light-rail and the constant danger that the riverfront presented. All week a brave and cautious work crew had erected fences along the shoreline.

Law had three deliveries to make, all last-minute calls. Ellen inquired about the possibility of chestnuts, Tiffani begged for *pesantiki*, and Trixie demanded apples. (Knowing Trixie, her demand was to cover her embarrassment for having to ask for help.) Without Bare Snow, Law would have never been able to gather everything on top of her enclave orders. She arrived too late to drive into Station Square proper; the long driveway was closed. She parked across the street in the old Hooters parking lot.

Law unloaded her Dodge into her two Radio Flyer cargo wagons. Brisbane tried to climb in with the McIntosh apples.

"No way. You won't eat just one. You get in the fish." Law used a slightly wormy-looking apple to lure him into the other wagon. He climbed in, complaining loudly. The porcupine was the size of a kindergartener and at times just as loud.

She started off with the apples and nuts, confident that Bare Snow would follow with Brisbane and the fish. They crossed the street that led to Smithfield Bridge.

The elf part of the festival had started several days earlier with setting up a temporary home for the religious shrines that guarded over the grounds. A wooden platform and roof had been handcrafted without any nails. Pennants flew overhead, mostly Wind Clan blue and Fire Clan red but with a sprinkling of Pittsburgh black and gold as a dodge around displaying Stone Clan color. The stiff plastic rustled in the wind like dozens of little people clapping.

An odd low roaring sound came from across the river. Law paused at the corner to look across the Smithfield Bridge. An elf with a bullroarer was leading a parade across the bridge. The instrument roared as he spun it in a wide circle.

"We're just in time," Law said. "Here comes the shrine."

"Gouni is coming!" Bare Snow clapped her hands and gave a little bounce of excitement. The autumn equinox was dedicated to the Goddess of Life and Harvest. Over the last week, it had become apparent that Gouni was the elf version of Santa Claus—if Santa Claus was a cheap bastard that only gave out blessings and roasted keva beans. Seriously, Law could not see the appeal but she knew that Bare Snow desperately wanted to be blessed by the priestess.

"They take forever to get the shrine into place," Law said. "If we hurry, we can be done to receive the blessing."

The old station building had been converted into a pub favored by the human train personnel. Law had spent many afternoons at the pub with her grandfather and other local retired railroad employees. It was a grand place with tall marble columns, an arched ceiling, rich detailed woodwork and beautiful stained-glass windows. It served killer bruschetta and Shirley Temple cocktails. It almost made her like being force-fed information on trains. Across the street from the station was the old Freight House that now housed several Earth chain stores, all closed due to Tinker destroying the orbital gate. It was no wonder that the pub leapt at the chance to host Oktoberfest.

The two-lane drive past the Freight House was closed to traffic. Booths lined it on either side. Bare Snow pointed in excitement at them. Jewelry. Handcrafted toys. Hot food. Games of chance. Everything locally grown and crafted.

The tenth booth in was Usagi's household. They were doing a simple ring-toss game with very cute, handmade, stuffed rabbits as prizes. All the half-elf kids were there, wearing rabbit hats that covered their pointed ears.

"Law!" The oldest, Moon Rabbit, bounded up to Law. The girl was going through a neon pink phase. She had on a bright pink rabbit onesie in lieu of a rabbit hat. "Law! Law!" She bounced up and down, making her ears and big cottontail flop. "Where's big sister?"

Law wasn't sure how anyone could miss the sexiest thing on two legs pulling a porcupine in a large red wagon. She could *hear* Brisbane complaining that he'd finished his apple. She glanced behind her and spotted the flash of red. "Right there."

The children launched themselves at Bare Snow and Brisbane with squeals of excitement that could shatter glass.

"You're here alone?" Law asked as Usagi hugged her.

"Clover is home with the two babies. Babs had a baby to deliver in the South Hills. Hazel is at work. The EIA worked some deal to get all the bakeries in town flour from the Westernlands. They're paying her in food that we desperately need. Widget got hauled off by a boy from the bakery; something about life and death and needing her computer skills."

It left Usagi outnumbered five to one.

"Do you need help?" Law felt she needed to ask even though babysitting wasn't her strong suit.

Usagi waved off the offer. "Hazel will take them home after she gets off work. I told them they could stay until dusk. They've been sewing rabbits for a week, it's the least I can do."

"They made these?" Law picked up one of the stuffed toys.

"The older kids did." She dropped her voice to a whisper. "The bunnies that the little ones made were really ugly so we're going to give them to any annoying drunks that win."

They had a solid barrier to prevent cheating, painted with happy bunnies to disguise the fact that it was a deterrent. A tape measure and graph paper showed that Usagi had left nothing to chance. She had everything carefully mapped out to maximize her profits.

"What do you expect to clear?" Law said.

Usagi looked slightly worried. "We need this to pay for

heat this winter. We were screwed out of a lot of money when we were cut off from Earth. July is our biggest jam production run and we collect on those deliveries in August at Shutdown." Which never happened.

Usagi picked up one of the bunnies. "Each bunny is a sock with some stuffing and two beads for eyes. The socks were free; the cuffs were frayed. I wasn't sure what I was going to do with six hundred pairs of socks but free is free. We're charging a quarter a game with a win ratio of four to one. I'm hoping to make close to a thousand dollars."

It was a drawback of living in a commune large enough to take Usagi's sprawling household of five women and their seven children. All the women pitched in money and time but it was Usagi that figured out how to make it all work. It would scare Law silly to have so many people dependent on her.

Law was good at rescuing damsels in distress. "If you want, we can rig up some kind of wood burner. They're not that hard to make. I can get you a cord of firewood before it starts to snow. It would be good to have, anyhow, in case the power goes off."

Usagi hugged her hard. "Thank you, Law. You're a lifesaver."

Law turned around to discover Bare Snow was passing out their fish. "What are you doing?"

"Little sister Moon Rabbit wanted a *pesantiki* but she didn't have any money to play the game," Bare Snow stated calmly. "And it would not be fair just to give one to her and not to the others. We have many. A few will not be missed."

The children had found clear plastic drinking cups and stood huddled around the wagon.

Law could not say no. Bare Snow had spent hours catching the fish; she had the right to give some away. Bare Snow liked playing big sister; it gave her the family that she'd always wanted. Law suspected too that it wasn't frivolous pretending. Moon Rabbit looked six years old when she was in her teens. If the children continued to age slowly, they'd need Bare Snow in a few decades.

The children "ooohed" and "ahhhed" over the little gleaming gold fish with large flowing fins.

"I'm sorry," Law murmured to Usagi. She'd learned long ago that it was a bad thing to give pets to children. Parents hated you for it.

"It's okay. I have a big aquarium somewhere in our basement. A biology student was throwing it out instead of taking it back to Earth. Free is free."

Law felt a little less guilty.

Bare Snow's long blue-black hair was up in Sailor Moon twin ponytails when they left Usagi's booth. They found Tiffani still struggling to hang the decorations on her booth.

"What a stupid time to break my arm," Tiffani complained.

"There's a good time?" Law took the banner and tacked it firmly into place.

"Don't make me hit you." Tiffani raised a thick cast on her right arm. She'd painted it with roses and thorns to match the sleeve tattoo that it covered. "It will hurt both of us more than we want."

"Are you going to need help to run your booth?" Law asked.

"Nah, once the decorations are up, it's just collect

the money, pass out nets, and wrap up winnings in plastic bags. I could do it in my sleep. Thanks for getting me fish. I would have been shit out of luck and fifty bucks."

Tiffani smelled strongly of marijuana.

"You sure?" Law asked.

"What? Oh!" She sniffed herself. "That! I only wish I was high at the moment. The hospital wouldn't give me anything for the pain. It's either moonshine or weed. Marijuana isn't any worse than Nyquil in terms of stuff like driving or cooking. Moonshine? Oh, that stuff kicks me on my ass."

"Nothing for pain?"

"They're saving it for when the fighting gets serious. I'm like 'Serious? What are you calling all the bodies piled up on the sidewalks?' And they're like 'That's just oni dead. We don't treat oni. We're talking human causalities.' What bullshit. Half of the EIA are oni. Whatever. I'm really hating this; the pain makes me a bitch on wheels. I'm going to be fun tonight with sixty zillion screaming little kids and drunk guys going 'I'll get you a freaking fish' and looking like assholes because they can't and being mad about it. After a while, I just want to stuff the fish down their throats."

"Are you sure you don't need help? I don't want to be bailing you out of jail again. You would have been deported if Johnnie Be Good had pressed charges."

"I am fine! And the pervert had that ass-kicking coming."

Law had to agree to that.

"I don't want to be high for this." Tiffani leaned close to whisper. "So far both sides are leaving humans out of the fighting but I figure that's only going to last so long. Beer, food and music in one place? Half of Pittsburgh is going to be here tonight. It makes for a damn big target."

Law's insides churned at the thought. According to the newspapers, the oni had kidnapped, tortured, raped, and eaten an unknown number of elf children. The Skin Clan troops fought on the sly, setting traps and using people as bait. She hated the idea of these people targeting the festival for no other reason than to pit the humans against the elves.

"I've got my escape route planned. I didn't park over there." Tiffani pointed toward the Hooters lot that served as main parking for the festival. Station Square's five-storied garage was slated to be a make-shift beer hall for all the microbreweries. "The way I figure it, everyone's going to either be running to their cars, or to the incline or to the light-rail and things will be all jammed up." She shifted to point at the low chain-link fence that ran alongside Station Square. On the other side was the Elfhome main line. A second temporary fence had been erected beyond the tracks to protect people from jumpfish. "The train tracks are right there, close enough to touch. I parked downriver at the freight yard and walked up to here. If the oni attack, all I need to do is grab my cashbox and go. Sorry, fish." She pretended to wave goodbye to the *pesantiki*. "You're dead meat."

Tiffani was right about the escape routes that the masses would take. Usagi would need to take the incline; it was the only direct way to get up to her place at the top of Mount Washington. There was a meandering back road on the other side of the ridge, but Usagi hadn't brought a car at the festival.

Law shifted uncomfortably as the possible targets shifted closer to her heart. She wanted to rage out into the city and make sure that no harm came to her close friends. "You've got my number. If anyone causes any problems or acts weird or you think that something fishy might be in the works, call me."

Ellen's tiny-house lunch counter was sitting on prime real estate across the street from the parking garage. Her trailer had been tucked beside the porte-cochere of the old Sheraton Hotel. She'd set up picnic tables under the porch roof and the scent of a wood grill was floating up from the back.

"Oh, please tell me that you found chestnuts!" Ellen said in greeting.

"Of course I did. Fifty pounds." Law lifted the five-gallon buckets out of the wagon. Elfhome and American chestnut trees had hybridized to create a larger, sweeter nut that ripened earlier. "I want my buckets back but I can wait until Monday."

"Here, taste this." Ellen held out a bratwurst in a bun.

It was an explosion of taste in Law's mouth. "That's good. Is that a honey mustard sauce? That's really good. What kind of bread is that?"

"Bean flour," Ellen cried. "I could not track down any wheat so I ground some dried navy beans. I'm allergic to wheat so I use it for myself all the time."

"It's good. Just different."

"I know it's good; I wouldn't sell it if it wasn't good. It's just that people don't like different; that's why I wanted the chestnuts. I need to sell something to make up the cost of the booth."

"People will buy it," Law stated. "Pittsburghers will

eat anything that doesn't bite them back. The rest will be too drunk to notice."

Ellen laughed. "I hope you're right. I'm short on money; all I have are ones and fives for the cash box. Can I pay you when you pick up your buckets?"

Ellen normally prided herself on paying up front. It had been a hard summer on everyone with the military lockdowns, but hardest on people like her. Between being cut off from their regular providers and their customers hoarding cash for the winter, small business owners were struggling.

"Sure, no problem," Law said

"How much do I owe you?" Ellen asked.

"Twenty bucks."

Ellen smacked her.

"Ow! What's that for?" Law cried.

"I am not a charity case. You've got two mouths to feed."

"We eat very well." Bare Snow had odd ideas as to what a proper diet was. Every meal had to have like thirty ingredients in it. Meat. Grains. Vegetables. Fruits. Spices. All mixed together into little froufrou dishes. "This morning, we had baked apples stuffed with bacon, onions and goat cheese."

"Oh, that sounds good. Get me the recipe."

The recipe seemed to be whatever strayed into Bare Snow's hand, but it was probably more premeditated than that.

"We're making money hand over fist off the enclaves," Law said. "We might be the only people in Pittsburgh currently doing well. I don't need to make a profit off my friends. Besides, if I charge you less, you can charge your customers less, and people will have more fun at the festival. Pittsburgh needs that."

Ellen hugged her hard. "You are a good person, Law. Thank you. These last few weeks have been an utter roller coaster ride. Everyone has been hunkered down in the South Hills, waiting to see if the worst is over yet. I've got all these bratwurst, no customers, and no way to freeze the bloody things. I would have been sunk if the Changs hadn't pulled out of the festival."

"They pulled out? Why?"

"I don't know. Vinnie called saying that one of the Chang boys had roughed him up for the money they put down last year to hold their normal slot."

The Changs traditionally sold meat-on-a-stick at fairs. They put their restaurant-honed skills to use by marinating skewers of chicken, saurus and wild boar in teriyaki sauce and cooking them on massive wood-fired grills. Because they could pump out large amounts of great-tasting food, they usually had the best location at any festival. It explained Ellen's prime real estate.

What Ellen obviously didn't know was that the Changs were half-oni. Law had only put all the clues together a few days before Tommy Chang threw in with the elves. She nearly had whiplash as her long history with the Chang family underwent a drastic rewrite.

What happened that made the Changs pull out of the festival? Had this happened after Trixie called demanding apples to candy? Or was this before, and thus the whole reason Trixie was suddenly scrambling to put together a booth at Oktoberfest?

The big eight-foot-long *zalituus* horns had reached the end of the bridge and started to blow, signaling that the shrine was nearing the end of its journey. Bare Snow started to bounce in place.

"I've got to go!" Law said. "See you Monday!"

The elves that were working booths drifted toward the front entrance, summoned by the horns. Most of the humans were like Law; if they had the time, they would go see the pageantry that the elves were creating. It wasn't their religion so they could easily miss it if they were too busy. A handful of humans countered with human traditions, plastering pilgrim hats and turkeys everywhere despite the fact it was only September.

Law pointed at the back of Ellen's tiny house. "Bare Snow, you can leave that wagon here and go see the shrine installed."

Bare Snow pointed away from the entrance. "No, I want to get funnel cake!"

"Funnel cake?" Law glanced up the street. Yes, three booths up, a bunch of high school students were drizzling batter into hot oil to make the tangled-ribbon cakes. Judging by the "Team Big Sky" banners and their remarks, the kids were younger siblings of the team members who were out looking for Oilcan. The team captain, John Montana, wisely decided that the search was too dangerous for the teenage kids.

"Moon Rabbit says funnel cake is heavenly and I should get lots," Bare Snow said.

And share it when they passed Usagi's again. In certain regards, Moon Rabbit was very much her mother without any brakes.

Law doubted that this funnel cake would measure up to previous years'. Just about anything fried and covered with sugar, however, would be heavenly to a child. "Go on. I'll deliver the apples."

Hopefully Trixie was somewhere ahead.

❖     ❖     ❖

When Law was nine years old, her parents had declared that she was too wild and unmanageable for them to handle. They sent her bouncing between various family members as they focused on throwing hissy fits of mutual selfishness that ended with their divorce. Years eleven and twelve she spent as an unwilling slave to her grandfather, up to her elbows in grease, rebuilding the Dodge and listening to his war stories of setting up the railroad on Elfhome. She ended her servitude by explaining in detail her budding attraction to girls.

She celebrated her freedom by roaming the city all summer, looking for someone to put words into deeds.

She found Trixie, hiding from the oni, not that Law knew that at the time. Trixie had been half-starved, physically scarred, shockingly knowledgeable about all things sexual, and desperately in need of saving. The girl tripped every trigger that Law didn't know that she had. Law fell hard but she was never sure where she stood in Trixie's heart. All the secrets that Trixie refused to tell Law seemed like proof that the girl didn't care about her.

It was embarrassing to realize that Trixie had been keeping Law safe from her own stupidity. Law hadn't been able to imagine anyone that she couldn't level with her fists or trusty "Lady Luck" baseball bat. The oni could have easily killed Law or worse. Law never even imagined worse; she had been too naïve.

Life since June had been an education on worse.

At the very end of the street, right before it opened up to the amphitheater space, Law found the Chang girls. Trixie and three of her younger female cousins were nervously pacing behind a makeshift counter. Hand-painted signs read CANDY APPLES $2.

"Where the hell have you been?" Trixie cried in greeting. She rocked a girly tomboy look with her black hair cut pixie-short, red tank top that flaunted her arm muscles, and tight faded blue jeans. She wasn't starving to death like when they first met, but her jeans made it obvious that she was still painfully skinny. "We couldn't heat the candy until we had the apples." She used her cigarette to light a propane burner. "After we coat the apples, we need to let them cool. We really needed an hour prep time and the shrine is already here."

Law ignored the bitchiness; Trixie was between a rock and a hard place. "I found a small McIntosh orchard that everyone missed." With an uncertain winter looming in front of them, everyone in Pittsburgh was gleaning abandoned farms for fruit. Law was needing to range farther and farther out. "I know this won't last you the whole weekend, but it should get you through today and tomorrow. I'll hit the orchard again and get you more."

Trixie flicked her cigarette onto the asphalt and ground it out with her red ballerina flats. "Tell me where it is and I'll send someone out to it."

"It's near the Rim..."

"They'll have guns." She picked up one of the apples. "If it was rice, it'd be no problem, but you try to explain the difference between McIntosh and Red Delicious to these idiots, you get a blank look."

Trixie meant her male cousins. Apparently she'd tried sending them out to get apples and hit a brick wall of ignorance. Trixie handed the apple to one of the girls that had been unloading the apples into large plastic bins. "Wash them and put them on sticks."

Said male cousins were nowhere to be seen. Whatever

went wrong and made the Chang family pull out of the festival, Trixie had set herself up as the only target.

"Are you okay?" Law whispered.

"We're fine."

"Are you sure? I could help you, if you just tell me . . ."

"Oh, stop!" Trixie kissed Law to silence her. She tasted of cigarettes and beer. With one kiss, they were back to thirteen, when Trixie had been Law's first everything. First crush. First kiss. First sexual fumbling on warm summer nights. First lost love. When Law wouldn't stop asking questions, Trixie enacted a silent treatment that made rocks seem talkative. They didn't break up so much as Law fled the silence.

If Law kept asking now, she risked the fragile friendship they'd built since then.

Law took a deep breath and plunged ahead. Silence was a small price if it kept Trixie from being killed. "Don't brush me off; I'm not thirteen anymore. I understand the danger now. I'm not going to go blindly charging into trouble. I can't help you, though, if you don't tell me the truth."

Trixie snorted in disbelief but didn't push her away. "There's nothing you can do. Tommy took Spot and went after Jewel Tear. He told the rest of us to lay low, but we're out of money and food. This is our one chance to get money before everything blows up in our face."

"Tommy knows where the oni took Jewel Tear?"

"No!" Trixie cried in frustration. She glanced at the girls washing the apples and whispered. "He's shooting blind. The timing was really wonky, so he thinks that the oni still have moles working the railroad.

The inbound trains are all loaded down with royal marines. The outbound, though, are empty except for the crews. It's three hundred miles to the East Coast. The oni could stop the train anywhere between here and there and no one would know."

Someone would know.

Tommy was right. The oni would need to have moles still in place to keep anyone from finding out.

At one time, Pittsburgh had been a mishmash of rail lines. There had been the Pittsburgh and Lake Erie, the Baltimore and Ohio, the Wabash, the Pennsylvania, the Erie Lackawanna, and probably a half-dozen others that Law had forgotten. At the time of the first Startup, the city had been a maze of active and rusty, abandoned tracks. While the humans on Earth focused on creating a massive quarantine zone around the metropolitan area, the people of Pittsburgh worked at consolidating the tracks into one railroad system that stretched out to the East Coast.

The hardest part of building a railroad wasn't laying track, it was creating a solid level track bed with a subgrade layer blanketed by ballast. Through the heart of seven mountains and across countless streams and rivers, the engineers were forced to lay only one track. Every place they could, however, they built sidings where a slower train could sit and allow a faster train traveling the opposite direction to pass.

Most people in Pittsburgh believed that there was only one train in motion at any given time: inbound or outbound. There were, however, always multiple trains incoming and outgoing. A fast-moving set of passenger cars might pass as many as five slower freight trains during its eight-hour trip. It was a little-known fact because the only humans ever to ride on the trains were the crews.

Communication was key when juggling freight trains carrying up to fifteen thousand tons of ore. The individual cars were carefully tracked from being loaded on the East Coast until they were handed off to Earth during Shutdown.

The tracking was done on the upper floors of the Union Station on Liberty Avenue. The building was a beautiful terra-cotta brick with turn-of-the-century charm. Downstairs was complete with a stunning rotunda built to allow horse carriages to unload out of the rain and snow. Ironically with Pittsburgh on Elfhome, the shelter had returned to its original purpose. Big cargo wagons pulled by large draft horses sat under the rotunda. Royal marines were loading tents and personal gear onto the wagons. The Fire Clan soldiers were fresh off the latest passenger train; they shouted in excitement when they spotted Law.

"It's a human! Look! A human!"

The marines crowded around Law.

"Maybe she's a human, maybe she's not," one tall male said. "Oni can disguise themselves so they look like humans. We should test her."

None of the marines seemed to notice Bare Snow skirting the edge of the rotunda. Law tracked her by the flash of blue in amongst the sea of red.

"Okay. Test me." Law put out her arm. She'd been tested earlier in the summer. The attack on the viceroy made the elves aware of the oni presence. As a food supplier to the enclaves, Law went to the top of the list of "humans we want to be sure are not oni." The

humans running the train and those employed by the
EIA were close seconds. All the moles should have
been ferreted out; unless the moles looked human.

Several of the marines pulled out a spell inked
onto a paper. There was a brief argument as to which
paper would be used. For a while, it seemed like all
of the spells might be applied. It was finally settled
by a furious game of rock-paper-scissors. (Although,
judging by the shouts, in the elf game "scissors" had
been replaced by "flame.")

The activated spell caused a ripple that felt like
static electricity to crawl over Law, spreading out from
her forearm to shoulder to scalp and then down her
back. Every hair on her body stood on end. Nothing
else happened.

There was visible disappointment on the marines'
faces when Law's appearance didn't change.

"Maybe it didn't work." The marine that lost the
rock-paper-flame game held out his unused spell.
"Maybe we should try again."

"No!" the rest cried out in a chorus.

An officer shouted from the front of the wagon.
"Stop talking with the native and get that wagon
loaded, you lazy slackers!"

*Native?* It was the first time Law had been called
that. She had been born on Elfhome, although if
asked she would have said she was born in Pittsburgh.

The marines loaded the last of the tents onto the
wagon. The driver flicked the reins to start the big
horses. They trotted out of the rotunda with the clatter of metal horseshoes on stone paving.

"Move out!" the officer shouted.

The marine still holding the unused spell paper

tried to stuff it away. The paper refused to cooperate. He finally thrust it at Law. "Here! For being patient."

*Free is free.* Law bowed. "Thank you."

The control room was a large, mind-boggling place. The longest wall was covered entirely by giant monitors showing the crazy spiderweb of tracks in Pittsburgh. Much of the tangle was the large freight yard at the foot of West End Bridge. From there were the dozens of dispersal lines that only led to Earth during Shutdown. A single thread leapt out across the room to a small web on the East Coast. Gleaming LED lights indicated train locations. Flickering indicated trains in motion. A vast amount of the network was dark, dormant, waiting on a miracle that would reconnect Pittsburgh to Earth.

A dozen workstations were positioned so they could see the wall in a single glance. Each had yet more screens, more buttons than God, and several computer keyboards. Law had been told countless stories about the room and how the controls had been greatly simplified for the elves. Law had assumed that she would *know* how to find what she was looking for.

"Yeah, yeah, just go and find out where all the trains are and where they've been," she whispered as she wandered through the room, eyeing the hundreds of buttons and switches. Where was everyone? According to her grandfather, it was vital that the tracks were continuously monitored to avoid any collisions.

The workstations were complete mysteries. She decided to ignore them and studied the wall instead. There were four trains showing on the board. One was the passenger train that had delivered the royal marines. It should be on its way to the freight yard in order to have its toilets emptied and the diesel engine refueled. It was just sitting at Union Station, idling. Law had heard that the railroad had been virtually stripped of human employees. It had left the elves too shorthanded to keep the system running smoothly.

Another train sat in the first siding beyond the Rim. Law couldn't see what it was waiting on. If the mystery train was outbound, then there was nothing in its way for a hundred miles. If it was inbound, it would take precedence over the empty passenger train.

It seemed unlikely that the oni used the mystery train to transport Jewel Tear; it was too close to Pittsburgh. The city roads ended at the edge of the siding. The oni could have driven to that point within an hour. A train sitting for days would have drawn more attention than one car, even out that far.

Law studied the other two trains on the board. One was on the East Coast, just pulling out of the distant station. The other was inbound but hours away. Judging by its speed, the incoming train was another passenger train loaded with marines. They had been arriving nonstop for most of the week, hundreds at a time. If either train had been used to transport Jewel Tear, the elf was no longer on it.

How was she going to find where the oni stopped the supposedly empty outbound train?

A slight noise made her turn. A male elf in Wind Clan blue walked into the room from a door she hadn't noticed.

"Who are you?" He came steamrolling toward her. "What are you doing here? This is a restricted area."

Law backpedaled to keep out of reach of him. "I'm Joe Casey's granddaughter. He's a safety inspector..."

"Casey is dead." He tried to catch hold of her arm.

Law dodged around one of the workstations. She pointed at the lone gleaming light on the wall. "I just wanted to know: what's that train there?"

He didn't even glance at the wall. "That is none of your business. You are not allowed in here. You must leave immediately."

Law decided to show some of her cards in a bid to get him on her side. "I think the oni have control of that train."

That made him pause. "Who told you that?"

She didn't want to name Trixie since the girl hadn't been identified as a half-oni, nor Tommy Chang, since it might poison the elves against anything she said. "What is that train? Is it supposed to be there?"

His body language changed from "I want you to leave" to "I don't want you to escape." He stalked forward, eyes narrowing. "Who knows about..."

Law realized she'd made a mistake. She'd backed into a corner in her attempt to keep from being thrown out before she had her say. *Okay, this is about to get ugly.*

He jerked to a halt as a flash of blue in Law's side vision announced Bare Snow's presence. His eyes widened as he recognized Bare Snow's blue-black hair and storm-gray eyes. He backed up, fear spreading across his face.

He *knew* that Bare Snow was an assassin when none of the elves at the enclaves did.

The only people that knew of Bare Snow's training were the ones that had tricked her into coming to Pittsburgh and tried to frame her for the attack on Windwolf.

He was Skin Clan.

Law punched him as hard as she could in a full roundhouse.

He went down and came back up with knives.

"Whoa!" Law jumped back. She hit the wall and tried to keep backing up.

He knew which one of them was more dangerous. He backpedaled, slashing at Bare Snow. His knives were human-made with blades of plain steel. Bare Snow parried his attacks. Made of magically sharped ironwood, her knives sliced through his. The steel blades went flying to land with a faint metallic ring.

With a hard lunge, Bare Snow nailed him to the wall with a knife through his right collarbone. The male cried out in pain. He started to curl around the blade but froze as Bare Snow pressed the tip of her other knife to his throat.

"Don't kill him!" Law shouted.

"Why? He's one of the Skin Clan's mindless drones."

"We need to ask him questions."

"He doesn't know anything," Bare Snow growled. "He does their busy work without even knowing their true plans, happy with his ignorance. If he does know anything useful, he'll die before he'll tell us."

"We could at least try asking him." Law needed to explain "good cop/bad cop" to Bare Snow at some point.

Bare Snow snorted in contempt. "For thousands of years, they've believed the lies that their master told them. That they are superior to their fellow slaves. That their fellow slaves are nothing more than disobedient furniture. That our people have no more right than a chair to say what happens to their bodies."

The male sneered at Bare Snow. "You worship at

the altar of the gods and yet you refuse the same loyalty to your creator."

"They're thieves!" Bare Snow cried. "They steal everything! They stole everything that the gods gave to us. Like petty little children, they sifted through everything they'd stolen, tossed what they didn't want into a dung heap, and then acted like everything else was their creation."

"Bare! Bare!" Law cried as the tip of the blade had drawn blood. "One question!" Law pointed at the track display. "You can save yourself if you just tell us what you know about that train. Why is it just sitting there?"

"Shut up, monkey!" the male growled. "You gibber away pretending to speak our language when all you're doing is aping the sounds. Nothing has been done to improve your people since you climbed down out of the trees. You still cling to the stupid idea of paradise after you're dead because you live short, disease-ridden lives. Your people are only good as a constant reminder of how much our lords have done for us. That they will do again. We will be gods and you will stay ugly little..."

"My Law is not ugly!" Bare Snow shoved the blade home.

"Bare!" Law cried. "No!"

It was too late; the male was dead.

"Oh jeez, Bare! We didn't find out anything."

"He did not want to tell us about the train." Bare Snow jerked out her knife to let his dead body slide down the wall. It left a smear of blood. "There are others of his ilk here. If the train were not important, he would have delayed us by answering all our questions in detail."

Law glanced at the wall. What was so important about the train that he was willing to die for it?

The Elfhome railroad followed the Monongahela, bending and twisting with the river, the track bed built up from the level flood plains. At Charleroi, it used a newly built bridge to cross over the river. Beyond that point, the right of way wound its way in a mostly eastward direction, cutting through empty towns and abandoned farmland. The Rim had taken out the little town of Wyano leaving behind a large level area to build a siding.

Law took old Route 70 to Wyano. At the exit ramp, she turned off her motor. The back roads were quiet places and the oni would hear her Dodge coming. She coasted down the long hill into Wyano. The Rim sliced across through the heart of the small town, a thin band of destruction backed by towering mature ironwood trees. The forest was overtaking the town with saplings overshadowing the Earth maples and black cherries.

Just shy of the Rim, Law pulled into a weed-choked driveway.

"We'll walk the rest of the way. It will be quieter." Law climbed out. Brisbane scrambled down from the cab. "You stay with the Dodge, Brizzy."

Brisbane complained loudly.

"You're too loud and you walk too slow." She pulled out a sack of wormy apples from the back of the truck. "I'll make sure you won't starve. You wait here."

He grunted in disgust but accepted the offering of apples poured into a small pile beside the Dodge. She tried to estimate what he might eat in an hour since she didn't want him wandering off; they might have to leave quickly.

She'd bought an illegal fully automatic Glock pistol in July. She never wanted to be on the losing end of a gunfight again. She belted on her holster and then checked the Glock's magazine. She made sure she had her Bowie knife, a fanny pack of zip-ties, and her stungun/flashlight combo.

Bare Snow stripped down to her lovely alabaster skin. In the leafy shadows, her white-ink tattoos were imperceptible. She stretched in all manner of distracting ways. It did all sorts of things to Law's heart to watch her. It had only been three months, but she couldn't imagine life without Bare Snow.

"We need to be careful." Law knew that it didn't need to be said; Bare Snow had "careful" beaten into her by her mother. Law had been the one who had gotten shot in their last big fight. Still it felt like asking for a blessing; things would be good because they spoke the words aloud.

"They won't know what hit them!" Bare Snow cried in English. Law wasn't sure where she learned the phrase until Bare Snow added, "In the name of the moon, I will punish them." She struck a Sailor Moon pose.

Walking with Bare Snow was like walking alone. Law knew that she was nearby but could neither see nor hear the female. Another person, she would have suspected of running ahead or falling behind, but she knew that Bare Snow worried for Law's safety and kept close.

They crossed the cracked pavement of the abandoned

street. Wyano had been a scattering of two-story wooden farmhouses on large lots. The paint on the homes had peeled off long ago and the exposed wood turned to gray. The houses hunched like ghosts in yards given over to ironwood saplings. Law picked her way carefully through the dead leaves, trying not to make noise and failing. Hidden sticks snapped and popped under Law's feet. Someplace nearby, Bare Snow walked silently. Law caught sight of her shadow once or twice and wished that she hadn't. It would be better if Bare Snow's invisibility were flawless.

The saplings became mature trees as they crossed the Rim. Another fifty feet of virgin forest and they reached the main line railroad tracks. Ironwoods overshadowed the track bed, keeping the berm free of underbrush. The twin shining rails came from the west in a straight shot. To the east, they disappeared around a bend as the track bed curved to avoid a steep hillside. Law's footsteps crunched loudly on the crushed rock ballast. She shifted over to the creosote-soaked wooden ties.

They'd walked for only half a mile before Law could pick out voices in the distance. She moved back into the shadows of the forest. The ironwood trees had been trimmed back to make room for the siding. The switch was set to let the main line trains pass. Because of the thick row of trees between the two sets of tracks, the passing trains couldn't see the mystery train sitting in the siding.

It was a twelve-car passenger train. Its wedge-nosed diesel engine purred in a rough idle, facing west toward Pittsburgh. Royal marines moved purposely in and out of the forest beside the siding. It looked as if all eighty-four seats of the passenger cars were full, putting the number of marines on board at a thousand. The last car was a general-purpose flatcar. It was stacked with the tents like the ones she'd seen the marines loading onto the horse-drawn wagons at Union Station.

Law crouched in the shadows, feeling relieved and disappointed. The mystery train was just another troop carrier bringing in more royal marines. The other two inbound trains were probably more of the same. Law couldn't tell why this one had stopped or what the marines were doing. Something felt very wrong but she couldn't put a finger on it.

She cautiously worked her way toward the trees where the marines were coming and going. Any time she'd dealt with the Fire Clan troops, they'd always been curious and nonthreatening, but that was in Pittsburgh, where they expected to find humans. They might not be so friendly if she popped up unannounced in the woods.

The marines had beaten a path through the bracken. Their footprints were deep, as if they had carried something heavy into the forest. She'd gone several hundred feet down the path before she found the naked body.

Law stumbled to a halt, covering her mouth to keep in a shout of dismay. It was a young male elf. His hair was Fire Clan red. His skin was a strange cherry color. Law tore her gaze from the body and scanned the area. Ahead of her lay hundreds of bodies, all naked, all cherry red. What in hell happened to them? Why were the marines dumping them here? Elves had a thing about cremation; they thought it freed the soul from the body. This was an abomination to them.

She stumbled deeper into the forest, trying to understand what she was seeing. She wasn't even sure what killed the elves. They appeared to be all in the same stage of rigor mortis, which meant they all died about three hours earlier.

An odd shift of shadows and the scent of bruised apples told her that Bare Snow was beside her.

"*Kyanos* poisoning," Bare Snow whispered. "I wonder how the oni poisoned them. It could not have been by something they drank or ate or they would not all have died at the same time. I know of no magic that could do this."

Traps were tricky things. A crayfish trap was only effective for a short time; given enough time, even brainless crayfish figured out a way to escape. How could you kill a thousand people?

"I don't know about this *kyanos* poison," Law said. "If it can be made into a gas, it would be a way you could kill this many people at once. The train goes through several tunnels. That would restrict the airflow. If they released a gas just as the train entered a tunnel, then it would remain trapped in the passenger cars. It would be like a mobile gas chamber. But why kill them? Who are they?"

"These are *laedin*-caste Fire Clan. These must be the real royal marines. What we saw were disguised oni in stolen uniforms."

"Are you sure?"

"How those others move is wrong. There is no cohesion. Their stride is too wild."

Law thought of the troops she'd seen in town.

Despite their fearless curiosity, the marines still moved like soldiers. They set guards that stood at parade rest. They unconsciously matched strides when they walked abreast. What's more, she had only seen males at the siding. The elves did gender equality in spades; between immortality and their low birth rate, females weren't restricted to support positions. The marines in town had been an equal mix of males and females.

"*Half of Pittsburgh is going to be here,*" Tiffani had said. "*It makes for a damn big target. I'm going to walk up to the train tracks...they're right there close enough to touch.*"

"Shit!" Law hissed. The oni were going to attack Oktoberfest dressed as elves! It would be a massacre. Anyone that survived would testify on the victims' grave that the killers were royal marines. Every human in Pittsburgh would take up weapons against the elves.

She had to stop that train. Somehow. She thought of the thousand armed oni dressed as marines. First she should warn someone, just in case she failed. She ducked behind a massive ironwood and took her phone out of her pocket. There was no signal. She waved her phone about, hoping to pick up something.

Who should she call? The EIA? She didn't trust them. Pittsburgh Police? No, getting more humans involved would just play to the Skin Clan's plan. It had to be elves. She needed to get hold of someone like Chili Pepper; he'd listen to her. The enclaves, however, didn't have phones.

Thinking of Chili Pepper reminded her of her conversation with Alton. The Kryskills had connections with the tengu; otherwise Alton wouldn't know where Jin Wong was or how to get hold of him. The elves trusted the tengu because they belonged to Tinker. Alton could get a message to Windwolf through the tengu.

One bar appeared in her phone's signal indicator. She tapped Alton's number. "Come on! Go through!"

Alton answered his phone with, "Who's this?"

"It's me, Law!" she whispered.

"Lawrie? Did you find Oilcan? Where is he?"

"Shut up and listen! The oni have control of one of the passenger trains."

"What? Say again?"

She risked talking louder. "The oni captured a passenger train! They have an inbound train."

There was a pause and she was afraid she'd lost her signal. After a moment, Alton said, "Roger that."

"Get a hold of Windwolf and the elves. They have to get to Station Square."

"Say . . ." The line went choppy. "Lawrie? Windwolf needs to go where? Union Station?"

She peeked around the tree toward the sidling. There were no oni in sight. She spoke louder. "Oktoberfest! Station Square!"

"South Side?"

"Yes! The oni are going to attack the festival!"

"Say . . ."

Her phone went silent. "Shitshitshitshit." The signal indicator was blank. She turned in a circle, trying to pick up a signal again. Nothing.

Hopefully Alton had gotten enough to do something. She swept her phone in a circle. She should call Usagi and the others and tell them to go home—

There was a loud metal clank from the direction of the siding. Law jerked around. The engine seemed louder than before. The air brakes hissed loudly as they released.

The oni were leaving!

Law took off running. Usagi and the kids! Ellen! Trixie! They would all be caught in the gunfire. If Alton didn't understand the message—if he wasn't connected as tightly with the tengu as she thought—if he wasn't the man she thought he was . . .

The consequences were sickening.

At the edge of the forest, Bare Snow caught her. She jerked Law to a halt still deep in the shadows. "Wait! They'll see you!"

The train was pulling away.

"We have to stop it!" Law whispered fiercely. She tried to tug free.

Bare Snow tightened her hold on Law's wrist. "They will kill you if they see you!"

"I have to try!"

"You will fail." Bare Snow was frustratingly calm. "I could hide from a thousand eyes, but you cannot. It would only take one oni with a gun and I'd be alone. I would not be able to kill them all and I cannot stop the train without you. We must find another way."

"There isn't another way!" Law wanted to shout, but locked her jaw against it. Bare Snow didn't know anything about trains. It was impossible to leap onto a train once it was up to speed unless you were moving at the same speed. The track bed was too wide to jump from a vehicle on the service road. Law could drive the Dodge onto the tracks, but the ties would make jumping from the hood to the back of the train iffy as hell. There was also the question of who was going to be driving while Law jumped. The same reason she could get the Dodge onto the tracks also meant it could easily go back off. Bare Snow knew the mechanics of driving but still constantly stalled the Dodge.

How else could they catch the train? Law tried to recall everything her grandfather told her about the tracks east of the city. There wasn't another siding until the split of the rails just before Station Square and that was too close to the crowd. If they derailed the train there, it could go flying into the Hooters parking lot.

There was the supply terminal. During Shutdown, barges on the Monongahela River offloaded rail supplies at Charleroi. Since there wasn't a service road for most of the tracks eastward, the railroad had a fleet of maintenance vehicles that could travel on the rails.

"We could get one of the hi-rails." Law turned toward the Dodge. "It's a pickup truck that can be driven either on the highway or tracks. The railroad has some Land Cruisers that have conversion kits mounted on them. They're also automatics with cruise control."

"They have what?" Bare Snow released her hold on Law.

"It will stay at the same speed by itself. You don't need to keep your foot on the gas. There should be at least one Land Cruiser at the terminal."

Once they had the hi-rail, they could ambush the train.

"Here it comes." Law gripped the wheel of the hi-rail.

She couldn't actually see the engine; they'd decided to hide the Land Cruiser behind the Charleroi Water Filtration Plant. The low red-brick building stretched for several hundred feet beside the tracks. Traveling at sixty miles per hour, the train had triggered the crossing on the next block. The automatic system clanged as it lowered its gate, blocking an intersection that most likely no one had used for years.

Bare Snow was on the long flat rooftop of the water filtration plant. She had Law's compound bow with her. Once upon a time, Law had cringed over how much money she had sunk into the top-of-the-line weapon. Now she considered it worth every penny.

The engine roared past Law's hiding space. She braced herself, foot on the brake, counting cars as they flashed past the filtration plant's driveway. "One. Two. Three." They were still too far out to pick up a cell signal in the river valley. She wished there had been time to break into the terminal building proper and use the landline. She was counting on Alton to act as backup when really she had no clue if he could. Did he get hold of Jin Wong? Did the tengu spiritual leader convince Windwolf to go to Station Square? Had anyone thought to disperse the crowds? Was Usagi still there with all the children? Usagi had promised the half-elves that they could stay until dusk which was still hours away. "Nine. Ten. Eleven." She gripped the wheel tightly. Over the whine and ringing of the steel wheels on steel track, she could make out Bare Snow's running footsteps.

The open car flashed past. There were bodies sprawled on the tents, arrows standing out like exclamation points. One warrior stood in the very back, bringing up his rifle as if he'd just become aware of the death around him. There was a whisper of bowstring and he fell. Did he shout a warning before dying? Would there be a welcoming party when they tried scrambling onto the train?

The Land Cruiser dipped slightly as Bare Snow landed on the roof. She slid into the open passenger window. "Go!"

Law raced the hi-rail down the block, keeping just out of sight of the oni in the last passenger car. They reached the crossing just as the gate came up. She hit the conversion switch. The Land Cruiser's AI took control of the steering wheel, found the tracks, positioned the SUV, and lowered the steel wheels into place. It only took twenty seconds but it seemed forever.

"Go! Go! They're getting away!" Bare Snow cried.

"We'll catch them!" Law hit the gas the moment she felt the car raise up, lifting the regular wheels off the ground. "We can go faster than them."

They caught up to the train in two minutes. Law eased up until the Land Cruiser's bumper was as close as she dared bring it to the train. "Get across and I'll follow."

A minute later, Bare Snow's blue hair scarf appeared on the back of the train. Tied to one of the tent poles, it fluttered in the wind. Law set the cruise control. She shouldered a backpack of tools and opened her door. The track bed was a blur of motion under the Land Cruiser.

"This would be a bad time to suddenly be clumsy." Nervousness rushed through Law as she scrambled up onto the roof of the SUV. Normally she enjoyed rushing into trouble to play knight in shining armor. This was different. This wasn't some muscle-bound idiot who would underestimate her until she landed her first hit. This was several tons of brute mechanical force. It wouldn't even notice her as it rolled over her body.

*Think of the kids. Moon Rabbit and the others. Trixie. Usagi. Ellen. Tiffani.*

Law steeled herself against the fear rushing through her. She took a deep breath. She charged down the windshield, across the hood and leapt.

There was a terrifying moment where she was sure that she wouldn't make it. The train seemed to suddenly lurch forward, out of her reach. And then Bare Snow had her by the wrist, hauling her onto the train.

Law scrambled wildly, hissing curses in fear. Wind blasted over her, trying to shove her from the flatcar. She found her balance, splayed out on the tent like a scared starfish.

"This is fun!" Bare Snow said.

"Fun as a barrelful of monkeys," Law grumbled.

"I'm not sure being in packed into a barrel would be fun for monkeys."

There was a dead body beside Law; the last "marine" that Bare Snow shot. The arrow had pierced his eye, killing him instantly. His blood stained the white canvas of the tents. Law pulled the spell paper out of her pocket. She took a photo of it with her phone and then used it on the body. She wanted to be sure these were actually oni before she tried killing them all.

It was a weird thing. Nothing seemed to change, and yet he appeared completely different. His hair stayed red and the general outline of his face remained square. His skin took on a reddish hue. His nose was flatter. He had nubs of horns.

"Oni," Bare Snow stated quietly.

It meant that Law was right about Station Square being the oni's target.

"Come on." Law picked her way across the bloodied tents.

The passenger cars had a windowed door at either

end. They were hooked together with flexible gangway connections. It meant that once she and Bare Snow were on the roof, they could travel the whole way to the front of the train without jumping. Getting past the first window while they scaled the door was going to be tricky.

Law explained the problem to Bare Snow. "There's a bathroom at the back of the car, so there's a buffer between the chairs and the door. If the chairs are all faced to the front, then no one should see us. See me."

"I'll check." It seemed like eternity before Bare Snow called simply, "Go."

Law leapt on pure faith that Bare Snow had moved out of the way and that the oni wouldn't see her. It was a fairly easy leap but the landing was a narrow sill. She gripped tightly to the gangway material. She ducked down when she landed. She rose slightly to peek through the window.

The seats faced forward. Most of the oni sat, seemingly bored after the long train ride from wherever they killed the marines. The few stood watching the passing landscape intently, as if waiting to see familiar landmarks. None were looking in her direction.

She stood up and caught hold of the upper sill of the gangway connection. She scrambled up to the roof as quickly as she could.

The train stretched out in front of her like a quarter-mile-long silvery snake.

She and Bare Snow had been moving at top speed since chasing after the train. The high span of the Elizabeth Bridge, though, was already in sight. It leapt from the ridges that lined both sides of the Monongahela River. Miles were disappearing faster

than Law wanted. She wanted to run to the head of
the snake and chop it off, but that courted disaster.
Unlike freight trains, the passenger car roofs were
rounded and smooth. No one was supposed to actually
walk across the top. The wind buffeted her, trying to
shove her off. If she fell, it would be like being hit
by a car moving at high speeds. There would be no
getting up.

She started forward, keeping an eye out for low
overpasses.

It was the hardest quarter-mile Law ever walked.
There was only a narrow invisible path down the exact
center of the cars where the roof was flat enough
not to start her sliding toward the edge. The train
lurched and swayed unpredictably. Every eighty feet,
she needed to scramble across the gangway connection. Three times she needed to duck down as they
passed under roads.

They were rounding the corner to Duquesne when
she finally reached the engine. Across the wide Monongahela River valley was Turtle Creek with the black
tower of the spaceship standing on end, covered with
the odd runes of dragon magic.

"I'm here." Bare Snow kept Law from bumping into
her. "There's no guard on the door."

The gangway connection hadn't been extended
between the engine and the first passenger car. When
the oni killed the marines, it would have been a way
to keep the engineer safe from any survivors long
enough for him to stop and pick up oni warriors.

"I tried to open it, I could not," Bare Snow said.

What had the Skin Clan done to the door?

Law's grandfather ranted often about the lack of security on the Elfhome railroad. The reasoning was that if the humans returned to Earth without warning—like they almost did when the orbital gate failed—the elves didn't want the humans taking all the keys with them. Law had been able to easily take the hi-rail because the keys had been left in the ignition.

The locomotives didn't have lockable doors. The Skin Clan must have added a lock of some type.

Law crouched at the edge of the roof. She couldn't see anything that would keep Bare Snow from opening the door. It must have been bolted on the inside. There were four other doors on the engine; they were flush with the sides to reduce wind resistance. Inset ladders gave access from the ground, but there would be nothing to hold onto from the roof down.

That left the windshield.

The engine's hatchet nose ended just short of its high narrow windshield. The thick glass was designed to take the impact of a cinderblock. Bare Snow's knives, however, were magically sharp and could cut through almost anything.

Law glanced at the passing countryside. They were almost to Rankin Bridge. Homestead was around the next corner and beyond it was South Side Flats. "Alton, if you screwed this up, I'm going to kill you. You'd better have gotten hold of someone by now. We're coming in hot."

"Law?" Bare Snow was learning English, but she hadn't followed what Law had said.

"Nothing. Come on." Law backed up and leapt across to the engine. At least its roof was wider and flatter. The huge diesel engine throbbed under their feet, a sound felt deep inside as well as heard. Once inside it would be a simple thing to sabotage the motor. It would stop the train, though, within a few miles of Station Square. The oni could reach Oktoberfest within an hour at a brisk walk. If Alton hadn't gathered a force that could stop the oni, then it would be a slaughter.

They needed to crash the train.

There were countless safety measures in place to keep just that from happening. Law needed to override them all. It was going to take time.

They were running out of time.

Law crouched down near the leading edge of the engine. From the vantage point, they could see the entire locomotive. She tapped her lips, wanting Bare Snow to lean close. Many engineers like riding with the side windows open; there was a chance they'd be overheard.

She felt Bare Snow's warmth beside her and then felt her soft hair against her lips. "Cut the right window in a cross with your knife. I will kick it."

"Kick it?" Bare Snow's doubt was clear even at a whisper.

"My boots will protect my feet from the glass."

"Are you sure this is wise?"

It took Law a moment to realize why Bare Snow doubted the move. The female was sure Law would fall. "Look, there's a wide lip at the top of the cowcatcher. I can brace myself against it when I kick."

"I see no cows. Why would they even be catching cows?"

"It's just a name for the nose guard thingy. Don't worry. Ready?"

"Go." Bare Snow vanished from her side.

Law slid down the left windshield to the snub nose. She caught hold of the five-inch-steep lip of the cowcatcher. There were three elves in the engine wearing Wind Clan blue. The one in the engineer's chair was pointing at the sudden fracture in the right-hand windshield. The one directly behind him shouted in surprise and dismay when Law appeared on the nose. She kicked hard at the cut glass.

The windshield shattered into pieces that cascaded into the cab.

Bare Snow killed the engineer before he could touch the controls; he jerked backward, blood spraying from his throat. The elf behind him had an assault rifle that he aimed toward the falling engineer.

"Down!" Law pulled her pistol and fired desperately. The gunshots thundered in the tight confides of the locomotive. Bullets ricocheted off the edge of the windshield by Law's head and smashed through the left side window. The elf went down, Law's three shots hitting him in the chest.

A third elf came running from the back of the locomotive and went down as if clotheslined. Law held her fire.

"Bare?"

"Clear!" Bare Snow called from somewhere far in the back of the engine. "Is this what makes it go?"

Law slipped through the window, careful not to hit any of the levers or buttons on the front dash. The floor was slippery with blood and the coppery smell mixed with hot diesel fumes.

Law stepped over the bodies to glance into the next section of the locomotive. The massive diesel engine took up most of the space, rumbling loudly. "Yes, that's what makes the train go."

A heavy latch had been installed on the metal hatch to the gangway connection. Through the window, she could see the first passenger car. Disguised oni warriors jerked open the opposing door. They obviously expected a passageway; the lead warrior fell out of sight.

Law ducked down. "We're going to get company. That door will only slow them down for a while."

An alarm sounded on the console. Law swore and dashed back to the engineer's chair.

"What is that?" Bare asked.

"Dead man's switch."

"They have switches for dead men? But he's an elf."

"It's a safety feature. Every fifteen minutes the alarm sounds and the engineer needs to indicate he's awake at the console by pushing the button." She hunted for said button. Luckily everything was neatly labeled in Elvish. She punched the button. "If he doesn't respond, the train will stop. We're lucky it's not every ninety seconds like on Earth or we'd be screwed. The elves didn't want the switch installed; they wanted to know if humans had attention spans of gnats."

"Don't we want to stop the train?" Bare Snow asked.

Law glanced up. They were passing the tall waterslides of Sandcastle. The South Side Flats started in five miles. "We're too close to the festival. We need to keep the train moving; we can't let the oni get off. Between Fort Pitt Bridge and West End Bridge is the Elfhome Freight Yard. The main line ends there. There's three sets of tracks out of it, but half a dozen switches need to be in the right position for a train this size to clear through it safely."

Bare Snow understood immediately. "Smash! In the name of the moon, I punish you!"

Law eyed the throttle housing. "We need to get this rigged so they can't change the speed, and then we need to get back to the hi-rail before the train hits the freight yard."

"Rigged?"

Law tapped the throttle as she examined the control. "This lever controls the speed. I want it so they can't move it."

Bare Snow sliced off the lever.

"Um." Law eyed the remains. "Well." She poked experimentally at it. She could see the shaft inside the housing, but she couldn't get her fingers onto it. If the oni could find a pair of needle nose pliers, they might be able to shift it, but they probably wouldn't have time to find a pair. Law pointed at the brake lever. "Do this one too."

Hot Metal Bridge appeared, marking the start of South Side Flats. They had ten minutes before the train hit the freight yard. She wedged the two sheared off levers onto the console so the horn blew in a continuous blast. "We have to go!" She shouted over the blare.

They scrambled out of the broken window.

Luckily, the oni had extended the gangway connection and Law crossed to the passenger cars unseen. She focused on moving as fast as she could, trying to ignore that they were speeding toward destruction with oni hot on their tail. South Side Flats was flashing past on the right as she ran. Twenty-first Street. Nineteenth Street. Thirteenth. Under the Tenth Street Bridge. Over the level crossing at Ninth.

She risked glancing behind her, knowing that Panhandle Bridge was coming up. While light-rail crossed high enough to let barges travel up the Monongahela River, its on-ramps started at street level. Did they have clearance?

No.

"Down!" Law shouted, hoping that Bare Snow heard her over the screaming train horn. She dropped down to all fours.

They flashed under the bridge, the steel support beams just a foot above her head.

A chaotic sea of bodies surrounded Station Square. Stone Clan black filled the Hooters parking lot. Alton had somehow roused the Harbingers. Humans fled in all directions, trying to leave the area before the fighting started. Where were Usagi and the kids? Had they gotten to someplace safe? Why was anyone still at Oktoberfest? Hadn't Alton warned anyone?

The trapped oni smashed out the windows of the passenger cars. They recognized shit hitting the fan when they saw it. Instead of bluffing it out while disguised, they'd decided to fight. Rifles bristled from the openings. The oni opened fire on the elves. The bullets came ricocheting back as they hit the Harbinger's shield wall.

With a sudden roar of deafening noise and searing heat, the first passenger car exploded into flame.

Windwolf was in the house.

Law ran faster as three more passenger cars erupted. "Oh shit, oh shit, oh shit."

This was going to give new meaning to "hit by friendly fire."

Law reached the last passenger car. Bare Snow was

somewhere ahead of her, still invisible. Smithfield Bridge rushed toward her, too low to clear. Three more cars erupted into flame. She couldn't duck down and wait for the bridge—she might become toast on the other side. She risked everything to dash forward and fling herself off the end. She felt the steel girders brush the spiked tips of her hair as she fell. She hit the white canvas of the tents stacked on the flatcar. There was another deep "whooof" as the last passenger cars went up in flame. She scrambled forward. Smithfield Bridge passed overhead, a momentary shield against the elf lord's power. The flatcar was only eighty-some feet but it felt like miles long as she stumbled over the bloody canvas, dodging dead oni bodies, trying to get to the safety of the hi-rail before the next flame strike landed.

She hit the end of the flatcar and leapt, landing on the hi-rail's hood. The windshield was gone; she had no idea when and where they'd lost it. She slid across the hood and into the passenger seat. "Bare?"

"Here!" Bare Snow called from driver's side.

"Brakes!"

Bare Snow stomped on the brakes. Law nearly flew back out the windshield. She caught hold of the dashboard and Bare Snow grabbed her. The steel wheels screamed in protest, metal against metal.

"Sorry!" Bare Snow cried.

The flatcar went up in flame. The fire licked the hood of the hi-rail.

Law swung back into the cab. She slammed the Land Cruiser into reverse. "Gas!"

They raced backward away from the burning train.

The burning train sped toward the Fort Pitt Bridge, shedding oni out the side doors. The laws of physics were not kind to them; they didn't move after tumbling across the track bed at sixty miles per hour.

There was another roar, deeper and louder, and an invisible force hit the locomotive. It tumbled sidewise like a child's toy, dragging the burning passenger cars off the rail. Fear flooded through Law. Where was everyone that she cared about? Had they gotten to safety? Were any of them in the path of the tumbling train cars?

With a deafening thunderclap, an invisible force hit the hi-rail. The world became a confusing tumble of smashing glass and crushing metal. All the airbags inflated in an explosion of white.

They landed upside down.

"Law?" Bare Snow whispered.

"I'm fine." Law wondered why they were whispering. *Oh, right, we just got taken out by the elves who are probably nearby.*

Play dead or bolt?

Considering that the concussion of the first hit had been absorbed by the now limp airbags, running would probably be good.

Law scrambled out the broken window.

The hi-rail was surrounded by elves.

She froze, hands up in what she hoped was the universal gesture of surrender. "I'm human! I'm Wind Clan!" Which probably wasn't the best thing to say, since the elves were all in Stone Clan black, but it was true. Since she was in a household with Bare Snow, she'd chosen her clan alliance.

A male *domana* came stalking through the *laedin*-caste soldiers that had rifles leveled at Law. All of the warriors were studies in brown, reminding Law of humans from India. Law wasn't sure if the elf lord was showing his clan pride or if he was one of those jerks who liked to appear menacing by dressing all in black. He succeeded better than most.

He gave Law a cold glance and turned away. "Kill it."

The air around Law changed and sounds muted slightly.

"Now, now, now, Cana Lily, you can't go killing everything." Forest Moss was unmistakable from his white hair to his missing eye. Last Law had heard, he'd gone mad, blown up a bunch of mannequins in Kaufmann's and then disappeared. While his hair was clean and neatly braided, dust still clung to his heavily wrinkled clothing. Mad or not, he was holding a shield spell around Law, protecting her. "You must take care, lest you harm our fair allies."

The other Stone Clan male snorted in contempt. "It is just some lowborn human trash."

"Hark! Hark!" Forest Moss put a hand to his ear. "I think I hear our cruel master's voice. Certainly that's the meter of his verse. 'Crush the weak and helpless under foot.' Yes, I recognize that sonnet. I think it continues with 'burn the newborns to blackened soot.'"

Cana Lily reared back as if slapped in the face. "Do you slander me?"

"Do you think that I meant you?" Forest Moss pressed a hand to his chest, seeming genuinely surprised and dismayed. "Why would you think that? Do you recognize yourself in those words?"

Forest Moss waved at the wrecked and burning train. "Look around you. See the chaos that our masters have caused. They've dressed their vile creations in our brave warriors' clothes and set them on our dear allies. Do you really need to see the evil in flesh before you can recognize it?"

"The Skin Clan are all dead," Cana Lily growled.

"Can you not see the way they still control us? Here, let me explain. Two bulls were standing in a field when a snake slithered up. One bull wisely ran away. The other stood still as the snake castrated it, put a yoke upon its neck, hooked it up to an over-loaded wagon and then cried out, 'Look at your lazy brother running away when there's work to be done! Is he not evil? Shall we not hate him forever?' The newly made ox took it to heart. He refused to listen to his free brother who called out, 'You're a hundred times his size, crush him under your hooves!' The ox carried the snake to wherever the snake desired, hating his brother instead of his master."

Cana Lily frowned in anger and confusion. "Are you calling me an ox?"

"I worry about you, Clansmate," Forest Moss said earnestly. "Hate has always been the blinder used by those who own slaves. It allows those they enslave to only see those who escaped the yoke, and not the one that sits holding the reins. The moment you hear anyone fear-mongering and pointing fingers, you should look for the shackle on your ankle."

"Don't belittle me, you mad idiot."

"Yes, yes, I'm very mad indeed. The Skin Clan gave me to their twisted beasts who burned all reason out of my mind along with my eye. It cast me into darkness that swallowed everything. But the sun has finally risen on my dark night and I will kill to keep that sun shining."

Cana Lily raised his hand as if to strike.

Law flinched. All her instincts were screaming to run but she didn't want to draw attention to herself just as these two started to brawl. All around her was evidence of the power that they wielded.

"Cana Lily!" Windwolf swept between the two. He had a dozen or more *sekasha* in Wind Clan blue arrayed around him. Among the elves was Jin Wong, the spiritual leader of the tengu, and several of his winged warriors.

Windwolf pointed angrily toward Oakland. "If you cannot keep your focus on the enemy, Cana Lily, then go, now, and get back on your gossamer. We are at war! Save your ire for the oni."

"That female was on that!" Cana Lily indicated the burning wreckage of the train. He apparently didn't know the name of the human invention.

"She supplies food to the enclaves," Jin Wong said quietly. Being that Law never interacted with any tengu, the only way he could know was via Alton Kryskill. "She is trustworthy. She was enlisted to help look for *domi*'s cousin. She called with news that she found this mess and warned of its coming."

That confirmed that the Kryskills had connections with the tengu; the whole way, up to the top ranks.

"The warning was wrong!" Cana Lily protested. "There were to be two vehicles colliding."

"Human technology has its weaknesses," Windwolf said. "The message was cut off in mid-transmission. We were warned that the oni had control of the incoming train; we prepared for everything that they could do with it."

"What was she doing on it?" Cana Lily pointed again at the train to make up for his lack of vocabulary.

Law opened her mouth to answer and then thought

better of it. Once she started to explain, everything might come out, including Trixie, Usagi's kids, and Bare Snow.

"Obviously keeping it from stopping," Windwolf said. "If the oni had control of the train, they would have slowed it to debark. How long are you going to stand there arguing with us while the real enemy escapes to wreak more havoc?"

Cana Lily glared at them and then spun on his heel to stalk away. "You keep monsters too close to your side, Wolf! They will eat your people when your back is turned."

"He just doesn't get it." Forest Moss gazed after Cana Lily with what seemed to be true sadness on his face. "We can't allow anyone to be treated like animals or the power-mad will use it against us. They alone will be glorified like gods and everyone else will be fodder for the beasts."

"Verily," Windwolf murmured. "We trod that line closely even before the humans arrived on our world. The half-caste or the mixed clan were treated like dirt merely because they weren't considered pure."

"Welcome to the new age!" Forest Moss cried in English and then lapsed back to Elvish. "Onward! I long to return to my sun and moon!"

He strode off, singing what sounded like "Radioactive" punctuated with explosions. They watched him go.

Windwolf waited until the Stone Clan *domana* was out of sight before giving Law a bow. "Thank you. You have saved more than the lives of those who were celebrating here. If the oni had been able to attack unchecked, then war would have broken out between the elves and the humans."

The elf had no idea that he owed even more to her and Bare Snow. It was nice, though, to be thanked for part of it.

"I have friends here," Law said. "Someplace. Or at least, I did." Usagi was the one Law was most worried about; she had been at Oktoberfest alone with five kids. Tiffani would have fled instantly. Ellen had a brother living nearby. Trixie was good at landing on her feet.

"My people started to vacate this area minutes after you called with the news," Jin Wong said. "Some stayed to fight, but those with children fled."

Relief nearly took Law to her knees. She breathed out and cautioned herself that just because everyone had been warned, didn't mean everyone reached safety.

Tiffani's fishing pool had been trampled. The water had drained to a mud puddle. The little gleaming fish lay scattered on the ground, long past saving. Law took the fact that they could find nothing of Trixie's booth as a sign that the Changs had packed up and left long before the oni arrived. Ellen's little house had been battened down with storm shutters and the charcoal grill drowned with water, so she'd beaten an orderly retreat.

All the little stuffed bunnies sat abandoned at Usagi's booth. Alarmingly, the cash box was still tucked under the counter, unlocked. Law picked it up, feeling sick with fear. Of course with five children to shepherd to safety, Usagi would have needed her hands free to fight or hold onto a kid. Had they gotten home safely? All Law could get on her cell phone was a Shutdown message of all connections busy. Everyone in Pittsburgh was trying to find out if their friends and family were safe.

Bare Snow whimpered and picked up something from the ground. It was a rabbit hat that belonged to one of the kids.

"I'm sure they got home safe," Law said. "Let's go check there."

Dusk bled to night as they rode up Mount Washington on the incline. Part of Station Square burned unchecked. Lightning occasionally struck out of the clear sky. Sudden eruptions of flame would follow seconds later.

Law picked her way down Usagi's toy-strewn sidewalk to knock on the door. "Usagi! Usagi! Is anyone home?"

There was the thunder of small feet. The door flung open and the entire herd of half-elves flung themselves at Bare Snow. The rabbit hats had been abandoned for a wide variety of wings.

"We flew!" Moon Rabbit shouted as she scaled Bare Snow. "We flew! It was awesome!"

The others hopped up and down and shrugged their shoulders to make their fake wings flutter. "We flew! We flew!"

And then Usagi was hugging Law tightly. "Oh, I've been so worried about you two!"

"Us?" Law hadn't told Usagi anything about chasing after oni.

"The tengu said you were the one that stumbled across the train while helping Duff look for Tinker's cousin."

Duff? Oh! Alton's little brother! He worked at the bakery with Hazel. Widget hadn't been dragged off to do computer work for the bakery; she'd been hijacked by the Kryskills to hack into the city's camera network.

"Widget sent the tengu to get you to safety," Law guessed.

"They didn't know how much time there was before the train arrived, so they just flew us straight up from Station Square."

"It was awesome!" Moon Rabbit cried.

"Scarier than hell," Usagi murmured. "At first I was angry, yanked away from all our work that way." She glanced toward the wall of windows overlooking South Side. She had a clear view of the train wreck. "I remember when you brought me Widget. She was still shivering from trying to swim the river in the middle of winter. I was afraid to take her in. You kept begging me and I was thinking 'you just don't want to be saddled with her.'"

That was true. Law didn't want the girl underfoot; Law walked too much on the dangerous fringe to have someone like Widget trailing along. "Sorry about that."

Usagi laughed and hugged her harder. "I'm thanking you! You were right. I was wrong. She's sweet and funny and smart and she saved all our lives today. Thank you. Thank you. Thank you."

"You're welcome." Law hadn't known it would turn out that way. She had only known that Widget needed help. She'd had no idea that Widget would someday be able to pay her back tenfold. She supposed that was the natural order. By lifting Widget up, Law had given her the power to help others. They were daisy-chained together; acts of goodwill looped back around. Law had saved Windwolf. He had protected her without even knowing how much he owed her.

Tinker saved the tengu, and they in turn protected Usagi and her children. Around and around, kindness being paid forward until it returned.

It was what Pittsburgh needed. What Elfhome needed; people helping one another without concern of clan or race or species.

# AFTERWORD

*Pay No Attention to That*
*Man Behind the Curtain*

Judging by the number of "Making of," some people like to know how their favorite stories and movies and such come into being. Judging by a handful of reviews on Amazon, some people don't. Apparently the people in the latter camp like to think that authors are godlike people that can spin out a vast complicated story arc across multiple books, writing millions of words about a cast of a thousand named characters, in one massive, preconceived plot that doesn't need to be tweaked or improved upon.

For those of you that enjoy such things, I've written down notes on the various stories. Why I wrote them, how I thought they were going to turn out, and how the plots were detoured to what you actually read.

For the rest of you, skip this. Trust me; you don't want to see behind the curtain.

## Stormsong

I'm going to talk about all her sections as a whole. The very first one I wrote for her was her meeting Tinker. I don't remember what inspired me to attempt it but I do remember that the story flowed. The scene came out with this amazingly strong voice. What surprised me most was that it was in first person and an attempt to rewrite it to third person failed.

I loved the bit but couldn't figure out what to do with it. The problem was that Stormsong doesn't actually "meet" Tinker until the middle of the first novel, and at that point she blends into the crowd. I couldn't extend the drabble into a story because it would go against canon; Tinker had no idea who Stormsong was and that couldn't change.

I wrote it after I'd finished *Wolf Who Rules* and have always wished I could have gone back and tweaked the novel to reflect the drabble. There is a slight but not glaring canon conflict that Stormsong doesn't mention this meeting while talking to Windwolf after the fight with Impatience. This can be dismissed by the fact that Stormsong didn't think it would be wise for Tinker to include her in her First Hand.

I wanted to write more from Stormsong's point of view, so I tackled her first meeting with Windwolf. Again, *boom*, the story flowed. Still there wasn't enough plot there to be standalone. I didn't have the time to invest into making it something bigger.

By this time I was working on *Elfhome* and I vaguely salvaged parts of the first drabble during the chapter Panty Raid.

The last bit I wrote for her was the journey to New

York, written soon after I'd finished *Wood Sprites*. I thought about expanding this into a complete story but that way lies madness. Stormsong couldn't find out more about the twins since she doesn't mention them for three books. Nor could she find out that Sparrow was a traitor. Coming up with a true story that didn't trip over those points would have been hair-pulling insanity.

## Little Horse

Fans kept asking me to write something from Pony's POV. I attempted to write something from after he met Tinker, but that didn't work. He's too on-camera during all the books. What ended up happening was simply a retelling of what the readers already knew. I was bored silly trying to write it. Everything that was interesting was too short to be called a story.

I decided to find a pivotal point in his life that didn't include Tinker. Once I approached the story from that mindset, it was obvious that the story would be about him deciding to accompany Windwolf to the Westernlands. I wanted some trigger event so that when the moment came for Pony to choose, it wasn't static "thinking" but an emotional response to some thrilling action.

Originally I started with Pony kneeling in the dirt, happy that he'd won the fight, but worried about the Wyvern's judgment. It became obvious that I needed to back up and show the cause of the fight: Clove and his weak eyes. The bonus to this was I actually showed the fight. Action is always a good thing.

## Lain

I had written that Lain's pivotal moment in her life after her accident was during the first Startup. The first scene flowed up to the point where Lain is shown the saurus. At that point, however, I lost the thread of the story.

I made a lot of random stabs at it. In one version, Lain rescued a soldier that had been trapped by a steel spinner spider. In another, Lain set up elaborate quarantine systems. In a third, she was rescued by Windwolf and was healed by magic to the point she could walk with crutches. At some point I decided that I wanted her to be isolated and forced to realize that her brains were what mattered.

How to get her alone? It didn't make sense with the setup I had in place that she would go into the forest alone. I didn't want her to be stupid. I decided that I could bring in Yves to give him more airtime, show off some of their relationship and explain how the empire of evil reacted to the first Startup.

Isolating her creates a new problem. The narrative becomes a monologue, which is difficult to keep tension high. Lain experiencing first contact with an elf also satisfied the idea that this was the first time elves and humans meet on Elfhome. I wanted Lain to have an actual conversation with the elf, so it limited who she could meet. I didn't want it to be either Windwolf or Stormsong since she obviously meets both of them for the first time in the first two books. Using Lightning Strikes allowed me to expand on Blue Sky's backstory and flesh out a character important to the series and yet never shown before.

Yes, the story does end slightly abruptly but Lain has had her epiphany. The reader of the series is sure to realize that Lain manages to get to Pittsburgh while it's cycling back and forth between Elfhome and Earth. Once there, she refuses to leave and sets up in her house on Observatory Hill.

## Wyvern

This was the first short story I'd ever sold. It was written after *Tinker* was released. Russell Davis had e-mailed me and asked me to write something to include in a DAW anthology he was editing called *Faerie Tales*.

I was in the middle of writing *Wolf Who Rules*. I didn't want to try to fit the short story's plot into the events of the main storyline (that insanity would come later). At first I thought I would do some first-contact stories with new characters. I started a few but they trickled off, not to be finished.

I realized I needed a character that I was comfortable with to build the story around because I was on a tight deadline. I pulled out an old character who originally had been a space marine. What would a space marine be doing on Elfhome? I decided that she could be a big game hunter. The bigger the game, the better, so I decided that she would go one on one with a wyvern.

I couldn't get a handle on it until I stumbled upon the idea that her "native guide" would be a *sekasha*. I had been raised on Tarzan movies where the big game hunter was always a brave, tall white guy and the "native guide" was this fearful, weak and small male that ran away at first sign of trouble. As a kid, I didn't realize how racist this was. Here was the chance to address that stance by making the two characters equal.

Unfortunately I didn't keep canon straight. Originally the female *sekasha* was Crow Song. In the books, however, I state that all of Windwolf's Hands are in Pittsburgh, that he had only lost Hawk Scream and Lightning Strikes, and only Stormsong speaks English. I decided to change the female to be Stormsong as the easiest way to match up all the elements. Certainly the female acts like Stormsong in the story. (So sorry for any confusion I caused people who read this in its original form.)

## Bare Snow Falling on Fairywood

Some stories are gifts from the muses. They just come. And sometimes they aren't, and you need to build them from the ground up. And sometimes they're a weird mix of both, stalling in some places and sprinting ahead in others.

When I moved to Hawaii, I started to meet very memorable people. A new friend impressed me in the complexity of her life. Her father is a professional Bigfoot hunter. Her mother was Hawaiian Chinese Portuguese mix that could have sprung from the pages of *Joy Luck Club*. She's an avid fisherman and into outdoor sports like snorkeling and kayaking, but she also loves to shop for clothes. Every time I talked to her, she had a story of great misadventure as she rushed out to save damsels in distress.

One night I had a dream that my friend was on Elfhome. Yes, she would fit right in! But what would her story be?

Fans had been asking about the Water Clan. I decided I would bring one to Pittsburgh; she would need a human defender in the face of all the technology. Still it wasn't clicking.

Around that time, Teddy the Porcupine videos were hitting my newsfeed regularly on Facebook. If you haven't seen these, go, now, watch them. They're a hoot.

One day the muse hit me with "a lesbian, an elf, and a porcupine walk into a hardware store." *Boom.* For some reason, adding a porcupine made all the difference in the world. Why? I don't know. I wrote the hardware store scene but it didn't have an inherent conflict in it that centered on Law. So I decided to back up. At Wollerton's, Law and Bare Snow were already a couple. How did they meet?

I made a few stabs at their first meeting being a totally random event. The very first attempt, Law left home on her eighteenth birthday and meets Bare Snow squatting out in the middle of nowhere. Yes, the story centered on Law, but lacked conflict.

In a different story, I'd played with the idea that Tooloo had tapped a hapless pawn and sent them off to do impossible things. Originally the pawn had been sent to Onihida to free Impatience from the oni. I realized that the story wouldn't be placed in Pittsburgh, would require massive world-building and wouldn't be a short story. I abandoned this project.

What if Tooloo called Law and arranged for her to save Bare Snow? Tooloo is quietly blocking the Skin Clan right and left. The fact that Bare Snow is Water Clan finally became vital to the story. If she's found in the wrong place, her presence could trigger the restart of the clan war. I wrote out Tooloo calling Law in the middle of fishing and had Law go off to find Bare Snow. Her location was a natural extension of canon: Windwolf had been attacked in Fairywood and gone on foot to Tinker's salvage yard. If you wanted to start a clan war, putting a Water Clan elf in Fairywood was a logical way of doing it.

Originally Bare Snow had been a normal, innocent female. I got as far as Widget hacking the DMV when I realized that wouldn't work. As a trigger to a clan war, there had to be more of a reason to suspect that she was behind the ambush. Also a normal person wouldn't chase after bad guys. Law had a history of going toe-to-toe with guys stalking women but her taking on an entire horde of bad guys didn't make sense. It needed to make sense that Bare Snow couldn't go to the Wind Clan with the news that Windwolf was going to be attacked. There was also the oddity of Bare Snow coming to Pittsburgh all by herself with no promise of joining a household.

At some point I remembered that I had set up that Windwolf's grandfather, Howling, had been assassinated. What if Bare Snow's family were the assassins? What if the Skin Clan had been behind it? At that point, it all worked. I rewrote the scenes so that Bare Snow was now a well-trained assassin whose mother had a price on her head.

But what was the story *really* about? The emotional heart of an action story is very difficult to figure out sometimes. For a long time, it eluded me. I nearly reached the end before I knew what it was. From Law's name to her profession to her choice of pet, I had gone with extremely quirky choices. (And yes, some of that reflected the inspiration.) Unconsciously I'd been having Law pick out things that were logical and wonderful for her, but that people around her hated. The heart of the story was staring me in the face.

## Pittsburgh Backyard and Garden

Sometimes it's hard to remember what triggered a story. I vaguely remember talking to June Drexler Robertson about wanting to do a story in Pittsburgh that didn't center on Tinker that dealt with the day-to-day life of humans trying to cope with magic and monsters.

I think if I had to list the very, very root of it, it was the scene in *Tinker* when Oilcan and Tinker are warning Ryan of the dangers of Elfhome's native life. They mentioned a list of safety rules posted at the observatory's dorms. (Don't leave doors open, report any strange animal no matter how cute and harmless it seemed, don't go into the swamp without a flame-thrower...) At some point later I tried to sit down and write out those safety rules. It wasn't as interesting as I thought it would be but it had promise of growing.

I don't remember how it went from "normal Pittsburghers" to a DYI TV show but I recall giggling madly. For some reason, the first thing I thought of was Alton Brown in a pith helmet. I allowed him to go a little manic, influenced by *MythBusters*, and freed from the constraints of "Don't try this at home." (Okay, so maybe a little Bob Ross too with "and a happy little tree lives here... and it's trying to eat you.")

Having gone off the deep end with Hal, I needed someone to balance him. Someone behind the scenes, calm to his manic, careful to his blithe enthusiasm, and heavily armed. I decided that Jane would be the opposite of everything that was Tinker. Tall, blond, intelligent but not a genius, liked to settle her problems with her fists, and had the world's most plain first name. (The last name of Kryskill comes from the family that actually built Hyeholde Restaurant.) She'd have a large, sprawling family: grandparents, mother, uncles, aunts, brothers, sisters, and cousins. She would even have a pet: a big, well-trained guard dog.

The idea screamed for a take on a "fish out of water" story. I wanted outsiders coming to Pittsburgh and the natives having to deal with the fact that the newcomers don't know how to deal with the local dangers. (Basically I cycled back to the seed idea of Tinker and Oilcan's explanation to Ryan.) I decided the Pittsburghers were doing a gardening show a la Elfhome and that the incoming crew was doing a more rarefied animal documentary.

Mind you, most of this was at a subconscious level and happened in the course of one afternoon during the conversation with June.

Nigel came from June telling me about Nigel Marven and *Chased by Dinosaurs*. She mentioned a segment of Nigel letting a poisonous spider walk across his face. I decided to name my naturalist in tribute to Marven, but I decided not to watch any video featuring him so that my Nigel wouldn't be a copy of him. I think Monty Python was more of an influence on my vision of Nigel. Riffing on the name *Chased by Dinosaurs*, I decided his show would be *Chased by Monsters*, which suggested a natural end to the story.

Just as I was working on the story, I happened to see the video of Aimee Mullins doing a TED Talk. Aimee was born in Pennsylvania with a medical condition that resulted in her lower legs being amputated when she was an infant. Despite this, she went on to be world-class athlete, actress and fashion model. She really inspired me. I decided that Nigel would have the same condition. It was only later that I decided to make use of his lack of feet: evil writer that I am.

With all that in the mix, I sat down and wrote the two obvious scenes. The first one establishes the *PB&G* crew, its show then unnamed, filming one of the monsters I've mentioned in the books but hadn't shown. The strangle vine had to be aggressive enough to warrant heavy weapons, thus the whole octopus plant on LSD came into being. Jane gets the phone call informing her of the babysitting job, and then in the next scene, she meets said newbies.

Originally I wanted Jane to be working on a show whose name was a riff on a real television series. The first one that leapt to mind was *Victory Garden*. I went off and researched it and decided it was totally not what I thought it was. So I went with *Pittsburgh Lawn and Garden*. While typing the show name for the twentieth time, I decided to abbreviate it. By changing "Lawn" to "Backyard," I could make it sound like a PB&J sandwich.

By the very nature of Pittsburgh on Elfhome, the arrival of Nigel and Taggart had to be on a Startup day. I couldn't bring them in after July since July was the last Shutdown. Bringing them in prior to July meant they wouldn't be struggling with the big world problem of the war between elf and oni, and that seemed pointless. Anything they discovered about the oncoming war would have caused problems with information already stated in the books. So obviously, *Chased by Monsters* arrived in July.

It meant that the *biggest* news story was Tinker's kidnapping.

It set up a "you're a genius" in terms of plot since I established that Mercy Hospital was the only human hospital in town and it's right beside where Tinker takes the nosedive during her kidnapping. By hurting Hal, I gave him front row seats to everything. Wow. Cool. The story just flowed out.

This triggered a problem though. By seeing Tinker kidnapped, why wouldn't this be the news story that the crew followed? Yes, it was out of their field, but a woman's life is at stake. As the author, however, I couldn't have them focusing on it because they couldn't influence the events. But by the same token, I wanted them to learn something big that justified doing a story from Jane's point of view.

I stalled around the Neighborhood of Make Believe scene, struggling to figure out how to make it a big story without stretching the fabric of the published book's universe. Eventually the "ah ha" light went on and I realized that Tinker's kidnapping had to be a catalyst for Jane to cope with the angst of a similar event in her life. Thus Boo was born. It was a kind of have your cake and eat it too setup.

## Blue Sky

In *Wolf Who Rules*, I wanted Tinker to talk with Tommy Chang prior to saving him from the Wyverns. I had in my mind that he would be a major player in Pittsburgh but I had the problem that he's not the sort of person Tinker normally would interact with. I made him the race promoter to give them a common element. Tommy seeks Tinker out to find out how much her being made into an elf changed her mentally. Like Maynard, he wanted to know where she stood in the political landscape. He couldn't, however, just ask her flat out like Maynard could, because that would indicate he was part of the conflict. The conversation about racing, then, was all just a cover.

At the time, I was ordering promotional materials through an online printing site. Their e-mails for proofs came from the address of Team Big Sky. It seemed too perfect not to use. In a throwaway line, I set up that Team Big Sky was John Montana and his little brother, the half-elf, Blue Sky.

Later I got to thinking about these two characters. Obviously they shared a mother. Who was Blue Sky's father? Did he know about his son? Did he care? It seemed likely that if the elves had so few children, they wouldn't be indifferent to a half-breed bastard. The two castes that created the most conflict for the world were *domana* and *sekasha*. Since Windwolf was the only real candidate for a *domana* father, I decided to go with *sekasha*. I wanted Tinker involved in the story, which she wouldn't be if the *sekasha* was alive, so I made his father be the male killed in the backstory told in *Tinker*.

## Peace Offering

I had wanted to do a story where Forest Moss found redemption in a human female. Originally I imagined that he would get mixed up with a woman that ran a brothel. She was a ruthless businesswoman and the arrangement was strictly for profit alone. I couldn't find a story in it; nothing to hang my hat on.

As I had wrapped up *Elfhome*, anti-abortion sentiments began to sweep the nation. It was tied tightly to people who wanted no sexual education in the classroom and no birth control given to young women. It triggered something in me and I felt I had to write my response to it.

My biggest problem with these purity pro-lifers is that they want to create school situations and laws that address only the perfect setting. In their perfect setting, girls don't need sexual education, birth control pills, and abortions because all they need is to say "no." In a perfect world, these purity pushers would be right. The world, however, is far from perfect. Horrible, terrible things happen. Things beyond a young woman's control. The most innocent event is that a massive wave of unfamiliar hormone-driven impulses get the best of them and suddenly they're faced with utter ruin. This gives them no Plan B except to spend the nine months carrying a child that they didn't plan, might not want, and have no way to care for.

In the United States, one in every five women has been raped, with forty-four percent of those rapes happening under the age of eighteen. In a high school class of three hundred students, thirty of the girls will be raped or sexually assaulted. Look at a graduating class (if the girl is so lucky to graduate) and in any cluster of ten seats, there sits a girl whose life is potentially destroyed by her attack. Add in the lack of morning-after pills and abortion, plus a society that tells her she's impure if she's not a virgin, and it's nearly sure that *the life she wanted* is over.

This purity-only mindset is like sending out warplanes without weapons or parachutes through enemy territory in broad daylight. Any intelligent person can tell you that is a stupid plan that will wipe out your military. Yet this is exactly what is being pushed for young women—go out among men with no knowledge or means to protect themselves and no way to save themselves if attacked.

I decided to write a story about a girl who lost the war. She fought hard but still found herself pregnant and on the run from an abusive man. She is the good girl who has been pushed to the edge of the cliff and is now out of options. Once I knew what I really wanted to address, the story wrote itself.

## Price of Peace

I left Olivia on a cliffhanger of being homeless with an insane elf in the middle of a war zone. I really wanted to get her to the point where she actually had someplace to live. I had fun running Olivia all over Pittsburgh, followed by mobs of elves. Perhaps too much fun. Eventually I started to wonder what the point of the story was. Originally Olivia ate at the O, went to the real estate agent's office and ended up at Phipps. Only after Forest Moss was called back to combat did she go downtown with Jewel Tear in tow. All interesting events but originally without a focus and thus not with a whole lot of building conflict.

Eventually I realized that I wanted to focus on two things, the first being Olivia's growing realization of all the strings attached to the deal she'd struck. The second was setting up what would be the bigger conflicts ahead for her. I shifted the order of the scenes and inserted all the scenes at the University of Pittsburgh and the shopping trip at Giant Eagle.

# Threads that Bind and Break

This story does a lot of heavy lifting in that it was written to tie together *Elfhome* and *Wood Sprites* and several of the earlier *Project Elfhome* stories and sets the stage for the next book, *Harbinger*. That's a lot of work for a novella.

I've discovered that fans refuse to acknowledge that characters lie or see events through different filters. For example, Windwolf states that he was "stunned" by the saurus and Pony states that Windwolf was "knocked unconscious." Fans claim this is a mistake, ignoring the fact that unconscious people don't realize they've been out of it for more than a few seconds and Pony couldn't actually have witnessed the events, else Tinker would remember a second *sekasha* at the scene. I didn't realize readers wouldn't follow this logic, or I would have made it clearer when Pony makes his claim. Having learned this lesson, I realized that the twins couldn't interact with any of the known characters prior to the end of *Elfhome* without fans calling it a mistake on my part.

This created a huge timing problem. I wanted the twins in Monroeville to witness the orbital gate crash and Earth's reaction to it at the start of August. If the Skin Clan had a back door to Elfhome, they would use it as quickly as possible. The elves had realized that oni forces were in Pittsburgh. Unless the Skin Clan reconnected their supply lines, their troops would be stranded without Earth's resources. The nestlings, however, would be killed shortly after the Skin Clan took them to Elfhome.

All these factors meant that the twins had to cross

worlds immediately. It left me with a gaping hole in my timeline. Where were the twins during the entire period represented by *Wolf Who Rules* and *Elfhome*? Because of the nestlings, if they'd gotten anywhere close to Pittsburgh, the tengu would know where the children were.

I either had to make the timeline unclear at the end of *Wood Sprites* or leave the nestlings' fate still in the balance. I wanted the twins to beat the oni decisively after everything they suffered, so I decided to be very vague on how long things took in the last chapter.

After *Wood Sprites* advance reader copies came out, fans started to piece together a timeline showing when certain events happened. They started to contact me wanting to know how the book fit into *Elfhome*. This got worse when I posted the first scene of *Harbinger*.

It became clear that I would need to firmly pinpoint events.

Sigh.

Hopefully this short story explains everything. If not, here is a timeline that more clearly spells it out.

Louise called the gossamer to the cave shortly after Oilcan was kidnapped. Tinker does not see the gossamer go because she's dealing with the chaos at Sacred Heart. When she finally pays attention to the airfield, the Wind Clan gossamer is already gone and only the Stone Clan airships are moored. Because of the Kryskills' connection to the tengu, they're some of the first outsiders involved. The phone call isn't Team Tinker enlisting Alton's help but the tengu asking him to contact Team Tinker and anyone else he knows that is trustworthy. (If you need a political reason for this, humans are considered neutral and thus could confront the Stone Clan elves without triggering a clan war. The tengu are firmly Wind Clan. They could only watch from a distance once Oilcan was found. Tinker had made it clear that she didn't want the tengu engaging Forge and Iron Mace on her behalf. Team Tinker is Riki's Plan B.)

As the gossamer heads out, Gracie is leading the tengu chasing after it. She knew via a dream that she was needed in Oakland. When the airship bolts, she knows that this was why she was in Oakland. Jin and Riki are caught up searching for first Oilcan and then Tinker. While the males are in Pittsburgh, they are out of contact with the people in the tengu village (which doesn't have a cell phone tower). When Gracie finds the twins, she decides that this is news that needs to be told face to face to Jin, not trusted to a phone that might be tapped. (And trust me, there's no code words to cover the twins and the babies and Joy.) It is Jin's place to tell Tinker, so the tengu settle the twins at the village and wait.

Meanwhile, all the elves are distracted from Tinker's side by the train on the South Side. Because of the bad cell phone connection with Alton, the wrong information is spread through the tengu. They believe that the oni planned to collide the inbound train full of elves with an empty outbound passenger train. Riki doesn't know what really is going on when Oilcan calls him, looking for Tinker. All he knows, from piecemeal reports, is that the *domana* are nuking the hell out of South Side and there's at least one derailed train.

Shortly after that, Tinker blows up Neville Island. Wind Clan elves show up to serve their *domi* and talk with one pissed-off Tommy. They don't tell the half-oni squat.

Tinker, being Tinker, ignores everything that doesn't connect to what she's focused on at that moment. Yes, she knows that the Harbingers have showed up; she doesn't think about them in the last chapter. Yes, she knows Jewel Tear was rescued by Tommy and is living with Oilcan; not a word about the battered female. She also knows that something happened involving the trains at Station Square. She doesn't think about that either. (To be fair, she didn't know that Oktoberfest was being held there and that loads of humans were in danger. She will freak once someone finally connects the two for her.)

*Harbinger* starts shortly after tea with Oilcan at the end of *Elfhome*. Jin has flown home and discovered the mess waiting for him.

# HARBINGER

## 1: Blackbird Singing in the Dead of Night

"*What?* Wait!" Tinker cried, cutting off the flow of Jin's explanation. She'd been awakened in the middle of the night to be told that the tengu's spiritual leader needed to speak with her immediately. The household staff had set out a formal tea in the dining hall and made themselves scarce but they were probably lurking in the deep shadows nearby, just in case she needed more tarts or, more likely, another pot of strong tea. A thunderstorm was rolling across Pittsburgh, flashing the courtyard garden into brilliance and then darkness. Rain drummed comfortingly on the dining hall's roof; the lightning was being generated from a non-magical source.

"I have what?" She was sure this would make sense if it weren't some ungodly hour in the middle of the night.

"Twin siblings." Jin looked exhausted. Since she'd seen him late in the evening, he must have flown to his village and back without stopping. "Six of them."

Tinker squinted at him. Maybe she was still asleep. "You're—you're kidding. Right?"

"No, I'm not." His great black wings rustled with his nervousness. "I know that technically they belong to Esme, but Gracie would love to adopt..."

"Back up. Back up. I have what?"

Jin sighed. "Twin siblings. Six of them."

"How can I have six twin siblings? Wouldn't they be six-something? Sextuplets?" No, that sounded like a porn video. "No, um, if I have six siblings then we would be seven. Seven...seven...seven..."

The conversation was in English, so only Stormsong was following her muttering. The tall warrior leaned over her shoulder to pour her more tea. "Septuplets, *domi*."

"Are you sure?" Tinker spooned several teaspoons of honey into the tea before gulping it. "September is the ninth month."

"It was the seventh month, but it changed to the ninth..." Jin sighed again and rubbed at the bridge of his nose. "It's a naming convention. I don't understand why they use these words, but when multiple eggs are fertilized, and then used at different times by different women, then the resulting children are considered 'twins' even though they have different families and are different ages."

He was talking about how she'd been conceived in vitro ten years after her father died. She vaguely knew the mechanics; Lain had explained them to her when she was very young. She'd alarmed Lain by talking about having a brother that lived far away. Only after Lain went through all the biology, Tinker confessed that she confused "brother" with "cousin." Lain had kept referring to possible siblings as "theoretical" until Tinker thought that the word meant "imaginary" because Lain indicated that it was quite impossible for such siblings to exist.

But Jin wouldn't wake her up in the middle of the night for imaginary siblings. Since Stormsong was quietly translating the conversation to the others of her Hand, Tinker switched to Elvish.

"Wasn't all that material stored at some place in New York City?" Tinker asked.

"It was," Jin said slowly and his wings rustled. "All of it has been used. To make children. Many children."

"Six of them?" Tinker said, just to be sure.

Jin paused before saying, "As far as I know."

She wasn't sure what she was supposed to do with the information. "Two more and we would have had a baseball team."

"*Domi*," Pony murmured. "Since both you and your cousin can tap the Stone Clan Spell Stones, we need to know where these children are located."

Tinker wasn't sure if he meant "we" as in her and her Hand or the *sekasha*-caste whose job was to keep tabs on the *domana*-caste. It made it suddenly clear why Jin was there, in the middle of the night, to report the news. She'd been thinking that this could have been handled by a phone call in the morning. To the elves, her siblings were potential walking weapons.

Jin was waiting for her to ask. His people were safe only because he'd promised to be her loyal servant. She was learning that everyone else understood that meant waiting for her to realize what the hell was going on and give the appropriate order.

"Where exactly are these ... Wait. Did you say children?"

"Technically two are children, and the other four are about to be newborns. They are at Haven."

The tengu village was someplace deep in the virgin forest, in a location secret even to her. The adults kept travel from Pittsburgh to where their children were hidden to the minimum, so many of the tengu that Tinker knew had an alternate home within the city. Jin had apparently returned home to discover he'd been invaded by an army of little Dufaes.

"That is not all," Jin added.

"This gets worse?" Tinker cried.

"In a manner of speaking—possibly. There is a third dragon in Pittsburgh."

Okay, a dragon was not a phone call in the morning.

"Malice-size?" She spread her hands wide as possible to indicate the massive dragon that Jin helped her kill a few weeks earlier. "Or Impatience?"

Jin put his hands together so that they nearly touched. "Her name is Joy. She has claimed all your siblings as her Chosen. We cannot do anything with the children without her approval. She is very protective."

Tinker snorted. "How protective can a pocket-size dragon get?"

"Very. She can and will summon help. We would be facing both Impatience and Providence in any attempts to go against her wishes."

Dragon tag-team fighting. Okay, that was a very scary thought. Impatience nearly killed Tinker and her Hand when they first met. He was fifteen feet of pure muscle, a mouth filled with razor-sharp teeth, and magical shields all backed with a genius that intimidated even her. Providence was dead and not-dead in a way that made her brain hurt. He was the guardian spirit of the tengu and they worshipped him as a god. It meant that in addition to fighting something that can't be "killed" it would push the tengu's loyalty to her to a breaking point. The elves considered the tengu a valuable ally because of Jin's alliance with Tinker. Otherwise, they would wipe the tengu out—adults and children alike.

*What Joy wants, Joy gets. Check. Assuming what Little Miss Pocket Dragon wanted was within reason.*

Gracie Wong had been married to Tinker's father and loved him deeply. There was little wonder that she would want to adopt...

"Wait—*about to be* newborn?"

"Yes, in about eighteen days." Jin's wings rustled loudly. "We think. Give or take a few days. Forgiveness, *domi*." He murmured the command to dispel his wings and they vanished from his back. The dining room suddenly seemed a lot less crowded.

"So there are two kids and a mega-pregnant woman about to pop? Or are we talking four women who are all pregnant? What the hell? Is someone on Earth giving out Dufae kids like lottery tickets?"

"It's—" Jin paused for a minute, obviously trying to find a safe, sane explanation. Considering Tinker's summer to date, there might not be one. Single-handedly, she'd managed to accidently change her species, rip a hole in the fabric of reality, kidnap a major US city, fall off the planet, crash a spaceship into Turtle Creek, kill a dragon...

Tinker was sure there was more but she was losing track of the weirdness. Not a good sign.

"It's—it's complicated," Jin finally understated. "Maybe I should back up." He paused again for several minutes, mouth open, eyes flicking back and forth as he tried to find a safe place to start. "There are two girls, Louise and Jillian Mayer. They are twins, and very much like you."

What did that mean? Short? Dark skin? Genius? Snarky? All of the above?

"Their father worked at the clinic where Leo's sperm was stored. Esme used it to fertilize a dozen or so of her eggs. Some number was used to create you and the rest were put into storage. Nine years ago, Mr. Mayer took some of the frozen embryos and implanted them into his wife. They raised your sisters as their natural-born children, and I gather they were very good parents."

"*Were*? Are they dead?"

"I don't know. Somehow, I'm not clear how it happened, your grandmother gained custody of them."

"Mine? I don't have a grandmother. A grandfather. Two, if you count Forge, but he's more like a great-great-great-something." She'd made peace with her elf ancestor that afternoon though he was still on probation with her for what he'd done to Oilcan. Forge was going to be ecstatic at the news that he had six more grandkids. If they were orphans, he'd probably want custody of them. She wasn't sure if this was a good thing or a bad thing. Certainly, it would make the *sekasha* happy if the babies were with a *domana*, but her siblings were still human. And she would prefer that they stay that way. No more of this changing species without warning.

"Esme's mother," Jin stated. When she looked at him confused, he expanded with, "Esme's mother is your grandmother."

"Oh! She's still alive?" Tinker tried to remember if Lain ever even talked about her family. Lain talked about Esme in terms of "my sister, the astronaut" but never anything else. Wait, there had been something recently about an Empire of Evil and Flying Monkeys. That didn't sound good.

"I—I'm not sure," Jin said. "I didn't actually talk to the twins; they were asleep and apparently very emotionally fragile after everything they've been through. I thought you should be told immediately. I didn't want to blindside you with any of this."

"This didn't count as being blindsided?" Tinker asked.

"This is still just us—and Joy—and the other dragons. I believe that the Stone Clan might want to claim the children. And there is Esme to be considered. I owe your mother a great deal; without her intervention none of this could be possible. You would not have been born. Everyone on my ship would have been lost. My people would still be enslaved. Biologically, the children are Esme's offspring. She did, however, abandon her genetic material when she left Earth. The children were carried by other women. Nor is Esme in a situation where she could take on the responsibility of raising six children, four of which are newborn."

"Yyyyeeeah." Tinker wasn't even sure where Esme was living since Tinker crashed her mother's spaceship into Turtle Creek. She knew Esme had spent several days in the hospital. Tinker had last seen Esme when they'd dropped her at Lain's. No, wait, the sisters had

come together to Poppymeadow's—later—sometime.
Tinker had totally lost track of time. It had been a
super-condensed-weird summer and wasn't officially
over yet.

Esme and six kids in Lain's house? With all those
deadly plants? Hell, Tinker had spent the first two
years of her life on a leash at Lain's to keep her
out of the reach of the various man-eating plants.
And there was a reason she'd not moved in with
Lain when her grandfather died. Lain was the type
of person that loved kids as long as she could send
them home. Tinker had lived with Lain the month
it took her grandfather to fetch Oilcan from Boston.
Life slowly degraded into a battle of wills that only
stopped before they reached open warfare because
her grandfather returned.

Esme had been distraught when she thought her
"son" had been killed. She'd been overjoyed when she
found out that Tinker was her real child. "But Esme
is capable of committing to crazy, impossible plans.
She might want to try."

*"Domi,"* Pony murmured, "by our laws, a child
belongs foremost to its mother, but then to its clan.
Who exactly qualifies as the children's mother might
be debated, since what your mother has done has
never been tried among our people. It means that
Stone Clan has the strongest claim, lacking a birth
mother. Sunder is currently head of Stone Clan in
the Westernlands."

Tinker growled in frustration. "We stopped being
Stone Clan ages ago. I have always considered myself
as Wind Clan."

"It was your right as an adult to choose a clan,

but children are not considered mature enough to decide this."

That was the same line of bullshit that Iron Mace used to justify what was done to Oilcan, despite the fact that her cousin was twenty-two. Forge had promised never to betray any of his grandchildren, so he might be the lesser of evils in this—if he could be trusted.

Tinker hadn't met Sunder yet; the three new Stone Clan *domana* had arrived while she was out playing hide-and-seek with Chloe Polanski. With a name like Sunder, though, he probably wasn't a pushover.

"But the children are only the tip of the iceberg," Jin said.

"Oh, good gods! What else? You didn't even talk with them!"

"They have been in Haven since you disappeared. I was focused on finding you and supporting Wolf Who Rules. It is our policy to maintain no communication between Haven and Pittsburgh, lest it would give away Haven's location. They arrived, however, with one of the *yamabushi* . . ."

"A what?"

"Forgiveness." Jin pinched the bridge of his nose. "I forgot you do not know the term. There is so much that we should share with you about ourselves, but there never seems to be time."

Tinker laughed tiredly. "Yes, I know. Story of my life lately." She needed a crash course on everything from the proper etiquette of "formal" meetings between clans to elf reproduction cycles. (The talk of babies reminded her that she wasn't using birth control and earlier conversations on the subject boiled down to "don't worry about that now." She really should find out *why* she didn't have to.)

"The *yamabushi* are what we call the blood guard of the Chosen One. They are descendants of Wong Jin's loyal servants who—" He caught himself with a grimace. "It's a very long story and most of it is not important right now. They arrived at Haven with a young male tengu by the name of Haruka Sessai. He's been trained since birth to gather information. He gave me a brief but concise report. I wanted to bring him but the girls wake often from nightmares and find his presence comforting. They trust him and Joy tolerates him, so he is keeping guard over them."

Tinker made a motion for Jin to move on to the important details. "What important details?"

"Your ancestor, Forge's son, Unbounded Brilliance, died in France during the revolution. Apparently, when he fled Elfhome, he had with him a spell-locked box, which we believe he'd stolen from Iron Mace, hence the reason that the warlord came to Pittsburgh. Iron Mace wanted to know if your family knew what was in the box. When Unbounded Brilliance was beheaded in France, his infant son was taken to America, but the box was lost."

It felt painfully wrong for something that happened over two hundred years ago to still be important, but Iron Mace had tried to kill Oilcan because of this box. "The only thing my family knows about it is some song." Oilcan had sung it to her while telling her about his kidnapping. "Knock, knock, open the box..."

Jin nodded. "The box was found in France and flown to New York. It was at the American Museum of Natural History. It was part of a traveling exhibit

that the humans put together of objects elves lost on
Earth."

Stormsong gasped.

"What?" Tinker asked.

"I've seen it. I was—oh—oh—oh sweet light—I've
seen one of your sisters."

"And you didn't think to tell me?"

"You were still human and we had not yet met. I
didn't recognize her at the time. She was just a little
human child, one of millions in New York City."

"How do you know it was my sister?"

"She was there at the museum, inside an invisible
paper box."

Was this "confound *domi*" night? "A *what?*"

Stormsong spread her hands. "I'm not sure how she
managed it, but she was using a spell to be invisible
so she could move through the museum unseen."

That did sound like something Tinker would do.
Knowing that Dufae's box was at the museum, it was
easy to guess why the twins were running around
invisible. "Was" obviously was the key word in this
story; the box wasn't at the museum anymore. The
only question was who ended up with it.

"What were you doing there?" Tinker didn't think
the elves ever went to Earth.

"I was with Sparrow. It was a diplomatic mission.
She had taken half of Wolf's First Hand because they
had been to Earth long ago, before the war with
the oni. Since I speak English, I was included—or
at least, that was the reason Sparrow gave for taking
me. It's obvious now that she took the people most
likely able to counter the attack on Wolf. When we
returned, Pony met us at the train station with news

that Wolf was missing and Hawk Scream was dead. The bitch ran us in circles all day until you brought him to the hospice."

Sparrow had been dead only a matter of days since it had been discovered that she was a traitor and had plotted the assassination attempt.

"And the box?" Jin asked.

Stormsong shook her head. "It didn't come with us."

"The humans believe that Sparrow claimed it," Jin said. "It was removed from the museum after you left."

"What was in the box?" Tinker asked.

"There were twelve magical devices inside." Jin took out what looked like a Fabergé egg done on a bowling-ball-size scale. "This is the one that your sisters took from the box. They could not take the other eleven that day and when they realized how important the contents were, it was too late. The box was gone."

"What is it?"

"It is a storage device. What is important was what was stored inside. Joy was in this one."

"Miss Pocket Dragon?"

"We do not know what are in the other eleven devices but we know that your ancestor referred to them as 'fully loaded.' It seems likely that there are eleven more little dragons inside the others."

Yes, twelve baby dragons and six siblings warranted an immediate visit in the middle of the night. And perhaps more house insurance.

"Where did Iron Mace get twelve baby dragons?" Tinker asked.

"I don't know," Jin said. "I will try to get the information from Joy. She—She—I'm told that she is quite difficult to work with. You should be aware that the spell that the greater blood used to transform my people—all of my people in a single transformation—was done using Providence's body. It was a test run of an even greater spell that they had developed that required his soul as well as his body. It is why he asked us to kill him."

"Oh." Tinker felt like someone had punched her. Eleven possible world-changing spells all locked into one deadly box.